Evelyn Hood Omnibus

A HANDFUL
OF HAPPINESS

THIS TIME
NEXT YEAR

Also by Evelyn Hood:

Evelyn Hood Omnibus

A HANDFUL OF HAPPINESS

THIS TIME NEXT YEAR

EVELYN HOOD

timewarner
paperbacks

A *Time Warner* Paperback

This omnibus edition first published in Great Britain
by Time Warner Paperbacks in 2003
Evelyn Hood Omnibus Copyright © Evelyn Hood 2003

Previously published separately:
A Handful of Happiness first published in
Great Britain in 1993 by Headline Book Publishing plc
Published by Warner Books in 1999
Copyright © Evelyn Hood 1993

This Time Next Year first published in Great Britain
in 1992 by Headline Book Publishing plc
Published by Warner Books in 2000
Reprinted 2000 (twice), 2001
Copyright © Evelyn Hood 1992

The moral right of the author has been asserted.

A CIP catalogue record for this book is
available from the British Library.

ISBN 0 7515 3501 X

Typeset by
Printed and bound in Great Britain by
Mackays of Chatham plc, Chatham, Kent

Time Warner Paperbacks
An imprint of
Time Warner Books UK
Brettenham House
Lancaster Place
London WC2E 7EN

www.TimeWarnerBooks.co.uk

A HANDFUL
OF HAPPINESS

Although Ellerslie is a fictitious Clydeside town, and none of the characters in this book bear any resemblance to people past or present, the Dalkieth Experimental Tank section is based on the Denny Experimental Tank, a section of the former Dumbarton shipyard owned and operated by generations of the Denny family. The Tank is now part of the Scottish Maritime Museum, and open to the public.

I would like to thank the following people for the assistance they generously gave me during the research for this book; the Scottish Maritime Museum staff in Irvine and Dumbarton, particularly Niall McNeil and Anne Hobin of Dumbarton; the staff of Dumbarton Library; Mrs Margaret (Peggy) Wallace, a former Tracer and Analyst in Hydro-dynamics in the Denny Experimental Tank, and Reg Wishart, a former Clydeside shipyard worker.

Evelyn Hood

To my sons, Alastair and Simon,
with thanks for the many years
of pleasure they have given me.
E.H.

1

'It's here! The letter from my Aunt Margaret's here!' Lizzie Caldwell, who was waiting impatiently outside the Experimental Tank department, squealed as soon as Jenny emerged. 'She says we can both start on the first day of December, me in drapery and you in hosiery. We're going tae Glasgow!'

Jenny's heart stopped as though an unseen hand had gripped it, then started to pump twice as fast. 'Let me see!'

'She says one of us is in drapery and the other in hosiery,' Lizzie said as she handed the letter over, 'but since it's my aunt that got us the places I should have first choice.'

Jenny pulled off the gloves she had just smoothed over her fingers so that she could relish the feel of the letter she drew from the envelope. In the four years since the beginning of the war, letters from men serving in the forces had become commonplace among the people who lived in the crowded shipyard tenements. Jenny's brother Maurice, stationed in France, sent letters to his mother, and once Jenny herself had received letters with her name on the envelope – but not now. Robert Archer was as dead to her now as though he had been killed in the fighting.

Maureen Malloy, who had come out of the office with Jenny, was squinting so closely at the letter that her chin dug into Jenny's shoulder. 'Stop starin' at it as if

1

you're expectin' it tae speak tae ye, and open the thing!' she ordered.

Like the envelope, the single sheet of paper was of fine quality, and bold black writing flowed imperiously across the page in neat lines. Although she wrote a good hand herself – fine handwriting was high on the list of qualifications demanded of the women employed in the tracing office – Jenny was impressed. This letter had been written by none other than Lizzie's Aunt Margaret, the stylish supervisor of the ladies' wear department of a large and important emporium situated in Buchanan Street, in the heart of the city of Glasgow. Aunt Margaret had, as Lizzie was fond of saying, 'pulled herself up by her own bootstraps.'

She repeated the phrase proudly, for the umpteenth time, when the letter was returned to her and the three girls began to walk home. By now most of the other Tank workers had gone and the street was empty. The double doors that led directly from the wax-model room on to the street had been closed and locked by Mr Duncan, the Tank superintendent.

'I don't see how anyone could pull themselves up by their bootstraps without draggin' the feet from under themselves and fallin' on their arses!' red-headed Maureen said, with a snigger. Maureen's parents had come over from Ireland as newlyweds; their many children, though born and raised in Scotland, had inherited their parents' easy-going Irish natures.

'That's all you know about it!' Lizzie shot back at her, her round, pale face flushing with anger. 'And that's why you'll always live in Ellerslie and probably stay in the tracing office until you get married and raise more brats than you can afford just because your priest says you should!'

2

'I can think of worse things tae dae,' said Maureen, unrepentant. 'All I want's for my Jacko tae come home from the war an' get back intae his old job in the shipyard. An' we like weans, both of us. I hope we have lots!'

'Please yourself.' Lizzie put her snub nose in the air. 'Me and Jenny'll be in Glasgow, learning to live like ladies.'

Maureen slipped a hand through Jenny's arm. 'You'll write tae me, won't you, Jen? When you can find the time tae let go of your bootstraps, that is,' she added, with a sidelong glance at Lizzie, who pretended not to hear her.

'Of course I'll write. And I'll send a fine christening present every time you have another brat,' Jenny promised, making Maureen giggle and Lizzie flounce by stressing the final word. She knew that it was wrong of her to tease Lizzie, but at that moment she was so excited that she wanted to pull off her hat and throw it into the air, to run and jump and swing round the gaslamp posts and sing for joy. She was going to Glasgow, to a huge city where nobody knew her, and there she could be whatever and whoever she chose.

She was getting away from Ellerslie and the overcrowded tenement flat where she had lived all her life, away from her father and his drinking and constant criticism, away from her faded, exhausted mother, who had never known anything but worry and who broke Jenny's heart with her continual fear of poverty and the workhouse. Away from Gran's twisted face with the spittle running down her chin.

As the girls turned on to the bridge that spanned the river running through Ellerslie they passed a small knot of people studying the billboards outside a newsagent's shop. 'Tide Turns For Allies!' said one of the boards, while the other proclaimed, 'Kaiser's Army Crumbling!'

'I wonder what'll come first – us going to Glasgow, or the war ending?' Jenny linked her free arm through Lizzie's so that the three girls were swinging along the footpath in line.

'It'll be a great way to end the year,' Lizzie's anger at the teasing had gone. 'Peace for the world, and a new life for you and me. For the three of us, with Molly and Jacko getting married,' she added magnanimously.

Jenny felt a twinge of guilt at the ease with which she would leave her family behind, but compensated by reminding herself that she would send money home to help them. The truth of it was that she would miss her job at the shipyard more than she would miss her family. She was proud to have been considered fit for a position in the Experimental Tank section – small though Dalkieth's shipyard was, it had been the first Clyde yard to install a tank where models of their designs could be tested before the actual ships were built. Only the mighty John Brown's Yard at Clydebank had followed suit so far.

A short distance along the riverside from the bridge the three girls reached their destination, four rows of tenement buildings in the form of a square. A hundred years earlier the son of the Dalkieth who had set up the shipyard had bought this land on the opposite bank of the river from the original town and built houses for his workers on it. He had built them in the form of a square surrounding a large back court, and had named the four streets James, George, William and Anne, after himself and his wife and two sons. Since then other tenements had sprung up around them, but the original buildings, now old and shabby, were still occupied by Dalkieth employees and their families.

Maureen said goodbye at the corner of Anne Street

and went off to the tenement building where she lived with her parents and countless brothers and sisters. Jenny and Lizzie, arm in arm, continued on along George Street, planning their dazzling futures.

'Just think— ' Lizzie squeezed Jenny's arm, 'we'll be in Glasgow in time for Christmas. We'll need tae give in our notices at the end of the month. Are you sure your da'll let you go?

'He'll have to for my mind's made up. And my mam'll be pleased for me. Alice has turned thirteen now – she can help with my gran as well as I can.' Though Jenny spoke lightly, guilt sparked in her again.

Alice, the clever member of the family, was still at school, and had a lot of studying to do. But she would manage. She would just have to manage, once Jenny was no longer there.

'Maurice'll mebbe be back home by the time I leave. Once he's back working in the shipyard again they'll not need my wages so badly.'

'D'ye think he'll marry that Lottie when he comes home?'

'He'll have to, now. He'd not leave wee Helen fatherless and he knows fine that she's his bairn.'

Lizzie's voice was suddenly self-righteous. 'My mother says Lottie's nothing but a slut.'

Jenny bit back a sharp retort. Lizzie was her best friend and she had just got her a new job in Glasgow. Anyway, Jenny herself had little time for her brother's sweetheart. Secretly she thought that Maurice could have done better for himself than Lottie, who was lazy and selfish. But that was Maurice's problem, not hers. She would soon be out of it all, living her own life in Glasgow.

She parted with Lizzie at the closemouth and ran up the dark, narrow stairs to the second-floor flat she had

5

been born and raised in, suddenly longing to share her good news. She would ignore any sarcastic remarks her father might make about it – she would soon be away from him and his ill-tempered tongue.

She lifted the door latch and burst into the tiny dim hall, calling as she went, 'Mam – the letter's come for Lizzie. There's places for both of us where her aunt works. We're starting in Dec— '

She stopped, suddenly aware that the place was silent apart from her own voice. At this hour of the day there was usually the sound of the hacking cough that was the legacy of her father's bad bout of pneumonia eighteen months earlier, and Helen's high, clear, little voice and a babble of talk from her mother and Lottie and Alice.

'Mam?'

There were only two people in the kitchen instead of the expected crowd; no smell of cooking, no bustle by the range where, for once, the pots were missing. Only the big kettle emitted its usual faint plume of steam. Marion Gillespie, Jenny's grandmother, was huddled as usual in one of the two fireside chairs, a shapeless mass of wool with an untidy white head at one end and scrawny ankles at the other. Faith Gillespie was in the other fireside chair, the one normally reserved for her husband, who was still the master of the house, though since his illness he had been demoted in the yard and now worked as a storeman instead of at his own trade as a fitter.

In her faded skirt and blouse, her hair well streaked with grey, Faith was almost unnoticeable, a shadow of a woman with little substance to her. 'Mam— '

Faith lifted her head and looked at her daughter with pale blue eyes.

'What's wrong? It's not Helen, is it?' Jenny, who adored her little niece, felt fear catch at her throat.

6

'It's no' the bairn.' Faith's mouth trembled. 'The poor wee bairn, that's never even seen her fath— '

Her voice broke. She held out a hand and with a twist of sudden fear Jenny saw that it held a crumpled buff form. She knew well enough what that meant. Many a home up and down the street had received one. Jenny's sister Bella had had one six months earlier, though in her case it had not been notification that her man was dead, but that he was being returned to her a cripple.

For the second time within half an hour she scanned a sheet of paper. This time she had to read it three times before the words sank in. 'Oh, Mam!'

Faith's head came up, her fingers reaching out to snatch the form back. 'He's not dead, only missin', it says that here,' she said fiercely. 'Not dead. He's comin' back tae us. It was just – a wee bit of a shock, that's all, comin' just when everyone's sayin' that the war's over and our men'll be home soon.'

Jenny wanted to put her arms about her mother, but the Gillespies weren't a touching family, so she could only stand over her mother helplessly, saying again, 'Oh, Mam!' while the pleasure of her own news leached out of her. 'Where's Alice and wee Helen – and Dad?'

'Alice took the bairn round tae Mrs Malloy's. I needed time tae think. I don't know where Lottie is, but yer da went out tae the pub.'

'He would. That's where he aye goes when he doesn't know what else to do.'

'That's enough,' Faith said, with only an echo of her usual sharpness. She allowed nobody to criticise her husband.

'I'll make a cup of tea.' Jenny fetched the old caddy, so well handled that its original picture had faded away, and measured tea-leaves into the pot, trying, as she worked, to come to terms with the news. Maurice, a young and self-conscious stranger in his uniform, watched her from the carved wooden frame on the sideboard. Behind his likeness she could see her own face in the small standing mirror and realised that she was still wearing her hat and coat. She took them off and put them over the back of an upright chair, automatically smoothing her already neat dark hair, which was drawn into a bun at the nape of her neck, straightening the collar of her ivory working blouse, finally meeting her own blue eyes in the glass and turning away quickly from the truth that she read in them, but didn't want to acknowledge.

'Someone should tell Bella.' Faith's voice fretted at her as she put cups out on the table. 'I didnae like tae ask Alice tae dae it, she's only a bairn herself.'

'I'll go to Bella's in a wee while.'

'What was it you were saying when you came in?'

'Nothing, Mam.'

'What was it?' Faith insisted. Jenny put the pot on to the brass stand that Maurice had made when he was an apprentice in the machine shop at the shipyard and turned to face her.

'I said that Lizzie had heard from her aunt. She's got places for us both in that big shop where she works in Glasgow.'

Faith stared for a moment, as though trying to make sense of the words, then a sudden flash of fear passed over her face. 'You'll no' leave us?' she said at once. 'You'll wait till Maurice comes home?'

Jenny swallowed hard. For as long as she could remember her mother had been afraid – of poverty, of illness, of the shadow of the workhouse. She had never known the luxury of security, even after marriage

8

rescued her from the home where she had been abused and half-starved. As a shipyard worker's daughter, then a shipyard worker's wife, Faith Gillespie had never known what it was to be free of insecurity and nagging financial worry. She had buried two sons in infancy, had almost lost her husband to pneumonia, had had to see her only surviving son go off to war, and had then had to take in his pregnant sweetheart when the girl's own parents threw her out.

She had spent most of her marriage being bullied by her strong-willed mother-in-law and, when the woman had succumbed to a stroke, it was Faith who had had no choice but to find room for her in her own over-crowded home.

'You'll no' go?' she said again, insistently, reaching a hand out to Jenny.

'Mam, the job's waiting for me. I'll send money home every week, mebbe more money than I'm getting just now—'

'Ye'll have tae wait – just till our Maurice comes back!' The words were wrung out of Faith's throat.

'Faith?' The latch lifted on the outside door and Mrs Malloy, a solid dumpling of a woman, came through the hall and into the room with a rush, filling it almost before she had cleared the door, her face heavy with the news she had just heard. 'Oh – Faith,' she said, and the old woman sleeping uneasily in the other chair stirred and woke with a whimper of fright as Mrs Malloy's passing rocked her like a small boat in the wake of a steamship.

'It's all right, Gran.' Jenny's arms went out automatically to support Marion as she slipped sideways and almost fell from the chair. Carefully, she eased her grandmother upright then fetched a cloth and wiped

9

spittle from her chin. Marion's eyes, which until short months before had had the ability to terrorise with one look, wandered for a moment then focused on Jenny. She gave a garbled grunt.

'She'll likely want tae use the commode, poor old soul,' Mrs Malloy whispered, then, raising her voice, she boomed, 'All right, hen, we'll see tae ye in a wee minute. I'll just make some tea first.' Although she still retained her Irish accent, Mrs Malloy's speech was pepped with Scottish words and phrases.

'It's already made.' Jenny heaved the large, battered teapot from the range with a skill acquired over the years. As she poured tea she heard her mother say behind her, 'He's not dead, Molly, only missing. He'll be home, just like he promised. He'll come home tae look after us all. He's not dead.'

Bella Kerr, Jenny's elder sister, lived a few closes further along George Street in 'single-end', a one-roomed flat on the upper floor. As Jenny climbed the stairs she could hear her brother-in-law's raised voice and her hands closed into fists in her pockets.

Patrick had been a riveter in the shipyard before the war, a cheerful young man who had swept quiet, timid Bella off her feet. While the early radiance of marriage still glowed in their faces, Patrick had been called up; then sent home a cripple with one foot badly damaged and all his zest in life replaced by a bitter resentment against the entire world. He could only get about with the aid of crutches now, and steadfastly refused to go outside where people could see him and pity him. Bella had to work hard, cleaning shops and offices, to support them both.

Silence fell behind the scarred wooden door as soon as Jenny knocked on it. After a moment Bella peered out, then stepped back as her sister pushed the door wide.

'What's amiss?'

'It's me that should be asking you that,' Jenny said bluntly, noting Bella's reddened eyes and the way she was rubbing at one wrist. 'I could hear you all the way up the stairs, Patrick.'

He glowered at her from the chair where he spent almost all his time. 'Mebbe they should've shot me in the throat, then. I wish tae Christ they had.'

'Pat, don't!'

Patrick Kerr turned away form his wife's anguished face, one hand plucking restlessly at the shabby rug over his knees, then looked back quickly at Jenny when she told them why she had come.

'God – poor old Maurice,' he said, his voice dull with shock.

Bella took her shawl down from its hook on the door. 'I'd best go round,' she began, then hesitated. 'Will you be all right, Pat?'

'I'm no' likely tae run away, am I?' The bitterness was back, in his brown eyes as well as in his voice, and the hand that had been fidgeting with the rug dug into the thin material, gripping at the crippled leg below.

'I'll stay if you— '

'For God's sake, woman, will ye stop moitherin' me an' go if ye're goin!' he shouted, so suddenly that Jenny jumped.

'But— '

Jenny's hand closed over her sister's wrist and then, as Bella winced, she relaxed her grip. 'Come on, Bella. Pat'll be fine on his own for a wee while.'

As they began to go down the hollowed stone stairs there was a noisy rush of water as someone flushed the cistern of the privy on the landing. The door opened and

11

Daniel Young, a widower who lived with his son on the ground floor, began to emerge then stopped abruptly at sight of the two young women, his jacket dangling from one hand. His pale thin face went beet red with embarrassment at being caught leaving a privy.

He ducked his head in acknowledgement then cleared his throat nervously, and began to descend towards his own flat, scrambling into his jacket as he went. Then he hesitated and looked back at Bella.

'Is something wrong?'

'It's our Maurice – there's been a telegram.' Her voice shook.

'He's missing, just,' Jenny put in swiftly.

'He'll probably be all right,' said Daniel, but his voice lacked conviction. They all knew that few missing men reached home. 'D'ye want me tae sit with Patrick while ye're out?'

'I'd be grateful. He's in a low mood.'

'I'll just tell the laddie, then I'll go up,' he said, and hurried on down before them.

'He's a good man, Daniel,' Bella murmured gratefully as the sisters passed his door. The brasswork on it was gleaming. 'Not many of the men Pat used tae work with bother now.' Tears brimmed up in her eyes and she wiped them away with a corner of the shawl as she stepped into the street. 'And now there's Maurice. This damned war, Jenny – will it never leave us be?'

'It's nearly over, they say.'

'Aye, but— ' Bella's voice broke. 'Nothing'll ever be the same again!'

'Lizzie got the letter from her aunt in Glasgow today.'

'What letter?' Bella asked blankly, then recollection flooded back into her small, pinched face. 'The place in Glasgow?'

12

'It's all arranged. I'm supposed to be handing in my notice at the end of the month.'

The same fear that she had seen in her mother's eyes came into Bella's. 'But things've changed now, Jen! We were counting on Maurice coming home. If he's— ' She stopped, then said, in a rush, 'Ye cannae leave us just now, Jenny. Not the way things are!'

'I'll mebbe not get the chance again.'

'But how'll Mam manage without your wage comin' in?'

'I can send money,' Jenny said desperately. Already the words were beginning to sound hollow to her own ears.

'Ye'd need tae be paid a lot tae afford tae keep yourself and send enough home.' Bella put a hand on Jenny's arm, her chilled fingers pressing into the flesh. 'Now that Dad's makin' less money workin' in the stores instead of on the ships there's not enough comin' in as it is.'

'He'll have to stop spending most of his money at the the pub, then,' Jenny said bitterly.

'You know he'll not do that. An' with Patrick not earning I can't spare anything. It's hard enough tae pay the rent as it is.'

'I need to get away, Bella!'

'Later, when things are better,' Bella's voice was pleading. 'You like your work in the tracing office, don't you?'

'Yes, but— '

'When things are better,' Bella said again, her hand tightening on Jenny's arm.

Looking down at the work-reddened fingers clutching at her sleeve, the broken nails and bony knuckles, Jenny knew that her sister was right. Despair washed over her; she felt like a prisoner about to start a long sentence for a crime that she hadn't committed . . .

13

2

It was a long, wearying evening. Neighbour after neighbour called to offer condolences as the news spread round the streets, each bringing something – a plate of home-made scones, a packet of biscuits, half a loaf, a 'scrapin" of margarine. Jenny and her two sisters were kept busy making tea, for it was the custom on such occasions to offer hospitality to every visitor.

Faith, still frighteningly calm and dry-eyed, assured each sympathiser, with growing determination, that her son would be found safe and well and sent home.

Alice had come back from the Malloys without little Helen, who had already been tucked into the wall bed that the three Malloy girls shared, and was to stay there for the night. Lottie returned home halfway through the evening, her red-gold curls and vivid tawny eyes lighting up the room as soon as she walked into it.

When the news was broken to her she looked blankly from one face to the other. 'Missing?' she asked at last. 'Missing in action? Maurice?'

'It means that they don't know where he is, Lottie,' Mrs Malloy said, and the girl glared at her.

'I know fine what it means!'

'It's all right, hen. He'll come back tae us,' Faith said for what seemed to Jenny to be the hundredth time. The neighbours exchanged furtive glances then nodded their heads vigorously. One of them put a gentle hand on Lottie's arm, but it was shaken off.

'And what if he doesnae?' Lottie demanded, dry-eyed. 'What's tae happen tae me then?'

There was a general hiss of indrawn breath from the group of women.

'Stop thinking about yourself for once,' Jenny said sharply, and Bella chimed in, 'What about Mam – how d'ye think she feels?'

'She's all right, she's got her man – and she's got you and Alice,' Lottie said sulkily. 'It's me that'll have no place tae go tae if Maurice doesnae come home the way he promised. He'd no right tae go off tae fight an' leave me with a wean!'

Jenny took a step forward, her hands fisting by her sides. Lottie had always been selfish, but until then none of them had realised just how deep her selfishness went. Jenny started to speak, then stopped, swallowing the bitter, angry words back, unwilling for her mother's sake to cause a scene at such a time.

'We'll see ye all right,' Faith was saying, 'You and the wee one. We'll look after ye till Maurice comes home.'

'Aye, no need for you tae fret, Lottie,' Mrs Malloy chimed in, a steely edge to her voice. 'I'm sure *you'll* land on yer feet, whatever happens.'

Lottie gave her a venomous look, appropriated a scone and a cup of tea that Alice had just poured for Faith, and announced that she was going to bed.

'An' don't you worry yersel' about yer wean – she's stayin' wi' me the night,' Mrs Malloy tossed the words after her but they were ignored as Lottie slammed the kitchen door behind her, leaving a shocked silence in her wake.

'I knew she was a hard bitch, but I didnae realise she

15

was as hard as that!' someone finally muttered, and Faith half-reared from her chair, roused out of her apathy by the need to defend her beloved son's sweetheart.

'It's the suddenness of it!' she snapped back, 'It's just the way it took her!'

'Ye're right, Faith, ye're right,' Mrs Malloy soothed, the edge gone from her voice as she stooped over her friend. 'Don't get yourself all upset, now.'

Behind Faith's back the other women exchanged looks that spoke volumes.

Long after Bella went home to Patrick, Teeze Gillespie lurched up the stairs and into the kitchen, drunk as a lord, loud-mouthed, aggressive, scattering the last of the well-meaning visitors and sending them off to their own homes.

'Make yersel' useful,' he commanded his wife thickly as the final caller fled, 'Get me somethin' tae eat!'

'I'll do it, Mam. You stay where you are,' Jenny said, but her mother had already scrambled out of the chair so that Teeze could sit down. Frying potatoes and onions on the range while Alice set the table and Faith fussed nervously around the sink, Jenny thought longingly about Glasgow, and the new life she had planned.

When the meal was ready and Teeze eating it the two girls helped their mother to pull the truckle bed out from under the bed in the alcove, then to undress and wash their grandmother. With the bed in the middle of the floor the kitchen seemed to shrink to the size of a cupboard. The corners of the low bed hacked unwary ankles as the three women manoeuvred the invalid out of her chair and worked over her.

It was a relief when Jenny was free to go to bed in the

small, narrow room that she had all to herself. It had been Maurice's room before he went off to the war and there was only space in it for the bed and a large orange box that Jenny used as both a table and a storage area for blouses and underwear. Her skirts and the one dress she owned were hung on nails hammered into the wall.

Most of the shipyard workers' houses boasted two or three handsome pieces of furniture, for the Dalkieths were, on the whole, good to their employees, and when a ship came in for refurbishment it had always been their policy to sell off the discarded furniture, made of the finest timber by skilled craftsmen, to their workers at nominal prices. Most of the other yards either sold the furniture to second-hand dealers or scrapped it.

Before the war, when Teeze and Maurice were both bringing in wages, the Gillespies had owned several pieces of furniture from the yard, including the handsome sideboard that still stood in the kitchen. But the fitting bay, open to the bitter winds that swept down the river had been well named 'Pneumonia Bay' by the men who worked there. Teeze Gillespie had succumbed to pneumonia about a year earlier, and the determined fight he had put up, insisting on going off to work day after day when he wasn't fit for it, had almost killed him and resulted in permanent damage to his lungs. Now he worked in the stores, sweeping floors and running errands and dedicating most of his reduced wage to the local pubs.

With Maurice fighting in the war and Alice still at school, money had become scarce; one by one the pieces Faith had delighted in and polished every day had been sold and replaced by orange boxes begged from local shopkeepers. Only the sideboard remained as a symbol of those better days.

Jenny blew out the candle – there was gas-light only in the kitchen – and lay in bed, thinking of her handsome, outgoing brother. It was hard to believe that he was dead but, unlike her mother, Jenny knew that they would never see Maurice again. Wee Helen would grow up without knowing her father.

The tears came unexpectedly and she wept for fatherless Helen, then for Maurice, and finally for herself and the way her hopes and plans had been dashed. There would be no going off to Glasgow for her, no new life. She knew that now.

One day, mebbe. But not yet. Not for a long time . . .

'Ye don't mean it!' Lizzie's voice was incredulous. 'Ye're surely not going tae turn down the chance tae get out of here and start a new life!'

'How can I, now that Maurice is – Maurice won't be coming home?'

Jenny, Lizzie and Maureen were crossing the bridge on their way to work. The sky overhead was threatening and, glancing over the stone parapet, Jenny saw that the water hurrying below on its way to the Clyde was yellowish grey and sullen. the weather suited her mood.

'She cannae leave her mam just now, Lizzie,' Maureen agreed. 'Mebbe in a month or two—'

'It'll be too late, then,' Lizzie snapped, walking faster, so that the other two had to run a few steps to catch up. 'I just need to get things settled here.'

'And you expect my auntie tae keep the position open for you, do you?'

'No, of course not. But mebbe there'll be another place later.'

'I don't suppose there will be. And you neednae think I'll stay here just because you're staying, Jenny Gillespie,' Lizzie said, sticking her chin out and increasing her pace until she was almost running. Jenny trailed miserably along behind her, swallowing back the tears. Life was so unfair. All she asked for was just a handful of happiness, but each time she grasped it, it ran through her fingers like sand.

'Ach, don't be so childish, Lizzie!' Maureen panted in exasperation when Lizzie finally slowed down and allowed the other two to catch up with her. 'Jenny's not doing it on purpose – she wants tae go tae Glasgow, but how can she, the way things are at home?'

They had reached the huge, wrought-iron main gates to the yard. The men started work half an hour before the office staff, so the steady flood of people crowding in at the gates had ceased. Now there was only the office workers and the inevitable knot of men waiting patiently outside the gate, anxious-eyed and shivering in the wind, in the hope of getting a day's work.

'Me childish? I like that! Who is it that's been fair desperate tae get out of Ellerslie ever since Robert Archer jilted her? Not me,' said Lizzie, and marched into the yard, leaving Jenny shocked and winded with the sudden pain of betrayal. She and Lizzie had been friends since their first week at school; they had grown up together and it was Lizzie who had helped Jenny through her grief when Robert had gone off to work in the English shipyards then chosen to marry an English-woman.

'I didn't – I don't care about Ro – about him,' she said feebly, but Lizzie had gone beyond hearing, stamping across the cobbled yard, her solid, broad behind swinging and swaggering beneath her blue serge skirt.

'She walks like one of they cows they drive through the streets tae the market,' Maureen said, but Jenny,

19

stricken, couldn't even manage a twitch of the lips as she moved on round the corner and along the street to where the yard's Experimental Tank section was situated.

'Ach, pay no heed tae her, hen.' Maureen caught up with her and slipped a hand into the crook of her elbow. 'She's just jealous because no man's ever looked at her. Why else d'ye think she's so set on goin' tae Glasgow? It's because she's heard that the men there arenae all that choosy!'

It was hard to stay downhearted for long in Maureen's company, and this time a faint, shaky grin tugged at one corner of Jenny's mouth as the two girls stepped over the wooden threshold into the wax room, which opened directly to the street. 'Maureen Malloy, you're terrible!' Jenny protested, her gloom lifting a little despite herself.

'I know that, but it's folk like me that keep the confessional frae gettin' dusty!' said Maureen.

The furnaces had been lit early to start the slabs of wax melting and the room was already cosy. Baldy Devine, one of the moulders, was working at the clay bed, the long trough where clay was shaped by wooden templates into a mould, then covered with canvas sheeting before liquid wax was poured in to make the finished model. He glanced up as the girls came in. Baldy was famed for having more hair on his wizened little face than his head; even his enormous grey walrus moustache exuded sympathy.

'We're all awful sorry tae hear about your Maurice, lass,' he said, and Jenny nodded.

'Thanks, Baldy.'

'Bearin' up, are ye?'

'I'm fine, Baldy.'

His brown eyes warmed in a smile. 'That's the ticket, hen.'

The model room was small, and there was only a narrow space between the clay bed and the large cutting machine where the exact measurements were cut into the models to guide the men who then shaved the surplus wax away, flake by flake. Neil Baker, one of the naval architects, was perched beside it on a small revolving stool, one plump hand resting on the lever that operated the sharp instruments within the machine. Although he was only in his early twenties Neil was already running to fat and his buttocks overhung the stool.

He glanced round, then leaned back as Jenny approached, ostensibly to study the plan pinned on the machine for his guidance. All the tracing office girls knew Neil of old. Normally Jenny would have squeezed past his broad back, ignoring his leer as their bodies were forced together by the narrowness of the passage, but this morning she hesitated.

'Sorry,' he drawled, and wiggled slightly on the stool, swinging it round so that her thigh would have to press against his knee as she tried to ease by him. 'There – you can surely manage past now.' His pale blue eyes ran deliberately over her and, despite her coat, buttoned to the throat, Jenny felt as though she had nothing on but her underclothes. 'You're not that fat.'

'No, but you are.' Maureen edged her way round Jenny then pushed past Neil, managing as she went to jab him in the ribs with an elbow, shoving him against the cutting machine. He opened his mouth to object, but instead let out an almost womanly squeak of outrage and leapt off the stool as Maureen unexpectedly reached down and grabbed a handful of his rump.

'You'd be worth a shillin' of anyone's money in the pork butcher's, Neil,' she said loudly then caught at Jenny's arm as Baldy and the other men in the room howled with laughter, pulling her past the naval architect, who was too busy coping with his own embarrassment to savour the brief contact between them.

'Bitch!' he snapped, crimson-faced.

'Bugger,' Maureen retorted calmly. Amused faces peered over the railings of the gallery above, where the joiners and cutters worked.

'Can I go next, Maureen!' someone shouted down.

'The first yin's free, the rest o' youse'll have tae pay for the pleasure,' she yelled back, laughing. 'Come on, Jenny. He's like a dirty old man, that one,' she went on loudly as they climbed the short flight of wooden stairs to the next level. 'Just because he's a naval architect and his dad's one o' the gaffers he thinks he's somethin' special.'

Before crossing to the stairs that led up to her own office Jenny paused and glanced down into the model room. The melted wax was beginning to pour in a pale gold river into the clay bed through the pipes leading from the two small heating tanks on one wall. Jenny had been working as a tracer for four years now, but she still found the process of model-making fascinating, and the work she did, analysing the results of the tests run on the wax models in the tank, made her long to know more about the whole complex business of designing and building ships.

She turned to glance at the tank itself, stretching three hundred feet away from her. The truck that spanned the water's breadth was on the move, backing up the length of the tank, with Mr Duncan, the tank superintendent and a naval architect by trade, standing on the small platform. Jenny lingered, waiting until it reached the far end. There it paused, then came clanking and rumbling towards her, driven by the steam engine at the far end of the tank, the model under trial clamped firmly on to the underside of the truck. As always, there was a breathless moment when it seemed that this time the truck would burst through the buffers at the end of the tank, then it came to a stop with a final bone-shaking clang as Maureen called her name from the second flight of stairs. Reluctantly, Jenny went to join her.

Senga, the third tracer, was already in the office and Miss McQueen, the supervisor, was hanging her jacket up carefully.

'Are you sure you should be at work this morning, Jenny?' she asked with unexpected sympathy. 'I heard about your brother. Could your poor mother not be doing with you at home?'

'She'd as soon everything was just as usual, Miss McQueen.' Jenny took her own coat off and hung it up, then reached for the smock that each girl wore to protect her clothes from the coloured inks they used.

The supervisor nodded. 'In that case, so would I – and that means, Maureen Malloy, getting on with the work instead of fidgeting with your hair,' she added with a sudden switch back to her usual tone. Maureen jumped, then scrambled up on to her high chair at the sloping desk running the length of the office wall as Miss McQueen doled out the morning's work.

Senga and Maureen were set to analysing the results of a series of trials carried out the previous day in the tank, which meant that they had to work their way through a great bundle of paper, collating the detailed results from each experiment on to four or five sheets which would then go back downstairs to the small

23

drawing office where the naval architects worked. Jenny was given the more precise task of finishing off a pencilled line-drawing, going over each line in coloured ink and tidying up the architect's scribbled notes.

It was the sort of elaborate task she normally revelled in, requiring precision and care. The details before her had to be meticulously recorded, as the completed line-drawing would be used by the designers, then the engineers, platers, boilermakers and everyone else involved in the building of the ship. Ever since Lizzie's final malicious comment about Robert her heart had felt as though it had been scrubbed with a hard-bristled brush dipped in strong disinfectant, a raw ache that slowly began to fade as she worked. It thrilled her to know that in the noisy, busy yard outside great sheets of metal would be bent to the correct shapes then riveted together on the massive stocks. Plate by plate, pipe by pipe, the ship would rise towards the sky until eventually it was completed. And she, Jenny Gillespie, would have played her part in its birth. Time flew past as she worked, then as she laid down a pen for a moment and stretched stiffened muscles Lizzie's voice intruded unexpectedly, 'Ever since Robert Archer jilted her— ' and Jenny knew that the pain that she thought had finally gone was still with her.

It was Robert Archer, Maurice's friend, who had first aroused her interest in the craft of boat-building, firing her with his own enthusiasm. Robert, himself a naval architect, had helped her to study for the examination that had won her a place in the tracing office. Their shared love of ships had turned to love for each other; or so Jenny had believed. But she had been wrong, she thought now, flexing her stiff fingers, trying to push the thoughts out of her mind, and failing.

24

An orphan who lived with an elderly relative, Robert had been made welcome in the Gillespie household, for Faith's sympathies were stirred by the way his knobbly wrists and large, strong hands stuck out of sleeves that were far too short for him, and by his cracked and battered boots, with string for laces.

'He's neglected, poor wee laddie,' she said, although Robert, who had grown up rather than out in his early teens, was already a good half-head taller than she herself. His burning ambition was to know everything there was to know about shipbuilding, and to be master of his own yard one day.

'I'll do it, you just wait and see,' he insisted firmly when Maurice and Teeze, both content to work for others, laughed at him. Jenny, looking at his determined young face, the glow in his grey eyes, had believed him.

At first he was almost unaware of her existence, for she was only Maurice's young sister and he himself, older than Maurice, was some seven years her senior. But as time passed and he completed his apprenticeship he became aware of her interest in anything he had to say about his work.

By that time, Jenny's talent and liking for arithmetic and drawing had begun to baffle her mother and annoy her father. 'What's the sense in a lassie knowin' how tae dae her sums an' paint pretty pictures?' her father taunted time and time again. Her attempts to justify herself usually ended in a boxed and ringing ear and, 'Ye want tae learn tae keep a civil tongue in yer head instead, girl! What man's goin' tae want tae marry a shrew?'

Only Robert understood. He began to encourage her and help her with her homework, sometimes even sitting at the kitchen table with her, patiently unravelling some

25

mathematical problem while Maurice, who like his father had little time for book learning, was out with this girl or that, enjoying himself. When she was about to leave school it was Robert who had suggested that she should sit the Dalkieth examination.

'They're good people tae work for. Willing tae encourage folk that work hard. You've got a sharp brain, Jenny – you should at least try the examination.'

The pattern of lines on the stiff paper before Jenny merged and faded as she thought of the day she heard that she had come top in the examination and been rewarded with a place in the Experimental Tank's tracing office. The day Robert had first kissed her. Dazed with success and excitement she had run to tell him and had found him coming down the stairs of the building where he lived. As he stepped from the final stair Jenny, scampering through the close, ran full tilt into him and he had to brace himself and catch her in order to prevent a collision.

'I did it!' she crowed into his chest, broader now that he had started earning a wage and justified better feeding. 'I came first! I'm to report to the tracing office on Monday!'

She looked up to see her own triumph mirrored in his normally serious face. 'Jenny, I'm proud of you!' He enfolded her in an unselfconscious bear hug, then held her back a little. 'What did your father have to say?'

Some of the pleasure left her. 'He just grunted.'

Robert, his hands still on her shoulders, shook her gently. 'He's just jealous – you know how the men in the yard are about the Tank. They all think the folk that work there are toffee-nosed.'

'I wish he could have been pleased with me, just this once.'

'Pay no heed. I'm pleased for you, Jenny. I'm proud of you,' said Robert, and then he kissed her, a light kiss that took them both by surprise. For a moment Jenny experienced sheer astonishment, then a great wave of happiness swept over her. Her arms tightened about him and he kissed her again, taking more time about it.

'That's never happened to me before,' she said shakily when he finally released her.

'Was it – did you not like it?'

'Of course I liked it, you daft lummock!' said Jenny, and he gave a yell of laughter that started a child wailing behind a nearby door, and a woman snapped her irritation. 'Come on— ' He took her hand and pulled her out of the close and along the street, not stopping until they reached the bridge—

'Are you not finished yet, Jenny?' Miss McQueen asked, irritated, her voice shattering the memory of the bridge, and Robert's arm about her shoulders. 'I promised Mr Duncan that drawing by noon. You're not usually so slow.'

'I'm sorry, Miss McQueen.' Jenny picked up a pen. It was a piece of malice on Lizzie's part, she thought as she worked; she had managed to forget Robert altogether, and now everything had come back to her, as vividly as though it had happened only yesterday instead of four years earlier . . .

Just before the threat of the coming war hardened into reality William Dalkieth, the owner of the shipyard and a man of great intelligence and ambition, had decided to send three carefully selected young employees to one of the yards in the North-East of England to learn more about shipbuilding for the eventual benefit of the Dalkieth yard.

Robert, one of the chosen three, had eagerly accepted

27

the offer. Sitting at the long, sloping desk, watching as one ink-stained hand held a ruler firmly in place and the other drew a blue line over the thick graph paper, she could hear his voice as clearly as though he, and not Maureen, was sitting on the neighbouring stool.

'If I stay here I'll be no more than an ordinary worker for the rest of my days. If I take this chance, who knows what could happen? We'll write to each other, Jen. It'll work out well for both of us, you'll see!'

There was one consolation – because of the work he was doing he was of value to the English yard and wasn't, to Jenny's relief, taken into the armed forces. But after six months his letters began to taper off. Then came the terrible day when he wrote to tell her that he wanted to marry an English girl he had met.

She had torn up all his letters then, put him out of her life and gone through the misery of knowing that everyone in the tenements and the Experimental Tank section knew that Jenny Gillespie had been jilted.

Eventually, the gossip had ended and somehow, she had survived.

3

In November a party was held in the big back court to celebrate the end of the war. Teeze got very drunk and tried to fight Mr Malloy then collapsed, and was carried upstairs by half a dozen men and slung into the alcove bed.

Before she went to her own bed Jenny stood at the narrow window in her room, brushing her long curly hair and looking out at the uneven pattern of lamplit windows on the other side of the court. Figures crossed and recrossed most of the windows, and she could hear the faint skirl of music, for the party had moved indoors, scattered through most of the tenement flats. With Maurice still missing, the Gillespies had little to celebrate, though Lottie had gone off with a group of revellers, leaving Jenny and Alice to put wee Helen to bed.

'Are you asleep?' Alice whispered through the bedroom door.

'No. Come on in.'

As Alice, barefooted and in her nightgown, a shawl wrapped around her shoulders, closed the door behind her the flame of the single candle in the room dipped and swayed. The moving light reflected brilliant colour from the mass of red and pink roses decorating a fat teapot on the orange box, the flowers seeming to move as though brushed by a summer breeze.

Alice perched on the edge of the bed. 'I couldn't sleep for Dad's snoring. That teapot's bonny, Jen.'

'It's for Miss McQueen. It's the first time she's ever asked me to decorate anything, so I wanted it to be specially good.' As a schoolgirl Jenny had learned the art of china painting from an elderly neighbour. She enjoyed the detailed work, which needed the same attention and precision as her job in the tracing office, and neighbours who couldn't afford to buy pretty china often bought pieces of plain white delft for her to decorate. She charged a nominal fee for her work, just enough to pay for the paints and brushes that she used.

'I wish I could paint like that,' Alice said wistfully. She knew better than to touch the teapot; it had to be left to dry, and then Jenny would bake it in the kitchen oven until the colours had set. 'Lizzie was fairly queening it at the party, wasn't she?' she added tartly. 'You'd have thought the whole thing was to celebrate her going off to Glasgow instead of the end of the war. Give me the brush.' She took charge of it and began to brush her sister's hair. 'You should've been able to go to Glasgow too, Jen, instead of being stuck here because of us. It's not fair – why did the war have to do this to us?'

'It's happened to thousands of folk. Even the Dalkieths lost Mr Edward in the fighting. Their money didnae protect him. When it came down to it, he was just the same as our Maurice.'

Her head bounced on the stem of her neck as Alice drew the brush again and again through her crackling hair. 'But Edward Dalkieth didnae leave responsibilities the way Maurice left us with Lottie and wee Helen. I'd not blame you,' said Alice fiercely, 'if you hated the lot of us for being so dependent on you. Lottie does nothing to help.' Her mouth, usually smiling, took on a downward droop. 'And it'll be almost a year yet before I'm old enough to leave school and get a job.'

Jenny took the brush back. 'You're going to stay on at school as long as you can. Maurice and me already decided that.'

'But that was before he— '

'Alice, you should still try for the scholarship to the Academy, the way Maurice wanted.'

'But the scholarship only covers the fees, not the uniform I'd have to wear, and mebbe the books as well.'

'We'll worry about that when the time comes. The first thing is to try for it. One day you're going to do better than any of us. You're going to get out of Ellerslie— '

'I don't want to, Jenny. I like Ellerslie.'

'At least you'll get out of this poky wee place and live in one of the grand houses— '

'With a garden and a drawing room and a maidservant?'

Jenny picked up a piece of wool and began to tie her hair back. '*Two* maidservants. And a carriage.' They slipped easily into the game they had played together for years and never tired of.

'No, a car,' Alice insisted. 'A big car, all gleaming and sleek. With a driver.'

'A handsome driver with black leather gloves— '

'I'll send him to fetch you for afternoon tea twice a week,' Alice offered grandly.

'I'll wear my furs and diamonds. But until I get them, lend me a bit of your shawl – I'm freezing.'

Alice giggled, and re-arranged the shawl so that they were both wrapped in it.

'That's better.' Jenny blew out the candle and they sat

31

in silence for a moment, looking out at the windows across the court.

'Jen,' Alice whispered at last, 'Shouldn't someone tell Mam that our Maurice's probably dead? Is it right to let her go on hoping?'

'Hoping's all she's got, pet. Let her hold on to it. She'll let go in her own good time.'

'But— ' Alice was stopped by a mighty yawn. Jenny began to unwrap herself from the shawl.

'Go to bed – and don't you fret about anything but yourself and your schoolwork.'

'Och, I can manage the work fine.' Alice stood up, adding wryly, 'Brains are all I've got.'

'Alice!'

'It's true – and I should know it because I'm the one with the brains. You're the pretty one of this family, and Bella's pretty too – or she was before Patrick got hurt. But me— ' Her hands gleamed in the light from the other windows as she indicated her sturdy body, her straight brown hair, her broad, freckled face. 'I'm brainy.'

When she was alone, Jenny got into bed. One by one the parties still going on in the crowded tenement flats came to an end, the revellers calling to each other as they crossed the dark courtyard on their way home, some laughing and some cursing as they stumbled over broken flagstones or walked into clothes-poles. The outer door opened and closed, marking Lottie's return.

Jenny fell asleep before the last of the lights in the windows opposite finally winked out.

The old year, the last year of the war that had brought heartbreak to almost every family in Ellerslie, died, and nobody mourned it. The womenfolk scoured and white-washed their homes as usual, to make sure they were clean for the start of the new year, and dumplings and rich, dark, fruity black buns were made for the New Year celebrations. There were fewer parties than usual, though, because so many of the tenement families were still in mourning for sons and brothers and husbands lost in the war.

1919 brought bitter winds that numbed the hands of the men working on the first peacetime ship in Dalkieth's yard. Teeze, searching for some way of gaining the stature he had lost when he had had to give up his trade, developed an interest in the problems faced by shipyard workers in general. Although trades unions were now commonplace on Clydeside none of the men who worked in the Dalkieth yard belonged to a union because it had always been the Dalkieth family's way to keep their employees informed of matters that concerned them, and to listen to grievances and deal with them at once.

But the war had changed many things. Men who had faced death defending their country were more determined than before to have their say. George Dalkieth, who now ran the yard, was a man who had never had the workers' respect, a man who was known for his lack of interest in anyone's opinions but his own. He was also a man who had stayed at home in safety while his brother and many of their employees fought in the front lines.

Since the war ended many of the Dalkieth workers had begun to feel that the time had come for the trades unions to represent their interest. A small group of men from the various sections in the yard fell, during that winter, into the habit of gathering in the Gillespie kitchen when the public houses closed, to talk about the business of the yard and argue over the changes that they felt were needed.

In the narrow streets by the river there was the usual outbreak of chest complaints, but at least they were spared the Spanish influenza that was still ravaging the country in the wake of the war.

'It's wary o' comin' here in case it catches somethin' worse than itsel',' someone said with a flash of irony one night in the Gillespie's flat.

A gust of laughter followed Jenny out into the hall when she went to answer yet another knock at the door. Daniel Young stepped into the hallway, muttering a greeting and dragging off his peaked cap. She stood back against the wall to let him pass; as she followed him into the kitchen she saw that the thin coat he wore was darkened over the shoulders with rain.

'Give me your coat, Daniel.' She took it from him and hung it up in the hall as Faith poured out a mug of strong black tea for him.

'Ye should have brought the laddie with ye, Daniel,' she said, lifting the condensed milk tin. Daniel stopped her with a raised hand.

'I'll have it as it is, Mrs Gillespie. The boy's got his schoolwork tae dae. He's fine on his lone.' The men gathered about the range eyed each other. Everyone knew of Daniel's burning ambition for his son, a clever boy who had never been allowed out to play with the other children. He took the tea with a nod of thanks and leaned against the high mantelshelf, as there were no more seats vacant. In contrast to the other men in the room, he was formally dressed in a neat shirt and a suit that looked as though it had been well brushed just before he came out. His straight dark brown hair was smooth against his skull and he wore a tie which was faded from many washings, but spotlessly clean. Even before he went off to join the Navy Daniel Young had been particular about his appearance. He went off to work each morning looking as though he was going to an office instead of a shipyard and he came back in the same neat condition at the end of the day. It was said that he visited the local public baths each afternoon before going home, to bathe himself and change out of his working clothes.

Jenny, who was working on a sugar bowl and milk jug to match the teapot she had painted for Miss McQueen, sat down at the table and picked up her paint-brush. Her gaze was drawn back to Daniel as she mixed more paint. He was talking with animation, using an index finger to underline the points he was making. His eyes glowed with enthusiasm and for once there was some colour in his thin face.

He glanced up suddenly and met Jenny's eyes. His voice faltered for a moment, then picked up as both of them looked hastily away as though caught committing some crime.

A discarded newspaper swept towards Jenny's ankles as she hurried down the street. It was a Saturday, and the week's work had just ended. She side-stepped out of the paper's reach then ducked in at the close, glad to be out of the cutting January wind that had scoured the street clear of the usual knots of men, women and children.

Coming up the stairs, she could smell the herring that they always had on Saturdays, dipped in oatmeal and fried with onions, then served with boiled potatoes.

In the warm kitchen Alice was setting the table for the midday meal while her mother attended to the pots on the range. Marion slept uneasily in one fireside chair and Teeze, home before Jenny, read his newspaper in the other, with Helen playing placidly between their feet.

'Jen!' Helen carolled the name joyfully as her aunt came into the kitchen. She scrambled up from the rag rug before the range, tipping herself on to her hands and knees, her round bottom sticking into the air, her face tense with concentration. She was fifteen months old now, and just learning to walk without holding on. Pushing down hard on her hands, she managed to rock skilfully on to her heels then, upright at last, she swayed for a moment before steadying herself and toddling across the floor.

'There's my clever girl!' Jenny lifted her, holding her close, burying her face in the silky-soft russet hair, then released her when Helen, who could rarely be still for a moment, squirmed to be set down again. The little girl toddled back to her rag doll, losing her balance at the last minute and collapsing on to the rug with a thump, tumbling first one way, against Teeze's ankles, then the other, brushing against Marion's stick-like legs.

'For Christ's sake, can a man no' get a bit of peace in his own house?' Teeze rustled the newspaper and scratched at one armpit. 'I'm surrounded by damned females!'

'Mind yer gran!' Faith Gillespie squalled at the same moment, rushing to move Helen six inches to the left, away from the old woman. Marion's body twitched as she woke suddenly, disturbed by the angry voices more than the bump she had received from Helen. She whimpered and struggled, and would have slid sideways if Jenny hadn't caught her shoulders.

'Come on, Gran, heave up a bit. That's better.'

Faith immediately brushed her daughter aside and

bent over the old woman. 'It's all right, Mam, I'm here. Ye're all right. We're get ye washed, will we, and then ye can have some broth. Alice, damp that cloth and hand it over here. Jenny, ladle some broth out for yer gran and yer dad.'

Marion Gillespie's bones had felt as brittle and delicate as a bird's; Jenny, watching her mother fussing around the old woman, recalled the way the colour had drained from Faith's face each time this same woman had marched into the house in the old days, her dark eyes cold, her back straight, her head, with its coronet of white hair beneath a black hat, held erect.

Marion had raised her son single-handed after her husband died young – possibly, quick-witted Alice claimed, his only way of escaping his wife – and from the day of Teeze's marriage she had done her best to make his wife's life miserable, visiting at least once a week, carping and fault-finding. Her domination had ended one day six months previously. While attending to a customer in the butcher's shop where she had worked since her husband's desertion she had paused, looked about her uncertainly, then dropped to the floor like a stone. She hadn't uttered an intelligible word since, or been able to do anything for herself. Faced with the shame of letting his mother go into the workhouse asylum, Teeze had had no option but to find a place for her in his own home. Having done his duty he ignored her, leaving her entirely to his wife.

Carefully, tenderly, Faith spooned broth into Marion, mopping at her chin between every mouthful. Alice fed Helen and Jenny saw to her father's needs, for Teeze never sat at the table for a meal, but stayed in his chair while his womenfolk danced attendance on him.

It wasn't until the rest of the family had been fed and

Helen and Marion washed and settled, the baby in her crib and Marion in her chair, that Faith and Alice and Jenny were able to sit down at the table for their own meal.

'Where's Lottie today?' Jenny wanted to know. When Faith shrugged she persisted, 'Is it not time she was staying in more, seeing to her own bairn?'

'For all the good she is, she's as well out of the way,' Faith said indifferently.

'But it's not right that she should be out enjoying herself instead of help— '

'Hold yer tongue or it's you that'll be out of here!' Teeze snapped.

'Aye, leave it, Jenny,' his wife said quietly. 'It's easier tae just see tae things myself than tae try tae make her dae them.'

Jenny, aware of the exhaustion on her mother's grey face and the way Faith pushed her food around the plate, too tired to eat it, subsided. But Lottie's laziness was beginning to rankle and, when the meal was over and the dishes washed and she had sketched some possible patterns for future china painting, she found that her annoyance over Lottie's selfishness made her too restless to concentrate on anything.

When Helen woke from her nap Jenny fetched the little girl's coat, noting as she pulled the buttons across Helen's tummy to meet the buttonholes that she would soon need a new one, then the two of them set out on a visit to Bella. It took some time to get as far as the close because Helen, proud of her new ability, insisted on going down the stairs on her own, one step at a time, clutching at the iron railings and breathing heavily in concentration.

Patrick was in bed and Bella washing clothes in the

38

small, stained sink. She wiped her hands on her sacking apron and drew the curtains that shut the alcove bed off from the rest of the room. 'He's had a bad day, poor soul.' She returned to her work, knuckling her hands round the collar of one of Patrick's shirts and rubbing hard.

'He's not the only one, by the look of you.' Jenny, peeling Helen out of her coat, eyed her sister with concern. 'Where did you get that bruise on your cheek?'

Bella bent her head quickly over the basin. It's only coal dust. I've just made up the fire.'

'Bella— ' Jenny began, then glanced at the curtained alcove. 'Come on out for a wee while. I've some things to get from the corner shop and you look as if you could do with a breath of air.'

Her sister finished scrubbing at the shirt and started to wring the water out of the heavy material. 'I'd best stay here. Pat might need me.' She shook the shirt out and hung it over the clothes-horse by the range.

'At least sit down and let me finish the washing for you. You look exhausted.'

'It's all right, I've only got my working skirt to do. You could mebbe unravel that for me.' Bella pointed, then paused to draw an arm across her face before returning to her work.

'That' was a man's jersey, shrunk and already coming apart at cuffs and waist. But the wool was good enough; all it needed was careful washing and drying and it could be used again.

'Mrs McColl gave it to me,' Bella explained as her sister picked up the jersey. 'She's awfy good tae me. She puts the word round her friends, and they pass their unwanted stuff tae her for me.'

'So she should be good tae you, you work hard

enough for her.' Bella spent one full day at week at Mrs McColl's big house, doing the heavy work. She also cleaned out Mr McColl's offices every Friday evening. Once, when the sisters were in the town together, Bella had pointed out Mrs McColl, a large well-dressed woman who looked far more able to do her own heavy work than thin little Bella.

'She pays me for what I do.'

'Not much.'

'It all helps. Don't you go criticisin' your elders and betters, Jenny Gillespie,' Bella said with a flash of spirit. She looked at Jenny. 'Ye're bein' awful nebby today.'

'I am not!'

'You're gettin' as bad as Miss Galbraith,' Bella teased, and they looked at each other and laughed. Miss Galbraith had been the terror of the local school when Bella and Jenny were pupils, an elderly woman with a permanent scowl and a voice that grated like a file on metal. Whenever one of the sisters tried to bully the other she was accused of becoming like Miss Galbraith.

'I wonder what happened to her?' Helen had settled down on the rug with a box of buttons. Jenny managed to locate an end of corrugated grey wool and started ripping at the jersey, winding the growing strand round her knuckles. 'You never think of what happens to your teachers outside of school do you? She's mebbe dead by now.'

Bella finished wringing out the skirt and spread it over the clothes-horse alongside Patrick's shirt, which had begun to steam gently in the heat from the range. The room smelled of wet clothes. 'If she is, she'll be giving them a hard time, wherever she ended up.'

As the dirty water gurgled noisily down the drain she dried her hands and arms and came to sit by the range, lowering herself into the chair carefully, as though she was an old woman with creaking bones. Helen immediately fisted her small hands over the legs of the chair and hauled herself upright, arms outstretched. Bella lifted her up and cuddled her, burying her face in the baby's rich red hair.

Lottie came into Jenny's mind, young and strong, drifting through life with never a thought for anyone else, even her own daughter or her missing lover, while Bella uncomplainingly worked herself into exhaustion for the sake of a man who had been damaged and embittered by the war.

'Her hair might be like Lottie's, but her face is that like our Maurice's,' Bella said over Helen's shoulder, her blue-grey eyes wistful. 'Lottie's lucky, having such a bonny bairn.'

'You're young yet, Bella, you'll have bairns of your own.'

'It takes love tae make bairns – an' money tae raise them,' Bella said almost inaudibly. The light from the window made the bruise on her cheek more noticeable, and Jenny felt a stab of helpless anger. Bella was a gentle soul who wouldn't harm a fly. It was wrong of Patrick to take his frustration out on his wife, she thought, but she had the sense to hold her tongue. Her interference would only upset Bella further. 'I got a letter yesterday from Lizzie,' she said instead.

'How is she?'

'If she's to be believed, Neilson's Emporium's as near as anyone'll get to heaven on earth.'

Her sister's small rough hand, still damp from the washing, reached over and touched her own.

'I'm vexed for you, Jenny. You should be in Glasgow too, away from all this worry.'

41

'Och, life was never meant to be a bed of roses for the likes of us. We're used tae disappointments.'

'You've had more than your share. First Robert, then— '

'Robert was a long time ago,' Jenny said sharply.

Bella stared at her sister over Helen's head. 'You sound different.' She leaned forward a little, then said, 'You look different. I've noticed it ever since we heard about Maurice. Harder, somehow.'

Jenny hauled viciously at the wool in her lap. 'Is it any wonder? Bella, if you hear of any other cleaners needed, let me know.'

'Ye're surely not thinking of givin' up workin' in the Tank, are ye?'

'It's not for me, it's for Lottie.'

Bella gave a yelp of laughter, a rare sound these days, '*Lottie?* I can just see her down on her knees scrubbin' floors!'

'It's time she earned her keep, and the bairn's. She can't expect tae sit around the house eating food bought with someone else's wages. I've tried hinting that she should think of finding work, but it does no good. She just ignores me and goes her own way. But now things'll have tae change whether she likes it or not,' said Jenny with determination.

'Is that what Dad says?'

'Him? He doesnae fret himself about how we're all tae live. He leaves that tae poor Mam – and she's too worn out tae take Lottie on. Bella – with Dad not earning so much now it's my wages that's making the difference at home. I don't mind supporting Helen and Gran, for they're helpless. But Lottie's well able to work. It's time she was doing her share.'

'Once Alice is old enough to leave school it'll be a help.'

'Alice should try for a scholarship in the spring. She could go on to the Academy – be a teacher, mebbe. She needs to get her chance – she's the clever one of the family.'

'So was Maurice.'

'Not clever enough tae keep himself frae gettin' killed.' Jenny picked carefully at a snarl in the wool. 'You'll let me know if you hear of any job that Lottie could do?'

'Aye.' Bella reluctantly began to loosen her arms from about Helen's warm little body. 'I'll make a wee cup of tea.'

Jenny put the shrunken jersey aside and stood up. 'No, I'll do it. I sit on my backside for most of the day.' She carefully measured a small amount of tea-leaves from the caddy then hoisted the kettle from the range and poured boiling water over them. 'You do more than you're fit for.'

They had kept their voices low, but even so Patrick Kerr, wide awake behind the thin curtain that hid him from their gaze, heard everything. He squeezed his eyes tight shut against the memory of the terror in Bella's eyes earlier, just before his fist had connected with her cheekbone, and against the frightening rage that had mauled him mercilessly over the past months.

But the anger still managed to force itself to the fore, filling his head, flooding the darkness behind his eyelids with a crimson glare.

4

Isobel Dalkieth stood in the big bay window of her drawing room. Although it was night outside and the room behind her was brightly lit by electricity the heavy blue velvet curtains were open and the dark window acted like a mirror, reflecting Isobel herself, straight-backed and handsome in unrelieved mourning black that would have overwhelmed most women but only served to complement her white hair, fine skin and clear green eyes. She looked past herself into the night, picturing in her mind's eye the terrace, the sloping lawn and the river beyond.

Like some of their own employees, the Dalkieths lived on the opposite side of the river from the main town, though in their case the surroundings were much more affluent. Isobel could see lights twinkling on the other side of the river and reflecting on the water; electric lights on the upper slopes where the wealthier townspeople lived, gas lamps nearest the shore where the tenements crowded together. She turned her head towards one of the side windows from where, by day, the bend of the river and a glimpse of the cranes and stocks of the Dalkieth yard could be seen.

'Here's to the first peacetime vessel in the yard, and a new beginning.' Fergus Craig, a quarry-owner, a member of the Dalkieth Board of Directors, and Isobel's brother, came to stand by her side. The window reflected him as an imposing man, also silver-headed, and tall enough to hold the extra weight brought upon him by increasing age and comfortable living.

Isobel accepted the glass he offered and sipped at her malt whisky appreciatively. She had never been one for wines. 'A poor beginning, Fergus.'

'Surely not. The order book's filled and the future looks secure. With the war behind us at last there's a new prosperity ahead.'

'With wages higher than they've ever been, and the spirit of anarchy in the country? Nothing'll ever be the same, or as good as before, you mark my words.'

There was a sudden pattering against the window as a shower of February rain slashed across the glass, distorting the lights opposite. Isobel shivered and turned back into the comfortable room as Fergus put his own glass down and drew the curtains together. 'It's natural for you to be in low spirits after what you've been through these past few years, my dear. But things'll change – and for the better.'

'Not for me. I've lost the best of them, Fergus. First my husband, then my son. George should have been the one to go to war.' Isobel's voice was harsh. 'But no, he insisted on staying behind to look after the yard when his father became too ill to oversee things himself.' She sank on to one of the two velvet-covered sofas flanking the fireplace. 'No matter that Edward was the better master. George was set on saving his own skin – and now he's all I've got left, God help me.'

'You're too hard on the boy. I remember a time when George was your favourite.'

Isobel shrugged impatiently. 'Edward was born to follow his father into the business, but George was mine, my little one. He wasn't raised for responsibility. That's the trouble, now that he's the only one left.'

'It may be the making of him.'

'Or the ruination of the yard. If I'd only known what was going to happen, Fergus.' Isobel stared into the flames. Her father, a quarry-owner, had himself been a director of Dalkieth's shipyard, and it had delighted him and the Dalkieths when Isobel and William Dalkieth married. Her ambition had matched her husband's and it had been a good marriage, a true partnership, until William's death from heart trouble only months before his elder son Edward was killed in France. Now, Isobel looked ahead and saw a bleak future for the shipyard that had meant so much to her husband.

'I will *not* let George destroy the yard, Fergus. Not after all that William and Edward did for it!'

'Then do as I suggest – as William himself would suggest. Bring young Archer back from Tyneside. Make him the office manager so that he and George will have to work in tandem and George won't get everything his own way.'

'But he's the youngest of the men William sent south; too young, surely, to take on such responsibility,' she protested.

'He's the only one available,' her brother pointed out. 'Grey died in an accident and McGarrity has no wish now to come back to Scotland, but Archer's willing. Sometimes age has little to do with it. William kept a close eye on the lad when he sent him to England, and I've continued to do so. He's learned a lot and given a good account of himself – and he's hungry for success.'

A frown tucked Isobel's finely shaped brows together. 'He's the same age as George.'

'But more – mature. Archer's had to make his own way in life, and he's done it with confidence.'

46

'I'll grant you that it would be good to have a man we could trust in the place. A man who'd look after our interests until such time as George matures – if he ever does.' Isobel took another swallow of whisky, then said, 'My real hope, I suppose, is that this new wife of his'll give him an heir, a boy I can train to take his grandfather's place. In the meantime, I must make sure that there's still a yard for such a boy to inherit.'

Fergus Craig eyed his sister warily. He had always been a little afraid of Isobel's iron-clad determination, which verged at times on ruthlessness. Though he himself had little time for his nephew George he was sorry for both the young man and his wife. Isobel set standards that few people could live up to. 'I'm sure that George will provide you with many heirs.'

'I sincerely hope so,' she retorted tartly. 'After going through the embarrassment of his divorce I deserve some compensation! Thank God his father wasn't alive to suffer the shame of it. But then, if William had still been alive, George and Catherine would never have been allowed to contemplate divorce.' She swirled the remains of her drink round in the glass, then asked, 'What d'you make of my new daughter-in-law, Fergus?'

'She seems suitable. I hope that George finds happiness this time.'

'Catherine was never the right woman for him. Her people had a lot of money, and that mattered to George far more than it should have. Fiona comes from more ordinary stock and she has a lot to learn, but at least she's got ambition, far more of it than George has. Harnessed properly, it could be put to good use. She may become an asset – if,' Isobel Dalkieth added slowly, 'she plays her cards well.'

The rain-shower returned to throw itself against the

47

windows again. Craig, eyeing his sister, judged that it was time to guide her thoughts back to the matter at the forefront of his own mind. He seated himself opposite her and leaned forward, elbows on thighs.

'About young Archer— ' he began.

'Me? Go out scrubbin' other folks' floors?' Lottie's voice was outraged. 'I'll do no such thing!'

'Then you'll have to find yourself something more suited,' Jenny told her. 'I'm not going to go on working to support the likes of you when you're well able to bring in a wage.'

'Hoity toity – just listen tae her!' the other girl mocked, throwing a glance at Faith, who clattered dishes in the sink, carefully keeping out of the confrontation.

'I'm tired of the way you just do as you please in this house without putting a penny into it, Lottie.'

'It's not my fault Maurice was killed,' Lottie said sullenly, 'If he'd come home— '

'Our Maurice hasnae been killed!' Faith spun round from the sink, eyes blazing. 'He's missing, that's all. He'll be on his way home now that the war's over – he'll be here soon.'

'We know that, Mam,' Jenny told her levelly. 'But until he does come home we need more money now that Dad's not earning what he used to. I'm making almost as much as he is now.'

And all my wage goes into the house, while he drinks most of what he does earn, she thought, but such things couldn't be spoken aloud in her mother's presence. Only Faith had the right to criticise her man's drinking, nobody else.

Alice came through from the bedroom where she had been studying. 'What's going on?'

'Nothing. We're just sorting a few things out, aren't we, Lottie?'

'Aye, well, if I must work it'll not be scrubbin' the floors under other folks' feet,' Lottie sulked. 'I'll find somethin' better.'

'You do that. If you don't, I'll go ahead and find something for you. And there's another thing,' Jenny went on relentlessly, 'I'm going to move into the big bedroom with you and Helen. Alice'll have the wee room, so that she can get on with her homework in peace.'

'I'm not sharin' a room wi' you!'

'Then you can find somewhere else to sleep.'

'But it's not fair on you, Jenny,' Alice protested 'I can manage fine.'

'You need peace to get on with your work. You need that wee room more than I do. And don't forget,' Jenny turned back to Lottie, 'if you haven't found work by the end of the week I'll find it for you.'

'Are you goin' tae allow her tae order us all about like that?' Lottie appealed to Faith. 'Next thing you know she'll be puttin' her old grandmother out in the street because she cannae earn her own keep.'

Faith picked up a shabby piece of towelling and began to dry her hands. 'Jenny's right. It's her wage that's keepin' us alive.'

Avoiding Jenny's eye, she shuffled in her down-at-heel slippers to tuck the blanket more securely round her mother-in-law's knees. 'Things have changed,' she said quietly. 'They've changed for all of us.'

Lottie flounced out in a rage and Jenny, inwardly shaking, went to the tiny room she had just given over to Alice. She sat down on the bed and began to pull the pins out of her hair, looking around at the claustrophobic, damp-stained walls as she worked, close to tears at the thought of having to give up her privacy and share a bed with Lottie.

Alice tapped at the door and came in, subdued. 'Jen, I can't take your room away from you.'

'Of course you can, it's all decided. We'll change over tomorrow – and not another word.' She began to comb her hair, then tutted with annoyance as the comb tangled in it.

'It's because it's curly,' Alice took the comb and began to ease it through her sister's tumbled dark-brown curls.

'Why can't it be straight, like yours?'

'Curls are better.'

'They're not.' Jenny took a handful of hair and tugged at it. Then, struck by a sudden thought, she bounced to her feet. The comb, pulled from Alice's hand and still caught in her hair, hit off her cheek as she knelt down to rummage beneath the bed, bringing out a tin box. She opened it, and produced the scissors she used for dress-making.

'Alice, I want you to cut my hair.'

'What? I can't do that!'

'Then I'll do it myself.' Jenny pushed her sister aside so that she could see herself in the room's small mirror.

'Jenny – what'll Mam say?'

'I doubt if Mam'll even have the time to notice. Anyway, it's my hair, not hers, and I can't be bothered pinning it up any more. It'd be easier to look after if there was less of it.'

Alice had one last try. 'You've got such bonny hair – it's a crime to cut it.'

Jenny pulled the comb free and tossed it on to the orange box, remembering, with a stab of pain, a night years before, just before Robert Archer left for England.

She remembered the wind rustling the leaves overhead, the lumpiness of the ground beneath her shoulders, Robert's hand loosening her hair, drawing it over her shoulders. She remembered the touch of his knuckles against her neck, the husky note in his voice. 'You've got such bonny hair, Jenny. Promise me that you'll never ever let anyone cut it off.'

'It's a crime to waste the time I have to waste on it every day, when there are other things to do,' she said now to Alice, and took a firm grip on a clump of hair, discovering how difficult it was to tell by her own reflection where she should position the scissors.

'Wait – I'll do it, if you insist,' Alice took the scissors from her. 'You'll only chop it and make yourself look ugly. Now— '

She turned Jenny's head to one side, selected a lock of hair, and began to cut. 'I just hope you won't regret it when it's too late.'

The noise of the scissors biting their way through her hair crunched in Jenny's ear. A dark curl fell to her hand and from there to the floor.

'I'll not regret it,' she said steadily. 'Times change, folk change. I'm different now, Alice, and it's time I looked different.'

Lottie sulked and pouted until the last moment, then found a job as a barmaid in a public house two streets away.

'It means I'll no' be here tae see tae the bairn at nights,' she pointed out triumphantly.

'I'll see tae her,' Jenny said, and added, catching and holding Lottie's gaze with her own, 'I usually do in any case.'

True to her word, she had changed rooms with Alice,

51

and now slept in the larger room, which reeked of damp and stale sweat and Lottie's cheap perfume. Alice, thrilled at having a place of her own to study in, had squeezed another orange box into her new room to use as a desk.

Jenny now had to keep all her possessions under the bed in boxes and bags, because Lottie's things were strewn about the small room; there were long red hairs each morning on both pillows of the bed they shared, and in little tangled clumps on the floor where they had been carelessly dropped after being pulled from the other girl's unwashed brush and comb. Gathering them up each day and carrying them into the kitchen to throw them on the range Jenny was glad that at least her own hair was now short and easy to keep clean and neat.

At the end of Lottie's first week at work there was another confrontation when she came in after everyone else had gone to sleep to find Jenny still awake in the bedroom.

'I'm waiting for your wages.'

Lottie glared, then said truculently, 'I'm no' givin' my money tae you.'

Jenny held her hand out. 'If you give it to Dad he'll only drink it instead of using it to pay the rent and buy food.'

'I'll give it tae yer Mam mysel', then.'

'No, I'll give it to her, since it was me that saw to it that you started earning your own keep,' Jenny said, and waited, her hand out, until Lottie sullenly handed over the money. Jenny pushed it around her palm with a forefinger. 'There's a shilling short here.'

'Four shillin's, that's all I get paid.'

'I went into the public house yesterday and asked the landlord. He says it's five. It's not Mam you're dealing with now, it's me,' Jenny went on as Lottie's mouth dragged itself into an ugly square.

'Ye're a right bitch, Jenny Gillespie!'

'Mebbe so, but I'll still have that other shillin' out of you.'

'How am I tae manage if I give ye all my wages?' Lottie whined, and Helen stirred in her shabby cot then settled again, thumb in mouth.

'You get tips from some of the customers. Think yourself lucky I don't take them, too,' Jenny retorted heartlessly. When Lottie had handed over the missing shilling she tucked the coins into a small purse, which she put beneath her pillow.

She gave the money to her mother the next morning and Faith took it without a word. Subtly, the balance of power had shifted in the crowded house. It was a small victory that gave Jenny little pleasure but, nevertheless, it was a victory.

The real battle came the following week, when Lottie deliberately handed her second week's wages to Jenny in front of Teeze, who was slouched in his usual chair. Soon he would take himself off to the pub and his wife and daughters would start on the ritual of the Friday night cleaning.

'The money's all there, just as you wanted,' Lottie said loudly, with a sly, sidelong glance at Teeze. His head came up with a jerk and Faith, spooning some left-over custard into Marion's slack mouth, mopping the resulting trickles with a well-stained cloth, let the spoon clatter back into the bowl, her eyes anxiously darting from her daughter to her husband.

'What's she givin' her wage tae you for?'

Jenny looked her father in the eye. 'Because I told her to.'

'Here, give it tae me.' He held out a large hand, scarred from a lifetime of working on the ships.

Jenny shook her head. 'The rent man'll be coming tonight and I want to make sure he gets what's due to him. Then the rest'll go to Mam. You'd not want to see us all thrown out on the street, would you?'

'That's my business, no' yours!'

'Jenny says it's hers,' Lottie put in, swaying over to the sideboard to study herself in the mirror.

'Hers? Since when did you run this family, madam?'

'With you not earning so much and Maurice not here I'm bringing in a fair amount of the money,' Jenny told him levelly. 'I'm going to make sure it goes where it's needed.'

The newspaper Teeze had been reading was thrown to the floor. 'I said give it tae me!'

'So's you can spend it in the pub?'

His eyes took on a familiar red glow and he lurched out of the chair, one hand beginning to swing up. 'Ye cheeky wee— '

Helen began to whimper and Alice snatched her up and held her close, her own eyes round with apprehension.

'Teeze, don't!' Faith put the bowl down and jumped up, catching at her husband's sleeve. With a growl, he pushed her away.

'Stop it, Dad!' Jenny's knees were weak with fear and the anticipation of the heavy blow, but she knew that the only way to save herself was to stand up to him. She forced back the memory of past beatings and took a step towards him although her instincts clamoured for retreat. 'We're both too old for that now. Hit me, and I'll hit you back.'

'By God an' ye'll no'!'

'I will. I mean it!'

His arm began to lower in sheer surprise. 'Lift a hand tae yer faither, milady, an' ye're oot o' this hoose,' he blustered.

'If you want me out I'll go, with pleasure. But I'll take all of my wages with me. How are you going to keep yourself and the rest of them out of the workhouse on what you're earning now – let alone keep the pub going?'

'Jenny!' Faith moved to stand in front of her husband, her tired face twisted with anger. 'Don't you dare talk tae your father like that in his own house! It's not his fault he had tae give up working in the fitting bay.'

'I know it's not – but it's happened, and now it's my wage that's mostly keeping us,' Jenny said mercilessly. 'So it's up tae me tae make sure there's money for the rent and the food from now on.'

Teeze's face, already red with anger, seemed to swell and throb as though it was going to burst. For a moment Jenny thought that she had gone too far and that her father was going to take a seizure, then, with a snarl he pushed his wife away from him so hard that she stumbled against Jenny, who had to catch her. He snatched up his shabby jacket and slammed out of the house, leaving a shocked silence behind him.

'Are ye satisfied now?' Faith asked her elder daughter at last. 'Did ye enjoy humblin' the man in front of everyone?'

'Mam, if he got hold of Lottie's wages you know he'd only drink the money away.'

'One day you'll be old an' past bein' able tae work as hard as ye once did. See how ye feel about it then!' There were tears in Faith's eyes.

Jenny picked up the bowl as her grandmother whimpered and pawed fretfully at the air. She dipped the spoon into the custard then Faith's hands wrenched bowl and spoon away from her, spattering the two of them.

'I'll see tae yer gran,' she said with quiet dignity. 'Ye'll not take everythin' intae your own hands – not yet. Ye can get on with yer work. And so can you two,' she added to Lottie and Alice.

'I've got my own work tae go tae,' Lottie said, and flounced out. Jenny fetched the tin of black-lead and the brush from the bottom of the cupboard and began to work on the range while Alice poured the last dregs from the teapot into the special enamel mug Jenny had decorated with bright flowers and fat, cheerful elves when Helen was born. She diluted the tea with warm water from the kettle, stirred in a spoonful of sugar and a spoonful of condensed milk, and handed it to the little girl, who received it in eager hands. Then Alice tipped hot water from the big kettle into the basin and started washing the good plates, those that were kept on show on the range of shelves on the dresser and only used for special occasions. Helen, well used to the Friday night ritual, retired out of harm's way underneath the table with her dolly and her mug.

When she had finished attending to Marion, Faith turned her attention to cleaning the sideboard. Nobody else was allowed to touch Maurice's photograph; each day she dusted it, and on Fridays it was thoroughly polished. A jug that Jenny had once decorated sat by the side of the photograph at all times, filled with bright paper flowers. The sideboard now had the look of a shrine.

'Why don't you sit down, Mam, and have a rest for once?' Jenny suggested, but the proferred olive branch was spurned.

'The day I'm no' able tae see tae my own house is the

day you can turn me out,' Faith snapped, and got on with her work. Marion, her fingers picking continually at a hole in the rug across her wasted legs, watched the activity going on about her with vacant eyes.

Throughout the warren of tenements the same routine of cleaning and scrubbing was going on. Although it was early March and dark outside, the sound of voices floated up from the courtyard, where women and children, working in the lights from the surrounding windows, were hanging up rugs and carpets so that the week's dust could be beaten out of them. Anyone who neglected her Friday cleaning was considered by her neighbours to be a dirty slut. Even the children had their own tasks, depending on their age and ability. Only the men were exempt from the Friday night cleaning as it was considered that they worked hard enough all week to support their families and were entitled to do as they wished during their time away from the shipyard. The fact that the womenfolk worked just as hard, some with outside jobs as well as families and homes to see to, was ignored.

When Jenny had finished with the range she was glad to escape with Alice to the back yard where they hung up the rugs on their washing line and took turns thumping the dust out of them.

'She did it on purpose – Lottie,' Alice said breathlessly as she wielded the carpet beater. 'She gave you the money in front of Dad just tae start a row.'

'She didnae win, though.'

'Not for the want of trying,' Alice said, but Jenny's attention had been caught by a lone figure struggling to hang a carpet over a rope at the other side of the court.

'Is that not Walter Young? He'll never be able tae handle that carpet on his own. I wonder where his father is?'

Since his wife's death Daniel Young had taken over all her housekeeping duties, even the Friday night work. Every week he and Walter were to be seen polishing windows and beating carpets, and Bella had told Jenny that Daniel even took his turn of cleaning the stairs and the communal privy.

'It doesnae seem right for a man tae have tae take on all that extra work after puttin' in a day in the yard,' Bella had said, her small face screwed up with concern. 'I've offered tae dae it, but he'll no' let anyone else help him.'

Walter's carpet, Jenny noticed, was getting the better of the struggle; with a brief word to Alice she hurried across the courtyard to help the boy. Between them they subdued the carpet and got it on to the line.

'Have you got more to bring out?' Jenny asked.

'Just the one from my room, and a wee rug.' The boy's face was flushed from embarrassment as much as from the struggle.

Jenny picked up the carpet beater. 'I'll start on this one and you can bring the others. Go on,' she said briskly when the boy hesitated, and he ducked his head and did as he was told.

'Is your father not here to help you tonight?' she asked when the other carpet and a smaller rug had been hung over the rope and she had relinquished the beater to Walter. At her urging he had rolled his shirt-sleeves up, revealing pale and stick-like arms. Daniel and his son were always immaculately dressed, and never usually had their shirt-sleeves unfastened, no matter how hot the weather may be.

'His head's awful bad. It happens sometimes, he'll be all right in the morning.'

'I'll help you to carry your carpets in,' she said when

they had finished, adding, as Walter started to protest, 'I'll tell you what – you help me and Alice upstairs with our rugs first, then we'll help you with yours in return. That's fair, isn't it?' She took his arm and led him across the yard, weaving around groups of women taking a moment to gossip and rest before getting on with their work.

Faith had swept the floors and was washing the cracked and faded linoleum when Jenny and Alice and Walter arrived. They stacked the rolled rugs on the landing, ready to be laid once the floors had dried, then went back downstairs to attend to the Youngs' carpets.

The two girls carried the large carpet between them while Walter hurried ahead with a rug under each arm. He erupted back out of the flat as they reached the door. 'I can manage fine now,' he started to say, but Jenny marched past him. 'We'll help you to lay the carpet.'

Daniel Young, his face ashen, his eyes dark shadows, sat on the edge of the wall bed. As Jenny and Alice edged into the room, the rolled carpet between them, he leapt to his feet, a duster falling from one hand, a brass candlestick clanging from the other. He made an involuntary move to pick them up then stopped short, clutching at his head.

'Lie down, man! You look like death warmed up.' Jenny dropped her end of the carpet and pushed him back on to the bed then gathered up the cloth and candlestick. 'Just sit still for a minute while we get this carpet down. Alice, you and Walter take that end and I'll unroll it— '

The room smelled of polish and black-lead and disinfectant. The few pieces of furniture had been pushed back against the walls in order to remove the carpet and wash the floor; all were glossy with care. Daniel Young's house didn't suffer from neglect even though there was no woman in it.

When the carpet and furniture were back in place Jenny plumped up the cushion on one of the two fireside chairs and went over to the bed. 'Come and sit down here, Daniel, and Walter can make you a cup of tea.' She looped her arm about him with an ease born of caring for her grandmother and helped him to his feet. His body was wiry beneath her touch, the muscles tense. 'Alice, you'd best go back and tell Mam I'll not be long. D'you get headaches often, Daniel?'

As Alice left, Daniel started to shake his head then thought better of it. 'Never like this. It's as though every bone in my face was aching like a rotten tooth.' His voice was muffled and he held his head in his hands as though frightened that it was going to fall off.

Walter was already pouring water into the teapot from the kettle that all the tenement dwellers kept simmering on the range. Jenny stopped him as he went to the sink to refill the kettle. 'Put some hot water into a basin first – this one'll do. Have you got a clean bit of cloth?'

She added a little cold water from the tap then tested the temperature with the tip of a finger. It was stingingly hot, but her hands could take it. She dipped the cloth into the bowl as Walter poured cups of strong tea then wringing it out she formed it into a pad. 'This is hot, but it'll help you.' She pressed the wadded cloth over Daniel's forehead and heard him draw in his breath with a faint hiss as the heat touched his skin.

'Hold that in place for a while, and don't talk,' she instructed, then blew on her tingling fingers before taking the cup Walter was holding out to her. She seated herself on the other fireside chair with a reassuring smile for the boy, who perched on the edge of one of the four upright chairs set round the table. He managed a nervous grimace in return.

Sipping at her tea, Jenny listened to the measured ticking of the clock and the sound of voices from outside, taking in the room in a series of casual glances. A landscape hung on one wall, and there were some ornaments around, including a china figurine and the pair of candlesticks Daniel had been polishing. On the dresser stood a photograph of Daniel in uniform, and another of him and his wife, their young faces solemn, Mrs Young seated, Daniel standing with one hand resting possessively, yet formally, on her shoulder.

Jenny remembered Molly Young only vaguely, for the woman hadn't mixed with her neighbours. The Youngs had always kept themselves to themselves, so much so that Bella was convinced that Molly might have been saved if only she had been able to bring herself to ask for help before it was too late. She had died of pneumonia about fifteen months earlier; Daniel, at sea at the time, had arrived home far too late for her funeral. The neighbours had scraped together what money they could spare to give the woman a decent funeral, for the tenement people believed in looking after their own, even those who hadn't mixed with them, and Bella had taken Walter in and cared for him until his father took over.

Daniel's breath hissed out in a tiny sigh of relief, and Jenny saw that he was sitting back more comfortably in his chair, his body relaxed.

'How do you feel now?' She took the mug from his hand and refilled it.

'It's getting better,' he said through lips that had

61

begun to regain some of their colour. His eyes were still closed; when she took his hand in hers and clasped his fingers round the mug the lids flew open and he stared up at her. She had never realised that Daniel's eyes were so dark, or, she thought when he swiftly glanced down at the mug, away from her, that his lashes were so long.

'Walter, away through and finish off your own room,' Daniel ordered, adding in embarrassment as his son went out, 'I wasnae able tae manage it. And now I'm taking up too much of your time.'

Jenny took her empty cup, and Walter's, to the sink. 'To tell the truth, it's nice to be away from the rest of them for a few minutes. There's times when they feel like an awful responsibility.'

'It's a shame that Teeze had tae take the pneumonia so bad. He was a good worker.' His words did more than anything else to make her feel ashamed of the way she had spoken to her father earlier. 'Leave the cups be, I'll see tae them.'

'I might as well rinse them through,' Jenny began, then stopped as his hand landed on her arm and she was firmly but gently drawn back from the sink.

'Ye've enough to do,' said Daniel evenly, one hand still clasping the cloth pad to his face, 'I'll not have ye runnin' after me an' Walter as well.'

She was glad to see that he looked and sounded stronger. 'I'll get back home, then. I don't want to leave Mam and Alice with all the work.'

'Aye,' said Daniel, adding awkwardly, 'Thank you for your kindness.'

As she went through the close and back into the courtyard she knew, without looking back, that he was standing in the doorway. She could feel the intensity of his gaze between her shoulder-blades.

5

On the stocks the first peacetime ship to be built in the Dalkieth yard for four years, a passenger steamer for a Far East company, was taking shape. Other vessels filled the slips, and the Experimental Tank was kept busy, as shipowners who had had to wait for pre-war orders to be filled or were anxious to replace tonnage either grown old during the war or sunk in battle clamoured for new stock.

Though there was still no word of Maurice, Faith Gillespie refused to give up hope. She devoted more and more time to her mother-in-law, and Jenny began to hurry home during her dinner hour in order to help with Helen and Marion. Lizzie still wrote now and again, telling of the wonderful new life she was leading in Glasgow, each letter finishing with words of sympathy for Jenny, stuck in Ellerslie.

Patrick became more and more withdrawn, reminding Jenny of a coiled spring that might, if it was triggered, lash out in all directions. Bella continued to maintain that the bruises she bore now and then were caused by her own carelessness, walking into a door, or tripping on the dimly lit stairs.

Sometimes Daniel Young was in the Kerr's single room when Jenny called, talking to Patrick about this and that, touching on each subject without digging too deeply, chatting easily without waiting for a reply. On these occasions Patrick seemed a little easier, even contributing some conversation himself, but as soon as the other man left he retired into his shell.

'He used to be so full of fun,' Alice said one evening when the sisters were walking home after a visit to Bella. 'I was jealous of Bella, being loved by someone like him, but now – it breaks my heart to see his unhappiness.' Her hand, through Jenny's arm, tightened. 'What if he's like that for the rest of his life? How'll Bella stand it?'

'Don't think about it, pet. We'll just have to take one day at a time and hope for the best.'

'Hoping's like wishing on stars – it's not going to change things,' Alice's voice trembled. 'Pat and Bella need more than hope.'

A gas light at the other end of the street flickered on, spreading a warm gold pool over the uneven and cracked paving stones below. The lamplighter with his long pole was a shadow in the gathering darkness, leaving the lamp and moving across the street. As another lamp burst into light Jenny threaded an arm round her sister's solid waist.

'Let's have a three-legged race,' she said on a sudden impulse, then, without waiting for Alice's reaction, 'One, two, three – go!'

Passers-by stared and some clucked their tongues at the rowdiness of youth as the sisters barged along the street, tightly linked, lurching on the cobbles, giggling breathlessly, their inner ankles fastened together by an invisible thong.

'That's the way, lassies!' the lamplighter called cheerily as they swung past him. They could hear his rusty laughter fading behind them as they swung round the corner, jostling in and out of the puddles of light, managing to keep the pace going until they reached their own close. There, they fell away from each other, laughing, leaning against the stone walls, dragging in deep breaths of night air before, at a more sedate pace, they went upstairs, Alice in the lead.

Someone else entered the close below and began to climb, taking the stairs two at a time. As they reached their own door and Alice put her hand on the latch a voice from the half-landing spoke Jenny's name.

Alice turned sharply at the sound but Jenny froze, staring at the scratched door panels without seeing them. She didn't need to look round; she knew that voice, would always have known it, anywhere.

'Jenny?' the man on the stairs said again, beginning to climb the final flight. Looking at her sister, seeing the shock on Alice's face, Jenny knew that it wasn't a dream. He was really there.

'I'll – I'll tell Mam we've got a visitor,' Alice said on a rush of words and slid into the house as Jenny finally turned, her body feeling strangely stiff so that she had to pivot round on her feet, shifting from heel to toe, heel to toe, until she was finally facing him.

He had reached the top step and was close to her by that time, older, better dressed, more assured, yet still the same.

'Hello, Jenny.' Robert Archer held a hand out to her, taking off his curly-brimmed bowler hat with the other hand. 'You're looking bonny.'

His grip was firm, dispelling her final doubt that he was really there, instead of down in Tyneside where he now belonged.

'You're staring at me as if I was a ghost,' he said, his square face breaking into a grin that showed the chipped front tooth which had always seemed endearing to her.

'I – I didnae expect to see you back here.' She had feared that her voice was going to fail her, but it didn't, though it shook a little.

'Bad pennies aye come back, did you not know that?' His eyes flickered beyond her to the open door. 'Are you not going to invite me in, then?'

The kitchen was a flurry of activity, with Faith and Alice darting about, scooping up toys and clothing. They stopped short when the door opened, their arms filled, their faces as guilty as if they had been caught robbing the place. Robert walked in as though he had been there only the day before.

'Mrs Gillespie, it's good to see you again.'

At the sound of his voice Faith's face wavered. For a moment Jenny thought that her mother was going to burst into tears, then a tremulous smile broke through and, thrusting a rag doll and a tattered basket of mending at Alice, who already had her arms filled, Faith took both Robert's hands in hers.

'My, ye're a sight for sore eyes, laddie! What are ye doin' back in Ellerslie? Ye'll have a cup of tea – Jenny, put the cups out. Take off yer coat, man, and sit yersel' down— ' In a flurry of words she led him to Teeze's chair and waited while he took off his thick topcoat. Taking it from him, folding it in her arms, she asked, 'Ye'll have heard about our Maurice?'

It was then that Jenny, taking off her own jacket and fetching the cups, realised why her mother was so pleased to see Robert in spite of the way he had jilted her daughter. He had been Maurice's best friend, and seeing him again was reassuring. If Robert could return to Ellerslie, so could Maurice.

'Aye, I heard.' His face was suddenly sombre. 'I'd have written, but I didnae know what to say.'

'He's only missing, not dead,' Faith told him hurriedly, putting his coat over the back of a chair and fetching the picture from the sideboard. 'He'll be back home before we know it.' According him a rare honour, she handed the photograph to Robert, who shot a swift glance at Jenny before taking the frame into his capable hands.

'Aye, I'm sure he will, Mrs Gillespie. Maurice was always one for waiting till the last minute. I mind when he was a first year 'prentice in the engine shop he was last in the gate so often in the mornings that come New Year's Eve everyone knew Maurice was bound to be the Skittery Winter – the last man in on the last day of the year.' His mouth softened into a smile at the memory and Faith leaned forward, hanging on his every word like a starving bird eyeing a crumb. 'I made some excuse tae be in the engine shop that mornin',' said Robert, his voice relaxing into the Clydeside accent, 'an' we were all waitin' for him – all set tae bang on metal sheets an' yell an' give him a red face. So the bold Maurice comes slidin' in quiet-like an' goes up along the side of the wall so's not tae be seen.'

Faith's face split into a beaming smile that took years off her. 'Aye, I mind that day as if it was yesterday – the mess he was in when he came home.'

'That's because he was just passing under the stairs leadin' tae the upper gallery when the rest of the 'prentices leaned over and emptied a pail of oily water over him.' Robert roared with laughter and Faith joined in, her laugh squeaky and stifled from lack of use. 'He'd never thought tae look up – but then, mebbe it was as well he didnae or he'd have got it in his face.'

Faith mopped at the tears that had come easily to her eyes then took the photograph back and set it carefully

67

on the sideboard. 'Och Robert, son, it's that good tae see ye! Are ye here for long? Where are ye stayin' now that yer auntie's gone?'

Robert took a cup of tea from Jenny, his grey eyes studying her face. She turned away, flustered, then to her horror she heard him say, 'I'm back home for good, Mrs Gillespie. The Dalkieth directors sent for me.'

'You're going to work in the yard again?' Jenny said in dismay.

'Aye. I see Mrs Dalkieth tomorrow. I'm staying in a lodging house until I know just what's to happen.'

'A lodging house? My, but that'll cost you a fair bit. You could— ' Faith started to say impulsively, then hesitated. 'We've no' got much room, son, but— '

'I'm fine where I am, Mrs Gillespie, don't you fret yourself about me.'

Marion woke with a sudden start, mumbling something. Faith was by her side in an instant.

'It's all right, Mam, it's just a friend of our Maurice's come tae see us. Alice, give me a hand here, we'll take yer gran through tae the other room,' she added hurriedly as Marion's mumbles grew louder and more urgent. Jenny would have helped, but her mother waved her aside. 'We'll manage. You stay with Robert.'

As she and Alice escorted the old woman out, Faith's free hand deftly scooped up the bucket Marion used as a commode. Then Jenny and Robert were alone.

'Who's that?'

'My gran.'

'The old bat that used to worry the life out of you all?'

'She'd a seizure nearly a year ago.'

'God,' said Robert. 'The poor woman.'

Jenny fussed with the teapot, pouring herself a cup of tea, but at last she had to turn round, to look at him

68

sitting at ease in her father's chair, his long legs stretched out over the rag rug, his eyes on her.

'You've cut your hair.'

She began to reach a hand towards her head then realised what she was doing and pulled it back. 'I didn't like it the way it was.'

'I did,' he said, his gaze intense. She wanted to look away, but instead she made herself meet his look boldly, returning it, studying him as he was studying her.

'It makes you look more – more grown up. You look well, Jenny.'

'So do you. Tyneside's treated you well.'

'They've got some fine big yards there. I learned more than I would have here.'

'Including all about marriage.' The words were out before she could stop them.

There was a pause, then, 'I was talking about ship-building,' he said gently. But now that the first shock of seeing him was over the thought of Robert living in Ellerslie again, where she might see him every day and be reminded of what might have been was beginning to hurt. She needed to gather all the pain up at once, like grasping a nettle, and get it over with once and for all.

'You should have brought your wife to meet us.'

'She's still in England.' Robert let the silence grow for a moment or two, then added, 'I'm ashamed, Jenny, of the way I behaved towards you.'

She was sitting on one of the upright chairs. Now she put her cup down abruptly and got to her feet. 'No need to be. You said yourself in your last letter that we were both too young to know our own minds.' She lifted the teapot, pouring out more tea for herself when he shook his head. 'You were right.'

'I was a fool!'

'Did you like the English shipyards?' she asked, abruptly changing the subject.

'Well enough, though the work was hard. They sent me from one department to another and filled my head with so much knowledge that I was fair dizzy at times. But I'm grateful to Mr Dalkieth for giving me the chance to better myself. I was sorry to hear of his death, and Mr Edward's.' He paused, shooting a glance at the closed door. 'And Maurice's,' he added quietly. 'You know he'll not come back, don't you?'

'I'm not daft.'

'And neither's your mother. She'll come round to the truth in her own time, poor soul. Mebbe it's easier on her this way.'

Another silence fell between them. Jenny risked a quick glance at Robert's brown herringbone suit, the striped shirt and neat blue tie, the watch-chain suspended across the front of his waistcoat. His clothes were smart and looked expensive, his hair well groomed and his face clean-shaven apart from a neat, dark moustache that made him look mature, and far more prosperous than he had before he left Ellerslie.

Through the wall they could hear Marion's squawking and Faith's soothing answers. Then to Jenny's horror there came the unmistakable sound of a full bladder being emptied into a metal bucket.

Robert cleared his throat then said, 'Are you still working at the Experimental Tank?'

'Yes.' Jenny spoke loudly to drown out the noise, which seemed to be going on and on. 'The Tank's very busy just now, we've got more work than we know what to do with. Miss McQueen's still the supervisor – and Mr Duncan's still in charge.' Dear God, Jenny couldn't ever recall Gran taking so long over the bucket before.

70

'I might as well tell you now, Jen – there's talk of me becoming the office manager.'

'What?' She had been fidgeting with her sleeve, unbuttoning and buttoning the cuff in order to keep her eyes from him, but now she looked up, full into his face. 'But you're a naval architect!'

'I told you, I've been a lot of things in the past four years.'

'Why you?'

The question was blunt to the point of rudeness, but it didn't seem to bother him. 'With Edward Dalkieth gone, they need someone who knows the shipbuilding business well, and knows Dalkieth's into the bargain. Apparently the old man had me in mind for works manager eventually, with Edward in charge of the office. But I understand that George Dalkieth holds that position.'

The embarrassing noises through the wall had stopped, but now the wail of a small child startled from sleep could be heard. Robert, who had borne Marion's ablutions calmly, tensed in his chair and stared at Jenny, colour surging into his face. 'That's – you've never— '

'It's Maurice's wee girl.'

'Maurice had a bairn? I didn't know that. For a minute there I thought it was yours.'

'How could she be mine?'

'It was possible – as I mind,' Robert said quietly, and Jenny felt her own colour deepen, this time with anger. She jumped to her feet.

'You've got a right nerve, Robert Archer!'

He cringed back into the chair in mock fear, putting up his arms to protect himself. 'And you've still got a temper, Jenny Gillespie,' he said. And, for a moment, a

71

dangerous moment, time dissolved and it was as though they had never been apart. Then Jenny gained control over herself and stepped back, moving away from him as far as possible, until she felt the edge of the table pressing into her backside.

'Lottie and wee Helen live here,' she explained stiffly. 'When Lottie's parents discovered that she was expecting they put her out. Maurice was going to marry her as soon as he came home, but— '

'How on earth d'you manage with them as well as your grandmother to look after? I heard that your father had had to move out of Pneumonia Bay and into the stores.'

'We manage fine,' she told him sharply just as Alice and Faith brought Marion back in. Robert got to his feet at once and hovered round the three of them until the old woman was settled.

'There, Mam,' Faith said. 'Jenny, away and see if you can get the wee yin tae sleep again.'

Alice had gone back into the hall. As Jenny, glad to be away from Robert's gaze, left the kitchen her sister paused at the front door on her way to the communal privy on the landing, bucket in hand.

'What's he doing here?' she whispered.

'Just visiting.'

'He'll be here tae see you.'

'Don't be daft, Alice, he's married!' Jenny snapped, and went into the bedroom, where Helen was struggling to climb out of her cot, her face flushed and wet with tears. As Jenny went in the baby managed to tread on the hem of her threadbare gown. There was a rending sound and a great rip opened down the front.

'Come on, lovely, you're all right.' Jenny swept the little girl into her arms and Helen pushed her warm, tear-wet little face against the hollow of her neck, clinging to her, stiffening when Jenny tried to put her back into the cot. Finally Jenny gave in, picking up the blanket and wrapping it round her to hide the tear in her gown before carrying her into the kitchen, where Helen took one peek round the room, saw that there was a stranger there, and buried her head in her aunt's neck again. Jenny sat down by the table and left her mother to deal with Robert.

Faith was telling him about Patrick and Bella when the outer door opened and shut then Teeze came into the kitchen on a familiar flurry of wheezy coughing.

'Teeze, will ye look who's here?'

'Eh?' He peered across the room, his drink-reddened eyes screwed up in an attempt to focus as Robert rose.

'It's Robert – you mind Maurice's friend Robert?'

'How are you, Mr Gillespie?' Robert held out his hand.

Teeze stared at it, then at the visitor's face. 'Get out of my house.'

'Teeze!'

'Hold yer tongue, you,' Teeze told his wife, taking a lurching step across the room, his gaze fixed on Robert. 'So ye're back, are ye – an' all dressed up like a gentleman intae the bargain.' The words were slurred but their delivery carried all the bitterness that had been eating into Teeze Gillespie ever since the pneumonia had taken away his strength and his self-respect. 'Ye jilt my daughter for some Englishwoman an' go through the war safe an' sound in the shipyards while better men than you die in the mud – then ye come walkin' in here an' expect me tae shake ye by the hand?'

Robert's face had gone white to the lips and his hand had fallen back to his side.

'Teeze Gillespie, you hold your tongue,' Faith screeched, trying to drag her husband back by the sleeve. He shook her off with a bull-like roar.

'Don't you tell me what tae dae in my ain hoose!'

'Dad,' Jenny said warningly, 'Robert's going to be the new office manager at the yard.'

'I don't care if he's goin' tae be Christ on a golden throne,' Teeze said thickly, 'I'll decide who's welcome in my own house – an' he's no' welcome! Get out afore I throw ye out!'

He drew his right arm back, his hand fisting, then swung at the man standing before him. Faith screamed, her own knotted fists flying to her mouth, and Helen let out a fresh wail, while Marion added a terrified keening to the noise. Robert fended off the wavering blow with ease and, at the same time, gripped his assailant's shoulder with his free hand, swinging round so that Teeze, caught off balance, suddenly found himself sitting in the chair that Robert had just vacated.

'I think he needs to get to his bed,' Robert said. 'I'm sorry about this, Mrs Gillespie, I shouldn't have come here. I'll not trouble you again.' And with a nod at Jenny and Alice he gathered up his hat and coat and gloves and walked out of the room.

As the outer door closed Faith snatched a dish-cloth from beside the sink and swiped at her husband with it. 'He's Maurice's friend! I wanted him here!' she screeched, then her thin body jerked as her husband reached up and caught at her wrist, digging his fingers in.

'I'm no' done for yet! I'm still the master o' this house, an' I'll say who comes intae it!'

'D'ye understand nothin', ye drunken fool? He's tae be one o' the bosses – he could lose ye yer job if he wanted tae.'

'I'll go down on my belly for no man!' Teeze roared back at her, then the coughing began and he let her go and doubled over, fists held to his face as the harsh barks of sound tore relentlessly from his damaged lungs.

'Alice, don't stand there like a sack of potatoes, fetch me a cup of water!' Gently, Faith dabbed at her husband's forehead with the towel. Her mother-in-law, startled by all the noise, began to flail the air with her good arm.

'It's all right, Gran, there's nothing wrong.' Alice crouched by the old woman's side, crooning soothingly.

When Teeze's coughing fit had subsided he pushed his wife to one side and got back on to his feet, his head swinging low on his shoulders as though his neck had collapsed, his eyes moving from one of his womenfolk to the other. Jenny was reminded of a bull she and Robert had seen once in a farmyard, glowering over a half-door.

'Christ almighty, will ye get tae yer beds, all of ye!' he ordered, and pushed past them to stump out of the flat and downstairs to the privy.

The glow generated by Robert's arrival had gone out of Faith. 'Jenny, put the bairn back in her cot,' she said in a flat voice, 'an' help tae get yer gran tae her bed.'

They could dimly hear a fist crashing against wooden panels and a familiar voice yelling. Some poor soul must be using the privy, and Teeze had never been patient when it came to waiting his turn.

In bed later, listening to Helen's soft, regular breathing, Jenny recalled the look on Robert's face when he'd heard Helen crying. She remembered the warmth of his hand clasping hers the Sunday before he left for England, and the way Ellerslie Water had looked, transformed by the setting sun into a ribbon of glittering gold as it hurried on its way from Loch Lomond to the

Clyde. Leaving the town behind, the two of them had turned aside from the path to where a thicket of rhododendron bushes stood, their great crimson blossoms brilliant against shiny dark leaves. They circled the clump of bushes until they reached a certain spot where Robert held a branch aside to let Jenny duck beneath it into a short leafy tunnel. At the end of it lay the special place they had discovered a few months earlier, a hollow in the middle of the apparently solid group of bushes.

He spread his jacket on the ground for her to sit on, then stretched on his back beside her. Sunlight shining through leaves tossed by a slight breeze cast moving shadows over his face and throat. 'I like this place,' he said. 'There's nobody fighting in the street outside or spewing into the gutter on the way home from the pub.' His hand sought and found hers, their fingers lacing together. 'One day, Jenny Gillespie, I'll build you a house in a quiet place like this.'

'How can you, when you're going away, and I'll never see you again?' Her throat was choked with unshed tears.

His free hand touched her hair and she felt him loosening the ribbon that held it.

'Don't be daft, of course I'll be back. Jen, I'm not going tae end up like most of the men here, watchin' the ships growing on the stocks and wondering if I'm going tae be laid off once they're finished, or waiting at the yard gates every morning in the hope of getting work. Worrying in case a gaffer takes a dislike tae my face, being dependent on someone else for the very bread I eat.'

'You'll forget me!' She began to get up and he pulled her down again, holding her as she struggled against him, his face firm and warm against hers.

'I could never forget you.' He kissed her, and her tears were wet on her face and on his as she stopped fighting him and instead tightened her arms about him, hungry for more kisses to remember when he was far from her.

When the kisses came she opened her mouth beneath his and felt a shock run through her as their tongues met and entwined. They rolled together on the ground, clinging, kissing. Her blouse came free of her skirt, then Robert's fingers were on her bare skin and she was moving against him, wanting to feel his touch all over her body, moaning when his hands finally covered her breasts.

They made love to each other clumsily, but with a shared sense that they belonged together and that there could be nothing wrong in their coupling. Later, as they wandered back along the riverbank, dazed with the wonder of what had happened to them, Robert said huskily, 'If I sent for ye, Jenny lass, would ye come to me?'

'I've got my own apprenticeship to go through,' she said reluctantly. Drunk with love as she was, dazed with the joy of what had just happened between them, she was still a shipyard worker, keenly aware of the value of an apprenticeship and the need to see it through.

'Aye, you're right. We'll have to wait a wee while yet.' Then, turning her into his arms, kissing her again, he added, 'But it'll seem a long wait.'

Lottie came home, blundering into the bedhead, cursing beneath her breath.

Jenny blinked as the other girl lit the stub of candle and began to undress, dropping her clothes carelessly on the floor. 'You're late.'

'Neil Baker was in the pub tonight. He walked me home.' Lottie stretched her arms above her head and the

77

candlelight outlined the curves of her semi-nude body and picked out the rich, red tints of her tumbled hair. 'There was someone else in the pub tonight, too, late on,' she said, a sly note in her voice. 'Robert Archer that used to live round the corner.'

'I know. He was here.'

'Oh aye? I heard that you used tae be sweet on him.'

'He was a friend of Maurice's,' Jenny said curtly. 'I left some water in the basin for you.'

'Ach, I'm too tired tae be bothered washing.' Lottie blew out the candle and flopped into bed. Her skin smelled of drink and tobacco smoke. She yawned loudly and tossed herself into a comfortable position before settling down. Within minutes she was asleep while Jenny, now wide awake, relived the fear she had gone through after Robert went away to Tyneside, the realisation of what might result from their loving, the tearful relief when her monthly bleeding came as usual.

Recalling again the shock in his face when he first heard Helen wailing she smiled wryly into the dark. Poor Robert, thinking that his past had suddenly jumped up at him like a jack-in-the-box. For a moment she wished that she had had the wit to frighten him, to make him think, even for a moment, that Helen was his child. Then another thought came to wipe the smile from her lips. If what he expected came true, Robert was going to be the new office manager. He would visit the Tank section often.

If only she had been free to go off to Glasgow with Lizzie, Jenny thought, turning over restlessly in bed. Then she would have been well out of the way by the time Robert came back to Ellerslie. But now it was too late. She was trapped like a mouse in a cage, with nowhere to hide, nowhere to go.

6

The door of the tracing office opened and one of the draughtsmen looked in. 'The ghost's walking,' he hissed, then withdrew.

Kerry Malloy, still in her first week, gave a shrill scream of 'Mammy!' and tumbled from her high chair, bringing a sheaf of papers down from the sloping desk with her. Senga only just managed to stop an inkwell from toppling over and spilling while Jenny scrambled from her own chair to scoop up the flurry of papers and Maureen hauled her sister up from the floor.

'God save us, ye eejit, what d'ye think ye're doin'?' she wanted to know, setting the girl on her feet and spinning her round to examine her overall for stains. Kerry's hair had come adrift from the black ribbon that was supposed to control it and her blue eyes were wide with fright. 'He said there's a ghost— '

'It's only something they say here in the Tank, Kerry,' Jenny explained, trying not to smile too broadly. 'It means that one of the bosses is in the building.'

'How was I to know th – ow!' Kerry squeaked as her sister brushed her down with a firm hand, pushing her about as though she was a sack of potatoes, then started to retie the ribbon round a handful of her red hair. 'I can do that myself – I'm not a wean!'

'Get on with it, then – and tidy that desk before Miss

McQueen comes back and finds the place looking like a bear garden,' Maureen fretted.

'The poor lassie's only been in the office for a matter of days, Maureen.' Jenny felt heart-sorry for Kerry, who was crimson with mortification as she struggled back on to her high chair.

'Who was it that begged Mr Duncan and Miss McQueen to take her on in my place now that Jacko's home and we're to be wed? It's me that'll be blamed if she's not suitable.'

'Of course she'll be suitable. Come on,' Jenny began to untie her smock as she crossed to the coat-rack in one corner of the small office. 'The launch party'll be downstairs any minute now and we want to get ready before Miss McQueen comes back. Down you get, Kerry – carefully, mind.'

Maureen gave her sister a final glare as Senga helped the younger girl to scramble from the chair she had only just settled into. Then, deciding that Kerry had been sufficiently humiliated, she smoothed her own fiery hair and reached for her jacket.

Although it was a working day there was a festive air about the yard. In honour of the first peacetime launch in almost five years the employees were to have a half-day holiday; already Jenny was picturing herself at the party to be held in the back court of the tenements, in the new yellow dress she had made for the occasion.

'Wait a minute – Kerry, have a peek outside and make sure old McQueen's not comin' yet,' Senga ordered. 'Maureen, mind what you said you'd do on the day of the launch?'

'Sure I mind – an' I'm not afraid to do it, so there!' Giving a final tug at her jacket Maureen hopped on to a tall chair that stood alone by the coat-rack, well back from the high angled desk where the tracers worked.

Kerry gaped from the doorway. 'What're you doin'?'

'Gettin' meself pregnant.' Maureen, beaming from her perch, swung her feet.

'That's surely not how you go about it?' asked fifteen-year-old Kerry, wide-eyed, and the three older girls collapsed in gales of laughter.

'Did you not tell her about the chair either?' Jenny asked when she could speak, wiping the tears from her eyes. 'They say that everyone who sits on that chair has a bairn within the next nine months, Kerry. That's why it's never used.'

'Aye – even Miss McQueen's terrified of sittin' on it by accident, an' she's fifty if she's a day, an' never as much as said yes tae a man in her life,' said Maureen, setting Senga and Jenny off again.

Kerry gazed from face to face with mounting suspicion. 'You're all having me on. It takes more than an old chair tae make bairns.'

'You mean you don't believe what they say?' Senga asked with mock horror, while Maureen jumped down and invited. 'Sit on it, then.'

As Kerry backed off, shaking her head, she turned to Jenny. 'You try it.'

'I will not. We've got enough in our house without another mouth to feed.'

'It doesn't really make you pregnant, does it?' Kerry left her post to reach out a cautious finger and stroke the broken shiny leather of the chair seat.

'You wait and see – I'll be bouncing a babby on my knee by Christmas.'

'I already know that, Maureen Malloy,' Kerry

retorted. 'But that's Jacko's fault, nothing tae do with you putting your backside on a harmless old chair!'

Maureen's face went scarlet. 'Ye wee midden, ye promised not to say anyth— '

She stopped abruptly as the door opened and Miss McQueen burst into the room like a ship in full sail, her plump face brilliant with two red spots over her cheekbones.

'The launch party have arrived. Quickly now, girls, line up and let me have a look at you.'

She fussed over her staff, tugging at a skirt fold here, settling the collar of a blouse there, until she was satisfied that they all looked presentable, then said briskly, 'Remember that this is a very important day for Dalkieth's shipyard. Are you ready? Follow me – and no noise!'

The clank and hiss of the steam engine on the floor below grew louder as they stepped out of the tracing office then filed in procession along the narrow corridor, forming, Jenny suddenly thought, a wake to Miss McQueen's sailing ship. A giggle bubbled its way up to her lips and was swallowed back.

'Wait!' A few steps down from the top of the wooden staircase the supervisor dramatically threw out an arm to stop them. The line broke up as the girls crowded forward, peering inquisitively over her meaty shoulders to the timber-floored area below. Jenny could only see a row of trousered legs and well-polished shoes, indicating that the drawing-office staff were already lined up to meet the launch party, and two men working self-consciously on an upturned twenty-foot model on the gallery just above the wax room, paring away the unwanted wax, curl by honey-coloured curl, to bring the hull down to the lines already cut into the model by the cutting machine. The floor round their feet was thick with shavings which would be swept up and returned to the melting tank to be used again.

From somewhere out of sight she could hear Mr Duncan, the Tank Superintendent, explaining to the guests in his slow monotone how the Tank itself worked. Then came the rapid swish of the truck racing up the length of the tank, followed by a clang as it came to a standstill and a subdued murmur of interest from the onlookers. Some of the excitement of the moment ebbed away from Jenny as another voice began to speak. She had forgotten for the moment that Robert, recently appointed office manager, would be with the visitors.

Mr Duncan's face, red with the stress of the occasion, peered up from the bottom of the stairs as he beckoned to Miss McQueen and her staff. The five of them flowed down the wooden staircase to the lower floor where they formed a line between the launch party and the stairs leading down to the wax-model room.

'In order to produce the best design possible the designer must study the environment in which the vessel will operate.' Robert's voice was clear and assured, and as Scottish as ever, though his pronunciation had improved. As she took her place in the line at the stairs Jenny risked a glance at him. He was elegant in a dark grey suit, seemingly not in the least overawed by the presence of the guests, who included Isobel Dalkieth, widow of the former owner, and her son.

'By testing a scaled-down design model several times under controlled conditions in the Tank we measure anticipated wave resistance, speed, and a number of other factors,' he was saying. 'This means that we can discover the flaws and strengths of each design before time and money goes into building the ship itself. As Mr

Duncan has told you, we can simulate any size or strength of wave in this Tank.'

Robert hadn't come back to the Gillespie house since Teeze had ordered him out and, although he visited the Tank section frequently, to Jenny's relief he had made no effort to single her out. He was apparently doing well in his new job, though she had heard that he had had to battle against an initial and understandable resentment from many of the men he had worked beside in the old days.

'It's not right for a man tae move out of his own class.' Daniel Young had voiced the opinion of many of the shipyard workers only the night before, when a group of them gathered in the Gillespie flat. 'George Dalkieth's a fool, I'll grant ye that, but he's got his mother tae keep him right – and he's a Dalkieth. It's not easy for men that mind Archer when he was no better than anyone else tae take orders from him now.'

Jenny had held her tongue for as long as she could, but finally her patience had snapped and she had rounded on Daniel and the others. 'What's wrong with a man working hard to better himself? Surely it's better to take orders from someone who's worked his way up and knows what he's talking about than from a man who's a boss just because he was born into the right family.'

They had all turned and gaped at her. Daniel opened his mouth to speak, then closed it again when Teeze growled from his chair, 'Ach, pay no attention tae her – she's altogether too big for her boots these days. An' I'd've thought,' he had added vindictively to his daughter, 'that ye'd be the last one tae speak up for Robert Archer, after the way he walked out on ye.'

Jenny's face burned as she remembered how first one

84

man, then another, had sniggered at her father's words, then they had returned to their discussion, shutting her out with their broad backs and hunched shoulders. Daniel had hesitated, eyeing her narrowly, then he too had turned away.

'These young ladies are our tracers and analysts, specialising in hydro-dynamics,' she heard Robert say now as he advanced towards the bottom of the staircase, the launch party following, the ladies in bright colours, the men sombre in grey and brown suits. 'Dalkieth's is the only firm in the country to train females for this work. They analyse the figures from the Tank experiments and draw up graphs of the results for the naval architect. They also see to the final line drawings – a highly-specialised skill. Miss McQueen— '

The supervisor bobbed forward in a flurry of excitement to meet the dignitaries and introduce her staff. Jenny was too interested in their clothes to feel nervous. Mrs Armstrong, wife of the manager of the company whose ship was being launched, wore a bright blue coat and skirt that did nothing for her sallow complexion, and a flower-pot hat in darker blue.

Old Mrs Dalkieth, straight as a ramrod and still strikingly attractive despite her silver hair, was immaculate in stylish black mourning. Mrs George, the second wife of the only Dalkieth left in the shipyard, also wore mourning, a smart two-piece black silk costume edged with rich ebony fur. She had added a dash of colour – a lilac blouse trimmed with pale grey beneath the jacket, and a pale grey drift of feathers about the broad brim of her hat.

Her blue eyes looked at and through the women lined up before her and, as she turned away, the presentation over, the delicate scent she wore lingered behind her and the feathers on her hat danced slightly.

'The wax model is made in a mould; you will see this process downstairs,' Robert took up his narrative skilfully as he led the party towards the joiners' section. 'It's then put into the cutting machine, where lines indicating the exact measurements are cut into the hull. These men— ' he had come to a halt before the workers on the gallery, 'then pare the model down carefully until they reach the depths indicated by the cutting machine. The model is then ready to be fastened beneath the Tank truck and tested.'

'She's beautiful, Mrs George,' Kerry said enviously a few minutes later as the four girls left the Tank building by a side door and set off in the direction of the launch area, leaving the guests to descend the wooden staircase to the wax room. 'And not a freckle in sight, lucky thing. My mam says Mr George divorced his first wife because she couldnae have any bairns to follow him into the business. I wonder if this one can?'

'You shouldn't gossip about your betters, Kerry,' Senga said crushingly.

'She's got a lovely slim figure, hasn't she?' Kerry rattled on.

'But a cold face,' Maureen put in. 'Come on, our Kerry, or we'll not get a good view of the launch.'

'You're not bothered about the launch, Maureen Malloy,' Kerry retorted. 'You're just wanting to make sure that you can stand beside Jacko!' As the other two girls forged ahead she hung back. 'Jenny, me and the rest of them at home have saved up and brought two cups and two saucers for our Maureen and Jacko's wedding gift. Could you paint them for us? I can bring them to your mam's tonight, after the party.'

'What d'you want on them?'

Kerry thought for a moment, then said, 'Bluebells. She loves bluebells. With green leaves.'

'And mebbe a butterfly, to add some more colour?'

'It sounds lovely. Could you do them in the time? I'd have got them sooner but it took a while tae make up the money.'

'I'll manage.'

'Thanks, Jenny.' Kerry squeezed her arm as they swerved to avoid one of the many puddles left by the night's rain. 'Look, she's found Jacko right enough. Come on— ' and she dragged Jenny over to where a group of men from the joiner's shop stood. Jacko, who had been one of the first to return to Ellerslie after the war and take up his old trade as a joiner in the shipyard, good-naturedly made room for them, one arm about Maureen. It was good, Jenny thought, to see her friend so flushed with happiness.

The town of Ellerslie had been built on both banks of the Ellerslie Water, a river spanning the half-dozen miles or so from Loch Lomond, its birthplace, to the River Clyde. Dalkieth's shipyard lay on the east bank, close to the mouth of the river, at a point where it broadened just before meeting the Clyde. The stretch of water wasn't large enough for the yard to compete with the giants of the Clyde shipyards, such as Fairfield's and John Brown's, but three generations of Dalkieths had gradually built up a reputable yard specialising in cross-Channel steamers as well as passenger and cargo boats, all of a size that enabled them to be launched safely from the yard.

Ship number 1462, the twelve-thousand-ton *Tanamura*, waited on the slipway, her great bulk supported by props, the Dalkieth house-flag, with its blazing gold 'D' against a crimson background, fluttering and snapping at the mainmast. After launching she would be towed round to Pneumonia Bay to be fitted out. Only when she was ready to leave the yard would she officially become the property of the company that had commissioned her and fly their flag.

The open ground beneath the vessel seethed with employees who had come to watch the launch; men black as night from the forge, their teeth and eyes gleaming white, dungaree-clad platers and riveters and caulkers and joiners, men from the engine and boiler shops, designers and draughtsmen and time-keepers as well as women from the offices and the upholstery and glass departments. In contrast to the dull colours of the crowd, all in their usual working clothes, the bunting and flags on the launch platform were all the colours of the rainbow under the May sun.

The buzz of excitement grew louder as the launch party finally emerged from the Tank section and made their way to the decorated platform, the ladies cautiously negotiating the wooden stairs. Mrs Armstrong named the ship in a voice that didn't reach Jenny's ears, then the bottle swept forward on the end of its lanyard and there was a cheer as it burst against the ship's stern with a sudden flowering of foam. There was a moment of breathless anticipation, then another, louder cheer ripped into the air as the vessel began to move, slowly at first, then faster as it neared the river.

The sky went black with caps tossed high as the *Tanamura* finally met with the water, her natural element, her bows lifting, then dipping, then levelling as the huge drag chains tightened to take the strain and slow the headlong momentum that would, if left unfettered, have allowed her to plough across the river and bury her bows in the opposite bank.

Jenny, cheering as lustily as the rest, felt tears pricking at the backs of her eyes as she watched the ship take to the water. In that moment the war that had killed and maimed millions and turned life inside out for millions more was truly over. Dalkieth's had returned, once and for all, to peacetime shipping.

When Jenny got home the kitchen was fragrant with the smell of baking and plates of sandwiches and scones covered the table. Helen, a tattered piece of towelling tied under her chin to protect her clean clothes, was noisily drinking from her decorated mug and Faith was scurrying between the range and the table, her hair wisping over her flushed face.

'Thank goodness you're back,' she said as soon as her daughter walked in. 'I'm fair distracted, tryin' tae get ready for the party an' tend tae yer gran wi' the wean under my feet. I tell you, our Maurice's goin' tae have his hands full dealin' with that yin when he gets back.'

Jenny lifted the lid on a huge cast-iron pot bubbling on the range; through a cloud of steam she made out the knotted corners of a cloth. 'A clootie dumpling!'

'I've tae dae my share,' Faith said shortly. Once she had been the best baker in the street, but all that had stopped when the telegram came about Maurice. Jenny hoped that Faith's return to her old skills was a good omen for the future.

Helen, who had become more difficult to look after since she found her feet, toddled over to the table and stretched inquisitive fingers up, groping for the edge of a plate. Jenny scooped her back just in time and found something for her to play with, then she made tea and persuaded her mother to sit down for a minute. 'Is Lottie not here to look after her?' she asked as she poured the tea.

'She was here – I didnae hear her go out. She must be somewhere about,' said Faith vaguely, her irritation eased slightly by the hot sweet drink. Jenny at once put down her own cup and hurried to the room she shared with Lottie and Helen. She had learned, since sharing a room, that it didn't do to leave Lottie too long on her own among other people's possessions.

Lottie, dressed only in a pair of cotton cami-knickers edged with dingy lace, jumped guiltily when the door opened and Jenny's new yellow dress fell from her hands to the floor. She stooped to pick it up but Jenny got there first, snatching the dress away from the other girl's avaricious fingers, clutching it protectively.

'What d'you think you're doing?'

'I was just lookin'.'

'I made this dress specially for the party and nobody else is going to have it.' Jenny's voice was hard. What Lottie saw, she wanted, and what she wanted she usually took.

Lottie's lip curled in a sly grin as she looked Jenny up and down. 'Who d'ye want tae look nice for? I doubt if Robert Archer'll be there – not now that he's such an important man.'

'Mind your own business!' Jenny examined the dress carefully and was relieved to see that it was unharmed.

Lottie picked up a lit cigarette from a saucer on the orange box and drew on it. 'Though I've heard that that wife of his still hasn't come to Ellerslie.' Smoke dribbled from between her lips and her tawny eyes danced with malice. 'Mebbe there never was a wife – mebbe he just made it up tae stop you from pesterin' him.'

Jenny snatched up the saucer, one that she had painted herself, and held it out. 'Take that through to the kitchen and wash the ash off it. I've told you before not to use my belongings.'

Lottie shrugged, and put a hand out for the saucer. As Jenny released it, it seemed to slip through Lottie's fingers and fell to the floor, breaking into two pieces a few inches away from one of Lottie's bare feet.

'You –!' Goaded beyond endurance, Jenny dropped the dress on to the bed and snatched at the other girl's shoulders, shaking her. Lottie gave a screech and dropped the cigarette, reaching for Jenny's hair. Jenny jerked her head back, out of harm's way, and the clawed fingers caught at her blouse instead, jerking it half-off Jenny's shoulder. A button rattled to the floor as the two of them teetered on the brink of falling over on to the bed.

The door flew open and Faith came storming in, squeezing herself between the girls, wrenching them apart and glaring from one to the other. 'What d'ye think ye're doin', the pair of ye – brawling like a couple of drunken sluts in the gutter!'

'She started it,' Lottie said sullenly, rubbing at her smooth shoulders, twisting her head to examine the red marks left by Jenny's fingers.

'She was going to take my dress – and she broke my saucer!' Jenny said at the same time. Faith, glancing down at the broken crockery, suddenly noticed the cigarette and swooped on it with an anguished wail.

'Look at my linoleum! For any favour, d'ye want tae burn the house down, and us all in it?' She licked a finger and rubbed at the burn left by the cigarette.

'Who's going tae see one more mark on that old linoleum?' Lottie demanded to know. 'It's me you

91

should be worryin' about. She could've burned my foot, makin' me drop my cigarette. And now I'll have tae wear somethin' wi' sleeves tae cover the bruises she's put on me.' She snatched the cigarette from Faith and flounced out, jostling Jenny as she passed.

'I'm sorry, Mam.' Jenny pulled the blouse back over her shoulder, angry with herself for having let Lottie provoke her.

'So ye should be. There's folk gatherin' in the back court for a party, an' you turnin' the house intae a bear garden – all over a wee saucer. One o' these days,' said Faith, getting to her feet, the pieces of china in her hand, 'ye'll mebbe know what it's like tae have real worries. Hurry up and get yerself ready then come and help me with yer gran.'

In the kitchen Lottie was washing herself at the sink, dabbing with excessive care at the fading finger-marks on her plump shoulders. She didn't look round as Jenny poured water from the kettle into a basin then carried it back to the bedroom, where she dragged the orange box against the door to keep it closed against unwelcome visitors before stripping and washing. Taking off her blouse she saw that it was torn where the button had been wrenched off. It would have to be mended before Monday.

She didn't know what had possessed Maurice to take up with the likes of Lottie Forsyth, she told herself furiously as she went down on her hands and knees to search for the missing button, which had skittered away under the bed.

Scrambling to her feet, the button clutched in her fist, she admitted to herself that she did know what had possessed Maurice. Lottie, full-breasted and slim-waisted, with her red-gold curls and her tawny eyes tilted up at the corners, was enough to tempt any man, and Maurice had always been easily tempted. Jenny, lathering hard yellow soap as best she could in the tepid water, scrubbing at her arms with the flannel, wished that he had been more selective in his choice of a sweetheart. But then Helen wouldn't have come into their lives, with her mother's lovely hair and her father's soft brown eyes and heart-stopping broad grin.

Alice tapped on the door just as she finished dressing. 'Can I come in and show you my outfit?'

Jenny pulled the orange box out of the way, and her sister came in, with Helen clutching her hand and guzzling happily at a crust dipped in tea and sugar. 'You stand by the window, Helen, and keep well clear of my skirt,' Alice warned, then pirouetted. She was wearing a pale blue muslin dress that Jenny had made over for her from a gown that Mrs McColl had given to Bella. Jenny had bought some cream-coloured lace and used it to trim the bodice and cuffs, with enough over to provide a mock fichu to fill in the low square neck.

'What d'you think?'

'It's lovely, though I say so myself.' The muslin softened the outlines of her sister's sturdy figure, and the colour of the dress complemented Alice's fresh colouring.

'Now let me see yours. Oh, Jenny, it's bonny!'

'D'you think so?' Jenny smoothed the skirt over her slim hips, comforted by her sister's admiration. The dress consisted of a strip of pale yellow crepe de chine that she had folded in two, cutting a round neck out of it and taking two strips from the side so that the dress formed a T-shape. Then, borrowing Mrs Malloy's old but reliable sewing machine, she had sewed along the sides and turned up a hem. Some dark blue braid on the neck and sleeves and a belt made from the surplus material edged with the braid completed the dress – her first new outfit since the beginning of the war.

'P'etty,' Helen said placidly. Lifting the edge of the smock she wore and looking down at her own little muslin dress, bought by Jenny, she said again, 'P'etty,' then returned to her crust.

'You don't think it's too short?' Jenny flattened the skirt against the front of her thighs and bent forward to examine the hemline. 'I feel as if my legs go on and on beneath it.'

Alice shook her head firmly. 'The new short skirt length suits folk like you, with pretty ankles.' Then she asked inquisitively, 'What's been going on? Lottie's moaning about being covered with bruises, though I couldn't see any. And Mam's in my room, getting ready for the party and looking more as if she's going to a funeral.'

'It was nothing.' Jenny was too ashamed of her burst of temper to admit to it. 'Just a wee argument between me and Lottie.' She ran a brush over her dark hair then fluffed it up so that it fell into soft curls round her face.

'Jen— ' Alice swallowed audibly then said, in a rush of words, 'I heard today that I got that scholarship.'

'What? Oh, Alice!' Jenny dropped the brush and hugged her sister, heedless now of the need to keep their good dresses free of creases. 'I'm proud of you!'

'Me too, me too,' Helen clamoured, suddenly jealous, and had to be gathered up into a three-way embrace.

'That means you'll be going to the Academy in September!'

'It means I'll have to find a uniform, too.'

'We'll manage.' Jenny, tears in her eyes, gave her sister another hug and Helen, caught between them, gave a muffled squeak of protest. 'Now we've got more than just a launch to celebrate!'

Alice wrinkled her forehead. 'I don't know if I'm doing the right thing, Jenny. Mebbe I should just leave school when I turn fourteen in August and get some sort of work.'

'You'll do nothing of the kind. You'll get another scholarship next year then when you're sixteen you'll be able to go to college and learn to be a teacher. We'll manage fine, you wait and see,' Jenny promised.

Alice nodded, then remembered, 'Mam wants us to help her to get Gran to the window so that she can watch what's going on down in the back court.'

'She'll not be interested.'

'I know, but it makes Mam happier to think she is,' said Alice with a wisdom beyond her thirteen years. The door opened and Lottie flounced in.

'If you don't mind, I'd like tae get dressed now. In private,' she said sullenly, ignoring their finery, even ignoring Helen when she proudly caught at the hem of her smock and hauled it up over her face to display her new dress.

'Look. P'etty,' her voice said, muffled by the smock, and Alice picked her up and carried her out at arms' length to avoid getting sticky from the remains of the sugared crust, still liberally plastered to Helen's mouth and fingers.

'You're the bonniest wee girl in the street,' she said, turning in the passageway as Lottie banged the door shut behind them to add under her breath, 'You'd think she'd at least say something nice tae the bairn.'

'Not Lottie – she never sees anyone but herself.'

Faith was back in the kitchen when they went through, dressed in the same 'best clothes' she had

had for many years – a dark green serge skirt and a high-necked blue blouse with carefully ironed frills at the neck and edging the three-quarter-length sleeves, a cameo brooch which had belonged to her mother pinned at her throat. She was carefully washing and drying her mother-in-law's face and hands. When Marion's hair had been brushed the three of them heaved and tugged until they managed to get her, chair and all, up to the window overlooking the courtyard.

'There, Mother, ye'll be able tae see everythin' now, won't ye?' Faith said cheerfully, ignoring the fact that in order to see out Marion would have had to get out of her chair and lean over the sink. The old woman's head lolled and a ribbon of saliva drooled from her slack mouth. Faith wiped it away.

'Mam, did Alice tell you her news? She's got the scholarship!'

'Aye, she said,' Faith said vaguely, then nodded to the table where the large round dumpling, rich with spices and raisins, released from its confining cloth and in pride of place, gently steamed. 'We'll have tae get this lot down tae the court. No sense in waitin' for yer father – he'll have stopped in at the pub.'

'But Mam, Alice— ' Jenny began, then as her sister frowned and shook her head at her she gave up. A thin thread of music rose from the back court outside and Alice dashed to the window, leaning precariously over her grandmother's shoulder. 'It's old Peter wi' his fiddle. Would ye look at the weans followin' him – he looks like the fattest Pied Piper anyone's ever seen!'

Jenny joined her, balancing herself with a hand on Alice's arm. For once, the open cobbled back court that served four rows of tenement buildings was free of a forest of lines of washing. The ropes and clothes-poles had been stowed away in the four wash-houses, one built against each of the buildings that made up the court, and the space they had left blossomed with trestle tables covered with a collection of multi-coloured table-cloths and bed sheets, each table decorated with jam-jars stuffed with wild spring flowers gathered from the fields outside the town.

Peter McLellan, a boilermaker in the shipyard, had come through one of the closes from the street and was marching between the tables, his face and his bald head shining from a recent thorough application of soap and water, his Sunday suit straining over his paunch, a battered old fiddle almost lost in the multiple folds of his chins. Behind him, hopping and skipping hap-hazardly as they came, was a ribbon of children, their faces split by grins of excitement.

Peter's music had called to more than the children. The court was suddenly busy with women bearing teapots, trays of mugs, covered dishes and bowls and jugs. The men followed, scrubbed and dressed in their best clothes, strutting a little as they walked. After all, hadn't they built the ship that was being honoured today? Didn't they have more right to celebrate than the Dalkieths and their fine guests who would at that moment be sitting down to lunch in the shipyard offices?

'Come on— ' Jenny turned back into the room to remove Helen's bib. 'Let's get you washed, milady. It's time to celebrate!'

7

The model gallery on the floor above the Dalkieth offices housed an impressive display of some of the vessels launched from the yard since its earliest years. On the *Tanamura*'s launch day most of the models had been cleared from the gallery to make way for four trestle tables, three running down the length of the gallery and the fourth placed across the room as a top table. Only a few of the larger models were left against the walls, handsome in their glass cases, for the interest of the male members of the launch party.

This was the first launch Fiona Dalkieth had attended, and so far she had found the whole business intensely boring. She saw no sense in having to climb a rickety ladder to stand on a crowded, breezy platform, one hand clutching at her wide-brimmed hat to keep it from being whisked off her head, while some simpering woman she didn't know or remotely wish to know tossed a bottle of good champagne at a ship. What was wrong with just letting the dratted thing slide quietly into the water by itself? And now she was forced to sit on an uncomfortable chair and listen to speeches before she could enjoy her lunch.

Even the pleasure of choosing new clothes for the occasion had been spoiled by Mama Dalkieth's insistence that they were still in mourning for George's brother and father. She stroked a hand down the skirt of her black silk costume. At least it was well made, and black suited her fair hair and pearly skin. And she had managed to add a dash of colour – her lilac and pale grey blouse and the cluster of grey feathers about the crown of her hat. George, who knew nothing of fashion and etiquette, had merely told her that she looked becoming, but Mama Dalkieth had looked at her very sharply when she walked into the drawing room of Dalkieth House on George's arm that morning.

Fortunately, their late arrival, carefully arranged by Fiona, had given the older woman no time to order her back to the modest house she and George shared on the outskirts of the town to find a more suitable blouse and remove the feathers.

A patter of applause signified, to her relief, that the speeches were over. The waitresses moved forward with plates of soup but even then there was a further delay while the Reverend John Stirling, no doubt as eager for nourishment as everyone else, delivered a mercifully brief Grace. But at last the company were finally able to relax with a clash of spoons against plates and the discreet hum of voices.

Fiona shifted slightly in her chair and noticed that her husband, several places along the table, was leaning forward and glaring at her. She glared back, and he made some strange circling movements around his forehead with one finger, repeating them as she stared at him, completely bemused.

'What?' Her lips shaped the word, but George's signals only became more agitated, his finger stabbing at the air above his own sleek brown hair.

'I think, Mrs Dalkieth, that your husband may be

99

trying to draw your attention to your hat,' said a quiet voice beside Fiona.

She turned to the man on her left. 'What's wrong with my hat?'

'Nothing at all. It's most attractive, but I think your husband may have noticed that every time you move your head one of the feathers connects with my eye.'

Before she could stop herself Fiona giggled, and was answered by a grin from her companion. 'The number of guests and the size of the room means that we're all rather close to our neighbours,' he explained.

I'm sorry, Mr— ' She looked at his place card. 'Mr Archer. Now I know why my mother-in-law chose to wear a small hat. I shall take mine off.'

'Not on my account,' he started to protest, but her hands were already busy with the hatpins, one elbow putting the man on her other side into imminent danger.

'Allow me,' said Robert Archer, deftly removing the second hatpin then the hat itself. Fiona took it from him and handed it to one of the waitresses after stabbing the pins through the material.

'Now some of the ladies look shocked,' said her companion.

'It's of no consequence. I don't see why women should wear hats at the table, it can be quite inconvenient – as you've just found to your cost. Also,' added Fiona as their soup plates were gathered in, 'it feels more comfortable, and I've just saved your eyesight. I think I may start a new fashion.'

The main course arrived and a waiter brought wine. The woman on Robert Archer's other side engaged him in conversation and Fiona turned to the man on her right. He answered her comments as briefly as possible, being far more interested in the food and drink before him, and she soon left him to his own devices, claiming Archer's attention again as soon as she could. He was vaguely familiar and, after a moment's thought, she recalled that he had been involved in the boring tour of the Tank section before the launch.

'Have you been with Dalkieth's for long, Mr Archer?'

He shook his head. There was silver over his temples and strands of silver glittering here and there in his thick dark hair, giving him a distinguished look, but his lean, strong face was still youthful. George's hair was an uninteresting mid-brown with no silver in it as yet, although his face was already beginning to fill out and take on a florid tinge.

'I've recently come from Tyneside to take up my duties here as office manager.'

'Indeed? You don't sound like a Tyneside man.'

He had just cut a piece of meat and put it into his mouth. Fiona had to wait while he chewed and swallowed without haste before he answered. 'I was born here in Ellerslie. I followed my father into the shipyard and was apprenticed as a naval architect in the Tank section. After I'd served my time Mr George's father sent me to a yard on Tyneside to learn more about shipbuilding. I came back only a few weeks ago.'

'Why should a naval architect be brought back as an office manager?'

He didn't seem the least offended by her bluntness. 'In the past few years I've come to know quite a lot about administration among other things, and the Board felt that it made sense to have an office manager with a good knowledge of the work carried out in the yard itself.'

There was a pause, during which he attended to the food on his plate and Fiona scrutinised him in a series of sideways glances. He was quite an attractive man, she decided, and not in the least afraid of women, so he was almost certainly married. 'Is your wife happy to come back to Scotland?' she probed.

'My wife is English, and she prefers to remain in her own country among her own people.' His voice was calm and unhurried.

'So she'll be hoping that you'll change your mind about settling here?' Fiona asked with increasing interest. 'And will you? Are you willing to risk your marriage for the sake of Dalkieth's?'

'If I am, I think my wife should be the first to know of it, Mrs Dalkieth,' he said in the same bland voice, and she gasped at his impertinence, then began to laugh.

'You're quite right, Mr Archer, it is none of my business. I am altogether too inquisitive.'

'Not at all. You're entitled to ask whatever you wish – just as I'm entitled to keep my own counsel.' Robert Archer cut another piece of meat with deliberate precision and Fiona, suddenly realising that everyone else had almost emptied their plates, turned her attention to her own meal, wondering why George had never spoken of his new colleague. She must see to it that Mr Archer was invited to dine with them soon. With his wife still in Tyneside the poor man was on his own and it was only right that she and George should make him welcome in Ellerslie.

By mid-afternoon the large back court was filled with men, women and children, many of them dancing on the cobbles to the music of old Peter McLellan's fiddle. The thin notes straggled into the summer air, as many wrong as right, but today nobody cared. Music was music.

Daniel Young and another man had helped Patrick Kerr downstairs and into the court, his arms round their necks, his twisted foot dangling helplessly. Now he was seated on an ordinary kitchen chair near his own close, with Bella hovering round him, the anxiety on her small face emphasising her resemblance to her mother. When Jenny went over to speak to him he looked at her sourly.

'God, Peter's playing gets worse by the day.'

'What we need is your mouth-organ, Pat,' Jenny said.

'I've got it here,' Bella dipped into her pocket and produced the mouth-organ that had once been Patrick's pride and joy.

'I've already told you – I don't want it!'

'Please,' Bella said softly. 'Please play something, Pat. Just for me.'

He looked at her in silence for a long moment, then as she said again, 'Please?' his mouth took on a wry, bitter twist and he held out a hand that was almost his trademark, the skin blue and permanently scarred, knotted in places by burns received from working with rivets still hot from the braziers. Before the war as a riveter in the shipyard, Patrick had scrambled sure-footed over scaffolding, high above the ground.

'All right, then, I'll play something just for you,' he said, and Bella's eyes lit up as he put the instrument to his lips. For a moment she looked almost radiant; then all the light died from her face as her husband pursed his lips about the mouth-organ and began to play the Last Post, the sad lament played over the graves of countless dead servicemen.

Heads turned and faces gaped as the heartbreaking refrain rose into the air, vying with the thin pipe of the old fiddle.

'No —!' Bella said on a sob, putting a hand out

103

towards him. He ended the lament on a harsh discordant note, and stared defiantly up into her stricken face.

'What's the matter, Bella?' he asked roughly. 'Why did ye no' dance tae my music? I'm sure ye could find plenty of new partners, men able tae whirl ye round and lift ye off yer feet. Here, you,' he added, beckoning to a lad who had pushed his way through the staring crowd. 'Catch.'

The mouth-organ flashed silver as it sailed through the air, to be caught deftly in the boy's grimy hands.

'Patrick—' Bella spun like a distracted top, torn between staying with her husband and retrieving the mouth-organ.

'I don't want it – I've told ye that, time and time again! Now mebbe ye'll believe me! Take it, son,' Patrick ordered, and with a yelp of 'Thanks, mister!' the lad disappeared into the crowd, the mouth-organ held high in triumph.

Patrick's face twisted into a scowl as he looked at the people who were still staring and whispering. 'What else d'ye want from me,' he asked roughly. 'A hornpipe?' His finger stabbed at his twisted lower leg and foot. 'Ye've had all the entertainment ye're goin' tae get from me – now clear off!'

They muttered their embarrassment, slowly turning away as Daniel Young pushed his way through, carrying two mugs of beer. His dark eyes took in the scene and he marched up to Patrick, holding out one of the mugs. 'Here ye are, man, drink it down. Bella, you go off and enjoy yourself,' he added. 'Patrick and me'll have a wee chat together.'

'Come on, Bella, come and get a slice of Mam's dumpling.' Jenny caught at her sister's hand and drew her away. 'Leave him to Daniel for a wee while,' she advised as they went.

'Ye'd think it was his head that had been hurt, not his leg,' Bella choked out, the tears spilling freely down her pale face now. 'Jen, what am I goin' tae dae if he doesnae get any b-better?'

Jenny put an arm about her and gave her a quick hug, remembering her sister's wedding less than two years before, and Patrick, home on leave and handsome in his naval uniform, dancing with Bella to the scrape of old Peter's fiddle. She recalled the tenderness in his eyes as he looked down at his slim young bride.

'Go and help Mam,' she said, giving Bella a gentle push towards one of the tables, where their mother was in the midst of a knot of neighbours. Some of the younger married woman were there, laughing and chattering. Perhaps they could help Bella to forget her worries for a few minutes.

A storm of harsh, familiar coughing came to her ears. Her father was with a crowd of men in a corner of the court beside two beer barrels, a donation from the Dalkieths. Too much talking and laughing had set him coughing, fighting for breath, almost bent double, the beer in the tin mug he held slopping over and splashing the cobbles. Jenny walked on, and came on Walter Young, Daniel's son, standing alone against one of the buildings, watching the proceedings. Although most of the youngsters in the courtyard were dressed in casual, comfortable clothes, Walter wore his usual heavy suit, complete with shirt and tie and polished boots. Hearing the violin music swing into a familiar tune Jenny impulsively held out her hand to him.

'Walter, you're the very lad! I've been looking for someone to partner me in a dance.'

105

He flushed scarlet and shrank back against the wall as though trying to push his way through the stones. 'I cannae dance!'

'I can – well enough for the two of us. It's easy, come and try it.'

He swallowed hard and looked about as though for assistance. When none came he gave a stiff, wretched little nod and put his hand into hers, allowing her to lead him to the edge of the area where Alice, her face red with exertion and enjoyment, reached out to him.

'Good for you, Walter – now we've got ourselves a set,' she shouted. Walter's hand twitched in Jenny's grasp, and for a moment she thought that he was going to wrench himself free and run, then the music started and the circle they were in began swinging round and it was too late for flight.

At first Walter's movements were nervous and jerky, but he soon picked up the rhythm of the simple dance and Jenny felt him relax. At twelve years of age, growing up instead of growing out, he was as tall as she was.

'You're doin' grand, Walter,' Alice shouted as they whirled together. Jenny laughed, her yellow skirt spinning around her legs like the petals of a flower, and awakened an answering smile on his perspiring face.

When the dance ended Alice tried to coax Walter towards a corner of the court where a group of lads were trying their prowess at walking a plank of wood set up between two barrels. The wood had been well rubbed with fat and the audience was squealing with helpless laughter at the walkers' attempts to reach the far end.

'You'd be good at it, Walter,' Alice said. 'I'd bet on you being able to run across that old plank like a mouse up a drainpipe.'

106

But Walter, blushing once more, shook his head and escaped back to his watching place beside the wall.

'It's a shame, so it is.' Kerry joined the two sisters as they watched him go. 'He should be havin' fun with the rest of the lads.'

'His father doesnae give him much time for playin',' Alice said. 'He's his heart set on Walter doing well at the school.'

'It's just his way.' Jenny felt she had to defend Daniel. 'He's a good man and he keeps that house of his like a new pin.'

'Aye, well, that doesnae seem tae me tae be man's work.' Kerry's voice was doubtful. 'My ma says it's time he was gettin' himself a new wife.' Then, after a quick glance over her shoulder to make sure that Maureen wasn't within earshot, 'I'll drop those cups and saucers in later on, will I?'

'Fine. I'd better go and see to Helen. It's not fair to leave her to Mam all afternoon.'

'Lottie's the one that should be looking out for her own bairn.' Then Alice's glance moved to a spot beyond Jenny and she added with a change of tone, 'Never you mind about Helen, we'll see to her. Come on, Kerry.' She grabbed at the other girl and pulled her away, into the crowd. Jenny, puzzled, began to turn just as a hand closed over her arm.

'Dance with me, Jenny,' Robert Archer said and, before she could protest, she had been swung into the midst of the dancers.

'You look bonny,' he said as he guided her over the cobbles, one arm about her waist. 'Is that a new dress?'

'What are you doing here?' She was aware of people staring as they danced by, nudging each other and pointing.

107

'I heard there was to be a street party to celebrate the launch, and I minded the fine parties we used to have.'

'That was in the days when you lived round here.'

Robert's arm tightened about her as he deftly swung her out of the way of an energetic couple who were in no mood to make room for anyone. 'I'm neither fish, flesh nor fowl, is that what you mean? Not one of the posh folk, for all that I'm working among them, and not one of the tenement folk any more. A traitor to my own kind.' His voice hardened. 'Your father made that clear the night I came to see you.'

'He shouldn't have spoken to you the way he did,' Jenny said into his shoulder. He smelled of tobacco and good soap.

'I suppose a man's got a right to speak his mind in his own house. I shouldn't have just walked in without finding out how he felt first.' Then Robert said, low-voiced, 'Not that his feelings concern me. It's yours I'm more interested in.'

'I have no feelings one way or the other, Mr Archer.'

'I wronged you, Jenny, I know that. But I was younger then, and my head was easy turned by everything that was happening to me.'

'I hear you've bought yourself a comfortable house.'

They were too close for her to see his face, but close enough for her to feel the laughter in his chest. 'At least you're interested enough to want to know what I'm doing. That's a good sign.'

She tried to step free of him, but he held her firmly and she had no option but to dance on. 'I'm not a bit interested, but I can't help hearing gossip now and again. And you've given the gossips plenty to talk about, coming back to Ellerslie.'

'In case you're wondering, I bought the house for my

own convenience, not my wife's. She's decided that she's going to stay in England.' The laughter had gone, and when she glanced up she saw the knot of hard muscle along the edge of his jaw. 'It was a mistake, Jenny, marrying her. When the word came for me to come back here to the shipyard I could have refused and stayed where I was. I wanted to be back with my own folk, back where I belong.'

She said nothing, staring at the lapels of his smart jacket. She had learned to live without him, had almost learned to forget him. It was wrong of him to come back now of all times, just when her own life had unexpectedly reached a dead end.

'I never thought to find you still here, still unwed,' he said just then, his hand tightening on hers.

'I should have been in Glasgow, but with Maurice gone I'm needed at home.'

'Mebbe it was meant for me to come back just when I did.'

Until then she had been confused and in turmoil at finding herself in his arms so unexpectedly. But now anger seasoned her emotions. 'Home to find me waiting for you, d'you mean? You're wrong!'

'Jenny— '

'There's nothing here for you, Robert Archer – not as far as I'm concerned.'

The music ended and she tried to pull away, but again his arm tightened about her waist. 'Let me be!'

'We've got things to talk about, Jenny. You owe me that, at least.'

'We owe each other nothing.' Turning her head away from him as the music started up again and she was drawn back into the dance she found herself looking at Daniel Young, skirting the group of dancers. His head turned at that moment, as if someone had called to him, and his eyes met hers. He began to shoulder his way towards her.

'Jenny, at least listen to— '

'Sorry I'm late, Jenny,' Daniel said, arriving by her side, ignoring Robert. 'I was talking to Patrick. You promised this dance tae me, did you not?'

'Yes – yes I did.' She stopped, and Robert was forced to stop as well, his arms falling away from her. 'Thank you, Mr Archer,' she said, and went into Daniel's arms.

'What's he doing here, pestering you?' he wanted to know as they moved away from Robert.

'He wasn't pestering me, but I'm glad you came along, Daniel.'

'He doesnae belong here anymore. Not now that he's one of the bosses. He'd have been better keeping away.'

Jenny said nothing. The last thing she wanted to do was talk about Robert. To her relief he didn't approach her again. She saw him talking to her mother, then dancing with Kerry Malloy; later he danced with Lottie, her red hair spilling over his jacket, her laughter ringing out above the noise.

She caught another glimpse of him over by the beer barrels, talking comfortably with the men, mug in hand, while Teeze stood nearby with another group, his back turned to the office manager. Then, to her relief, he left the party, shaking hands with former neighbours and school friends on his way out.

'He's not a bad fella at all,' she heard Mr Malloy say as she walked past the men later, Helen toddling along by her side. 'Not a snob, like some I could mention. If ye ask me, it's good tae see one of our own kind gettin' on in the world.'

8

Kerry, as promised, delivered two plain white cups and saucers after the street party, carefully wrapped in newspaper. When the evening chores were done on the following day Jenny put her precious box of paints and brushes on the kitchen table and started work.

Alice was doing schoolwork at the other side of the table, Lottie was at work, and Helen slept soundly in the cot in the larger bedroom. Teeze, home for once, was sprawled out in his chair by the stove, his stockinged feet on the home-made hearth-rug, his head tipped back, mouth open, snoring. Marion puffed and grunted and bubbled in the truckle-bed, which took up most of the kitchen floor.

Faith sat opposite her husband with a pile of darning on her lap, her chair turned to catch the best light from the gas mantel above her head. Her needle flashed in and out of the material in her hands, getting dangerously close to her face as time wore on and her tired eyes became less able to focus on what she was doing. She badly needed spectacles, but couldn't afford them. Instead, she wore her mother-in-law's when the old lady was asleep, and refused to believe her daughters when they tried to tell her that someone else's spectacles might not be suitable for her eyes.

The gas mantel on that wall wasn't strong enough for

111

the delicate work Jenny was doing, so she fetched one of the two paraffin lamps that usually sat on the big dresser flanking Maurice's photograph. As the extra light flooded the table Alice lifted her head and gave a vague smile of gratitude before returning to her work.

Alice would make a good teacher, Jenny thought as she got on with her own work. She was conscientious, and she got on well with children. It was right that she should get the opportunity that she deserved. They would manage, somehow, to get the uniform and find the extra money she would need.

Kerry had stipulated bluebells for her sister's wedding gift. Jenny dabbed deep blue paint on to the old saucer she used as a palette, dipped a fine brush into it, and started work, then her hand stilled for a moment as she realised that Alice would eventually have to go to Glasgow to attend college. She would be the one to make the journey that Jenny had so dearly wanted to make. A sudden stab of envy and resentment shot through her, startling her with its intensity. She drew in her breath sharply, and Alice looked up.

'What's wrong?'

'Just indigestion,' Jenny said mildly, and with a determined effort she concentrated all her attention on her work.

An hour ticked by, then another. Faith's hand slowed and stilled, and she began to nod over her darning. Jenny put down her brush and clenched then straightened her stiff fingers just as her father's snores stopped dead. Across the table, the sisters' eyes met.

'One – two – three— ' Alice mouthed, and had reached fifteen before Teeze gave a great shudder then sucked in his breath again with a choking snore that brought Faith's head up with a start and almost, but not quite, wakened Teeze himself. He shifted in his chair, then relaxed again.

'Lucky you weren't painting then,' Alice murmured. 'You'd have run that butterfly straight into one of the bluebells. He'll forget to breathe in again one of these nights.'

They grinned at each other like conspirators, then Jenny picked up the cup she was working on, blessing her sister's impish sense of humour. Life would be intolerable without Alice.

When the first cup was completed she edged round the truckle-bed and put it on to the mantelshelf where it could dry safely before being fired in the oven. The gas-light emphasised the delicate blue of the flowers, the twining fragile green stems and leaves, the sudden rainbow burst of the butterfly, hovering above one of the blossoms.

Jenny was cleaning her brushes when Lottie came in, blinking in the light. Her hair was tousled, her eyes sleepy and cat-like, and her mouth had the full, almost bruised look that spoke of a man's kisses.

'I'm parched. Is there any tea?'

Teeze choked into silence in mid-snore and woke up, yawning and stretching and scratching himself. The old woman in the truckle-bed stirred and Faith, brushing her darning into the old basket that had held her sewing and knitting for all the years that Jenny could remember, shushed Lottie, rising stiffly from her chair and tiptoeing to lean over the bed, her body shading the old woman's face from the light. When she was satisfied that her mother-in-law wasn't going to waken she straightened up, easing her back carefully as though it hurt her.

'Clear the table, you two, and we'll have a cup of tea before we get to our beds.'

Alice, knowing that a protest would only bring a thump on the ear from her father, began to gather up her books and Jenny carried the lamp back to the dresser. As she set it down its light washed across Maurice's elaborately framed photograph. The telegram that had come from the War Office, already yellowing, was tucked into the frame of the mirror behind the picture.

Looking into the mirror, seeing Faith's tired, worried face reflected in the glass, the lines and hollows deepened instead of softened by the shadows from the gas mantels, she wished that her mother had had the comfort of a strong religion. But the Gillespies didn't believe in religion, only in the here and now and in folks' ability to stand on their own feet, and so Faith had to settle for a handful of flowers beside the likeness of the only one of her three sons to achieve adulthood.

On the afternoon of Maureen's last day at work Miss McQueen, unable to bring herself to join in any unseemly rowdiness but equally unable to put a stop to tradition, discreetly left half an hour early, pleading toothache. As soon as the door had closed behind her the other girls pounced.

Maureen, squealing with excitement, tried to take shelter in a corner but Kerry and Senga dragged her back and held her while Jenny pinned streamers of coloured paper to her blouse and skirt and sleeves, finishing off with a large red paper heart over Maureen's left breast and a paper baby-bonnet, all carefully made at home by Senga and herself and brought in that morning.

'There!' With a flourish she completed the dressing-up by hanging a baby's bottle round Maureen's neck on a string, then stepped back and eyed the result with satisfaction.

'I'm like a dog's dinner, so I am!' the bride-to-be lamented, beaming.

'You're lovely,' Jenny told her, pushing a battered old top hat into her hand. 'Come on, then.'

Giggling they dragged her down the narrow stairs to where the men were already waiting. On the floor by the joiners' area stood a large chamber pot filled with salt. Even Mr Duncan shared in the fun, beaming broadly as he stood by his office door and watched the age-old traditional 'bottling' of the bride-to-be.

'Jump ower the chanty, hen,' Baldy shouted. 'Jump high, for yer man's sake!'

There was a roar of appreciation as Maureen, a rustling rainbow now that her plain white blouse and black skirt were festooned with paper ribbons, lifted her skirt higher than necessary to show plump calves and dimpled knees before skipping over the chamber pot to a cheer of approval from the men.

'Ye'll hae a hooseful o' bonny babies noo,' someone shouted and Maureen yelled back, 'God, I hope no'!' before the men advanced to claim their bridal kiss, each one dropping a coin into the top hat as his contribution to the wedding. Then they lifted the bride-to-be by the arms and legs and carried her, shrieking and displaying more black stocking than was seemly in a young lady, down the stairs and through the wax room and out to the street where a kitchen chair waited, tied to a trolley and decorated with scraps of coloured material.

Passers-by stopped to watch and laugh as Maureen, her bonnet askew on the side of her head, was pulled through the streets to her home in style, waving grandly to either side and having the time of her life. Most of them waved back and shouted out their good wishes, some even tossing a coin into the top hat on Maureen's lap. Children with nothing better to do trailed along after the procession, fighting over the occasional penny that missed the hat and chinked on to the pavement close to their bare toes.

'It'll be your turn next, Jenny,' Maureen called down from the trolley and Jenny, running alongside, shouted back sarcastically. 'Aye, that'll be right! Who'd want me when they'd have to take on my whole family?'

As was usual with weddings in their neighbourhood, the happy couple had a private religious ceremony with only their bridesmaid and best man present before returning to Maureen's home for a meal attended by the immediate family. Friends and neighbours, some of whom had donated tea or sugar or milk or baking for the wedding breakfast, came in afterwards to pay their respects.

Old Peter McLellan had arrived by the time Jenny and Alice reached the flat, and was already busy scraping at his fiddle. The furniture had been pushed against the walls and the centre of the small kitchen was crammed with dancers, so tightly packed together that they could only jump up and down on the spot.

On the sideboard, a handsome piece of furniture from the Dalkieth yard, the presents the couple had received were laid out for all the guests to admire. There was a condiment set from a well-to-do aunt of Maureen's, a pair of dish-towels, a pretty caddy full of tea, a home-made tea-cosy, hand-embroidered pillowcases. And, in pride of place, the decorated cups and saucers, only just completed in time and delivered first thing that morning.

'Jenny!' Maureen, in her best blue dress, fought her way through the crush and hugged her friend when Jenny and Alice squeezed themselves into the crowded room. Her face was crimson with excitement and heat; although the window had been wedged open with an up-ended brick from the yard below the room was stifling. 'Thanks for painting my cups and saucers, they're that bonny! Jacko's sister's fair purple with jealousy. I'm goin' tae put them in my china press – when I get one.'

'Mam baked some scones for you. I'll give them to your mother.' Alice pushed her way further into the crowded kitchen as Maureen towed Jenny to the table by the window. 'Have a drink,' she invited proudly.

Two rows of thick, plain tumblers stood on the table, the larger holding lemonade or beer, the smaller with amber whisky in them. Jenny selected a glass of lemonade and backed into a corner as Maureen was claimed by her new husband for a dance. He, too, was red-faced and perspiring, and more than a little drunk, but even so there was something touching about the protective way he smiled down at his bride as they bumped and pushed their way round the crowded floor, colliding with other would-be dancers.

'Here's a seat for you.' Jenny turned to see Daniel Young indicating the chair he had just left.

'Thanks, Daniel.' She seated herself and he loomed over her so that she had to tip her head back to look up at him. 'Is Walter not here?'

'He's got homework tae do. This isnae a good time tae let his studies fall by the wayside.'

'But the school's closed for the summer holiday, surely?'

'I always arrange for his teachers tae give him work tae dae over the holidays,' said Daniel. 'He cannae afford tae fall behind. He's got himself work at the dairy in Denny Street for the holidays, and he studies in the evenings.'

'There's surely no danger of him falling behind. From what I hear, he's a clever lad.'

Daniel's long serious face lit up. 'He is that. His teachers are fair pleased with him. The headmaster wants him tae go tae the Academy. He'll sit the examinations next April. I hear that your sister's goin' there?'

'Yes, she is. We hope she's going to be a teacher.'

Daniel nodded his approval. 'Folk with brains should be encouraged to better themselves – even lassies,' he added.

If anyone else had spoken so disparagingly about women, Jenny would have challenged them indignantly. But somehow Daniel was different. He would defend his beliefs hotly, and a wedding party was no place to start an argument. So she merely said, 'So Walter's not going into the shipyard, then?'

He had leaned one shoulder against the wall so that his body cut her off from the rest of the room. Now his mouth tightened. 'He is not. That's no life for a lad with brains. He's not going to have oil and filth beneath his fingernails.' His own nails, she noticed, glancing away from his face to ease the ache that had begun to nag at the back of her neck, were very short, square cut and spotlessly clean.

A shrill scream came from Maureen as Jacko swung her up into his arms, scattering dancers to right and left. Startled, Daniel turned and as his body eased away Jenny saw her friend held close to the low ceiling, almost above her new husband's head, her skirt ballooning out to reveal rounded thighs. Daniel looked away hurriedly, his face reddening.

More and more people were crowding into the already packed room, for the Malloys were a popular family in the tenements. When Alice reappeared a few minutes later Jenny drained her glass and stood up, anxious to get into the fresh air. Daniel immediately emptied his own glass and accompanied the two of them. As they went downstairs, Alice dawdling behind them, he began to ask Jenny about her work in the Tank section. By the time they reached the street, meeting people on their way up to the Malloy house as they descended, she found herself talking easily. Daniel was a good listener, though a stilted conversationalist.

'It's amazing to think that a young lassie like you can tell just what speed a ship'll make, and how it'll ride the water,' he marvelled. 'It's a rare talent ye've got.'

'We just work it out from the information sent to us from the Tank. I liked drawing at the school, and mathematics, and I find the work easy enough. I wish women could go into the drawing office at Dalkieth's, though, I'd like to have done work like that,' Jenny told him as they stepped out of the close. It was late afternoon; the slice of sky above the roofs and chimneys was a clear blue and a group of chairs was clustered about every closemouth so that men and women could sit out in the sunlight for a while, the men smoking, the women with basins and bowls on their laps so that they could peel potatoes or scrape carrots for the evening meal. Without realising it, Jenny and Daniel's feet slowed on the cobbles and, by the time they reached the Gillespies' close, Alice was ahead of them. Daniel touched his cap and began to turn away then hesitated and looked back.

'I wondered— ' he began, low-voiced, and hesitated, giving a sidelong glance at the people sitting nearby. Then in a sudden rush of words he said, 'I thought I'd take a walk out to the edge of the town later this evening, to get away from all this for a wee while.' One hand indicated the grey walls crowding in on them, the cobblestones underfoot, the people. 'Mebbe ye'd be free tae come with me?'

Sheer surprise confused her. 'I'm – I'm not sure if I'll find the time,' she stammered. 'There's my gran to see to, and— '

'I'll be at the corner there at about eight o'clock. If you don't come by the time the church clock strikes the quarter I'll know you've got too much to do,' said Daniel hurriedly, and strode off before she could say another word.

Alice had been loitering in the close, listening open-mouthed to every word. 'You're not going to meet him, are you?' she asked, popping out of the close at Jenny as soon as he walked off.

'Why not?'

Alice's snub nose wrinkled. 'He's awful dull.'

'He's a nice kind man and don't you forget it,' Jenny told her sister with enough of an edge to her voice to make the girl's eyes widen. She had had no intention of meeting Daniel that evening, but all at once she decided that maybe she would. It wouldn't do any harm and, after all, there was no sense in hurting the man's feelings.

His disparaging remark about Alice's intelligence came back to her mind, and was dismissed. It would be unfair of her to refuse to go for a walk with him because of a chance remark made without thought.

After all, they were only going for a walk, not courting each other.

120

9

After their wedding George Dalkieth had brought his new bride to the house he had bought for his first wife. It was modest in comparison with the large residence he had been raised in by the river, but it was in a select neighbourhood, and a staff of two maids, a cook and a gardener looked after the young couple very well.

Isobel Dalkieth had suggested that George should sell the place, with its memories of a failed marriage, and bring Fiona to Dalkieth House, where they could have their own suite of rooms, but they had declined; George because he had no wish to live under his mother's watchful eye, Fiona because she had made up her mind that when she moved into the big house it would be as the sole mistress, not a companion dependent on Isobel's bounty. Besides, she could control George much better while they lived on their own.

A few weeks after the launch George burst into their bedroom, waving a crumpled newspaper at his wife, who was still in bed.

'Look at that, dammit!'

'What, dear?' Fiona, who had been enjoying a leisurely breakfast, accepted the paper and studied it vaguely. He snatched it from her and folded it again and again, then thrust it back at her, his handsome face purpling, one finger stabbing at a small announcement. He had thrown himself on to the bed beside her, so close that every time he gave an angry huff she was acutely aware that he had had kippers for breakfast again. George liked to start the day with a hearty meal, which was one of the reasons why he and his wife breakfasted apart.

Fiona peered at the item that kept disappearing beneath his accusing finger and, despite the fire that she insisted be lit in the grate every morning, even in the summer, the blood chilled in her veins. Captain Harold Beasley and Mrs Catherine Beasley of Ashford House, Dunfermline, were happy to announce the birth of their first child, a daughter, to be named Alexandra Catherine. Mother and child were both well.

As she struggled to find the right words the newspaper was snatched from her hands and thrown across the room. 'The bitch!' stormed George, getting up from the bed and pacing the room. 'The bitch! Refusing to give me an heir, then she's not married to that bounder for five minutes before she's shedding brats!'

'Perhaps— ' Fiona began, then stopped short, hit by the enormity of what she had almost said.

'Perhaps what?'

'Nothing. I just – nothing.'

'Fiona,' said George through his teeth. 'I give you notice here and now – I mean to have a son, and I mean to have him soon!'

'Have I ever denied you your rights?'

'No, but we've been married for long enough.'

Now that the first moment of panic was over Fiona's mind had begun to function. 'We've not been married for a year yet. In my opinion it shows vulgar haste to have a family within the first two years of marriage.'

'I,' said George tightly, 'do not agree. You hear me, Fiona? I want an heir!'

'You shall have one, but first I would like to finish my breakfast.'

'Be damned to your breakfast!' snarled George. For a moment he stood in the middle of the pretty bedroom, which Fiona had had redecorated entirely when she moved in, his feet apart, hands fisted on his hips, then, to his wife's horror and outrage he advanced and snatched up the tray containing her lightly boiled egg and pot of weak China tea, setting it on a nearby table with a jingle of agitated china. Stripping off his jacket and unfastening his waistcoat then his trousers he moved back to the bed.

'George! What do you think you're – the maid might come in!'

'She knows better than to walk into a room without permission,' said George Dalkieth, hauling the bed-clothes aside and climbing into bed. Once again Fiona was surrounded by the aroma of kippers. With a rending sound the fine lace on the bodice of her night-gown gave in to his clutching fingers.

'At least give me time to— '

'Dammit I've not got time, I'm due at the yard!' snapped George, pushing her down against the pillows that had been carefully piled up to support her back. She slid down the heap until she was lying flat on the mattress and George impatiently batted toppling pillows out of the way as he followed her, dragging what was left of her gown up around her hips. Without further ado he rolled on top of her, ignoring her breathless objections, crushing her with his weight. The strong smell of kippers filled her nostrils, and her lungs when she opened her mouth to protest further. She shut it again. Not that there was much sense in protesting, for he was already rocking and plunging on top of her like a demented bull.

123

A few minutes later he was out of bed and getting dressed while Fiona, clutching the sheet to her chin in a belated attempt at modesty, was still considering whether anger or hurt would have the most effect on him. Since anger hadn't done much previously, she opted for hurt, catching her breath and squeezing a tear into her eyes.

It had no effect. Without glancing at her, without apparently hearing her sniffles, her husband completed his toilet, anxiously consulted the handsome watch on his watch-chain, and muttered, 'I'm going to be late.'

'George— '

Impervious to the tear that she had now managed to trickle on to her cheek, he picked up the discarded tray and put it back on the bed. 'I mean it, Fiona – I want an heir. Catherine refused to give me one, but you won't, if you're wise.' Then he left the room, and she was alone – sore, humiliated and furious.

She well knew that word of his ex-wife's child would quickly spread round the town. Everyone would know that the woman George Dalkieth had divorced because she was apparently unable to give him children had borne a daughter to her second husband with quite indecent haste. People would snigger, and no doubt wonder if George would be prepared to divorce a second wife if she, too, remained childless.

Fiona had no intention of allowing that to happen. Her father owned a large and successful emporium in Glasgow and his family had enjoyed a comfortable life, but, when all was said and done, her father was only a tradesman compared to the Dalkieths, and Fiona's marriage to George had been quite a triumph. She wasn't prepared to be sent back home in disgrace.

Despite her protests about the vulgarity of having

children too soon, there was no reason why she shouldn't have been pregnant before this. There might well be a sinister warning in the fact that George's first wife hadn't had his child, but had conceived easily with her second husband.

Fiona lay among the rumpled mess of her formerly comfortable bed and thought hard. She knew that George wouldn't consider even the most carefully worded suggestion that he himself should have a talk with the family physician. To men like George the ability to father children was a God-given right, a fact. Without that ability they couldn't consider themselves to be men.

Fiona wasn't particularly interested in children herself, but the Dalkieth money meant that they could afford a good nursery staff and she had a vague idea that children brought their own blessing and that she and George would, when the occasion arose, make devoted parents.

There was still plenty of time, she'd thought, after all, he was only twenty-seven years of age and she was five years younger. But now, with the birth of a daughter to his first wife, the situation had become serious. Time was running out. If she didn't become pregnant soon she might find herself with problems.

She began to sit up then realised that George had dumped her breakfast tray back on the bed in such a way that she was almost lying underneath it. Because the sheet was over her shoulders and arms she couldn't free her hands to lift the tray away. She squirmed this way and that, but there was no way of freeing herself, other than heaving her body over and sending the entire tray, with its cold toast and egg and tepid tea crashing to the floor and ruining the expensive carpeting she had chosen personally.

She had no option but to lie still, a prisoner, until the maid tapped on the door and entered, in answer to a terse command, to find her dishevelled mistress lying flat on her bed, pinned beneath her breakfast tray, with pillows strewn over the floor and the bed looking like a battle-ground.

The widespread admiration that Maureen's painted cups and saucers had caused on her wedding day brought more work for Jenny, and filled up what little spare time there was left after she had put Helen to bed and helped her mother.

Whenever possible, she went out in the evenings for a breath of fresh air when the old woman and the baby were settled, walking down by the river most of the time, following the path that led away from the ship-yard and out into the country around the town. Sometimes Daniel Young walked with her; he said very little about his own work, but was always interested in Jenny's. Despite herself, she was flattered and soothed by his admiration.

Often they walked in silence; at first Jenny, used to people talking all the time, found this uncomfortable, but soon she realised that with Daniel there was no need to talk all the time. She came to appreciate the freedom his silence gave her to concentrate on her own thoughts.

She was taken aback when Maureen, meeting her in the street one day, referred to Daniel as her sweetheart.

'He's nothing of the sort!'

'You walk out together.'

'That doesn't make us sweethearts,' Jenny protested, and her friend winked.

'It's the way me and Jacko started out – it's the way every couple starts out.'

'We just happen to meet sometimes, and if we're walking in the same direction we might as well walk together.' Jenny retorted, and was exasperated when Maureen smirked.

Daniel, she soon noticed, only mentioned the shipyard when they visited Bella and Patrick, and then he talked generally, apparently unaware of the tension that always seemed to crackle through the small room, never saying anything that would remind Patrick too strongly of the work he had had to give up because of his war wounds. Patrick became more animated whenever Daniel was in the room.

'You're good with him,' Jenny said as they stepped out into the street after one of their visits. Patrick had been unusually relaxed and animated that night, and Bella's face glowed with happiness as she watched him. 'I never know what to say to him. He's so – locked in. Patrick was never like that before.'

'He's had a rough time of it. You'd need tae have been there tae know how bad it was. I tell you one thing, if it ever comes tae another war I'll not let my son go,' Daniel said with iron in his voice.

'It'll never come to that again.'

'I hope not. They asked enough of us the last time, and took more than most of us could afford tae give – and little thanks we've had for it.' The iron was still there, bitter in his throat. Looking sideways at him, she saw the sinews standing out on his neck. 'Look at young Pat back there – what sort of gratitude have they shown him? Robbed him of the right to work and given him nothin' but a pitiful pension in exchange. They'll not ever do that tae my boy – he's goin' tae be one o' the bosses, not one o' the slaves!'

*

In September Alice donned the grey skirt and blazer, the blue blouse and grey-and-blue striped tie worn by the Academy pupils. She had managed to buy the uniform from a second-hand shop, with money earned by working during the summer holidays at a local bakery.

Her father stared the first morning she walked into the kitchen, self-conscious in her uniform. 'What the hell's she dressed like that for?'

'It's her clothes for the Academy,' Faith was explaining nervously when Jenny came into the room.

'Academy?' Teeze said the word as though it was dirty, and Alice flinched.

'You know fine that I won a scholarship, Dad.'

'I know nothin' of the sort!'

'I told you myself,' Jenny cut in. 'You grunted and went on reading your paper.'

He stabbed a thick finger in Alice's direction. 'She should be out workin' for her keep, like the rest of us!'

'You're right there,' Lottie remarked from the table, where she was drinking a cup of tea, her eyes still puffy with sleep and her uncombed hair in a tangle.

Alice flushed and opened her mouth to speak, but Jenny, putting a reassuring hand on the girl's arm, said, 'She'll do better for herself getting an education.'

'And who's tae support her while she's gettin' it?'

'I will,' Jenny told him. 'It's my wages that do most of the supporting round here anyway.'

She heard her mother gasp at her impudence, but Jenny held her father's gaze, refusing to be the first to look away.

He crumpled the newspaper he was reading and threw it on to the floor, then stamped out of the room, leaving Jenny more determined than ever that, no matter how hard it was, she would see that Alice got the opportunity for advancement she had had to deny herself.

Jenny's struggle to find the money to keep her sister at the Academy received unexpected assistance a month later. She was called to Robert Archer's small but comfortable office in the shipyard's main office block and offered the job of supervisor in the tracing office.

'But – but Senga's surely the one who should take over from Miss McQueen!' she protested, after a stunned silence.

The pen in Robert's hand tapped at the blotting paper before him, flipped over, tapped again. 'You both started on the same day. There's no question of seniority.'

'She's two months older than I am.'

'But you're the one that Miss McQueen recommended,' he reminded her, adding with a lift of an eyebrow, 'Unless you think you're not capable of taking on the responsibility?'

'Oh, I am!' She had no doubt of that. And suddenly she realised that promotion meant more money and a slight easing of the family's financial situation.

'That's settled, then. Mr Duncan agrees with me that when Miss McQueen retires next month you'll become tracing office supervisor – with an increase in wages, of course.'

'You're not— ' she began to say, then hesitated, reddening.

'Not what?'

'You know fine what I mean. You're not giving me the job just because of— '

His mouth tightened and the pen dropped to the desk. 'You think I'd have favourites? I told you – Miss

129

McQueen recommended you and Mr Duncan supported her. There's no favouritism about it, although I have to say that I think they've come to the right decision. You're good at your work, Jenny. You deserve this chance.'

She got to her feet. 'Thank you, Mr Archer.'

'You can surely use my given name when there's nobody else about.'

'Best not,' she said, and left the room. Scowling, he picked up his pen, dipped it into the inkwell and started to write, then laid it down again and got up, crossing restlessly to the window. Below him, as he stood on the upper floor of the office block, was the woodyard with its huge piles of timber. The angle-iron smithy lay beyond them with the joiner's shop to the left and the tidal basin to the right. The river itself was hidden from his view by an intricate mass of scaffolding and half-completed ships. Dalkieth's yard had eight building berths, and now, in September 1919, seven of them were occupied. George Dalkieth and his mother had every right to be satisfied with the way things were going, yet uneasiness gnawed at Robert's gut.

He glimpsed movement below him as Jenny, neat in her white blouse and dark skirt, came out of the shelter of the office block and began to flank the woodyard on her way back to the tracing office. Watching the set of her shoulders and the tilt of her head with its short, dark hair Robert felt a sudden sense of loss. For all her quiet demeanour, Jenny Gillespie had her pride. He had no way of knowing whether it was only pride that had made her keep him at arms' length since his return to Ellerslie, or genuine indifference. He remembered the feel of her in his arms as they danced together at the back-court party on the day of the first peacetime launch, close and yet remote, willing to turn away from him and step into another man's embrace without a backward glance. It was possible that she would never forgive him for having betrayed her after his move to England. He had heard that she was walking out with someone else now; perhaps, Robert thought, the time had come to accept that he had lost her for good.

His lips tightened as he watched her move out of sight, then he turned back to his desk, telling himself that Jenny wasn't the only woman in the world. There were others, including one as erect and slender as Jenny, but with hair like silky corn framing a blue-eyed face that could slip from haughtiness to a beguiling smile in an instant.

Tonight he was due to dine at Fergus Craig's house, and no doubt Fiona Dalkieth would be there. Since his return to Ellerslie he had received a number of invitations to soirees and supper parties. His first inclination had been to refuse, for he had little interest in such goings-on, but Isobel Dalkieth had reminded him gently but firmly that he represented the shipyard now and was no longer free to please himself.

So he had attended this event and that, and each time Isobel's daughter-in-law was there, growing increasingly friendly towards the new office manager as her husband grew increasingly sullen. Fiona Dalkieth, Robert soon realised, was something of a flirt. Now that he had settled back into life in Ellerslie and had got the measure of his new appointment he was beginning to hunger for feminine company. He had enjoyed and appreciated the physical side of marriage and the warmth of a woman in his bed. He wanted that woman to be Jenny – but if she had indeed lost interest in him, then he would have to look elsewhere. Time was

131

passing; he was in the prime of life – and his hunger was growing.

At Elspeth Craig's dinner table that evening the conversation, dominated by the men, mainly concerned shipbuilding. One of the guests, Malcolm McWalter, was an ageing man who owned a small shipyard adjacent to the Dalkieth yard. On occasion the two yards had helped each other out, but now McWalter felt that it was time for him to retire and he was anxious to find a buyer for his business. It was clear from the way he introduced the subject – and from the reaction he got from George Dalkieth – that the man had already approached George unofficially, and George was in favour of taking over the smaller yard.

'Are you sure that this is the right time to think of expanding?' Robert Archer enquired, and George gave him a withering look across the table.

'When could we find a better time? Our order books have never been so full and our profits are up. This is when we should invest and expand. Clyde shipbuilding is respected all over the world.' George thumped a fist on the table for emphasis.

'And how do we pay for this expansion? Robert asked mildly. Isobel Dalkieth took her eyes from her son and looked at him. 'During the war years the Government subsidised shipbuilding because we're an island nation and our warships were vital. They're not going to continue to subsidise us now that peace has been restored.'

There was a murmur of agreement around the table but George shrugged it off as though it was a speck of dust on his lapel. 'We borrow from the banks. Our name's good.'

132

'Only while business continues to be brisk.'

McWalter, seeing his chances of selling out to the Dalkieth yard under threat, cut in sharply. 'Why should it not continue?'

'At the moment importers and exporters all about the globe are rushing to replace ships either sunk in action or too old to be of use for much longer,' Robert explained. 'Commercial shipbuilding has stagnated during the past five years and there's a great need for it at the moment—'

'My point exactly,' George interrupted, his voice triumphant. Archer didn't even bother to give him a look, concentrating instead on Isobel Dalkieth and Fergus Craig, seated near each other.

'And what happens when that need has been met? That won't take long because shipyards all round the world, not just here in Britain, are working flat out to satisfy it. We must also take into consideration the captured enemy tonnage that's being handed over to commercial traders to take the place of ships commandeered for the war effort then lost.'

'That's only a stop-gap business,' George told him impatiently. 'The enemy ships are old and battle-weary; they'll all have to be replaced by new stock.'

'And once they are, there must be a lull, a recession. Mark my words,' said Archer insistently, 'Shipping companies aren't bottomless wells. Once they meet their targets the orders will slow down and the result for us may well be empty berths, men being laid off – and profits dropping.'

'Only for those yards that have refused to move with the times,' George trumpeted, his face reddening with anger. 'You're talking like a cautious old woman, Archer!'

A flash of anger brightened Robert Archer's eyes. His fingers, absently caressing the stem of a glass, tightened on its fragility. 'I was brought back to the Dalkieth yard because of the knowledge I gathered on Tyneside. There's little sense in me holding my tongue when I hear wild talk about expansion and spending money at a time when we should be consolidating what we have and planning for the future.'

'You were brought back because of your experience as a shipbuilder,' George snapped at him. 'You've little enough knowledge of the financial side of things, for all that you've been pushed into the post of office manager.'

Archer's face reddened at the deliberate slight. 'No man who's had to live on what he earns, and do without when there's no money coming in, can be accused of knowing nothing about finance,' he said, looking his tormentor full in the face. 'It's those who only know how to live on wealth earned for them by others who have little knowledge of its value.'

He knew as soon as he had said it, as soon as a rustle of movement and the sound of indrawn breath eddied around the table, that he had gone too far. George Dalkieth was by no means the only person present who had been born into money, or made his comfortable living through the efforts of other men on comparatively low wages.

'Ladies – ' Elspeth Craig rose from her seat abruptly in response to a glance from her husband. 'Shall we withdraw and leave the men to their port?'

'I agree. We've been sitting here overlong.' Isobel got to her feet and swept from the room, her head high. Fiona's eyes met Robert's as she rose from her seat, and he saw sympathy in them.

'I'm afraid you spoke out of turn, Mr Archer,' she murmured later when the men had come into the drawing room. Robert was standing on his own near the windows and slowly, moving from one person to the next, she had contrived finally to reach him.

'I only spoke my mind, Mrs Dalkieth.'

'How very refreshing – and how dangerous.' Her blue eyes held his for a long moment and the corners of her full mouth flickered into a conspiratorial smile. 'I find that my husband prefers people to speak *his* mind, not their own.'

'Indeed? Are you speaking his mind now, Mrs Dalkieth?'

'George's opinions are boring. I prefer to make up my own mind about things. And,' she added, 'about people.'

'Indeed?' said Robert. Then, in a faintly mocking echo of her own words, 'How very refreshing.'

10

'You didn't have much to say for yourself this evening,'
George Dalkieth complained when he and his wife were
on their way back to their own house in their chauffeur-
driven car.

Fiona cast him a sidelong look. 'I'm not interested in
chatter about clothes and the problems of finding and
keeping good servants. And I'm even less interested in
shipbuilding.'

He grunted and said nothing more until they reached
home. In the hall Fiona reached up to kiss her husband's
cheek. 'Goodnight, dear.'

'I'll be up in a moment.'

She sighed as she began to mount the stairs. She had
no doubt that he would be up in a moment. She was still
not pregnant, and George was still hell-bent on proving
to himself and his former wife that he was a virile man,
capable of fathering a brood of children on the right
partner.

A bedside lamp had been left on and Fiona's nightgown and George's pyjamas had been laid out on the
satin quilt. Fiona prepared for bed swiftly and climbed
in, switching out the lamp and hoping against hope that
George would settle down in the library with his newspaper and a glass of whisky and delay coming upstairs
until he was too tired to make love to her.

Her heart sank when she heard his heavy tread less than five minutes later. By the time he switched on the overhead light she had buried her head beneath the quilt and was giving every sign of being in a deep and peaceful slumber. The floor creaked and he grunted once or twice as he stripped his clothes off, leaving them where they lay. He had been raised by nursemaids and had never had to learn how to fold his clothes or put them away.

The light clicked off and he muttered a subdued curse as he fumbled his way towards the bed. A draft of cold air assailed her back as he thumped into it, then his hands reached out for her, tugging at her shoulder, wrenching her round to face him.

'George— ' she protested, but his fingers were busy with the bows of her gown. Her own hands came into contact with cold, naked skin and she jerked back in disgust. 'George, I do wish you'd put your pyjamas on! It's vulgar to come to bed naked. Only working-class men do such a thing!'

'How do you know about working-class men?' he mumbled, his fingers busy.

'George!'

'Anyway, pyjamas get in the way.' He found the hem of her gown and started to haul on it. She pressed her hip against the mattress but he levered her up and continued to peel her as though she was a grape.

'I'm tired!'

'I'll not take long.'

She knew that only too well. The bed squeaked in protest as the nightdress was hauled as far as her armpits and George Dalkieth triumphantly claimed his reward.

'All you have to do is become pregnant,' he panted as

he rolled her over on to her back and covered her with his own body. 'Then you can sleep till the brat's born if that's what you wish!'

'Women can't just become pregnant by wanting to!' The words came out in a series of jerks as Fiona's ribcage was crushed and released like an accordian.

'Yes they can – Catherine proved that, the secretive bitch that she is. Anyway— ' George gave a wheezy, coarse chuckle, 'I'm doing my bit.'

While he did his bit, Fiona lay stiffly beneath him, her teeth sunk into her lower lip, praying that this time she would conceive and get the whole messy business over with.

Robert Archer suddenly came to mind, with his lean body, his narrow face, handsome in its own way, those grey eyes that seemed to hold a promise of – something that Fiona would like to find out more about. Deliberately, she conjured up an image of him lying alone in his bachelor bed, perhaps staring into the darkness, thinking of her. As George pumped and puffed the picture in her mind changed until she could imagine her own fair head on the pillow beside Archer's dark one, see his eyes gazing into hers, feel his arms about her, his hands—

She whimpered and gave an involuntary shudder just as George, with a final muted roar, collapsed on top of her, almost squashing her.

'You see?' he murmured smugly into her ear, tickling it with his whisky-laden breath, 'You enjoyed it, too. That means you'll probably fall pregnant.'

It was all she could do not to heave herself round bodily and toss him out on to the carpet.

At the Board meeting a week later Robert Archer was not surprised to find himself out-voted on the decision to buy over the neighbouring yard and expand Dalkieth's with the assistance of a bank loan.

When he made one last attempt to argue against the motion put forward by George Dalkieth, Isobel said clearly and coldly. 'I feel, Mr Archer, that you're erring on the cautious side. A commendable quality, but one that has to be tempered by a degree of adventure now and again. I agree with my son that we should make an offer for the McWalter ground.'

During the four weeks Miss McQueen was training her into her new post there were times when Jenny almost gave in to the temptation to go to Robert's office and ask him to change his mind and give the position of supervisor to Senga. The thought of being in charge of the tracing office, being responsible for the quality of the work done there, terrified her. If she hadn't had so many problems at home she would have relished the thought of promotion. But sometimes she felt as though being the new supervisor was just one more weight on her shoulders, and more than she could cope with.

But once October came and Miss McQueen departed for Paisley, where she was going to take over as housekeeper to her brother, a widower and church minister, Jenny discovered that she loved her new position. With the shipbuilding industry flourishing, Dalkieth's Experimental Tank was in great demand from shipbuilders up and down the reaches of the Clyde as well as from its own yard and the tracers and analysts were kept busy from morning till night.

It took fifteen minutes for the water in the Tank to settle after each experiment, but as soon as it did, off the truck went again, backing up to the end of the Tank then surging forward with a clatter and rattle of machinery to clang to a sudden halt that almost sent the naval architect balancing on the small platform reeling. After each set of experiments another fat roll of paper was carried up to the tracing office, bearing another series of figures to be worked out and analysed by the girls.

As well as dealings with the model trials the tracers worked out the likely results before each Dalkieth ship left the slips to run the measured mile over the stretch of water off Skelmorlie, and analysed the actual results once the trials were over. Often they were working on a ship's performance while it was still running the mile, for a 'doo-loft', complete with pigeons and caretaker, was part of the shipyard equipment. An apprentice was sent aboard each ship due to run the measured mile with a basket of fluttering cooing birds that were released at intervals to fly back to the loft with information fastened to their legs. As each bird returned to the loft the message it carried was brought at once to the tracing office.

Jinnet Harper, a woman in her thirties who had left the tracing office to get married during Jenny's first year there, was brought back to make up the team of analysts and tracers. The war had treated Jinnet badly; her husband had been killed in action and her only child had later died of Spanish 'flu. She was pathetically grateful to Robert Archer, who had remembered her from his own days in the Tank section as a naval architect, for seeking her out and offering her her old job back.

Thanks to Jenny's promotion and increased salary the Gillespie family's financial worries had eased a little. Alice was settling in well at the Academy, while Lottie, for all her sulking and complaining, seemed to be enjoying her work at the public house, and Teeze had said no more about her paying her wages over to Jenny.

Faith fretted just as much as before and fussed over her mother-in-law as she waited, with heart-rending patience, for Maurice to come home.

'You'd think the truth would have dawned on her by now,' Alice said as she and Jenny and Bella worked together in the brick wash-house early one Monday morning, a good hour before the shipyard siren was due to sound. The sisters had taken to combining their washing and dealing with it before they had to go about their day's duties, and while Patrick was still asleep.

Alice was turning the big mangle while Bella and Jenny fed the sheets through it one by one. Grey scummy water cascaded from the tangle of wet linen into the tub on the floor as the two of them tried to keep the folds of the material smooth so that it wouldn't bunch up and jam the rollers.

'Mebbe someone should say something. It's not right that she's still waiting. It might be better for her to face the truth,' Bella was volunteering when the door opened, letting in a waft of fresh air and Mrs Malloy, a cigarette dangling from the corner of her mouth and her arms filled with laundry.

'God, but ye're early birds, so yez are! I'll just use that water when ye've done if ye've no objections. No point in throwin' out good hot water.'

'It's very dirty, Mrs Malloy.'

'Ach, that'll no' bother me, Alice hen. Sure, my old man's dungarees are that filthy they could stand on their own. I could send them tae wash themselves if they

werenae as thick as he is when it comes tae followin'
directions.' Kerry's mother laughed wheezily. 'Any
water'll be clean enough for them.'

The sisters exchanged looks. Mrs Malloy was notorious for 'borrowing' other people's water to save herself
the trouble of cleaning and refilling the big copper.

'If that's what you want, Mrs Malloy,' Jenny said,
and the woman dropped her load on the floor and
began to sort through it, her huge, rolling behind
straining against the confines of an old tweed skirt.
They could see the stitching in the seams being pulled
apart.

'Who did yez say would be the better of knowin' the
truth?' the woman demanded as she worked. Nothing
was a secret as far as Mrs Malloy was concerned, but
there wasn't a malicious bone in her entire body and
many a neighbour in need had benefited from her casual
generosity in the past.

'Our mam,' Alice's round face was screwed up with
concern. 'We're thinking it's bad for her to go on
waiting for Maurice when we all know he's not coming
home.'

'Who says he's no'? Did he send ye a telegram, then?'

'After all this time— '

Mrs Malloy fisted her shiny red hands, already
showing signs of winter hacks, on to her hips, the
washing forgotten. 'Listen tae me, lassies – for all yez
know yer poor ma might be right. He might be safe an'
well.'

'But— '

The woman stopped Jenny with one look. 'God has
his own ways, hen, an' don't ye forget that. Mebbe this
is his way of helpin' yer poor ma tae get used tae the
idea of losin' her only son. Leave her be, that's what I

142

say. Leave her with her hopes. Ye've no way of knowin' what harm ye might do if yez try tae make her see things different.'

'D'you think our Maurice is going to walk through the door one of these days?' Bella challenged, and Mrs Malloy swung her turbanned head with its fringe of escaping greying hair in her direction.

'No – but that's my opinion, no' Faith's. She's no' daft – she'll make up her own mind in her own time. She'd not thank ye for tryin' tae interfere – an' neither would I,' she added. 'So think on. Yer ma's been a good neighbour tae me an' I'll no' see her heart broken by a thoughtless word. Here— ' she advanced on the boiler and reached into the hot water without flinching to haul a fistful of sheet out. 'Get that through the mangle or yez'll all be late an' my water'll be stone cold.'

'How's Maureen?' Jenny remembered to ask as they worked together.

'Like a house-side, an' wishin' she'd never let Jacko cuddle her so hard in the spring.' Maureen's mother cackled. 'But that's what we all think when we get tae her stage. Next thing the bairn's squawlin' in a cot an' there we are, daft as ever, lookin' for another cuddle.'

'Tell her I'll visit her soon.'

'She'd like that, hen. Ye've got a lot o' sheets, surely?'

'Mrs McColl that I work for gave me some old ones,' Bella said breathlessly as they all struggled to get the final sheet, a renegade, out of the water and through the mangle. 'What with Gran not bein' able tae hold herself in any more, Mam needs extra sheets.'

The Irishwoman shook her head. 'I mind the way yer gran used tae lift her feet high when she came walkin' down the street tae visit yer ma, for all the world as though there was some infection hidin' in the gutters, an' the look on her face when she had tae pick her way through the bare-arsed weans playin' in the street. Her ladyship, we used tae cry her.'

'My Mam hated her then,' Bella remembered.

'Ach daughters-in-law an' mothers-in-law never get on well thegither. Look at me an' our Tom's Rosie, stuck-up wee bitch that she is,' said Mrs Malloy without rancour. 'But for all that ye cannae fault the way Faith looks after the old woman now that she's in need.'

'I don't know why Mam's so good to her now, after the way Gran used to talk to her.' Jenny retrieved the old wooden and metal clothes tongs from the floor by the boiler and started to fish in the water for any smaller clothing that might be hidden in the steamy yellowish depths.

'One day when ye've done a bit o' livin' yersel', hen, ye'll understand,' said Mrs Malloy. 'Now – will ye let me at that water while there's still a wee drop of heat in it?'

At the end of October, just after Helen's second birthday, trouble flared at the shipyard when a section of the workforce threatened to down tools over the sacking of a lad who had been caught making tea for his 'gang'.

Daniel, who had been involved in the row, spoke at length about it at an unofficial meeting in the Gillespies' house that night, his thin face tight with anger. As well as the usual six or seven men who had got into the habit of calling in at Teeze Gillespie's home every week there were a half-dozen more, some sitting on the floor, some leaning against the walls. Tonight there was tension in the small crowded room, and an air of purpose that had never been present before.

Jenny, sitting in a corner, doing some darning for her

mother, let the work drop to her lap as she watched Daniel and listened to the words that poured from his lips.

'The gaffer came by an' took a kick at the brazier. It was that swine Baker, the one that has a son workin' in the Tank section. Sent the whole thing over, he did, an' if the poor lad makin' the tea hadnae jumped back he could've been burned, or scalded by boilin' water. Red-hot coals all over the place – an' the tea-leaves lost. It cost money tae buy that tea.'

There was a growl of anger from his listeners and one of them said, 'Any decent man, even a gaffer, would've given the lad a warnin' an' let the men have their hot drink. From what I heard, it was so cold that the fire had been lit tae melt the oil in the machines.'

'You're right,' Daniel told him. 'I went there mysel' afterwards, tae talk tae them. The wind was blowin' up from the river sharp as a knife, an' they were all shakin' wi' the cold. Poor Jamie that got intae trouble had only a thin jacket on over his shirt.' He looked round the circle of faces. 'We all know Jamie – he's only a simple-minded laddie that earns what he can by doin' whatever he's told tae dae. He was in such a state o' fear in case he lost his job that they had tae stop him from putting the hot coals back intae the brazier with his bare hands. Then Dalkieth himsel' sent word that the lad was tae be turned away, an' him wi' no chance o' gettin' work anywhere else. The men that know Jamie best went tae his office tae ask him tae give the lad another chance, but it was no use.'

'It was George Dalkieth's father that gave Jamie the job in the first place,' Teeze said, ' 'cause the laddie's own father had been a good worker in his time. I mind the day he died in an accident in that very yard.'

145

Daniel nodded. 'When we heard word o' what was goin' on we put our heads together then sent word tae the office that we was goin' tae down tools if Jamie was turned off.' His mouth was grim. 'It's no' right that a man like Dalkieth should have the power tae take another man's livin' from him without a word of protest spoken. The men that first saw Mr George were level-headed creatures with the right words in their mouths, yet they couldnae get him tae see reason – him that never missed a meal in his life or was ever threatened wi' bein' put out o' his fine house because he couldnae find the rent.'

'If it had been left tae him we'd all've walked out and be damned tae the consequences, an' mebbe more would've followed us,' the other man said. 'But Robert Archer stepped in just then, an' he up an' took Jamie's side.'

Jenny saw her father's mouth tighten at the words of praise for Robert. Daniel nodded, and gave a bark of laughter. 'I don't know who was the most surprised, Mr George or ourselves. Archer said it wasnae worth losin' time ower a can o' tea. I hear he gave that bastard Baker a right tongue lashin'.'

He looked round the circle of faces. 'If you ask me, it's high time the unions were in that yard. George Dalkieth's no' the only yin that's entitled tae his rights.'

Around the range, heads wagged in vigorous agreement.

11

At that moment Robert Archer, sober and neat in a brown suit under a warm topcoat, skirted George Dalkieth's gleaming new motor car, which stood at the foot of the broad sweep of steps leading to the front door of Dalkieth House.

An elderly butler admitted him into a large square hall dominated by a massive painting of the wife and children of George Dalkieth, the founder of the shipyard. Archer laid his hat and gloves on a gleaming table and was ushered into the library where Isobel Dalkieth waited for him behind a huge desk, her hands clasped on the spotless blotter before her. Her face was expressionless but George, who occupied a chair opposite his mother, looked sullen.

'Well, Mr Archer, you know why you're here?'

'I'm here because you asked me to call, Mrs Dalkieth.' Archer put an extra feather of weight on the word 'asked' and knew by the way her eyebrows tightened slightly that she had noticed it.

'I – asked you to call because I want to get to the bottom of an incident that occurred in the yard this morning.'

'It was an internal matter and it has been dealt with, Mrs Dalkieth.'

Isobel stopped him with a raised hand. 'I understand

147

that there's talk of the unions being involved with our yard because of it. This makes it more important than an internal matter. I would like to hear your side of the story, if you please.'

Archer's eyes flickered towards George Dalkieth, who was scowling at the carpet and pulling at his lower lip. So the fool had gone whining to his mother for support, had he? He glanced at the empty chair near George, then back at Mrs Dalkieth. He was damned if he was going to stay on his feet like a schoolboy in the wrong.

'Sit down, Mr Archer.'

'Thank you.' He took time to settle himself before telling her calmly about the foreman who had come across a man making tea and had kicked the brazier over, tea-can and all.

'I understand that the man in question was only doing as he was asked by others. The fire was already there, and it was bitterly cold in that part of the yard. There was no harm— '

'The men know the rules about making tea in the company's time,' George snapped.

'Even so, they still make tea. I did it myself when I was working in the yards.'

'Then you should have been dismissed for it.'

'I made certain that I was never caught, Mrs Dalkieth. But the lad concerned in today's trouble didn't have the wit to avoid being caught. He was only doing as his workmates asked.'

'If he's bright enough to earn money, he's bright enough to know the difference between right and wrong,' growled George, while his mother said crisply. 'I trust you're not adopting too lenient an attitude towards the men, Mr Archer.'

'I can assure you that there's no danger of that.'

'You soon knuckled under when a group of them threatened to walk out,' George cut in.

'I saw no sense in making an issue of something as unimportant as an illicit can of tea.' Archer heard a thin note of anger come into his voice and swallowed it back. 'If the men had walked out it would have held up production. Others might well have joined them. The nature of the situation didn't call for that.'

'The working man is becoming altogether too aggressive these days,' Mrs Dalkieth said coldly. 'If we're not vigilant we'll be done for.'

'The working man has just won a war, Mrs Dalkieth. He's not in the mood to see things return to the way they were before he was wrenched from his home and his family and sent away to risk life and limb for his fellow countrymen.'

'That's a dangerous attitude for a manager to take!'

'On the contrary, I think it's a practical attitude. Men give better service to a company that recognises their self-respect.' Robert Archer stood up. 'I can assure you that I'll not allow anything to bring Dalkieth's yard into disrepute, or to interfere with the work. If you intend to bring this matter before the Board of Directors I shall be happy to justify my actions to them.'

A trace of colour stained the woman's cheeks. 'In other words, you're wondering why I chose to deal with the matter myself instead of bringing the other directors into it. I happen to agree, Mr Archer, that today's disturbance was trivial and can now be laid to rest. I merely wanted to hear your— ' She stopped short, but she and Archer both knew that she had been about to say, 'your side of the story.'

'If you have no more need of me,' he began as the door opened and Fiona Dalkieth swept in.

'George, I can't wait any longer. I promised Mrs Tennant that I would call and it's getting late. I can send the car back for you.'

'Thank you, Mr Archer,' Mrs Dalkieth said evenly, as much in reproof to her daughter-in-law as to the office manager, who inclined his head and left the room, catching the scent of lily-of-the-valley as he walked past the newcomer.

He collected his hat and gloves and stepped out into the chilly, windy evening with a sense of relief. The house behind him was altogether too oppressive and luxurious for his liking. So George had gone running to his mama to complain that the new office manager had overstepped himself, he thought, striding down the drive. From the very first, Archer had had no doubts of the other man's antagonism. He even understood it – George had worked with his father and his brother, and now they were both gone and an outsider, a man from the tenements and a former apprentice in the yard, had appeared in their place. It was natural for George to feel that his nose had been put out of joint.

But Robert Archer also knew why he had been appointed. George was the weak link of the shipping family and Robert had been brought in as a counterbalance, someone who knew more about shipyards than George ever would. Someone who would keep the yard going while George reigned as crown prince.

From the moment Archer had met Isobel Dalkieth he had recognised her ruthlessness and ambition, her burning love of the company and her desire to keep it solvent. She had all the strength that her surviving son lacked, but it wasn't a woman's place to run a shipyard.

She needed Robert Archer's knowledge and experience to keep the yard from going under when the slump came, as come it must.

And he needed the yard just as much as she did. He had worked hard for such a position, had dragged himself up the ladder inch by inch, working by day and studying by night, living hand to mouth to pay for books and tuition. He had toiled in atrocious conditions and had had to learn how to use his fists as well as his tongue and his brain. He had worked on his accent, his appearance, his bearing, and now his efforts had paid off.

And, by God, he swore to himself as he walked, he wouldn't let a wealthy, arrogant know-nothing like George Dalkieth take any of it away from him.

A thin, icy drizzle had began to fall, and he turned his coat collar up as he swung through the Dalkieth gate and on to the pavement. He had only gone some ten yards when he heard a car turning out of the driveway behind him, then a voice called his name. He turned to see that George's handsome car was keeping pace with him, the uniformed chauffeur staring straight ahead as though disassociating himself from his young mistress, who was waving from the rear window.

'Mr Archer, can I offer you a lift?'

'I'm only going to Park Street.'

'I'm driving in that direction. Stop, McFee,' she ordered, and opened the door as the car halted.

'Thank you.' Archer ducked his head and climbed in as she moved across the seat to the other side. The interior smelled of leather and lily-of-the-valley.

'You don't have a car yourself?' she asked as he seated himself beside her. This time her hat had a narrow oval-shaped brim, and she wore a coat of silky black fur. Her small face glowed like a pearl against her large fur collar.

'I've never felt the need for one.'

'Park Street, McFee.' She gave Archer a sidelong glance as the car moved forward. 'Do you rent rooms there?'

'I have a small house.'

'For your wife, when she comes North.'

'My wife has decided that the Scots are too fierce for her. She will not be joining me.'

'Oh? I'm sorry.'

'No need to be, Mrs Dalkieth.'

She let the silence grow between them, and Robert did the same, until finally she probed, 'So you live on your own?'

'A housekeeper comes in every day.'

'It must be lonely in the evenings and at the weekends.'

'I've not found it so.'

'I shall tell George to invite you for dinner one evening.'

'If you'll forgive me for saying so, Mrs Dalkieth, that wouldn't be a good idea. Men who have to work together see quite enough of each other without being expected to socialise as well.'

She pouted. 'So I must do without your company just because you and George are tired of the sight of each other?'

He smiled. She was pretty and flirtatious, and he was enjoying this little interlude, locked into the small leather-smelling space with her, behind the chauffeur's rigid back. 'I doubt if my company would be of any great interest to you,' he said, wondering what on earth such a pretty young woman could have seen in a lumbering ox like George Dalkieth – other than his money and his family's prestige.

'I don't agree.' Fiona leaned forward as the car came to a standstill, rubbing at the window with a gloved hand. 'Which is your house?'

Archer found and operated the door handle while the chauffeur was still reaching for his own handle. 'The third on the left.' He got out, then turned and said into the car's interior, 'Thank you for the lift.'

'We'll surely meet again, Mr Archer.'

'I look forward to it.' He shut the door and stepped back, watching as the car moved away. He had heard the town gossip about George's disastrous first marriage, and wondered if the people who forecast the same ending to his second marriage were right.

As he opened his front door and stepped into the narrow hall he seemed to catch the scent of her perfume again . . .

Fiona smiled to herself as she trailed her gloved fingers over the leather seat where Robert Archer had been sitting. He was the sort of man who grew more interesting with each meeting, she thought. It was a pity that George had taken a dislike to him, not that Robert – in her mind, she was already calling him by his first name – would let that bother him. He wasn't like George, who fussed and worried over every imagined insult and slight.

Fiona had already heard all about the silly business in the yard that day, over and over again. There had been no arrangement to visit Mrs Tennant, but having been left alone for far too long in her mother-in-law's drawing room she had suddenly decided that she had had enough. It seemed, from the glimpse she had seen of

George's face when she walked into the room, that his mother hadn't, after all, given him the support he had looked for. Which meant that he would probably start complaining again when he came home. Then – the worst thing of all – they would have to go to bed.

Fiona shifted uneasily on the car seat at the thought. She was beginning to feel like a mare that had been put to stud. Night after night she went to sleep feeling sore and stiff and woke up feeling sore and stiff, with only her monthly bleedings affording her any peace. Not that she was allowed to enjoy her few brief nights of freedom, for George spent the time railing on at her about her inability to conceive.

Fiona was becoming increasingly aware of the fact that she was not going to fall pregnant. And, as the weeks and months passed, she grew more and more certain that the fault didn't lie with her, but with her husband.

The hands of the clock over the tracing office door stood at six o'clock. The truck on the floor below was still working, the whine and rattle of its engines only dimly heard by Jenny, who was alone in the tracing office, bent over a library book on shipbuilding, referring now and again to a line-drawing on the desk beside her.

In her anxiety to give a good account of herself she often put in extra hours at the tracing office, sometimes arriving earlier than the others, sometimes staying behind to finish a piece of work. She would happily have worked during her midday break, when the truck was finally stilled for an hour and the place was quiet, but she had to go home then to help her mother, snatching a quick meal as best she could.

By chance she had found the books on shipbuilding in the local public library and had started taking them out, trying to marry ship design as she knew it with the facts and figures in the textbooks.

After her father found one of the books and sneered at her for sticking her nose into men's affairs 'just because ye've been made up tae gaffer over a parcel o'lassies in thon place where they play wi' toy boats', she began to hide the books from his sight, and take them into the office with her. On evenings when the naval architects were working late and the other girls had gone home she could read the books without fear of interruption.

The drawing she was puzzling over reminded her of one she had seen earlier that day, pinned to the cutting machine on the ground floor. Clutching the open book Jenny made her way quietly out of the office and down the darkened stairs, meaning to slip downstairs without being seen by the men working at the Tank. But as she stepped off the final stair Neil Baker called her name, sauntering towards her. 'Are you looking for me, Jenny?'

'I was just going down to the wax room. I didn't mean to disturb you.'

'I was coming over for a drink anyway. My throat's dry.' He picked up a bottle from a nearby bench and held it out to her, saying when she shook her head, 'It's only ginger – I'd not be fool enough tae bring strong drink in here.'

'I'm not thirsty.'

He shrugged then drank from the bottle, his throat muscles moving as the liquid went down.

'What are you doing here?' he asked, capping the bottle. 'I thought everyone else had gone home. What's that you've got?'

The book was plucked from her hands and he flipped it over and studied the gilt lettering on the front. His eyebrows rose.

'Ship-design?' She had expected him to laugh, but to her surprise he asked mildly, 'Interested in design, are you?'

Jenny swallowed. 'I'd like to know more about what happens outside my department.'

'Mebbe I can help you.'

She stared at him. 'D'you mean it?'

'Why not? You only needed to ask. Here— ' Neil jerked his head towards the Tank. 'D'ye fancy a shot on the truck? Nobody would know but me and the engineer, and he'll say nothing. Come on and I'll show you how it works.'

It had been a dark, brooding day, and now a wind was rising. Jenny could hear it gusting against the solid stone walls of the model room.

'I should be getting home,' she protested, but half-heartedly, her gaze moving past him to where the truck waited, a wax model slung beneath it. She had always wanted to ride on the truck.

'It'll not take long. We were just going to do a run. Watch how you go, you don't want to fall into the water.' Neil took the book from her and put it down on the bench beside the bottle then drew her towards the waiting truck. She edged after him along the narrow walkway then he jumped up on to the truck platform and reached a hand down to help her up.

'You'll have to hold on tight, there's not much space.' Neil swung himself up beside her and signalled to the engineer at the far end of the Tank. The area where the models were shaved to size retreated as the truck started its glide along the Tank, the dark water below ruffling in their wake like deep grey satin. As they went Neil briefly explained about the system of weights and counter-weights, indicating the roll of paper and the four coloured pens attached to it, waiting to record the results of the test run.

'Watch them when we're making the run. The one on the left's for control, it maintains the margin. The others show the true speed, the resistance, and the calculated speed. Take it carefully, Frank, we've got a passenger tonight,' he said to the grinning engineer as they reached the far end of the narrow Tank. Then, reaching round Jenny and taking hold of the rail so that she was tucked securely within the protective loop of his arm he grinned down at her. 'Hang on, Jenny, here we go.'

The truck accelerated fast, swaying from side to side like a tramcar; the pens connected to the mechanism holding the model fast scrawled rapid coloured lines over the revolving roll of paper and, looking down, Jenny could see the water being thrown to either side as the model knifed through it. She clung tightly to the railing, the wind generated by their speed ruffling her hair, grateful for the support of Neil's arm about her as they rocketed along. It was the most exhilarating experience she had ever known.

'Hold on,' he shouted, his mouth close to her ear, then released the rail and pulled her tightly against his body as the truck reached the end of the Tank and stopped with a jerk that seemed to rattle every tooth in her head and might have toppled her from her perch if he hadn't been holding her.

Despite herself, she shrieked at the sudden stop, then turned to laugh up at him, half in embarrassment at her own foolishness. 'That was wonderful!'

'I thought you'd enjoy it.'

'You're lucky, doing that every day.'

'Ach, it gets to be monotonous. And if ye're not feelin' too well, it can be downright unpleasant.'

'I can imagine that. Thanks, Neil.' As she began to turn towards the walkway his arm tightened, holding her back.

'Stay an' have another run,' he said into her hair.

'It's time I was going home.' She tried again to move away from him and realised that his body was pinning her against the rail and one of her arms was trapped in his embrace.

'Neil, let me go.'

'You can surely spare a minute or two.' His free hand landed on her shoulder, the thumb travelling down towards her breast.

'Frank'll be wondering what's going on,' she said, and Neil laughed.

'Don't bother your head about him. It's dark down here, he can't see us.'

She tried to pull away and realised that the rail was biting into her back. 'Mebbe not, but he'd hear me well enough if I shouted.'

'You'd not be so daft— ' said Neil, then ducked his head suddenly, his mouth searching for hers. Furious with herself for having been so naive, Jenny jerked her own head away then swung it back, hard, aware of pain shooting through the back of her neck as her forehead collided with his mouth. He gave a muffled exclamation and released her so suddenly that she stumbled and almost fell from the platform. One of his hands flew to his lips and came away smeared with blood.

'You bitch!' He lunged after her as she scrambled from the truck. Fingers clamped round her wrist and she was spun round to face him. She tried to pull away, the planks that formed the walkway bouncing beneath her feet. Beneath them the water, still disturbed by the passage of the truck, lapped noisily.

'Let me go!'

'Not till you've made up for hurting me,' Neil panted.

She was bending her head in desperation to bite at the hand holding her prisoner when the side door leading out to the shipyard squeaked open. Neil's fingers fell away from Jenny's wrist and she stumbled, off balance and convinced that she was going to topple into the dark water below. Her outflung hand caught at the truck as Robert Archer walked out of the shadows.

'What's going on here?' he asked, then as he came forward and got a clearer view of the two people by the truck he added in a sharper voice, 'What's happened to your mouth, Baker?'

There was a brief silence, then Jenny said swiftly, 'I – it was my fault. I didn't realise the truck stopped so suddenly. My head bumped against Neil's mouth.'

'You both know that only the naval architect is allowed to ride the truck.'

It was enough that she had let herself fall for Neil's lies, without causing further trouble by telling Robert the truth. If Neil was to lose his job, Jenny realised, he would make a bad enemy. His father, being a gaffer, had power in the area. Her life was difficult enough without adding to her problems.

'I asked Neil to let me try it,' she told Robert. 'I thought that since there was nobody else here to know it would be all right. Isn't that so, Neil?'

The naval architect muttered something, his voice muffled by the handkerchief he had pulled from his pocket to staunch the blood. Jenny put a hand to her

159

dishevelled hair. 'I'd best be getting home. I'll just get my coat.'

Silently, his eyes on Neil now, Robert stepped aside to let her pass. Furious with herself for having been caught in such an absurd situation, she hurried upstairs and collected her hat and coat, jumping when Robert spoke coldly from the doorway behind her.

'I thought you'd have had more sense than to ask a man like that for favours.'

'I didn't— ' she began, then stopped abruptly, realising that she was in danger of contradicting her earlier story. His eyes narrowed.

'You'd not lie to me, Jenny – would you? If Baker's been pestering you— '

She made herself meet his eyes. 'He hasn't.'

He studied her in silence for a moment, then said, 'From what I saw when I arrived you were fortunate I happened to come through from the yard when I did. What are you doing here at this time of night anyway?'

'I was finishing off some work.'

'You're not paid to work late,' he said curtly. 'I'm paid to work all the hours that God and the Dalkieths send, but you're not.'

'I don't mind staying on if something has to be finished.'

He put the book she had left behind down on the desk. 'Baker tells me this is yours.' One finger traced the lettering on the front. 'You're wanting to learn how to be a naval architect now?'

Jenny snatched the book up from beneath his hand and held it close. 'Are you laughing at me, Mr Archer?'

'I'd not dare do that, Miss Gillespie,' said Robert, straight-faced.

'If you must know, I only wanted to find out more

160

about how ships are designed. I was going down to compare one of the drawings with the sketch on the cutting machine— '

' — and you fell foul of Baker instead. You should have asked me. I'd have explained it to you.'

'You're the office manager.'

'Does that make me an ogre? Show me the drawing you're talking about.'

She would have liked to refuse, but instead, reluctantly, she opened the book and found the page. Robert took the book from her and studied it, then reached for a pad of paper and a pencil, drawing them towards him as he settled himself on one of the high stools and motioned her to sit beside him.

'The first thing you have to know in ship design is how the water deals with any object that's put into it— ' began Robert. Below, the truck clanged into action again.

The Tank area was dark and silent when they finally went downstairs, the library book beneath Jenny's arm, her head spinning with facts and figures. In the model room, still warm from the furnaces that had been switched off when the men went home, tools were laid out neatly in readiness for the next day and the clay bed was empty, waiting for a new model to be started in the morning. A wax hull lay snugly in the cutting machine.

'I like this room when everybody's gone home for the night.' Robert paused and put one hand on the rim of the clay bed. Looking at that square, capable hand, she suddenly recalled the days before the war, and the warmth of his palm against her cheek, and glanced away from him in a flurry of confused emotions.

Outside, he locked the door and put the key in his pocket. 'I'll walk you home.'

'I can manage fine.'

'For God's sake, Jenny, d'you have to be so distant? We used to be friends.'

'I can manage,' she said again, still bothered by the sudden memory of times long past. 'Thank you for your help.'

She walked quickly away, pulling her coat closely about her against the wind. If things had been different – if old Mr Dalkieth hadn't sent Robert away, if he hadn't met someone else on Tyneside – they might well have been walking home together. But not now. The past was past, and it couldn't ever be brought back.

A figure leaning against the wall a few yards further on, cap pulled low over his forehead, hands thrust into his coat pockets, straightened up then moved towards her. As he stepped beneath a lamp-post she saw that it was Daniel Young.

'I called in at the house and your mother said you were workin' late.' He fell into step with her. 'I thought I'd wait for you and walk you home.'

'There was no need,' she protested.

'I wanted to,' said Daniel.

12

The spring of 1920 seemed to be sulkily reluctant to take over from winter. In April wintry winds swept through the tenement buildings, which were old and unfitted to keeping out the cold. It became common-place to hear children, day and night, choking and wheezing with the croup that had always been prevalent in the damp, low-lying west of Scotland. The elderly grew silent and bitter-mouthed, plagued by the constant ache of rheumaticky joints.

Teeze Gillespie took a bad bout of bronchitis but struggled out to his work every day, insisting that it was only a wee cold.

'That's what you said before, and it turned out to be the pneumonia,' Faith reminded him, her face drawn with worry, and he rounded on her fiercely.

'It's my body – I know what ails it, woman! Will ye stop worritin' at me an' gie me peace?' he bellowed, setting off another fit of coughing. Faith, gnawing at her bottom lip, said no more, even when Teeze had to give in and take to his bed. There was no point in recriminations once the harm was done. Instead she set herself to nursing him, boiling kettles in the hope that the steam would help to improve his breathing until the kitchen became permanently foggy and the other members of the family felt as though they were suffocating in the damp, humid air.

Jenny, taking her turn of rubbing her father's chest with turpentine liniment to try to ease his discomfort, feeling the rumbling and wheezing of tortured lungs vibrating through her fingers, saw the weary acceptance in his eyes and remembered with sudden pain the pride he had had in his strength when he worked in Pneumonia Bay. True, he hadn't hesitated to use that strength to subdue his children and his wife with unnecessary harshness at times, but Jenny took no pleasure at all in seeing him weakened and humbled. Energy and good health were the most valuable possessions a tenement dweller could have and, when they ebbed away, as they must in time, there was nothing left – no dignity, no self respect, no hope.

'Here ye are, Teeze—' Faith pushed past her, a steaming linseed poultice in her hands. Jenny, her palms stinging and burning from her ministrations, stepped aside and watched as Faith laid the poultice in place over her husband's hairy chest. Teeze sucked in his breath sharply.

'Is it too hot?'

'No.' He ground the word out. 'It's fine.'

Faith drew the edges of his clean but tattered pyjama jacket together. 'Try tae get some sleep now,' she urged, drawing the blankets up to his neck, her hands as gentle as her voice. He grunted and closed his eyes, turning his head away from the two women.

'Should we mebbe get the doctor in?' Jenny ventured as they moved away from the bed. Her mother gave her a withering look.

'An' what dae we pay him with? It's hard enough tryin' tae feed us all an' pay the rent an' keep the place warm for him an' her— ' she nodded at Marion, dozing by the range, ' — without throwin' money intae the doctor's pocket an' a'.'

It was true. With Teeze ill and not earning, every penny was needed. Thanks to Faith's expertise they managed to get by on vegetable broth and bread and stove potatoes, a nourishing dish cooked with margarine and oatmeal. The big fear shared by people who lived from hand to mouth was being unable to pay the rent, for a roof over the family's head had to take precedence over everything else. The money that Jenny and Lottie brought in between them managed to do that, but not to stretch to medicines or the sort of luxuries Teeze needed to tempt his appetite.

Once or twice, lying awake in the night, worrying, listening to Lottie's snoring and the occasional huff of indrawn breath from Helen and her father's continual coughing on the other side of the wall Jenny made up her mind to approach Robert Archer and ask for help, perhaps an advance on her wages, to tide them over. But in the cold light of day the pride that had kept her going after he had jilted her, and again when he came back and she had to face the sly murmur of the gossips once more, kept her silent. Anyway, an advance would have to be paid back and that would cause further hardship. They must just manage as best they could.

Alice wanted to leave school and get a job, but Jenny held out against the idea. 'If you give the Academy up now you'll be sorry for the rest of your life.'

'But I feel so useless,' the younger girl protested. 'At my age I should be bringing money into the house.'

'Think of what you'll earn when you're a teacher.'

'And think of how long it'll be before I'm earning it,' Alice said gloomily.

'It'll be worth waiting for.' Jenny knew now why Daniel was so insistent that his son should stay on at school. Her own determination that Alice should do well was becoming more important, perhaps because it seemed to justify the sacrifices that Jenny herself had had to make. 'Promise me that you'll stay on,' she coaxed, and Alice bit her lip, then nodded.

'All right, if it'll make you happy. But in return you'll have to promise that if you can't manage any longer you'll tell me so and let me look for work.'

The day came when Teeze was so bad that Faith *had* to call the doctor in. He sounded his patient's chest and asked a few brief questions, then left a prescription and instructions on the sort of diet Teeze should have.

'Send for me if the coughing persists,' he said as he was leaving, and gave a shrug of the shoulders when Teeze said huskily, 'There was no need tae call ye this time. Women are aye over fussy. I'll be back at work by next week.'

To Teeze's annoyance, his illness put a stop to his cronies' weekly meetings in his house, though a few of them continued to visit him, bringing news of the shipyard. Daniel Young was one of the most regular visitors, often bringing a bottle of beer for the invalid and making time for Teeze despite his own growing commitments as a shop steward.

Since the business when young Jamie had almost lost his job after being caught brewing tea, the demand in Dalkieth's yard for proper representation to ensure the workers' rights had accelerated. The purchase of the adjoining yard and the setting up of more machinery there added fuel to the fire. If George Dalkieth was set on the yard's growth, he must be reminded that the men

166

who toiled to bring in his profits deserved consideration.

The unofficial gatherings that had begun in the Gillespie kitchen and in other kitchens around the town swelled during the first months of 1920 into meetings large enough to be held on open ground in the town, or in local halls run by committees sympathetic to working men. Union representatives travelled to Ellerslie to talk to the men and many of them, Daniel in the forefront, became trades union members. The pressure on George Dalkieth and the Dalkieth Board grew until by April, to George's fury, the unions were established in the yard. Daniel was one of the first to be voted in as a shop steward.

He bore his new appointment with quiet pride, and flattered Teeze by asking his advice and listening solemnly to what the older man had to say.

'Sure and there were some that were against the man because he's never mixed in with the rest,' Mr Malloy told Teeze when Daniel's appointment was confirmed. 'But he risked his job by joining the union, and he's got a good head on his shoulders.' He tamped tobacco down into his pipe and added thoughtfully, 'Mebbe it's not a bad thing that your man's a loner – there'll be no favouritism from Daniel Young, not for any of the workers or any of the bosses. We'll all know where we stand with him.'

Jenny silently agreed with what he said. Daniel's kindness to Patrick and her father and his fierce determination to gain justice for his fellow-workers had earned her respect.

'You know that your father'll mebbe never be able tae work again?' Daniel asked her quietly one Sunday afternoon when he had persuaded her to go out for a walk along by the railway line. The banking, bright with wild flowers in the summer, was dank and drab, but at least the air was breathable after the stuffy little kitchen with its smell of linseed oil and turpentine.

'I know.'

'He might manage in the summer,' Daniel went on, 'but come the bad weather he'll fall sick again. His lungs are in a bad way. It's sad tae see a good worker like Teeze turned intae an invalid before his time.'

His sombre voice, saying things that Jenny had known for weeks but refused to allow herself to brood over, suddenly filled her with despair. Life had been hard since Maurice's death, but now they were in danger of experiencing the bite of real poverty, the continual grinding struggle just to put enough food on the table, the worry of dependents like her grandmother and Helen, and now her father, the terror of hearing the rent man's steps coming through the close below and mounting the stairs, step by step.

Far away a train whistle shrilled, mocking her with the memory of the life she might have been living in Glasgow at that very moment if things hadn't gone sour. She fisted her hands deep into the pockets of her jacket and veered away from Daniel, struggling up the railway embankment, digging the toes of her best shoes into the sour-smelling winter vegetation to prevent herself from slipping back.

She heard Daniel calling her name, heard the pounding of his feet below her as she reached the top and stopped, inches from the shining rails, gulping in air, staring across the railway line to the fields and trees beyond. The train whistle shrilled again, nearer this time, and she felt the ground trembling beneath her feet in warning of its approach.

168

'Jenny, for God's sake!' Daniel's hand clutched at her, and she felt herself being pulled back down the slope, stumbling on the rough ground, dragged back into Ellerslie and all her problems. Above, the train whipped past them, screaming, throwing its shadow over them, going far too fast for Jenny to make out the faces behind the windows. The wind of its passing dragged strands of hair across her face and pressed her skirt tight against her legs; then it was gone, dashing along the tracks to the outside world, a free spirit, leaving her and Daniel behind.

'What d'ye think ye're doin'?' he demanded to know, his voice rough with fright. His hand on her arm was shaking, she could feel the tremors through the sleeve of her jacket. 'I thought for a minute ye were goin' tae fall under the wheels!'

'I was all right,' she started to say, then one eye began to sting, and she was blinded by sudden tears. 'My eye— '

Daniel whipped off his cap and tilted her chin up, peering into her face, pushing her hands away when she tried to cover her burning eye in an effort to ease the pain. 'Look at me,' he ordered brusquely.

She obeyed, squinting at him with one eye because the other was a blur of burning moisture. His breath was warm on her cheek. She had always thought of his eyes as deep brown or black, but in fact they were blue, though so dark that they were almost navy blue.

'It's a cinder, I can see it. Hold still, now, and I'll lick it out.'

'What?' She tried to draw back but his hands tightened on her shoulders, holding her still.

'Don't fret, I do it often in the yard. Men are always gettin' things in their eyes there. Just open yer eyes as wide as ye can and trust me.'

His face came very close, so close that it blotted everything else out. She felt the tip of his tongue probing at her eyeball, gentle as a night-moth's wing, then it flicked swiftly across the surface and away as he drew his head back. He glanced to one side, spat into the grasses by the side of the path, then peered into her eyes again. 'That's it.'

Released, she blinked cautiously once, then again. The burning pain had gone. 'You've done it! I've heard of some men in the shipyard being able to do that, but I've never met one till now.'

'It's not everyone can do it the right way,' he said with casual pride, bringing a spotlessly clean handkerchief from his pocket and mopping gently at her wet face. 'D'ye feel better now?'

'I'm fine.' She smiled up at him.

'Marry me, Jenny.'

'What did you say?' She was stunned.

'I said, will ye marry me? I admire you, Jenny, more than any women I know. It's been hard for ye since Maurice was lost, and with Teeze ill now it'll only get worse.' Daniel spoke hurriedly, the words pouring out as though once he had begun he couldn't stop. 'It's too much for ye tae manage on yer own. If ye kept on with yer work at the experimental tank we could support your family between us. And they'd have more room if ye moved in with me and the boy.'

Taken completely by surprise, she sought for the right words. 'It's too much, Daniel. I couldn't ask anyone to take on my whole family.'

He shook his head. 'I'm not makin' the offer lightly. It's something I've had in my mind for a while now, and it'd not be all the one way, Jenny. There's Walter, needin' a mother. And – there's me,' said Daniel, his voice suddenly low and unsure. 'I've been long enough without a wife, a woman about the house. I'd be honoured if ye'd take me for your husband.'

Dazed, she turned and began to walk swiftly back to the town. He fell into step with her and she was grateful that he made no move to touch her. 'I'd not expect an answer right away, it wouldnae be fair on you.'

'I don't know, Daniel— '

'Just say ye'll think about it an' give me yer answer in a day or two. If it's no,' said Daniel steadily, 'I'll accept it and not bother ye again. Ye've got my word on that.'

'Aye,' said Jenny, still so confused by the sudden turn events had taken that she didn't know what she was saying. 'In a day or two.'

When they parted at her closemouth he took her hand in his and shook it formally then turned and walked away without looking back, his shoulders square. He hadn't put his cap on again and his dark head, still bare, was held high.

She didn't love Daniel, Jenny thought as she tossed in her bed that night. She had known love with Robert; fleetingly, it was true, but she could still remember the sweetness and the joy of it. But, on the other hand, Robert had also taught her the bitterness and emptiness of rejection.

It was well past time for the public houses to close, but Lottie hadn't arrived home, so she wasn't there to grumble at her bed-companion's restlessness. Jenny moved her pillow to a more comfortable position and knew that she couldn't marry Daniel. It wouldn't be fair on him – there were other women who would make better wives, women who wouldn't burden him with their own responsibilities.

Through the wall her father began another series of deep lung-tearing coughs. She heard her mother's voice, then a faint whimper from Marion. Jenny eased herself from the bed, the linoleum icy beneath her naked feet, and reached for the old coat that hung from the nail on the door.

In the kitchen the light from the single candle on the table gave the shadowy, crowded room a bleak appearance. Faith was kneeling on the bed, spooning some of the soothing syrup Jenny had bought for Teeze into his mouth and Marion was flailing about in the truckle-bed, grunting and trying to get up.

'All right, Gran – I'll help you.' Jenny stooped over the bed and drew the blanket back, relieved to find that for a mercy Marion hadn't wet the bed. The old woman floundered like fish in a net, her nightdress caught up. Jenny's hand brushed against naked, skinny thighs, then she got Marion in the firm but gentle grip that she and her mother had learned by a hit and miss method and levered her into a sitting position. Faith joined her and together they managed to get Marion on to the shabby commode that someone had loaned them.

'Thanks lass,' Faith whispered across her mother-in-law's tangled head. Her own hair was lank about her face, her eyes sunken shadows in the candlelight. 'Och, leave it be till the morning,' she said when they had got Marion back into bed and Jenny was lifting the bucket from the commode. 'We don't want tae waken the neighbours at this time o' night.'

Teeze had turned to face the wall and was asleep, breathing noisily. Jenny picked up the bottle of syrup and held it to the light before putting the stopper back in. It was almost finished. If she bought more, would their supply of oatmeal and potatoes last out until the end of the week, when she and Lottie got their wages? Was there enough milk left to do Helen and Gran tomorrow?

Faith took the bottle from her. 'Go back tae bed, hen. You've got your work tae go tae in the mornin'.'

'Mam, Daniel Young's asked me to marry him.'

Fear poured into Faith's eyes. Her mouth trembled, then she asked huskily, 'What did ye say tae him?'

'Nothing, yet.'

'Jenny, lass— ' Faith put a hand on her daughter's arm. 'D'ye want tae marry a shipyard worker an' stay in the tenements for the rest o' yer days, aye worryin' about lay-offs an' the rent an' feedin' the weans?' Her fingers tightened. 'It'll no' be long till Maurice comes back an' then ye can go off tae Glasgow the way ye wanted tae. Once Maurice comes back— '

'Mam— ' Jenny put her own hand over her mother's icy fingers, suddenly realising what Faith was thinking. 'Daniel's thinking about all of us, not just himself. He says that if I could keep on my place in the tracing office, between us we'd be able to look after all of you, and Walter.'

'He said that?' Jenny could see the tension draining from her mother's stooped body. 'He's a good man, Daniel. Ye could dae a lot worse than accept him.' There was little doubt about the reply she wanted Jenny to give Daniel now that she knew of his offer to help to support her family.

'Mam— '

Teeze snuffled like a bull and heaved himself over in the bed, 'For Christ's sake, it's like a madhouse in here. Get tae yer beds, the pair o' ye!'

Tired as she was, Jenny's thoughts started racing again as soon as she returned to her own room and she realised that she was as far from sleep as ever.

Daniel's face seemed to hover against the grey square of the window, his eyes boring into hers. She recalled his casual comment at Maureen's wedding party about Alice's intelligence, and how angered she had been at the time. Then she thought of his offer to help to support her family as well as his own if they married, and the sudden hope on her own mother's face when she heard about it. Not many men could bring themselves to be so generous.

She blinked, and Daniel's image fragmented and was reshaped into Walter's anxious young features.

'There's Walter needin' a mother,' Daniel had said. It was true. The lad did need a woman in his life, softening the edges of his father's ambitions, making a proper home for him. If she married Daniel, Walter would be her stepson. And there might be other children eventually, when they could afford them. She wanted children, had always assumed that one day she would have babies of her own.

Lottie came in, stripping off her dress and clambering into bed, bringing with her the usual stink of alcohol and tobacco smoke and another aroma that often hung about her body when she returned very late – a musky, vaguely unpleasant smell. She dragged at the blankets, settling herself into the lumpy mattress with all the grace of a pig in a mudhole. In the morning, Jenny knew, her face would be clown-like with the smudged make-up that she rarely washed off before going to bed.

Jenny moved as far to her own side of the bed as she could, and remembered that marriage to Daniel would mean an end to having to share a bed with Lottie.

It was still dark when she stepped out of the back close early the next morning on to cobbles damp with the night's rain. Figures crossed and recrossed the lit windows of the surrounding tenements as the people inside prepared for another day's work. Daniel, his face puffy with sleep, his shirt open at the throat, his braces dangling, opened the door in answer to her soft knock. At sight of her he reddened and began to haul his braces up over his shoulders.

'Jenny? Is there anythin' wrong?'

'I came to give you my answer.'

'At this time in the morning? It could have waited till – come in.' He stood aside then said as she hesitated, 'The boy's out on his milk round. I'm just gettin' his breakfast ready.'

'I'll not keep you.' She stepped past him, along the hall and into the kitchen. The table was set for two and a pot of porridge bubbled on the range; even at that early hour the kitchen was neat and spacious compared to the Gillespie kitchen, where the truckle-bed would still be in the middle of the floor. Textbooks and exercise books were stacked carefully on the sideboard beside the photograph of Daniel and his wife. She turned to face Daniel and saw the apprehension in his eyes.

'D'ye want a cup of tea?'

'No. I just came to say that I'd be honoured to be your wife, Daniel.'

The colour ebbed from his face, then flowed back. His eyes widened and he swallowed hard, his Adam's apple bobbing beneath the skin of his throat. She had never seen Daniel without a collar and tie before; his open shirt and loosened cuffs gave their meeting an air of intimacy that suddenly embarrassed her. She glanced away from him, at the school-books, the photograph of Daniel and the solemn, dead girl whom she was to replace and, finally, at her own fingers, twisting nervously together.

His own hand came into her line of sight and took one of hers. She thought for a moment that he was going to embrace her and turned to him, relieved that he had taken the initiative, to discover that just as he had done the day before, he proposed only a formal handshake.

'I'm – pleased,' said Daniel gruffly. 'Will I make the arrangements, then?'

'Mebbe you should.'

'I'll call on Teeze after work an' ask his permission. I like tae dae things properly,' said Daniel, releasing her hand.

They stood for a moment, as awkward with each other as strangers, then Jenny said, 'I'd best get back, then.'

'Aye.' He opened the door and waited for her to pass him. On an impulse she rose on tiptoe and kissed him, feeling him flinch back slightly in surprise as she put her hands on his upper arms. His face was smooth and clean-shaven, his lips cool and firm.

'I'll do my best to be a good wife, Daniel.'

'Aye,' he said, then she was out in the close again, making her way back to the home that she would soon leave as a bride. Suddenly, in the space of a few hours, she was a woman on the threshold of marriage.

13

Teeze Gillespie was highly pleased by the news, for Daniel was one of the few men he respected and he considered that his daughter had done well for herself.

'Ye're more fortunate than most,' he told Jenny when Daniel visited him that evening to ask formally for his approval of the marriage. 'Ye've got a fine man here – see an' be a good wife tae him. Alice, away out tae the pub an' get a few bottles o' beer. Here— ' He reached into his pocket then hesitated, his face tightening.

Jenny, watching the shame beginning to touch his eyes, opened her mouth to offer to pay for the beer and was forestalled by Daniel's easy, 'Man, it's my place tae provide the drink tonight, no' yours. I'll give the lassie the money – an' this is a special wee gift for yourself.'

Teeze's face, sagging with relief, brightened as he accepted the small bottle of whisky. Faith even managed a slight smile as she hurried to fetch glasses and speed Alice on her way to the public house. The word went round the tenements almost immediately and when the public house closed men began to congregate to drink the health of the engaged couple. Wives arrived, led by Mrs Malloy and Maureen, who had put on weight since the birth of her son and looked more like her mother than ever.

'I never thought you'd end up with Daniel Young,'

she whispered, drawing Jenny into a corner, her eyes bright with curiosity. 'Are ye sure ye're doin' the right thing? He's such a quiet man.'

'There's nothing wrong with being quiet. God knows we could do with more like Daniel in this town.'

'I know, but even so— ' Maureen began.

'I'll have to help with Gran,' Jenny said hurriedly, squeezing past her.

Marion had to be taken through to the bedroom and tucked into the bed shared by Jenny and Lottie because the kitchen was too crowded for her own bed to be hauled out.

'Anyway, folk would keep steppin' on the old soul,' Mrs Malloy said in a loud whisper as she helped to ease Marion into the room where Helen already slept in her crib. Lottie, who had just arrived home from work, came to see what they were up to and gave a yelp of horror.

'She'll pee the bed! I'm no' sleepin' in a wet bed because of her!'

'Ach, she's been on the bucket, hen,' Mrs Malloy assured her, and the girl sniffed.

'That's no consolation. I've known her tae wet her drawers as soon as they were pulled up again.'

'Listen tae Lady Muck here! What d'ye want us tae dae – wring the poor old soul oot like a floorcloth? Fetch Teeze's coat, someone,' Mrs Malloy ordered, 'We'll slip it under the sheet tae save the mattress if she has a wee accident.'

Alice brought the coat that Teeze had used in the shipyard, stiff with age and smelling of rubber. Ignoring Lottie's grumbling, Mrs Malloy flipped it under Marion then tucked the old woman in securely. 'There she is – snug as a bug in a rug,' she proclaimed, taking Faith's thin arm in her huge hand and propelling the other woman out of the room. 'Come an' drink tae the happy couple, hen.'

'She's never at a loss for words, is she?' Alice murmured as she and Jenny followed the others into the kitchen, 'I'll never forget her throwin' up the window an' shoutin' "It's a laddie!" before Maureen's cord had even been cut.'

Jenny giggled at the memory. 'And poor Daniel and Walter beating away at their carpet down in the back court. I thought Daniel was going to die on the spot with the shame of it.'

'Ye'll be all right wi' Daniel,' Teeze, glowing with drink, told his daughter for the umpteenth time as his womenfolk tidied the empty kitchen after the wellwishers had gone home. He belched, and scratched his stomach with the base of the glass clutched in his hand. A dribble of beer, unnoticed, ran down his chin.

'An' he doesnae spend all his wages in the pub,' Faith added under her breath, clashing crockery in the sink. 'Ye're blessed there, Jenny.'

The summons to the boardroom was delivered by the Tank superintendent himself. 'Three o'clock, Mr Archer says.'

'I thought he'd have left things to you.'

Mr Duncan shrugged. 'New brooms like tae dae their own sweepin', I suppose. I told him that as far as I was concerned I'd be happy for ye tae stay on after ye're wed. Ye've done well so far, lassie, and I've nae doubt ye'll dae even better, given the time.'

As the time of her appointment drew nearer Jenny became more and more nervous. She should have confirmed that she could stay on in the tracing office before telling Daniel that she would marry him, she fretted, the line plan on her desk neglected. Again and again she looked up at the clock; sometimes the hands raced towards three, and at others she had to listen for the steady deep ticking to make sure that it hadn't stopped.

Although the boardroom lay directly beneath the tracing office Jenny had never been in it before. Nervously she descended the stairs just before three o'clock, giving herself enough time to pull at her cuffs and run her hands over her neat hair before tapping at the door at the bottom of the staircase.

'Come in.'

The boardroom was small, but luxurious in comparison with the rest of the Tank section. It was carpeted, and the wooden wall panels where hung with portraits of past directors. A highly polished oval table ringed by tall, oval-backed chairs dominated the room. Robert Archger stood by the small window overlooking the yard, his hands clasped behind his back. He turned as Jenny entered, the planes and lines of nose and jaw and mouth and forehead looking as though they had been carved out of grantie.

'Sit down.' He repeated the words impatiently as she began to shake her head, drawing a chair out for her. She had no option but to go to it and sit, straightbacked, her hands clasped tightly. To her relief he moved away as soon as she was seated, walking to the other side of the table.

'Mr Duncan tells me you're of a mind to marry. Who's the fortunate man?'

Jenny drew in a deep breath, praying that her voice would be steady. 'Daniel Young.'

'Young?' Robert's voice was astonished; his brows

rose, then drew together. 'I've had occasion to deal with him once or twice. He's one of the men that came home from the war with new ideas about the way things should be.'

'He's surely got the right to speak up when he feels that injustice has been done.'

'Some take it too far – and he's one of them. Why, Jenny? Why him?'

'I don't see that that's any business of yours.'

He studied her, his eyes seeming to dig into her heart. Finally he said, 'It's surely not love. There was once a glow about you that I've not seen since I came home. I don't see it now.'

Jenny turned her face away from his scrutiny, biting the insides of her lips, wanting nothing but to get out of the room and away from him.

'Is it for your family's sake? Is that it? For God's sake,' Robert said explosively, 'if it's help you needed for them why couldn't you come to me? You surely know that I'd do anything I could for you.'

'All I'm asking, Mr Archer, is to be kept on after – after my marriage. Mr Duncan says that he's agreeable.'

He tried to catch her eye but she stared over his shoulder, carefully studying every line of the whiskered face in the portrait behind him. Finally Robert said, 'You know I'd not refuse you that. As Mr Duncan says, you're a good supervisor.'

'Thank you.' She got to her feet. 'May I go, Mr Archer?'

His voice was as formal as hers as he said, 'Of course, Miss Gillespie.'

Her hand was on the handle of the boardroom door when he spoke again from just behind her, 'He's not the right man for you, Jen.'

Suddenly angry, she spun round on her heel. 'What right have you to say such a thing?'

'I still care for you, Jen. I'd not want to see you made unhappy.'

'You'll never see that,' she told him, and left the room.

Halfway up the staircase she had to steady herself for a moment with one hand against the wall before she could go any further.

Jenny had started to hate Maurice's photograph. Not a day passed without Faith showing it to little Helen, telling her, 'That's your daddy, hen. Kiss Daddy.' The little girl carefully planted her mouth against the cold glass, which was then re-polished and put back.

When the photograph was taken Helen hadn't been conceived, and Marion and Teeze were both fit and well. On the day Maurice had strutted into the photographer's studio Patrick had been walking on two good legs and Robert and Jenny were still writing to each other, with no thought, on her part at least, that the love between them could so easily wither and die.

It seemed now, to Jenny, that she could detect a smugness in the likeness of her brother's self-conscious young face, as though Maurice had known, even then, that his King and country asked only that he fulfill his duty to them and after that he wouldn't be expected to go on to take the responsibility for his own people.

She held her tongue for as long as she could, then one day, when Faith and Helen were going through their usual ritual, it became too much to bear. 'You shouldn't do that, Mam,' she protested. 'Helen never knew Maurice and there's no sense in trying to pretend that she did.'

Colour rose in her mother's face. 'I'm makin' sure that she'll know him when he comes walking in that door. I'll not have his own daughter treating him like a stranger when he comes back tae us.'

'But he's not— '

'Hold your tongue!' Faith shouted. 'You just keep your mouth shut or I'll – give him to me, Helen,' she added sharply as the little girl reached up and got a firm grip of the elaborate photograph frame. 'Don't touch! Now look what you've done – you've made a mess of Daddy's nice picture frame!'

She smacked the little girl's fingers until they released their grip then pulled the duster from the pocket of her pinny and started to rub frenziedly at the frame. Helen's eyes filled with tears; her mouth opened into a square and she began to howl her outrage at the unexpected and unwarranted attack. Jenny gathered her up, holding her close and crooning to her as Faith was crooning to the photograph of her son.

Marion, a silver web of spittle between bottom lip and chin, watched the scene before her impassively.

Jenny and Faith walked down the street together, stopping to have a word with some of the women sitting outside their closes. Helen, sure on her feet now, impatient of delays, ran on ahead of them, disappearing into their own close with a whisk of her skirt. When they reached the landing halfway up the stairs she was already sitting on the top step, beaming down at them.

'C' mon, Gran, she shouted, her voice echoing in the stairwell. 'C' mon, Jen!'

'She's lookin' more like her daddy every day.' Faith rested a hand on the damp wall and paused to gather her breath before she started the final climb.

'Give me your bag, Mam.'

Faith held tight to the worn leather shopping bag, its handles mended so often that there was more string than leather now. 'I can manage,' she said, and started toiling up the worn stone steps.

Teeze was well enough now to visit the pub and Marion was alone in the kitchen, slumped as usual against the arm of her chair, her chin sunk on her chest.

'Mind ye don't sit on yer Gran's feet, Helen,' Faith said automatically, putting her shopping bag on the table and reaching for the rag she used to wipe Marion's chin. 'Sit up now, Mother, an' let me get you comfy, then we'll all have a nice cup of— '

She stopped, then broke into a sudden strange keening wail that chilled Jenny's veins and startled Helen into a frightened whimper.

'Mam?'

Faith's knees had given way and she had sunk down on to the floor beside her mother-in-law's chair, her hands clutching at the old woman. For a terrifying moment Jenny thought that her mother, too, had taken a seizure. It was only when she tried to free Marion from the grasping hands and settle her into a more comfortable position in the chair and her hand touched a cold and lifeless face that she realised that her grandmother was dead.

All the life seemed to go out of Faith after Marion's funeral. She spent most of her time huddled in the chair that her mother-in-law had used, Maurice's photograph in her lap, staring into space and scarcely eating or drinking. Now and again she roused herself to answer the women who called to pay their respects and show their sympathy, relapsing back into her inner world when they left.

'She's in shock,' Mrs Malloy diagnosed. 'Sure, she's worked hersel' tae the bone tae look after that old woman an' now she doesnae know what tae dae wi' hersel' '. She looked over her shoulder at Faith, who was staring at the range as though trying to memorise every knob and every hinge. The ball of one thumb moved ceaselessly over the smooth cold glass covering Maurice's face.

'I'll damned soon show her what tae dae wi' hersel',' Teeze snarled. 'She's got a house tae see tae the same as she always had, an' if she doesnae get on with it I'll want tae know the reason why!'

Mrs Malloy was afraid of nobody. It was rumoured in the tenements that Mr Malloy, big man though he was, had only tried to hit her once, in the early days of their marriage, and had got a black eye and a bruised head for his trouble. 'Yer should be ashamed o' yersel', Teeze Gillespie,' she snapped back now. 'Yer own mother no' cold yet an' you foul-mouthin'!'

He glared at her then took refuge, as usual, in the pub. Lottie, as was to be expected, was of little use in this time of crisis, and it was left to Jenny and Alice to keep the house going as best they could.

A week after the funeral Jenny and her mother were alone in the kitchen when a sudden uproar in the close below, the clatter of feet, a man's deep laugh, brought Faith to her feet, her eyes wide, her hands clutching at the air. The photograph that had been lying in her lap fell to the floor.

'Mam?' Jenny had been sitting in her father's chair

185

with a pile of darning, and the work fell from her hands as she scrambled to her feet. Faith was already hurrying to the door and out into the small hall; by the time Jenny reached her she had opened the outside door and was staring out at the landing, one hand fisted at her throat. Two pairs of booted feet were coming up the stairs and someone was whistling 'Tipperary'.

'He's here, Jenny – he's come home and he's brought one of his pals with him.'

'Who?'

'Maurice – who else?' Faith asked impatiently, taking a step on to the landing.

A shiver ran though Jenny, as though something unspeakable had just walked across her grave. 'Mam— '

Two youths swung into sight at the top of the stairs, jostling each other – young Tommy Lang, who lived with his parents in the flat opposite the Gillespies, and one of his friends. When they caught sight of Faith, her hair tousled, her eyes huge and brilliant in the gloom, the whistling faded. They stared, startled, then scurried up the last short flight of stairs, crowding together as they arrived on the landing as though trying to keep as far from Faith's stricken face as possible. Tommy's hand fumbled with the latch, the door opened, and the two of them tumbled inside, almost falling over their feet in their haste to get out of sight. The door slammed and there was a burst of raw, relieved laughter from behind the scarred panels.

Faith's shoulders had slumped at the sight of the youths. She allowed Jenny to draw her back into the house and close the door. In the kitchen, she bent and picked up the photograph. The fall had broken the glass, and a crack ran raggedly across Maurice's solemn young face, distorting his features. Faith's finger traced the crack.

'He's no' comin' back, is he, Jenny?' she said, her voice empty.

'No, Mam, he's not coming back.'

'She was a wicked old bitch, all the years we knew each other. But I thought that if I took care of her, if I was good tae her, my Maurice'd be sent back tae me.' She sank into her chair and looked up at Jenny, struggling to be understood. 'It was as if I was bein' tested, d'ye see? I thought— ' The hand holding the photograph began to shake, then a violent trembling took hold of Faith's entire body. Tears pattered down on to Maurice's features and he continued to smile uncaringly through them.

'Oh, Mam!' Jenny dropped to her knees and, for the first time in her life, she put her arms round her mother and held her while she wept, understanding at last why Faith had been so devoted to the woman who had tormented her all her married life.

At last the shuddering and gasping stopped and Faith drew back, her face swollen with grief. 'I'm fine now. Make us a cup of tea, there's a good lass.' She scrubbed the last of the tears away with a piece of faded cloth that Jenny recognised as the rag she had always kept for Marion, then got up and used the poker to lift one of the iron lids on the range. She dropped the rag into the flames, then put Maurice's photograph back on the sideboard and picked up the jar of artificial flowers that had always stood beside the photograph.

'Put that up on the mantelshelf, will you? It doesnae look right there.'

'Mam, mebbe Daniel and me should put the wedding off for a wee while,' Jenny ventured a few minutes later as they sat on either side of the range, cups in hand. Faith's face was still swollen with weeping, yet there was something about the serenity in her eyes and the set of her thin shoulders that indicated that she had at last reached the end of a long hard journey and had come to terms with what had happened to her over the past years.

'Why should ye do that?'

'With Gran dying – I should mebbe stay here for a bit longer. I'm sure Daniel would understand.'

'No,' Faith said swiftly. 'Your Gran would've wanted you to go on with your own plans.' She leaned forward and put a hand over her daughter's fingers. 'Daniel's a good man, and it wouldnae be right tae keep him waitin.'

Jenny shifted uneasily in her chair, well aware of the meaning behind her mother's words. Now that Faith had finally accepted that Maurice would never come home, Jenny's wage – and the support that Daniel had promised – was all the more important to her.

'All right, Mam,' she said quietly, and Faith relaxed and handed her empty cup over to be washed.

Getting up and taking both cups to the sink, Jenny wondered about the impulse that had made her offer to put the marriage off, and couldn't be certain that it had been done solely for her mother's benefit. She knew that she herself wouldn't have minded the postponement, the chance to put off her future for a little longer.

Carefully, she rinsed both cups under the running tap and put them on to the draining board, trying to ignore the panic that fluttered deep in her heart like a bird trapped in a net.

Daniel was a good man, she reminded herself. Trustworthy, conscientious, hard-working. There was no doubt of that. And her decision to marry him had already been taken. If she was to voice any doubts now she would only upset her mother, anger her father, and shame Daniel and herself in the eyes of the community.

There was no going back. And there was no other path, now, to take.

14

In May the weather changed for the better. Suddenly summer arrived, marked on the hills around the town with flowering clumps of golden broom, and in the narrow streets beside the river by the familiar smell of poor drains and overcrowded housing.

It was Jenny's turn now to be dressed at work by Kerry and Jinnet and Senga in brightly coloured paper streamers and to jump over the chanty of salt. The faces of the joiners and moulders and clay-workers scratched hers as they took turns to kiss her, and the coins they contributed to the wedding festivities jingled into the old top hat she held. As she was carried through the town on the trolley more coins flashed in the sun as they soared from the hands of the onlookers into her lap. She waved and laughed and did her best to enjoy her moment of fame, acutely aware that none of this harmless nonsense fitted in with the grave solemnity of the man she had promised to marry.

Daniel had insisted on contributing some money to her wedding outfit. 'I know you've got more than enough tae do with your own wage,' he said earnestly when she tried to refuse. 'But it's your wedding day, and I want you tae get somethin' that pleases you.' She gave in, and bought a new costume, a pleated skirt and long, loose-belted jacket striped in bronze and soft rose pink with white collar and cuffs. After a great deal of searching she managed to buy some bronze material to make a blouse and a ribbon to put round the crown of her straw Panama hat.

She and Daniel were married in the vestry of the parish church on a sunny day a month after she had accepted his proposal, with Alice and one of Daniel's workmates as their witnesses.

Afterwards they walked further into the town to a photographic studio where they had their likenesses taken, Jenny sitting erect on an uncomfortable wooden chair, Daniel standing behind her, one hand resting on her shoulder. Then they went back to the Gillespie flat for high tea with Jenny's family and Walter, who was almost inarticulate with shyness in spite of Alice's efforts to winkle him from his shell.

Helen, in a new frock that Jenny had made for her, scampered to the door to meet the wedding party then fell back shyly, intimidated by her aunts' smart clothes and the presence of the two men, and tried to hide herself in her mother's skirt. With an exclamation of disgust, Lottie pushed her away.

'It cost me good money, this dress. Don't touch it!'

'Come to me, Helen.' Jenny lifted the little girl up and Helen threw her arms about her and buried her face in her neck. Lottie shrugged and turned her attention to Daniel's best man.

Neighbours came and went, most of them bringing items of food or drink for the wedding party. They drank the health of the bride and groom, and with each toast Teeze grew more inebriated. Daniel, Jenny noticed, only sipped at the glass of beer before him, and quietly but firmly refused to let Teeze refill it every time he filled his own glass. Sitting by his side in the crowded

191

room, aware of the warmth of his shoulder against hers and the clean fresh soapy smell from his skin, she felt a moment's panic as he realised that when he left the house she would go with him as his wife. She swallowed hard and glanced down at the wedding ring on her finger. Her life would never be the same again . . .

Helen fell asleep under the table, and when Jenny would have scooped her up and taken her off to her room, Alice got there before her. 'You stay where you are, Mrs Young,' she said, smiling, and Jenny watched the little girl being carried off, head lolling, relaxed as a contented cat against Alice's shoulder.

Not long after that Daniel got to his feet and courteously thanked his new in-laws for their hospitality. 'It's time we were on our way,' he said, and Walter immediately rose.

To Jenny's horror her father clapped a large hand on Daniel's wrist to detain him. 'Now you look after my wee lassie,' he slurred. 'She's one o'the best an' ye'll no' find a better. See an' look after her, man.'

'I will, Teeze, I will.'

Faith touched Jenny's hand. 'Ye'll be all right, hen?'

'Of course, Mam. I'm only going to be at the other side of the back court – you'll see me every day.'

It was a relief when the three of them finally got out of the place. To mark the solemnity of the day they walked to Daniel's home through the streets instead of crossing the courtyard, stopping every few yards to talk to neighbours who came to closemouths or leaned from open windows to wish them well. Jenny walked with a hand on her husband's arm, while Walter stayed two steps behind them all the time.

Daniel had refused to let Jenny help to prepare his two-roomed flat for its new mistress, insisting that he and Walter could see to it between them. The place was spotless and the shabby suitcase Daniel had collected from her parents' home that morning stood neatly against one wall.

'Walter, away tae yer bed,' Daniel said as soon as they were inside.

'Would you not like a cup of tea first, Walter?'

'He needs sleep more than tea. He's tae be up early in the morning for the milk round.' Daniel led the way into the kitchen and opened the door of a tall narrow closet in one corner, beside a small chest of drawers. 'I'll see tae the tea. I've made room for your clothes in here, and there's two drawers freshly lined for ye.'

He made tea in silence while Jenny hung up her clothes. She opened the wrong drawer by accident and caught a quick glimpse of spotlessly clean, neatly folded long johns and vests before she shut the drawer hurriedly, warmth rising to her cheeks.

The tea was hot and strong; Jenny clutched the cup for comfort, wondering if Lottie would be able to rouse herself if Helen woke in the night, and whether or not Alice would have trouble trying to keep up with her homework without Jenny there to see that she got peace to work on her books.

Daniel washed his empty cup at the sink, dried it and put it away before reaching for his cap. 'I'll just take a turn outside,' he said gruffly.

'What time does Walter have to be up for his milk-round?'

'Five o'clock. He gets himself up so there's no need for you tae rouse yourself on his account.'

'He'll need to eat something before he goes out.'

'He breaks his fast when he comes back.'

When he had gone she hurried to wash and dry her

own cup and put it away in a cupboard that was clearly cleaned thoroughly once a week. Then she stripped her clothes off and put them neatly over a chair before washing herself and putting on her new nightdress.

Finally she drew back the curtains that masked the wall-bed from sight and stood for a moment staring at the patchwork quilt, the sheet folded back neatly over it, the two pillows, side by side. Her fingers ran admiringly over one of the pillowcases. At home she had often had to do without the luxury of a pillowcase and the few that the Gillespies owned were patched and darned and permanently stained, no matter how hard they were scrubbed, from Marion's dribbling and Lottie's habit of tumbling into bed without washing the make-up from her face. But Daniel's pillowcases were snowy white and well ironed, made of the best linen, each case edged with a frill.

Jenny turned back the covers and climbed into the high bed, settling herself carefully so as not to crumple the bedding or tangle her newly brushed hair.

A few moments later Daniel tapped lightly on the kitchen door and waited until she called to him to come in. He glanced swiftly at the bed then looked away, saying gruffly, 'I always set the breakfast table last thing.'

'I'm sorry, I didn't know— ' She began to sit up, but he said at once, 'Stay where you are, I'll do it.'

Embarrassed by her first mistake, she watched as he prepared the table then took off his jacket and waistcoat and shirt, handling each item carefully and taking time to fold it.

'I left enough hot water for you in the kettle.'

'I always use cold water,' said Daniel, turning one of the gas mantels off. The soft light of the remaining mantel glanced off his muscular arms and neck as he worked at the 'jawbox' – the small sink set beneath the window – and Jenny felt a thrill of anticipation tingling deep within her. Unbidden, the memory of Robert's loving just before he left for Tyneside came back to her. Shocked though she was at herself for thinking of another man's lovemaking on her wedding night, the memory refused to go away once it had arrived. A wave of warmth ran through her body and she moved restlessly, stretching her legs down towards the foot of the bed until her toes were blocked by the sheet tucked tightly round the mattress.

Daniel turned off the second gas mantel and the dark room was filled with the whisper of his movements, his breathing, the rustle of his underclothing being slipped off. Jenny heard a drawer squeak open then shut again, followed by a crisp, hissing sound as Daniel's nightshirt was slipped over his head. She moved in the bed again and ran her hands over her own body, testing the flatness of her stomach, the swell of her hips, the softness and fullness of her breasts beneath the thin material of her gown. She let her fingers slide along the warm valley between her breasts and hoped that she would please Daniel.

There was a flurry of cool air against her calves as the blankets were lifted, then the mattress dipped as her husband slid in beside her. She waited, holding her breath, for his touch. Waited and waited, the air silently, slowly drifting from her lungs. Then, to her astonishment, Daniel said, 'Goodnight, then,' and turned over, his back to her.

For a moment Jenny lay still, unable to believe that he was going to go to sleep, then she raised herself on one elbow. 'Daniel?'

He grunted.

'Daniel, did I do something wrong?'

'No. Go tae sleep.'

'Daniel— ' She laid her hand on his cotton-clad shoulder then drew it back with a gasp of fright as he suddenly threw himself over in the bed to face her.

'For pity's sake, woman, have ye no decency?' His voice was a harsh whisper. 'D'ye expect me tae take ye when my own son's lyin' eighteen inches away from us?'

'But— ' Jenny glanced into the darkness behind her, in the direction of the wall that divided them from Walter's room, ' — he'll surely be asleep by now. He'd not hear us.' She pushed away the memories of herself and her brother and sisters as children, awake in the darkness, listening to the sounds from the kitchen wall-bed, the creaking of the bedframe, the grunting, the thudding of her father's large body against the wall until sometimes they feared that he would burst through it, covering them with plaster. She remembered them nudging each other, biting the blanket to stifle their giggles – remembered, too, the undercurrent of nervous fear. In the tenements the walls were thin and the houses so small that every child grew up wise to the facts of life. But Daniel wasn't like her father. He would be gentle and – quiet.

'There'll be no fornicating in this house,' Daniel hissed at her. 'Not in my son's presence. Now go to sleep.' And he turned away from her again, hunching himself to his side of the bed.

She lay awake for a long time, tormented by her own wanting, knowing by his shallow breathing, the tension that she sensed even though their bodies weren't touching, that Daniel, too, was awake.

196

The Gillespie flat faced on to the back court but Daniel's flat fronted the road and, now and again, the night was disturbed by voices or footsteps, even the squeaking, once, of a perambulator or a handcart. A group of drunks, women as well as men, on their way home from a public house staggered along the street, their voices loud and threatening in the night.

Jenny moved to ease a cramp in her calf and her bare foot brushed lightly against Daniel's. He flinched away and she hurriedly eased her body closer to the wall to avoid any further contact. A tear rolled slowly from beneath one of her lids and eased itself down her cheek. She felt its wetness drip from her to lose itself in the linen pillowcase.

When she woke in grey dawn she didn't know where she was or what had roused her. Then she heard a stealthy sound from the adjoining room and began to push the blanket back so that she could go to help her mother. It was only when her fingers hit against the wall instead of sweeping through thin air that she recalled that she was in Daniel's home, in Daniel's bed. She was Daniel's wife – in name, if not in body.

Memories of his rejection the night before rushed back to her as she lay still, listening to his even breathing. The door of Walter's room gave out a faint squeak of hinges; she heard the boy tiptoe along the hall then the close door opened and closed. At once Daniel startled the life out of her by suddenly bounding from the bed and into the hallway. He was back in the kitchen while she was still struggling to sit up.

'He's gone,' he said, then the bed coverings were thrown aside and he was kneeling over her, his hands reaching for her, pushing beneath the pretty nightgown with its coloured bows, exploring her, claiming her.

'God, ye're bonny,' he said huskily, 'My bonny Jenny!'

Jenny, still struggling to come fully awake, felt as though she had been swept up by a sudden storm and was being tossed and turned in its wake with no time to catch her breath. 'Daniel – ' She tried to catch his hands in hers, to make him slow down, but he ignored her. Her nightdress was pushed up as far as it could go and Daniel moved swiftly to straddle her; the ceiling was blotted out by his body as he moved into her swiftly, insistently.

When she cried out in pain and protest at the suddenness of the assault he muttered breathlessly into her ear, 'It's all right, it always hurts the first time.'

A wave of chill realisation swept down Jenny's spine at the words. The first time. Even thinking about Robert the night before, while she was waiting for Daniel to come to bed, it hadn't occurred to her that she was no longer the virgin that Daniel had naturally expected her to be. If he had heard anything of her affair with Robert all those years before he would have assumed, as everyone else had, that it was long over and forgotten. Only she and Robert knew that their love had been consummated.

Daniel rolled away from her, panting, then almost at once he got out of bed, leaving her alone. She swiftly covered herself and the rumpled sheet with the blanket, but he kept his back to her as he pulled on his underdrawers then turned on the tap and began to sluice his hands and face and chest. The storm of his passion had passed as suddenly as it had arrived.

He dried himself and hauled his singlet on, then she heard the clatter as he opened up the range and stirred the embers within into life, followed by the brisk sound of the wooden ladle stirring the oatmeal that had been left to soak in water overnight. He pushed the iron pot over the fire and scooped the rest of his clothes into his arms.

'The laddie'll be back soon. I'll dress in his room,' he said, then the door closed behind him. Jenny jumped out of bed then hurriedly dragged the undersheet free of the mattress, bundling it up to hide the absence of the blood that should have been spilled on it.

By the time Daniel tapped on the door she had washed and dressed and brushed her hair, and was stirring the porridge. The blanket and the patchwork quilt had been smoothed neatly over the bed, and she saw his eyes flicker to the bucket in the corner, where the sheet, and her nightgown for good measure, were soaking in cold water.

'The boy'll no' be long,' he said, whisking the curtains shut to hide the bed from sight. He looked just as he had looked on the morning she had arrived to tell him that she would marry him, though this time even his braces were in place.

'God, but I'm hungry.' He sat down at the table and fingered one of the plain white cups. 'I was thinkin', Jenny, could ye mebbe decorate them a bit when ye've got the time? Just for us,' he added with unexpected, touching shyness, his free hand reaching out to touch hers briefly. 'Tae commemorate us findin' each other?'

Jenny's hopes that she would be able to draw Walter out of his shell once she was his stepmother were soon dashed by Daniel. From the day of his son's birth he had mapped out the boy's life and he was firmly opposed to any attempt she made to ease Walter's regime.

When she tried to encourage her stepson to spend a little time each day on recreation Daniel said that Satan found mischief for idle hands and he'd not have his son lounging on street corners and learning bad habits. When Jenny suggested that the milk round was too much for the boy on top of all the studying he had to do Daniel said, thin-lipped, that Walter had to learn that everyone had to learn to pay their way.

'Don't spoil the boy,' he said impatiently when Jenny made treacle scones, knowing that they were Walter's favourites.

'It's no bother to make a few scones, Daniel. And he's been working hard at his homework all evening. He surely deserves a treat.'

'He knows that the reward for working hard lies in getting good results in his examinations, not in treats.' Daniel spoke the final word scathingly and Walter's long thin hands, busy spreading margarine thinly on a scone still warm from the oven, faltered.

Jenny could have wept for the boy as she watched him force the scone down, bite by bite, all the pleasant anticipation scoured from him by his father's cruelty. She didn't make treacle scones again, knowing from her own experience that Walter would probably hate that particular delicacy for the rest of his life.

The intimate side of her marriage continued to follow the pattern that had been set immediately after their wedding. Daniel appeared to be totally indifferent to her while his son was in the house, but as soon as they were alone he behaved like a starving man falling on a feast. She grew to accept his loving – if what happened between them could be given such a name – but for her there was no joy in it, not even the pleasure of knowing that she had satisfied her husband.

During the day she and Daniel were at work and Walter at school, so their swift couplings only took place in the early mornings. On the rare occasions when she and Daniel were alone at home during the day he eagerly took advantage of his son's absence, whisking her to the bed no matter what task she might be busy with. Confused by the situation, she didn't dare say anything to anyone about it, even to Bella, and was left to wonder if this was what most men and most marriages were like.

At least the tracing office and its familiar, comforting routine were still part of her life. She had heard that some of the yards on the Clyde were beginning to see a drop in orders now, but Dalkieth's Experimental Tank was in use all day and every day, and Jenny and her staff were never short of work. Now and then, hurrying to collect a drum of paper from the truck or to deliver an analysis to Mr Duncan she encountered Robert Archer. Each time, afraid that those searching eyes of his might look deep into her mind, she stared at the floor. She couldn't bear the thought of Robert, of all people, guessing the truth about her bewildering marriage.

But, to her relief, he behaved towards her as he would behave towards any other employee, wishing her a crisp good morning or good afternoon each time they met, then passing her by.

15

Robert Archer was too wrapped up in his own problems to brood over Jenny's marriage. The conflict between himself and George Dalkieth had worsened, and it had become increasingly clear that Isobel Dalkieth was not going to be able to bring herself to vote against her son when he and Robert clashed. Already work had begun on the land they had bought from McWalter. Some of the Dalkieth buildings had been extended, and new machinery, bought with a substantial bank loan, had been brought in.

From his office window Robert stared down at the yard and wondered if the time had come for him to leave Ellerslie once again. Some of the yards on the Clyde were already beginning to feel the first waft of chill air from the economic storms lurking on the horizon, and the same thing was happening to a greater extent on Tyneside. He knew all about it for he kept a close watch on what was happening to shipbuilding all around the globe. But there was still time for a sensible company to evaluate and use its own strengths, to hunt out and eliminate its weak spots. Given a less prejudiced platform where his opinions would be listened to, he could perhaps do some good somewhere else. At the very least he would retain his own self-respect and not let George Dalkieth drag it down together with his own.

Robert Archer didn't believe in brooding over the past and what might have been. He had hoped, on hearing from Tyneside that Anne had plans for marriage to another man, that once his divorce came through and he was free he and Jenny might come together again. But Jenny was married now, and any dreams he had had of winning her back were over. He himself had no strong ties with Ellerslie, no family, and certainly no lingering affection for the place. Shipbuilding was all he cared about, and he could pursue his career in any yard, anywhere.

He ran a finger over his moustache as the idea of killing two birds with one stone came to him. He would suggest to the Board that he should travel to Tyneside soon to get some idea of the problems facing the yards there. What happened in England always affected Scotland later. If he found evidence of trouble on Tyneside that could, with foresight, be avoided here in Ellerslie, surely Isobel Dalkieth wouldn't brush it aside whatever her son might say to the contrary. And he could use his visit to find out which yards might be interested in offering him a post.

Jenny had been used to a household where the men came in filthy from the shipyard. Every working day her mother had dragged out the old hip-bath and put so many pots and kettles of hot water on the range that the kitchen was like a steam-room by the time Teeze and Maurice came home. Teeze, as head of the household, always got first use of the bath and Maurice followed him, while Jenny and her sisters were banished to the other room.

She vividly remembered the day Maurice had rebelled over the filthy state of the water he was expected to step into. Teeze had swung a fist at him, and for the first time Maurice, his muscles developed by a year of hard work at the yard, had retaliated. The resulting uproar had brought Jenny and Bella and Alice running from the bedroom to see, through clouds of steam, two naked bodies, one thick-set and white, the other slim and boyish and still dappled with shipyard grime, grappling with each other while poor Faith knelt at their feet, holding tightly to the bath, which was in danger of being tipped over and flooding the kitchen floor and house below, screaming at her menfolk to behave themselves.

Bella, Jenny recalled with amusement, had clapped her hands over Alice's eyes, but not quickly enough.

Many lessons were learned that day. Teeze discovered that his son was too strong and too old for physical chastisement, and the three sisters, pooling their observations when they were alone in bed later and going into intensive though giggling discussion, had learned quite a lot about the male anatomy. Poor Faith had learned how humiliating shame could be for a previously respectable woman, for the uproar had been so alarming, even in the tenements where fights were commonplace, that the people who lived below had sent for the police.

From then on Maurice had made do with two basins of water in his tiny bedroom, and a head-to-toe scrub each day when he came home from the yard.

The rumours about Daniel Young's visits to the public baths after each day's work turned out to be true. Every morning when he set out for the yard, as clean and neat as an office worker, he carried a shabby carpet bag containing his dinner and his working clothes. Every afternoon he came home in the same spotless fashion, his overalls and working shirt and even his underwear rolled up and stuffed in the bag.

'It's my job to have hot water ready for you, and the tub out,' Jenny argued in the early days of their marriage, but Daniel scowled and shook his head.

'I'll not walk through the streets and in at my own door like a tink,' he said shortly. 'I'll not have my son seeing me like that. The day he was born I swore that he'd never have to do it, either. He'll have work that he can be proud of, clean work.'

'Shipbuilding's a craft to be proud of.'

'Aye – to those that don't have to put up with the noise and the dirt and the humiliations,' Daniel retorted, and refused to change his ways.

He had looked after all his clothes well, including his working clothes, which were darned and patched over and over again and, unlike many of his colleagues, he had managed to get together two sets so that he could change in the middle of the week as well as on Mondays.

Between that, and his insistence that he and Walter changed their shirts more often than most men, Jenny's washload was just as large as it had been in her parents' home, and she took to washing clothes occasionally in the evenings. Although it meant more hard work at the end of a busy day, she enjoyed being in the wash-house at a time when it was quiet. It reminded her then of rainy days spent happily in that same wash-house with the other tenement children, the girls playing at wee houses, or at shops on the broad windowsill, using pebbles for goods; the boys playing with toy soldiers or swinging from ropes suspended from the two hooks set in the ceiling, one at each end of the room. The hooks had been set into the ceiling to take a drying line in wet weather, but they weren't used much, for the wash-house was usually too steamy to allow clothes to dry.

Alice often gave her a hand with the washing and, now and again, if Daniel was out at one of his union meetings and Walter had finished his homework, the boy offered to help. It was during one of those washing sessions, on an August evening a few weeks before she and Walter were due to go back to school, that Alice announced that she had given up her Saturday work in the bakery and found work instead in a local pawn-shop.

'And I'm going to start evening classes in book-keeping and typewriting,' she announced. 'Mr Monroe that runs the shop says he'll help to pay for them. He says I've got a good head for figures.'

There were four of them in the wash-house that evening – Jenny, Walter, Alice, and Helen, who was toddling around, dragging a piece of wood tied to a string. This was Helen's doggie, and her favourite toy of the moment.

'Oh, Alice! You were doing fine at the bakery. Why give it up?' Jenny plunged Daniel's dungarees into the hot scummy water yet again, rubbing them fiercely against the ribbed washboard.

'The work was awful dull, Jen. I did nothing but sell potato-scones and wee cakes, and the flour made me sneeze.'

'But a pawnshop! Could you not have found some-thing more – more respectable?' Jenny gave a tut of impatience as she reached for the cake of harsh black soap and it skittered off the bench and across the floor. 'Fetch that, will you?'

Alice dropped to her hands and knees to scrabble on the floor for the elusive slippery tablet. Over her shoulder she said breathlessly, 'It's a very respectable pawnshop, and Mr Monroe's a respectable employer, but his chest's bad since he got gassed in the war and he's finding it all too much for him.'

'Poor soul, it's a pity he's got no wife to help him.' Jenny straightened up for a moment, stretching her back and arms. She recalled Alec Monroe, a thin young man who had been invalided out of the army after being gassed in the trenches. At that time his widowed mother had been running the pawnshop, but not long after he came back home she died, leaving the shop and the flat above to Alec.

Alice captured the soap and handed it over. 'At least he's got me now. I'm a great help with the books, he says, and the work's interesting.'

'I'm not certain that I'm happy about you taking on nightschool as well. Your schoolwork'll suffer.'

'Not at all,' said Alice firmly. 'Book-keeping's arithmetic, and the typewriting's interesting.'

Walter was wiping the mangle down with a rag to clear the dust from the rollers before the wet clothes went through. 'I wish I could get another holiday job,' he said over his shoulder. 'It's dull, scrubbing down floors and walls in the dairy.'

'Look for something else, then,' Alice suggested, but he shook his head.

'It was my father that got me that job and he'd not like me looking for something else. Working in a pawnshop's certainly a way of meeting people.' A grin lit up his face as he paused to turn the cloth over in search of a dust-free area. 'I only get to meet cows.'

Seeing the way his whole face changed when he smiled, Jenny resolved to make sure that it happened more often. Already, in his fourteenth year, she could see that Walter was going to grow up to be a fine-looking young man. He would set many a lassie's heart dancing in another few years or so.

'Oh, it's interesting, right enough.' Alice deftly side-stepped round Helen, who had suddenly veered in front of her, and returned to the tub where she was plunging shirts in fresh rinsing water. 'Mind that Miss Galbraith from the school, Jenny? She came in last Saturday morning and she just about keeled over when she saw me standing behind the counter. I knew the minute I saw the look on her face that she minded me from when I was in her class. She just stuck there in the doorway and didnae know whether to come on in or fight her way out, so I said to her, easy-like, "Good morning, madam, d'you require us to look after your valuables for the week?" When I said it like that, as if it was a sort of favour she was doing us, in she came and not a word was said about us recognising each other.'

'Poor soul, she must have fallen on hard times. What did she pawn?'

'Mind your own business,' Alice rapped back at her. 'And me and Mr Munroe'll mind ours.'

Jenny laughed, knuckling a particularly filthy patch of cloth against another patch so that she could rub harder and deciding that when the washing was finished she was going to give her hands an extra going over. She kept a mixture of glycerine and rosewater in the house at all times, for she had to look after her hands to keep them supple for her work in the tracing office.

'I wish my father would let me do something different,' Walter said.

'Fathers are all the same. My dad's doing everything he can to make me feel foolish about going to night-school, but he'll not win,' Alice told him. 'And neither should yours. The way I see it, you're the one that's doing all the studying so you're the one that should decide what you want to do with your life, not your father.'

Walter stopped what he was doing and gaped at her as though expecting her to be struck dead on the spot for uttering such sacrilege. Then he said, wonderingly, 'You're right.'

'Of course I'm right.' Alice lifted the lid of the boiler and a cloud of steam enveloped her. Helen, enchanted, giggled and dropped her 'doggie's' string and started windmilling her arms vigorously to disperse the hot damp cloud descending on her.

'Now don't you go putting ideas into Walter's head,' Jenny told her sister nervously, 'Daniel wouldn't like it.'

Walter was leaning on the mangle now, the rag dangling from his hand, staring through the steam at Alice's wavering outline. His eyes were glowing with what Jenny could only think of as hero-worship.

'I'm not putting ideas into anyone's head. I'm just saying what I think.'

Jenny looked at her younger sister as the steam began to break up and realised that Alice was growing up. Her sturdy, solid body was beginning to take on a womanly shape, even wrapped as it was at that moment in a sacking apron. Wisps of brown hair with a curl to it fell over a face rosy with heat and exertion, and the lingering steam softened her strong features. Alice might never be pretty, but one day she was going to be attractive in her own way.

The steam from the boiling water, together with the fire beneath the copper, was making the small room unbearably hot and stuffy. Jenny went to open the door and take a few breaths of fresh air before returning to her work.

'What I'd really like to do,' she heard Walter say as she stood in the doorway, 'is work on a ship. In the engine room.'

Dragging an arm across her damp face, Jenny turned in dismay, 'But Walter, your father's set on you working in an office.' It had never occurred to her that Walter himself might have other ideas.

His shoulders slumped. 'I know. It's all I ever hear from him – but what I really want is tae be an engineer.'

'Just mind what I said – it's your life, not your father's. The shirts are done,' Alice said. 'Fetch the pole, Walter.'

He obediently handed her the long wooden pole that had been leaning on the wall and she plunged it into the boiler, twisting it with deft flicks of the wrists so that the clothes would wrap themselves around it. 'Careful Helen pet, the water's burny. Take your wee doggie over to the door so's it doesnae get splashed. Ready, Walter? One-two-THREE!'

Her voice ended on a shriek and Walter jumped to add his strength to hers as she hoisted the pole out of the copper. It came free with a tangle of sopping, steaming material clinging to the other end and water cascading over the floor as they swung round, working in unison, and deposited their load in the waiting tub of cold clean water.

Walter eased the pole free. 'To my father, engineering's black work, an' he says I'm never going to have to put on dungarees and get my hands oily.' He used the pole to poke the shirts down into the rinsing tub. 'Mebbe when the time comes I'll get him tae change his mind.' He spoke without much hope, and Jenny, returning to the washboard, knew why. Daniel held fast to a dream that had been born on the same day as Walter himself, a dream he would not easily relinquish.

'Nobody should be allowed to decide what someone else should do with the rest of his life. We've only got one each,' Alice said briskly. 'Now then, Walter Young, are you going to stop clinging to that pole like a monkey on a stick and help me to get the rest of the stuff out of this boiler?'

16

The wooden doors between the Palmers' parlour and their dining room had been folded back to accommodate the large number attending their musical soiree. Fiona Dalkieth, who had been there for half an hour and was already bored, drifted from one group to the other, eyeing herself in every mirror she passed, admiring the way the low waistband of her new, deep red gown, embroidered with a pattern of black and silver beading, showed off her figure to advantage. As she paused before one of the mirrors to put a hand up to her hair her sleeve, full from the elbow, fell back from her soft white forearm and tiny diamonds in the gold bracelet clasped about her wrist sparkled in the light from the chandelier.

The expression on her lovely face was one of aloof boredom, but in truth Fiona was becoming more nervous with every day that passed. George was even more determined to father a child and the week before, when she had had to admit to him that her monthly bleeding had started, he had accused her of using some sort of preventative. When she protested that she would never do such a disgusting thing he had snapped back at her, 'Then you must be barren!' Since then he had made one or two veiled references to divorce.

She would not be sent back in disgrace to her family

in Glasgow, Fiona vowed as she fidgeted her way round the room, nodding to acquaintances but reluctant to be drawn into idle chatter. Papa had money, but he disliked parting with it unless there was good reason. He had made it very clear to his only daughter that his only reason for spending a fortune on her clothes was so that she would attract a wealthy husband; the thought of his reaction if she returned to the family home, divorced and disgraced, was quite unbearable. To use his own words, she would be shop-soiled goods.

Fiona had quite forgotten where she was and had reached the stage of picturing herself as a poor relation, farmed out to some distant cousin as a companion or, even worse, a housekeeper, when a voice said from behind her, 'You're very solemn tonight, Mrs Dalkieth. I take it that you're missing your husband?'

Fiona turned quickly, her face lighting up. 'Rob – Mr Archer! I didn't know you were coming here tonight.'

'Nor did I. I had expected to be in Tyneside this week.' There was a decided edge to Robert Archer's voice.

'With George? He left for England this morning. He was looking forward very much to visiting the yards there.' And she herself had been looking forward very much to several days of freedom.

'Instead of George,' he corrected her. 'The visit to Tyneside was my idea but, unfortunately, it was felt that I was needed here to deal with some problem that one of our clients has raised.'

Fiona beamed up at him. 'Well I for one am delighted that— ' she began, but just then Mrs Palmer decided that her guests should move to the library across the hall to be entertained by the singer she had engaged for the evening.

213

Fiona paid scant attention to the musical entertainment, for she was busy making plans. While the cat was away, she thought . . . and felt a delicious squiggle of excitement run through her body. She risked a sidelong glance at her companion, thinking how strange it was that, although he came from the working classes, he wore his clothes with more of an air than George. He seemed to be completely unaware of her appraisal; his gaze, and apparently all his attention, was fixed on the singer.

'You seem to be quite taken with the lady,' she whispered under cover of a polite pattering of applause.

'I was thinking of a cat my aunt once had,' he murmured, his face expressionless. 'Given a hairpiece and a gown that cat would have looked just like her. It would even have sounded like her.'

Shocked, delighted, Fiona clapped a gloved hand over her mouth, but not swiftly enough to smother a peal of laughter. Heads turned in their direction and the singer, about to start her next song, paused.

Robert patted Fiona on the back then took her arm and led her back to the drawing room, where he seated her on an upright chair. 'A sudden fit of coughing,' he explained above her head to Mrs Palmer, who had followed them. 'A glass of water, perhaps?'

By the time it arrived Fiona was recovered and dabbing at her eyes with a lacy handkerchief. She sipped at the water and when their hostess had returned to the library she looked up at Robert reproachfully. 'I doubt if I shall ever be invited here again.'

'Will you mind that?'

'Not in the least.' As he took the glass from her and put it on a nearby table his hand came in contact with hers and the thrill of excitement returned.

The musical interlude ended and the others came in for supper. To Fiona's annoyance she and Robert became separated; occasionally their eyes met and each time they exchanged smiles. When Mrs Palmer began rounding up her guests after supper and sending them back to the music room to hear some violin solos, Fiona, unable to bear the thought of staying a moment longer, made her excuses, pleading a headache.

As the front door closed behind her she paused for a moment, drawing her sable-trimmed coat more closely about her, then walked along the short drive, the sound of violin music becoming more distant until she stepped on to the pavement and it faded away altogether.

The night was pleasantly cool and the roadway quiet. Fiona slowed her steps and had strolled as far as the lamp-post at the corner when she heard someone coming along behind her. She waited until the footsteps were close before turning.

'Mr Archer – we meet again.'

He looked up and down the empty road. 'Hasn't your chauffeur arrived after all?'

'My chauffeur is no doubt sitting snugly in his room reading his newspaper. I told him that someone else would drive me home.'

The light above them revealed amusement in his grey eyes. Usually Robert Archer was serious but, when he smiled, Fiona thought with pleasure, he became almost handsome. 'At times like this I regret that I don't own a car. I could have offered you a lift.'

'I recall you telling me once that you prefer walking. I believe I shall try it for myself,' said Fiona, and placed a gloved hand on the arm he offered.

It was delightful to stroll through the quiet night with someone other than George, who puffed if he had to walk any distance at all and spent most of his time grumbling about something or other.

They reached a corner and he moved towards the kerb, ready to cross the road, then paused when Fiona stopped. 'Isn't this the road where you live?' she asked, the flutter in her throat making her words sound quite breathless.

'Yes, but I intend to walk with you to your own gate.'

'Couldn't we— ' She moistened her lips with the tip of her tongue, 'Couldn't we perhaps stop for some refreshment? I feel quite parched.'

'D'you think that's wise, Mrs Dalkieth? I live alone.'

Fiona looked up and down the quiet road. 'There's not a soul here to see us. You surely wouldn't deny me a glass of water to sustain me for the rest of the journey?'

In his hall, she gazed about with interest before following him into a small comfortable parlour.

'A glass of water?'

'I would prefer sherry wine, if you have it,' said Fiona, unfastening the large buttons on her coat. The silk material rustled as he drew the garment from her shoulders and tossed it over his arm. Slowly, her eyes fixed on his, Fiona withdrew the pins from her hat and handed it to him, then peeled off her gloves. He waited, expressionless, until she had handed hat and gloves over, then said, 'Please sit down,' and went back into the hall. Fiona wandered around the room, pausing to examine the bookcase, which held a collection of technical books on shipbuilding. To her disappointment there were no photographs to study.

When Robert came back into the room he was carrying a salver containing two filled glasses. She accepted one and sank on to the comfortable sofa, watching as he removed the guard from before the fireplace and knelt to poke the fire, which had been banked up in readiness for his return, into a blaze. Then he drew the curtains, enclosing the two of them in intimate, flame-splashed darkness for a moment as he crossed the room to switch on the electric light.

'You said that you hadn't intended to visit the Palmers tonight. Did you change your mind because—?' Fiona let the sentence linger unfinished on the air and sipped her wine slowly, watching him over the glass.

Robert Archer hesitated before answering. The directors' decision to send Dalkieth to Tyneside instead of himself had infuriated him. The man knew nothing of the questions that should be asked, the observations that had to be made. He would believe anything he was told and would almost certainly return to Ellerslie with a totally erroneous picture of the economic situation in the Southern yards. Robert had gone to the soiree because he knew that if he stayed at home his anger would gnaw at him until it drove him into a pointless, frustrated rage. At such a time it was never a good idea to be alone. Looking up, looking into Fiona's wide long-lashed eyes, he realised that he had been alone too often lately.

Fiona took his silence as a reluctance to commit himself. 'It was because you guessed that I would be there, and knew that George would not.' She got up and moved with short swift steps to the curtained window, the fringed hem of her elegant gown swirling about her calves. The neckline was cut straight across from shoulder to shoulder and she had recently had her hair bobbed; her skin was very white against the rich red of the dress and, as she bent her head, the nape of her slender neck looked touchingly fragile and vulnerable. 'I'm tired of pretending, Robert,' she said in a rush of words. 'Pretending to be happy with George when I'm wretchedly miserable, pretending that I enjoy going to one silly party after another and seeing the same people all the time. Pretending— ' She swung round and the light turned the tears in her blue eyes into sapphires. 'Pretending that I don't care— ' She stopped herself with a hand pressed tightly to her lips.

'Fiona— ' He put his untouched glass down and went to her and she moved to meet him without hesitation. When he put his arms round her, her hair was soft and smooth against his cheek; she lifted her face to his and her mouth fluttered and opened beneath his, the point of her tongue flickering, warm and moist, along his lips.

The coals of restless anger that had been smouldering in him since he heard that George was to go to Tyneside collapsed and became a consuming heat, and it took all his control to push her gently away from him, his hands on her shoulders.

'Fiona, are you sure?'

She closed her eyes and the tears, caught now among her long fair lashes, became diamonds. 'Yes,' she said. 'Oh – yes!'

Fiona was an avid reader of romantic novels. Before George entered her life she had day-dreamed of being wooed and won by handsome, virile lovers but, even so, her feet had always been kept firmly on the ground and she had assumed that such dreams were no more than the stuff of imagination.

But lying in Robert's bed she discovered that dreams could, after all, come true. After months of celibacy his own needs were urgent, and Fiona found herself swept up in a passion that she had never even dared to dream of, kissed and stroked and coaxed into moaning abandon and surrender that at times became almost too much to bear.

When at last they lay exhausted among the tangled sheets, their limbs still twined round each other, she whispered, 'I'm so glad that you decided to attend the soiree after all.'

'So am I.' Robert, sated and at peace, turned his head lazily to kiss her earlobe. They lay in contented silence for a few moments before his body tensed and he said with sudden urgency, 'I hope to God I've not – we haven't— '

'Sensible women know how to take precautions nowadays,' Fiona murmured reassuringly. 'Any child I bear will be my husband's, I can promise you that.'

As she felt his body relax again in her arms she smiled slowly, lazily, thinking to herself that a man with the ability to pleasure a woman as Robert had pleasured her must surely also have the ability to father on her the fine healthy son she so badly needed . . .

George stayed in Tyneside for longer than he had intended, sending back word that he had important business to see to.

'What sort of business?' Robert demanded anxiously of Fiona when she visited him.

She shrugged. 'He just said that it would be of benefit to the yard.'

'But— '

Fiona pouted. 'Don't let's talk about George, or the yard,' she said, going to him, moving her body against his. A shiver of desire shook him; she sensed it and smiled, a cat-like smile of anticipation. 'Let's just be glad that he's given us more time together,' she murmured, her small soft hands busy with the buttons of his shirt. At the touch of her fingers against his skin Robert shuddered again, then swept her off her feet and into his arms.

She was right – he would know what George was up to soon enough. In the meantime, he had urgent business of his own to see to.

But when George Dalkieth came home the news he brought was far worse than anything Robert had imagined. He had become acquainted with a group of English businessmen who had formed a consortium for the purpose of investing in a number of industries, including shipbuilding. On a wave of euphoria at what he saw as his astute business capabilities George smugly informed the Board that he had agreed to make the Dalkieth yard part of their group.

When Fergus Craig, speaking a mere second before Robert, protested, 'But Dalkieth's has always been an independent yard,' George told him loftily, 'And a number of small independent yards like ourselves are going to the wall in England at this very moment. This way we can prosper on new money, investors' money we can use to buy more modern machinery.'

'And in return you lose control of Dalkieth's.' Robert Archer's voice was like ice.

'Not at all. We benefit by an exchange of shares, including shares in a steelworks. We showed a net profit of two hundred and fifty-four thousand pounds last year,' George told his fellow directors, 'We're on the crest of the wave and by God we're going to ride it! Good shipping's still in demand— '

'For the moment,' Robert put in, but George ignored him.

' — and will be for many years to come,' he continued stiffly. 'We paid out a good dividend to our shareholders last year and all the indications are that we shall be able to do so again this year. Why would the consortium want to invest in us if we were about to fail?'

'Because they know nothing about shipbuilding,' Robert Archer said stubbornly. 'They're only interested in making profits – and if they start to lose money they simply sell out as fast as they can and walk away, regardless of the suffering they might leave behind them. If we become linked to other businesses, companies we have no control over whatsoever, it means that if they fail we fail.'

'The consortium is run by men with good business experience,' George blustered.

'Experience in investing money, not in shipbuilding!' Robert looked round the table, his eyes lingering on Isobel Dalkieth. Her gaze dropped before his and he knew, with dismay, that once again George had gone to her first. She had already pledged her support for this mad scheme.

Fergus Craig hurriedly cleared his throat. 'I can see reason in both arguments. As George says, this may seem like a good time to expand, but on the other hand we don't know what the next few years may bring.'

'By that time we'll have money coming in from businesses outwith shipbuilding to keep us going, thanks to the share-exchange scheme. We ourselves use coal, timber, iron and steel, machinery,' George rushed on, expanding on the shining future that had been spread before his delighted gaze in England. 'Linking this yard with associated companies not only saves cost on materials but shares the incomes of these other industries. Look at the Experimental Tank – it has more work than it can comfortably handle from other yards, let alone from our own. We were the first yard to have such a tank. My grandfather had the foresight to invest hard-earned money in that project and it's paid for itself a hundred times over.'

'The Experimental Tank is specialised, in a category of its own. And your grandfather,' Robert added in a voice that would have cut through iron, 'was a man of vision. He didn't choose to spend his money on consortiums or associated industries because he realised that the more entangled a family business like this becomes with outside interests, the less control it enjoys. Has it ever occurred to you how easily this wonderful consortium could collapse if anything out of the ordinary occurred?'

Isobel Dalkieth's head came up suddenly, her eyes meeting Archer's. He saw the doubt in her gaze and said slowly, deliberately, to her alone, 'Ask yourselves how strong their understanding is of the world-wide problems affecting shipbuilding today. And ask yourselves if this is the right time to hand our future success over to men who have never in their lives built ships.'

Her lips parted, but at that moment George thumped a fist on the table, his face purpling. 'Dammit, man, they have controlling interests in Tyneside yards far larger than Dalkieth's! I can assure you that they know their business better than any jumped-up naval architect!'

Robert was on his way round the table to where George sat before he realised that he had got to his feet. George flinched back in his chair as Fergus Craig reached out to clamp a restraining hand on the office manager's arm.

'Gentlemen!' Isobel Dalkieth's voice cut through the room like a whip. 'I will not allow this meeting to turn into a bear-garden!'

There was a pause during which the air crackled and the men around the table shifted uneasily, their eyes flickering from works' manager to office manager and back again. Then Robert Archer jerked his arm free and returned to his own seat.

'I beg your pardon, Mrs Dalkieth. I would like to record my objection – my strong objection – to the matter of the consortium.'

'Your objection is noted.' Isobel's voice was cold as she called for a vote. It was evenly divided, half the directors agreeing with George Dalkieth, half with Robert Archer.

'Yours is the casting vote, Isobel,' her brother told her, his voice husky with apprehension.

She stared down at her hands. The clock on the wall ticked out sixty seconds before she looked up again to say levelly, 'I vote that we agree to an exchange of shares with the consortium – but I suggest that we restrict the number of Dalkieth shares to a level that leaves control in our hands.'

The crack as the pencil between Robert Archer's fingers snapped rang through the small panelled room. When the meeting ended he walked out without speaking to anyone, almost bumping into Jenny. She stumbled and he caught at her arm to steady her, staring down at her as though she was a stranger.

'Robert? Are you ill?'

Recognition came into his grey eyes but the anger was still there, bright and hard.

'I'm sick to my stomach, Jen.' His voice shook with rage. 'I wish to Christ that I'd never set foot in this damned place!'

He released her and walked away with long, angry strides, moving fast, his shoulders hunched and his head pushed forward, throwing himself through the side door into the yard and out of her sight.

George Dalkieth couldn't be trusted to run a wheelbarrow down the middle of a street, let alone run a shipyard, Robert thought savagely as he sat in his small house that evening, a bottle of whisky by his side and a glass in his hand. George was a fool and, thanks to him, Dalkieth's yard was in danger of slipping into the hands of a group of men whose only interest lay in making money, switching fortunes around at will, pledging the assets from one company under their control to raise funds for another. They played a dangerous game and Robert wanted no part of them.

He emptied the glass then refilled it. 'To your damnation, Mrs Isobel Dalkieth,' he said aloud, and half-emptied it with one swallow.

There had been a moment at the meeting when he had seen doubt in the woman's eyes and thought that perhaps this time she would listen to him; then George had managed to rouse him to unwise fury and the scales had tipped in the wrong direction – just a fraction, but enough. She was well aware that her son had no business sense at all but, even so, her maternal instinct was stronger than her undoubted ability for business. As long as George had his mother's support, albeit reluctantly, Robert Archer might as well save his breath to cool his porridge.

He could still walk out, leave the Dalkieths, mother and son, to their own devices and return to Tyneside. He emptied the glass, put a hand to the bottle, then changed his mind. He would need a clear head in the morning.

A sudden delicate waft of lilies-of-the-valley brushed his nostrils as he got into bed an hour later – Fiona's scent, caught in the threads of the pillowcase, teasing him with the memory of her last visit to his bed, only the day before.

He closed his eyes and her lovely body was imprinted on the darkness behind the lids; he could almost feel its silky nakedness against his own skin. His fingers tightened on the pillow at the memory.

He had assumed that George's imminent return would make this their last time together, but to his surprise Fiona had disagreed. 'There are ways and means – we can go on meeting and George won't find out, I promise you.'

She refused to argue, and Robert soon gave up trying to make her see reason, though he knew in his heart that, for everyone's sakes, the affair couldn't be allowed to continue. But now, finding himself clutching at the pillow that bore her scent like some weak, lovesick youth, he knew that the matter was out of his hands. He wanted her – and if the occasion arose he would not be able to deny himself.

There was, too, a certain satisfaction in knowing that, in one way at least, he was getting the better of George Dalkieth.

17

The old man who lived opposite the Youngs grew too feeble to look after himself and, in September, when he was taken off to a married son's home, Bella and Patrick managed to secure the tenancy of his flat. Although Patrick no longer worked at the yard the fact that he had been injured fighting for his country, coupled with his wife's family's history of employment with Dalkieth's, meant that he and Bella were allowed to continue as tenants.

The new flat was only a single room, the same size as the home they already had, but at least there were no stairs to prevent Patrick from getting outside.

'I'm sure he'll be much better once we make the move and he can start getting out and about again,' Bella said, but without much conviction, rubbing hard at the filthy window-pane. She and Jenny had taken on the task of scrubbing the place out before Daniel and Walter white-washed the walls.

'You should try to get him to apply for one of those special boots to help him to walk.'

'He wouldnae agree tae it before – but mebbe now that he's had time tae think about it— ' Bella stopped as the scrubbing brush slithered from her sister's wet hand and Jenny rose and walked unsteadily towards her. 'Jenny?'

'I'm – I'm fine. It's just the heat of the place— ' Jenny brushed Bella aside and struggled with the sash, managing to open it an inch. 'I'll ask Daniel if he can put in a new cord to make this easier for you,' she said automatically, then managed to smile at her sister. 'It was just the heat,' she said again.

'But it's cold in here.' Bella eyed her closely. 'Are you sure you're all right?'

'Of course I'm – oh, Bella,' Jenny clutched at her sister's hand. 'It cannae be a bairn, can it?'

'You'd know that better than me.'

'But we've not been married all that long!'

'Four months. Long enough.'

'I've been worrying about it for the past week. I didnae mean to fall wi' a bairn for a year or more, not till things got a bit easier,' Jenny said in a panic.

Bella's gaze held a mixture of pity and envy. 'What's for us won't go past us. And if it's true, you'll manage. Folk always do. Away home and sit down for a wee while. I'll finish off here.'

'You'll do nothing of the kind. I'm fine now,' Jenny drew a deep breath and went back to her work, plunging her hand into the bucket to retrieve the brush. 'There's no need to treat me like an invalid.'

'Is Daniel pleased?'

'There's plenty of time yet.' She rubbed the cracked yellow soap vigorously over the brush's worn bristles.

'You've not told him? I'd have told Pat the first minute I suspected. We both wanted bairns before – before he was hurt.' Then Bella asked shrewdly, 'You're not scared tae tell Daniel, are you? He'll be pleased, Jen, even if it's happened sooner than you meant it to. Look how proud he is of Walter— '

'If you'd talk less and rub that window harder mebbe

227

you'd get it clean,' Jenny snapped, scrubbing at the floor as if she was trying to force the brush through the planks.

It was precisely because of Walter that she had put off telling Daniel her suspicions about a baby. She was afraid that, wrapped up as he was in his ambitions for his son, he wouldn't want the responsibility of raising a second family. But, if she was indeed pregnant, Daniel would have to know, sooner or later.

She sighed, decided that there was no point in fretting until she had to, and concentrated instead on applying herself to forcing years of ingrained dirt out of the worn floorboards.

The move turned into a festive occasion, with the Malloy clan joining in. Even Teeze was there, making up for his inability to carry anything heavy by directing operations. When his chronic bronchitis had finally forced him to leave the shipyard his wife had feared that he would spend most of his time and what little money he had in the public house where Lottie worked. But Teeze had proved her wrong. At first he lay in bed most mornings until midday and spent the afternoons loitering with his cronies at the corner of the street. Then, to everyone's astonishment, he took to helping a former workmate, now retired, who had an allotment near the river.

As far as his family was concerned he was as surly and uncommunicative as ever, but at least he spent less money on drink, and now and again he stamped into the house to toss a small turnip or greens or a handful of potatoes, the earth still clinging to them, on to the table with a grunted, 'I'll have that wi' my dinner.'

Although he no longer worked at Dalkieth's yard, his

experience and knowledge was still sought after, and the fact that his son-in-law was a union representative gave him a certain standing at the meetings, official and unofficial, held on at least one evening every week, usually in a large room in the Burgh Halls.

Jenny and Alice were convinced that their grandmother's death had something to do with the change in Teeze. Marion had dominated him all his life; even when she was a helpless invalid her very presence in his house had unsettled him. It was sad, Jenny thought as she watched him oversee Daniel, Walter and Maureen's husband Jacko struggling to ease the Kerr's bedframe out on to the upper landing, that anyone should be so hated and feared that their death meant liberation for others.

Lottie was the only member of the family who didn't help with the move. Helen was there, scurrying about, wild with excitement and getting in everyone's way.

'Careful, pet, you'll get hurt,' Jenny cautioned as her niece ran across the room and almost collided with the bedframe. She lifted the little girl out of harm's way, cuddling the warm wriggling little body in her arms.

'Here, give her tae me.' Faith ordered, taking Helen from her. 'You go down and make some tea – they'll all be parched by now. Go on,' she added as Jenny began to protest. 'You need a rest, ye shouldnae be doin' too much at a time like this.'

'What's Bella been— '

Faith eyed her daughter, and a faint smile softened her mouth. Since the day she had finally accepted that Maurice would never come home a new understanding had developed between her and Jenny. Not open affection, for the Gillespies weren't an affectionate family, but an almost sisterly rapport, the sort of special

229

relationship that only women can share. 'Bella's not said a word, but I'm no' daft. I've had six of my own and I know the signs.'

When the furniture was in place Mr Malloy sent two of his brood out to the public house for some beer and his wife and Faith produced sandwiches and home-made scones and tea. Bella's habitual air of exhaustion and worry was gone for once and she looked as happy as she had on her wedding day, when the future had been spread out before her like a carpet of crimson and gold. Jenny glanced from her to Patrick, clutching a glass of beer, smiling over something Jacko was saying to him. It was only a shadow of the grin that used to split his handsome young face almost in two, but it was a beginning.

Cautiously, Jenny let herself hope that this move would be a new beginning for them all, and that they were finally going to emerge from the shadows of the war that had so cruelly ripped their lives apart in different ways.

'Walter and your sister seem tae know each other well,' Daniel said a few hours later when they were back in their own home and Walter had been packed off to his bed.

'It's just a friendship, Daniel.'

'Aye, well, just you mind that the boy's got a long road tae go if he wants tae get on.' In one gulp he drank down half the scalding tea Jenny had just poured out.

'For goodness' sake! Alice is working hard at school herself, she's got ambitions of her own.'

His dark deep-set eyes studied her suspiciously. 'You think so? Lassies know they can aye get married, but a man has tae make his own way. I'll not have anyone encouraging Walter tae take time away from his books.'

Jenny felt irritation well up and tried to quell it. 'My sister's not interested in marriage.'

'She'll change her mind as soon as she finds some man tae look after her.' He emptied his cup and pushed it over for a refill, wiping his mouth with the back of his free hand. 'Just mind that it's no' goin' tae be my Walter.'

'So you're even going to deny him marriage, are you?'

'He'll find the right wife at the right time. But first he's got the university in front of him.'

Jenny, about to pour more tea into her own cup, set the pot down carefully on the range. 'Daniel, have you ever wondered if Walter wants to go to the university?'

'Eh? What laddie wouldnae want it?'

'He might not be clever enough— '

'He is!' Daniel said fiercely. 'I know he is! I'm warnin' you, Jenny, don't you or yer sister try tae make him think otherwise.' He drained his cup again and got to his feet. 'I'll away an' take a turn round the back yard.'

'Before you go, I've something to tell you.' Jenny smoothed her apron carefully over her flat stomach, suddenly nervous. 'I'm – I'm going to have a bairn.'

He stared, his pale face dismayed, then said, 'Ye're sure?'

'I'm sure.'

'Oh, God.' Daniel sank down into the chair he had just left. 'I thought you said you knew how to take care of that sort of thing.'

'I tried, but— ' She had intended to make use of sponges soaked in vinegar and pessaries of water and flour, but she couldn't tell him that his refusal to make love to her with his son in the house, the hurried, urgent

231

couplings whenever Walter happened to be out, gave her little chance to make use of the knowledge she had gleaned from the other tenement women.

'Ye'll have tae stop work, then.'

'Not for a while. I'll not let on to anyone at the Tank until I have to.' She hadn't even thought of having to leave the tracing office, and Daniel's reminder sent a pang through her. She loved her work.

He went without another word and stayed out for longer than usual; Jenny was in bed long before she heard his step in the close. He put out the remaining gas mantel as soon as he came into the room, undressing in the dark, and when at last he came to bed they lay silently apart from each other as usual. She longed to reach out and touch his hand, but didn't dare. Instead she said after the clock on the wall had ticked several minutes by, 'Daniel, are you vexed with me?'

'Go tae sleep,' he said. Then, after another silence, 'No sense in frettin' yerself. We'll manage.'

She released her breath in a long sigh of relief, and was drifting off to sleep when Daniel spoke again, his own voice drowsy, 'This new one'll have Walter as an example. It means I'll have two sons tae be proud of.'

Suddenly sleep fled and Jenny lay awake far into the night, worrying about the child she was carrying, while beside her Daniel slept.

The contract with the English consortium was signed and a generous slice of the Dalkieth shares were relinquished in return for shares in Tyneside yards as well as an iron and steel works. Flushed with success, George paid a second visit to Tyneside in October to cultivate the new friends he had made there.

'As far as I'm concerned he can go to England as often

as he wants,' Fiona said happily, making use of her husband's absence to visit Robert.

'The thing is, what harm's he doing while he's there?'

Fiona curled up in the corner of the sofa, tucking her slim, silk-clad legs beneath her and smiling at her lover possessively. 'I don't care, as long as he's doing it elsewhere.' She had never been happier. With George out of the way she was mistress in her own home, freed from his unwelcome attentions, able to visit Robert whenever she could manage to slip away. 'Stop talking about George, and come here.'

Robert, leaning against the mantelshelf, looked down at her. She wore a misty blue tweed suit, the jacket lying open over a cream silk blouse that followed the curves of her breasts. The top button was unfastened, giving a glimpse of smooth skin below the soft hollow at the base of her throat. Her eyes were as blue and clear as a summer sky and her skin glowed. The sulky pout she had always worn when he first knew her had vanished.

'You look more beautiful each time I see you.' He took her hand and let her draw him down to her side.

'That's because I'm happy.' Fiona's hand cupped his face, and he turned and let his mouth nestle into her palm. 'Leave him, Fiona,' he said against her hand. 'Come to me.'

'Leave George? I couldn't do that!'

'Why not?'

'He's my husband.'

'Divorce him.' Robert took her into his arms and kissed her. He hadn't meant to say it so soon, but being with her again, knowing that it couldn't be for long, had given him impetus. Stupidly, he had lost Jenny to another man by leaving Ellerslie and entangling himself in a disastrous marriage, and now that he had found

233

love again he didn't want to lose it in the same way. 'Let him divorce you.'

'But the scandal— '

'We don't have to worry about the scandal. Let Ellerslie topple off its foundations with shock – we'll be far away, you and I. We could start a new life in England, or even abroad. I could find work anywhere.'

Fiona appalled, pushed him away and sat upright. 'Robert, I couldn't possibly. The Dalkieths – my f-father— ' Dismay entangled her tongue. This was not part of her plan.

'Your father and the Dalkieths be damned! Fiona, I mean it. I could make you happy, you know I could.'

Fiona liked to be in control of situations, and this one was slipping away from her. She fought to regain it, drawing Robert's head back down to hers, letting her lips flutter against his face as she spoke. 'Please, my love, give me a little time to think about it. Surely that isn't too much to ask?'

Her fingers skilfully loosened his waistcoat, slid between the fastenings of his shirt to stroke his chest. His need for her flared up in him like a forest fire and, with a soft moan, he buried his mouth in the hollow at the base of her throat.

Just over a mile away, on the other side of the river, another fire blazed, this time in the grate of the drawing room in Dalkieth House.

Fergus Craig stretched out his feet and sipped the last of his whisky, drawing comfort from the warmth of the flames and the spirit's excellent bouquet. Isobel paced the room, moving restlessly between fireplace and window, then back again. Her upright figure was clothed, as usual, in black, but even so her silk and wool dress was stylish, cut straight across at the neck from shoulder to shoulder. The bodice was embroidered with jet beading echoed on the three-quarter-length sleeves and the sash at the low waist of the dress was caught by a large square jet buckle. Her diamond and sapphire ring flashed as she fingered her long pearl and jet necklace

'It was a mistake to bring Robert Archer into the company,' she announced. 'A mistake, Fergus! I wish I'd never let myself be persuaded into it.'

Fergus thought longingly of his own comfortable drawing room. He and his wife had intended to have an evening at home together, Elspeth busy with her knitting, he himself studying a new book on ornithology which had been delivered that day from his bookseller. He had been unwrapping it when Isobel's summons had arrived. 'He's proved himself to be very able.' He wrenched his mind from what might have been and forced it back to the present.

'Oh, I grant him that,' Isobel said impatiently, pausing to pick up her own glass and toss down a mouthful of whisky. 'But he and George – they're like chalk and cheese, oil and water. They've each got their own ideas and neither will budge an inch. It's causing confusion to the other directors and considerable worry to me. The Dalkieth Board has always been used to strong leadership, Fergus – always! Now look at us – the minute you put George and young Archer into the same room they're at each other's throats. Dear God, the directors' meetings have become more like dog-fights than anything else.'

'You agreed at the time that we needed a balance of views, Isobel.' He looked down into his empty glass, wondering if he could help himself to more whisky.

Isobel was usually very generous with the decanter but today she was in such a pet that she seemed to have forgotten her duties as a hostess. 'George has the family background, and young Archer possesses a very good brain, not to mention his experience. One gives his views, the other counters with his – and the Board weighs up both opinions and makes the final decision. That's what we planned.'

'That might be what we planned, Fergus,' said his sister in ringing tones. 'But in reality if one of them says black's black the other's sure to insist that it's white – while the rest of the directors sit there in utter bewilderment like a flock of hens scared to open their beaks in case either George or young Archer turns on them.' She emptied her own glass and refilled it from the decanter on a side table then stoppered the decanter and banged it down so hard on its silver tray that her brother fully expected the crystal to crack and the whisky he desired more strongly with each passing moment to spill all its goodness into the carpet below.

'The Board members are often waiting for your decision, my dear. They rely heavily on your judgement.'

Isobel passed a hand over her smooth white hair. 'And I find it more and more difficult to make a judgement.'

'I can see that if George wasn't your son, it would be easier for you to form a – more detached opinion of his arguments,' Craig said delicately.

'Fergus, I'm shocked! I have never let favouritism sway me in the slightest and I never will!'

'I didn't say that you favoured the boy, Isobel, I merely said— '

'Besides, you know that I myself can't stand George.

He irritates me more and more – and there's Fiona, as flat in the stomach as ever she was with still no sign of a child yet,' Isobel said, off on a tangent. 'Next thing we know the young fool will be talking about divorce again, and how I'll cope with the shame of that I don't know. It's just that— ' she stopped, staring down into her glass, her brow furrowed, then said, 'George is family, Fergus, even though he is a fool. And Robert Archer may be very clever – I certainly can't fault his behaviour apart from an occasional abrasive lapse that I'm generously willing to overlook – but when it comes down to it, one can scarcely oppose one's own flesh and blood, not to mention one's own class.'

There was a slight pause before she said more briskly, 'And then there's the unions.'

'The unions?' asked Fergus Craig in bewilderment, then flinched back into the cushions of his chair as his sister suddenly swooped down on him. Memories of nursery fights of sixty years before, when Isobel had been known to use teeth and nails ruthlessly in order to get her own way, suddenly flooded his mind and it was all he could do to suppress an involuntary yelp of fear.

'My dear Fergus, you've clearly had more than enough to drink,' said Isobel, whipping the empty glass from his fingers and returning it to the tray with another crash. 'Your mind's all fuddled, just when I'm relying on you to help me sort things out. Never before have the unions been in Dalkieth's yard – never. Edward and his father must be birling in their graves. It only happened after you talked me into making Robert Archer office manager.'

'Isobel, the war changed the face of Britain. The unions were bound to come in sooner or later.' Privately, Fergus thought that if George had been in sole charge the unions would have run riot over the yard by this time. Thanks to young Archer's level-headedness unions and management worked better together in Dalkieth's yard than in many others, and were set to continue doing so.

'And the workforce expects so much these days,' Isobel was saying. He was glad to note that the whisky's mellowing effect was beginning to show and some of the fire was going out of her. 'They never used to be so demanding, Fergus. They knew their place in the old days, and they were grateful to employers for looking after them. Look at the fine tenements the Dalkieths built for their workers on this side of the river. They cost a great deal of money, but nobody ever stops to think of that when they're talking of labourers being worthy of their hire.'

'Times change, my dear. And, talking of time, I ought to be going.' Craig began to struggle to his feet. His stomach was bothering him again, as often happened when he spent too much time in Isobel's company. And there was a very fine malt waiting for him in a cupboard in his library.

'Can't you stay a little longer?'

Fergus consulted the handsome silver watch slung across his stomach. 'Elspeth will be expecting me back.' His voice was almost pleading.

'The truth of the matter is, Fergus,' his sister sank into a chair, her voice slow and subdued, 'It's all such a burden, and we're none of us getting any younger, are we?' Her fingers caressed her left hand, lingering on the magnificent engagement ring and the worn plain gold band beneath it. 'I wish William was still alive – and Edward. They would know what should be done.'

She looked up, and Fergus saw that her blue eyes

sparkled, not with impatience now, but with tears. Isobel had always been undeniably beautiful, and at that moment she was also vulnerable, a mixture of the impetuous child she had once been and the old, rather tired woman she had become. Strangely, his own eyes began to sting a little. He subsided back into the chair he had almost freed himself from.

'Perhaps I can stay – for a little while,' he said gently, round a lump that had begun to form in his throat.

18

'D'you realise the chances you're giving up? You could have been a schoolteacher yourself – anything you put your mind to,' Jenny said in despair. 'Why didn't you tell me that you were planning to leave the Academy?'

'Because I knew you'd talk me out of it. Why else d'you think I waited until I'd got Mr Monroe to agree to take me on full time before I said a word to Mam?' Alice was unrepentant. 'Anyway, I'd never have made a decent teacher – I've not got the patience, for one thing. I'd have become a grumpy old witch by the time I turned twenty-five.'

'You've given up your schooling because of me, haven't you?' Jenny felt guilt settle heavily on her shoulders. 'Just because I'm going to have to stop work. But we've talked about it, me and Daniel, and we can still manage to— '

'It's nothing to do with your baby, so don't start fretting about that. It's what I want to do, Jen. I just wish Mam hadnae told you.'

'But don't you see— '

'Ach, leave her be,' Faith advised from the sink, where she was bathing her little granddaughter. 'Will you keep that towel on, Helen? You'll catch your death of cold!'

Naked, and seemingly oblivious to the cold early December air that blew through the cracks in the ill-fitting window frame beside her, the little girl sat on the draining board with her feet in the sink, bent double so that she could dabble her hands in the water. When Faith tried to tuck the towel more securely round her shoulders, she shrugged it off. 'Don't want it!'

'Well don't expect me tae fret over you when you start coughing,' her grandmother warned. 'Jenny, our Alice was always one tae go her own way and you'll just tire yourself out arguin' with her. Shut your eyes, now, Helen.'

She poured a jugful of warm water over the child's head to rinse the soap out of her hair. Helen squeaked and gurgled then gasped, inhaling water. Alice, laughing, went over to wrap the towel round her plump body then scooped her up, carrying her to Teeze's empty chair where she sat down, the little girl in her lap.

'You're a right water baby, aren't you?' she said as Helen's face emerged from the folds of the towel, blinking.

'I'm not a baby!' three-year-old Helen said indignantly.

Jenny lifted the small patched gown from the wooden clothes-horse before the range, where it had been airing and sat down on Faith's chair. 'Come and sit on my knee, Helen, and I'll help you to put your wee gown on.'

'She's awful heavy now,' Alice said doubtfully.

'Tuts, I'm not made of glass! The bairn's not due until May – I'm scarcely showing yet.'

'Here she comes, then, big heavy lump that she is.' Alice jumped up and with an exaggerated heave swung Helen, squealing with excitement, into the air then down on to Jenny's lap.

'Again!' Helen demanded, holding out her arms and wriggling like an eel in Jenny's arms.

'You behave yourself, young lady, or I'll send you to bed without any supper,' Alice told her, her face twisted into a scowl. 'See, Jen? I'd make a terrible teacher. I'd have all the weans in tears.' Then, dropping back into her chair, she said with a sudden change of voice, 'Anyway, I never wanted to teach.'

'But you never said— '

'It was Maurice's idea, then yours, but never mine,' said Alice. 'I just wanted to please the two of you, but now I've decided that the person I should really try to please is myself.'

Looking at her sister over the damp curls that had already begun to spring back into place on Helen's head, Jenny realised that seemingly overnight her little sister had grown up. Now that Alice was no longer a schoolgirl she had drawn her brown hair into a bun at the back of her head and, under her apron, she wore a black skirt and striped blouse instead of her usual school clothes. There was a new air of purpose about her.

With a sense of shock, Jenny realised that she – and Maurice, when he was alive – had fallen into the same trap as Daniel. Because Alice showed signs of being cleverer than the rest of her family, they had tried to steer her along the path that they themselves might have wanted to take, had they had her abilities. But Alice had had the strength of character to make her own decisions. Would Walter have the courage to do the same?

'If you ask me, it's time this young madam had a good starving anyway,' Alice said just then, prodding Helen in the stomach and making her wriggle so hard that she tumbled off Jenny's knee and on to the floor, howling with laughter just as her mother came into the kitchen on a waft of sharp, cheap scent, her red hair fastened on top of her head, glittering earrings dangling from her ears.

Helen, the nightgown half on and half off, picked herself up and ran over to her, to be pushed away.

'For goodness' sake, don't paw at me like that! Go and get dressed. This place sounds like a bear-garden,' Lottie said, and Alice sniffed loudly then fanned the air, winking at Jenny.

'Funny, that's not what it *smells* like,' she commented blandly. 'I'd say it smells like a bro— '

'That's enough from you, miss!' Faith interrupted loudly while Lottie, slipping her arms into a new coat, glared.

'I'll mebbe be late back tonight,' she told Faith then walked out without a further glance at her daughter. They heard the outside door banging, then Lottie's heels clacking down the stairs.

The laughter had vanished from Helen's face. It crumpled, then was straightened with a visible effort of will as she began to work at pushing her arm into an empty sleeve.

'She'll mebbe not be back at all.' Alice took a small bowl down from a shelf and began to break stale bread into it.

'You mean she stays out all night?' Jenny asked, horrified. 'You never told me about this, Mam.'

'Because it's none of your business,' Faith said brusquely, with a warning glance at the little girl.

'Go and fetch my brush, Helen, and I'll do your hair for you,' Alice suggested. When the three women were alone, she took the weighted muslin cover off the milk jug and stirred milk into the broken bread. 'Lottie does stay out all night sometimes,' she told Jenny, scattering a spoonful of sugar over the mush in the bowl. 'And she never does a thing for that poor wee soul.'

'Is she still walking out with Neil Baker?'

'Aye.' Faith emptied the teapot into the sink then reached up to the high mantelshelf for the caddy. 'He'll be waitin' out in the street for her, tae walk her tae work.'

'It was him that bought her that coat. I just hope they get married.' Alice poured some hot water on to the bread and milk mixture then relinquished the kettle to her mother before adding, 'We'd all be glad to see the back of her.'

'And what'll happen to Helen then?'

'I'd keep her here in a minute,' Faith said at once.

'So would I,' Alice agreed, 'for she's a pleasure to be with. But she's Lottie's bairn, Mam, not ours. And mebbe it would be good for her to have a proper father.'

Helen hurried back into the room just then, the gown now on, though twisted round her plump little body. 'I'll do it myself,' she announced, and started swiping at her own head with the brush.

'And after it's done you'll have to eat up all this bread and milk, because we're fattening you up for Christmas, so that we'll have something nice to eat,' Alice told her, and Helen giggled against the outspread fingers of her free hand, then yelled as the hairbrush got caught up in a tangle of red hair.

Although it was only three o'clock in the afternoon the lights were on in George Dalkieth's drawing room, illuminating the silver tinsel that decorated the large Christmas tree in the bay window.

Robert Archer, striding up the driveway, his booted feet splintering thin ice and splashing heedlessly through puddles, ignored the pretty picture that the tree made. He rapped sharply on the front door, then descended the two curved stone steps and paced up and down the drive, impervious to the thin snow that was beginning to fall, spinning round when the door opened to glower at the maidservant.

'Tell Mrs Dalkieth that Robert Archer would like to speak to her,' he snapped, striding up the steps. The girl faltered back and he marched past her into a narrow hallway.

'I'll see if madam— '

'On a matter of some urgency,' said the caller grimly, and the maid, who had begun to hold out her hand for his hat, gave a muffled squeak and let her arm fall back to her side as she turned and scuttled through an adjacent doorway. Archer dropped his hat on to a half-moon table set against one wall and was peeling off his gloves when the girl reappeared.

'This way, sir.'

In the drawing room a fire blazed in the grate. The room was bright with paper chains strung from the light-fitting in the centre of the ceiling to the four corners, and smelled strongly of fresh pine needles. Fiona stood beside a large and handsome sideboard which held a small cardboard box and the model of a stable, together with some figurines. In her hand she held a small plaster statuette of the Madonna, her painted robe the same colour as Fiona's soft woollen dress.

'Mr Archer, this is a surprise.' Her eyes flickered past him to the maid, hovering in the doorway. 'My husband isn't at home— '

'It was you I called to see.' He stood stolidly in the middle of the room, an alien presence in the midst of the cheerful Christmas preparations.

'Indeed? You'll take some tea?'

'No thank you.'

'Then you can go, Margaret,' Fiona told the servant calmly. As the door closed, leaving them alone, her tone sharpened.' What are you doing here, Robert? You know you sh— '

'Is it true?'

'Is what true?'

'Don't play games with me, Fiona!' said Archer coldly. Her colour deepened and her eyes slid away from his. She fidgeted with the figurine. 'Are you expecting a child?'

Fiona put the Madonna down very carefully. 'As a matter of fact, I am expecting George's child, but— '

'You're sure that it's his?'

Her gaze was suddenly cold and direct. 'Of course.'

'Are you certain it's not mine, Fiona?'

Her hands flew protectively to her waist. 'I told you – I always took precautions!' Then, as he said nothing, she added defensively, 'I was going to tell you— '

'You haven't come near me for weeks!' He wanted to take hold of her and shake her, but, mindful of the servants nearby, he kept his hands fisted by his sides.

'I – it was difficult for me to get away. And I didn't know how to break the news to you that it must end between us.'

'So you decided to let me hear it from my house-keeper!'

Fiona ran the tip of her tongue over her lips and then, aware of the way his eyes followed the movement, turned away and dipped into the open box, bringing out a crib complete with baby. 'So it's all over the town already?'

'Of course it is. This town delights in gossip, and George Dalkieth seems to be a rich source,' he said bitterly. 'Everyone knows he divorced his first wife because she didn't give him an heir. Everyone knew about the child she later bore her second husband.'

Fiona carefully positioned the crib before the stable, then placed Mary and Joseph behind it so that they looked down on the child, Joseph kneeling, Mary standing, serenity painted on both faces.

'Your mother-in-law must be delighted with your – success, Fiona.'

'Robert, I know I should have had the courage to tell y— ' Her words ended in a gasp as his impatience got the better of him and he caught her arm, swinging her round to face him. She smelled, as always, of lily-of-the-valley and, beneath the woollen sleeve, he could feel the fragile bones of her elbow, the warmth of her skin.

'I've already asked you to come away with me. I've not changed my mind on that,' he said, his voice low and intense. 'If this child you're carrying is mine, there's no need for you to be afraid to tell me. I promise you that I'll welcome it and love it and care for it— '

'There's no question of it being yours! Is it my fault that my husband's first wife didn't conceive his child, while I did?'

'Swear to me, Fiona, that it's his child you're carrying, and not mine?'

'I will!' She looked up at him, her blue eyes wide and sincere. 'On a Bible, if you wish.'

'That won't be necessary,' he said quietly, and released her.

'Robert – Robert, you were a good friend to me when

I badly needed a friend.' She was anxious to keep a pleasant façade between them so that there would be no comment about any sudden hostility towards her on his part on future social occasions.

'I'd hoped I was more than that, Fiona.' He swung out of the door and into the hall, snatching up his hat and gloves, wrenching the front door open.

As he stepped through the open double gates and turned to walk back to his own home a car came towards him, slowing to take the turn into the driveway he had just left. Glancing at it he saw Isobel Dalkieth staring at him through the side window. He nodded to her and walked on, wondering indifferently what explanation Fiona would give for his visit.

No doubt she would think of something, and frankly he didn't care what it was. He was sick with the humiliation of discovering that he hadn't meant as much to Fiona Dalkeith as he had fondly imagined.

The latch of his wrought-iron garden-gate stuck the first time he pushed at it, and he jabbed his hand down again, impatiently, releasing the latch but tearing the skin down the side of his thumb. The wound stung, and when he was inside the house with the lights on he saw that blood dripped from his hand. He sucked it away, and more welled up as he opened the whisky decanter. Impatiently, he held his hand over the hearth and poured whisky on to it, drawing his breath in through set teeth as the alcohol burned through the torn skin. Then he sloshed a generous amount of whisky into a glass, and threw himself down on to a chair.

Three times he had genuinely cared for a woman, and three times he had suffered. His marriage had been a mistake on both sides, and when he and his wife had finally agreed to end it he had known only relief. He had lost Jenny through his own selfish stupidity, and had perhaps lost her again when he returned to Ellerslie because, absorbed in his new career with the Dalkieth shipyard, he hadn't taken the time or the trouble to woo her as he should, to overcome her natural resentment at his earlier desertion.

And then, older and wiser though he should have been by that time, he had fallen for Fiona, believed her when she said that she truly loved him.

She had never intended their affair to be anything but an affair, he told himself bitterly as he refilled his glass. No matter what she thought of George Dalkieth she valued the social position she enjoyed as his wife. Robert, born in the tenements, could never offer her anything as grand as the Dalkieth name.

As for the child – he emptied his glass and got up to fill it again – what did it matter who had fathered it? Clearly Fiona had decided that it would be born a Dalkieth, and there was an end of the matter.

His hand still throbbed, but at least the alcohol was beginning to dull the anger, and the humiliation. A man knew where he stood with a good malt whisky, Robert thought with muzzy satisfaction as he fetched a fresh bottle from the cupboard.

In the first weeks of 1921 one of the building berths in the Dalkieth yard fell vacant unexpectedly, due to the last-minute cancellation of a vessel that had been ordered by one of their major customers. The clients, a firm of shipping merchants in the Far East, were hit by an unexpected world-wide drop in freight charges, and were not the only company to find themselves forced to take a second look at their order books and cut back on planned expansion.

George Dalkieth promptly committed the empty berth to a steam yacht commissioned by an industrialist he had met in Tyneside, a member of the consortium.

'But everyone knows that Dalkieth's yard builds commercial vessels, not pleasure boats!' Daniel fretted to Jenny. 'What are they thinking of, giving up valuable space to pleasure boats?'

It was a Saturday afternoon, with the week's work over, and a pile of ironing to be tackled. Jenny placed two flat-irons on the range where they would heat up quickly. 'It's surely better to use the berth than let it lie idle, Daniel.'

'Aye, but— ' A frown puckered his brow, 'They're sayin' that the market's beginnin' tae fail, and surely this is a sign of it. Even George Dalkieth wouldnae give up a good berth tae some rich man's toy if there was the chance of a better order. And I've heard that some of the larger yards down South are askin' their men tae take a cut in wages.'

'That'll not happen up here, surely.' Jenny, spreading a protective blanket over the kitchen table, tried to sound confident, but Daniel's concern worried her, for he wasn't one to fret over unfounded rumour and gossip. She poured water into a bowl to damp the clothes during the ironing.

'I hope not.' He reached for his jacket. 'I'm away tae a meetin'.' It seemed to Jenny that he was always at some meeting or other these days.

When he had gone she made sure that the irons were heating then wrapped a heavy shawl about her head and shoulders and, fetching a basket, went out to the darkening back court, festooned as usual with clothes-lines. It had been a cold day, but dry, and like all the other women in the tenements, she liked to get her washing out in the fresh air whenever possible.

Every item on the line, shirts and blouses, socks and trousers and Daniel's and Walter's vests and long johns, was frozen solid and she had trouble folding them to get them into the basket. The ice through the fabrics crackled and snapped, and her hands were soon numbed with the cold. Bending to push a mutinous pair of trousers into the basket Jenny was suddenly swept by a wave of dizziness and had to clutch at the nearby clothes-pole until the courtyard stopped swinging about her like a carousel and swayed to a standstill.

She heard boots skittering over the cobblestones, then Walter's voice asking sharply, 'Are ye all right? D'ye want me tae fetch Bella?' His hand was firm beneath her elbow, his young face concerned.

'I'm fine.' She blinked and smiled into his steady dark eyes, so like his father's. 'It must have been all that bending and stretching.'

'Sit down for a minute.' He steered her towards an upturned orange box then went back and finished taking in the washing, working swiftly and deftly. When the frozen clothes had all been subdued he scooped the basket under one long arm and came back to ease her to her feet and escort her into the welcome warmth of the kitchen, where he put the basket down near the range to let the clothes thaw out.

'I'll make a cup of tea then see tae the ironin' – you sit down and rest.'

'I'll do nothing of the kind. I'm over it now,' she told him firmly, taking the cups from the dresser.

Walter hesitated, fiddling with the stiff corner of a shirt that poked over the edge of the basket. Watching him from the corner of her eye as she moved about the kitchen, Jenny was aware of a wave of affection for him. In the seven months since her marriage to his father she had come to love Walter, a love born out of pity for the boy who carried such a burden of responsibility and paternal ambition on his thin shoulders. Only ten days away from his fourteenth birthday, Walter was still gawky and awkward, in some ways touchingly young for his age, yet in other ways, such as his concern for her, quite mature.

He had, as was expected, done very well in his scholarship examination, so instead of leaving his schooldays behind he would be moving to the Academy at the end of the month. Then, Jenny knew, Daniel would expect even more effort from him.

'Have you finished your homework?'

'Long since.' The material between his fingers was limp and damp now, and Walter blew on his numbed fingers to warm them.

'Why don't you go out for a wee while, then?'

'My father— '

'Your father's off on union business and he'll not be back for a good hour or more. You can have some time to yourself and be back at your books long before then.' She studied him and saw that although his cheeks and nose were bright red from being out in the yard, his face was pale and he looked tired. 'It's not good for a laddie of your age to be sitting over school-books all the time.'

Hope gleamed in Walter's eyes. 'If you're sure it'd be all right— '

'I'm sure. Go on now – but keep moving, I don't want you to catch cold.' Jenny measured tea-leaves into the pot then added water as Walter ducked into the hall. He reappeared almost at once to say shyly, 'Jenny?'

'Aye?'

'I'm – I'm pleased you're living here.' His face was flushed now with embarrassment. 'And I'm pleased about the bairn. I hope it's a wee lassie.'

'Your father wants another son.'

'Well, I think a wee sister would be nice,' he said with an almost conspiratorial grin, and went. She caught sight of herself in the mirror on the mantelshelf and saw that there was a broad smile of pleasure on her face.

She had come to realise that giving Walter some freedom when his father was away from the house was the only way in which she could help the boy. The attempts she made to stand up to Daniel on Walter's behalf since her marriage had resulted in him accusing his son unfairly of trying to hide behind a woman's skirts.

Walter was no sooner gone than he was back again. 'There's a visitor for you,' he said, and hurried off to make the most of his unexpected hour of freedom as Lizzie Caldwell walked into the kitchen, smiling self-consciously.

'I'm down from Glasgow for my sister's wedding – you mind Annie? – and I thought I'd just look in and see how you are. I can't stay long.' She took off her stylish woollen coat then settled herself in a chair by the range, glancing around the kitchen. Jenny, hanging the coat behind the kitchen door, was uncomfortably aware of the underwear suspended from the overhead pulley and the ironing blanket spread in readiness over the table. She swooped on the basket of thawing clothes and pushed it under the wall-bed out of sight, then took the cups and saucers down from the shelf.

'This is a pretty cup – did you paint it yourself, Jenny?' Lizzie asked as she accepted her tea. 'It's unusual.'

Daniel had been so pleased with the cups and saucers

Jenny had painted at his request that she had gone on to decorate the entire set, teapot and all, using bold bright colours in a mixture of geometrical shapes she had found in one of Walter's mathematics books.

Lizzie surveyed Jenny over the rim of the cup as she took a sip, then returned it to the saucer and said, with a glint of amusement, 'You've – grown.'

Jenny laughed and put a hand to the small bulge below her apron, then looked enviously at her friend's trim figure. 'And you've shrunk!'

Lizzie looked down smugly at her beige skirt and dark green knitted top. Her hat was also beige, like her coat, a small-brimmed cloche trimmed with a green feather. 'To tell you the truth, I'm wearing one of the emporium's best corsets, though I've lost weight since I left Ellerslie. Now that I'm in charge of ladies' under-wear I like to look smart for our clients, so I watch what I eat.' She smoothed her skirt. 'I bought this from the emporium, too – I get a discount on clothes there, being a supervisor.'

She wore a discreet touch of lipstick, Jenny noticed, and her thick eyebrows had been plucked out and new brows, delicately arched, pencilled in. They gave her ordinary face a slightly sophisticated, quizzical look that suited it.

'I heard about your gran. Your mother must have taken it hard. I mind how well she looked after the old woman.'

'She's over it now. And our Alice is out of school and all but running Munroe's pawnshop,' Jenny said proudly. 'She's got a great head for business.'

'You didn't do so badly yourself. Supervisor at the tracing office, no less.'

'I'll have to finish there soon.'

Lizzie sipped her tea, then turned the cup round slowly, studying the design. 'I'll need to get you to do a set for me some time.' She accepted more tea, then launched into a vivacious account of her work in Glasgow and the clients who insisted on asking for her personally each time they came in.

'You'd have done well, Jen, if you'd only come with me. Are you sorry you didn't?'

'A wee bit,' Jenny said, then, aware that the words sounded disloyal to Daniel, she added quickly, 'but I'm happy enough in Ellerslie.'

'Are you? Lizzie's eyes beneath the elegant new brows were bird-sharp. 'I heard that Robert Archer's back at the yard,' she added casually, taking cigarettes and matches out of her leather bag.

'He's the office manager there.'

'That's someone else who's done well for himself. Was it not difficult for you, him coming back to Ellerslie, I mean?'

'The past's past,' Jenny told her shortly. 'Anyway, he got married in England – as you no doubt heard.' Lizzie's sister Annie was an incurable gossip and Lizzie must have been kept well informed of everything that had gone on during her absence.

'I'd heard he was divorced and living in a nice house with a housekeeper to look after him.' Lizzie blew out a plume of smoke, the cigarette propped elegantly between plump but well-manicured fingers. 'When you think of him all those years ago, always looking as if that aunt of his didnae give him enough tae eat— ' Her genteel tones began to blur at the edges as she slipped smoothly into local gossip.

'Lottie's walking out with Neil Baker these days. D'ye mind him?' Jenny asked.

'That naval architect that couldnae keep his hands tae himself? She's setting her sights high. D'ye think she'll manage tae catch him?' Lizzie asked, diverted. Her voice rose and fell and when Jenny finally looked up at the clock she realised that time had gone by faster than she had thought. Walter hadn't yet returned and Daniel would be home soon.

Lizzie interpreted her glance and got to her feet. 'I'd best go – I told Annie I'd not be long. It was nice seeing you again, Jenny,' she said as she slid her arms into her coat sleeves then drew on her beige kid gloves. 'If you're ever in Glasgow come and visit me.' She reached into her bag and brought out a flat parcel. 'I brought this for you from the emporium – it's a remainder of some of our best material,' she added casually as Jenny unfolded the brown paper and exclaimed with pleasure over the fine cream muslin sprigged with tiny pink and blue flowers. 'I thought you could mebbe make a wee gown for the bairn.'

'More than one – this'll do two or three.' Jenny stroked the material. 'Oh thank you, Lizzie, it's kind of you.'

'It's nothing,' said Lizzie airily. At the close door she said, suddenly wistful, 'I wish you could have come with me, Jen. You'd have loved Glasgow.'

'I'm happy as I am,' Jenny said firmly.

Lizzie's gaze swept over her friend's swelling, aproned figure. 'Well – if it's what you want— ' she said, and went off along the close, her heels tapping crisply on the stone flags.

Back in the kitchen Jenny studied herself in the mirror on the mantelshelf. She looked pale and tired; wisps of hair fell across her face, and there was a downward droop that she hadn't been aware of at the corners of her mouth. She was beginning to look like the other housewives in the tenements, the women who had had to struggle all their lives, making ends meet, scraping the rent money together week after week, only just managing to keep themselves and their families going with nothing left over for luxuries.

The latch on the outer door rattled, and Walter hurried in. 'I met some of the lads from school and the time just sort of slipped past,' he said anxiously. 'Is he— ' The fingers of one hand fumbled with his jacket buttons as the other whipped off his cap.

'No, but I thought you were going to – quick,' Jenny urged as she heard familiar footsteps in the close. 'Into your room with you!'

Walter didn't need telling twice. He peeled the jacket off and pushed it into her hands as he slid past her. When Daniel came in the jacket was hanging on the back of the door and Jenny was stacking the used cups on the draining board, already scolding herself for getting into a panic just because he had almost caught Walter in his outdoor clothes.

'Where's the boy?' he asked, as he always did.

'In his room, working at his books. Where else would he be?' She hesitated, then said, 'Daniel, d'you not think that Walter should be out in the fresh air more often?'

'He gets fresh air every day, on his milk-round, then going to and from the school.'

'But that's not much, is it? The other laddies get out to play football or play along the riverbank— '

'Has he been whinin' tae you again?' Daniel wanted to know, his voice tense. 'Because if he has I'll soon teach him tae— '

'No!' She caught at his arm as he got up from his chair and began to move towards the door. 'Of course

257

he's said nothing – Walter would never complain! It was just – every boy needs to get fresh air and exercise, Daniel. Maurice used to be out and about all the time, and I'm sure you were too, when you were Walter's age.'

Under her fingers, the muscles in his arm were like steel. 'Aye, I was out in the streets all the time – because my father was a drunkard who cared nothing for his weans. And what happened to me, eh?' He glared down at her and her hand fell away from his arm. 'I'm nothin' but a slave now, dependent on the likes of George Dalkieth for the money tae keep me and mine alive.' His voice rose. 'My son's goin' tae have a better life than I ever did, Jenny. He'll be the one tae give the orders, no' the one tae take them. And until then he'll dae as I say – so don't you try turnin' him against his work with talk of playin' football and runnin' wi' the other laddies that are goin' tae follow their fathers intae the yard. Heed me now, Jenny, for I'll be master in my own house!'

She had never known Daniel to raise a hand to anyone, but she knew now that there was no need for it – his anger was so intense that it radiated into the room from every inch of him and seemed to take on a shape of its own. Its heat scorched Jenny and, trying to contain her shock, she moved away from her husband, back to the stove.

'I've had a visitor.' Despite herself, her voice shook, and so did her hands. 'D'ye mind Lizzie Caldwell who used to work in the yard office? She's in Glasgow now, working in a big store. She brought some bonny cloth to make gowns for the baby.'

'Oh aye?' Daniel said without interest, sitting down and unlacing his boots. The anger had gone out of him almost as suddenly as it had sparked, and he started to talk about the meeting he had just left.

The baby kicked and she put a comforting hand on her swelling belly. She wanted only the best for the child she was carrying, but surely Daniel, too, would want the best for it. After all, it was his child as well. She suddenly recalled Walter saying earlier that he hoped that she would have a daughter.

A cold hand brushed against the skin between Jenny's shoulder-blades at the memory. Had the boy said that because he knew only too well what would be expected of a boy rather than a girl? And if – when – that happened, when Daniel started imposing his own thwarted ambitions on the new baby just as he had done with Walter, would she have the strength to resist him, Jenny wondered. Even for the sake of her own child?

19

Apart from bouts of morning sickness in the first few months Jenny continued to enjoy good health, and she was able to keep on working until March, just over two months before her baby was due.

'I'll be sorry tae lose ye, lass,' Mr Duncan said on her final day at the Experimental Tank. 'Ye've been a grand supervisor.'

'I'll be sorry to go,' Jenny's voice shook. Now that it was coming to an end, she knew that her work in the Tank section had meant more to her than she had realised. She had to swallow hard to keep back the tears when Senga, who was going to take her place as supervisor, presented her with a parcel of baby clothes knitted by the tracing-room staff.

Mr Duncan, with much clearing of the throat, gave her a handsome glass vase, bought by a collection gathered from the other departments in the Tank and, at the end of the day, Robert Archer summoned her to the boardroom. He closed the door, shutting out the clang of the truck, enclosing the two of them in the dusty opulence of the carpeted room.

He had changed, even in the time since he had come back to Ellerslie. He had aged, she realised, looking more closely at him. There was an air of tension about him now, disillusionment in his steady grey eyes, a sharpening of his lean features. Jenny felt a moment's pang for the ambitious young man she had once loved, then reminded herself, briskly, that she too had changed. It was inevitable. Their lives, once apparently destined to be woven together, had taken separate paths after all, and they had grown away from each other in a way that she would never have thought possible in the days of the rhododendrons. There was no sense, now, in thinking about matters that were over and done with.

But when he said, 'How are you, Jenny?' she knew by the tone of his voice that for him, too, the past couldn't be denied. Alone together, with nobody else to overhear, Robert wasn't merely talking to an employee.

'I'm very well.'

His eyes travelled slowly over her face. 'And are you happy?'

'Daniel's a good husband to me.'

'I'm pleased to hear it. You deserve happiness, Jen,' he said gently, then on a more formal note, 'You'll be missed here. Your loyalty and your hard work have been appreciated.'

Carefully, avoiding contact between their fingers, Jenny took the stiff white envelope he proferred, reminded of the envelope that had arrived from Lizzie's aunt, the letter that had fleetingly offered her the chance to leave Ellerslie. If she had been able to take that chance she wouldn't have seen Robert again, wouldn't have married Daniel.

She opened the envelope and gasped as she read the fancy lettering on the treasury note inside. 'Ten pounds? It's too much!'

'As far as Dalkieth's is concerned you've been worth every penny of it. And if ever you need any help— ' again, the formality had gone, and it was Robert himself who was speaking, studying her with that gaze that seemed to have the ability to read her very soul, ' — remember that *we're* still friends, no matter what's happened between us.'

'Thank you, Mr – thank you, Robert.' She held her hand out and, for a long moment, he took it in his own warm, strong clasp, putting his other hand over their clasped fingers.

'Jen— '

'I must go— ' She pulled away from him, and he let her hand slip from between his. As she turned towards the door she heard him say her name again, but she had found the handle, and she opened the door and went through without looking back.

It was too late, now, to think of looking back.

As the weeks passed the routine of Jenny's new life began to take up all her attention and the tracing office was gradually relegated to her past. She was able to take some of the burden from Bella's shoulders now that she was at home all day. She could keep an eye on Patrick and give him his midday meal, saving Bella many a hurried journey across the town to feed him and then rushing back to work.

The move to a ground-floor flat had had little impact on Patrick Kerr after all. He still refused to use the crutches he had been given when he first came home, or to have a special boot made to enable him to walk more comfortably. When Jenny took tea or a meal to him she always found him crouched in a chair, staring at the walls that held him as securely as any prison cell. He scarcely looked at her or answered her when she spoke and, without realising it, she herself started behaving like a gaoler, putting the food down near the edge of the table, within his reach, and withdrawing without a word.

Bella was working as hard as ever to support the two of them. She was up early in the morning and in bed late at night.

'You're killing yourself, d'you know that?' Jenny asked bluntly one day when she had managed to coax her sister to come in for a cup of tea.

'I'm as strong as a horse.' Bella fidgeted, turning away from her sister's scrutiny. Her wedding ring was almost lost in swollen, reddened flesh and Jenny could hear the rasping noise her roughened fingers made as they twisted together.

'Horses are sometimes worked until they fall down in the street, then they're shot,' Jenny pointed out, and Bella laughed.

'You think I'm ready for the catsmeat man, do you?'

'I think that's all you'll *be* fit for, the rate you're going.'

'Ye're havering, Jen.' A strand of hair fell over Bella's wan face; she put her hands up to push it away and one sleeve fell back to reveal an ugly blue and green bruise on the soft inner skin of her thin arm.

'I see you've run into another door,' Jenny said dryly. 'You should try opening them some time.'

Bella flushed crimson, dropping her arm back into her lap, dragging the sleeve down over the tell-tale bruising. 'Mind your own business!'

'It *is* my business. D'you think I want to see you turning yourself into an invalid? What'll happen to Patrick, then?'

Tears flooded at once into Bella's eyes. She put her cup down and made for the door.

'Bella— '

'Patrick'll be wondering where I've got to.' Bella fumbled with the latch of the outer door with shaking hands, taking so long over it that Jenny, large and clumsy as she now was, had time to follow her into the narrow hall.

'Bella, I'm only trying to— '

Bella rounded on her, sobbing freely now. 'Patrick didnae ask tae be turned intae a cripple, Jen! I loved him before, and I love him now. And if I do end up as catsmeat,' she added, her voice rising as the door finally opened for her, 'it's only what he would have done for me if it had been the other way round!'

Then she plunged across the close, disappearing into her own flat and slamming the door in Jenny's face.

On the following day when Jenny took food in to Patrick he was in his usual chair, a discarded newspaper crumpled on the floor by his side. He didn't bother to acknowledge her when she went in. Seeing that the fire was almost out she put the tray down on the table and hurried to replenish it.

'You could surely have managed to keep the fire going, Patrick. Bella left enough coal in the scuttle for you.'

'I'm warm enough.' He glanced at her indifferently. He was thin, pale with lack of fresh air, and unshaven, and his hair needed cutting.

'Mebbe so, but there's a cold wind blowing outside and Bella'll be in need of the fire when she comes home,' Jenny said breathlessly. Stooping over the range was an effort now that the birth of her baby was only a few days away, and when she straightened her back gave a painful twinge.

'Bella's not sitting indoors all day with a blanket over

her legs like some people, Patrick. Anyway, she'll be tired enough when she gets back without having to set to and light the range. She works hard to keep the two of you – or haven't you noticed?'

With a sweep of his hand Patrick tossed the blanket to the floor to reveal his twisted foot, covered by a thick sock. 'I'm a cripple,' he said bitterly, 'or haven't you noticed?'

Jenny hadn't had a chance to talk to her sister since Bella had rushed out of her house in tears. She had spent an uncomfortable, sleepless night fretting over the things she had said, wishing they had been left unsaid. Guilt honed the edge of her voice. 'I've seen men in the streets every day since the war with crutches and false limbs. There's a man that sells newspapers in Dreghorn Street who has to go about on a wee sort of cart because he's got no legs at all!' She picked up the tray and put it on a stool beside his chair, so that he could reach it. 'You're fortunate compared to him.'

Patrick's lips pulled back from his teeth in a snarl of rage. 'Fortunate? What d'you know about the way I'm suffering?'

'How did our Bella get those bad bruises on her arm?' Jenny countered and colour stained the skin stretched tightly over his cheekbones.

'Runnin' girnin' tae you, was she? Whinin' for sympathy?'

'Our Bella's got more self-respect than that. She didn't mean me to see, but I did, just as I've seen the black eyes and the bruised mouths. Why should you take your bitterness out on her? It wasn't her that sent you to the war, Patrick. And at least you came back – Maurice didn't, and neither did thousands of other men.'

His hands, still powerful, gripped the wooden arms of his chair, the knuckles white. 'Where's the sense in a man comin' back if he's no' whole any more?' He ground the words between his teeth. 'Who wants a cripple?'

'Our Bella does, for one! She loves you so much she'd have welcomed you home no matter how bad you were hurt. But that doesn't matter to you, does it? All you want is to make her stop loving you and start hating you instead, so that you can feel even sorrier for yourself. You're more crippled in your head than your leg, Patrick Kerr,' said Jenny with contempt, 'and it's time someone had the sense to tell you the truth of it.'

'Get out of here, you bitch! Mind yer own business!'

'You're just a poor, pathetic, creature, Patrick, without the guts of a flea.'

With a wordless yell he launched himself at her. If he had reached her the two of them would have gone crashing down, but in spite of her added weight Jenny was able to step aside, though, as she turned, she felt a sudden tearing sensation in her back. Patrick's hoarse roar turned to a thin scream of pain as his weight was thrown on to his twisted foot and it buckled beneath him. He caught at the table cover as he went down and an empty bowl and a vegetable knife Bella had left there spun down after him. He measured his length on the rug before the fire, the side of his head narrowly missing the leg of the other fireside chair. He escaped further injury when the falling knife landed on its handle and bounced away from him. The bowl spun into a corner and the tablecloth drifted down to cover his head.

To her own astonishment, Jenny began to laugh. She stood clutching at the corner of the table while her crippled brother-in-law writhed on the floor at her feet, clawing the cloth away from his face, wave after wave of hysterical mirth washing over her.

'Get me up, damn you!' Patrick yelled.

'Get yourself up, if you're still man enough.' Laughing was giving her a stitch in her side and she managed, with an effort, to get it under control as she went to pick up the bowl. It was still intact; Jenny put it back on the table but decided against salvaging the knife and the tablecloth for fear that Patrick might catch at her ankle and pull her off-balance.

At the door she turned. 'The men begging in the streets'd rather let the folk see the poor, maimed things they've become through no fault of their own than let their wives slave for them. Think about *that*, Patrick Kerr.'

Inside her own flat she leaned against the panels of the outer door. She dearly wanted to sit down but she was shaking too much to make her way into the kitchen. She had done a terrible, cruel thing. She should go back to make sure that Patrick was all right, she told herself, then thought of the sharp knife lying within his reach. If he had managed to get to his feet, if he had the knife, there was no telling what he might do if she went back.

But if Patrick killed himself, it would be her fault, she thought. Then she remembered the ugly bruising she had seen on her sister's arm the day before, and all the other bruises Bella had had.

The shaking had eased off a little. She pushed herself away from the door and into the kitchen, trying to think. Someone should go to make sure that Patrick was all right, but Daniel was at work, Walter at school. She wondered if she could ask her mother if she would look in on him, making some excuse for not doing it herself.

There was no harm in admitting that she had angered him without saying anything about his fall or the sharp knife that had tumbled from the table. It was the thought of the knife, temptingly close to his hand, that was worrying her more than anything.

She was reaching up to take her coat from the back of the door when a huge, strong hand seemed to take hold of her body, gripping her cruelly round the back and belly.

She gasped and curled one arm protectively round her body, the other hand catching the back of a chair, clutching it tightly. When the pain finally ebbed she lowered herself cautiously into the chair, moving as though she was an old woman, and sat still until she got her breath back.

It was only a touch of cramp, she told herself, getting up to fetch a glass of water and sipping the cold liquid slowly, standing by the sink. Then the tumbler dropped from her fingers to shatter against the tap as the pain struck again and she bowed herself over, trying to hold it in and control it, frightened in case it began to control her.

When it was over she went as quickly as she could to the outer door, ignoring her coat, aware only of the need to get help quickly. The elderly woman who had moved into Bella's old flat was on her way downstairs when she opened the door, a shabby shopping bag in one fist. She nodded, then looked again at Jenny.

'Ye're awful white, hen. Is it the bairn?'

'I think so. But it's not supposed to come for a few days yet.'

'Bairns don't use calendars,' the woman said, dropping her bag and guiding Jenny back indoors. 'You go and lie down and I'll fetch yer mother.'

By the time Faith arrived at a run, accompanied by Mrs Malloy, Jenny had managed to heave her swollen clumsy body on to the bed.

'Sure an' this one's in a hurry tae see the world, is it no'?' the Irishwoman said almost at once. 'It'll be a lassie – the laddies arenae half as nosy.'

Patrick Kerr lay where he had fallen for a long time after Jenny walked out, his cheek pressed painfully into the cracked linoleum, and wept like a child, noisily, angrily, the frustration pouring out of him in a torrent of self-pity that was bitter with salt when it trickled into his mouth.

When, at last, the tears slowed and dried to a snuffling and gasping, he stayed where he was for a while then finally reached out and managed to catch at the leg of Bella's chair. Painfully, laboriously, he pulled himself to his knees, whimpering like a dog when burning needles of pain shot through his wounded foot, which had twisted beneath him when he fell. It took several attempts before he got his good foot under him and stood up, then turned himself about, gripping now at the table, and finally fell back into his chair, his twisted leg throbbing each time it was bumped against the furniture.

He rubbed the sleeve of his jersey across his face again and again until the angry tears and the mucus which had run from his nose were scrubbed away, before realising that one hand was gripped tightly about the wooden handle of the knife that had fallen from the table. He turned it over to let the light from the window kiss the blade into life, running the ball of one thumb over the cutting edge, his breathing still ragged, with the occasional shoulder-heaving gasp. The knife was sharp.

Patrick tested the point against the inside of one wrist, where a blue vein was clearly visible just under the white skin.

There had been a man in the trenches, a friend, who had cut his wrists. It was an easy death, someone had said. Patrick pressed a little harder, then pulled the blade away as a glistening bead of blood welled up. He lifted his wrist to his mouth and licked the blood away. He wasn't afraid to die; it would be easy, it would be more fitting than to spend the rest of his life a cripple – but that bitch Jenny had probably left the knife near him on purpose, and he'd not kill himself just to please her! He turned the blade over again, thinking longingly of the pleasure it would give him at that moment to drive it through his interfering sister-in-law's throat.

A piece of driftwood lay on the hearth, a lump of timber that Bella had found on the river shore and brought in to be used as kindling for the range. Patrick bent over and managed to curl the fingers of one hand round it and hoist it to his lap. He stabbed the knife into it savagely, dislodging a flake of wood that fell away, revealing the pale, grained interior. He stabbed again, then again, the breath whistling in his throat. More flakes tumbled down to the floor by his wounded foot and he wielded the knife again, this time with direction and purpose, the neat handle fitting comfortably into his palm. Five minutes later the lump of wood in his hands had taken on the rough shape of a woman, short haired and with a swollen belly. He turned it over, examining it closely, then grinned and twisted the point of the knife deep into the swelling.

'That's done for you, Jenny Young,' he muttered, then paused on the point of tossing the carved figure down and uncurled his fingers to expose it lying in the palm of his hand. He turned it around, studying it from all angles, his mind stirring with memories that had long since been pushed out of sight. Finally he lifted the knife again, this time using the blade carefully to start paring the swollen stomach away, flake by flake, turning the blade deftly this way and that, slipping back into an old and soothing routine.

By the time Walter arrived home from school, Jenny was in the final stages of a short and swift labour, and had forgotten all about Patrick. Her hands gripped her mother's as the pain came and went, advancing a little further each time it came, receding a little less each time it ebbed, until it seemed to be a part of her that would never leave. Dimly she heard Mrs Malloy in the hall, instructing Walter to go round to her house until he was sent for.

'Should I mebbe run to the yard and tell my father?' The boy's voice was high-pitched with tension.

'No! Jenny forced the word through the wall of pain surrounding her, knowing full well, even in the midst of her torment, that Daniel wouldn't want his son to see him at work.

'Best not,' Mrs Malloy told Walter. 'He's played his part – let him come back in his own time. It'll be over by then.'

She was right. By the time Daniel arrived home, scrubbed clean and smelling of carbolic soap as usual, his daughter, also washed and smelling of soap, though in her case a flowery soap that Jenny had saved for the occasion, was gowned, shawled, and asleep in her crib.

'She's healthy lookin',' he said awkwardly, staring down at her.

'Ye're a fortunate man, Daniel. A clever son, an' now a bonny wee daughter,' Faith told him. He nodded, but Jenny, watching from the shadow of the alcove bed, saw the disappointment in his face. He had set his heart on another son.

'Where's Walter?'

'I sent him tae my house. He was best out o' the way,' Mrs Malloy said serenely, and at once he made for the door.

'I'll fetch him,' he said, and hurried out. Mrs Malloy made a face at the closing door.

'An' what's troublin' the man?' she asked with good humour. 'Scared his laddie'll be enjoying himself, for once? Or scared he'll catch somethin' in my house?' Her rich laugh boomed out, filling a room that seldom heard laughter.

'It's just his way,' Jenny found herself defending her husband. 'He doesn't mean anything by it.'

'Now don't you go thinkin' I'm bothered, child. Don't I know Daniel Young well enough by now?' Mrs Malloy said calmly, then, as the baby snuffled, she swooped down on the crib and scooped her up, blankets and all. 'An' no need for you to fret, bonny wee thing that ye are,' she instructed, depositing the sweet-smelling bundle in Jenny's arms. 'Now then, just you enjoy yer wee daughter an' have a good rest. Sure an' ye've earned it.'

The baby had translucent skin like white porcelain, and a lot of soft, black hair. Her wide, serene eyes were dark blue, staring up at Jenny, who held her close, marvelling over the lightness yet compactness of the small body in her arms. She had let Daniel down, she knew that, but, deep in her heart, she was glad that she had given birth to a daughter. This baby would be free to grow up without the responsibility that lay so heavily on poor Walter's young shoulders . . .

Bella came in an hour later, her exhausted face radiant, to croon over the baby.

'Oh Jen, she's beautiful!'

Jenny, more rested now, suddenly remembered the scene in her sister's flat earlier. 'How's Patrick?'

'He's fine. In fact, he's better than fine. You'll never guess what he did today, Jen! He got hold of my wee vegetable knife and a bit of wood I'd brought in for the fire and he started carving a lovely wee figure, just like the sort of things he used tae make before the war. It's like a wee figurehead for a wee toy sailing ship. He was so busy with it he forgot all about eating that dinner you made for him.'

She laughed, and cuddled the baby close. 'Tae think I was worried about leavin' any knives near him in case he hurt himself. It was a daft thought. I should have encouraged him, not tried tae protect him so much, but Jenny, I never thought tae see him workin' away like that again.' She dropped a light kiss on the sleeping baby's forehead. 'Mebbe this bairn's brought luck with her. Mebbe things are goin' tae get better at last!'

20

As Daniel felt that it was unseemly for his son to be in the same house as a woman recovering from childbirth Walter was dispatched to the Gillespies' flat, where he slept in Alice's room. Daniel moved into Walter's room and Alice shared the alcove bed with Jenny so that she was at hand to help with the baby during the night. Faith came in every day, bringing Helen with her.

They had wondered how Helen, the only child in the family for the past three years, would react to her new little cousin. At first sight of the new baby she tossed her faded, battered rag doll out of its 'perambulator' – an old wooden box with rickety wheels and a wooden handle that had been passed to her from the youngest Malloy child – then smoothed out the scrap of blanket in the bottom of the box. Briskly pushing back her sleeves in imitation of the women she had seen about her all her life she confidently held her fat little arms out.

'My babby,' she announced, and her lower lip trembled when Bella, who was holding the shawled bundle, shook her head.

'It's not a dolly, pet, it's a real wee girl, and we've tae be very careful with her. See— ' Bella drew a fold of shawl away from the tiny face, and Helen approached on tiptoe to stroke the baby's cheek with a wondering finger, then tugged at Bella's skirt in a sudden fit of jealousy.

'Me now,' she demanded, trying to scramble up on to her aunt's knee, forcing Bella to hand the baby over to her mother and pick Helen up.

'I doubt we've spoiled her over much,' Faith commented, shaking her head.

'Ach, she'll be all right.' Bella cuddled the little girl. 'We'll just need to be sure that she doesnae feel left out of things.'

For the first few days after her daughter's birth Jenny was content to lie back and be cossetted for the first time in her life. She listened to Helen's contented chatter and watched Faith moving competently about the kitchen, marvelling over her mother's renewed energy now that she was free of Marion and had come to terms with Maurice's death.

'He's a nice laddie, that Walter,' Faith said more than once. 'Grateful for everything ye do for him, and awful good with Helen. A nice, quiet laddie.'

'Too quiet, for his age,' Jenny said, sadly.

'Not when him and Alice get together. She'd get a stone tae turn noisy, that one.'

'Is he keeping up with his schoolwork?' Jenny asked anxiously.

'He does more than he should if you ask me.' Faith removed Helen's clutching hands from the side of the crib. 'That's enough kissin' for now, pet, let the babby get some sleep or she'll grow up crabbit.' She cast an approving glance at her new granddaughter. 'Have you and Daniel thought of a name yet?'

'We both like Shona.' Jenny had had several names in mind, but Daniel had shown little interest, saying to each suggestion, 'Whatever you want.'

'Shona.' Faith tried it on her tongue, then nodded. 'It suits her.'

Bella came in every day to linger over the crib and, if the baby was awake, to hold her and croon over her. There had been no new bruises and she had lost some of her usual tension. Alice and Walter had been combing the riverbanks in search of pieces of timber for Patrick, who had indeed rediscovered his interest in wood carving.

'He's got talent,' Alice told Jenny. Since starting work in the pawnshop she had become quite an expert where ornaments and jewellery were concerned.

Not all Mr Monroe's customers pawned their best clothes – the more affluent survived from month to month on the proceeds of vases and statuettes and even family heirlooms passed down from one generation to the next. Alice had discovered a collection of books on antiques in Alec Monroe's flat and she was working her way through them, one by one, with increasing interest. 'I've told him that I think he might be able to sell some pieces if he works hard enough.'

'What did he say to that?'

Alice shrugged. 'He just gave me one of those looks of his. You know Patrick – he's never got much to say for himself now. But at least he's doing something. I'll keep at him,' she added thoughtfully. 'There are folk that come into the shop sometimes to see what's for sale, not to pawn their own stuff. I'm sure they'd be interested in his carvings. And in your painted china, too,' she added, eyeing her sister.

'D'you not think I've got enough to do now that she's arrived?' Jenny ran a finger gently over the dark fluff that covered her daughter's neat skull and looked down at Shona's tiny face pressed into the curve of her breast, her cheeks rounding then emptying as she sucked strongly.

'Just remember what I'm saying when you do have the time,' Alice said quietly.

Ten days after Shona's birth Jenny was up and about and well enough to gather the reins of the house back into her own hands. Walter came home and was immediately captivated by his tiny half-sister. Shona was a placid and undemanding baby, and the household routine reshaped itself easily to accommodate her.

Robert Archer strode down the cobbled street, skirting groups of toddlers playing in the gutters, tipping his hat to the women who stopped their gossiping at the close-mouths to stare as he went by. It had been a good while since he had lived among them but they all knew who he was. He turned in at one particular close and rapped on a ground-floor door with the head of his cane. It opened after a moment and Jenny Young stared at him in astonishment.

'What brings you here?'

'I'd business in the area,' Robert lied blandly. 'And I thought that since I was here I'd pay my respects. Have I called at a bad time?'

'No. I was just putting the bairn down.' She led him into the kitchen, which was neat and bright and welcoming. 'You'll take a cup of tea?'

He nodded and went over to the crib, where the baby lay, wide-eyed. Robert put a finger into a tiny hand which gripped it with surprising strength. 'What are you calling her?'

'Shona.'

'It's a bonny choice.' He stayed where he was, reluctant to break the grip on his finger, while Jenny moved about the room. Her surprise at his arrival was so strong that he could almost taste it. 'She looks like you.'

'I think she's got Daniel's mouth.'

He looked at the tiny rosebud mouth, and disagreed, but silently. To his eyes Jenny's daughter was Jenny in miniature, with her neat little face and her solemn and steady blue-eyed gaze. If things had been different, this could have been his daughter, he thought, and knew why he had suddenly decided to call. He was still smarting over Fiona Dalkieth's sudden rejection and from the suspicion, which had never left him in spite of her denials, that she had made use of him. It came hard to a man with Robert's sturdy independence to think that he had been taken for a fool.

When the tea was ready he carefully eased himself free of the baby's grip and watched Jenny pouring his tea. Her face and body were still softly rounded from childbearing, and there was a new maturity in her blue eyes. 'You look well,' he said, then, catching them both unawares, 'Are you content, Jenny?'

'Yes.' She said it quickly, perhaps too quickly, then, as he stretched out to take a scone from the proferred plate. 'And you?'

The scone had a crisp outer shell, but inside it was light and fluffy, melting on the tongue. Robert laid it carefully on his saucer. 'I suppose you could say that I've got what I deserved.'

'What does that mean?'

He looked up at her and was warmed by the concern he saw in her eyes. 'It means that I'm fine.'

'You don't look it.'

'Does that matter to you?

'Of course it matters! We were good friends, you and me.'

'More than friends.'

She flushed slightly. 'Once, mebbe. But I'd always want your happiness, even though we took different roads.'

He looked round the kitchen, then at the baby, still awake. 'I sometimes wonder if I took the wrong turning altogether.'

'You did what you wanted to do.'

'What my head wanted, Jenny.'

Jenny smiled faintly. 'Your head was always stronger than your heart,' she said.

'I suppose so.' He was silent for a moment, then, 'Things are busier than ever at the Tank.'

'So I hear. Senga and Kerry visit me.'

'You're missed, Jenny.'

'What about the yard?' she dared to ask. She knew that Daniel and the others were worried about the yard. There were rumours that orders were hard to find and men might be laid off.

He shifted uneasily in his chair. 'Business could be better than it is. It's the same in every yard just now.'

'But Dalkieth's surely won't fail. Not with the good name it's always had.'

'You heard what happened to the steam yacht George Dalkieth undertook to build?' Robert asked wryly, and she nodded.

'The whole of Ellerslie's heard about it.'

A month after George Dalkieth commandeered the empty dock for his friend's steam yacht an urgent order had come in from a regular client for a passenger steamer to replace one that had been badly damaged in a storm. The yard had no available space and the lucrative order had gone instead to a rival. Not long after that the man who had commissioned the yacht left the country abruptly – one step ahead of his personal creditors, according to the rumours – and, after a fruitless search for another buyer, the half-completed yacht had been abandoned and was now rusting in some corner of the yard. George Dalkieth had shrugged the matter off, refusing to take any blame for it.

'Have you heard of a whipping boy, Jenny? In the old days, when the prince did anything wrong another boy, a commoner, was punished in his place because nobody could be allowed to chastise a member of the royal family.' Robert got up, putting his cup down on the table and walking to the window, where he lifted the neat net curtain aside and stared out at the street without seeing it. 'I sometimes think that that's why I was brought back from England – to take the blame for George Dalkieth's mistakes.'

'But everyone knows who took on the yacht,' Jenny protested. 'They know you'd never have done anything as foolish as that.'

'I work hand in glove with the man. That means that in the eyes of those who matter I'm tarred with the same brush.' His voice was hard, bitter. 'And Mrs Dalkieth has one great weakness – she can't help favouring her own flesh and blood. The other directors follow her blindly because George's a Dalkieth and it sticks in their craws to listen to anyone less well-born than he is.' He swung round and, even though his back was now to the window and his face in shadow, she knew that impotent anger was stamped on it. 'And when George leads them into a pickle, what happens? They can't chastise *him* in front of his mother, so they look for a whipping boy. They're outraged because I let him blunder.'

'Are things going badly for Dalkieth's?'

'What does your husband say?'

'He's concerned,' Jenny said honestly. 'They all are.' She joined him at the window, putting a hand on his arm. 'All the yards are having problems just now, but I'm sure Dalkieth's is strong enough to weather the storms. And so are you. Don't lose heart, Robert.'

The clock ticked on and, from the crib, came a soft snuffling sound. Robert noticed that Jenny's hair, close to his shoulder now, shone in the light coming through the net curtains. She smelled of fresh baking.

He was aware of a great sense of loss. This could have been his – Jenny, the neat, clean kitchen, the baby in the crib. But instead, his damned self-centred ambition had led him to reject her and everything she could have given him. The longing to turn the clock back was suddenly so strong in him that he felt ill.

Her fingers tightened on his arm and concern came into her eyes. 'Robert? Are you all right?'

He wanted to put his arms about her, to bury his face in her hair and to just hold her for the rest of his life. Instead, with an effort, he turned away.

'I'm fine. I'd best get back.' He had already ruined her life once, and he had no right to give in to his own weakness and do so again.

'If you're not happy working for the Dalkieths, mebbe you should go back to England,' she suggested as she handed him his hat and cane.

'Would it matter to you whether I went or stayed?'

'You've not got the right to ask me a thing like that, Robert. Not now.'

'I'm asking you anyway.'

'And I've not got the right to answer you.'

'I suppose not,' he said. 'Thank you for the tea.'

When he had gone Jenny lifted Shona from the crib and sat down, rocking her daughter in her arms, remembering the expressions that had chased each other across his face as they stood together at the window, and her too-swift answer to his question about her contentment. Daniel was a good man, but his continual tension, his treatment of Walter, meant that living with him was like walking on a knife-edge.

Robert, too, was an ambitious man – ambitious for himself and for Dalkieth's. There was a similarity between the two men although their situations – Daniel a worker, Robert one of the 'gaffers' – put them on opposite sides of the fence. It seemed strange, Jenny thought, that the two men in her life were so ambitious in their different ways, when all she herself wanted was to have the right to grasp a handful of happiness, just one handful, and be able to keep it close for always.

'Mebbe folk like us were never meant to be happy,' she said to Shona, her lips moving against the baby's silky little skull. 'Mebbe just making the best of what we've got is our happiness.'

Isobel Dalkieth had been insistent that her first grandchild must be born in Dalkieth House. It took little pressure to get her son's and daughter-in-law's agreement; George because he heartily disliked the thought of childbirth and felt that, with his mother in charge, he himself would be free to continue to live a normal life, and Fiona because it was an extension of the pampering she had been smothered with ever since she had announced the glad news. Since that day, her mother-in-law had been much kinder to her, and her determination to enter Dalkieth House only as its mistress no longer applied.

282

To her great relief she and George were given separate bedrooms. He was established in his old room while Fiona was given a large and comfortable bedroom, refurbished to her own taste, at the front of the house. Two rooms on the top floor overlooking the back garden were lavishly fitted out as day and night nurseries, and an experienced nanny and nursery-maid had been appointed. Isobel's own doctor, the most respected medical man in the area, had eased Fiona through the waiting months, and she glowed with health and well-being.

Even so she was apprehensive about the ordeal that lay before her and, as soon as the first pains gripped her, she took to her bed and ordered her maid to fetch Doctor Baillie at once. The maid, acting on instructions from the woman who paid her wages, went first to Isobel Dalkieth.

When the door opened and her mother-in-law appeared, Fiona raised herself on her pillows. 'Where's the doctor?'

'Everything's being attended to, my dear.'

'Have you sent for George?'

Isobel seated herself on a chair near the bed, her hands folded in her lap. 'What use will George be at a time like this? You surely don't want him cluttering up the place.'

'He should be in the house.'

'He'd be of more use at the shipyard, trying to undo some of the harm he's done with his stupid ideas. I've been hearing, though not of course from George, that this combine he insisted on bringing in seems to be having little success and more than a few problems in England. Has he said anything to you about that?'

'George doesn't talk to me about business matters,'

Fiona said sulkily from among her pillows, and Isobel raised her eyebrows.

'You mean you don't encourage him to do so? Oh, my dear, you're making a great mistake. A man – any man, but particularly a buffoon like George – needs guidance from his wife. I always thought of you as having the sense to realise that.'

Fiona gaped at the older woman then said in feeble protest, 'Mrs Dalkieth, I cannot listen to you talking of your own son like that! How can you bring yourself to— '

'Don't try to pretend that you're shocked, my dear. George is a buffoon – you know it, and I know it, and we don't have time to waste on pretence. Now – has he said anything to you about this combine he's embroiled us with?'

Fiona shifted uneasily in the bed. 'The shipyard is George's concern, not mine.'

'You should make it your concern. In fact, you *must* make it your concern from now on. I shall insist on it.'

'Mrs Dalkieth— '

Isobel fluttered one hand at her daughter-in-law. 'My dear Fiona – please! You must learn to call me Mother, now that you're about to give birth to my grandchild.'

' — when do you think the doctor will arrive?'

'In plenty of time. I recall that Edward took ten hours in the birthing and, as for George— ' Isobel shook her head and tutted. 'A full twenty-four hours. George always was slow to come to a decision.' She fingered her magnificent engagement ring then said bluntly, 'Between ourselves, Fiona, I blame myself for the mess George has made of the yard. I have allowed the fondness I felt for him as a little boy to linger on and, because of that, I've turned a blind eye to his faults instead of dealing with them. I hoped that once he was in charge of the yard he would take his responsibilities more seriously, and that was very foolish of me. I hope that you will never make the same mistake.' She sighed, staring down at the ring. 'And now we're in trouble, Fiona. I've given George his head once too often, and I persuaded the whole Board to support him. I should have listened to Robert Arch— '

She rose quickly and went to the bedside as Fiona's swollen body suddenly went into a spasm, her hands gripping at the quilt. Isobel consulted the small fob watch that hung round her neck by a gold chain then, as the pain receded and Fiona relaxed, she picked up a bottle of Eau de Cologne from the bedside table and dabbed some on to a lacy handkerchief, smoothing it over the girl's forehead.

'Rest, my dear, and gather your strength. You're going to need it before this business is over. So now I must make amends for my foolishness,' she went on, regaining her seat, folding her hands. 'For the sake of Dalkieth's yard, Fiona, I must go to Mr Archer and eat humble pie. It won't be easy, but if we're to have a shipyard for this child to inherit it must be done. What do you think of Robert Archer, Fiona?'

Fiona's blue eyes widened, then, as Isobel looked back steadily at her, she turned her head away. 'I – I scarcely know the man,' she said fretfully. 'Isn't the doctor here yet?'

'There's plenty of time yet. Archer comes from common stock but he talks a great deal of sense and I believe that he genuinely cares about Dalkieth's, just as I do.' Isobel rose and walked to the window to stare down at the driveway.

'Can you see his car coming?' There was a note of panic in Fiona's voice now. Isobel ignored it.

'George doesn't care about the business, not the way he should. He assumes that because it has always been there and always been successful nothing can harm it. He thinks that everything he does and says must be right just because he is a Dalkieth.' She began to move back across the room to the bed. 'But we have to face facts, Fiona, you and I. George is useless.'

Fiona raised herself up clumsily and reached for the bell-rope that hung at the bed-head. Isobel reached it first, tucking it out of her daughter-in-law's reach.

'What are you doing?' Fiona asked, alarmed.

'You mustn't exert yourself, my dear. Everything's under control.' She sat down again. 'There's a difference between being a Dalkieth and having the Dalkieth name, Fiona. George is a Dalkieth by blood but he has no notion whatsoever of what's best for the yard. I, on the other hand, am a Dalkieth only by marriage, yet I've spent all my adult life in the service of the business.'

She studied Fiona, ignoring the tumbled hair, the flushed face, the frightened eyes, seeing only the self-centred ruthlessness that she knew lay beneath the surface.

'Your child, Fiona, will inherit everything. Given proper guidance in his formative years he could do more for the shipyard than George ever will. And he'll have full rights to the Dalkieth name. Whether or not,' she added calmly, 'there's Dalkieth blood in his veins.'

'What do you mean?' Fiona demanded shrilly, forgetting her own problems for the moment, 'Of course he'll have the Dalkieth blood! He'll be your own son's child!'

'Will he? I've been thinking a great deal over the past

few months, Fiona, and it seems to me that George's blood may well be altogether too thin to spread to another generation.'

Fiona began to speak then gasped, her hands reaching out, her body stiffening beneath the satin quilt. Isobel hurried to her side again and put her hands in Fiona's, setting her teeth against the pain as the girl's fingers gripped and tightened like bands of steel, her nails digging in. By the time the contraction eased away the backs of Isobel's hands were scored with deep red weals.

'Where's that damned doctor?' Fiona moaned as the dampened handkerchief mopped beads of sweat from her crimson face.

'Don't fret yourself, I'll get word to him in good time,' Isobel said soothingly and her daughter-in-law's blue eyes, which had been screwed tightly shut, flew open in horror.

'You've not sent for him?'

'I thought we should talk first.'

'For God's sake —!' Fiona tried to struggle out of bed and was pushed back on to the pillows.

'Don't upset yourself, my dear. It's bad for the baby.'

'Fetch George! I want George!'

'Only a fool would want George,' said his mother. 'And you're no fool. I've come to realise that over the past few months.'

'You're going to kill me!'

'Nonsense! You're a healthy, well-nourished young woman. If you were a peasant woman in some other country you would think nothing of birthing your baby in a ditch then getting on with your work.'

Fiona lunged up, a hand stretched up towards the bell-rope, but failed to reach it. She dropped back on to the mound of soft pillows like a beached whale, gasping with effort and fear. 'You're trying to destroy my child!'

'On the contrary, your child is extremely important to me. But I need your co-operation, and I need to know the truth.' Isobel moved to sit on the side of the bed, catching her daughter-in-law's wrists in her own strong hands. 'Tell me, Fiona – who is the father of this child?'

'It's George – George – George!' Fiona's voice rose to a scream. 'Who else could it be?'

'There's no sense in shouting, dear,' Isobel told her calmly. 'The servants all know that I am with you and that I can be trusted to decide when the doctor should be sent for.'

'Fetch the nurse!'

'When I'm ready. I pay her wages, Fiona. She'll wait, like the rest of them, until I give her her orders. It can be very useful, holding the purse-strings. You'll learn that in time.'

'George— '

'Forget George,' Isobel advised crisply. 'We don't need him. You were about to tell me who you chose to father your child, weren't you, my dear?'

Tears, born more of anger than fear, glittered in Fiona's eyes. 'Damn you!' She spat the words out, trying without success to free herself from the older woman's grip.

'I already know what it's like to be damned, my dear, and it holds little fear for me now. I've made some very discreet enquiries, Fiona, and I believe that I already know the answer to my question. But I must hear it from you. I must know that the parentage is acceptable. Until I do,' said Isobel Dalkieth clearly, 'there will be no nurse, and no doctor. Do you hear me, Fiona? If necessary, we'll deliver your child together.'

'I'll tell them— ' Fiona panted, against the beginning of the next pain.

'And I'll tell them that it all happened more quickly than either of us thought it would. My word will stand against yours. Tell me his name, Fiona,' Isobel added as her daughter-in-law caught desperately at her hands again. The rings on the older woman's fingers hurt them both as Fiona struggled against the contraction. When it finally receded, Isobel said again, mercilessly, 'Tell me!'

'Ro – Robert Archer.' The name came out in a wail, and Isobel nodded her head.

'I was almost certain. A good choice, my dear.'

'Please – the doctor— '

'One more thing before I send for him. No doubt you've had some ideas about holding the truth about your child's parentage over my head or my son's head one day.'

'No!'

'Don't lie to me, Fiona. We're going to need each other from now on. Between us we'll rebuild Dalkieth's for my grandchild – my son's child. But there's to be no thought of using what you know in order to feather your own nest. Do you understand me?'

'Oh God – it's coming—!'

Isobel managed to free one hand and swept the bedclothes aside. 'You're nearer your time than I thought,' she acknowledged. 'Listen to me, my dear – if you are planning to blackmail George or myself in the future then I might well save myself a lot of trouble by letting you and your baby die here and now. Do you understand me?'

'Yes – yes! Help me, you old witch!' Fiona screamed as her mother-in-law moved away from the bed. In a moment Isobel was back, thrusting a leather-bound

Bible into the girl's hands. Fiona clutched at the book, sweat breaking out on her forehead.

'Swear to me on this Bible that nobody but the two of us will ever know the truth. Nobody!'

Fiona Dalkieth looked into her mother-in-law's cold green eyes and knew that the woman meant everything she had said. There would be no assistance until Isobel got what she wanted.

'I – I promise!' She forced the words through gritted teeth and felt a cool hand brushing the hair back from her forehead.

Then the door opened and she heard Isobel's voice, far away, calling urgently to the servants.

21

In August Alice, who had, as her mother said, turned into a right wee organiser since she started work, hit on the idea of arranging a trip on the River Clyde for the people living in the tenements.

'One of the women that comes into the pawnshop regularly was telling me the other day that they used to do that sort of thing when she was wee,' she told Jenny. 'We'd a back-court party to celebrate the end of the war, and one when the first peacetime ship was launched – is it not time we were celebrating again?'

Walter's eyes lit up, but Jenny said cautiously, 'I'm not sure there's much to celebrate just now. Daniel says that these folk in England who put money into Dalkieth's are in trouble and two of their yards have had to close down. If it happens here— ' She let the words trail away, her eyes drawn to the crib where three-month-old Shona, who had just been fed, lay kicking.

'All the more reason to have something to look forward to just now,' Alice argued, and Walter nodded eager agreement.

'If there's bad times coming we'd at least have something good to remember. I mind once when I was a wee laddie my mother and father took me on a steamer trip down the Clyde. It was grand.'

'I've never been on the river in my life,' Alice put in.

'It's time I tried it, and it's long past time Walter here went on a voyage, since he's set on being a ship's engineer.'

'Alice— ' Jenny warned, mindful of the way Daniel would react if he heard such talk. Alice jumped up to croon to the baby, avoiding her sister's eyes.

'It should be a paddle-steamer,' Walter said, his face glowing. 'You can see the engines on a paddle-steamer. You stand at a rail, and they're right there in front of you.'

'You can explain it all to me,' Alice told him as she returned to the table.

'There's nothing much to explain.' He flipped through the exercise book spread open on the table then snatched up a pencil and started drawing diagrams on the inside of the back cover. 'It's all so simple and sensible, that's the beauty of it.'

Alice shuffled her chair round the corner of the table to get a better view of the drawing.

'The steam's forced through here, intae the cylinders there, d'ye see?' Walter talked on, his pencil flying easily across the page. Looking at his absorbed face, the light in his eyes, Jenny was reminded of the way Robert had been before he went off to Tyneside.

'Who'd have the time to organise an outing like that? It'd take a lot of work.'

'No it wouldn't.' Alice assured her sister briskly. 'I'll see to it myself. I'll put a poster up in the pawnshop and mebbe get one in the wee corner shop window too, to make sure everyone gets to hear about it. You'd come, wouldn't you, Jenny?'

'It would depend on what Daniel says. And there's Shona to think of. She's too little to take on a steamer.'

'We'll think of something. And even if Daniel won't

go there's no reason why you and Walter shouldn't come along.'

'What about the cost? The folk round here haven't got money to throw away.'

Alice, the bit between her teeth, tossed every objection aside. 'They can bring bread and jam to eat, and bottles of lemonade. Old Mrs Smillie said they all kept back something special to pawn when it was time for the annual outing. Which means,' said Alice airily, winking at Walter, 'that it'll not do our shop any harm either, if I can get everything arranged. We've got almost five weeks before the end of September, I'm sure I can have it all seen to in the next three— '

They were so involved in what they were discussing that for once neither Jenny nor Walter heard Daniel's step in the close and the sound of the outer door opening. When he walked into the kitchen the three of them looked up with a start; Jenny's darning needle missed the heel of the sock she was mending and stabbed into her thumb, and Walter swiftly closed his exercise book, hiding the engine sketch from view as his father's eyes settled on him.

'Walter, have you not got homework to do?'

'He's been working all afternoon,' Jenny rushed to Walter's defence. 'Alice has been helping him with his mathematics.'

'Can you not manage it without help?'

Walter went crimson, opening his mouth to reply then shutting it again when Alice said calmly, 'It was just some problems I was going over with him. Sometimes two heads are better than one.'

'And sometimes peace and quiet are sufficient,' Daniel told her curtly. He jerked his head towards the door, and Walter, the tips of his ears afire with humiliation, scrambled to his feet, gathering his books together. One of them slipped to the floor; Alice and he both stooped to pick it up and for a moment their fingers touched.

'I'll see you again, Walter,' she told him, then turned to Daniel as the boy slipped out of the room. 'I was just telling Jenny and Walter that I'm thinking of arranging a trip down the water. Walter says he went with you and his mother once and fair enjoyed it.'

Daniel grunted noncommittally, taking his jacket off with abrupt movements and hanging it on the nail at the back of the door so sharply that Jenny thought for a moment that the material was going to tear.

Alice raised her eyebrows at her sister behind his back, then, in answer to the silent appeal in Jenny's face, said, 'I'd best get home. Mam'll be wanting me to see to Helen while she gets the dinner ready.'

'What was she doing here?' Daniel wanted to know as soon as she had left. Jenny put her darning aside and dropped to her knees to fetch some potatoes from the box beneath the wall-bed. It still felt good to be able to kneel again after the months of carrying Shona, when she had been too stout to move freely.

'She's my sister and Shona's auntie. She often calls in.'

'And does Walter come into the kitchen every time she calls?'

'No, but I don't see why he shouldn't be allowed to talk to her now and again. He works hard, Daniel, and he doesn't have anything like the freedom the other laddies of his age have.'

'That's because the other lads' parents don't care about their futures. I told you, Jenny, I'll not have him distracted from his studying.'

294

Daniel unfolded the newspaper he had brought in with him, shaking the creases out of it noisily. Shona, unaware of the tension between her parents, stared up at her own bare toes, flailing through the air, and let out a squeal of amusement at their antics.

Her father tossed a glance at the crib, the first time he had looked in its direction since coming into the room, then turned back to his newspaper.

'Another thing,' his voice said from behind the printed sheet. 'You shouldnae let that bairn lie there with nothing over her legs when Walter's in the room. It's not seemly.'

Jenny said nothing, but her grip on the handle of the potato-peeler tightened until her knuckles stood out sharp and white beneath the skin.

Alice lost no time in going ahead with her plans. With Walter's help, when his father was at work and well out of the way, she called at every single flat in the area, and soon had a healthy list of families eager to take a trip 'doon the water'.

To her delight, Robert Archer looked in at the pawnshop when he heard about the proposed trip, and donated a generous sum from his own pocket. Part of it was used to subsidise the cost of the outing, but Alice kept enough back to pay for a generous boxful of sweeties for the children.

Even Isobel Dalkieth got to hear about the river trip, and offered, in a letter addressed to Alice, to pay for two charabancs to transport the Ellerslie party to Helensburgh, where they were to embark on the paddlesteamer.

Alice brought the letter to Jenny with a gleeful grin. 'I'm going to keep this letter for ever, Jen. Would you listen to the way she's worded it?' She held the paper at arm's length and read aloud in the manner of a herald reading a proclamation, ' " — I have pleasure in making this donation to mark the birth of my first grandson, William Dalkieth, in the month of July in the twenty-second year of this century." Have you ever heard such a pompous way of saying that the bairn was born in July 1921?' Alice demanded to know, lowering the letter.

'I suppose the Dalkieths always have to sound different from the rest of us.' Jenny hung one of Shona's small gowns on the clothes-horse to air before the fire.

'At least she gave us money, and I'm grateful for that. I invited Robert to come along with us,' Alice went on, 'but he thought he'd better not. He said most of the folk would want to get away from the yard, not be reminded of it. You know, I like Robert. He might be one of the bosses now, but he's still human.'

Teeze sniffed when he read the letter from Mrs Dalkieth. 'George Dalkieth himself's too mean tae put his hand in his pocket. He had tae leave it tae his mother.'

'He'd no' want tae waste good money on the likes of us,' Daniel agreed. 'I hope the boy grows up tae be a better man than his father.'

Excitement gripped the tenements as the appointed date approached. Bella offered to look after Shona, who was now bottle-fed and, by waiting until the right time and choosing her words carefully, Jenny managed to persuade Daniel to take herself and Walter on the trip.

'I can pay for it out of the money I got from Dalkieth's when I left,' she offered eagerly. Daniel had refused to take the ten-pound note Robert had handed to her, advising her to put it into the bank in case she ever had need of it.

Again he turned down her offer. 'I've not reached the stage where I have tae be dependent on my wife for money,' he said stiffly. 'And God willing, I never will. I'll pay for the trip myself.'

Once his father had committed himself to going on the outing, Walter relaxed and talked of nothing else, although when Daniel was present he was careful to behave as though the occasion held little importance for him.

It wasn't fair on the boy, Jenny thought, noticing the way Walter hid his thoughts and feelings from his father instead of feeling free to express himself. She was determined to see that he enjoyed every minute of the outing, and that there would be other treats for him in the future, no matter what his father thought.

'Gonny come with us, Walter?' Jamie Preston coaxed for the tenth time. 'It'll no' take long, honest.'

'I'm supposed to go straight home,' Walter argued, though he yearned to go with the other boy.

'Ye will be, in a way. It's on the way home – well, nearly,' Jamie wheedled. 'Look, just down there an' not far intae the yard.'

They had met on the street corner on their way home, Jamie from school, Walter from the Academy. In one direction lay the street that led to the bridge, in the other lay the Dalkieth's shipyard. Walter eased the leather strap holding his school-books on his shoulder and his eyes followed Jamie's grubby finger, pointing towards the forbidden land.

'Can you no' go on your own?'

'Aye, but I'd as soon have comp'ny.'

Walter's eyes flickered towards the road he should be taking, then back to the road he wanted to take. 'You're sure your uncle said it would be all right?'

'I told ye!' An impatient note was creeping into Jamie's voice. He shifted his weight from one booted foot to the other with a rasping sound. 'My uncle's put in a word for me tae be taken on as a 'prentice, an' Mr Osbourne telt him tae tell me tae go tae the yard an' see him mysel' – och, for any favour, man,' he added, the impatience bursting forth, 'the hooter'll be soundin' if we stand here much longer. I'll go on my lone!'

He started down the street, his cracked boots scuffing over the paving stones and, after one last moment of doubt, Walter made up his mind and scampered after him. The opportunity to step inside the yard, even a little way, was too tempting to be resisted.

'I'll come – but we're not tae stay long.'

'I don't suppose Mr Osbourne'll have it in mind tae treat us tae tea an' biscuits,' Jamie said sarcastically, stopping in front of the yard entrance. He scrubbed an arm over his face then spat on his hand before passing it over his tousled hair. 'Here – take these, I don't want tae look like a school-wean.'

He tossed his books, clumsily bundled together with a piece of old string, at Walter, who took them without argument, too busy staring up at the shipyard gates to object.

They were enormous, wide enough to take two lorries side by side, each gate a masterpiece of scrolled black iron, curved at the top in such a way that when they were closed they formed an arch, spiked at the top. The letters D-A-L-K, picked out in gold and a good twelve inches high, marched up the half-arch of the left-hand gate, while I-E-T-H ran from top to the bottom of the right-hand arch. When the gates were closed the name would be laid out like a golden rainbow straddling the sky.

'Come on!' Jamie tugged at his friend's sleeve, almost dislodging the two bundles he carried. Walter dragged his eyes away from the black-and-gold splendour, tightened his grip on the books, and followed the other boy through the gates and over the cobbles, trying to look everywhere at once. Until then, his only sight of the shipyard had consisted of glimpses of the tops of cranes and derricks from the surrounding streets and the occasional illicit trip along the opposite riverbank. From there the building berths could be seen, with the vessels in them under construction.

Most of the shipyard workers' children had a better knowledge of the yard than Walter; occasionally, if a man forgot to take his midday 'piece' with him one or other of his children had to take it to him. Youngsters whose fathers were given to drinking or gambling their wages as soon as they received them were used to gathering outside the gates with their mothers on Fridays so that desperately needed money could be claimed before the man who had earned it squandered it in the public house nearest to the yard. But Daniel never talked of his work at home, other than to rail at the bosses for their injustices, and Walter had learned early in life that questions about his father's workplace were inevitably answered with, 'That's no place for you. You'll never have tae seek yer living in any shipyard – not while there's breath in my body!'

Once, and only once, he had dared to disagree, pointing out that shipbuilding, particularly on the Clyde, was a hard-learned skill to be proud of. Daniel had rounded on him, tense with anger.

'What d'you know about it? The noise and the filth and the – the degradation of it all!'

In the face of his rage Walter had fallen silent and never dared to broach the subject again, though the word 'degradation' had told him more than his father realised. It told him that in his past, a time that was never mentioned, Daniel Young must have been a scholar, and he guessed that somehow his father's academic thirst had been denied and suppressed. He was trying, Walter realised from then on, to quench that thirst through his son. But knowing that, understanding something of his father's motives, had given Walter no consolation. Daniel had once wanted what Walter had, but ironically Walter craved what his father had – the chance to serve his apprenticeship in a shipyard, then eventually go to sea as a ship's engineer.

At the rickety wooden gatehouse just inside the yard Jamie was talking earnestly over the closed lower half of the door. The watchman leaned out, one arm gesticulating as he gave directions, and Jamie nodded then jerked his head at Walter and set off at a trot.

'I'll be watchin' for yez comin' back,' the watchman shouted as Walter scurried past. 'None o' yer loiterin', mind. An' nae pilferin', or I'll spifflicate yez!'

'It's the machine shed we're lookin' for,' Jamie panted when Walter caught up with him. 'Down on the right he says, across from the berths— '

The rest of his words were drowned out by a thunderous clanging from deep inside the huge building they were passing. Both boys shied away in sudden panic, Jamie clapping his hands to his ears and laughing shamefacedly at his own fright. Walter, hampered by the books he carried, felt his head ringing with the merciless racket of machinery hammering metal into shape.

'Christ—' Jamie shouted as they cleared the building, 'Nae wonder hauf the men that work here are deaf!'

A handcart piled high with copper piping came wavering towards them, the front wheel bouncing from one cobblestone to another and being deflected each time so that the entire cart zig-zagged from side to side as well as inching forward. They skipped out of the way and, as it went past, Walter saw that it was being pushed by a youngster less than half the height of the load which towered above him, threatening all the time to burst the ropes that lashed it to the cart. A large peaked cap of the type all the shipyard workers wore, known as 'doolanders', was jammed down over the boy's ears and almost rested on his nose. Beneath it, what could be seen of his face was purple with effort, his lips drawn back in a grimace and his teeth clenched.

As they went deeper into the yard the clanging from the shed they were leaving behind gave way to a mixture of other sounds – saws ripping their way through timber, hammers bouncing and echoing on metal, men yelling, the hiss and thump of steam-driven machinery. The place was as busy as Ellerslie High Street on a Saturday afternoon, and the broad strip they walked along was edged with great piles of timber, its fresh, sharp, resinous smell enfolding the boys before becoming absorbed in the general smell of heat and metal and oil as they moved on. Great sheets of iron and steel were piled along the roadside, too, and there was even a massive boiler, large enough to hold the Young's two-roomed flat, resting on the cobbles like a whale driven ashore on a beach.

Walter's head swivelled from side to side as he trailed after Jamie, trying to take in everything at once. The sheer size of the place, the activity and even the noise, enthralled him. He detoured, skipping over rails and abandoned scraps of metal as he went, to peer in through a cavernous door larger than the yard entrance. A massive machine rose up into the shadows of the roof, dwarfing the line of men who tended it. The smell of oil caught at his lungs; he sneezed, a sound drowned by the machine's rumbling, and turned away to follow Jamie, realising that they had almost reached the first of the building berths. The first three vessels were in their early stages; within the stocks their shapes were outlined in sturdy timber that from a distance, had a delicate, lacy quality. The metal sheets that would be put in place later were piled on the ground before each berth, sacrificial offerings to heathen gods. Sheer-legs and cranes clustered round the ships and men worked everywhere – on the ground, on the skeleton vessels high above, on the stocks themselves. It seemed to Walter that there were more men in the part of the yard he had seen so far than there were in the whole of Ellerslie.

As they walked further along, jostled out of the way now and again by cursing, hurrying men, more vessels came into view, great ribbed monsters with their graceful sweeping outlines supported on timber struts. One was almost completed, clothed in metal armour, her upper decks already railed in, one propeller in place. Walter stared up at the vast, curved underbelly of the ship, the part that would be below the surface when the vessel was in the water, and knew what an ant must feel like when it looked up at the raised foot of a passing human being.

Jamie, suddenly remembering what he was there for, tugged at his sleeve. 'What was it the man said?' he bellowed in Walter's ear. 'Across from the berths?'

'I don't know,' Walter shouted back, his eyes greedily travelling over the ship. 'I didnae hear him.'

'We'll have tae ask,' Jamie roared, and pulled again at his arm. Reluctantly, knowing that now that he had seen the yard for himself he would never be content to spend his life in an office, Walter lowered his gaze, staggering slightly as dizziness washed over him. The nape of his neck, which had been bent right back while he gawked up at the ship, reproached him with a twinge of pain and he had to move his head cautiously from side to side to loosen cramped muscles as he followed Jamie away from the building berths and in through another enormous opening. He stepped into the noisy darkness and stopped, appalled.

In the early days of the war Walter's mother had started taking him with her on Sundays to a religious service in a small hall where a powerfully built man with iron grey hair and a thick beard had talked for hours on end about the eternal flames of hell, where the sinful and the damned would toil and burn and suffer for eternity. Daniel Young had a strong mistrust of religion, and so Walter's mother had made him promise not to tell his father when he came home on leave.

The man had painted such a graphic word picture of the torments of hell that Walter, drinking in and believing every word, had started to suffer from nightmares. Unfortunately one of the nightmares occurred while his father was home and Daniel discovered what his wife and child had been up to in his absence. Furious, he had forbidden visits to future services.

The nightmares had gradually stopped after that and Walter had forgotten about them as the years passed, but now, stepping inside the building opposite the berths to be struck by a blast of heat, he was

303

transported back in an instant to the world of eternal hellfire.

Before him lay a huge, dark cavern, splashed by scattered patches of crimson and gold flames from roaring furnaces tended by shadowy figures glimpsed only sporadically against the fires. The merciless crash of hammers beating on metal resounded through the place. It looked and sounded as though a vicious thunderstorm had been trapped inside the building and was crashing round and round, roaring endlessly, fruitlessly, for freedom.

Near the door two men stripped to the waist, their arms and torsos black, worked over an anvil, taking it in turns to hammer at a sheet of metal held in place by a third man. One of them saw the two boys hesitating just inside the doorway and broke the pattern of his work, lowering his hammer to the ground and leaning on the long, sturdy handle. His partner paused, looking round to see what had caused the interruption, his eyes rolling like pale marbles in his filthy face.

The first man's teeth flashed in the gloom as he shouted something at the boys. Jamie, intimidated, stumbled back a step, bumping into Walter, seizing the sleeve of his jacket and urging him forward. 'Tell 'im we only want tae know where the machine shop is,' he said nervously as the second man dropped his hammer and strode towards them.

Walter clutched the books to his chest, his mouth dry with fear, the nightmares flooding back into his memory. This was exactly what the preacher had talked about. Surely hell couldn't be any worse than this place and the Devil himself couldn't be any more terrifying than the man who was now standing over him?

His nerve broke. He dropped the books and turned to

run, wanting only to get away from this place and out into the blessed cool air. A hand, black and oil-shiny, caught at his shoulder and he was spun back towards the flame-shot, thunderous blackness of the place.

'Walter! What the hell d'ye think ye're up tae?'

He would never have known, if he hadn't heard that familiar voice, that the filthy, half-naked devil looming over him, reeking of oily sweat, was his father . . .

22

'What's that on your jacket?' Jenny peered at the material. 'It looks like oil.'

Walter, who had returned home from school later than usual that day, mumbling something about having had to stay behind to help one of the teachers, pulled the sleeve round and inspected the greasy smudge. His face went red. 'I – I must've leaned on a wall.'

'Take it off and I'll see what I can do with it. Are you all right?' she asked as he obeyed, his head lowered so that his face was hidden from her.

'I'm fine.' He handed the jacket over and went to his room.

'Where's the boy?' Daniel wanted to know as soon as he came into the kitchen an hour later, clean and neat as always, but with a suppressed anger, a deepening of his usual tension, that frightened her.

'Working on his books, the same as he always is at this time. Is there something wrong?' He ignored her, striding to the door and calling his son's name.

Walter came at once. 'I only went because— ' he began as soon as he came into the room, but his father interrupted him, his voice thick, the words forced out of his throat.

'You disobeyed me.'

Walter swallowed, then said, 'Jamie Clark had tae see one of the gaffers about work in the yard. He asked me tae— '

'I'd forbidden ye tae go near that yard, and ye deliberately disobeyed me!' The room crackled with menace.

'Daniel,' Jenny said nervously, then flinched back as he rounded on her, his dark eyes blazing.

'You keep yer neb out o' this, it's between me and my son!' he told her harshly.

Walter was white to the lips but he held his ground. 'Is it because I saw you? Is— ' his voice suddenly broke and faltered, and he took in a sharp, steadying breath, his eyes still locked with his father's. ' — is that why you're angry with me?'

Daniel's hands clenched into fists and for a moment Jenny thought that he was going to hit the boy. Instead he said, his own voice scarcely above a whisper, 'Aye, ye saw me – ye saw how yer own father has tae earn his livin', in filth and sweat. Now ye know why I'll not have ye settin' foot in that place!'

'What's wrong with working with your hands?' Walter's voice was thin but desperate. 'Where's the shame in it? It's surely more honest than letting other men work tae earn for you— '

'Get back tae yer books,' his father told him roughly. 'Ye don't know what ye're talking about!'

'I do! I'm fourteen now, old enough to be out of the school. Old enough tae know what I want.'

'Walter— ' Jenny warned, but he paid no heed.

'What you want doesnae come intae it – it's what I want that matters!' Daniel snapped, but Walter obstinately struggled on.

'I want tae leave the Academy and go intae the yard. I

want tae learn tae be an engineer, then go tae sea,' he told his father, whose lips thinned with rage.

'Workin' in the filth an' the noise of the engine shop at Dalkieth's, then goin' tae sea buried in the bowels of a ship, at everyone's beck an' call? There'll be none of that for my son!'

'It's my life we're talking about! You can't make me live it your way.'

Daniel's fury had reached white-heat. 'I'll have a bloody good stab at it,' he snarled.

'I want tae be an engineer,' Walter insisted, his hands folded tightly into fists by his side.

'Ye'll dae as ye're told!'

They faced each other, Walter only half a head smaller than his father, both of them whip-thin, though Daniel's body was muscular and strong, Walter's still boyish and unformed. If Daniel chose, Jenny thought fearfully, he could beat the boy into a bloody pulp. Walter must have known it, too, but he had gone too far to back down.

'I'll not always be under your control,' he said, his voice, in the throes of breaking, only just managing to avoid rising to an absurd, childish squeak.

'Ye're under it for now, an' ye'll dae as ye're told! I'll not be crossed! D'ye hear me? I'll not be argued with in my own house!'

Daniel's thin chest was heaving and he was beginning to spit the words out breathlessly between foam-flecked lips. Jenny, suddenly afraid that he was in danger of going into a fit, put a hand on his arm, only to have it violently thrown aside.

'D'ye hear me?' Daniel demanded again. There was a brief pause, then Walter, paper-white but still in control of himself, nodded.

'Aye, I hear ye. But the day'll come, Father, when I'll be old enough tae walk out of this house an' go my own way. And I'll mebbe never come back. You just mind that.'

Daniel gave a strangled yelp and his hands moved swiftly to the buckle of the broad leather belt round his waist. Jenny stepped between father and son again, her own hands reaching to cover his.

'No, Daniel! I'll not have you beating the boy!'

He growled, trying to shake her off again, but she held tight, and he had to give up, glowering at her, so close that she felt his breath warm on her face.

'Have it yer own way,' he said at last, then, looking over her head at Walter, he added, 'But ye can forget about goin' on the steamer trip next week.'

Jenny heard the boy catch his breath with a gasp that was close to a sob. Turning, she saw his eyes flare as though he had just been struck in the face.

'Daniel! You can't do that to the laddie!'

'He went intae the yard when I'd forbidden him tae go near the place. You'll not let me give him the beatin' he deserves for defyin' me, so he'll have another punishment instead. Now get back tae yer books,' he growled at his son.

Walter turned and went without a word. As the door closed on his skinny back Jenny said, 'How could you be so cruel? He's been looking forward to the trip for weeks.'

Daniel picked up his cap. 'Ye've spoiled him long enough, you and that sister o' yours. It'll be her that's put these daft notions intae his head.'

'It wasn't Alice at all. Walter's wanted to be an engineer for a long time.'

His eyes were accusing. 'So ye knew about it all along, did ye?'

309

'He mentioned it one time.'

'An' ye kept it a secret from me? From now on,' said Daniel viciously, 'Mind yer own business and leave the raising of my son tae me. You've interfered enough!' And he stalked out of the house.

Jenny's hands shook as she made a cup of tea and took it into the narrow, airless little room where Walter spent most of his time. He was staring down at his books, pencil in hand, and didn't look up when she tapped on the door.

She set the saucer down. 'He doesnae really mean it – about you not going on the trip.'

'Aye he does.' Then he added, low-voiced, 'I wish I'd just taken the beatin' instead.'

'I'll talk to him— '

'Leave it!' He looked up and she saw the angry tears glittering in his eyes. 'The harm's done, and you'll make it worse for yourself.' Then he added more gently as she began to argue. 'I don't want you tae get intae bother because of me. And I'll not have the two of us sidin' against him. It'd not be fair.'

'Walter, why did you have to go to the yard when you knew he was so set against it?'

'Jamie asked me tae go. Anyway, I've wanted tae see inside that yard since I was wee. It doesnae do any good,' said Walter with adult wisdom, 'tae deny things tae children. It just makes them hungry tae know more. Mind that when wee Shona starts askin' ye questions.' He stared at the pencil between his fingers. 'It was me seein' him that he couldnae stand. Seein' him covered with the filth of the place, runnin' with sweat.'

Jenny looked at the situation through his eyes and knew why, after what Daniel had done, his son could still find the compassion to understand and pity him.

'Daniel hates dirt. He must hate having to work in it every day.'

'I just wish he was man enough tae understand that I'm proud of what he goes through tae keep me – and you, and the wee one,' said Walter. As she was going out of the room, he added, 'I meant what I said – as soon as I can, I'll be out of here. And I'll no' be back.'

Daniel and his son scarcely spoke to each other after the quarrel. Walter spent all his time in his room when his father was at home, coming into the kitchen only for meals, which were eaten in silence. When Daniel was out Walter played with the baby and helped Jenny as before, but there was a change in him, a withdrawing that worried her.

Alice, too, noticed it, and was furious when Jenny told her what had happened. 'How could Daniel be so hard on him? Walter's always done all he could to please his father.'

'And now he's gone back into his shell. It's as if he's rebuilt the wall that he always had round him.'

'I'll break it down,' Alice said confidently, but even she couldn't reach Walter; this time his defences were impregnable.

Jenny's hopes that Daniel would relent came to nothing. Anger at being defied by his own son continued to burn deep within him and, not content with banning Daniel from the trip on the River Clyde, he introduced a series of other, small punishments. He insisted on being shown the boy's homework every evening, and he was never satisfied with what had been done, demanding that it be re-worked. Walter began to eat most of his meals in his own room, or go without, because Daniel decreed that he couldn't spare the time from his books. Even the boy's milk-round was carefully timed, with Daniel waiting impatiently at the closemouth for his return, and imposing one small punishment after another each time he considered that the boy was later than necessary.

Walter seemed to shrink back into himself, suffering the continual tyranny without complaint, refusing to talk about it to Jenny. When she tried to protest to her husband, she was told shortly that matters between himself and his son were none of her business.

Ashamed to tell anyone, even Alice, what was happening, unable to offer either comfort or hope to her stepson, Jenny felt helplessly that the whole business was slipping out of control.

September had started off as a wet month, the air damp and heavy with reminders that the summer was over and autumn had arrived. But when the Saturday chosen for the trip arrived the clouds were gone and the sun was out. It was clearly going to be one of those perfect autumn days rarely seen in that part of the world.

All morning the streets round the tenements were busy with women darting in and out of closes, borrowing and exchanging pieces of finery, packing food, hurrying to the shops for items that had been forgotten until the last moment, tripping over the excited children who scurried about like frantic mice, unable to stand still for more than ten seconds at a time.

By the time the midday hooter blew in the yard the women and children were dressed and ready and there was scarcely a kitchen where the window wasn't already opaque with steam from the tin bath waiting in front of the range, with soap, towel, clean shirt and freshly pressed suit close to hand.

Walter had taken little Shona to his room, so that Jenny could get on with the housework. When she went in to fetch the baby he looked up, startled, and her heart ached when she saw his red-rimmed eyes and the track of tears on his cheeks.

'She poked her finger in my eye,' he said hurriedly, handing the little bundle over and scrubbing at his face with his sleeve. 'It was watering.'

'Mebbe your father'll change his mind about the trip, now that the day's arrived.'

'Mebbe.' Walter bent over his books, his voice muffled. 'If not, don't go blaming yourself. It's my own fault. I shouldnae have gone tae the yard.'

She cuddled the baby, trying to find some words of comfort. 'Time passes, Walter. You'll soon be old enough to do as you want.'

The hooter shrilled from the yard, signalling the end of the Saturday shift.

'I tell myself that,' Walter said as Jenny stepped out into the narrow hall. 'But there's times when I wonder if I'll ever really be free of him, or if he'll be with me wherever I go, no matter how old I am.'

Before the sound of the hooter had died away the first of the men came pounding over the cobbles. Along the streets they poured, peeling off to disappear into this close and that close like rabbits fleeing down their burrows before a fox.

In Jenny's kitchen there was no need for the tin bath. She had to wait longer than the other women for her man to return home but when he did he was clean and neat, already dressed in his best brown suit and clean white shirt. She looked up hopefully as he came in and saw at once that he hadn't changed his mind. For weeks she had looked forward to the outing, but now that

Walter was staying home the pleasure had all gone. She would happily have stayed behind to keep the boy company, but when she suggested it, using a sudden concern over leaving Shona as an excuse, Daniel insisted on her going with him. 'You went tae enough trouble tae get me tae agree in the first place,' he said implacably. 'An' we're both goin'. The bairn'll be fine with Bella.'

By the time the menfolk were ready the charabancs had arrived, almost filling George Street from footpath to footpath. As the people poured out of their closes and clambered into the charabancs children were passed from hand to hand and grans and grandpas were cheerfully 'punted' up the high stairs by those queuing behind them. Alice rushed between the two vehicles, exercise book in hand, ticking off names to make sure that nobody was left behind by mistake or, even worse, that no dishonest person had managed to sneak aboard in the hope of getting a free ride.

The loaded buses jerked forward to a great burst of cheering from the loiterers who had gathered to see them off. Faces bobbed at the windows and hands flapped vigorously at those being left behind.

'Ye'd think we were emigratin' tae the other end of the world,' giggled Maureen, sitting by Jenny, her boisterous toddler bouncing on her lap. Helen, only weeks away from her fourth birthday, eyed him disapprovingly from her own seat on Jenny's knee. She wore a new blue dress Alice had made specially for the outing and a straw hat freshly trimmed with a row of little blue silk flowers was perched on her red-gold curls. Lottie was on the outing, but she and Neil had vanished into the other charabanc without a backward glance and Helen, used to her mother's neglect, had watched them go without complaint then slipped her hand in Jenny's.

Helensburgh, a residential town long popular with rich Glasgow industrialists in search of an attractive riverside area where they could build summer houses well away from the smoke and grime and factories that brought them their wealth, was a graceful town of wide streets and smart shops and an air of serenity. As the charabancs turned from the main street and made for the pier the lusty singing that had started up before they had cleared Ellerslie was replaced by a whoop of excitement at sight of the paddle-steamer, 'Lucy Ashton', waiting for them by the pier.

'Look!' Helen pointed at the trim little steamer, smart in the colours of the North British Fleet. Her hull and paddle-boxes were painted black, picked out in white. Her white deck-saloons shone in the sun like cake icing, and smoke plumed from the single red funnel with its white band and black top. The Union Jack fluttered from the steamer's bows and the house flag, a red pennant with the Scottish thistle inside a white circle, flew from the top of a slim flagpole almost twice the height of the funnel.

'I'm going up there,' Helen shrieked into Jenny's ear, indicating the open upper deck, where wooden seats were laid out in rows for the convenience of passengers. At the upper rail the steamer's ports of call were listed in white letters on a polished wooden notice board. 'Hunter's Quay, Kirn, Dunoon, Rothesay.'

The River Clyde was on its best behaviour as the 'Lucy Ashton' moved serenely across the mouth of the Gareloch. The sun made the water sparkle like a handful of diamonds and the white water in the steamer's wake turned to glittering snow for several yards before breaking up into fine lace and eventually reverting back to water again. Clearing the Gareloch they passed another opening, this time to Loch Long, that narrow, deep stretch of water edged on both sides by heavily wooded hills that plunged down into and below the water like Norwegian fjords.

Daniel, in company with most of the men and boys, went down below at once to watch the engines working. Jenny patiently trailed over every inch of the steamer with Helen, who finally settled for the upper deck where she could wrap her arms around the rail, her red-gold head angled out and down so that she could watch the water sliding past the ship's flank.

'It's spoiled, isn't it, with Walter not being here?' Alice settled on the bench beside her sister.

'I'm trying to remember everything so that I can tell him about it.'

'So am I, but it's not the same,' said Alice, sadly.

At the first three destinations they only stopped for long enough to land some passengers and pick others up. The longest stop was at Rothesay, on the Isle of Bute, where the passengers had just over an hour to spend as they pleased. Some explored the shops and a few, including Lottie and Neil, hired bicycles and set off to explore the island. Jenny and Daniel, the Malloys, and Alice and Alec Monroe, her employer, elected to have a picnic on the beach then the men and boys launched themselves into a noisy game of football. Alec, his lungs injured by gas during the war, couldn't join them, but Alice roped him in as her assistant and the two of them took the smaller children to the water's edge to paddle in the sea. Jenny would have been content to watch, her back comfortably settled against a convenient rock, but Mrs Malloy would have none of it.

316

'Hold my skirts down, lassie,' she ordered, slipping her shoes off and glancing swiftly from side to side to make sure that nobody was watching her. Jenny did as she was told, and after scuffling discreetly beneath her skirt for a moment Mrs Malloy triumphantly flourished a pair of thick, much-darned stockings.

'I'll hold your skirt now. Come on, our Maureen, we could all do with gettin' a bit of salt water round our feet.'

The water was cold and they stood in a huddled group for a moment, shrieking in various sharps and flats each time a small wave broke round their ankles until the chill of the water eased as their skin became used to it.

'Come on, then,' Mrs Malloy boomed, hoicking up her skirt and petticoat to reveal thick, well-muscled calves, so generously roped with bunches of swollen veins that they looked like carved, slightly bent pillars in an old church.

The women followed her, venturing in until the water reached their knees. All too soon the steamer gave a long, mournful bellow on its siren, the signal that it was time for its passengers to return.

'It sounds as sorry to go home as I am,' Alice said as they straggled back along the beach. Wisely, she had decided to hold the sweets, bought with Robert Archer's money, back as a final treat for the homeward journey. She was still close enough to her own childhood to know what was popular, and there were squeals of delight when Alec and Jacko opened the boxes that had been stacked in the purser's office, out of reach of inquisitive fingers, to disclose a rich harvest of boiled sweets, sherberts, 'soor plooms', chews, aniseed balls, midget gems, liquorice straps, toffees, cinnamon sticks, and even toffee apples.

As the steamer headed for Helensburgh on the last lap of the journey Jenny glanced at Daniel, leaning now on the railing and looking towards the land that was creeping nearer with every turn of the paddles. He had caught the sun and there was a faint blush of colour over his forehead and cheekbones and nose; he had taken his jacket and tie off and loosened the collar of his shirt. His body, as he leaned over the railing, was relaxed. He turned, caught her eye, and turned away again without speaking or smiling. She wondered if he was regretting his harsh decision to deny this trip to Walter. But regrets weren't enough, she thought, sad for the man as well as the boy, knowing that unless Daniel, by some miracle, learned to unbend, there was little hope for a future relationship with his son. In a few short years, as she had reminded Walter, he would be old enough to live his own life, and if Daniel insisted on continuing down the path he followed now he might never have the chance to know his son as a man.

Jenny shivered as across the water Helensburgh grew from a blurred mass to a collection of roofs and steeples. What did the years ahead hold for her, and for Shona? At some time in his past Daniel Young must have suffered deeply, to have so much bitterness burned into his soul. He was a good provider, an honest man, and she still cared for him, despite his rigid attitude towards Walter. But she knew that now her caring had come to have more pity in it than love.

She was Daniel's wife, she had promised to stay by his side for the rest of their lives, and it was not a promise made lightly. But she had begun to fear for Shona. She couldn't bear to think of her baby being subjected, like Walter, to such a harsh regime as she grew older. Jenny had seen enough of life to know that children brought up without love very often found it impossible to give love themselves, and she didn't want that to happen to either Walter or Shona.

A group of children thundered past, screaming with excitement, and she came out of her thoughts with a start to realise that she could clearly make out the pier and the charabancs waiting to take the Ellerslie party home.

Moments later they were bumping gently against the timbers of the pier as the great pistons in the engine room below slowed, reversed, then stopped. The paddles came to rest and the water beneath the paddle-boxes calmed.

Once the steamer was safely roped to the pier the gangplank was put into place and the passengers began to surge down it, children's heads bobbing in sleep on their fathers' shoulders, their mouths sticky and stained with raspberry and lime and orange and lemon and liquorice. Daniel, carrying Helen, was loose-limbed with the pleasure of the day as he strode sure-footed down the gangplank, Jenny at his back.

As they stepped on to the pier two uniformed policemen stopped Jacko, several yards ahead, and spoke to him. He turned, his little son sleeping on his shoulder, his cheery face suddenly puzzled and concerned, and indicated Daniel.

The police officers advanced, solemn-faced, drawing Daniel and Jenny out of the throng to tell them, with rough gentleness, that Walter had hanged himself that afternoon from one of the hooks in the back-court wash-house . . .

23

As soon as Robert Archer walked into the general office the supervisor rushed over to him, almost dancing across the floor in his agitation.

'Mrs Dalkieth's been sitting in your office for the past twenty minutes,' he whispered, 'I said you were in the Tank section, and she said she'd wait.' His moustache bristled with anxiety. 'I'd have sent someone to fetch you, or at least taken her to the boardroom where she'd be more comfortable, but she'd have none of it.'

'I'm sure it'll do her no harm to sit on a hard chair for once.' Robert turned away from the man's shocked expression and went towards the door of the small room that led off the general office. George Dalkieth used the comfortable office adjoining the counting house that his father and grandfather had had before him and Robert had had to make do with what was left.

Isobel Dalkieth, straight-backed in an upright chair, extended her hand to him when he went into the room and he took it briefly in his.

'Good afternoon, Mrs Dalkieth. You wish to see me?' He seated himself behind the desk, making no reference to the time she had had to wait. He was in no mood to be pleasant or self-effacing.

'I've come to apologise to you, Mr Archer,' Isobel Dalkieth said flatly, then, as he gaped at her, she allowed herself a slight smile. 'Well may you look surprised. It's not often that I apologise to anyone.'

'Particularly someone so much further down the social scale than yourself.'

'You sound bitter.'

'I believe I have a right to be bitter, Mrs Dalkieth.' He gave her a level look.

'I can understand that.' Isobel smoothed her expensive gloves in her lap then looked the office manager in the eye. 'Mr Archer, my husband was a man of vision and intelligence, and he recognised two things many years ago. One was that, of his two sons, the elder was fit to follow him into the business while the younger was not. The other was that at some time in the future, the yard might have need of a man with experience, intelligence, and a sense of loyalty. Brilliant though he was, I doubt if he could have foreseen the coming of the war and our elder son's tragic death.' She paused for a moment then said more briskly, 'Be that as it may – he looked around for a suitable candidate to fill that need, should it arise— '

'And settled on me,' Robert interrupted, impatience in his voice. 'You mentioned intelligence; I've got enough of that to be aware of my own history, Mrs Dalkieth.'

Her mouth tightened, then she nodded. 'You're quite right, I was being condescending. And I now realise that, without stopping to think of the harm I was doing, I've all but ruined my husband's plans by insisting on keeping control of the shipyard and letting my maternal affection – my natural maternal affection,' she stressed slightly, 'take precedence over my sense of the rightness of William's intentions. In that sense I've done you a grave injustice.'

Robert dismissed the final sentence with a wave of the hand. 'I'll not wither away and die from your lack of understanding, Mrs Dalkieth, but the business might. You may already have delivered it a mortal blow – you and your son and the other Board members.'

'You're being very harsh, Mr Archer.'

'As I'm not a gentleman I see no point in mincing my words.' Robert opened a drawer, rummaged among some papers and withdrew an envelope which he tossed over to her side of the desk. 'I was about to hand this to your son, to be read out at the next Board meeting. You might as well take it.'

'Your resignation?' She made no attempt to pick the envelope up. 'Your decision to desert Dalkieth's?'

His eyes glittered at her from the other side of the desk. 'Don't bother trying to make me feel like the rat deserting the sinking ship, ma'am. I did my best to save this yard and I was thwarted at every turn. My sense of loyalty towards the Dalkieths vanished some time ago.'

'I'm quite aware of that.' Isobel's tone was enigmatic but, as he looked up sharply, she went on, 'However, what's done is done and I'm not here to rake over the past. Do you intend going back to Tyneside?'

'Perhaps – if I can find a place there. It's more likely that I'll have to seek work abroad. I have no ties and I'll go wherever I must.'

She rested her elbows on the wooden arms of her chair and linked her long, slim, fingers together. 'Mr Archer – how, in your opinion, can this yard escape closure?'

His answer was prompt. 'It must break loose of the combine that's strangling it.'

'In order to do that we would have to buy back the shares they hold.'

'Which means applying for a considerable bank loan and running yourselves into a great deal of debt,' he agreed. 'But that is your only hope. You must also look closely at the interests this company holds in other businesses. Some will be worth keeping because they'll pay for themselves with careful management. Others will have to be sold off, if that's possible.' He spoke swiftly and decisively, like a man who had already given a great deal of thought to what he was saying. She watched him, frowning slightly, but not interrupting him.

'You must try to sell off the additional land your son insisted on buying, and try to sell a large part of the new machinery, possibly abroad. It'll never be used here anyway – there won't be enough work coming in to warrant it – and at the rate things are going,' he pressed on ruthlessly, 'you'll be bankrupt in two years. There's no point in letting good machinery rust away to scrap when you might get something back on it. Not as much as you paid, but a few pounds are better than nothing. The Experimental Tank's giving a good account of itself, but you'll have to fine down the main yard, possibly close some of the berths and lay off more workers. Offer to build vessels at more competitive prices.'

'That would leave us very little profit,' she protested.

'Indeed, and it'll lead to bitterness among the workers and the unions. Nobody,' said Robert with feeling, 'likes to see men thrown out of work through no fault of their own. It will also lead to panic among your shareholders; they would need to be carefully handled and assured that if they can stand behind you and give you their continued support they'll get their money back eventually. The market will recover, Mrs Dalkieth.

I don't know how long it'll take, but it must recover eventually. All Dalkieth's can do at the moment is try to survive until then.'

'Do you believe that it can be done?'

'Not,' said Robert flatly, 'unless the Board changes its way of thinking.'

'If I guarantee that that will happen— ' Isobel picked up the sealed envelope and held it between the tips of her fingers, ' — if I give you my word that from now on you will be listened to and your advice will be followed, will you reconsider your resignation?'

'To be honest, Mrs Dalkieth, I doubt if you could bring yourself to vote against your son when it came to it.'

She jutted her chin and said, her voice hard, 'I can do anything I put my mind to.'

He leaned forward, propping his elbows on the desk, steepling his fingers. 'Why should I believe that you mean what you say? Why the change of policy now, when it's almost too late?'

'I have my grandson's future to consider now. He may only be a few months old, but I fully intend that he shall inherit the yard one day. If that is to happen the company *must* keep going. I also intend to make certain,' she added, 'that he will be a worthy successor to my husband. But I can't do it alone, Mr Archer. I need your help.'

'Mrs Dalkieth, I've tried to give you assistance in the past and been spurned. Your grandson is no concern of mine, so why should I be willing to put my own interests aside in favour of his?'

She gave him an oblique look from beneath her lashes. 'Give me one year to prove that what I promise, I will do. And, during that year, do all you can to guide the company along the lines you've suggested.'

'You're asking me to act in what the workforce will naturally see as a ruthless manner. Once again I'll be the villain – only this time it'll be more than just the Board opposed to me.'

They eyed each other warily, no longer the elegant lady and the man from the tenements, but equal adversaries, both ruthless, both determined. 'What salary would it take to persuade you to give me that year?' Isobel Dalkieth asked at last, and he gave a bark of impatient laughter.

'You couldn't afford to pay me what I'd deserve, Mrs Dalkieth. Not with the financial problems the yard has at the moment.'

She smiled faintly, and shrugged. 'You're right. Nor can I appeal to your loyalty, for you already offered me that when you came back to Ellerslie – and I threw it back in your face.'

She got up, walked round to the side of the desk, and deliberately dropped the envelope into the wastebasket.

'I can only ask, in the name of my late husband who gave you a chance many years ago – and in the name of my grandson, who deserves the opportunity to prove himself.'

Robert hesitated. 'I like the idea of a challenge.'

'I thought that you might. I *hoped* that you might.' She smiled, a genuine smile, and held out her hand. Her fingers curled about his, strong and bony. 'I promise that you'll not regret your change of heart, Mr Archer.'

As he opened the office door for her she added, 'You will receive an invitation tomorrow morning to my grandson's christening celebration. I promise you that it will be the last unseemly exhibition of wealth in the Dalkieth family until such time as we can celebrate the rebirth of the yard and the end of the downturn in the market. I hope that you will accept. Indeed, I would particularly like you to be present.'

Daniel went through the formalities of arranging his son's funeral impassively, not even uttering a word of protest when he was told that Walter, a suicide, must be buried in a far corner of the parish churchyard instead of being laid to rest beside his mother in the plot that Daniel had bought for himself and his family.

'It was his fault – if he had been kinder to Walter, the poor lad would still be with us,' Alice said fiercely, her own eyes red with weeping as she and Jenny watched Daniel walk alone from the grave without a backward glance. 'He stood there as if he didn't care one whit— ' Her voice broke and Jenny put her arms round her sister, holding her as she longed to hold Daniel.

'Ssshh, pet. He's grieving in the only way he knows.'

Alice dug into her pocket for a handkerchief and blew her nose hard. 'We were getting to know each other, Walter and me. I feel – it's as if we'd just managed to touch each other's fingertips. If I'd only had the time to take a good grip on his hand he'd not have fallen the way he did!'

'I know.' Jenny watched her husband's retreating back. 'I know.'

'You must never let him do the same thing to Shona.' Alice pushed the handkerchief back into her pocket. 'Whatever happens, Jen, don't let him!'

On the day after the funeral Daniel got up at the usual time and dressed, not in his good street clothes, but in his dungarees. He went off to work without a word and returned soon after the siren blew to mark the end of the working day, still filthy from the foundry. Jenny, who had half-expected this to happen, said nothing, but fetched the hip-bath from the hall cupboard and filled it with water from the pots she had been heating on the range, just in case. When Daniel stripped and climbed into the bath she helped him to wash, scrubbing his back as her mother had scrubbed her father's and Maurice's at the close of every working day.

When he was clean Daniel dressed and sat down to his meal, leaving her to empty the bath pailful by pailful before drying it and putting it away. Now that Walter was gone there was no reason for him to hide the truth about the work he did.

From then on he only spoke to her when he had to, and paid no attention at all to Shona, even when she crowed and laughed and held out her chubby arms to him. Lying awake by his side in the night, knowing full well that, like her, he was sleepless, Jenny longed to reach out to him. But he made no attempt to touch her, and on the only occasion when she tried to put her arms about him he flung himself violently from the bed and blundered out of the kitchen without a word and into Walter's room. From that night on, he slept in his dead son's room, with Walter's books laid out on the little wooden desk and Walter's coat hanging below his on the nail on the back of the door.

'I can't reach him,' Jenny said miserably to Bella after several weeks had passed and it had become clear to her that Daniel had no intention of letting their lives return to normal. 'If he'd talk about the laddie, or even let himself grieve naturally – but he'll not do it.'

'It's strange the way grief takes different folk. Look at my Pat, now – just when I'd given up all hope of him ever coming back tae himself he began tae change. Mebbe it'll go that way with Daniel.'

'Mebbe you're right, mebbe he just needs time,' Jenny agreed, but without much hope.

It was ironic that just as Daniel was retreating from this world Patrick Kerr had begun to regain something of his old self. He had asked Jacko Livingstone, who worked in the joinery shop at the shipyard, to make him a decent pair of crutches, and had started to go out again. He arranged to be fitted with the special boots he had refused when he first came home from the war, and already Alice had sold about half a dozen of his carvings in the pawnshop and had taken in a few orders for more. He used scraps of discarded wood Jacko brought to him from the shipyard, and driftwood that Bella and Alice found on the shores of Ellerslie Water.

Some of the strain had left Bella's face and she had started to smile again. Nobody seemed to have noticed that Patrick never spoke to Jenny or looked at her. She knew that although her outburst on the day Shona was born was probably responsible for his improvement he would never forgive her for what she had said to him, and the way she had laughed at him as he lay sprawled on the floor at her feet.

Sometimes, when she looked at herself in the mirror and realised that she was still young, only twenty-three years of age, panic rose into her throat, threatening to choke her. The thought of spending year after year in the same small flat with a husband who had become a stranger terrified her. On these days she wanted to gather Shona up and walk out of the house, out of Ellerslie, to a place where the two of them could start a new life. But she couldn't leave Daniel; without her there to cook his meals and keep his house clean and wash his clothes, what would become of him? And how could she cope in a strange town with no friends or family and a small baby to care for?

Fiona Dalkieth studied the people milling round the large drawing room at Dalkieth House and smiled contentedly. This was what she had worked for, planned for. The guests, among them some of the most important and influential people in the district, were all here to attend her son's christening party and, as his mother, she was indispensable and free of any fears that she might be cast aside by George and sent back in disgrace to her father, who was at that moment standing by one of the windows, champagne glass in hand. Beside him, George gulped from his own glass as though trying to slake a burning thirst, although Fiona knew for a fact that he had been drinking steadily since their return from church.

Not that it mattered now if he drank himself to death. She stroked the silky pale fur on the cuffs of her cream and brown brocade jacket and glanced casually to her right, where she could see herself reflected in a long wall mirror. She had lost most of the soft plumpness left by child-bearing, and the long jacket and straight, matching skirt below skilfully slimmed the last lingering traces of excess fat out of existence. Her cream shoes, square-heeled with sequins scattered over the brown rosettes at the insteps, were flattering to her ankles and calves, while the sapphire earrings just seen beneath her brown and cream turban matched her eyes admirably. The earrings, and the bracelet on her right wrist, were a gift from George, to mark his gratitude at the birth of his son.

Fiona's smile widened as she remembered the fuss George had made over the cost of the sapphires. His mother had over-ruled him, telling him sharply that he had waited long enough for this son and heir and that his wife deserved only the best. She herself had paid for Fiona's brocade and fur suit, summoning representatives of a well-known and respected Glasgow fashion house to Ellerslie so that her daughter-in-law could choose the materials and pattern in comfort. Isobel had also decreed that now that a new member had been born into the Dalkieth family the time for dressing in black to mourn the dead was over, and she herself was dressed on this auspicious day in lilac and pale grey.

Fiona moved through the room, assuring a group of gushing women that small William, the guest of honour, would indeed be brought to the drawing room as soon as he had wakened from his afternoon nap, stopping to talk with studied condescension to her father and mother and brother, pausing to rest a hand on George's arm and reach up to kiss his cheek.

'Eat something, my dear,' she breathed into his ear as she did so. 'If you don't you'll probably fall over and you know how displeased your mama would be if that happened in front of her guests.'

She smiled sweetly into his angry eyes and moved on to another group, confirming that yes, the house she and George had lived in until recently was to be sold.

'We've decided to settle in with Mother Dalkieth,' she explained. 'She's been lonely in this large house on her own and, of course, she wants William nearby.'

'I'd not care for the thought of living with my mother-in-law,' one of the women said, and other heads nodded their agreement.

Fiona's blue eyes widened. 'But George's mother and I get on very well indeed. We understand each other perfectly and we both want the same things for George and William.' No need to point out that here, in Dalkieth House, there were enough servants to ensure that Fiona need never be troubled by any of the tiresome duties of motherhood, and enough room to ensure that she and George need never again share the same room, let alone the same bed. She had done her duty by him and now she was about to reap the rewards.

There was a stir as the nurse came in, her arms filled with the imposing christening gown Isobel had bought for her grandson. The baby was carefully laid in his mother's arms, staring solemnly up from beneath the white swansdown trimming of his christening cap at the cooing women who flocked from all sides of the room. Fiona was moving in slow procession down the centre of the room, smiling graciously at the well-wishers, when someone in front of her moved away and she saw Robert Archer standing by the door, watching her.

The breath caught in her throat and her arms tightened protectively round her son as she was transported back to the moment when Robert had stormed into the house she had shared with George to confront her. They hadn't met since that day.

'I'll take William now, my dear,' Isobel said in her ear, and Fiona relinquished the bundle of silk and lace as Robert walked towards her.

'May I offer my congratulations, Mrs Dalkieth?'

'Mr Archer,' she said graciously, offering him her hand. Then, seeing that Isobel had moved away and they weren't being overheard, she added low-voiced, 'What are you doing here?'

'I received an invitation.' His eyes, cold and grey as a misty day, searched hers and he smiled thinly, recognising her panic. 'Afraid that I'll speak out of turn? My dear Fiona, gentlemen aren't always born in mansions and boors aren't always born in tenements. But I don't suppose you'd realise that.'

Looking round to make sure that they were still not overheard Fiona saw that Isobel, sitting on a sofa with the baby in her arms, was watching her closely. She realised that Robert's invitation was the older woman's way of discovering whether he was likely to be a threat to the Dalkieth family.

She took a deep breath and smiled up at him. 'Thank you for your good wishes, Mr Archer,' she said, her voice clear as a bell. 'Excuse me, I must have a word with Mrs Palmer . . .'

24

Isobel Dalkieth kept her word. Despite her son's opposition she had Robert Archer appointed to the Board of Directors and saw to it that he was given the freedom to carry out the changes he had insisted were essential if the Dalkieth yard was to survive.

The results of the ruthless decisions he had to make rocked the town and led to a considerable number of men being laid off from the yard. Daniel Young was one of them. He walked through the yard gates for the last time in the middle of January, 1922.

In the four months since Walter's death Daniel had spent most of his evenings and weekends away from the flat, only coming home to eat and sleep. After being turned away from the shipyard he stayed at home, day and night, staring into space, making no attempt to seek other work and worrying Jenny with his refusal to talk about their future.

It was common knowledge in the town that George Dalkieth had more or less given up all pretence of running the shipyard, and spent most of his time brooding in his office or at home, while Robert Archer had taken over the reins. As a result, Robert was blamed for what was happening in the yard.

'Good men bein' turned off after giving years o' their lives tae the company an' others havin' tae take cuts in wages,' Teeze rumbled, his big scarred hands tightened into knotty bunches on his thighs. 'But whatever happens the Dalkieths'll not go without, ye can be sure of that. An' Archer's done well for himsel', has he no'? The bastard thinks nothin' o' climbin' on the backs o' his own folks tae dae it.'

'It's not Robert's fault,' protested Faith, who still had a soft spot for her dead son's friend. 'All the yards are having a bad time.'

Teeze coughed, then spat with a skill born of years of experience between the bars of the range. The burning coals behind the bars hissed briefly. 'There's no danger o' him bein' turned off, though, is there? He's seen tae that.'

A week after Daniel was laid off Jenny and Robert Archer came face to face in the street. She would have ducked past him with a nod and hurried on but he stopped directly before her, laying a hand on her arm. 'Jenny, I'm vexed about your husband having to be turned off, especially after what happened to the boy. But I've no power to choose that one man should go before another.'

She was uncomfortably aware that the passers-by were staring at Robert, some of them with antagonism. Under the shawl she wore she tightened her arm protectively about Shona, slumbering against her breast. 'I don't blame you for what's happened, I know that all the yards are in a bad way just now.'

He nodded. He looked tired and there was grimness in the set of his mouth. Jenny felt sorry for him. He was basically a good man and she knew that he would take no pleasure in the harsh steps he was having to take to safeguard the yard.

'If Dalkieth's isn't pruned back now it'll be finished

once and for all,' he said sombrely. 'I'd as soon see the place staying open and mebbe being able to take the men back eventually than have it closing down and everyone thrown out on to the street. But that's no consolation to men who have no work to do and no pay coming in. But Jenny, there's a place in the main drawing office. It's yours, if you want it.'

'The drawing office?' For a moment excitement leapt up in her, then she came back to earth. 'I don't know how Daniel would feel about that. Then there's the bairn to think of.'

'It'd be a wage coming in. You've got a good, skilful hand, Jenny, and I'm not offering the work out of charity. They could fairly do with you in the drawing office. Can you not speak to Daniel about it?'

'I could try, I suppose . . . I must go, Robert, he'll be wondering where I've got to.'

He touched his hat to her. 'Think about my offer,' he said as she turned away. 'Let me know.'

She thought of nothing else as she hurried home. Since Walter's suicide there had been times when the resentment she had experienced when Maurice's death had forced her to give up her plans to move to Glasgow came flooding back; each time she fought it down, for there was no sense in brooding over what might have been. She tried hard to concentrate instead on keeping the house nice for Daniel, who neither noticed nor cared, and tending Shona, who was growing into a contented affectionate baby. Without her daughter, Jenny knew, life wouldn't be worth living.

But now Robert's offer of work, the sort of work she had always wanted to do, put temptation in her way once again. As she made her way automatically through the streets she tried to think of the best way to put the offer to Daniel. They desperately needed the money she would earn, but she doubted if Daniel would agree to being supported by his wife. He certainly wouldn't consider a reversal of roles, with him looking after the house and caring for Shona. He had done that after his first wife's death, but he had done it all for Walter, and what little interest he had shown in his daughter had died along with the boy. If – Jenny scarcely dared to even think the word – he agreed to her going back to work, she would have to pay Bella or her mother to look after the baby. Lottie had married Neil Baker in the previous November and she and Helen were now living in a smart little tenement flat several streets away, so Faith would be free to take Shona during the day.

But there was another problem. Daniel knew that Robert had been Jenny's sweetheart before going to England, but it was obvious from remarks he had made in the past that he considered the relationship to have been a childish affair, one that was over and forgotten long before Robert's return to Ellerslie. Since then he had grown to dislike Robert simply because he was 'one of the gaffers', and as such he was allied in Daniel's eyes with the Dalkieths. Like Teeze, Daniel put the sole blame for his dismissal at Robert's door.

Walter's short life and tragic death bore witness to the fact that Daniel Young was a man who looked on his family as his possessions rather than human beings with rights of their own. If he was ever to discover that his wife and Robert Archer had been lovers, Jenny thought, there was no telling what he might do. And the very fact that it was Robert who had offered the job to her might be enough to stir suspicion in his mind.

She had no choice – she must turn down Robert's offer of work. But with every step she took she wanted the drawing-office job more and more. She had the ability to do it, they needed the money – by the time she turned in at her own close she had convinced herself that if she was patient, if she waited for the right time to speak, if she used the right words . . .

There was a lightness in her step and a smile on her lips as she lifted the latch and stepped into the tiny hall.

She had left Daniel huddled by the range in the kitchen, but now the room was empty. She put Shona down in her cot and glanced in at Walter's room. It had been left just as it was when Walter walked out of it for the last time, with one of his school-books open on the small table, a pencil lying on top of it. Sometimes Daniel sat in there, but today it, too, was empty.

Jenny returned to the kitchen and was about to see to the baby when she noticed a page torn from one of Walter's exercise books lying on the kitchen table. She read the few words scrawled over it in disbelief.

Daniel wrote, in a scrawl quite unlike his usual neat script, that he had gone to look for work, away from Ellerslie to where nobody knew him. There was no mention of keeping in touch with his wife, or sending for her and his daughter when he could. There was no word of assurance or affection. Just his formal signature, 'Daniel Young,' at the bottom of the page.

At first Jenny was afraid that Daniel planned to kill himself, just as his son had done. Over the next week she attended to Shona mechanically, hurrying to the door every time she heard footsteps in the close, lying awake night after night listening to the wind howling round the building and wondering if he was out in the open, perhaps sleeping rough, or ill and unable to get help. She called on all the men Daniel had worked with, but nobody had seen him or heard from him. She even went to the police station, where she was assured that there had been no word of an accident involving an unknown man, and the river hadn't cast up any bodies.

'There's plenty of poor souls on the roads just now, missus, looking for work,' the police constable told her gruffly. 'Yer man'll probably come back tae ye, and with any luck he'll have found a place for himself. He's mebbe not wantin' tae face ye until he can bring a wage in again.'

Confused and bewildered, Jenny waited for two days, then three, then four. When a week had passed without any word from her husband, she knew that she could wait no longer and she must face up to some hard facts.

She didn't love Daniel, at least not in the way that a woman should love her man. He had been a conscientious husband but as a father he had shown little interest in Shona, and his behaviour towards Walter had been so ambitious and self-centred that he had destroyed the boy. As for Jenny herself, the fact that he had made no attempt to contact her or to find out if she and Shona were managing showed that he had little genuine feeling for her.

She no longer wanted to live with him again, but for Walter's sake more than anyone else's, she needed to know that Daniel was safe and well, that he hadn't, in his misery and guilt over the boy's death, decided to follow the same path and take his own life.

In the past few days, waiting in vain for word of him, she had been haunted by the memory of Walter, wounded beyond bearing by his father's continual bullying, insisting through ashen lips, 'I'll not have the two of us sidin' against him. It'd not be fair.'

If Walter was here, he wouldn't rest until he had

made sure that his father was alive, and safe. Since he could no longer do that, Jenny must do it for him, if only to atone for the part she herself had played in his death by standing by instead of finding some way to convince Daniel that he was being unfair to his son. And when she had done her duty by Walter's memory, when she had made certain that Daniel was all right, she would be free to shape a new life for herself and her child.

She wrote at once to Lizzie Caldwell in Glasgow, and when she got Lizzie's reply she took it across the close to show to Bella. Her sister's small face crumpled with dismay as she read the letter.

'Why did ye want tae go askin' her tae find you a job in Glasgow?' she wanted to know. 'This is where you belong.'

'I'm certain now that that's where Daniel's gone, to the big shipyards there. I have to try to find him and I need to support myself while I'm about it.'

'But it's a big place – how could you find one man there? And what about the house, and Shona? Ye'll no' be able tae pay the rent here as well as pay for lodgings for yerself.'

Jenny had thought it all through. 'I'll have to let the house go. Daniel didn't give a thought when he left as to how I was going to manage to keep it on. We can always get somewhere else to live when I find him – we might settle in Glasgow, if he gets work there. As for Shona . . .' She touched the little girl's soft brown hair, knowing that parting with her daughter, even for a short while, was going to be hard. '. . . I'll ask Mam if she'll take her for a wee while. I've still got the money I got when I left the tracing office – that'll help me to pay Mam and keep myself until I get started in the job

Lizzie's managed to find for me. It'll not be for long,' she added hopefully. 'Mebbe Daniel's got a job already and he's writing to tell me at this very minute.'

'Jen, let me take Shona,' Bella said on a rush of words, her eyes hungry.

'You? But –' Jenny glanced at Patrick, intent on carving a cat. Before him on the table lay a photograph; obviously someone had put in an order at the pawnshop for a wooden model of a favourite pet. As usual, he hadn't looked up when Jenny came into the room, only grunted a greeting and gone on working.

Bella's hands twisted together in her apron. 'Mam can help out while I'm at Mrs McColl's and anyway, I don't have tae go out working so much now that Pat's bringing a bit in. I'd like tae look after the wee one for you, Jenny.' She went over to the table and put her arms about her husband. 'What d'ye think, Pat? We could manage, couldn't we?'

He laid down his knife – a sharp, small-bladed knife Alice had given him, easier to work with than the vegetable knife he had started with – and looked up at her in silence for a moment. Then he shrugged and went back to his work.

'If that's what you want,' he said indifferently, and Bella looked up at her sister, her face radiant. As far as she was concerned, the matter was settled.

Robert called at the flat and did his best to persuade Jenny to stay in Ellerslie.

'I've already offered you work – take it, and stay here so that when your husband comes back the house'll still be here,' he urged, but she shook her head.

'I'm sure he's in Glasgow and it's not right that he should be alone at a time like this. I need to know he's all right,' she said firmly, and he finally gave in, insisting on accompanying her to the station on the allotted day.

The air was rancid with the lingering remnants of the night's fog and the ground was slippery underfoot. Their breath met and became one white cloud as Robert stood on the platform, still in Ellerslie, while Jenny looked down at him from the carriage, feeling that already she was on foreign ground, almost in limbo.

'D'you think you'll find him?' he asked.

'I must.'

'I think you're frightened in case he's taken his own life, as the boy did.'

'No!' Shaken by his perception, she almost shouted the word out. A man hurrying past paused and stared at her in confusion, then scurried on his way.

'I think you're both sick with guilt over the laddie's death, Jen, you and Daniel,' Robert persisted, and when tears blurred her eyes he reached up and laid a gloved hand over hers where it rested on the window ledge. 'His fault, mebbe, but never yours. Don't go blaming yourself for other folks' wrongs, my dear.'

Further down the snaking train a door slammed, the sound echoing mournfully.

'It seems to me that the man just wants to be on his own,' Robert went on. 'If I'm right, he'll not thank you for the trouble you're taking.'

'Mebbe.' She blinked the weak tears away and his face came into view again, upturned to hers. 'But I have to be sure of his feelings before I can think of trying to make another life for me and Shona.'

'Remember, if there's anything at all that I can do you only have to let me know.'

'I will. Thank you, Robert, you've been a good friend to me.'

A shadow clouded his eyes. 'Not such a good friend in the past,' he said. 'But I intend to make up for that in whatever way I can.'

The whistle blew and as the train jolted forward sudden terror swept over Jenny at the thought of going off to the city on her own. She wanted to open the carriage door, to jump out and bury her face in Robert's shoulder and stay there until, somehow, her world came right again. Instead she waved from the window until he was hidden from her by smoke from the funnel and it was too late to do anything but follow her plans through.

Lizzie was already waiting at the ticket barrier in Queen Street Station, a welcome sight to Jenny, who was quite demoralised by the clamour of the place, including the noisy chirruping of birds in the great iron arches far overhead. With an air of calm confidence Lizzie beckoned to a lad and ordered him to carry Jenny's case.

'I can manage,' she protested, but Lizzie frowned and shook her head.

'You're a Neilson employee now,' she said, her mouth shaping the words primly, like a buttonhole slipping around a button. As they stepped out of the station entrance she pointed proudly to the open square on the opposite side of the street. 'That's George Square, with all the statues. And over there— ' her finger stabbed in the direction of a handsome building with pillars and an upper balcony overlooking the square, ' — that's the City Chambers.'

The streets round the square were busy with trams and cars and bicycles and horse-drawn carts. Jenny scarcely had time to get used to the noise before Lizzie hurried her away, the boy with the luggage trailing a few steps behind.

'You'll be able to see the emporium on the way to your lodgings in Oswald Street. This is West George Street we're in just now. I've managed to get you into the china and glass department on the first floor. I work on the ground floor myself. The woman you'll be lodging with used to work in the millinery department but she's retired now, and recently widowed. Very respectable. You'll be able to walk to work.'

Lizzie herself, it transpired, lived in a boarding house for young ladies in Tollcross. 'It's very genteel – I was fortunate in getting a room there. I was recommended by Miss Blake, who supervised the drapery department before me. I'd have got you in there, but there are no rooms vacant just now. There's Neilson's down there – see?' They had rounded the corner into Buchanan Street, and she indicated a tall building halfway down the hill. They were on the opposite pavement; as they got nearer Jenny could see the words, 'Neilson and Son' in large gilt letters over the three glassed double door-ways in the centre of the building, between two rows of huge display windows.

As they crossed the street and walked along the frontage of the store, admiring the toy window, the two ladies' fashion windows, the gents' clothing window, and the millinery window, Lizzie bragged about the navy and gold canopies that were pulled out over the windows each morning. Then they walked round the corner of the store and into an alleyway so that Jenny could familiarise herself with the staff entrance, not nearly as grand as the front entrances which were reserved for customers and the more superior staff members, such as the floor-walkers.

At the end of Buchanan Street they turned into Argyle Street where they were separated briefly by a group of people advancing along the pavement towards them. Jenny swerved towards the kerb, the youth with the case following her, while Lizzie moved the other way, towards the shop windows. Reunited, the three of them waited at the junction with Union Street until a policeman held back the traffic for them, then after crossing they plunged beneath the railway bridge known, Lizzie informed Jenny, as the Highlandman's Umbrella because the Gaelic-speaking Highlanders who had flocked to Glasgow for work tended to meet there. At the far side of the bridge they crossed the road again and turned into Oswald Street, where Jenny was to lodge.

Mrs McLean lived in a spotless close where the stairs, even those from the pavement to the close itself, were neatly edged with fresh white pipe clay and the lower sections of the close walls were covered with shining bronze tiles edged with small blue flowers. Her door on the first-floor landing was a poem in flawless varnished wood, with brass knocker, nameplate, letter-box, handle and bell-push gleaming as though they had been fashioned from pure gold. While Lizzie rang the bell, Jenny dug in her purse for a coin for the station lad, who handed her case over, skimmed down the stairs, and was whistling his way through the close by the time Mrs McLean opened the door.

The landlady was very small and slight and dressed in black silk with white lace at collar and cuffs and a black apron. Her grey hair was skewered high on her small head by long pins topped with black jet knobs that matched her bright black eyes almost exactly.

'You buy your own provisions,' she said as she led them along the hall. 'I will cook your breakfast and tea each day, and lunch on Sundays but I don't care for folk in my kitchen. And I do *not* permit gentlemen callers.'

She opened a door and stepped back. 'I hope the room's to your liking, Mistress Young.'

The room allocated to Jenny had highly polished linoleum on the floor with a small, handmade rug by the narrow bed, a wardrobe, a chest of drawers, one chair, and a small marble-topped table bearing a flowered bowl and a matching soap dish and water jug.

'It's grand, Mrs McLean, thank you,' Jenny said warmly.

The grey head bobbed briefly in acknowledgement. 'The bathroom's the next door along,' said the woman, and withdrew.

Lizzie sat down on the bed, taking her hat off and looking round. 'It's not bad.'

'It's very nice indeed. Imagine – an indoor bathroom!'

'Glasgow's very modern,' said Lizzie complacently, getting up to tidy her hair before the mirror. 'Jenny, d'you know how difficult it's going to be for you to find Daniel in this city?' she asked as she worked, her voice muffled by a hairpin gripped between her teeth.

'It'll be like looking for a needle in a haystack, but I've got to try. I couldn't just stay in Ellerslie, not knowing what was happening to him.'

Lizzie removed the hairpin from her mouth and stabbed it back in place, then patted her hair. 'There's thousands of places where he could have found lodgings. Are you certain he's in Glasgow at all?'

'I don't even know that. But I have to try,' Jenny repeated, fully aware of how hollow the words sounded.

'Well, I'd better get back, and you'll be tired. You're sure you'll remember how to get to the emporium in the morning?' she asked anxiously as she pinned her hat on.

'Of course I will. If I forget I've got a good Scots

tongue in my head,' Jenny said firmly. She was growing a little tired of her friend's patronage.

'If you have to ask anyone for directions, make sure you speak to someone respectable. Mebbe I should come round early tomorrow and walk to the store with you.'

'You'll do nothing of the sort! If I can't manage to find a big place like Neilson's on my own how am I going to find Daniel? I'll need to get used to the streets and I might as well start tomorrow. You've done more than enough for me already.'

At the door Lizzie said anxiously, 'You'll remember to be at the staff entrance at eight o'clock sharp?'

'I'll remember. Goodnight, Lizzie,' Jenny said, and after she had closed the door she took a quick look at the bathroom before going back to her own room. She was gazing in wonder at the white, claw-footed bath, wash-hand basin, and lavatory bowl boxed in with varnished wood when a door further down the hall opened, making her jump guiltily.

'You'll take a cup of tea and a wee bit shortbread with me before you go to your bed?' Mrs McLean suggested.

'Oh, that would be very nice,' Jenny said, gratefully.

'It'll be ready in the kitchen in five minutes,' said the landlady, and Jenny went back to her own room to take a new white blouse and a black skirt out of her case and hang them up in readiness for the morning.

Tired though she was when she went to bed she lay awake for a long time, tossing restlessly in the strange bed, wondering how Shona was settling in, and if she was fretting for her mother as much as Jenny was fretting for her.

By the time the clock in the hall chimed midnight she had made up her mind that she couldn't spend another night away from her baby, and fell asleep on the decision to catch the first train home in the morning. She slept fitfully throughout the night, but by morning her commonsense was restored, and she knew that she had to stay in Glasgow, at least for a while. Shona would be safe with Bella, and Faith was nearby to help out if needed. Lizzie had gone to a great deal of trouble to find a job and a room for Jenny, and she couldn't go back to Ellerslie until she had at least made a good attempt to find Daniel.

She took up her position in a corner by the staff entrance of Neilson and Son's Buchanan Street emporium well before eight o'clock, keeping out of the way of the people who poured down the narrow lane and in at the entrance. They flocked in, some alone, others in groups of two and three, chattering and laughing, some yawning, some of them throwing her inquisitive glances as they swept past her and in at the modest wooden door. She wondered, as they flooded by, if one day soon some of them at least would be known to her.

Lizzie bobbed out at her from the middle of a group. 'There you are,' she said as though she had been searching for Jenny everywhere. 'Come on!'

It was like being five years old all over again, going to school for the first time. Even Jenny's first day in Dalkieth's hadn't been as nerve-wracking as this, because there had been some familiar faces in the wax-model room and Senga, whom she had known well at school, was as new and as nervous as Jenny herself. Here, she knew nobody but Lizzie, who was enviably confident of her surroundings as she showed Jenny where to put her coat and where she could tidy her hair.

'I forgot to say last night that I'd be grateful if you'd call me Eliza from now on,' she murmured as they stepped from the ladies' cloakroom into a narrow corridor. 'Lizzie's too common, now that I'm supervising my own department.'

'D'you think I should call myself Janet, then?' Jenny asked in amusement, but Lizzie – Eliza, Jenny reminded herself – was quite serious.

'Oh no, Jenny'll do. After all, you'll just be a sales-girl.'

As they made their way along the corridor they were jostled by women in crisp white blouses and neat dark skirts and men in smart suits. Some of the older men wore grey striped trousers, stiff high collars, and frock-coats.

'Are they customers?' Jenny asked in a whisper, and her friend gave her a withering look.

'Not at all – they're the floor-walkers. They oversee everyone and make sure the customers are kept happy.' Colour flooded her plain face as one of the frock-coated men paused on his way past to greet her by name. 'That's Mr Scott of Gents' Suits,' she murmured as he passed on. 'He's very genteel.'

'Is he married?'

'His wife died two years a – what d'you want to know that for?'

'You went as red as a poppy when you saw him.'

'Don't be daft!' Lizzie snapped, her colour deepening, reminding Jenny of carefree days in the school playground when romance was still something to be dreamed about and whispered over. 'Come on – I've got special permission to take you into the foyer before we go to our departments, but we'll have to be quick because the customers'll be coming in soon.'

They turned down a short corridor, leaving the bustle of incoming employees behind, then Lizzie opened a door and Jenny followed her into a dazzle of light and space. She had never in her life seen such a handsome place as the entrance foyer of Neilson and Son. Marble flooring stretched from where she stood to the huge plate-glass doors some distance away, and five galleries rose overhead, each supported on huge pillars garlanded with wreaths of gilded flowers. The galleries culminated in a great glass cupola high above, and the overall effect was one of light and space and opulence.

In the summer, Jenny realised, natural light would pour in through the glass frontage and the cupola, but on that late February morning it was still dark outside, and the place was lit by chandeliers on every floor and suspended from the roof.

'This is my department,' Lizzie said proudly, leading Jenny forward. 'Neilson's started in drapery and it's always been one of their main departments.'

The space in the middle of the huge foyer was empty, but to the sides, beneath the first gallery, ran a series of long, polished counters with shelving on the walls behind them. Between the shelves stands draped with materials blazed with jewelled colour, from shell-pink to crimson, pale lilac to royal purple, soft cream to burning orange. As well as self-colours there were floral patterns and stripes and polka-dots, and every type of material from thick warm velvet to delicate summery muslin. Women, neatly dressed in blouses and skirts, were beginning to come through the small baize door behind Jenny to take their places behind the counters, each murmuring, 'Good morning, Miss Caldwell,' as she slipped past. Lizzie greeted each one by name, giving stiff little nods of the head almost as though she was royalty.

'My staff,' she explained.

'Did you arrange all those stands, Li – Eliza?'

'Of course not, they've got folk specially paid to do that, and the windows too.'

Craning her neck Jenny saw that a wide marble staircase rose from the foyer, directly opposite the entrance, dividing at the back wall to lead off left and right towards the first gallery. The pillars edging the stairs were draped in generous swathes of material in shades of green varying from a deep woodland green at the bottom of the stairs to a delicate pale shade at the landing, each swathe draped as though it was a wide sleeve being held up and out to indicate the way to the floor above.

Lizzie's voice brought her back to the foyer itself. 'These are the lifts – for customers and management only.' She indicated two tiny apartments, one at each side of the foyer, well lit by electric lighting, the walls padded with pleated gold cloth. Wrought-iron sliding doors had been folded back, and a uniformed white-gloved page-boy in Neilson's navy blue and gold colours stood beside one of the lifts. Three doormen in uniforms heavy with gold braid stood conferring by the main doors from the street.

'It's all – beautiful!' Jenny said in awe. A scamper of feet came from behind them and a second page-boy, still fixing his pill-box hat in position, swept past to take his place beside the unattended lift.

'Come on, it's almost time to open and I've to see you settled in first.' Lizzie – *Eliza*, Jenny reminded herself – led the way back through the discreet baize door and into the plain narrow corridors that the store's customers never saw, to a flight of narrow wooden stairs that the customers would never be expected to use.

25

In the china and glass department the brilliance from a battery of skilfully placed electric lighting was echoed again and again in glass drops and prisms, crystal and cut-glass vases on the stands and tables. At the other side of the gallery tables covered with snowy napery were placed strategically in such a way that they allowed ample room for customers to move between them, each table set with a different china display. More china stood on stands between the counters which, as on the ground floor, were placed against the walls. The whole gallery was radiant with colour and pattern and reflections.

'My God,' said Jenny without thinking, 'I'd hate to see what a clumsy person could do in a place like this!'

'Ssshh!' Eliza was shocked. 'Our customers are never clumsy – and neither are the staff, if they know what's good for them.'

She led Jenny over to a grey-haired man, immaculately moustached and dressed in a grey frock-coat, grey-striped trousers, a snowy shirt with a grey bow-tie, and immaculate white gloves, and introduced her to the floor-walker, Mr Davidson. He inclined his head then said, 'You may go to your own department now, Miss Caldwell.'

'Yes, Mr Davidson,' Eliza said demurely, and slipped

back through the baize door, leaving Jenny with the floor-walker. A very superior-looking lady standing behind one of the counters was introduced as Miss Lang, the china supervisor.

Her voice was frosty. 'What experience have you had in retailing?'

'None – but I worked for years as a tracer and analyst in a shipyard. A very delicate touch was needed for that – and a sense of responsibility. I learn quickly.' Jenny was determined not to be intimidated.

'Hmmph. Well, you'll assist Miss Ballantyne.'

Miss Ballantyne was an angular young woman of Jenny's own age, with curly red hair, more carrotty than the red-gold of Helen's and Lottie's hair. 'You'll be fine with me,' she said reassuringly when the supervisor had left them alone. 'Just don't knock anything over, and don't let Miss Lang get you down. Her bark's worse than her— '

She stopped abruptly as Mr Davidson, who had been standing by the low wall and looking down on the foyer, turned with one hand raised, palm out, the other reaching for the handsome watch chained to his waistcoat. The assistants behind the counters, mainly women, straightened their shoulders, their eyes fixed on the floor-walker.

Jenny sensed anticipation sweeping through the department, brushing against her, then moving on and upwards. She was suddenly keenly aware of the staff on the gallery above, and the galleries higher up, all standing to attention, all waiting for some signal. After a moment Mr Davidson nodded slightly, returned his watch to its pocket, and began to parade slowly round the gallery, hands clasped behind him.

'That's us open for the public now,' Miss Ballantyne

said on an outgoing breath. 'They'll not start arriving for a while yet – this isn't the sort of store where the folk rush in as soon as the doors are opened. At least, not unless we're having our Christmas Bazaar. Now just watch me and remember that the customer's always in the right, even if she's a nasty old cat out to make trouble. And keep a smile on your face if you don't want Miss Lang or Mr Davidson giving you one of their looks.'

Within the hour the public had begun to invade the department, some using the marble staircase, others preferring to be whisked from floor to floor by lift. At first Jenny stood well back, watching and listening as her companion dealt with the ladies who approached their counter; later, when the department had become quite busy, she stepped forward nervously and managed to achieve her first sale without offending the customer or dropping any of the merchandise. As the woman walked away Miss Ballantyne gave Jenny an encouraging smile. 'You did fine. Now— ' She nodded up towards the overhead wires, 'Let's see if you know how to work the cash system.'

Jenny had intended to spend every spare moment searching for Daniel, but at the end of her first day at work her feet and legs were so sore that it was all she could do to make her way downstairs, collect her coat and hat, and walk the short distance to her lodgings, where Mrs McLean awaited her in the kitchen with a cup of strong tea and a basin of hot water and mustard for her feet.

'I mind what it was like on my first day,' she said briskly, stirring the tea and handing it over. 'You'll get used to it – everyone does. Take your stockings off, my dear, there's alum and zinc in there to ease your feet, and I'll give you a recipe for some soothing powder to sprinkle inside your stockings in the mornings. You'll be fine inside a week.'

Jenny, gratefully flexing her stiff aching toes in the basin, doubted it. She was used to standing for hours at a time on the stone floor of the wash-house at home, but had had no idea that standing on carpeted flooring while wearing the smart shoes demanded by Neilson and Son could be so exhausting.

But her kindly landlady was right – after her first week the fatigue eased off and she began to settle into the store's routine. Under Kate Ballantyne's placid supervision she learned how to cope confidently with the customers, even the more difficult and arrogant of the women who came to their counter. She was fascinated by the girl's ability to speak 'pan loaf' to the clients then lapse easily into her own plain Glaswegian accent when there was nobody near enough to hear her but Jenny.

The plainer crockery on show at their counter meant that most of their clients were ordinary working-class women like themselves, but now and again wealthier clients, used to begin treated with servility, would step from the lift – in some cases like a crab emerging from a pretty shell, Jenny thought privately – and advance on their counter.

'They're no' daft, the Scots wifies,' Kate said candidly when Jenny remarked on it. 'Those that don't have much tae spend want the best value for their money. And most of them that have plenty only have it because they wouldnae spend a penny more than they had tae. That's why you'll often get someone with a big house at Kelvinside and furs on her back walking past all the good china and coming to our counter. They want the best they can get – but they want it for as little as they have tae spend. And even our plain stuff's good quality, the Neilsons insist on that.'

Jenny learned to cope with the sophisticated pneumatic cash-carrying system, tucking money into hollow cups with screw-tops, sending them flying off along the overhead tracks to the change desk, and receiving the receipts and change by the same route within minutes. She learned how to recognise the 'tabbies' – the women who were only in the store to look, and had no intention of buying – and to give them enough attention to keep them happy without wasting too much time and energy on them. She absorbed the art of watching everything that was going on without seeming to watch, and how to keep a discreet look-out for kleptomaniacs.

'Not that we have many of them in this department, but some folk just can't keep their fingers to themselves,' Kate told her. 'Not just the poor-looking souls either – we've had real ladies trying tae slip a wee figurine into a pocket before this.'

For the first week it was all Jenny could do to keep up, let alone start looking for Daniel. By the second week she had begun to feel more confident about her own ability and had stopped crying herself to sleep every night, though not a minute went by, sleeping or waking, without her thinking longingly of Shona. She wrote to Bella almost every day and to her mother and Robert once a week, posting the letters on her way to work in the mornings.

'Now that I've settled in and stopped falling asleep every time I sit down I am about to start my search for Daniel,' she wrote to Robert at the end of the first week, her stomach turning over with nervousness as she re-read the words. Now that she was actually in the city, and had seen for herself now huge and how busy it was, she knew that she had little chance of finding her husband. But she had to try. She licked the envelope then sealed it, thumping the flap down with a determined fist to make certain that it was properly sealed.

She began her search in the area where she was lodging, for Oswald Street was close to the river and Daniel just might be nearby. She knocked at lodging-house doors, went into little corner shops, and summoned the courage to make enquiries of the men hanging about at street corners. There were plenty out of work in the city, gaunt men with little hope in their eyes, standing about in groups of anything from three to a dozen, clustered together for comfort. Many of them had fought all through the war, only to find on coming home that Lloyd George's promise of a land fit for heroes to live in was an empty boast as far as they were concerned. By day, every street had its share of maimed ex-servicemen begging for coins, and at night they slept in doorways.

Jenny, passing their huddled shadows on her way back to Oswald Street after yet another fruitless search, had to fight back the desire to shake each shoulder, peer into each wan face, to make sure that Daniel wasn't among their number. She couldn't bear to think of him reduced to such poverty and homelessness. When the rain hissed outside, or the wind beat against the sturdy tenement walls, she lay awake, dividing her time between worrying about Shona and worrying about Daniel.

She began to get up early, tiptoeing out of the house and down the stairs, joining the flow of men on their way to the shipyards, asking here and there if anyone knew Daniel Young. Nobody ever did, so she extended her search to the yards themselves on Sundays and Tuesday afternoons, her only time off, travelling on the trams that rocked self-importantly through the city streets, swaying from side to side like land-ships – or drunk men, Jenny often thought as she stood at the stop, hand outstretched, watching a tram speeding towards her, sparks shooting from the harness connected to the overhead rail.

She confided her real reason for coming to Glasgow to Kate, who at once circulated Daniel's name round her family and friends in the hope that someone might have heard of him. 'You must really love him, to leave your own folk and your bairn behind,' she said wistfully.

'He's my husband,' Jenny said and left it at that.

Letters arrived regularly from Alice, assuring her that everything was fine at home and that Shona was happy and being well looked after. 'Bella dotes on her and Patrick's taken to her as well,' she wrote. 'When I visited them last night Shona was on his knee while Bella got her supper ready.'

Robert, too, kept in touch with her. Seeing his confident handwriting on the first envelope that arrived from him Jenny was swept back over the years to the day when she had received that final short note from Tyneside, telling her that he was to be married. She remembered the disbelief, the heartbreak, the terrible sense of loss. She hadn't experienced any of these emotions when Daniel left her, she now realised, and tried to tell herself that that was because she was older and wiser.

She sat holding the envelope for a while, tracing her name, written in Robert's hand, with the tip of a finger, before finally opening it.

Robert wrote that he thought that he had managed to turn the tide of misfortune, and the yard may well be saved. 'I wish you were here in Ellerslie, among your own folk,' he ended the latest letter. 'But knowing you I realise that you have to make your own decisions.'

Occasionally Eliza or Kate, insisting that Jenny needed to take some time to herself, persuaded her to go window-shopping or to take a tramcar ride to one of Glasgow's handsome large parks. She enjoyed herself on these outings, but while she was admiring the fine clothes in the windows of Fraser and Sons or Pettigrew and Stephens or Treron & Cie, or hurtling along the streets in a swaying tramcar, or walking by the boating pond in Queen's Park, she was also searching the faces around her, hoping against hope that one of them would be Daniel's.

When she went to the music-hall with Eliza she even scanned the people in the gods when the interval came, though she knew full well that unless he had changed a great deal her husband wouldn't frequent such a place, with its comedians and jugglers and bosomy singers. Then she remembered, wryly, that she herself had enjoyed the first half just as much as anyone else, though not all that long ago she would have claimed that she had no interest in such frivolity.

'What are you grinning at?' Eliza wanted to know, and laughed when Jenny told her. 'I mind being shocked the first time someone asked if I'd like to come here. But there's something about the atmosphere of the place, and everyone else enjoying themselves.' She rummaged in the paper bag of boiled sweets she had brought with her, selecting one and passing the bag to Jenny. 'Would you look at that hat over there? I'd not even take it home for the cat, let alone be seen in public underneath it!'

Kate had taken Jenny home in the first week to meet her family, and since then Jenny had become a regular visitor. The Ballantynes, almost as large a mob as the Malloys in Ellerslie, lived in a two-room-and-kitchen; Mrs Ballantyne was as bony and as placid as her daughter, and always managed to find room for someone else at her table. The vicious 'flu epidemic that had ravaged the country just after the war had carried off her husband and two of their younger children. Kate was the second eldest, and she and three others who were also working supported the rest. A brother worked in an abattoir and Evie, just out of school, was behind the counter of a local greengrocer's shop. Evie was the artistic member of the family and would have liked to stay on at school to gain some extra qualifications, but her father's death had ended her hopes. Jenny, remembering her own frustration when she had to stay in Ellerslie after Maurice went missing in action, sympathised with the girl. Doris, Kate's elder sister, was a clippie on the trams.

'She got the job near the end of the war when they were glad enough to get women to do the work,' Kate explained proudly to Jenny. 'And she was so good at it that she managed to keep it on. And why shouldn't women be as good as men? Just because we sit down to pee it doesnae mean we're stupid.'

Four members of the family were still at school, though the two older boys were shop messengers in their spare time and the girl helped behind the counter of a nearby baker's shop. The youngest child, Timmy, was only six years old, and it was some time before Jenny realised that Timmy was Kate's own child and not a brother.

'His dad and me was going to get wed but he got killed. He was a builder and he lost his footing one day,'

Kate said without a shred of self-pity. 'I was working in Fraser's then, but I lost my job when they found out that Timmy was on the way. Nobody at Neilson's knows about him, so keep it to yourself.'

Kate herself turned out to be ambitious; she was determined, one day, to become a floor-walker.

'Why not? We'd two lady floor-walkers in Neilson's during the war when I first started, replacing men who'd gone off to fight. One of them, Miss Cameron her name was, was good to me, she taught me how important it was to speak right, and how to look after my clothes properly. But both the men came home and they'd been promised their jobs back, so the ladies had to go. Miss Cameron went to Stirling to look after her brother's family because his wife was poorly, so I didn't see her again.'

For a moment she looked sad, then she squared her shoulders and picked Timmy up for a cuddle. Jenny watched enviously, thinking of Shona. 'But she was good at her work, Miss Cameron,' Kate went on, 'and there's no reason why Neilson's shouldn't start taking on women again, one day.'

The Ballantyne household re-awakened Jenny's homesickness, and she broke her own rule and managed a swift trip back to Ellerslie, travelling home after work on the Saturday evening and returning on the last train on Sunday. The sight of Robert waiting on the platform when she stepped down from the train at Ellerslie brought a strange mixture of happiness and guilt – happiness at the sight of him, guilt because she hadn't told him that she was coming home.

'Alice told me,' he said before she had a chance to speak, taking her bag from her. 'Otherwise you might have come and gone without me knowing a thing about it. Fortunately I've got into the habit of looking in at the

pawnshop now and again to exchange news about you.'
He put a firm hand beneath her elbow and led her from
the station to where a hansom cab waited. 'Get in.'

'I could easily have walked,' she protested as he
joined her in the leather-smelling interior, and he let
his face relax into a faint smile.

'You've only got a short time, remember? No point in
wasting some of it by walking home. Besides, you spend
enough time on your feet, what with your work and the
search for your husband.' He sat back in the opposite
corner and studied her. 'You look tired.'

'I'm managing. How's the shipyard?'

'Holding on, now that George's grip's broken at last.
I think there'll be something for Mrs Dalkieth's precious
grandson to inherit after all.'

When they reached the tenements he ordered the
driver to stop. 'I don't suppose you'll want to be seen
driving up to your father's close in my company.'

Jenny reached for the door, but Robert stretched a
long arm past her and she pulled her fingers hurriedly
from beneath his. As he opened the door she was aware
of the masculine smell that came from him of soap and
tobacco and hair-oil . . .

Her mother and two sisters were waiting for her in
the flat, Faith washing dishes at the sink, Alice working
at the table, once spread with homework, now with
what looked like account books, and Bella nursing
Shona by the fire.

'Jen! Look, pet,' she lifted the baby, turning her
round towards the door. 'Here's your mammy come
tae see you.'

To Jenny's dismay Shona's brows puckered uncertainly, then she let out a whimper and burrowed into
Bella's neck.

'They forget fast at that age,' Faith's voice was brisk. She dried her hands and reached for the teapot on the range. 'Give her a minute tae get used tae ye. Ye'll be ready for a cup of tea.'

Jenny sipped obediently at her tea, answering Alice's questions about Glasgow without really hearing them, waiting in an agony of impatience to hold her daughter again. After a few minutes Shona got over her shyness but, even so, she twisted her head round to make sure that Bella and Faith were within reach when Jenny at last gathered her into her arms.

'Oh, lovely, you've grown since I saw you last! Look what I've brought for you.' She held out the little cloth kitten she had bought from Neilson's toy department and Shona's eyes widened. She reached for the toy, then, a few minutes later, discovering that the cat was inedible, tried to claim the biscuit her mother was eating. Faith cut a thick crust from the end of the loaf and dipped it in tea, then in sugar.

'I'll take her now,' Bella offered. 'She'll get your nice skirt in a mess.'

Jenny clung to her baby. 'That doesn't matter.'

Faith fetched a cloth and tucked it round Shona's neck. The baby submitted impatiently, then grabbed at the proferred crust.

'She likes tae fill her belly, that one,' Bella said fondly.

'You're sure she's not too much for you, or a nuisance to Patrick?'

'Not a bit of it. She's given him a new interest in life. And you'll never guess— ' Bella's face lit up; she looked very like the happy young girl Patrick Kerr had courted and married. 'The gatekeeper at the yard's retiring, and Robert Archer's offered the job tae Patrick. He's tae start at the end of the month.'

'Bella, that's grand! Will he manage all right?'

Her sister nodded. 'He'll not have a lot of walking to do once he gets tae the yard, and there's a seat, Robert says, for when he's not havin' tae talk tae folk going in and out. That special boot's made it much easier for him tae get out and about.'

'He'll still have to go on with his carving,' Alice put in. 'You've no idea how much folk like them. I can sell as many as he can make.'

Shona gradually settled down in her mother's embrace while Jenny talked about her work in the emporium and her fruitless search for Daniel. It was amazing that there was so much Ellerslie news for her to hear in return after an absence of only four weeks. Maureen was pregnant again, and Alice was of the opinion that she and Jacko were determined to have just as many children as Maureen's parents had had. Jacko had managed to keep his job at the yard and so had Neil Baker. Lottie was becoming more and more stuck up and hadn't visited for several weeks.

'I don't bother about her, but I miss wee Helen,' Faith said wistfully.

Alec Monroe's gas-damaged lungs had been giving him trouble, forcing him to spend a week in his bed in the flat above the pawnshop. 'But he's back on his feet again,' said Alice, who had not only coped with the shop on her own but had managed to find time to look after Alec as well.

There was a rumour going around that George Dalkieth was drinking more than was good for him. He wasn't seen around the yard much, which was a blessing as far as the workers were concerned, and Robert was taking on more to do with the running of the place than ever before. Bella had met a former schoolfriend now in service at Dalkieth House, who told her that the two Mrs Dalkieths, matriarch and daughter-in-law, were real cronies these days, though they'd scarcely looked at each other before.

'It's the bairn,' Faith said wisely. 'A bairn can either heal trouble or cause it.'

'There's no doubt that the wee one's the centre of that family,' Bella agreed. 'Annie tells me that his mother and his gran dote on him, though his father doesnae bother his backside.'

'Mebbe his nose is out of joint,' Alice put in. 'He was aye his mother's favourite, from what I've heard.'

Shona's eyelids had begun to droop and her head was heavy against Jenny's arm. Now she yawned, and Bella reached over and gently took the half-chewed crust out of her fingers. 'I'd best get her home and intae her bed.'

'Can she not sleep here tonight, with me?'

'Her wee crib's not here,' Bella said. 'It's no' fair at her age tae expect her tae chop and change. I'll bring her back tomorrow morning.'

Reluctantly, Jenny handed the sleepy baby over, winding Bella's shawl about the two of them. Her arms felt strangely light and empty without Shona.

'I wish I could find Daniel then come back home,' she said later when she and Alice were lying together in the double bed she had once shared with Lottie. Alice had elected to desert her own small room for the night so that she and Jenny could talk. Through the wall Teeze, who had reacted indifferently to Jenny's presence when he came home from the pub, was snoring loudly.

'If it's Shona you're fretting about, she's contented enough. Bella and Pat are both good to her.'

'I know that,' Jenny said. 'It's me that's missing her . . .'

26

It was even harder to leave Shona a second time. By Sunday afternoon the baby had spent so much time with her mother that she wailed and held her arms out to Jenny when she was handed over to Bella.

Jenny's own eyes filled as she blundered out of Bella's house and through the close where she had once lived. She walked past Robert, waiting for her at the end of the street, without noticing him, and he hurried after her and put a hand on her arm. 'What's wrong?'

Jenny rubbed at her face with the heel of her hand and sniffed as he relieved her of her bag. 'It – it was just having to leave the wee one.'

He shook his head, frowning. 'Stay with her, Jen, and I'll find someone to look for your husband.'

'I can manage,' she said curtly, marching ahead of him, angry that he had seen her weakness.

'That's your trouble, Jenny Gillespie,' he said from behind her. 'You're altogether too independent.'

'I've had to be. And my name's Young, not Gillespie. Give me my bag, I can— '

'I know,' he said dryly. 'You can manage.'

The next day started badly in the store. Among the people at Jenny's counter was a plump, well-dressed woman with a discontented mouth who insisted on seeing every decorative wall-plate poor Kate could find, and turning up her nose at each and every one of them.

'It's ridiculous,' the customer complained, 'All I want is something simple and you can't supply it.' Her gloved finger stabbed at one offering after another and her voice became shrill with impatience. 'This shape is right but the pattern is wrong, while this pattern's more what I'm looking for, but the colours aren't right.'

'There are other wall-plates over at that counter, madam,' Kate told her hopefully.

'I'm aware of that, but the prices on that counter are ridiculous.'

'What about this one?'

'Aren't you listening to me? I already told you, the colour is wrong.'

'You said yellow, madam.'

'Precisely. I said yellow, not orange. These flowers are orange.'

'They're daffodils, madam, and daffodils are yellow,' Kate pointed out and the woman stared at her then turned towards her companion, who was half her width but just as sour looking.

'Come along, Muriel, we'll try Dallas's. Perhaps the staff there will be more helpful. As for you, miss, I shall be complaining about your impudence, make no mistake about that,' she added sharply to Kate. 'Mrs Neilson happens to be a friend of mine and she'll hear about this.'

'But— '

Jenny broke in hastily, realising that her friend had been driven to the end of her tether and was about to make matters worse for herself. 'I believe that madam was thinking of pure yellow flowers, Miss Ballantyne. Pansies, for instance.'

'Pansies – exactly.' The woman swung round to look at her.

'Yellow pansies, with velvety-brown centres?'

'That would match my dining room. You have a plate like that in stock?'

'I could make one up.'

'You? Make one?'

'If madam would choose the right shape,' Jenny indicated a shelf of plain plates, 'I could paint it for her.'

'How long would it take?'

'We could have it delivered to you on Saturday morning, madam.'

The woman hesitated, then said grudgingly, 'Very well – but I'll come in myself on Saturday. If I'm not satisfied I'll not buy it.'

'Of course not, madam.'

'Are you daft?' Kate wanted to know as the two women walked away.

'I can do it, I used to paint china at home for people and I've got my paints with me.'

'But Mrs Provan's terribly hard to satisfy,' Kate protested. 'You'll get yourself into trouble.'

'At least it's kept her from complaining.'

'She'll probably have us both out of work on Saturday,' Kate predicted gloomily. 'What about Miss Lang and Mr Davidson? What are you going to tell them?'

'We'll wait to see what happens. I'll pay for the plate out of my own pocket for the moment. Can I paint it in your house? I need an oven and my landlady'll not let me use hers.'

For the next three evenings all thought of looking for Daniel had to be put aside while Jenny worked at the Ballantyne's kitchen table. The family watched, enthralled, as a cluster of yellow pansies, fringed with leaves and with deep brown hearts began to fill the centre of the plate, with the yellows and browns of the blossoms echoed round the rim, mingled with leaf-green in a series of feathery outlines.

'Imagine having a talent like that!' Mrs Ballantyne said in awe, and Evie, the thwarted artist languishing behind the counter of a greengrocer's shop, watched every stroke of the brush with rapt attention.

Seeing her interest, Jenny showed the girl how to paint one of her mother's saucers, which could be used to test the oven before the pansy plate was entrusted to the heat. The girl picked up the idea quickly and chose an imaginative design of green leaves.

On Thursday afternoon Mrs Ballantyne did a baking and, by the evening, Jenny judged the oven section of the range to be at just the right temperature for the saucer. She tested the design with the tip of a finger to satisfy herself that the paint was dry then slid the saucer into the oven and closed the door.

'If it's too hot the colours'll lose their freshness and if it's too cool they'll not bake in properly, then they'll be spoiled when the saucer's washed,' she explained, a worried frown tucking itself between her brows. It stayed there until the saucer was brought out half an hour later, the pattern baked firmly on to it, the leaves Evie had painted looking fresh and green.

'They're so real they look as if you could just pick them off,' Kate marvelled, and Evie flushed with pride and pleasure as she gazed at her own handiwork.

Mrs Ballantyne willingly did another baking on Friday afternoon, and that evening it was the pansy plate's turn to go in to the oven. While she waited to see the results Jenny's tea cooled in its cup and she was too nervous to do more than nibble at the scones Kate's mother had made that afternoon.

'Oh, Jenny— ' Kate whispered when the moment came and the oven door was opened. 'Then, 'Oh, Jenny!' she squealed as the plate emerged. 'It's beautiful!'

Jenny gazed down at the pansies, bright and pure, half-hidden by the cloth she was using to protect her fingers from the heat. 'The thing is – what will Mrs Provan think of it?'

As soon as Jenny produced the plate on Saturday Mrs Provan's friend, the woman who had been with her on Monday, gave a squeak of delight. 'Marion, it's awfully bonny!'

Mrs Provan withered her with a look, then studied the plate carefully, peering at it then holding it at arm's length, turning it this way and that to catch the light before finally saying in a grudging voice, 'Mmhhmm, it's quite nice. Certainly more like what I had in mind in the first place. How much is it?'

Jenny, who had been hiding her nervousness behind an impassive face, felt such a wave of relief wash over her that she almost had to clutch at the edge of the counter to keep herself upright. She named the sum that she and Kate had earlier agreed would be fair and acceptable.

'Though it's my belief that you could charge a lot more,' Kate had said. 'It's worth it.'

Mrs Provan handed the money over without protest, left instructions for the plate to be delivered to her house that afternoon, and sailed away, her friend bobbing in her wake.

'You'd have thought she could have carried it herself,. 'Jenny said as she deftly packed the plate in tissue paper.

'That sort wouldn't carry a bite of food to their own mouths if they could get someone else to do it for them,' Kate told her, adding, 'I still think you should take the difference between the price of the plate the way it was before and the price Mrs Provan paid.'

'It wouldn't be right to take some of her money.'

'But it means that Neilson's is getting more than the original plate cost and you're getting nothing for your work,' Kate argued, but Jenny was adamant.

'If they found out, I'd not want to be accused of taking money from them. But your mother should get something for the use of her oven.'

It was Kate's turn to shake her head. 'You're not going to pay her out of your own pocket. We all did well out of the extra baking.'

They were still arguing about the matter when Mrs Provan's friend came back on her own, scurrying across the carpet with an occasional guilty glance over her shoulder, for all the world like an escaped fugitive, to ask Jenny if she would decorate a plate for her as well, 'Any flowers you like, as long as they're in different shades of red,' she murmured, and scuttled off.

Over the next few weeks word began to spread among the customers. A third order came in, then another, and Jenny was soon in a quandary. Evenings that should have been devoted to looking for Daniel were spent instead working in the Ballantynes' little kitchen. Evie was pressed into service to do some of the plainer work and Jenny had to buy more paints and brushes and was therefore forced to take some money to cover her own expenses and pay Mrs Ballantyne for the extra fuel needed to keep her oven at the necessary temperature.

'It'll have to stop,' she told Kate when the work began

to spill over into the weekends. 'I've got a bairn waiting for me at home and I'll have to get back to her soon. And there's still Daniel.'

'You'll have to tell Miss Lang what's going on.'

'And lose my job?'

'Jenny, you're beginning to bring custom to Neilson's. We're getting folk in that I've never seen before, looking for hand-painted china because they've seen your work in someone else's house. You'd not lose your job, not now.'

'She'll not be pleased at me keeping it quiet all those weeks, nor will Mr Davidson. It's ridiculous,' said Jenny, shaking her head. 'I ran my own department at Dalkieth's, I'm a married woman with a child, yet I'm scared of Miss Lang. She's like all the schoolteachers I ever had rolled into one. But you're right, Kate, I'll have to tell her.'

But Kate wasn't listening. Instead she was gaping at a tall, fair-haired young man who was making his way across the carpet towards their counter. 'That's Mr Matthew!'

'Who?'

Miss Lang and Mr Davidson had seen the newcomer and were converging on him from different points of the gallery. But he moved faster than they did, and Kate just had time to hiss, 'Matthew Neilson, Mr Neilson's son,' before he was standing in front of them, looking from one to the other and asking with interest, 'Which of you paints plates?'

'I – I do,' Jenny confessed, horrified that he knew.

Clear blue eyes settled on Jenny's face. 'And you are Miss—?'

Miss Lang, only just beating Mr Davidson to the counter, supplied the information in a voice fluting with nervousness. 'This is Mrs Young, Mr Matthew. She's been working with us for about six weeks now. Is there— '

' — anything wrong, sir?' Mr Davidson took up the sentence as he arrived.

'Nothing wrong,' Matthew Neilson said crisply. 'I want a word with Mrs Young, that's all. In my office, if you can spare her for a while.'

'I gather,' he said dryly a moment later, as he and Jenny left the counter, 'that your superiors know nothing about your – activities?'

She kept her eyes on the door leading to the back stairs, not daring to look up at him. 'I was just about to tell Miss Lang.'

A firm grip on her elbow turned her towards one of the lifts. 'This way,' Matthew Neilson said, and within moments the three of them – Jenny, the lift attendant, and the store owner's son – were caged in a padded silken box and the china department was dropping away from them. Jenny tensed and the fingers still holding her elbow tightened slightly. 'Your first time in a lift?'

'Y-yes.'

'Don't worry, it's quite safe.'

Ladies' Fashions and Gents' Suitings flashed by, moving disconcertingly from top to bottom of the latticed iron doors enclosing the lift, then the tearoom appeared and, after a slight bounce, the floor settled and the gates rattled open.

'This way.' Matthew Neilson led her past the tearoom, through a door marked 'Private' and into a short corridor with more doors to the left and right. He opened one and ushered her into a fairly small, plain room dominated by a large desk.

'Sit down, Mrs Young. You'll have a cup of tea – or would you prefer coffee?'

'Neither, thank you.'

He grinned. 'Even a condemned murderer gets something,' he told her, opening an inner door. 'Muriel, could you bring tea for two, please?' he asked someone out of Jenny's line of vision, then returned to lean against the edge of the desk.

'My parents and I dined with friends of theirs last night,' he said conversationally. 'I believe you've met Mrs Provan?'

'She's a good customer of Neilson's,' Jenny said nervously.

'She showed us a handsome new wall-plate that had been specially designed and painted for her and congratulated my father and I on our new service to customers. We had to confess that we knew nothing about it. Nor, I gather, does anyone else.'

Jenny took a deep breath and launched into an explanation about Mrs Provan and her insistence on a plate with a yellow pattern, pausing when an efficient-looking woman brought a tea-tray from the inner room.

When the secretary had returned to her own office Matthew Neilson picked up the teapot. 'I understand from Mrs Provan that you've painted plates for other customers,' he said, pouring tea as though accustomed to it.

'One or two ladies who saw Mrs Provan's asked me to decorate plates for them. I didn't like to refuse.' Jenny accepted the cup he held out to her. The tea had a refreshing, slightly lemony scent; she sipped at it appreciatively, then said, 'I've charged the customers the same price they would have paid for a decorated plate, and only kept back enough to cover the cost of the paints

373

and the fuel Mrs Ballantyne used. I've not taken a penny away from the store, Mr Neilson.'

His eyes were on her wedding ring. 'Are you a widow, Mrs Young?'

'No.'

'A deserted wife?'

Jenny's face grew hot. She got to her feet, carefully setting the cup and saucer on the tray. 'That's none of your business, Mr Neilson.'

'As an employee— '

'I am no longer an employee,' she told him.

'And what about the people who are still waiting for orders to be completed? What about Mrs McNeill? She's a very good customer of ours and she was at Mrs Provan's last night too,' he added as Jenny, confused, stared at him. 'She asked me if Neilson's could supply a specially decorated tea-service for her. I said I'd see to it.'

'Then you must employ a china-painter.' Jenny opened the door, determined to retain her dignity. She would not allow this inquisitive young man to dismiss her, order her from his father's store. She would leave of her own free will.

'That,' said Matthew Neilson, 'is an excellent idea. Will you accept the post, Mrs Young?'

She turned to face him, astonished. 'Me?'

'You're a china-painter, aren't you?'

Yes, but— '

He came round the desk, closed the door, and led her back to her chair. 'I see no reason to look for someone else when you've not only got the talent to do the job, but the sense to recognise the gap in our services to our customers. Naturally there will be a considerable increase. After all, you'll be starting a new department for us.' He took an ornate box from the desk and offered it to her. 'Cigarette?'

She shook her head, still bewildered by the turn the interview had taken.

'My father,' he explained, lighting a cigarette for himself, 'is always looking for new ways to please our clients and there seems little sense in advertising for a china-painter when you're right here. You'll have your own workroom, of course, and if you give me a list of the necessary paints and so on I'll see that they're supplied.'

Jenny felt as though the world was spinning too fast. 'I haven't said that I'll do it,' she said faintly.

'Why let someone else make money out of your idea, Mrs Young?'

Jenny thought of Ellerslie, and Shona. She wanted to go home to her baby, but she still hadn't found Daniel; leaving Glasgow now would be like turning her back on him. If the job that Matthew Neilson was offering paid well enough then maybe she could find some way of bringing Shona to Glasgow for the time being. And her evenings and weekends would be free again now.

'Well?' His voice nudged at her. The smell of cigarette smoke was sharp in her nostrils.

'I accept,' said Jenny.

27

A former store-room off the china department, well-lit by a row of windows looking down on Buchanan Street, became Jenny's workshop, and within two weeks Matthew Neilson saw to it that the room was freshly painted and well equipped with everything she needed, including a compact gas-fired oven.

At Jenny's request Kate's sister Evie was brought in as her assistant and, to Matthew's delight, the handsome posters he set up in the foyer and in the china department advertising the store's new facility for its customers resulted in a lot of interest in the new department from the start.

'I knew we'd do well,' he exulted, strolling round the workroom, examining a row of plates waiting to be fired.

Jenny took time to complete an ivy leaf, the tip of her tongue between her teeth as she concentrated on the work, then she laid down her brush. 'I didn't. Anyone can paint china; I can't think why folk should want to spend good money getting someone to do it for them when they could easily do it for themselves.'

'You've not got the right commercial attitude.' He picked up a book of flower plates that she had bought and flipped through the pages. 'People with money prefer to have things done for them. Which is fortunate for Neilson's, and for you, too, Mrs Young.'

The last words were delivered in amused tones. He had taken to calling her by her first name almost at once, but when he thought that she was being too serious and stuffy he reverted to her title. The two of them had worked together on renovating the work-room, Jenny planning it and Matthew Neilson making sure that everything was done just as she wanted it. During that time he had tried to find out more about her, but Jenny had calmly but firmly declined to answer his probing questions or volunteer any information.

She liked him, but his conviction that money could buy anything troubled her. If he knew why she was in Glasgow he would be quite likely to offer to pay some-one to find Daniel for her, and she had no wish to expose her husband to that sort of prying.

She picked up a fresh paint-brush, wishing that Matthew would go back to his office and leave her to get on with her own work. Instead he said suddenly, 'Let's go out for a drive this evening.'

'What?' She was confused.

'It's a lovely day outside. You need a break, and I'm looking for an excuse to give the car a spin.'

'I'm sure you don't need to find an excuse.' Jenny loaded her brush with paint and turned back to her work. To her annoyance, her fingers shook slightly and her heart had speeded up; his interest in her was certainly flattering.

Two large, well-cared-for hands were planted on the table in front of her and he said from above her head, 'Be a sport, Jenny. There's no fun in driving about on my own.'

'Mr Neilson, I'm an employee of your father's.'

'And a married woman. I'm only suggesting a drive, not an elopement.'

'Surely you can invite someone more suitable?'

'I can't think of anyone else that I particularly want to spend the evening with. Besides, you need to get some fresh air after slaving away all day.'

Jenny put the brush down again and rested her elbows on the table, glancing out of the window. The sky was hidden from sight by the building opposite, but it had been a clear blue when she went out for a breath of fresh air during the midday break and the sun sparkled back at her from the windows across the road.

She had intended to take a tram out to Govan that evening and walk along some streets near the shipyards in the hope of catching sight of Daniel.

'The snowdrops and crocuses and daffodils are coming out in the parks. Jenny, you're forever painting flowers – you should really have a good look at the real thing now and again,' the voice above her head coaxed.

'It would be nice, but— '

'Good! I'll pick you up at eight,' Matthew said, and whisked out of the room.

Jenny had fully intended, once she was earning more money, to find a place of her own so that she could bring Shona to Glasgow. But when she suggested it in a letter home Alice wrote back that the family were opposed to the prospect.

'Shona would have to spend her days with a stranger while you were at work, and how could you look for Daniel when you'd have her to see to in the evenings and at weekends?' Alice wrote. 'I think Mam and Bella are right when they say that she's best left where she is, with people she knows. The sooner you find Daniel, or decide that you've done all you could to find him, the sooner you'll be back here, with Shona.'

Jenny read the letter over several times, and knew that her family was right. Shona was best left in Ellerslie.

The days and weeks had rushed past while she was busy setting up the new workshop. Unable to bear too many partings from Shona she had decided that it was best if she didn't return to Ellerslie frequently, electing, instead, to spend her weekends searching for word or sight of her husband.

By April her outings with Matthew had somehow become weekly events, usually visiting one of the many beautiful parks within easy reach of the city centre. As their friendship developed she steadfastly continued to refuse to say much about herself and where she came from, knowing full well that he would insist on meeting her family or, even worse, would turn up in Ellerslie uninvited when she had gone back there. Good company though he was, there was a possessive side to Matthew's nature that bothered Jenny. They had all but quarrelled one Sunday evening when, returning footsore and tired from another fruitless search round the streets by the river, she found him comfortably settled in her landlady's parlour, with Mrs McLean bright-eyed with excitement, plying him with fruit loaf and tea out of her best china cups, taken from the display cabinet for the occasion.

'I thought we might discuss a new pattern I've had in mind,' he said blandly, smiling up at Jenny as she stopped in the doorway.

'I told Mr Matthew you'd not be long,' Mrs McLean chirped, pouring out fresh tea for Jenny before refilling Matthew's cup.

'Did you not tell him that gentlemen callers aren't encouraged?' Jenny asked with a slight edge to her voice, and her landlady coloured and tutted.

'I didnae mean Mr *Matthew*,' she said reprovingly, and Matthew himself added, 'Besides, I'm not a gentleman caller. I'm here on business.'

'Sit down here, my dear. I'm just off to evening service, so you can have some time on your own,' Mrs McLean gathered up her own cup and plate and whisked out of the room with a final girlish simper in Matthew's direction.

'Mr Neilson— '

'It's usually Matthew out of shop hours, Jenny.'

'You said you were here on business,' she reminded him. 'Though I'd prefer it if you didn't call at my lodgings.'

'I wouldn't have to, if you'd only agree to see me more often.'

'We see quite enough of each other as it is. Anyway, I'm too tired to talk business tonight.' She had come back feeling dispirited after yet another fruitless search, and had been looking forward to going to bed early.

'You shouldn't walk so far, then. Mrs McLean said you go out walking a lot when you're not at work. Maybe we could take walks together.'

'I don't think so.'

'Why not?' Matthew wanted to know, maddeningly.

'Because— ' Jenny stopped abruptly as her landlady popped her head, now topped by a black straw hat with a bunch of daisies pinned to the brim, round the door.

'Don't trouble to put the dishes in the kitchen, dear,' she said brightly. 'I'll see to them when I get back.'

' — because I like to walk on my own sometimes,' Jenny finished when the landing door closed and they were alone.

'Come for a drive.'

'I'm not in the mood for a drive, Matthew! Why don't you take your mother out for a nice run in the car?'

He scowled, sliding down in his chair and stretching long legs across Mrs McLean's brown and red carpet. 'My mother has other fish to fry. My sister's honoured us with one of her rare visits. She's brought the infant with her and there are nursemaids and cribs and toys all over the place. I barked my shins on a perambulator this morning. Walked out of the drawing room and almost fell over the damned thing in the hall, waiting for his majesty.'

'You don't care for children?' Jenny thought of Shona, never far from her mind.

'Oh, they're well enough in their proper place, which is the nursery, with the door closed. That's where we lived until we reached an interesting age. But this brat's the first grandchild and my parents are besotted. Everywhere I turn there he is being passed from hand to hand and fussed over.'

Jenny was glad that she hadn't said anything about Shona. Not that Matthew's opinions would have been of any importance.

'At least her husband's not with her,' Matthew said. 'He's a terrible bore. I can't think what she ever saw in the fellow.' Then he brightened. 'They're going to have a party on Tuesday evening for some friends. Why don't you come along as my guest?'

'Don't be ridiculous, Matthew. I'm an employee.'

'But a special kind of employee. You started up a new department for us.'

'That doesn't mean that it would be fitting for me to visit your parents' home as a guest.'

'You got on well enough with my father when he had a look at your workshop. You impressed him.'

'We met in the emporium on business terms, not

social.' James Neilson, a smaller, stockier man than his son but with the same thick hair and moustache, except that his was grey instead of fair, had asked a number of practical questions and listened carefully to the answers, studying Jenny with eyes that were shrewd, though kindly enough.

To her relief, Matthew finally took no for an answer, and left before Mrs McLean came back and invited him to stay for supper. Washing the good china carefully in the kitchen after he had gone Jenny shook her head over his naive assumption that his mother would willingly play hostess to one of her husband's employees. Besides, Mrs Neilson was sure to ask questions about her, questions which couldn't be fobbed off the way Matthew's were.

As April gave way to May Jenny felt that she had travelled on every tram in Glasgow and walked through every street, but still there was no sign of Daniel. He had made no attempt to contact her or anyone else in Ellerslie, and even the Ballantyne clan had found nothing out.

She managed to get a few days off from the store, making the excuse that there was illness in her family, and went home for Shona's first birthday, taking with her a handsome baby doll complete with cradle, bought from Neilson's toy department. After such a long time apart it took Shona, who had taken her first shaky steps only a week before, longer to get to know her mother again; at first she held tightly to her grandmother and aunts, particularly to Bella, and when she finally came to Jenny and allowed her to cuddle her she soon wanted to get down on the floor, where she was eager to toddle around, holding on to the furniture.

382

'They don't stay babies for long,' Faith said, watching the little girl stagger from table to chair. Her voice was wistful with the memories of her own babies, some dead, the others grown now.

'I know that,' Jenny agreed, and wished that she had stopped to think before sacrificing months of Shona's precious babyhood to the search for Daniel.

She was kneeling on the floor, helping Shona to put her new dolly to bed, when Patrick came in, pausing briefly in the doorway to clutch at the frame for balance after the journey upstairs.

'Hello, Pat', she said. 'You're doing well.'

'Well enough,' he said shortly. He had discarded the crutch and was using a stick now; he swayed from side to side as he walked into the room, reminding Jenny of the Glasgow trams, but for all that he moved confidently and without pain.

Shona, who had been intent on her doll until then, glanced up and saw him. Her pretty little face broke into a broad grin and she held her arms up to him.

'Pat!'

'Here, here, let me sit down, hen. Don't rush at me like a bull at a barn door,' he said, his face softening as he looked down at the baby. She caught hold of the table leg and scrambled to her feet as he lowered himself into a chair, then toddled over to him, swaying from side to side much as he had done, the doll dragged along by the skirt after her. Patrick leaned down to her, hoisting her into his lap and she held her new present up to be admired. Solemnly, he studied the doll's golden curls and the tucked and embroidered muslin dress, then his eyes, following Shona' pointing finger, travelled to the lace-covered crib in the middle of the kitchen floor.

'Aye, it's bonny,' he said and Shona, satisfied, scrambled down from his knee and went back to the crib.

'It must have cost a fair bit, too,' Patrick added almost accusingly, his gaze moving to Jenny's face then down over the striped green crepe de chine blouse and matching skirt she wore.

She flushed, keenly aware as usual of his dislike and his resentment.

'It's grand to see Pat and Bella getting on together,' Alice said as she and Jenny set out for Lottie's flat the next day. 'He's got his self-respect back now that he's earning again, and he's good to Shona, so you've got no reason to worry about her.' Then she added with a sidelong glance at her sister, 'He seems to have some bee in his bonnet about you, though.'

'What makes you say that?'

'His mouth tightens whenever your name's mentioned, and he goes quiet when you're in the same room as him. Did the two of you quarrel?'

'Why should we?' Jenny asked evasively. As far as she knew nobody, not even Bella, knew about the confrontation between herself and Patrick on the day Shona was born. And nobody would ever hear as much as a hint of it from her.

As they turned the corner into Mayfield Street she changed the subject, eyeing the three-storey greystone tenements. 'Lottie's fairly come up in the world. But I can't see her down on her knees taking her turn of scrubbing the stairs.'

'Neil pays a woman to do the heavy work, I believe.' Alice's voice was heavy with disapproval. She turned in at a close tiled like Mrs McLean's and added, as Jenny followed her up the stairs, 'I come here when I can, for Helen's sake, but Lottie doesn't make any of us welcome. She doesn't like to be reminded of us, or our house, now that she's done so well for herself.' She knocked on the door then said as they waited, 'You'll – you'll see a difference in Helen.'

'She'll be quite grown up now – she'll be five in October,' Jenny replied as Lottie opened the door, a cigarette smouldering between the red-tipped fingers of one hand, her red hair frizzed on either side of her carefully made-up face. She led the way into the 'drawing room', where a low table had been laid for afternoon tea.

When her guests had been supplied with tea and shop-bought gingerbread Lottie dropped into a comfortable armchair and tapped the ash from her cigarette into a convenient ashtray, studying Jenny openly. 'You look smarter now that you're living in the city,' she said at last.

'You look very smart yourself, Lottie.'

The other girl glanced complacently down at her low-necked, knitted blue jumper and slender black calf-length skirt, with fine pleats at each side. She stretched out one slender leg, twisting her foot this way and that to admire her buckled, wedge-heeled shoes and silk stockings.

'Neil makes a good wage.'

'Is Helen in?' Alice wanted to know, and Lottie's red mouth turned down in a scowl.

'She's been a right pest all morning, so I sent her out to play. Thank goodness she'll be old enough to go to school in September. Mebbe I'll get some peace from her then. She likes attention, does that little madam,' she said impatiently, then began to question Jenny about Glasgow, the people she met there, the clothes the women wore.

'I've been to Glasgow with Neil several times and he's promised to take me to Edinburgh soon for a holiday,' she remarked, stubbing her cigarette out and selecting a fresh one from an ornate box. She lit it and blew a smoke ring across the room. 'I thought mebbe your mother would take Helen while we're gone. There'd be no pleasure in trailing her round the shops, listening to her whining all the time.'

Alice and Jenny exchanged glances as a gentle, tentative tapping was heard at the door of the flat. Lottie, ignoring it, went on talking. When Jenny finally interrupted her to say, 'I think there's someone at the door,' she frowned.

'It'll be Helen, I suppose. That lassie never gives me a minute's peace.' She got up, sighing ostentatiously, and flounced out into the hall. The sisters exchanged glances, and Alice raised her eyes to the ceiling.

'Well – come in if you're coming,' they heard Lottie say crossly. 'Don't hang about on the landing letting me catch my death of cold.' The door shut then Lottie reappeared, looking back over her shoulder. 'Come and say hello to Mama's visitors. Come on,' she added sharply, 'D'ye want them to think you're a naughty little girl?'

Helen edged into the room, sliding her small body round the doorframe as though trying to keep as far as possible from her mother. Jenny stared, shocked, at the little girl's pale face. The soft brown eyes that had once sparkled with life were now wary and guarded.

'Helen! My, what a big lassie you are now.' Jenny got up, holding her hands out to the little girl, who took a swift step back, her own hands tucked behind her pink silk frock.

'D'you not remember me, Helen?' Jenny asked, dismayed.

'Of course she does,' Lottie said sharply. 'She's just being silly as usual. Shake hands with your Aunt Jenny the way you've been taught,' she ordered her daughter and Helen did as she was told.

'How d'ye do?' she murmured. For a moment her small hand rested submissively in Jenny's, then it slid away. When Alice held out her hand she went over to her at once to lean against her knee.

'She's never seen you looking so grand, Jenny, that's what it is.' There was malice in Lottie's voice.

Jenny ignored her. 'Your hand's cold, pet.'

'So it is.' Alice rubbed the small fingers. 'You should have put a coat on her, Lottie.'

'It's her own fault, she refuses to run about like the other children.' Lottie poured more tea for herself. 'Just stands in a corner like a daftie. She's needing to go to the school – they'll mebbe learn her some sense there. They take the strap to naughty little girls there,' she added, raising her voice.

'Mebbe Helen should have some tea to warm her up,' Jenny said, suppressing her anger, and Lottie shrugged.

'Fetch your mug, then,' she told her daughter. Helen obediently scurried from the room and it was all Jenny could do to blink back tears when she returned clutching a familiar tin mug, the elves and flowers painted on it still visible, though the colours had faded over the years.

'She's still got the mug I painted for her!'

Lottie shrugged. 'She'll not be parted from it. Anyway, it keeps her from breaking my good stuff,' she said carelessly as Alice poured a little tea into the mug then topped it up with milk and stirred in some sugar. 'Don't you go messing up that frock, mind,' she added sharply as Alice proferred the plate of gingerbread. Helen's reaching fingers fell back to her lap, empty, and she sat down on a pouffe near her mother, the mug in her two hands.

Jenny waited until the little girl had finished her tea before handing over the brightly wrapped parcel she had brought. 'This is for you, Helen. It comes from the big shop where I work in Glasgow.'

Shyly, prodded forward by her mother, Helen accepted the parcel with a whispered 'Thank you,' and turned it over, her wide eyes greedily devouring the gay pattern on the wrapping paper.

'Hurry up and open it, then,' Lottie told her daughter impatiently, then snatched the parcel out of Helen's hands. 'Oh, I'll do it – we'll be here all day if we wait for you.'

She ripped off the paper that Jenny had chosen so carefully and withdrew a clockwork bear. 'Very nice, I'm sure,' she said.

Jenny took the bear from her and knelt on the carpet to wind it up. 'He's got his own little key in his back, Helen – see? You turn it like this, then he plays on the drum.'

She set the bear down and they all watched as the arms moved jerkily. Helen gave a giggle of delight, and when the tapping on the drum slowed to a standstill Jenny handed her the bear and showed her how to turn the key. Carefully, she wound the bear up and when it started beating its drum she smiled up at Jenny with genuine pleasure, a smile that died away when Lottie, crossing her legs and swinging one foot idly, remarked, 'We'll need to see if we can get a key to put in your back, won't we, Helen? Mebbe then we could get you to move a bit faster.'

'I'm having a wee party for Shona's first birthday tomorrow,' Jenny said as she and Alice prepared to go. 'I'd like Helen to come.'

The little girl's face lit up. 'Oh yes!' she said, then added, with a swift glance at her mother, 'Yes – please.'

'I'll come round and fetch her at two o'clock,' Alice offered.

'Or you could bring her yourself, Lottie. You'd be welcome,' Jenny lied with a small, polite smile.

'If she's going to be out of the way for the afternoon, I'll make the most of it and go to the shops in Helensburgh,' Lottie said.

'That poor wee soul!' Jenny exploded when the sisters were out in the street again. 'She used to be such a happy bairn!'

Alice's normally cheerful face was troubled. 'I'm quite sure they're not cruel to her, Jen. She's always got pretty clothes on and she seems to be fed well enough. It's just that Lottie has no patience with her.'

'She never did have. Mam's house might not be as smart as Lottie's, or in such a good neighbourhood, but at least Helen had plenty of love in it.'

'Mebbe it'd have been better for the wee soul if Maurice had come home. Though I doubt if he'd've been able to stomach Lottie for long,' Alice said. Then, as they walked over the bridge spanning Ellerslie Water, she cautioned, 'Don't say anything to Mam, Jenny. She frets over Helen enough as it is.'

When Helen arrived at the Gillespie flat the next day she had exchanged the pink silk frock for a pretty handembroidered dress in pale cream muslin with a broad sash and frills round the hem. Lottie had sent a stuffed toy rabbit for Shona.

'She says to tell you,' Alice whispered, wrinkling her nose, 'that it's not much but we can't all buy our toys from a big Glasgow store.' Then, raising her voice again, she said cheerfully, 'Now then, Miss Helen, I'm going to put one of my aprons round you so that you can eat the birthday cake your gran made and the nice jelly Auntie Bella's brought without having to worry about your pretty dress.'

It took a full hour before they could persuade Helen to relax. Comparing her tense little face with Shona's beaming grin, Jenny felt helpless anger against Lottie and Neil. Helen had brought the clockwork bear with her and, throughout the afternoon, she kept a tight hold of it, shaking her head and backing away when Shona, well aware that on that day she was the centre of attention although she was too young to know why, reached out an imperious hand and tried to take it away from her.

Lottie had told Alice that Neil would call after work to take Helen home. When five o'clock came and the town's hooters began to shrill, Helen jumped and her eyes grew moist. Bella, talking cheerfully all the time, washed her face and hands and combed her hair, and when Neil came tramping heavily up the stairs, she was buttoned into her coat and all ready to go home.

It was the first time Jenny had seen Neil since his marriage. Always inclined to plumpness, he had become downright fat, with the slight thickening of advancing years already beginning to overlie his good-looking features. Like Lottie, he was complacent and self-confident and his pale blue eyes roamed over Jenny from her short hair, which had been styled, to her ankles.

'Glasgow suits ye,' he said, then added with a sly grin, 'Or is it bein' fancy free again that's doin' it?'

'I've still got Daniel's ring on my finger,' she retorted tartly, the memory of Neil's clumsy attempt to force himself on her on the night she had ridden the Tank truck flooding back.

He grinned, then looked down at Helen, who stood meekly before him.

'Come on then, home tae yer ma. Here—' he stooped and put a hand on the clockwork bear. 'Give that back.'

Her eyes darkened with alarm as she locked both arms tightly about the bear, pressing her lips together with such determination that they almost disappeared.

'That's Helen's bear,' Jenny interceded swiftly. 'I gave it to her yesterday.'

'Did ye?' Neil's voice was indifferent. 'Come on, then,' he ordered his stepdaughter, who followed him without a backward glance. Her tears had been blinked back fiercely while she was being helped into her coat.

Faith's face was shadowed as she watched them go and Jenny could almost feel her mother's longing, just like her own, to catch Helen up and refuse to let her go back to Lottie. As the door closed she picked Shona up without thinking, her mind on her forlorn little niece. It was only when the baby squeaked a protest that she realised she was clutching her almost as tightly as Helen had clutched the toy bear.

'I think Neil's kind enough to Helen,' Alice said later, when the sisters were in bed. 'It's just that he doesnae know anything about bairns. He'd probably be just the same with his own.'

'For the bairns' sakes,' Jenny said into the darkness, 'I hope he and Lottie never have any.'

28

'Daniel might not even be in Glasgow,' Robert said as the door closed behind his housekeeper.' Have you thought of that?'

'I know.' Jenny poured tea for him, then herself. Shona, sitting on the rug at her mother's feet, stared round Robert's parlour with open curiosity.

'He might have gone to Tyneside. You're surely not going to start looking down there, are you?' Robert accepted his tea and went back to stand by the mantel-shelf. 'Jenny, you've done all you can. That place in the drawing office is still yours, and I'm quite sure this young lady would be better off with you at home instead of coming and going like a visitor.'

Shona began to haul herself to her feet, using her mother's skirt for support, and Jenny put out a hand to stop her. 'Mind the teapot, pet.'

'Here's something for you to play with.' Robert discarded his cup and knelt down beside the little girl, unfastening the silver watch from his waistcoat then holding it against Shona's ear. 'Hear that?' The baby listened, wide-eyed, then reached for the watch and chain.

'Don't let her touch it, Robert, she might break it,' Jenny protested.

He laughed, relinquishing the watch. 'If she manages

to do that it won't have been very good to start with. Anyway, it's only a possession. No, like this,' he explained gravely to Shona, who was frowningly pressing the watch-face against her cheek and wondering why there was no sound from it. 'Against your ear. This is your ear, round the corner.' He tickled the tiny lobe and Shona giggled, tucking her head against her shoulder.

'I never realised you were so good with children,' Jenny said, surprised.

'I might be a hard taskmaster at the yard, but I'm not an ogre. I like bairns well enough.'

'You'd make a fine father.'

'I'd like that,' he said, looking up at her. His face was on a level with Jenny's and, as his eyes caught and held hers she felt herself flush.

'Get up before you ruin your nice clothes,' she scolded him, busying herself with Shona, who was trying to eat the watch.

He did as he was told, brushing the knees of his grey trousers. 'As I was saying, the place in the drawing office is still yours.'

'It's kind of you, but I must go back to Glasgow. I've got work to do there and, now that the lighter nights are in, I can spend more time looking for Daniel.'

Robert frowned. 'Does he still matter so much to you, Jen?'

She was saved from having to answer when Shona, deprived of the watch, began to protest noisily.

'She's getting tired, we'll have to go home,' Jenny said hastily.

'When are you going to let me drive you to wherever it is, and meet your family?' Matthew Neilson wanted to know when Jenny returned to work.

'I'm not.' Eliza and Kate and Evie were the only people in the store who knew Jenny's story, and she had made them promise that they wouldn't say a word to anyone, particularly Matthew, about Ellerslie or Daniel or her reason for being in Glasgow.

'Does that mean that I'm not good enough for them?'

'It's got nothing to do with that. I just like to keep my private life and my working life separate.'

'But I want to know you better.'

'I don't see why.'

'Don't you?' They were alone in the workshop, and he put a hand over hers as she reached out to pick up a fresh brush. 'I like you, Jenny Young. I like you very much. I want to meet your family and your friends, and see the place where you grew up. I want to show you off to my friends and take you to see my home.'

'Matthew— ' Gently, she removed her hand from beneath his and picked up the brush. 'I've got work to do, and so have you.'

He sighed, then straightened up. 'You're a hard woman, d'you know that?'

'I'm a working woman.'

'Come out with me tonight.'

'I can't, Matthew.'

'We'll go to a music-hall and join in the songs,' he murmured, leaning over her as she worked at the table. 'We'll laugh at the comedy acts and ooh at the dancing ladies kicking their legs, then we'll go somewhere pleasant for supper and I'll get you home at a respectable time. What do you say?'

Jenny put her brush aside. On the previous evening she had grown more and more depressed with each turn of the wheels as the train carried her away from Ellerslie, and she had scarcely slept all night. She knew that she would more than likely sit in her room that evening thinking about Shona and Helen and home instead of forcing herself out to look for Daniel.

'Yes?' Matthew coaxed, sensing surrender, and she looked up at him and smiled faintly. At times she found his self-assurance and his conviction that life held nothing but comfort and enjoyment quite insufferable but, on the other hand, he was kind, and good company.

'Do we visit the music-hall tonight, or do I go and toss myself off Kelvin Bridge with a brick in my pocket and a note saying that Mrs Young drove me to it?'

'It would take more than me to send you off Kelvin Bridge!' Jenny laughed.

'It would be quicker than dying of boredom, which is what I'll catch if I don't have anywhere to go. Yes or no – and if it's yes, I promise you I'll leave you in peace for the rest of the day.'

'In that case,' she said, smiling at him, 'It's yes.'

When he had gone back to his office and she was alone again she wondered if she had done the right thing in giving in to him. Clearly, he was reading more than he should into their friendship, and perhaps she should be warding him off rather than agreeing to go out with him. But at that moment, missing Ellerslie and Shona, worrying about Daniel and now Helen, she had enough to do without fretting over Matthew as well.

After three months Jenny felt that she had covered most of the area round the river without even a hint of success.

'I keep thinking that mebbe Daniel's turning the corner into a street just as I'm turning the far corner out of it, or that he left a shop five minutes before I went into it,' she told Kate and her mother. 'I'm losing hope.'

Mrs Ballantyne reached across the kitchen table and put a warm work-roughened hand over hers. 'Mebbe it's time tae think o' yer bairn now, hen,' she said gently. 'Ye've done yer best by yer man, an' nob'dy can say otherwise. Ye've got yer future tae consider.'

'Mebbe you're right,' Jenny agreed. Without letting Matthew know what she was doing she began to organise the china-painting department so that it could go on without her. The work was flowing in and she suggested to him that it was time they brought in another worker – someone with experience.

'Evie's talented and she's going to be very good for the department, but she still has to take time over her work. It should be easy enough to find someone like me.'

'I don't agree at all about that,' Matthew told her, his voice and his expression serious for once. 'As far as I'm concerned you're a very special lady, Jenny Young.'

She felt colour flooding into her face, and turned away from him, fidgeting with her brushes. 'I'm talking about someone who's done china-painting at home for some time and knows what she's about.'

Miss Beckett, a former schoolteacher who had had to give up work to nurse ageing parents through their final illnesses and was now alone in the world, proved to be just the right person. She was a talented painter with a flair for colour and an eye for design and, within two weeks of her arrival, Jenny was able to leave her to get on with her work unsupervised, confident that the finished produce would be of a high standard.

'I've had an idea,' Matthew said one evening when they were out together in his new car, a racy American sports car known affectionately as 'The Wasp' because its bodywork was bright yellow picked out in black and it was useful for buzzing about in. 'My sister's brat's heading for his first birthday and, of course, Uncle Matt's expected to come up with a decent present. D'you think you could paint a set of nursery dishes for him?'

'Of course.' They were driving near the river and Jenny, as usual, was watching the passers-by, just in case. She dragged her attention away from the pavements to glance at him. 'What sort of design would you like?'

He swung the car round a corner and blared the horn at a group of youngsters playing football in the centre of the street. They scattered, grinning and cheering, some whistling shrilly, fingers in their mouths, as the car swept past them.

Matthew gave the lads a lordly wave and parped the horn again. 'Oh, whatever you think the kiddy would like. Something with lots of colour – I'll leave it to you.' He had to raise his voice above the noise of the wind rushing past them as he put his foot down on the accelerator. They had reached a wider road and the tenements were being left behind.

'When do you want it for?'

'The beginning of July – can't remember the exact date,' said the fond uncle. 'My mama's going to visit them for the actual birthday and she can take my gift with her. My sister's coming back to Glasgow with her for a couple of weeks later in the month.' He groaned loudly, then said, 'If I know my mama, she'll want another celebration here for the kid. The house'll be full of brats and I'll probably be expected to be there playing the jolly uncle. And I expect it'll mean a second present – I shall raid the toy department for that.'

The wind had strengthened now that there were fewer high buildings to hold it back. It caught at Jenny's hair and she was glad that she had kept to the short style she had decided on so suddenly several years ago. It was becoming fashionable now and more and more young women were having their hair bobbed.

'You could have the party in the toy department itself instead of the house.' The suggestion was put idly, but Matthew's reaction was instant, and enthusiastic.

'By Jove, Jenny, that's a terrific idea! We could hold it on a Tuesday afternoon when the store's shut. Pack everything away except some toys for the kiddies to keep. Some of the staff might be willing to come in and help get the place ready, and we could get people in to see to the food.'

'You'd have to offer the staff extra payment for giving up their free time.'

Matthew grinned. 'The old man won't like it, but Mother'll make him toe the line.'

A man was tramping along the pavement ahead of them, thin-backed, shabbily dressed, his shoulders rounded against the wind. Jenny felt her throat tighten; she twisted round as they drew level then passed him, straining to see the face beneath the peaked cap.

'Someone you know?' Matthew yelled cheerfully.

'No.' She turned to look through the windscreen again, the familiar dull ache of disappointment and anti-climax nagging behind her breastbone. 'Nobody I know . . .'

Jenny's casual suggestion about the party was taken up enthusiastically by Mrs Neilson when Matthew passed it on. On the day of the birthday party staff members who had agreed to stay behind flocked to the toy department as soon as the glass double doors below closed behind the last customer.

Everything was packed away except a selection of less expensive toys so that each small guest could be given something to take home at the end of the party and, upstairs in the tearoom, the hired caterers started laying out sandwiches and cakes, jellies and trifles.

'It's like watching Santa Claus's little gnomes at work.' Matthew surveyed the army of workers, some packing toys and dismantling display stands and spiriting them out of sight, others setting out small gilt chairs for the children and larger chairs round the sides of the department for nannies and nursemaids.

A gramophone was brought in, together with a pile of records. Ladders appeared and, in no time, the large room became bright with paper streamers suspended from corner to corner across the ceiling and paper bells and balls hanging from the chandeliers. Kate and Evie Ballantyne, pink with excitement, were among those who had offered to help, though Miss Beckett, announcing that she was altogether too elderly for such goings on, had departed homewards. Jenny would have preferred to spend the afternoon doing the rounds of the shipyards, asking the gatemen if they knew anything of Daniel, but Matthew had insisted on her being in the store. 'It was your idea,' he told her, 'and you're going to be there. Besides, I'll finally get the chance to introduce you to my mother.'

'Who's that?' she asked now as one of the lift doors rattled back and a tired, elderly man shuffled out as though his feet hurt him. He was carrying a large carpet bag and the woman who followed him from the lift had a shabby, bulging suitcase. Matthew's secretary, who had undertaken to organise the party, scurried over to the new arrivals and led them into a sideroom.

'It must be the magician.' Matthew shook his head.

'The brat's only a year old. He can't walk or talk yet – how's he going to appreciate a magician?'

'The other children will.' Jenny had been told that there would be about thirty small guests up to four or five years old. Looking at the bustle before her she wondered at people who thought nothing of spending at least a year's wages for the average shipyard worker on celebrating the birthday of one little boy . . .

As the lifts brought the first guests up with their nursemaids Jenny slipped through the discreet baize door and down the plain narrow staircase to her workroom, where she settle down at the table. The party preparations for Matthew's nephew had brought back memories of Shona's birthday tea; the wonder on her baby's small face at first sight of the birthday cake Bella had made for her: the way Helen had clutched the clockwork bear throughout the afternoon, and cried when it was time to go home. Remembering that day, Jenny had no wish to be part of the party for the pampered, wealthy children upstairs.

She had almost completed an elaborately decorated teapot for a customer; she put it on a high stool and studied it from all angles for some time, then slipped a smock over her blue-and-white striped blouse and blue skirt, and started work, her sudden bout of homesickness eased and comforted by the work.

A full hour passed before the door opened and Matthew said, 'There you are! I thought you'd taken fright and run away. Come on, my dear mama and my sister want to meet you.'

'Can't you tell them I've gone home?'

'No, I can't. Come on,' he said insistently.

Reluctantly, Jenny put the teapot aside and unfastened her smock, hanging it on the row of pegs by the door then pausing to take a quick look in the mirror.

'You look fine.' Matthew's hands fell gently on to her shoulders and he turned her round to face him. 'I tell a lie – you look lovely,' he said, then drew her into his arms and kissed her. Taken by surprise she yielded for a moment, lifting her arms to hold him, letting her mouth soften and part beneath the gentle pressure of his lips. It had been a long time since a man had kissed her. Too long. But as his own arms tightened about her and the kiss began to intensify she came to her senses and pushed him away.

'Matthew! What d'you think you're doing?

'Kissing you.' He tried to draw her back into his embrace, but this time she resisted, pulling back and almost stumbling against the corner of one of the work tables.

'You've no right— ' she said feebly.

He raised his brows, amusement mingling with the tenderness in his eyes. 'You seemed to be enjoying it as much as I was.'

'I – I thought you wanted me to meet your family.'

'Oh – we've got five minutes before we go up,' he said, advancing on her. 'Maybe even ten.'

'For goodness' sake, Matthew— ' She pushed him away again, confused and alarmed by her own response earlier. 'We're in your own father's store!'

'If that's all that's fretting you we can easily arrange to go some where less – businesslike,' he teased, but she was already at the door, turning the handle, stepping out into the china gallery, which looked more like a large cluttered room than a store department now that the chandeliers had been switched off and the place was only lit by the afternoon light from the large windows. She made for the door leading to the back stairs but

Matthew got to it first, brushing past her and holding the door open for her.

'Come out for a drive tonight,' he said as she passed him.

Jenny started up the stairs. 'I've got things to do tonight.'

He arrived on the toy department landing a fraction of a second behind her, catching at her hand as she reached for the handle of the door. 'Please, Jenny. I want to talk to you.' His voice had lost its teasing note now and his eyes were serious when she looked up at him. She felt shaky, and unsure of herself.

'I'm a married woman, Matthew, it's not seemly for us to— '

'A married woman lives at home with her husband,' he said sharply. 'Where is *your* husband? Why isn't he looking after you? It's time I knew more, Jenny.'

'There's no reason for you to know anything,' she protested defensively.

'Oh yes there is, my dear,' he said, with the slightest catch in his voice. For a moment she thought that he was going to kiss her again and a tingle ran, unbidden, through her body. She put her hands behind her back as though to prevent them from betraying her and reaching for him. But Matthew stepped back and turned towards the door.

'Oh yes there is,' he said again, under his breath, and opened the door. She walked past him into a clamour of noise, music blaring from the gramophone mingling with squeals of excitement from the children who sat in two circles on the floor. A large parcel was being passed quickly round each circle.

'Wait here,' Matthew said, his lips brushing the lobe of her ear as he spoke, then he made off, his tall figure, elegant in a well-cut blue suit, skirting one of the circles and blending into a group of women, some in nannies' uniforms, gathered round a long table set with refreshments.

The small guests were all beautifully dressed, well-fed, confident, so unlike the children Jenny had been used to all her life, many of whom were undernourished and grimy, some with legs bowed by rickets and heads shaved because of ringworm or lice. She wouldn't have wished any of that on the children here, but the contrast was painful . . .

The music suddenly stopped and a plump toddler seated near her gaped in dismay at the parcel in his hands then tried to push it at the girl beside him. She resisted fiercely and, as Jenny took an involuntary step towards them, a grey-clad woman swooped.

'Now then, Master Kenneth, out you come like a good little sportsman.'

'Nooooo!' screamed Master Kenneth, kicking fat little legs. The music started up again and the game went on as the nurse gathered her charge up and carried him off, kicking and screaming, to the other end of the room.

Smiling, Jenny turned away and was suddenly and unexpectedly transported back in time to Dalkieth's Experimental Tank section and the first peacetime launch and the line of tracers waiting at the foot of the wooden stairs to be presented to the official guests. On that day Fiona Dalkieth had worn mourning black. Today, walking with Matthew towards Jenny, she wore a leaf-green silky dress with long loose sleeves and a skirt that drifted in layers about her slim calves. A broad, dark green girdle was fastened about her hips by a glittering clasp and a boa of pale brown feathers was draped casually over her shoulders.

Young Mrs Dalkieth's soft fair hair was now cut fashionably short, and the discontented look had left her lovely face, replaced by self-satisfaction and determination. For the first time, seeing her close to Matthew, Jenny recognised the strong family likeness between brother and sister.

One thing hadn't changed – Fiona Dalkieth was as indifferent to Jenny now as she had been at their first meeting. Then, as now, Jenny was merely an employee and of no importance. Matthew was angered by his sister's attitude; Jenny could tell it by the tightening of his jawline, the sharpening of his voice as he said, 'It was Jenny who painted the nursery china I gave to young William.'

'Indeed?' Fiona murmured. It was left to Mrs Neilson, plump and fair and far more friendly than her daughter, to say how sweet the china was and how pleased William would be with it when he was old enough to appreciate it.

Matthew, who had moved away from his sister and mother to stand by Jenny, slid a hand beneath her elbow. 'Come and have a cup of tea with us,' he said firmly. She would have preferred to return to her workroom but, when she started to say so, he ignored the words, steering her towards the long table with Mrs Neilson trotting after them. Fiona drifted off to where a nursemaid stood holding her son.

Jenny, teacup in hand, answering Mrs Neilson's questions about where she had learned to paint china, noticed the way Fiona's face softened as she took the child from his nurse and kissed his brown hair. She settled the baby on one hip and picked up a wafer biscuit with her free hand, offering it to her son, who grabbed at it.

'He'll ruin his suit,' her mother pointed out, and Fiona shrugged.

'He's got plenty of clothes.'

The game of pass-the-parcel had ended and the other children were being shepherded to the opposite end of the room, where the little gilt chairs waited in rows before a small stage.

'Do you and your husband belong to Glasgow, Mrs Young?' Mrs Neilson asked.

'I've not been able to find that out,' Matthew's voice was lightly mocking. 'Jenny guards her privacy jealously – don't you, Jenny?'

His mother's eyes sharpened with curiosity. 'Don't be silly, dear, I'm sure Mrs Young has nothing to hide – have you, my dear?'

There was a burst of ragged applause as the magician stepped on to the stage, resplendent in an evening suit, crimson-lined cloak, and shiny top hat. He looked quite unlike the tired, shabby man Jenny had seen earlier.

'You were saying, Mrs Young—?' Matthew's mother said, raising her voice slightly above the noise.

'We – I came to Glasgow this year.'

'Oh? Where did you live before then?'

One of the lift gates rattled open and Fiona squealed as little William Dalkieth, startled, dropped his sticky, half-eaten biscuit on to the bodice of her smart dress. His head, capped with soft brown curly hair, swung sharply towards the noise in a movement that seemed to Jenny to be oddly familiar.

'Look what he's done!' Fiona wailed, holding the baby at arms' length and staring down at the wet smear on her dress. 'Take him, someone!'

Automatically, Jenny put her cup down and lifted the baby into her own arms. Fiona snatched the folded

405

handkerchief from her brother's breast pocket and began to dab at her dress then stopped, staring at the two men advancing across the carpet from the lift, one in the Neilson uniform, the other in a dark lounge suit. Following her gaze, Jenny saw Robert Archer striding across the carpeting so quickly that the doorman accompanying him had to run to keep up with him.

'This gentleman insisted on being brought up to see you, Mrs Young,' the man said breathlessly when they arrived within earshot. 'I told him that— '

'Robert?' Fiona stepped in front of him, putting a hand on his arm. 'What on earth are you doing here?'

His dark head snapped round in a swift, surprised movement. It was the second time within a minute that Jenny had seen that distinctive turn of the head.

'Fiona?' Robert said, puzzled, briefly diverted, then looked back at Jenny, continuing unchecked towards her, his momentum brushing Fiona's hand from his arm. 'I've come to take you home, Jenny,' he said.

There was a burst of clapping and cheering from the other end of the room and the baby in Jenny's arms joggled up and down, his round head – the head, she now realised, that had just the same way of turning in surprise as Robert's – bumping against her chin. The magician, who had produced a large bunch of paper flowers from thin air, bowed to his audience, his crimson-lined cloak swirling wide.

'I've come to take you home, Jenny,' Robert repeated. 'It's Daniel – he's come back to Ellerslie.'

29

The tenement Daniel was staying in was near the quarry. It was old and damp and smelled of neglect and cats and too many years of human habitation. In some places the stone stairs were almost worn down to the level of the tread below and Jenny had to ascend cautiously through the semi-gloom, putting a hand from time to time on the slimy, flaking walls for balance. She had refused to allow Robert or Alice to accompany her. This was a meeting she knew she had to face on her own.

She reached the landing, hesitated, then knocked on the centre door. Daniel himself opened it. For a long moment husband and wife looked at each other, then he said, without surprise, 'You'd best come in.'

The door opened into a single room, much the same as the room Bella and Patrick lived in. There was scarcely any furniture – a table, a shabby sideboard, and a single upright wooden chair. Daniel drew it forward for Jenny.

'It's no' much,' he said, indicating his surroundings. 'But – it'll do for the short while I'm here.'

He was clean and neat, as always, but his face was positively gaunt and, as he moved restlessly to the small window, she saw that his dark hair was streaked with grey.

'Patrick told me you were in Glasgow, looking for me. There was no need.'

'I had to make sure you were all right.' Then, when he said nothing, she added, 'Shona's well. Bella's been caring for her. Patrick mebbe told you that?'

'Aye.' He had gone to the tenement where they had lived and, finding strangers in his former home, had knocked at the door on the opposite side of the close and had spoken briefly to Patrick. Jenny knew from what Bella had told her that he *had* been in Glasgow, working in one of the smaller yards, until suddenly deciding to return to Ellerslie.

'I'd have brought the wee one with me today, but I thought it might be best to wait until the next time.'

He shook his head. 'I'm not staying in Ellerslie. I'm moving on.'

'Where?' She was confused.

He ignored her. 'I had tae come back tae see— ' He swallowed hard, ' — tae see the lad's grave. But I cannae stay.'

'But what about me and Shona?' she asked, and he looked at her as though she was a stranger.

'We should never have got wed, you and me,' he said coldly. 'Me and Walter should have stayed as we were. I thought it was my duty tae give him a mother, but I was wrong.'

She stared at him, shocked, then asked quietly, 'Is that the only reason you wanted me to marry you, Daniel? To be a mother to your son?'

He glanced away, refusing to meet her eyes. 'We should never have got wed,' he said again. 'We were all right until you came intae the house an' started tae encourage him tae rebel against me.'

Jenny's nails dug into her palms. The man's injustice and self-centredness suddenly infuriated her. 'Don't try to blame me for what happened to Walter,' she began, then stopped. There was no sense now in quarrelling over the past, and it was clear that Daniel had turned his own feelings of guilt around in an attempt to clear himself of blame over his son's death.

'But we did get wed,' she said instead, 'and Shona's the result. What's to happen to her?'

He shrugged, an impatient twitch of the shoulders. 'She's your bairn. I only wanted Walter.' His voice broke on the name, and when Jenny, suddenly full of pity, tried to put a hand on his arm, he turned away from her, dragging the door open with one of the abrupt, jerky movements she remembered so well. 'Ye'd best go.'

She made one last attempt. 'I'll come back tomorrow and we can talk about— '

He looked at her as though they were strangers. 'We've got nothin' tae talk about,' he said, and she knew that he meant it, and that her marriage was over, once and for all.

At the end of the street she turned the corner, walking fast, head down to hide her tears from passers-by, and walked into a man standing there. As she rebounded he caught at her arms to steady her and she stared up at him through a mist, then said on a half-laugh, half-sob, 'You keep turning up at the most unexpected times, Robert Archer!'

'I followed you,' he admitted, 'and waited just in case.'

'In case of what?'

He shrugged impatiently. 'Are you all right?'

409

'Why wouldn't I be?'

'Oh, no reason,' said Robert. He brought a neatly folded white handkerchief from his pocket and lifted her chin with his free hand so that he could dab at her eyes. 'What did he say?' he asked, his tone softer.

She took the handkerchief from him. 'I can manage,' she said sharply and began to walk away. He caught up and fell into step beside her.

'What did he say, Jenny?'

'He's going off again, on his own. He doesn't want me, or Shona. She's his child, and he doesn't even care about what happens to her. I should never have married him, Robert!' she said on a sudden wave of anguish, and he put a comforting arm about her shoulders.

'We all do things we shouldn't. It's just the way folk are, though knowing that doesn't make it any easier,' he said. They walked on together in silence for a moment before he asked, 'So what are you going to do?'

'I don't know,' said Jenny. 'I just don't know.'

'Why didn't you tell me?' Matthew asked two days later, hurt in his voice. 'I'd have helped you to find this husband of yours if you'd only had enough trust in me to tell me the truth.'

Jenny had dreaded this meeting, but she had had to return to Glasgow to talk to him face to face. 'It was my business, I had to see to it alone.' They were in his office, untouched cups of tea cooling on the desk between them.

'What sort of man would go off and leave his wife to fend for herself the way he did?' he asked angrily. 'And how can you think that you owe him any duty after that?'

'I told you – he didn't know what he was doing after his son died. He was out of his mind with grief.'

'And now you're going back to Ellerslie, back to him.'

It would have been easier to let him think that, but he deserved the truth. 'No, I'm not going back to him. Daniel's left the town. He wants to be on his own from now on.'

Hope flared in Matthew's eyes. 'That means that you can stay here, in Glasgow, in the store— '

She shook her head. 'I only came to Glasgow to look for Daniel. My family are in Ellerslie, and my daughter. It's where I belong, Matthew.'

'And how are you going to support yourself?' he demanded. 'You've got a job right here; you can bring the child to Glasgow.'

'She's best where there are folk she knows. And so am I,' Jenny said, getting to her feet. 'I've had a word with Miss Beckett – she can run the workroom just as well as I did, and Evie's a good worker. They can manage fine without me.'

'And what about me?' He got to his feet and came round the desk to her. 'What about me?' he asked again. 'Jenny, I love you, and you love me, I know you do.'

'I'm not sure if I know what love is, Matthew.'

'I'll teach you,' he offered eagerly. 'I promise you that I'll wait until you're sure, then we can be married, once you're free.'

'I don't know if I'll ever want to marry anyone again.' Jenny felt very tired, and unsure of her own feelings. 'All I know at the moment is that I need to go back to Ellerslie, back to Shona.'

'And what about me? I don't want to lose you.'

411

'You'll manage fine, Matthew,' she said gently. 'We all have to manage as best we can.'

A week later she left Glasgow for the last time and returned to Ellerslie. Sitting in the train, her gloved fingers twisted together in her lap, she stared into the future, with little idea of what it would hold for her. She had been asked to continue doing some work from home for the store, and she had agreed, for she was going to need all the money she could earn. She was going to live for the time being with her parents and take up Robert's offer of work in the yard's drawing office, but she must find a flat for herself and Shona as soon as possible. She had no intention of settling back into her parents' home, becoming a daughter again instead of a mother and an independent woman.

'Are you all right, my dear?' the elderly woman on the other side of the carriage asked, and Jenny suddenly realised that she had raised a hand to her forehead in an attempt to ease the beginnings of a headache.

She summoned up a smile, assured the woman that she was quite well, and stared out of the window to avoid further conversation.

Robert met her at the station and this time he told the cab driver to take them both right to her parents' closemouth. Ignoring the stares of the children playing in the gutters and the women loitering in gossiping groups he assisted her from the cab and carried her case into the close.

'My father might be home— ' she warned.

'To hell with your father!' Robert tossed the words over his shoulder as he mounted the stairs ahead of her. 'He'll have to get used to seeing me around – and so will everyone else,' he added, raising his voice as the door opposite the Gillespies' opened a crack. It closed at once, on an offended sniff.

A mixture of expressions flitted across Faith's face when she opened the door to them. 'Teeze is in,' she faltered, then fell back as Robert stepped into the hall.

'Good,' he said calmly. 'I'll have a word with him before I go.'

Teeze, reading his newspaper in his favourite chair, glanced up, his face stiffening when Robert appeared in the doorway.

'I told you no' tae come here again!' He tossed the paper aside and began to struggle to his feet.

'Teeze— '

'Don't fret yourself, Mrs Gillespie.' Robert put Jenny's case down and faced the older man. 'It's time you faced facts, Teeze Gillespie. Whether you like it or not I'm here, and I'm here to stay. Jenny's forgiven me for the wrong I did her all those years ago, and it's time you forgave me too. As to Maurice, I'm sorry he's dead, but I'm not going to go on apologising to you just because I'm still alive.'

He held a hand out but Teeze struck it aside.

'I'll not take the hand o' a traitor tae his own sort,' he roared. His other fist, bunched and knobbly with age, but still strong, came up fast and sailed past Robert's ear as he stepped aside. Before Teeze could recover his balance his outflung arm was twisted behind him, and he was spun round.

'Call me a traitor again, Teeze, and I'll ram your teeth down your throat,' said Robert as he forced the older man towards the sink. 'I've worked bloody hard for what I've got. I've taken that shipyard out of the gutter where George Dalkieth put it and made it whole again and by God, I'll get the respect I'm due from now on!'

'Robert!' Jenny dragged at his arm. 'He's an old man!'

'Who are you callin' old?' Teeze yelled as he was forced down over the sink.

'Mind your own business, Jen,' Robert grunted, pressing down hard on the back of Teeze's grizzled head with his free hand. 'This is between your father and me.' Teeze, bellowing like a bull, tried to kick back and only succeeded in losing his balance. Robert's fingers curled into Teeze's hair and prevented his face from smashing into the sink, while with his elbow he managed to jerk the brass tap on. Cold water jetted out, hit the back of Teeze's head, and sprayed into the room, soaking Robert and Jenny and Faith, on either side of him now, trying to break his grip.

The older man's roar turned into a gurgle. 'Ye'll drown him!' Faith screamed, beating at Robert's shoulder with frenzied fists.

'It'll take more than a wee bit water to drown this old devil,' he told her grimly, and held his victim down for a further moment before hauling him upright and releasing him. Teeze clutched at the edge of the sink, water and mucus spraying from his mouth and nose as he wheezed and choked and blew.

'Now then,' said Robert, shaking his own head so that drops flew from his hair, 'If it's further humiliation you want we'll go downstairs and I'll deal it out to you in front of the whole street. But speaking for myself I'd as soon shake you by the hand then buy you a pint.'

Teeze, still unsteady on his feet, glowered at the younger man, clearly considering another lunge at him.

'For pity's sake, don't be such a stubborn old fool!' Faith snapped at him with a vigour unusual for her. 'D'ye want him tae drown you altogether? The matter's settled, so away and have a pint and stop your nonsense!'

Teeze, accepting the wisdom of her advice, gave a mighty sneeze and dragged his arm across his face, then pushed wet grey hair out of his eyes. 'Ye'll buy me a whisky,' he growled.

'A whisky, then,' said Robert, and walked out of the kitchen. Teeze, pawing Faith aside when she tried to mop with a towel at his wet shirt, took his jacket from behind the door and followed the office manager. Alone, Jenny and her mother looked at each other.

'What would ye dae with them?' Faith finally asked helplessly, and for the first time in a week Jenny felt a smile pull the corners of her mouth up.

'Nothing,' she said. 'Nothing at all. Let them sort it out over a drink, Mam.'

As she fetched a cloth and got down on her knees to mop at the puddles on the linoleum her thoughts moved from Robert to the moment at the birthday party in the store when little William Dalkieth had reminded her so sharply of him.

As office manager Robert would often meet Fiona socially. He was an attractive man and she was a beautiful young woman. And like everyone else in Ellerslie Jenny knew of the rumours that George Dalkieth had been unable to father children on his first wife.

If her suspicions were correct and Robert had been Fiona Dalkieth's lover, how did matters stand between them now? Rinsing the cloth at the sink, she told herself that whatever had happened between Robert and Fiona Dalkieth, and whatever might happen in the future, was none of her business.

Shona was almost ready for bed when Jenny went into her sister's flat. She was newly washed and in a clean gown, and her blue eyes, almost as dark as her father's, were heavy-lidded with sleepiness. From her seat on Patrick's knee she looked up at her mother with wonder at first, a slight frown between her brows. When Jenny spoke to her the frown cleared and she smiled, showing two tiny white teeth. Jenny stooped to take her and Patrick let the small warm body go with some reluctance then picked up a half-carved piece of wood. Bella took his knife from a drawer and carefully laid some sheets of newspaper about his chair to catch the shavings. She had put on weight and her shoulders had straightened; her movements, as she knelt at Patrick's feet, smoothing the newspaper out, were deft and controlled instead of jerky and nervous. The little room was spotlessly clean and cosy, with an air of serenity about it, and Jenny suddenly felt uncomfortable.

'Will you not be sorry to leave Glasgow, now that you've made a place for yourself there?' Patrick wanted to know, his eyes intent on his work. Tiny pale shavings dropped from beneath the knife-blade, reminding Jenny of the pale gold wax shavings that had lain thickly on the floor of the Experimental Tank section beneath the tables that held the models.

'Glasgow's not my home.' Once she had wanted so badly to get away from Ellerslie, but now she knew that it was where she belonged – for the moment at least.

Shona yawned and her eyelids drooped. Bella immediately held out her arms. 'I'll put her down.'

'I'll do it. No sense in disturbing her more than we have to.'

Bella lifted back the crib blankets. 'She gives us a goodnight kiss,' she explained as Shona wriggled and girned when Jenny began to lower her into the crib. 'First Pat, then me.'

416

Jenny carried her daughter over to Patrick and watched as he was kissed soundly on the cheek.

' 'Night, 'night, pet,' he said gruffly. The ritual was repeated with Bella, who then said encouragingly, 'A wee kiss for yer mammy now, hen.'

Shona's mouth, butterfly soft, brushed Jenny's cheek, then she allowed herself to be tucked into the crib.

'Where'll you live, Jen?' Bella wanted to know when the clothes-horse, draped with an old bit of sheeting to shut out as much light as possible, had been angled beside the crib. She drew the curtain across the single window and lit a taper at the range then reached up to light the two gas mantels. They came to life with a soft popping sound, the flames moving quickly from blue to steady gold. 'How'll you support yourself?'

'I'm going to work in Dalkieth's drawing office, and the store where I worked in Glasgow's offered to sell any china I can paint for them in my spare time. I'll stay with Mam and Dad for now, till I find somewhere to rent for me and Shona.'

'Did Mam tell you that Lottie and Neil are going to Edinburgh for a week soon? Mam's going to look after Helen while they're away. You'd best leave Shona with us until after that.' Bella's fingers pleated the folds of her skirt. 'It'll be too much of a crowd in the one house and you don't want to move Shona round too much.'

'You've had her for long enough, Bella – it's time I took over.'

'Bella's right,' Patrick said unexpectedly, his eyes on his work, his hands sure and quick. Beneath his fingers a dog was emerging from the block of wood, one paw delicately lifted, head turned, ears sharp, as though its nocturnal prowl had been alerted by an unexpected sound. It looked for all the world as though the animal

417

had been imprisoned in the block and Patrick was freeing it. 'No sense in unsettling the bairn when she's contented with us.'

Walking back to her parents' flat along the darkening street later, hands pushed deep into her pockets, Jenny thought of how well Shona got on with her aunt and uncle. When the time came for her to take Shona back it would hurt Bella. The prospect nagged at Jenny. Her sister had suffered enough, and Jenny didn't want to inflict more pain on her. But on the other hand, Shona was all that she had left of her marriage, and she ached to be reunited with her own child.

As she walked through the close and began to ascend the stairs she wondered if she was being selfish in wanting Shona back. Should she put Bella's happiness before her own, and accept the fact that the little girl was contented where she was?

Then her thoughts flew to the years ahead, to Shona growing up, discovering that her father had deserted her without a backward glance, and her own mother had handed her over to someone else to care for. And as she stepped into her parents' home she knew that she could never let that happen. Shona's place was with her, in a home of their own, a haven where they could shut out the rest of the world and make their own happiness.

30

George Dalkieth's initial triumph at fathering a healthy son and heir had been quickly soured by what he saw as his mother's betrayal – her sudden and inexplicable tendency to rely more and more on Robert Archer's advice and to vote in his favour at the Board meetings.

'The man's a damned upstart and yet you listen to his every word and vote for him over me,' he complained bitterly again and again.

'Mr Archer knows a great deal about shipbuilding and I've come to realise that what he says makes sense,' Isobel retorted crisply, then added, her voice noticeably chilling, 'As for those precious friends of yours, the English yards they invested in are in trouble. They're selling the machinery off and putting men out of work. That's not what I want for Dalkieth's.'

'But we'd not be out of pocket if it happened here,' her son protested mulishly. 'The machinery and the ground are worth a fair amount. If the yard did have to be sold off we could live comfortably on the proceeds.'

'That,' said Isobel, disgusted, 'is not what your father and grandfather – and your great-grandfather, too – intended. Don't be so selfish, George. You've got a son to think of now. You want him to inherit the yard, don't you?'

George wasn't so sure. Some of his new-found friends

had introduced him to the delights of shooting parties and fishing parties in the North of England and the Scottish Highlands. He had had a taste of the life that the landed gentry led, and he liked it. If he had money he could buy himself a small estate, with a house grander than Dalkieth House as well as fishing and shooting rights. He could invite his friends to stay and Fiona would make an ideal hostess. Such a life would be much more convivial than the existence he led now, living under his mother's roof, being expected to make the shipyard the centre of his world, and continually having to put up with Robert Archer's cool manner and insufferable self-importance.

He put this proposition to Fiona but, to his astonishment, she didn't agree with him at all. Wrapped up in caring for her beloved son, basking in her new-found and very welcome rapport with her mother-in-law, pampered by servants and soothed by her comfortable life in Dalkieth House, Fiona was happy at last. She had no desire to give everything up in order to become a hostess to George's boring hunting, shooting and fishing friends.

Another problem had arisen for Fiona, a problem that she couldn't discuss with her mother-in-law. Rampaging across the moors and splashing into rivers, killing defenceless creatures, or at least trying to kill them with gun and fishing-rod, seemed to go straight to George's loins. He came back from his hunting forays with renewed desire for his wife's company, and Fiona's hopes that he might lose interest in her once she had presented him with an heir had come to nothing.

It would have helped, she thought wistfully, if he had found some female companionship on his longer trips and at least learned some of the niceties of lovemaking but, as she already knew from bitter experience, the women who took part in these country house parties tended to be large and hearty, with few feminine subtleties.

Often, lying in George's arms, Fiona recalled Robert Archer and the passion she had known with him. Once or twice she even considered approaching Robert again, but she knew that that was impossible. Believing that she had no further need of him she had ended their affair in a tactless and humiliating manner – and Robert wasn't the sort of man who would easily forgive and forget. She couldn't even tell him the truth about William, for she had made a solemn promise to Isobel.

It was a relief to Fiona when George came home from one of his trips wheezing and sneezing and had to take to his own bedroom with a chill, leaving his wife in peace. She showed her gratitude by pampering him, feeding him calves' foot jelly and insisting on his staying in bed until the chill was completely cured. As he slumped against a mound of pillows and announced his intention of being up and about in time for the following week's launch Fiona eyed him critically. He had put on weight since their marriage, mainly by dint of self-indulgence and comfortable living, and not even his half-hearted scrambling over heather moors had done much to trim him down.

'We'll see what the doctor says, dear,' she told him firmly.

'Nonsense! My own wife has been invited to launch this vessel and I shall be there to support her.' George took her hand, which almost disappeared into his beefy palm and Fiona patted his cheek with her free hand in a maternal way.

'We'll see,' she said lightly, and began to free herself

421

from his hot, moist grip. He tugged unexpectedly, and Fiona, taken unawares, lost her balance and fell on to the bed, against him.

'George!'

'Dammit, Fiona,' said George Dalkieth, his mouth soft and rubbery against her cheek, his free arm tightening about her waist, 'it's damned lonely in this bed all by myself.'

The drawing office was a large, airy room with windows along three of the four walls and counter-balance lamps hung from the ceiling above large, flat tables. At first there was some awkwardness among the draughtsmen as Jenny was the only woman in the place but, as far as she was concerned, she was there purely to work and, to her relief, the men soon accepted that.

She loved the precision and fine detail of the work she was required to do, relishing the sight of a great, empty sweep of paper laid out before her, waiting for her pen to enrich it with detail and colour and purpose. She loved the way an entire ship could come into being in theory beneath her hands from sketches and drawings passed from the naval architects.

There was always plenty to do during her free time. She went round to Bella's at least once every day to help with Shona and, now that Neil had taken Lottie off to Edinburgh on the trip he had promised her, there was Helen to see to at home. Neil's parents didn't want to take her in. They disapproved of Lottie, Alice told Jenny, and would have nothing to do with Helen, born out of wedlock.

The child, who had once scampered cheerfully about the tiny flat dressed in cut-downs made out of old blouses and skirts that nobody wanted, now wore pretty clothes, and sat silently in a corner, watching and listening, flinching if anyone tried to talk to her. She had just had her fifth birthday, and had started attending school the month before. She slept on the truckle-bed Marion had once used, set up in the larger bedroom which she shared with Jenny; she often woke screaming from nightmares and they had had to put a waterproof sheet over the mattress because Helen quite often wet the bed. Slowly, patiently, Jenny and Alice worked on her, coaxing her to go out with them, reading to her, teaching her games. Shona, now sixteen months old and becoming more steady on her feet every day, often came to the flat with Bella, but even her company had little effect on Helen.

'It's as if she's tied into knots and she's scared to unloosen them in case she falls apart,' Alice said one evening as she and Jenny left the house together. 'Mam asked me to fetch her home from school the other day, and when I got there she was just waiting in a corner of the playground on her own, with all the other children playing round her.'

'I never thought I'd see Helen so quiet and timid,' Jenny agreed, her voice concerned. 'She used to be so lively.'

'It's that Lottie, always nagging at her and criticising her. Sometimes she puts me in mind of Gran before she fell ill.' Alice bounced the bundle of the account books into a more secure position beneath her arm as she walked. She had brought them home from the pawn-shop and worked on them at the table while Jenny decorated a plate she was working on for the store. It had been like old times again. When she had finished, Alice, gathering the books together, had suggested that Jenny should walk round with her to deliver them.

'I'd as soon get them back where they belong, and we could both do with a breath of fresh air. And you've not had a look at the shop since I started in it, have you?'

They left Helen sleeping and Faith darning by the range. It was early October, and dark outside. 'D'you mind the times we used to pretend to run three-legged races down the street?' Alice asked, tucking her free arm into Jenny's.

'I do – but if you've got it in mind to try it now you can forget it. These cobblestones are in a terrible state.'

'Ach, they're no worse than they always were,' Alice countered blithely. 'It's us that's getting older, and more scared of breaking our legs. Getting older's sad, isn't it?' she said from the lofty heights of seventeen.

When they reached the shop she produced a bunch of keys on a ring. 'If I knock, Alec'll come hurrying down to open the door and that'll start him coughing, poor man. He can come down the stairs in his own good time when he hears us.'

While her sister unlocked the door, Jenny studied the two small shop windows where once there had been a clutter of dusty items on view. Now there were far fewer, all neatly laid out, including a group of familiar wood carvings varnished to a high gloss.

'These windows've changed a lot. It looks like a proper shop now.'

'There was no sense in holding on to goods that hadn't been redeemed.' Alice said over her shoulder. 'When they're laid out properly folk are more interested in coming in to buy.'

A bell tinged as she opened the door and led the way inside. 'Wait until I've lit the mantel,' her voice floated through the darkness. Jenny heard the rattle of matches in their box, then there was the scrape of a match-head and a tiny flame blossomed. She looked around when Alice had lit the mantles. 'My – there's been a lot of changes here!'

'It was high time. The place was so crowded that it had almost come to a standstill. We still get plenty of stuff brought in every Monday to be redeemed on Fridays but now it's all stored in the back, out of sight.'

Jenny looked round, remembering the days when she had often scurried into this same shop to pawn her father's Sunday suit on a Monday or redeem it on a Friday night. During the war, when Maurice was in France, his best suit had lived here, being redeemed every three months to ensure that it wasn't lost for ever, then instantly re-pawned, brought home only when Maurice was due home on leave.

'D'you mind the time Maurice came home without letting us know and giving us time to redeem his good suit?'

Alice giggled. 'How could I forget? He was furious because he'd to go out in his uniform until we got it back.'

'Do folk still pawn the same thing, week in and week out?'

'Of course. It's usually the only item they can spare,' Alice told her. 'When folk you know keep bringing in the same thing it fairly colours your thinking towards them. There's one poor soul I can't pass in the street now without seeing her as a big chanty covered with bright blue flowers.'

Even Alec Monroe, who came slowly down the stairs from the upper flat while the two of them were laughing, had changed. Although he was only a few years older than Jenny he, like the shop, had always seemed to her to be dusty and grey and rather sad. But now his

425

movements were more brisk than she remembered, and he looked quite smart and cheerful. When he asked her, 'What d'ye think of the old place now?' his voice was confident and he looked round with a complacent air.

'It's changed a great deal, Alec.'

'For the better, thanks to yer wee sister here. When she first marched in here and told me I should give her a job I nearly sent her packing, d'ye know that? Deciding tae give her a chance was one of the best things I ever did.'

'Ach, away with you,' Alice said calmly. 'He's an awful flatterer, this man.' She fixed her employer with a stern eye. 'Have you finished up that soup I made yesterday?'

'He fancies you,' Jenny teased when they were on their way home, and stopped dead in her tracks when Alice said calmly, 'I should hope so, for I think I'm going to marry him.'

'What? I never heard anything about this!'

'Neither has anyone else, including Alec, so I'd be grateful if you'd say nothing for the meantime.'

'Alice, you're only just seventeen years of age! And the man's ailing, he always will be.'

Alice's expression, as they stepped out of a pool of shadow into the light from a streetlamp, was serene. 'All the more need for a wife to look after him.'

'He's a lot older than you are.'

'He's only thirty. I'm not going to rush into anything,' Alice said practically. 'I'm only thinking about it – I'll give it another year before I make up my mind.'

'You could do better for yourself.'

Alice snorted and gave her sister an old-fashioned look. 'I've no wish to marry someone of my own age and a raise a brood of children and worry about feeding and clothing them like Mam's always had to, hoping my man doesn't lose his job or spend all his pay in the pub. Alec's gentle and caring – and I'm no oil painting, Jenny. It seems to me that we could be contented together.'

They walked in silence for a moment, then she added, 'If we do get wed I'll do my best to keep him alive for as long as I can, but if it turns out that we don't have all that long together – well, at least we'll have been happy. And I'll inherit the shop, for he's not got any other family to worry about,' she added with self-mocking amusement, then was serious again. 'I think a good partnership and a proper understanding of each other's more important than romance for folk like us.'

As the day of her mother's return from Edinburgh approached, Helen, who had begun to emerge slightly from her shell, grew quieter again. She followed Jenny about the small flat like a shadow, accompanying her tearfully to the door when she went to work, waiting on the top step for her when she returned, as though she hadn't moved from the same spot all day.

Clutching the clockwork bear, her favourite toy, she watched as Jenny, talking cheerfully all the time, packed her few belongings.

'I'll visit you often, pet, now that I'm back in Ellerslie. And we'll go to the park sometimes, you and me and Shona and Aunt Alice.'

Helen sucked in her lower lip and wriggled her back against the wall, as though trying to burrow through the flaking plaster.

'It's breaking my heart to see her,' Jenny confided low-voiced to Alice as the two of them waited outside the landing privy for the little girl. She was old enough now to go to the lavatory on her own, but insisted on someone – Jenny, if she was available – going with her and waiting outside for her.

'I don't think they're bad parents. I mean, I don't think they beat her,' Alice's brow was furrowed with concern. 'If you ask me, Lottie and Neil see her as a nuisance, and that's a terrible burden for a wee girl to carry.'

The cistern flushed and, after a moment, Helen came out, the bear jammed tightly beneath one arm. She took Jenny's hand and together the two of them, with Alice following, climbed the stairs back to the Gillespie flat.

Darkness came, and there was no sign of Lottie or Neil. The hands of the clock on the mantelshelf ticked past Helen's bedtime and her small body relaxed a little as Jenny washed her, dressed her in the new nightgown she had bought to replace the well-worn, too-tight garment Helen had brought with her, and put her to bed. A few hours later Helen, screaming in a nightmare, woke the entire household, and most of the other folk in the building. Jenny took her into her own bed, risking wet sheets and, long after Helen had fallen asleep, clutching her aunt tightly, her entire body convulsed every now and then with a massive shudder, Jenny stayed awake, thinking about Shona, asleep now in Bella's house. Would she, like Helen, change from a contented baby to a frightened little girl because of the changes in her young life? Bella was right – it was best to leave Shona where she was until Jenny could find a home for them both.

She longed to turn over and re-settle the pillow, which had bunched itself uncomfortably beneath her neck, but Helen's grip was so strong that she couldn't break it without wakening the child. So she suffered the discomfort and lay still, fretting over Shona, wondering how long it would be before she could claim her own baby back.

In the morning Robert came into the drawing office, frowning, to ask Jenny if she knew why Neil Baker hadn't turned up for work on his first day back.

'Mebbe his father's heard from him.'

Robert shook his head. 'His father knows no more than you do,' he said irritably.

'D'you think there's been an accident?'

'I think,' said Robert, 'that the two of them are too busy enjoying themselves to give a thought for anyone else.'

Two more days went by without a word from Lottie, then Jenny came home from work to find Faith sitting in the kitchen, empty-handed for once, staring at the gleaming black-leaded range as though she had never seen it in her life before.

'Mam?' Memories of the day the telegram about Maurice had arrived from the War Office swept in on Jenny. Her heart seemed to falter then patter on its way twice as fast as usual.

'Neil's been here.'

'For Helen? And I wasn't here to tell her I'd be sure to visit— '

'Lottie's left him, Jenny. He says she's staying in Edinburgh and she's not coming back. He was in such a taking – I'd not give much for her chances if she ever does come back,' said Faith. 'Not with the look he had on his face.'

'What about Helen?'

'He doesnae want her, and neither does Lottie. He told her that to her face, poor wee fatherless bairn that she is— '

'Where is she?'

'Through there,' said Faith with a jerk of the head. Jenny hurried at once to the bedroom. Helen, spurning her own small bed, had climbed into Jenny's and was sound asleep there, sprawled on her back instead of in her usual tight knot. Her mouth was soft and full and her hands, relaxed and half-curled like little shells, lay on either side of her face. The clockwork bear, carefully tucked up, lay close to her, but out of her arms for once, with its bright-eyed, furry head on Jenny's pillow . . .

31

For once, Jenny gave her reflection in the mirror more than a brief glance as she pulled off her close-fitting hat and ran her fingers through her short hair to fluff it up. The glass, a pleasant oval within an elaborate gilt rim, reflected a woman thinner in the face than before, with serious eyes and a mouth that had been firmed by the events of the past few years.

Deliberately, she smiled at her reflection and was relieved to see that the mirrored mouth still curved easily and a light came into the blue eyes. Then the smile faded, and the serious look returned.

As she turned away from the mirror and moved to the sofa, drawn up before a welcoming fire, Robert came into the little parlour, balancing the tea-tray on one upraised hand like a butler.

'Tea, m'lady?' He set the tray on the small table before her, and sat in the armchair opposite. 'My housekeeper's rheumatism's bothering her today so I said I'd bring the tray through. I'm afraid I'm going to lose her – she's talking of giving up work. I'd be grateful if you'd see to the rest. I'd probably spill it into the saucers.'

As she poured the tea and handed a cup to Robert she took time to study him. He looked tired and there was an almost grim set to his mouth. She had heard from

Teeze that, while she was in Glasgow, there had been serious fears in the town over the future of the Dalkieth shipyard, but now the orders were coming in again and the yard was beginning to recover, unlike others on the Clyde hit by the sudden backlash after the war. It was generally agreed, though grudgingly in some cases, that Robert Archer had been instrumental in the yard's survival.

'How's Mr Dalkieth?' she asked. Robert shrugged. 'Back in his bed as far as I know, and being cossetted by his womenfolk.' His mouth turned down in derision. 'His mother claims now that he always had a weak chest. As far as I'm concerned he can stay where he is. Running the yard's easier when he's not around the place issuing counter orders and getting everyone's backs up. When he came in for that launch last week he caused nothing but trouble.'

'You know, Robert,' Jenny said, shaking her head, 'we never dreamed when you used to run around with Maurice that one day you'd be in charge of the shipyard.'

'We've both found ourselves on unexpected roads, haven't we?' Robert asked, then, as she glanced down at the gold band on her left hand he said, with a slight bleakness in his voice, 'Are you still fretting over Daniel Young?'

'I wonder at times what's happened to him.'

'He wanted to be on his own, Jenny, and you could do nothing about that – just as you could do no more than you did to prevent the boy's death,' he added with the uncanny knack he sometimes had of reading her mind. 'There's no sense in wishing that you could turn the clock back and change what's happened. We all wish that now and again, but it's not possible. You've got a child of your own, now. All you can do is try to give her a good life.' Then, leaning forward to look more closely at her, 'Is there something wrong with the wee lass?'

Jenny put her cup down carefully. 'She's fine. It's just— ' she hesitated, then said in a rush of words, 'I'm beginning to wonder if she's still mine, Robert, or if she's Bella's child now.'

'Your sister's only looking after her until such time as you've got a place of your own.'

'That's what we all say, but it's been over seven months since she and Patrick took Shona in. That's a long time in a wee girl's life.' Jenny's fingers pleated the material of her grey woollen skirt. 'There's me and Mam and Dad and Alice in the house I was born in – and now Helen's back with us and it's as if I've never been away, never married Daniel or had Shona or gone to Glasgow.' She stopped, then said, 'The other day we were all in my mother's kitchen when the bairns came in from playing in the other room. Helen came straight to me, the way she always does, and Shona went to Bella. And nobody seemed to think anything of it. A bairn for me, a bairn for my sister.' She swallowed hard, then said, low-voiced, blinking tears back, 'I love Helen – but she's not Shona.'

'Jen— ' He came to sit beside her, putting a hand over hers. 'I didn't realise it was so hard for you.'

'Nobody does, and that's what's worrying me. They're all beginning to accept things as they are.' Then she squared her shoulders, forcing a smile. 'But I should be doing something about it instead of sitting here girning and grizzling at you like a bairn that's been left out of a game.'

She leaned forward to pick up her cup, but Robert

moved his grasp from her hand to her arm, stopping her. 'There's more than enough room in this house for you and Shona. Hear me out, Jenny,' he went on swiftly as she started to speak. 'I've already said that we can't turn the clock back, but we can change the course of our lives if we put our minds to it. I still want to marry you, Jenny, more than ever before.'

'I've already told you that— '

'And what about what's best for Shona?' he interrupted impatiently. 'You want to be with her, don't you? You could bring her here tomorrow – today, if you want. Jen— ' He reached out to her. It would have been so easy to lean towards him, to go into his arms and stay there, but instead Jenny got to her feet with an abrupt movement. Letting Robert look after her and Shona for the rest of their lives would be too easy. She had made the decision to manage on her own, and she would stay with it.

'You're wrong, Robert. What's over is over and there's no sense in thinking otherwise.'

His face darkened as he stood up. 'Am I to be condemned for ever because of a mistake I made eight years ago?'

'I'm not condemning you, Robert. We're good friends and I hope we always will be. But we're nothing more than friends.'

'You know that's not so,' he said quietly. 'But you'll just not admit the truth to yourself. You've been badly hurt, Jen, but don't let that spoil the rest of your life – and mine.'

'It's time I was off home.' Jenny went into the hall. The breath was catching in her throat and she felt a desperate need to get out of the house, away from the man whose hand reached past her and took her coat from the stand.

'You said yourself, we've travelled roads we never

434

thought to travel, you and me. Our paths crossed once before and it seems to me that they should cross again, Jenny.' His hands lingered on her shoulders as he helped her on with her coat.

She stepped away from him and opened the front door. 'It wouldn't work, Robert, not now.'

'You're too independent for your own good.'

'I've had to learn to stand on my own feet and I'll go on doing it,' Jenny told him from the bottom step. 'It's safer that way.'

'And lonelier,' she heard Robert say as she fled down the path. Walking along the pavement on her way home, listening to the brisk tapping of her heels on the hard stone, she told herself that she was right in what she had said to him – she had to be right. She had trusted in Robert once before and she had trusted in Daniel, too, and both times her trust had been destroyed. For her own sake, for Shona's sake, she must retain her independence, even if it meant, as Robert had said, leading a lonely life.

Fergus Craig got to his feet as quickly as his girth and age would allow as the door opened and his sister came into the room.

'How is he?'

Isobel crossed to the window. November was halfway through and winter was on the other side of the glass; remnants of the fog that had smothered the town since early morning still hovered in wisps over the river and the lawn was patched with frost. In the flower beds beyond the terrace the pruned rose bushes were skeletal and soggy.

'He's dying, Fergus,' she said without looking round.

'Surely not! He's still a young man – he's strong enough to fight off a bout of pneumonia.'

'George,' said his mother, 'was never strong. I always said so, but people thought that I was being over-protective. D'you remember that rheumatic fever he had as a child? Doctor Harkness has confirmed that his heart was damaged at the time.' She turned to face her brother. 'I always felt that George wasn't meant to make old bones. Edward now – he was different. Much stronger in every way. It's strange that the war took him first when I thought he'd have been the survivor.'

Fergus, his normally ruddy face pallid with shock, put a hand on her shoulder. 'Come over to the fire, my dear, it's too chilly by the window.'

'George's room's so warm,' Isobel said, allowing herself to be drawn to the fire. 'I needed to look out at the cold for a minute.' Her rings flashed as she spread her hands to the blaze.

'Brandy— ' Fergus bustled over to the table that held the decanters, but his sister shook her head.

'Not for me.'

'I need one,' he said bluntly, picking up the decanter. 'George should never have insisted on attending that last launch while the chill was still on him.'

Isobel shrugged. 'I tried to tell him that, and so did Fiona, but George is never one to listen to advice when his mind's made up, as you well know.'

Her brother downed his brandy in two gulps then set the glass down as the door opened again, this time to admit the younger Mrs Dalkieth, slender and graceful in a drifting grey dress with rose-pink panels.

'My dear— ' he hurried to take her hands in his. 'Isobel has just told me – dreadful news, dreadful! If there's anything I can do, you only need to ask.'

She smiled faintly. 'Thank you, Uncle Fergus.'

'How is George?'

'Asleep now, with the nurse in attendance. The doctor's just leaving, Mother Dalkieth. He'll be back this evening.'

'Thank you, my dear.' Isobel held her hand out and the younger woman went to her.

Fergus hesitated, then said, 'Perhaps I should have a word with the doctor— '

'By all means,' his sister said, and he escaped thankfully. Fiona sat down beside her mother-in-law, who retained her hand.

'We must be very brave, my dear,' she said at last.

'Yes, Mother Dalkieth.'

'And be grateful that at least George has been blessed by a healthy son to follow him in the family business.' Isobel's voice was serene. In Fiona she had found a daughter she could both admire and cherish; who had given her a grandson she loved as much as she'd ever loved his supposed father.

Fiona raised her blue eyes to her mother-in-law's face. They had grown to respect each other a great deal in the past fifteen months or so. 'Yes, Mother Dalkieth,' she said.

32

Although few people had had much time for George Dalkieth as a person, his family background decreed that his funeral would be a splendid affair. The shipyard was closed down for the day and most of the workers, under the watchful eyes of the foremen, lined the streets to watch the funeral procession pass by on its way to the cemetery, where George was to be buried in the family lair. The hearse, drawn by two black horses, their plumes dancing in the wintry sunshine, was piled high with flowers.

Isobel and Fiona Dalkieth, both in unrelieved mourning black and both veiled, led the cavalcade of mourners, with Robert Archer in the second car.

Robert had always hated funerals, despising what he saw as the hypocrisy often shown by mourners who didn't, in truth, care a whit about the dear departed. But he had been summoned to Dalkieth House on the day before to be instructed by Isobel Dalkieth herself on the part he would be expected to play in the ceremony.

'You will be one of the cord-bearers, Mr Archer,' she told him, standing erect before the drawing-room fireplace, dressed in black from throat to ankle, a piece of fine veiling over her white hair. 'My brother will stand by my side during the service at the cemetery, and I would like you to stand beside my daughter-in-law.'

'Surely, Mrs Dalkieth, her own father or brother should support her.'

'They will also be cord-bearers, of course, but as our office manager I feel that you should be the one to stand by George's widow,' she told him, her voice clear and firm.

As the minister's rounded syllables rolled over the assembled mourners Robert stared up at the massive white marble statue towering above them all, solid against the browns and golds of the autumnal trees beyond, and set about with columns and angels. The name DALKIETH arched across the large facing panel in ornate black and gold letters, very similar to the letters curving over the main gates of the yard. Below the surname were listed the names and dates of the past three generations of Dalkieths, ending in William and Edward, George's father and brother.

This, Robert realised, was the third family funeral Isobel Dalkieth had had to attend in recent years. First her husband, then her elder son, and now her younger son. He stole a sidelong glance at her; even the black veiling over her face couldn't hide the sharpness and strength of her profile.

A heavy, sickly scent rose from the wreaths piled to one side, waiting to be laid over the black scar of the filled-in grave, and above it wafted the delicate perfume of lily-of-the-valley, bringing Robert's mind sharply back to the slim young woman who stood unmoving by his side. She had been dressed in black the first time they had met, he recalled, but this time her hat was small and neat and heavily veiled.

Two years had passed since their brief, passionate affair. Since then they hadn't seen each other very often, and never alone. Their most recent meeting had been

439

during the last launch from the yard, a month earlier. On that day, Robert remembered, Fiona had looked into his face for the first time since she had ended their affair and, to his consternation, he thought he had glimpsed a faint stirring of the warmth and intimacy she had once shown towards him. But now, although he couldn't see her face, he could tell by the way she had tensed beneath his touch as he helped her out of the car at the graveside and by the way she stood erect, alone, not deigning to rely on him for support, that he was no longer part of any plans Fiona Dalkieth might have for the future. Now that she was widowed, she would be aiming her sights higher than an employee, a man who had come from humble beginnings. If there was to be another man in her life it would be someone with money and position.

A grim smile brushed his mouth at the thought and he stepped forward at a nod from the minister to grasp one of the cords supporting the casket that held George Dalkieth. The other cords were held by Fergus Craig, Matthew Neilson and his father, a Dalkieth cousin who had travelled from the Borders for the funeral, and one of the foremen, a burly man who had worked for the Dalkieths for over forty years.

As the cords were laid down on the sides of the grave, their work done, Isobel Dalkieth stepped forward and picked up a handful of soil. As it pattered on to the lid of the casket below, Fiona stooped gracefully and picked up a handful of soil in her turn. She opened her gloved fingers to release the earth, then dusted her hands together to dismiss the final stray fragments of soil.

Isobel Dalkieth, who had stood straight-backed throughout the ceremony, put a hand on her brother's arm as she turned to where the cars waited on the wide gravelled drive. From where he stood Robert could see that for once the woman was leaning heavily on her escort. But Fiona, following her mother-in-law, walked alone.

The people who thronged the Dalkieth drawing room were, to a large extent, the same guests who had gathered not much more than a year before to celebrate the christening of William George Dalkieth, heir to the shipyard. Then they had worn bright colours, now they were all in black, milling across the rich Persian carpet like a flock of crows about to take wing.

At first, gathering in the dining room for refreshments on their return from the cemetery, they had been subdued and solemn-faced, keeping their voices down to a discreet sorrowful murmur. Time had passed since then; stomachs were comfortably filled, the funeral lay behind them and, as the servants, magpie-like among the crows in their black and white uniforms, circulated with trays bearing glasses filled with clear or amber-coloured liquids, the noise had risen to an animated chatter of voices, with here and there a cry of recognition and greeting, and even the occasional laugh.

That, Robert thought, standing alone in a window-bay, sipping at his whisky, was what he disliked most about funerals. No matter how dearly the deceased may have been loved the predominant emotion once the interment was over tended to be one of relief that it was someone else who had had to be left behind in the cemetery and that, for the rest of them, life was still there to be lived. He watched Fiona, making her way through the room group by group, accepting condolences with her usual composure. She had folded her veil back on returning to the house; within its sombre folds her face was like a flower, her mouth pale.

She had come to him not long after the funeral party returned to the house to thank him formally for his presence. Her voice and eyes had been cool and her gloved hand had barely brushed his. As she turned away from him Robert had noticed Isobel Dalkieth watching the two of them, her face expressionless.

'Mr Archer— ' Isobel's voice broke into his thoughts now, harsh and steady. 'I wonder if I might have a word with you?'

In the small, book-lined library across the hall, the door closed against the noise of her guests, she motioned Robert to a chair then moved behind the large desk. Waiting for her to sit down before he took his own seat he remembered the last time he had been in this room, the night that Fiona had driven him to his home. George had been present at that meeting, lowering and sulking, picking at his lower lip, his pale blue eyes sliding between Robert and his mother.

Isobel folded her hands, still gloved, on the desk before her, and plunged into business without wasting any time. 'Mr Archer, at the next Board meeting you will be invited to take on the duties of general manager, with a new office manager and a works manager to be appointed by the Board with your approval, to work under your supervision. I'm telling you now because I want you to have time to make your plans.'

Robert gaped at her for a moment. He had expected to stay on in the yard, but not to be offered full control. 'You're inviting me to take over the entire shipyard?'

'I am.'

'But surely the Board should be consulted over such a step.'

She waved his protest aside. 'The matter can't wait until then. Decisions have to be made as soon as possible. Now that I've lost both my sons I have to think of my duty towards my grandchild. In any case,' she added calmly, 'I'm confident that the Board will do as I say. They always have. And as I said, I want you to be able to present your plans as soon as the position is offered to you.'

'Mrs Dalkieth, if I am to be offered and accept the appointment you suggest,' he said levelly, putting a faint emphasis on the word 'if', 'I must point out that from that I will not necessarily do as you wish. I will make my own decisions.'

'So I would hope. You've got a sensible head on your shoulders, Mr Archer. I know I haven't always acted on your suggestions,' she went on, her mouth curving in a dry smile that didn't reach her eyes, 'but I believe that we can still work together. Will you accept?'

'If you don't mind, Mrs Dalkieth, I'd rather be approached by the Board officially before I give my answer.'

Irritation swept across her features. 'You're being very cautious.'

'I don't believe in getting my fingers burned twice,' he told her bluntly.

'Let's suppose the Board does make the proposals I've just put to you. Will you accept them?'

'I may well accept them – and that's as much as I'm prepared to say for the moment.'

'Very well, I'll accept that – for the moment.' She put her hands on the edge of the desk and got to her feet slowly and a little stiffly.

Robert went before her to open the door. 'Thank you for your faith in me.'

Isobel Dalkieth paused and looked him up and down, the dry smile lingering again on her pale mouth.

'Not at all, Mr Archer,' she said at last. 'After all, we do owe you a debt of gratitude. And I have always paid my debts.'

Then she went out of the room and across the hall, back to her guests, with Robert Archer following behind, puzzling over the debt of gratitude, and her use of the word 'we'. Was the old woman, he wondered, quickening his pace to pass her in order to open the drawing-room door, beginning to get delusions of grandeur? Had she taken to using the word 'we' in its Royal sense?

As the yard was closed on the day of George Dalkieth's funeral Jenny had decided to work at the kitchen table on a set of decorative plates for Neilson's store. Her mother and father were out and she had covered the linoleum floor with newspaper and set Shona and Helen, smocks covering their clothes, to some painting of their own. Helen was working on a doll's teaset Alice had given her while Shona was busy lathering paint from her brush on to some unwanted wallpaper Jenny had found in a cupboard.

When the doorknocker rattled, Jenny tutted with annoyance and put her brush down carefully then hurried to the door, the children squeezing into the hall after her. She threw open the door then stared up at the dark-suited young man on the doorstep.

'I've been attending my brother-in-law's funeral, Jen, and you don't think I'd come to Ellerslie without calling in on you, do you?' Matthew Neilson said.

Flustered, pulling at the ties on her overall, Jenny was suddenly aware of two heads, one dark, one auburn, poking inquisitively round her legs. 'Into the kitchen, the pair of you,' she ordered, backing along the narrow hall so that Matthew could step inside. In the kitchen he smiled down at Shona and Helen.

'I thought you had one child, not two.'

'This is Shona, my daughter, and this is Helen, my niece. Say good afternoon to Mr Neilson,' Jenny instructed the little girls, who backed away, hand in hand. 'Watch where you're putting your feet or you'll get paint on your shoes,' she added to Matthew, who picked his way across the sheets of newspaper towards the table where the half-finished plates lay.

'They're good.'

Jenny filled the kettle, feeling, as Helen and Shona both clamped a fist on her skirt, like a liner escorted by two reluctant tugs.

'They should be finished in another three days. They're a special order for Miss Beckett. Sit in that armchair, it's the most comfortable.'

He sat on Teeze's chair and Jenny snatched sidelong glances at him as she bustled about, gathering up the newspaper from the floor, picking up discarded toys. She saw by the expression on his face as he studied the room that he was taken aback by the shabbiness of the place, and longed to tell him sharply that it might not be much, but it was clean and respectable, but held her tongue.

'How's the workroom getting on?' she asked instead. She was dismayed by his unexpected appearance, and irked with herself for not realising that he would be attending the funeral. If she had thought of it, she would have made a point of keeping out of the way.

'Well enough, but we could do with you back in charge.'

Jenny measured tea into the pot and wished that her mother was there. She could have done with someone to take the children off her hands. Or, to be more exact, off her skirt. 'I'm sure Miss Beckett and Evie are managing fine.'

'Maybe they are, but I'm not,' said Matthew. She ignored him, concentrating her attention on making tea and persuading the little girls to go back to their painting. Free of them at last, she set out cups and saucers, moving her work carefully aside.

'Are your parents not in?' Matthew asked.

'Not just now.'

'I was hoping to meet them.'

Jenny, thinking of Teeze's probable reaction to her visitor, was glad that he, at least, wasn't at home. 'How is your sister, and Mr George's mother?'

'Remarkably calm. They seem to have built up quite a strong bond since the boy's birth.'

'Will your sister go back to Glasgow now?'

'Good lord, no. She intends to stay in Dalkieth House and bring the child up within sight of this precious shipyard of theirs.' Matthew sipped at his tea, then put the cup down. 'Are you happy, being back home?'

'It's where I belong.'

'People shouldn't belong anywhere,' Matthew said firmly. 'They should be free to go wherever they want.'

'That takes money.'

'So you'd not stay here if you had the money to move?'

'I didn't say that. Careful, Shona— ' Jenny, uncomfortable under the intensity of his gaze, bent down and guided her daughter's paint-brush away from the linoleum and back towards the paper, now slashed with bright colours.

When she straightened up again Matthew said, 'I miss you, Jenny. Come to Glasgow – for a holiday.'

'I've got my work to do.'

'You could surely arrange to get some time off. You work at Dalkieth's, don't you? I'll arrange it for you, if you like.'

The sheer arrogance of the man almost took her breath away. She began to speak, but he swept on enthusiastically. 'Bring the child with you.'

'You don't like children, Matthew.'

'I didn't say that.' Matthew's voice was hurt. 'I said I didn't care for Fiona's. Yours would be different. I know you think I'm too easy-going, Jenny, but I've had time to think things over since you ran away.'

'I didn't run away, I came back to Ellerslie because my husband was here.'

'And where is he now? You're young yet, Jenny. You deserve the chance of happiness with someone else, someone more worthy of you. And what about your daughter – doesn't she deserve a good future?'

Irritation flashed through Jenny. She had heard enough. 'Yes, Matthew, she does, and I intend to see that she gets it.' She got to her feet. 'But I'll manage it on my own, without having to be grateful to anyone else. And now, if you've finished your tea, I'd like to get on with my work,' she went on, removing the cup and saucer from his hands.

'But— ' Matthew spluttered, scrambling with difficulty out of Teeze's shabby chair.

'You're a nice enough person, Matthew, but you and me come from different worlds,' Jenny told him ruthlessly. She had tried to tell him politely that she wanted to get on with her own life, but men like Matthew could only understand the blunt truth. 'You think that just having plenty of money gives you the right to do anything you want and get whatever – or whoever – you want. But you're wrong.'

'But Jenny, I only – oh, blast!' Matthew said as the latch was lifted on the outer door.

Helen, followed by Shona, ran to open the kitchen door as Robert, dressed, like Matthew, in funeral black, stepped into the kitchen. He halted abruptly at the sight of Jenny's visitor.

'Archer— ' Matthew's voice was cool.

Robert nodded curtly to him, then as Shona clutched at his trouser-leg he bent and swung her into his arms. 'Is this a bad time to call?' he asked Jenny over Shona's bobbing head.

'Not at all. Mr Neilson was just about to go back to Dalkieth House. I'll see you out, Matthew.'

At the landing door, Matthew said, 'Are you rejecting me because of him?'

'It's got nothing to do with Robert. I told you – we're not suited, you and me.'

He left without another word, his mouth turned down at the corners in the sulky pout Jenny had come to know well. It was an expression he and his sister shared.

Robert, who was admiring Shona's painting, looked up as she went back into the room. 'Sorry if I chased your admirer away,' he said, his voice heavy with sarcasm.

She ignored the jibe, asking automatically, 'Will you have some tea?'

'I've had enough tea today to launch a ship.' He got to his feet and inspected his trousers for paint smears.

'How's Mrs Dalkieth?' Jenny asked.

'They're both fine. I get the feeling that there's not much sorrow there. I never liked the man myself but he was entitled to more grief than his wife and his mother showed today. I believe his son's of more importance to them than

George ever was, poor soul. Fathering that child was the only thing he did right, in his mother's eyes.'

The final sentence brought back her earlier thoughts about the child's true parentage. Still unsettled by Matthew's unexpected and unwelcome appearance she asked, before she could stop herself, 'How well d'you know Fiona Dalkieth, Robert?'

Taken aback by the question, he looked up at her with the familiar twist of the head that the baby had used on the day of his birthday party in the Neilson store. And she knew then that her earlier suspicions had been correct.

'What made you ask a thing like that?'

'That day when you walked into the store I saw— ' she hesitated, then said carefully, 'I saw the way she looked at you. She thought you'd come to see her.'

'Is that why you refused me when I asked you to come and live with me?' Robert asked levelly, 'Because you think there's something going on between me and Fiona Dalkieth?'

'I gave you my reasons and they have nothing to do with her.' Then she said again, 'Robert, how well d'you know her?'

He looked for a moment as though he was going to protest, then shrugged. 'I don't like keeping secrets from you of all people, Jen. It happened after you got married. I was lonely, and so was she. It only lasted for a month or two.' His mouth twisted wryly. 'If it gives you any satisfaction to know it, she jilted me, just as I jilted you. She threw me over when she discovered that poor George had managed to give her a child after all.'

'Are you so sure that the wee boy is George Dalkieth's son, and not yours?'

There was a pause, then Robert said, his eyes holding

hers, 'She swore to me that the child was her husband's. Whether he is or whether he isn't, he's a Dalkieth and I have no claim on him whatsoever. As you've said yourself, Jenny, the past is past.'

'But Fiona Dalkieth's free now, and so are you,' Jenny pointed out, and his brows rose.

'Are you trying to match-make?'

'I'm just – wondering.'

Robert gave a bark of laughter. 'You've been reading too many romantic novels, Jen. I told you – it was loneliness on both sides, and mebbe it amused her to deceive her husband with someone he couldn't stand. It meant very little as far as she was concerned, though at the time I foolishly chose to believe that I was – important to her.' His voice was self-mocking. 'There you have it – the truth about what a fool I've been. But believe me, we'd not look at each other now if we were the last man and woman alive.'

Shona toddled over to Robert and he put a hand on her head, smiling down at her absently as Jenny picked up Matthew's empty cup and took it to the sink. She was so intent on her thoughts that she turned the tap on too hard.

A jet of water deflected off the cup and shot up to soak her hair and face and the front of her painting smock. The little girls squealed with startled laughter as she reeled back from the sink and Robert snatched at a towel hanging over the back of a chair then reached through the spray to turn the tap off.

'Mercy,' said Faith from the doorway above the children's squeals, surveying her dripping daughter and the puddles on the linoleum round the sink. 'Are ye no' content wi' almost drownin' my man, Robert Archer, without trying tae drown my lassie as well?'

450

33

'The two pennies first, then the wee bar of chocolate, then this,' Alice instructed, handing over a tiny flaxen-haired doll. 'Then the tangerine on top so that it's the first thing she sees.'

It was Christmas Eve and she and Jenny were busy making up a stocking for Helen, sound asleep in the next room.

Christmas, well celebrated by the English, was a festival that passed by almost unnoticed in Scotland, other than with small gifts for the children.

Pushing the golden tangerine down into the stocking, Jenny remembered her own childhood Christmasses and the breathless excitement of pulling a knobbly stocking down from the range and plunging greedy fingers into its depths. In a good year she and her brother and sisters could count on the sort of stocking she was making up now for Maurice's daughter, but there had been a few bad years as well.

'D'you mind one Christmas when Dad was out of work and our stockings were padded with cold ashes from the range with a penny poke of sweeties sitting on the top?'

'I'll never forget it,' her sister said with feeling. 'I cried and cried, for I'd set my heart on a wee teddy-bear I'd seen in a shop window.' She reached over to touch

Jenny's hand lightly. 'Next Christmas you and Shona'll be in a place of your own, you'll see.'

Jenny sighed and shook her head. 'I'm beginning to wonder about that. She's getting more and more settled with Bella and I don't seem to be any nearer finding somewhere for us both. I need to go on working, and it means getting someone to look after her while I'm at the shipyard.'

'You will,' Alice said with conviction. 'It'll all work out. It has to.'

New Year was the special celebration in Scotland, with the yards and quarries and factories closing down for the day. Every house had to be cleaned from top to bottom so that the new year could get off to a good start, and every range or stove in the town was put to good use as the women made the traditional rich fruity 'black bun' or dumpling. Both Robert Archer and Alec Monroe first-footed the Gillespies, arriving together on the landing as the church bells began to ring 1922 out and 1923 in, each man with a piece of coal for good luck in one hand and a bottle of whisky in the other, much to Teeze's delight. There was more whisky flowing on New Year's Day itself, when Kerry Malloy became engaged to a riveter in Dalkieth's yard.

It was as well that Jenny was staying with her parents, for both Teeze and Faith suffered poor health during the early wintry months of the new year. Jenny was kept busy looking after her parents as well as seeing to Helen and working in the drawing office. Bella helped as much as she could, for Alice had her hands full keeping the pawnshop going and nursing Alec Monroe, who, like Teeze, was unable to cope with cold wet weather.

At the end of March, when the three invalids were on their way back to health, Alice announced that she and Alec were to be married on the same April day as Kerry and her sweetheart, with a joint back-court party after the ceremonies.

'Mebbe you could bring Shona to live with you once I'm wed,' she said to Jenny. 'The bedroom's big enough for you and the two bairns, or you could mebbe sleep in the wee room if you wanted to be on your own.'

'Never mind me – are you sure you're doing the right thing? You're not eighteen yet, Alice. You told me you'd wait till then to decide.'

Alice surveyed her sister defiantly. 'I know that, but Alec's chest was awful bad this time and— ' she stopped, then went on slowly, 'I'm sure enough to know that if he's only going to be with me for a short while I don't want to waste the time we have. Me and Alec are going to reach out and take what happiness we can, while we can. That's what we decided together.'

'Your sister might still be very young but she's got her head screwed on the right way,' Robert said a week later as he and Jenny walked out along the riverbank with Helen trotting between them, one small hand firmly gripping Jenny's fingers.

'It's strange to think that in a few weeks' time she'll be out of the house and I'll be the only one left with my parents.'

He walked on in silence for a moment, then with a sidelong glance he said, 'D'you mind me telling you my housekeeper had decided it was time she gave up working for other folk? She's leaving at the end of this week, though she's been good enough to arrange for someone to take her place. It seems that she's got an extra room in her house and she's been thinking of taking in a lodger. I wondered if you'd be interested. She lives in Chapel Street.'

'I'd need a place where I could have Shona with me.'

'As to that, Mrs Kennedy's fond of children. In fact,' said Robert casually, 'we've talked about it, and if you became her lodger she'd not be averse to looking after Shona while you're working.'

Jenny stopped so quickly that Helen almost fell over. 'Does she mean it?'

'I've never known Mrs Kennedy to say anything she didn't mean. I told her you'd go along and see her tomorrow evening.' He glanced over at Jenny and grinned at the look on her face. 'I thought you'd be pleased,' he said smugly, catching Helen's free hand in his. 'Come on then – one, two, three – and up we go!'

Helen squealed as the two adults swung her forward between them and up into the air. 'Again!' she demanded as soon as her feet thumped back down on the earthen path. An elderly couple approaching them sedately, arm in arm, beamed at the little girl's pleasure, and the woman said to Jenny as they passed, 'I mind when we used to do that with our wee lass. Make the most of her while she's still a bairn. They grow up too soon.'

'We will,' Robert assured her, his grin widening. 'Won't we, dear?'

'You're impossible!' she hissed at him as the older couple moved on.

'That's only because I don't know any better. One, two three—'

As they walked on, swinging Helen between them, it was Shona that Jenny was thinking of, and the wondrous possibility that all the days and weeks and

454

months they had been apart might at last be coming to an end . . .

Mrs Kennedy lived in a neat little terraced house with a wrought-iron gate leading from the pavement into a minute front garden.

'My man was a supervisor in Craig's Quarry,' she told Jenny proudly as she led her into the hall. 'He saved for most of his life tae buy this house, and managed tae leave enough tae let me keep it on after he died, together with the money I earned looking after Mr Archer. I'd not like tae have to sell it after all those years, and when Mr Archer came up with the idea of renting out the spare room it was a godsend.'

'I didn't realise that it was Mr Archer's idea.'

'Oh yes, indeed.' said Mrs Kennedy innocently, putting a plump hand on the gleaming banister and beginning to mount the stairs. 'He's a good man, Mr Archer,' she said over her shoulder as she went.

The room she was offering to rent was a good size, furnished with a large polished walnut wardrobe, matching chest of drawers, and a double bed as well as a small fireplace. The flowered wallpaper was fresh, with no sign of the damp patches Jenny had been used to all her life, and cream lace curtains hung in the bay window. Heavier cretonne curtains, also flowered, could be drawn over at night. There was even electric lighting.

'My son saw tae that,' Mrs Kennedy boasted, clicking the switch on and off. 'He's an electrician tae trade. He's married now, and living in Dumfries. My daughter's in Paisley, and I don't see them or their families all that often, so it would be nice tae have a bairn about the place.' She looked round the spotless room. 'This was ours when my man was living and the bairns were at home. I sleep downstairs now that the rheumatism's settled intae my knees. The wee one'll be no bother tae me while you're at work, Mrs Young, and I've got a folding bed that can be set up for her.'

She led the way back on to the small square landing and opened another door. Jenny, craning past her, saw a lavatory seat, a tiny wash-hand basin, and a small bath. Her eyes widened and Mrs Kennedy, watching her closely, beamed.

'I can see why you don't want to sell the house,' Jenny said, admiringly.

'Oh, my man was away ahead in his thinkin',' the older woman said. 'There's still the privy out the back door, an' I just use that myself. But it's grand tae have a bath in comfort when I want one, without havin' tae heave buckets of water up and down the stairs.'

'As to the rent— ' Jenny ventured as Mrs Kennedy started back down the stairs.

'Och, don't fret yourself about that, my dear, I'm sure we can come tae some arrangement. Come down tae the kitchen and we'll talk about it over a cup of tea.'

As she followed Mrs Kennedy into the cosy kitchen, where steam plumed gently from the kettle waiting on the range, Jenny knew that whatever the rent might be she would find it. At last she had discovered a home where she and her baby could be together.

Alice prudently took Shona and Helen out for a walk so that Jenny could tell Bella her news without the distraction of the children underfoot. Bella and Patrick heard what Jenny had to say in silence, then Bella said slowly, 'You mean you're going tae take Shona away from us?'

'That's why I've been looking for somewhere to live, so that we can be together.'

'But— ' Bella looked at Patrick then back at Jenny, her fingers twisting together, her small face stricken. 'You've got your work tae do. You'll not be able tae be with her during the day. Who'll see tae her then?'

'Mrs Kennedy's raised a family of her own and she likes bairns. Shona'll be fine with her.'

'But she doesnae know this woman, Jen!'

'She's met her at Robert's house and they've always got on well together.' Jenny's heart chilled within her as she saw the look on her sister's face.

'It's one thing being friendly on a visit, an' another bein' left alone with someone she doesnae know!' Bella said, desperation in her voice. 'Shona's used tae being here, with us. It's wrong tae move her again, just when she's settled.'

'Bella, I have to have my baby with me,' Jenny said, her voice pleading for understanding.

Bella moved away from her sister, going to stand by Patrick, who reached out a hand and clasped hers. He struggled to his feet and shoulder to shoulder they confronted Jenny, faces set.

'That's not what ye thought when ye went off tae Glasgow after Daniel and left the bairn behind,' Patrick said belligerently, his brows drawn together.

'Oh Patrick, I had to make sure Daniel was all right. You knew it was only for a wee while, didn't you, Bella?'

'But it wasnae for a wee while, was it? It was more than a year ago.' The hostility Patrick had only covertly shown towards Jenny since Shona's birth was out in the open now, twisting his mouth, hardening his eyes. 'A whole year Bella's looked after that wean like a mother while you've been busy with your own life!'

Jenny tried to speak but his voice rose, drowning her out. 'An' now you come walkin' in here, bold as brass, an' expect us just tae hand her back tae you as if she's of no more importance than – than a piece of clothing ye'd loaned us!' Patrick spat the words out.

'Let her stay, Jenny,' Bella begged. 'She's been happy with us. Let her stay – until ye're settled in, just.'

'And then you'll find another reason and another reason why I shouldn't take her back.' Looking at her sister's stricken face, Jenny felt as though she was being cut in two, but at the same time she was keenly aware that she was on the verge of losing her baby, the only person who truly belonged to her.

'What about Helen?' she heard herself saying. 'She needs parents to love her and look after her. Why don't you— ' She stopped as she heard the latch on the outer door being lifted.

'It's not Helen I want!' Bella's voice was shrill with pain. 'It's Shona, not *Helen*!'

'For God's sake!' Alice swept into the middle of the room, her face tight with anger as she glared round the small circle. 'Keep your voices down, will you, you could be heard out there in the close!'

She left the room quickly and Jenny and Bella stared at each other, appalled.

'Ye don't think the bairns heard us?' Bella whispered through stiff lips.

'Ach, they're too wee tae understand what we're sayin'. And if they did, it's her fault!' Patrick stabbed an accusing finger in Jenny's direction then snatched his jacket from the nail hammered into the door and caught up his stick. He pushed his way past the sisters, ignoring

Bella's pleading, 'Pat— ' and disappeared out of the open door.

After a moment Alice re-entered, Shona and Helen trailing after her. The little girls' faces were dark-smeared round the mouth and in their hands they each clutched a half-chewed liquorice strap.

Bella immediately stepped forward and scooped Shona up into her arms. 'Look at the state of you,' she scolded lovingly, rubbing with the ball of one thumb at the corner of Shona's mouth as she sat down by the range, the child in her lap.

Jenny held out a hand to Helen, who hovered by the door, looking from one to the other of the adults. 'Come to the fire and get your coat off, love.'

Alice's voice was determinedly bright and cheerful, though above her smiling mouth her eyes were still stormy as they surveyed her older sisters. 'They were desperate for a sweetie, so I thought it wouldn't hurt, just this once. We'd a grand walk, didn't we Helen?'

The little girl nodded, clambering on to Jenny's knee.

'Horsie.' Shona wriggled on Bella's lap, reluctantly allowing the shiny black liquorice sweet to be prised from her fingers so that first one arm and then the other could be freed from her coat sleeves.

'That's right, we saw a big horsie pulling a cart, and a blue motor car. Didn't we, Helen?' Alice dampened the corner of a towel at the kitchen tap and brought it to Jenny, who used it to wipe the stickiness from Helen's face.

Bella spat efficiently on a corner of her handkerchief and wiped Shona's face and hands. Shona turned her face away impatiently, squirming down from Bella's lap and reclaiming the liquorice strap. She toddled over to Jenny and offered her the sweet.

'Thank you.' Jenny bent her head and was about to pretend to nibble at the liquorice when Helen, with a sharp cry of 'No!' leaned forward on her knee and struck it out of Shona's hand, at the same time aiming a kick at the smaller child.

A week later Jenny moved herself and her daughter into the Chapel Street house. At first Shona pined for Bella and Patrick and the single end that had been the only home she remembered. Walking the floor with her when she refused to settle in her new bed, reading stories and reciting nursery rhymes and listening to her over-tired daughter crying for Auntie Bella and Uncle Pat, wondering if she had done the right thing after all, Jenny came close to despair. She had been looking forward to being on her own with her baby, but now all the pleasure had gone out of it.

'I feel like a murderer,' she said shakily to Robert when he called on her a few days after she moved in. They were in Mrs Kennedy's front parlour; his former housekeeper had just brought some tea in and borne Shona off with her to the kitchen. 'You should have seen Bella's face when I picked Shona up and carried her out of the house. She looked as though I'd just slapped her.'

'You've got every right to have your own child with you.'

'That's no consolation to Bella – or Patrick. Mebbe they're right, mebbe I'm being selfish and putting myself first instead of thinking about what's best for Shona.'

Robert took her by the shoulders and gave her a little shake. 'The best place for Shona is with her own mother. There are times when we have to stop thinking about other folk and pay heed to what we want ourselves,' he lectured. 'She's all that's left to you of your marriage. If you hand her back to your sister you'll not just break your own heart, you'll be turning your back on your own flesh and blood and giving away months and years out of your own life.'

He released her with one final, admonishing shake. 'And what would she think in the years to come when she heard that her own mother had walked away from her and left someone else to raise her?'

She stared at him, astonished. 'I never thought I'd hear you say things like that.'

'Just because you know me better than most it doesn't mean that you know me well,' said Robert. 'Don't forget that I was raised by an aunt and I've got no happy memories of it.'

'That's because your auntie was a hard kind of woman, not like Bella at all.'

'Perhaps,' said Robert, his mouth grim. 'And perhaps a lot of my unhappiness in those days was knowing that my own parents hadn't cared enough to keep me.'

'But your mother and father died— ' Jenny began, and he held up a hand to stop her.

'Enough! Will you stop talking, woman, and pour out my tea before it grows stone cold?'

34

'This,' said Alice, 'is going to be the society wedding of the year – at least as far as the Dalkieth tenements are concerned. Have you not finished with my hair yet?'

'Nearly – and I'd be done if you'd stop jumping about,' Bella said through the hair-grip between her teeth. She took it from her mouth and pushed it into the soft knot of hair at the nape of Alice's neck, then stood back. 'There.'

Now it was Jenny's turn. She took Bella's place, and carefully placed the blue cloche hat, the same colour as Alice's eyes, on her sister's head. The brim dipped at one side; Jenny tugged it slightly to a rakish angle before skewering it in place with two pearl-topped hatpins then adjusting the cream-coloured bow at the side. Alice peered into the cloudy mirror and nodded, then swung round on the chair and stuck out her feet.

'Come on, slaves – put my shoes on.'

Shona, in a pink embroidered dress, bustled importantly forward and squatted to push a smart fawn shoe on to one of her aunt's feet, but Helen hung back, the other shoe dangling from a limp hand.

'Come on, slowcoach.' Bella tried to pull her forward, then, as Helen resisted she shook her head. 'I don't know – you're a big schoolgirl now, not a baby.' Impatiently, she took the shoe from the little girl and knelt to fit it on to Alice's foot herself. Helen watched, the hand that had held the shoe fidgeting with the skirt of the new yellow dress Jenny had made for her.

'There! How do I look?' Alice jumped up and pirouetted as well as she could in the small space between bed and orange box.

'You're lovely,' Jenny said sincerely. The fawn silk and wool dress Alice had chosen to wear at her wedding fell from the neck to the loosely-belted dropped waist-line, then to mid-calf, in straight folds that had the effect of slimming down the girl's solid body. There was blue bead embroidery on the bodice and along the edges of the loose sleeves, and the high-heeled shoes, each with a shining silver buckle, made the most of Alice's surprisingly slender ankles, her best feature. Blue pendant earrings gave added length to her neck, and a long necklace of blue and cream beads cascaded down to the loose-fitting sash round her hips.

'You look so – lady-like,' Bella chimed in, her eyes dampening.

'So I should hope, on my wedding day. Now don't you go crying, Bella, or I'll have to slap you, and I don't want to have to go hitting people on a day like this, do I, girls?' Alice demanded of her nieces.

Bella sniffed hard, and blinked. 'I still think you should have had your own special day instead of sharing it with Kerry.'

'Not at all. This way I get to have a big party in the back court. The Malloys know how to do these things in style. Come on, young ladies, and we'll see what Gran thinks.' Alice whisked out of the room, and Shona followed, catching at Helen's hand and dragging her along.

Bella took a handkerchief from the pocket of her

knitted jacket and dabbed at her eyes. 'I know I'll not be able to stop myself from crying. She's still so young.'

'She'll be fine.' Jenny put a tentative hand on her sister's arm, half expecting to have it shaken off.

Instead, Bella put her own fingers, still roughened by hard work, on top of hers.

'I hope so.' Bella gave her eyes a final dab then said shyly, 'Jen, I think I'm expectin.'

'What? Oh, Bella!'

Bella's eyes, still damp, were blazing with happiness. 'It's early days yet, and I've said nothing tae anybody else, but Pat. But I feel – different. I'm sure in my own mind that we're to have a bairn of our own. Just when I thought it would never happen, too!'

Jenny hugged her, and Bella returned the embrace warmly. 'Now I know how you must have felt about wee Shona,' she murmured into Jenny's ear. 'For there's nobody ever going to be allowed to take this bairn away from me!'

They beamed at each other, both on the verge of tears, then Bella gave a loud sniff and put the handkerchief away. She picked up her hat, a brown felt cloche. 'Come on,' she commanded briskly, 'it's nearly time tae go tae the church.'

Alice and Alec had asked Bella and Patrick to be their witnesses. 'You don't mind, do you?' Alice had asked Jenny anxiously. 'I'd sooner have had you to stand by me, but Alec and me both felt that it would be a kindness to Bella and Patrick.'

'Of course I don't mind,' Jenny had assured her, and meant it. Alice was being married by the same minister who had performed the ceremony for Jenny and Daniel, and she had no wish to be reminded of the past. Instead, while the small marriage ceremony was taking place,

464

she was kept busy hurrying up and down the stairs, helping to set out the tables in the back court, spreading tablecloths and linen sheets over them, anchoring the material with jam-jars crammed with wild flowers. The weather had decided to bless the double wedding day and the sky overhead was the same blue as Alice's eyes.

By the time the happy couples had arrived, Kerry and her new husband from the Catholic church, Alice and Alec from the Protestant manse, where they had been married in the minister's parlour, Peter McLellan's fiddle was piping away and the men, led by Teeze and Mr Malloy, had already broached the bottles of whisky and barrel of beer bought for the occasion, in spite of their womenfolk's scowls of disapproval.

Robert Archer arrived halfway through the festivities, long after the last crumb had been eaten. He brought some bottles with him, and was noisily welcomed by Teeze and his cronies. When at last he was free to search Jenny out and draw her into the group of dancers there was whisky on his breath.

'They look very happy.' He indicated the newly married couples, standing together in a group of young people. Kerry had tossed her hat aside and her red head flamed in the sun; Alice, with Alec's arm looped possessively about her shoulders, was radiant. 'Does it not put you in the notion for a wedding of your own?'

'I've already had my wedding, Robert Archer, and so have you.'

'We both made a mistake. Mebbe,' said Robert, holding her back slightly so that he could look down at her, 'we're the sort of people that need to learn the hard way. The next time'll be better.'

'There won't be a next time for me,' Jenny told him firmly, but he had drawn her back against him, his arm

465

hard about her, and she was talking into his jacket. She doubted if he heard her.

When the dance was over she noticed Helen standing against the wall, alone, watching the revellers, just as Walter had stood years ago, alone and aloof. Jenny left Robert and went to the little girl, taking her hand, leading her to where the other children, Shona among them, were playing a noisy game of Blind Man's Buff. Helen stood back, watching them, and when Jenny moved away, she followed like a small shadow, staying close to her for the rest of the afternoon.

The party continued after Kerry and her new husband and Alice and Alec left, then gradually the adults began to withdraw from the court, small children drooped over their shoulders, sound asleep. Jenny gathered Shona up and bent down to smooth the tumbled red curls back from Helen's face. 'I'll need to take Shona home to bed now, pet. You go and find Gran. Go on,' she urged as Helen shook her head. The little girl went, step by step, looking back over her shoulder.

'D'ye think she's all right?' Bella murmured from behind Jenny. 'I mean, in her head?'

'Of course she's all right! She does well enough at the school,' Jenny told her sharply.

'She's got no life in her any more. Well, mebbe she's sickening for something.'

'She's just – unsettled, with Lottie deserting her. She'll be fine,' Jenny said, but she was worried as she watched Helen disappear into the crowd.

At home in Chapel Street she settled Shona in her crib and went back down to the kitchen to make a cup of tea for herself. Mrs Kennedy was in Paisley, looking after her daughter and her new baby, and she had the house to herself. The room was warm and peaceful, the clock's ticking soothing, and she was almost asleep in her fireside chair when the doorknocker rattled, making her jump.

Bella stood on the doorstep, still in her wedding finery, her brows knotted with worry.

'Jenny, is Helen with you? She's gone,' she went on as Jenny shook her head. 'Mam thought she'd mebbe followed you.'

'I've not seen her since she went off to look for Mam. Are you sure she's not just put herself to bed?' Helen had taken, lately, to going to bed without a word to anyone.

'It was the first place we looked.'

'The river— ' Jenny felt her heart constrict.

'There's folk looking by the river and all over. The Malloys are out helping, and Robert. He was still there when Mam discovered that she was missing. I'd best go to Mam – she's in a right state about it,' Bella said hurriedly and turned towards the gate.

'I can't leave Shona. Let me know if you – when you find her,' Jenny called after her.

'Aye— ' Bella was already out on the pavement, hurrying off into the night. Jenny shivered, realising that although it had been a lovely day, there was frost in the air. She closed the door and went upstairs to look at Shona, who was sleeping peacefully, then prowled restlessly about the ground floor, hurrying to open the back and front doors now and again, fancying that she heard a child crying, or a light scratching on the panels. But there was never anyone there.

The clock's ticking had a menacing note now, each second extending the time since Helen had last been seen. Jenny was tormented by mind-pictures of the

467

small figure trudging slowly, reluctantly, away from her, into the crowd.

She paced from parlour to kitchen and back to the parlour again, thinking of the fields edging the town, where a little girl could easily be lost, and of the river, deep and cold and fast-running. Sometimes there were tramps and beggars around the area, unknown people who just might take it into their heads to harm a little girl, or steal her away, if they found her wandering alone.

Several times she put on her coat then took it off again, knowing that she couldn't leave Shona on her own. She was pacing the parlour for the hundredth time, wishing that tonight of all nights Mrs Kennedy could have been home, when the doorknocker crashed against its metal plate.

Although she had been praying for contact from the outside world Jenny screamed at the sound, then almost fell over a large horse-hair chair in the darkness in her haste to reach the front door. As soon as she opened it Robert swept in on a wave of frosty air, shirt-sleeved, his jacket wrapped about the bundle his arms.

'She's fine, she's fine,' he said at once. 'I found her huddled under a bush down by the shore and she wouldn't let me take her anywhere but here.'

'Helen?' With trembling hands Jenny unfolded the jacket to reveal a familiar tumble of red curls and a dirty, tear-streaked face pressed against Robert's arm.

'She needs to go to bed,' he said, low-voiced. 'You lead the way.'

'No, let me take her.' As Jenny gathered Helen into her arms the little girl woke with a yelp of fright, then recognised her aunt and started to cry, wrapping her arms tightly around Jenny's neck.

'It's all right, love, you're all right,' Jenny told her over and over again. Forgetting Robert, forgetting everything but the joy of holding Helen again and knowing that she was safe, Jenny began to climb the stairs.

When she came back down half an hour later the house was silent and she thought that Robert had left. But he was in the kitchen, sprawled back in one of the cushioned chairs by the range, sound asleep, his legs stretched out across the rag rug. Carefully stepping around them, Jenny made fresh tea then put a hand on his shoulder. His grey eyes opened at once, blinking up at her as he struggled upright in the chair. 'The warmth must have got to me,' he said, yawning. 'How is she?'

'Sound asleep in my bed. Does Mam know she's safe, and Bella?'

'I sent word to them that she was fine and that I was bringing her here.'

She put a mug of tea into his hands and sat down opposite him.

'What did she think she was doing, Robert? Mam's always loved her, there was no reason for her to run away.'

He swallowed some tea and knuckled the last of the sleep out of his eyes, then ran a hand through his hair, lifting it into tufts all over his head. 'She doesn't belong,' he said simply. 'Bella's got Patrick, Shona's got you, and now Alice has her own husband. Helen doesn't have anyone.'

Jenny remembered the day Bella had shouted at her, 'I want Shona, not Helen.' The little girl must have heard, after all. 'Did she tell you that?'

'She didn't need to tell me. I know what it feels like

469

not to belong.' He emptied his mug and held it out to be refilled, grinning ruefully at her. 'I ran away more than once when I was about her age, but I wasn't very good at it, I kept being brought back.' The grin faded. 'That's why I was so eager to be Maurice's friend, to be part of his family for a while. Then I made the greatest mistake of all. I ran off again to Tyneside when old Mr Dalkieth gave me the chance.'

He drained his cup and went to the sink to rinse it out, speaking over his shoulder. 'I don't know who my father was. My mother apparently went off with someone else when I was about a year old and left me with my aunt.' He turned to face her, wiping his hands on a towel. He looked tired. 'The shame of it haunted her for the rest of her life – though, as she kept telling me, she did her duty by me. But children need love, Jen, not duty.'

'You've never told me anything of this before,' she said, stunned. 'Not even when we were courting. I thought I knew everything about you in those days.' The thought of the misery he must have suffered, the secret he had locked away from everyone, horrified her, even though it had happened so long ago.

'Why should I? I didn't want your pity – I didn't want anyone's pity. I'm telling you now because I know how Helen feels. It's you she wants, Jen. Not your mother.'

'I know that. And I'm going to keep her.'

'Good,' said Robert, then was overcome by a huge, jaw-cracking yawn.

'It's time you were in bed. In your own bed,' she added swiftly as he raised an eyebrow at her.

'You're a hard woman, Jenny Young. You've only just decided to take one orphan in, and now you're throwing another out into the street.'

'You're old enough now to look after yourself,' she told him, taking his jacket from where she had laid it over the back of a chair, and holding it out to him. He sighed, but took it, shrugging it on.

'One day,' he said, 'I'll get the answer I want. I'll let myself out.'

The kitchen door closed quietly behind him and she heard him go along the hallway, then the front door opened and closed. She was alone, apart from the two little girls sleeping above.

Jenny picked up her own empty mug and took it to the sink, telling herself that she had done the right thing in sending Robert away. She had responsibilities now, and it wouldn't be fair to burden anyone else with them.

Then, as her hand tightened on the tap, Alice's voice seemed to ring out in the silence of the room. 'Me and Alec are going to reach out and take what happiness we can, while we can,' she had said, when she announced her forthcoming marriage.

Jenny hesitated, her fingers falling away from the tap. Young as she was, Alice had had the sense to recognise where her own happiness lay. And she had had the courage to grasp at it firmly, to hold for as long as she could and to remember for always. Alice, Jenny realised suddenly, had the right way of it.

She hurried out of the kitchen, along the hall, towards the front door, fumbling with the latch, the sense of urgency, of time slipping away from her, suddenly strong.

The cold night air hit her as she went through the door and out on to the little path. The wrought-iron gate was so cold beneath her clutching fingers that they felt as though they had been burned.

She had dithered for too long; the street was silent

and empty. Still holding on to the gate she looked one way then the other, a sense of loss welling up in her, then spun round as Robert said from the doorway, 'You'll catch your death of cold standing out there.'

'Where were you?'

'Sitting on the stairs, waiting for you. I decided it was too cold to venture outside. I was certain,' he said reproachfully, 'that you'd have caught up with me before I reached the front door, but I was wrong. As I said before, you're a hard woman, Jenny Young.'

'Robert—'

'Don't say another word. Just come here, to me.' He held out his hand and Jenny's own arm lifted as she went towards him along the paved path, glittering with frost in the light from the hall. She put a foot on the first step, then on the second step, and then she was within reach and Robert's fingers closed about hers, warm and strong, driving away the chill left by her contact with the gate.

The heat from his hand spread like a fire up her arm and deep into her body. Her own fingers tightened about his as he drew her into the light and comfort of the hall, his free hand swinging the door shut behind her, closing out the darkness and the cold . . .

THIS TIME
NEXT YEAR

Some Greenock geographical and historical facts have been slightly altered to suit the needs of the story line.

My gratitude goes to Alice Robertson for generously giving me access to her research material into the history of Greenock's sugar refiners.

E.H.

1

'I think he's dead.'

A steamer out on the River Clyde bellowed mournfully as though in agreement and a chill draught breathed against Lessie's cheek as she straightened, stepping back from the bed, the fingers that had brushed the cooling grey face automatically rubbing at her skirt to rid themselves of the touch of death. Rain had started pattering against the small ill-fitting window that lit the room.

Incongruously, she smelled roses, and realised that it was Anna McCauley's scent. Cheap and sharp though it was, it made a pleasant alternative to the smell of damp and decay and generations of human residence that permeated the weary old tenement building.

'Oh Jesus,' moaned Anna, one fist clenched against her chin to stop its trembling. 'Don't say that!'

'What d'you want me to say?' Lessie snapped, her own nerves in shreds as she held the small mirror, innocent of any clouding, out to the other girl. 'The man's not breathing, is he? Where's the sense in saying he's fine when he's not?'

'What the hell's he doing dying in my bed?'

Lessie's voice was tart when she said, 'You know that better than I do.' But Anna was deaf to sarcasm or criticism. She stood on the broken blackened linoleum, swaying back and forth, moaning.

Lessie, fighting back the urge to slap her, stared round the room, wondering what in God's name was to be done. A portrait of the ageing Queen Victoria as a young woman, neat beneath a coronet, incongruous as the smell of roses in the bare room, looked back at her from behind

Anna's tangled red curls. The royal eyes were disapproving. And no wonder, Lessie thought. The poor woman must have witnessed sights in this place that no personage of blue blood should ever witness. But surely this was the worst scene of all.

'How could he no' have waited till he was out in the street afore he did it? How could he no' have—' Anna managed to bite back the self-pitying tirade, then said in a rush of panicky words, 'They'll say it was me that killed him. They'll take me to the Bridewell and h-hang me.'

Her own panic honed Lessie's voice to an edge that would have sliced through iron. 'They'll not hang you! It'll have been his heart that did it.' His heart, and overstrenuous exercise on the narrow, grimy, tumbled bed, she thought, but kept that to herself, saying only, 'I'll have to get back. The wean's on his own.'

'You'll no' leave me?' In her agitation Anna snatched at Lessie's arm. The movement dislodged the coat she had hurriedly wrapped about herself before rushing out onto the tiny landing in search of help when her bed companion had suddenly departed – in spirit though not, unfortunately, in body.

There was a flash of long slender limbs, the curve of a perfect pink-tipped breast before the coat was scooped back into place.

'I've got tae see that Ian's all right.'

'But you'll come back?'

Lessie would have given anything she had, except Ian, to stay away, but it was clear that her neighbour wasn't going to let her escape easily. Donald, she silently asked the memory of her dead husband, Donald, what did you think you were doing, bringing me to this street, then dying and leaving me alone to deal with the likes of Anna McCauley?

Aloud she said as she moved to the door, 'Get yourself dressed. I'll be back in a minute, then we can decide what to do about – ' she paused, then flapped a hand at the still figure in the bed, ' – him.'

'You're sure you'll be back? I couldnae—'

'I'm sure!' Lessie snapped and closed the door of

Anna's flat behind her to the sound of a low moan of anguish from its living occupant. For a moment she leaned against its panels and drew a deep, shaky breath.

The basket of still-damp washing she had been bringing up from the crowded little back yard stood by her own door on the other side of the landing. She had dumped it there when Anna, wild-eyed and wrapped in the coat, rushed from her flat just as Lessie reached the top step. Picking it up she went into her own living quarters, suddenly anxious about the silence. By this time Ian, fretful after a bad night, should surely have been bellowing out his loneliness and his fear of being deserted.

To her relief he was asleep, still tied firmly into the fire-side chair with a long woollen scarf. His head had sagged against one shoulder, his small pale face was streaked and dirty round the mouth, and a fist still clutched the well-chewed remains of the sugared crust she had put into it to keep him happy for long enough to let her hurry down to the back yard before the threatening rain started. There was a sharp tang of urine hanging in the air around him and she was glad she had thought to put a napkin on him. Ian, not long past his first birthday, was learning how to use a chamber pot and learning well, but ill health had caused a reversion.

At the sight of him, all thought of the dead man in Anna McCauley's bed vanished from Lessie's mind, swept away by her burning, overwhelming love for this sickly scrap of humanity, this living proof of the happiness she and Donald had shared for one brief year before pneumonia took her young husband from her.

She bent over the baby, careful not to wake him, and listened anxiously. His bout of whooping cough had given them both disturbed nights for weeks but now, thank God, he was breathing easily. Better to leave him where he was, wet backside and all, than to disturb him by moving him to the shabby cot against the inner wall of the room, as far away as possible from the draughts that always found their way in, no matter how much she tried to plug the gaps in the window frame.

In the meantime – Lessie's heart sank at the thought

3

– Anna McCauley was waiting for her. If only she had been two minutes earlier bringing in the washing she might have been safely inside her own door by the time Anna, violet-blue eyes wide with horror, had burst out onto the landing. Instead she had been right there, to be caught by the wrist and dragged into the woman's flat and into her problem.

The whole building – the whole of the Vennel, come to that – knew how Anna McCauley made her money. Lessie had been shocked to the core, once she worked out why there were so many men coming and going up and down the hollowed-out stone stairs, to realise that she was living on the same landing as a prostitute. Her husband had promised her that as soon as he was made up to foreman in the shipyard they would move out of the Vennel and find somewhere better to live. Poor Donald had not lived to keep his promise.

Lessie, a respectably married woman, had always carefully avoided contact with Anna apart from the occasional word of acknowledgement if they happened to meet on the stairs or in the close leading to the street. But now it seemed that she was burdened with Anna and the wages of her sins, for the moment at least. If she didn't go back across the landing now, the woman would no doubt come banging on her door and then Ian would be wakened.

With a sigh dragged up from the soles of her cracked shoes, Lessie gave one last glance at her son and crept from the room.

Anna was waiting anxiously, one bright eye peering through a crack in the barely opened door. As Lessie appeared, the door opened wider and she was almost hauled through it. It shut behind her with a firm click and Anna, her voice still tremulous, said, 'Now what are we to do?'

'You must fetch a policeman and let him deal with it.'

'And have myself taken off tae the polis station and questioned till I don't know what I'm sayin'?' In a panic Anna seized at Lessie again with a grip that would raise bruises by nightfall. While waiting for Lessie's return she had dressed herself and pinned up her hair. It glowed a vibrant russet colour in the dim grey room.

'What else can you do? A man's dead in your bed; either you have him taken away or you let him be. It's up to you.'

'D'you no' know who he is?' Anna waved a hand towards the bed and Lessie took advantage of the movement to prise herself loose from the other's grip.

'How should I know him? He's nothin' tae do wi' me.' She had looked at the dead man as little as possible. All she knew was that he was middle-aged, scrawny and unattractive, probably in life as well as in death.

'I thought everyone did. It's Frank Warren!'

Lessie gaped at the bluish sunken face on the shabby pillow, then at Anna. 'One of the sugar folk?' Her sister Edith was a maid in the elderly Warren brothers' house, and to hear Edith talk, Mr Frank and Mr James were on nodding terms with God. Lessie had occasionally glimpsed one or other of them walking or driving in the town, on their way to or from their successful refinery, but that was the nearest she had ever come to them, until now.

'Aye, one o' the sugar folk!'

'What's a man like that doing here?' The question was blunt, but Anna was too upset to take umbrage.

'He liked coming here,' she said simply. 'We could have taken a room at one of the hotels or even gone out of the town tae somewhere like Glasgow.' She gave a sniff and a gulp and scrubbed the back of one arm over her face. 'But he liked tae come here wi' a scarf over his face so that nob'dy would recognise him – the selfish bastard,' she added, glaring at her dead lover.

Lessie could see now why Anna could scarcely tell the police that the man had died in her bed. God knew what the townsfolk would say if they found out. Although the Warrens meant nothing to her, the sense of duty towards her betters that had been instilled into her at school wouldn't allow her to see them humiliated.

She bit her lip in thought for a moment. 'We could dress him and sit him in the chair.' The idea developed in her mind as she went along. 'Then you could fetch a policeman and tell him that – that Mr Warren took ill in the street and you saw him there and brought him in tae rest for a minute. And he just up and died before you could fetch help.'

Anna was looking at her as though she had just come down from a mountain carrying God's words carved on tablets. 'Aye! They'd think he was just goin' through the street on his way tae the sugar warehouses on the harbour, wouldn't they? Here, help me!' Spurred into action now that a plan had been formed, Anna scooped up the clothing lying over her one and only chair, dumped it on the floor by the bed, then pulled back the sheet that covered the dead man. Her nose wrinkled and she reeled back. 'Christ, he's fouled my bed, the dirty bugger that he is!'

'He can't help that, can he? It happens when folks die.' In the days before her withdrawal from the world, Lessie's mother had done her share of laying-out. Lessie had helped her on a few occasions. 'You can wash your sheets afterwards,' she told Anna brusquely, anxious to get out of the place as soon as she could and get back to Ian. 'Come on, the sooner we get it done the better. He'll stiffen up if we waste any more time and then we'll not be able tae dress him.'

It was a long and difficult task. Frank Warren, naked as the day of his birth, wasn't a big man, but in death it seemed that every limb had doubled its natural weight. It was like coping with a huge, unwieldy rag doll. Both women were slender and, in Lessie's case at least, under-nourished, but they were young and used to hard work. Even so, they were breathless by the time they had dragged the dead man from the bed, dressed him on the floor to the accompaniment of a flow of muttered curses from Anna, then heaved him into the chair, a sagging piece of furniture with broken springs that twanged their protest as the body was dumped on them. All the time Lessie kept one ear open for a sound from her own flat. If Ian should waken before they were finished she might have to fetch him in, and she had no wish to let him see what his mother was up to, even though he was still too young to ask questions or to talk about what he saw.

'Thank God,' Anna panted when they finally got the corpse settled and had stripped the bed, covered it with the old stained coverlet and put the sheets to soak in a bucket of cold water brought from the sink on the landing. Most of her hair had escaped from the pins to lie in tendrils about her neck and her lovely face was red with exertion. Lessie knew that she herself must look just as hot and exhausted.

'Now you'll have tae run down and fetch a policeman,' she started to say, but Anna interrupted her, dropping to her knees to reach beneath the bed.

'His wallet.' She waved it as she got up again. 'Lucky I saw the corner of it peeping out. They'd have had me for theft if I hadnae.'

She flipped open the leather wallet, riffled through it, and extracted more crisp notes than Lessie had ever seen at one time. Dampening one fingertip on her tongue, Anna removed two of them with decisive flicks of the finger and held one out. 'Here, take this for your trouble.'

'I'll do nothing of the sort!'

'Och, go on!' Anna pushed the money into Lessie's hand and stuffed the remaining note down the bodice of her own blouse. Putting the rest back and stowing the wallet into the dead man's breast pocket, she said over her shoulder, 'It's only what he owed me. He'd finished when he went an' died so it's mine by rights. An' God knows you're entitled tae half o' it.'

'I don't want it.' Lessie put the money down on the table.

'Don't be daft! You're no' goin' tae tell me that you don't need it, an' you wi' a bairn to raise.' Anna tried to push the money back into Lessie's hand and for a moment there was a brief struggle which ended with Lessie spinning away towards the door, leaving the crumpled, rejected note on the cracked oilcloth.

'I don't want it! Now go and fetch a policeman,' she said over her shoulder, and left the room.

Anna caught up with her in the gloom of the tiny landing, clutching at her once again. 'Lessie, come wi' me tae speak tae the polisman; he'll believe you more than me.'

'It's got nothing to do with me!'

'It wis your idea to—'

A wail followed by an ominous bout of coughing from her own flat gave Lessie the strength to wrench herself free of Anna's clinging fingers, her mind filled with thoughts of Ian. 'It'll look suspicious if there's two of us. Go on now, I've my bairn tae see tae!'

Ian, his small face purpling, was struggling against the scarf that held him in the chair while choking sounds tore their way out of his chest and his lungs laboured to suck in air. Lessie jerked the ends of the scarf apart and lifted him into her arms, carrying him to the window. His fists beat at her in misery and fear, then the first terrible crowing whoop came and he stiffened in her arms, pulling away from her so that she had to put one hand on the small of his back to prevent him from toppling from her arms. The veins in his neck stood out with the strain of trying to breathe. His blue eyes, the same vivid, far-seeing blue as Donald's, were bulging, suffused with tears. His nose began to run and still the attack went on.

'Dear God . . . ' She felt so helpless, guilty because her own lungs were drawing in life-giving air while her child suffocated. Then suddenly, when she felt that he could stand it no longer and she could bear it no longer, Ian sucked in air again, falling against her and vomiting the half-digested crust he had so enjoyed earlier down the front of her blouse.

'There, my wee dove, you're all right now, Mammy's got you safe,' she whispered, pacing the small room with him, rocking him while the panic-stricken weeping that always followed an attack shook his small body. How could you tell such a tiny bairn what was wrong with him? How could you assure him that in two weeks, three, six maybe, he would recover?

'As long as his lungs stay clear,' young Dr Miller had told her when she first took Ian to him. 'Keep him warm and away from draughts. And see that he gets nourishing food. A spoonful of tonic wine once a day, perhaps, and cod-liver oil to build up his strength.'

Looking at the thin fair young woman before him, seeing the little frown lines that worry had already engraved between her brows, knowing full well how hollow his words were to the likes of her, he had added, without hope but bound to say it, 'Chicken soup, if you can afford it.'

Lessie hadn't known whether to laugh or cry. It was hard enough just feeding the two of them and her brother Davie, who had been sent by their father to live with her after Donald's death so that there would be a wage coming in. Not that a young laddie like Davie earned much. Certainly not enough to buy chicken soup and tonic wine and cod-liver oil. Unless, she thought ironically as she wiped Ian's sticky tear-stained face with the wetted corner of a towel and put him back in the chair, she used the rent money and risked eviction. At least Ian would be the best-nourished child in the gutter.

'It's all right, Mammy's no' goin' away,' she reassured him as he whimpered and held his arms out to her. 'She's just getting you somethin' tae eat.'

She had saved the last few spoonfuls of a pot of broth made the day before with a good piece of bone she'd coaxed from the butcher. She heated it now, wishing as she stirred at it that Davie hadn't eaten so much of it the night before. But he put almost all of his wages into the house and he was a husky, growing lad. It would be wrong to ask him to deny himself nourishment when he had such hard work to do on the docks. It was different for her – women in Lessie's world were used to going without so that their menfolk and children could eat.

When the broth was at the right temperature for Ian she put a little into a bowl and coaxed it into his mouth, drop by drop. By the time he had finished his eyelids were drooping.

'Poor wee scrap, you're worn out wi' all that nasty coughing.' She changed his napkin, ignoring his girning and his fretful, irritated swipes at her busy hands, and laid him down in his cot. Then she found a clean blouse for herself. As she took the soiled blouse off, something fell to the ground. Lessie, who had a hatred of the cock-roaches that infested the old building, choked back a scream and shied away. But the object on the floor didn't scurry away to the safety of the ill-fitting skirting board. Cautiously she picked it up and found herself holding the pound note Anna McCauley had tried to force on her earlier, folded into a tiny square.

'That besom!' She remembered how the girl had followed her out onto the landing and clutched at her – in a panic, Lessie had thought at the time. But instead Anna had been making sure that the money she took from the dead man was shared between them, making them partners in conspiracy.

'I'll show her!' Lessie said to a drowsy Ian as she struggled into the clean blouse. She wrenched open the door then closed it again at once. The door of Anna's flat was half open and a man's voice was rumbling in the room beyond. A second man was on his way in, his back to her, a small black bag in one hand.

Quietly, like a thief in her own house, Lessie tiptoed away from the door, back into the centre of the room. She opened her fist and smoothed out the note. The very look of it was opulent, with its crests and whirls. The words 'Pay on Demand' jumped off the paper at her. She closed her fist, feeling the money crinkle and rustle in her palm. Twenty whole shillings. Biting her lip, she glanced at Ian, who was breathing easily now. With the money she held she could buy the cod-liver oil the doctor had recom-mended, another bottle of cough mixture, and a small boiling fowl to make more broth and provide at least two dinners for the three of them. Ian needed the nourish-ment.

She laid the note down on the table then picked it up again and smoothed it out. She wouldn't be keeping the money for herself, but for her bairn, poor wee fatherless morsel that he was. It wasn't his fault that he had been born in the oldest and shabbiest part of Greenock instead of in one of the better tenements, or even one of the villas along the shore with his own nurse and everything his little heart could want.

Lessie chewed at her lip again; she knew that she wouldn't return the money. Not now, at any rate. Later, when Ian was well again, she would repay every penny, no matter how many stairs she had to scrub or how many floors she had to wash to earn it.

She would have to pay it back, because until she did, the money forged a silent, sisterly bond between herself and Anna. And Lessie Hamilton was an independent woman. She always had been independent, even as a child. She wanted a bond with no one, especially the likes of Anna McCauley.

2

Not many of the men crowding the streets on their way home from the docks were given to talking, mainly because after a day's work they were too tired. The predominant sound was the clatter of nailed boots on the cobbles and paving stones, with the occasional farewell grunt as this man and that peeled off to vanish into dwelling houses or along narrow side streets. Larger groups turned into one or other of the public houses, where drink would help to ease tired muscles and loosen tongues.

Archie Kirkwood and his younger son Davie, walking almost shoulder to shoulder, said nothing because they rarely had anything to say to each other. Stealing a sidelong glance at Davie, Archie saw the tired droop of mouth and shoulders, the way the boy's booted feet scuffed along. He didn't have the stamina needed for a docker, this one. Didn't have the muscle and gumption. Too fond of reading and thinking. Engineering, for Christ's sake! A man never knew what was going on in that dark head, or behind the cool grey eyes. Archie felt much more comfortable with Joseph, his firstborn. He was a real chip off the old block, was Joseph, never out of mischief and trouble. It was a pity he'd refused to become a docker. He was strong, like his father.

When they reached Dalrymple Street, the parting of the ways, Davie would have swung off towards the tangled knot of crowded old streets where Lessie lived with no more than a murmur of farewell, but the older man said gruffly, 'Is our Lessie goin' out tonight?'

'No.' Davie hesitated then said, his voice defensive, 'It's my night-school night.'

Archie's mouth gave an involuntary downward twist of derision, but he only said, 'Tell her I'll mebbe look in later.'

'Aye.' Davie loped off, his step quickening now that he was moving away from his father.

'God,' thought Archie Kirkwood in disgust as he walked on, turning away from the Clyde and moving deeper into the town. 'Night school!' That was no place for a man. In his own young day he would have been one of those marching into the pub, or gathering on a street corner, but not now. Not since—

He pushed the memory out of his mind but it came creeping back, as it always did, to haunt him as he turned in at the mouth of the close, climbed the stairs to the first floor, and opened the door of his home. The smell of cooking and polish, the smell at once both warm and cold that meant home, enfolded him as he stepped across the lintel.

'Dadda!' Thomasina, dark like him, just past her twelfth birthday, came skipping to meet him at the kitchen door, trailing the shabby rag doll her eldest sister Edith had made for her when she was a toddler. She beamed up at him, clutching at his jacket then pushing her short stubby fingers into the pockets in a way that the others had never dared. Thomasina wasn't afraid of him as her brothers and sisters had been at her age. She loved everybody and expected everybody to love her. With a squawk of delight she found the orange he had brought for her and ran to show it to her mother.

'There wis a fruit ship in,' said Archie, and at once hated himself for trying to make conversation with his wife. He was always trying, and always being rebuffed.

'Give it to me, lovey, and I'll cut it for you,' Barbara told her daughter gently, then with a change of voice she said over her shoulder to her husband, 'Wash your hands then sit at the table. Your food's ready.'

One knife, one fork, and one spoon awaited him on the scrubbed table. He always ate alone these days. Barbara and Thomasina ate when he was out of the house, as though taking nourishment was something shameful, to be done in secrecy.

As his wife brought the steaming soup plate to the table, Archie caught the faint smell of whisky. Ironically, while he had never touched a drop in years, Barbara, a strict teetotaller through all the years of his intoxication, couldn't get through the day now without drink. There was always a bottle hidden about the place.

A plate of meat and potatoes, also steaming, followed the soup. While he ate in silence, Barbara moved about the kitchen, rubbing at spotless surfaces, washing his soup plate and spoon the moment he had finished with them, always busy. Thomasina sucked and chewed noisily on her orange. Juice glistened on her chin and Barbara swooped on her, crooning, to wipe it off.

Archie cleared his plate and pushed it away. It, too, was immediately claimed and washed while he moved to his fireside chair and opened the newspaper he had brought in with him. Home was the loneliest place in the world. In the past twelve years Barbara had only spoken to him when it was necessary. When Edith and Lessie married and moved out, Barbara had left the marriage bed and taken over their room. She slept there now with Thomasina. Joseph still used the wall bed when he was home, but more often than not he was out God knew where with his cronies or some woman or other, or in the jail. As soon as he was old enough, Joseph had taken up his father's abandoned mantle of drinker and fighter.

Thomasina, sitting in her relaxed, boneless way on the rug before the range, discarded the last sucked-out quarter of orange peel and scrambled to her feet to claim her place on her father's lap. None of his other children had ever tried to sit on his knee but Thomasina always did and Archie, aware of Barbara's eye on him, didn't dare reject the girl.

Christ, he thought as she wriggled into a comfortable position, pushing the paper aside, her head bumping painfully against his lip, the faint smell of orange juice mingling with the scented soap that Barbara washed her with every day, it was embarrassing for a man, so it was, to see a near-grown lassie behaving like a wee bairn.

He caught Barbara's eye and saw by the chill look in it that she was reading his thoughts. Thomasina wasn't going to change because Thomasina, through no fault of her own, was simple. Guiltily, carefully, he rearranged the newspaper so that he could hold it and support the girl's body at the same time, narrowing his eyes to squint at the newsprint across the silky head that nestled confidingly on his shoulder.

'What's going on across the landing?' Davie wanted to know as soon as he walked into the house. His voice was anxious. 'A polisman was coming out just now. Is there something wrong with Anna?'

'How should I know?' Lessie asked tartly. Davie had been fascinated by Anna McCauley since the moment he had first set eyes on her, and Lessie sometimes had nightmares about what might happen if she didn't do all she could to keep him away from the woman. Anna was a man-eater and Davie was only seventeen. She felt responsible for his welfare.

'For God's sake, Lessie, you don't have the polis visitin' for nothin', ye know that. They were at our house often enough after our father, then Joseph.' He half turned towards the door. 'Mebbe I should go an'—'

'You'll do nothing of the kind! Anna's fine, I saw her myself earlier. Anyway, we should mind our own business.' Lessie stirred hard at the pot on the stove then tutted as a splash of broth flew out and landed on the cuff of her clean blouse. 'Now look what you've made me do!'

'Your mammy's in a terrible mood, young Ian,' Davie told his nephew, picking him up and nuzzling into his midriff. Ian, who was tickly, gave a screech of laughter and wriggled.

'Here, is that chicken I can smell?' Davie suddenly forgot about the policeman. Working on the docks, out in the open most of the time, he had a hearty appetite.

'I did a bit of extra cleaning for Mrs Hansen today,' Lessie lied. 'I thought we'd have a treat, for once.'

'Chicken!' He put the little boy down. He took his

jacket off and hung it neatly on the nail in the back of the door.

'Och, I forgot tae fetch the water for you.' Lessie left the stove and picked up the bucket.

'I'll do it.' Davie took it from her. 'You look tired out.'

'So do you.' He always looked exhausted after a day at the docks.

He grinned at her, elated at the prospect of the meal ahead. 'I can manage to carry a pail of water.' She heard him whistling as he went out to the stone sink on the landing. Davie was good company and she didn't know how she would have managed without him. Quiet and withdrawn at home, where his mother had no time for anyone but Thomasina and his father thought him a weakling, Davie had blossomed since he came to live with her in the Vennel.

To the accompaniment of the clanking of ancient protesting pipes and the gush of water from the landing, Lessie set out bowls on the table then ladled broth into them, carefully stepping over Ian, who was sitting on the rug, poring over a battered rag book someone had given him and telling himself a story in a singsong nonsensical babble. The fine wispy red hair at the nape of his neck, hair the colour of his father's, made her heart turn over with love.

She cut some thick slices from half a loaf and arranged them on a plate, then suddenly realised that Davie was taking his time about coming back inside. Hurriedly she went to the door and her heart sank as she saw Anna by the sink with a pot in her hand, one shoulder leaning against the scarred streaked wall, her hip jutting. Davie had filled his bucket and turned the stiff old tap off; his hand still rested on it and his attention was given over entirely to Anna.

'I don't know what I'd have done without your sister,' she was saying as Lessie got to the door.

'Lessie?'

'Aye, did she no' tell ye? I ran oot screamin' like a lost hen.' Anna's clear laugh rippled out; she had turned her earlier terror into an amusing story for Davie's benefit and even in the gloom of the landing Lessie could see her eyes sparkling up at him. 'An' it was Lessie who—'

'Davie, your food's spoiling!'

He jumped at the interruption and looked round at Lessie guiltily. Anna laughed, then moved to take her own place at the sink as he hefted the battered bucket.

'Ye're a strong lad, Davie Kirkwood. Lessie's fortunate tae have someone tae lift full buckets for her.'

Davie glanced at his sister then said quickly, 'I could fill a bucket as easy for you as for Lessie if you left it outside your door each evening.'

Anna's eyes, slightly tilted at the outer corners, moved over him, then rested lightly on Lessie, standing watchfully at her door. 'Och, I'm strong enough tae dae my own carryin'. I've aye had tae fend for myself. But thanks for the kind offer.'

She turned on the tap and held the pot under it. Her sleeves were folded back and her arms, bare to above the elbow, were smooth and slender. Lessie saw Davie's eyes linger on them and wished that she could dip a hand into her apron pocket and take out Anna's pound note and hand it back. But she had already spent it on a bottle of tonic wine and a large bottle of cough syrup, not to mention the chicken.

'Davie!'

He came at last, with one final glance at Anna, who smiled back at him.

'Why did you no' tell me what had been going on?' he wanted to know when the door was at last closed, leaving Anna outside.

'It wasnae something I'd want tae talk about, least of all tae you,' she snapped. Ian had come toddling to the door to find out where everyone was and she shooed him ahead of her into the kitchen. 'Get yourself washed or you'll never finish your meal in time to go tae the night school.'

'God, Lessie, anyone'd think I was the same age as wee Ian here,' her brother burst out, pouring water into the basin and stripping off his shirt. He reached for the harsh yellow soap. 'I know fine how Anna earns her keep.'

'Then you'll know why I'm not interested in talking about her. D'you think I like living in the same building as a . . . a . . .'

Davie lifted cupped handfuls of water to rinse his face. Watching him, Lessie realised that her little brother was a man now. Healthy though he was, Davie, when matched with his father and brother, had always seemed slight and frail. But six months' hard work on the docks had added muscle to his arms and shoulders.

'Folk have tae feed an' clothe themselves, an' pay the rent.' He spoke indistinctly, bent low over the basin to prevent the water splashing everywhere, but even so she could hear every word. 'Anna has nobody tae fend for her.'

'There are better ways of earning money.'

Davie reached for the towel and buried his face in it, then emerged to say bitingly, 'You're great at moralising, Lessie. Mebbe if you hadnae been fortunate enough tae find a good man like Donald you'd be more understanding.'

'Understanding?' She stared at him, deeply hurt by his criticism. 'How can you try tae defend someone like Anna McCauley?'

Davie gave his arms a final rub, ran his fingers through his hair and went into the tiny narrow room where he slept. He came back almost at once, pushing his arms into the sleeves of the clean shirt she had left hanging on the back of the door for him. 'Someone has to. You helped her this afternoon, from what she told me.'

'I'd no choice. She caught me on the landing, else I'd not have had anything to do with what was going on.' Lessie became aware that Ian was listening, his small face turning from one to the other, his brow furrowed. He was used to laughter and harmony, for Lessie and Davie got on better together than any other members of the Kirkwood family.

'I'll just say this, Davie, before we sit down at the table. If you ever take up with Anna McCauley you're out of this house.'

He smiled without humour. 'I couldnae afford Anna,

an' you know it.' Then he pulled his chair out and sat down, picking up his soup spoon. Lessie stared down at him, chewing her underlip. She loved Davie, loved his quick smile, his warmth and compassion. She fretted for him because she knew how much he hated working on the docks. She was proud of the way he had started night school in the face of jeers and taunts from his father and brother. She desperately wanted him to do well in life, to be happy, to have all the good things that he deserved. And at that moment she also wanted to slap him, to shake him, to force him to promise that he would never, ever lie with the likes of Anna McCauley. Davie deserved a good woman, a woman he could be proud of. Slowly, unable to say all these things, she sat down opposite him and picked up her own spoon.

The soup was good, the chicken was tender and succulent, the potatoes were served in their jackets the way Davie liked. But the meal had been spoiled for them both by their quarrel and they ate in unaccustomed silence. Pushing pieces of chicken around her plate, tasting them without pleasure, Lessie reminded herself bitterly that the food had been bought with ill-gotten money. Everything to do with Anna McCauley was defiled, even the chicken.

Once or twice she sensed Davie glancing at her, but when she looked up, ready to smile, his eyes hurriedly slipped away. He spoke now and again to Ian, feeding the little boy chicken from his plate. When Lessie protested half-heartedly that he'd had his share, Davie shrugged and said, 'The laddie needs it. He's got a lot o' growin' tae dae yet.'

When they had finished, he went into the tiny hallway to fetch his jacket and came back. 'Here's my wages. An' I brought this for the wean. I thought it would help tae ease his cough.'

The orange lay on his palm, round and golden, a captive sun.

'Och, Davie!' Lessie felt tears pricking at the backs of her eyes. She knew how much he hated the way his father and the other dockers looked on a percentage of any cargo they unloaded as their rightful due. The big hooks they used in their work might, by accident, breach a barrel or damage a crate and the contents find their way into pockets or empty bottles. One crate or barrel out of hundreds was never missed, but Davie, who, as his father scornfully told him, had been born with enough of a conscience to do for the whole world, would never take part in sharing out the spoils. Lessie knew how much it must have cost him to take that one orange.

Ian, wide-eyed, reached up with both hands and took the fruit from his uncle, lifting it at once to his mouth. He bit into the skin then blinked rapidly and dropped it, rubbing at his lips and grimacing.

Davie laughed and scooped him up. 'Ye're supposed tae take the skin off first, daftie!'

'I'll give it to him tomorrow.' Lessie retrieved the orange, then said softly, 'Thanks, Davie.'

He grinned at her and suddenly the quarrel was over. Davie wasn't one to nurse his anger. He glanced at the clock on the wall and picked up the books that were always kept at one end of the mantelshelf. 'I'd better go or I'll be late. My father said he'd mebbe look in on you.' Davie didn't refer to his parents as Mam and Da like the others. He made them sound as though they were distant beings, and for years – ever since Thomasina's birth had changed both his parents – he had managed to avoid giving them any title when speaking to them.

Archie Kirkwood arrived an hour later, when Ian, rosy and clean after a good going over with cloth and soap, was being dressed in the tattered jersey and trousers kept for night-time wear. Lessie heard his heavy footsteps on the stairs and was at the door, the baby riding comfortably on one hip, by the time Archie reached the landing.

He didn't hear the door opening; he curled one big scarred hand round the corner at the top of the stairs for support and paused, head down, drawing a deep breath. He looked, Lessie thought with compassion, like an old man. Then he lifted his head, saw her, straightened his shoulders, and became his usual self.

It was raining outside; his jacket was black with moisture but he shook his head when she told him to take it off. 'I'm used tae a drop o' rain. This past winter I've worked in it day in an' day oot. Whit is it they say?' A creaky, little-used smile tugged at the corners of his mouth. 'April showers? By God an' they seem jist as harsh as they were in January an' February an' March.'

His voice filled the small room. As a child Archie had been regularly beaten by a violent stepfather and by the time he was old enough to fight back, the hearing had completely gone in one ear and was impaired in the other. He hated his disability and did all he could to hide it from others. His loud voice and his way of staring intently into the faces of those speaking to him so that the movement of their lips helped him to grasp what they were saying intimidated people who had no knowledge of his deafness. The hidden impediment had also run him into many a fight in his younger days, for if men spoke and laughed with their faces turned from him he was quick to suspect that they were making mock of him.

Lessie made strong black tea and he drank it thirstily, the cup almost hidden in his fist, and nodded when she questioningly lifted the teapot. 'Aye, lass, I've a thirst on me tonight. How's the wean?'

'He's doin' fine.' Out of habit she spoke clearly, shaping the words so that he could read as well as hear them.

'An' yersel'?'

She refilled her own cup and sat down opposite. 'I'm fine too.'

He nodded, then stared into the glowing embers in the grate. Used to his silences, Lessie picked up her sewing basket and started darning a shirt of Ian's. Ian himself squatted contentedly on the rag rug between their feet, staring like his grandfather into the fire, picking at the little balls of fluff that bobbled his faded, too-tight jersey.

Archie visited every two weeks or so now, visits that had started not long after Donald's death. At first Lessie, unused to attention of any sort from her father other than a fair number of slaps when she was younger, had been uncomfortable when he came into her home; but gradually she came to realise that it was his way of conveying sympathy over her early widowhood. He never spoke much, and he never called when there was a chance that Davie might be in.

She put down her sewing, stooped to gather up the neat little pile of fluff balls Ian had amassed, then picked up the baby, who was beginning to nod drowsily.

'Say goodnight to your granda.'

Ian tucked his head into her neck, overcome with sudden shyness, and she carried him to the cot that Donald had worked hard to earn, noting as she tucked him in that he was getting too long for it. She would have to look round for something more suitable soon.

By the time the teapot was empty, Ian was sound asleep. The medicinal syrup she had bought that day seemed to have done the trick, for apart from one chesty bout of coughing that didn't, mercifully, turn into gasping and whooping, he had had a good evening. Lessie prayed that it would stretch into a good night; being startled awake at frequent intervals wasn't fair on Davie, who had a long hard day ahead of him. Not that he had complained; that wasn't Davie's way.

'I'll make more tea.'

'No, I'd best get back.' Archie levered himself to his feet then dipped a hand into his jacket, which had added its drying aroma to the mixture of smells in the house – dampness, the disinfectant Lessie scrubbed the floor with in an attempt to deter the cockroaches, the general smell of an old, uncared-for building – and brought out an orange. 'This is for the wee fella.'

'Oh Da, that's good of you!' She took the fruit from him, thankful that she had put Davie's orange away, out of Ian's sight. It wouldn't do to have Archie finding out that his wasn't the first gift.

'Tell Mam I'll look in on her soon,' she said as she stood at the open door watching him pull his cap down over his bristly grey hair before stepping onto the landing. The tap was dripping as usual; Archie gave it a wrench as he passed the sink and the dripping stopped. Lessie knew that she was going to have a struggle to get it on again.

As he paused at the top of the stairs to accustom his eyes to the poor light of the flickering gas mantle on the landing, his shoulders slumped again and his first tentative step looked like the tottering of an old man.

Watching, she felt pity for him. It was a disturbing emotion. All her life she had feared him; if there was love there, it was hidden so deep that she was unaware of it. True, a strange rapport had grown up between them since his visits began, but she had thought of it as a grudging, unvoiced mutual respect.

It saddened her to realise that on her side it was only pity.

3

The corner shop was busy. Shoulder to shoulder, Mr and Mrs McKay worked hard weighing and parcelling, calculating totals with brows knotted and fingers scribbling invisible sums on the scarred old counter.

Waiting in line, Lessie noted that Mr McKay's face was grey with fatigue, though it wasn't yet midday, and his lips had a blue tinge to them. His wife kept darting anxious glances in his direction. When it was Lessie's turn to be served and the old woman was dropping broken biscuits, cheaper than whole ones, into a paper bag on the scales, she said below her breath, 'Could ye mebbe gie me an hour or two this afternoon, lass?'

'I'd need tae bring Ian with me.'

'Och, he's no trouble at all. Geordie had a bad night,' the wrinkled bloodless lips mouthed the words so that there was no danger of Mr McKay overhearing, 'an' I'd like him tae have a bit o' a rest after his dinner.'

'I'll be here by two o'clock.' Lessie dug into her purse and offered her halfpence in payment for the biscuits, but Mrs McKay said, 'Tuts, lassie, put your money away,' and shooed her from the shop.

Ian, strapped into a battered old perambulator that someone had given Lessie in exchange for a few days' housework, was waiting outside, thumb in mouth, watching the people around him. The Vennel was a noisy, busy place at all times. By day the street echoed to the clamour of voices, children's shrill yells, and the incessant clop of hooves on cobbles and the rumbling of iron-bound cart wheels; by night, when the carthorses were in their stables and the children in their beds, drunks

25

cursed and shouted and quarrelled their way up and down the footpaths.

Lessie tucked the biscuits, a special treat for her mother and Thomasina, into a pocket where Ian's busy fingers couldn't get at them, and began to bump the perambulator carefully over the uneven pavement. The pram had been shabby when she first got it, but Davie had mended the broken wheels for her and lashed the handle back together with string; Lessie dreaded the day it disintegrated for good, because Ian was getting heavier and she was fortunate to have transport for him.

For a few hours' work in the shop this afternoon she would get the biscuits and perhaps a bag of barley and split peas for soup, or porridge oats. In return for scrubbing stairs and doing housework she was very often given some child's cast-off clothes for Ian, or something for herself. Bartering was popular in the world she inhabited, and at times it was a more sensible method of payment than money.

Before going to her mother's house she had work to do, scrubbing the stairs in a tenement in Cathcart Street. She hurried there, the pram wheels squeaking with every turn. The bobble on Ian's woollen hat, knitted from a ripped-down shrunken jersey that had once belonged to Davie, bounced cheerfully as she bumped the baby carriage up the step into the close. She knocked on the door of one of the ground-floor flats and it opened almost at once.

'I was watching out for you.' Miss Peden, erect as ever in spite of her snowy hair and her wrinkled-apple little face, backed along the hallway before the pram. 'Come in, come in.' Her kitchen, spotless as usual, was warm and smelled of baking. 'You'll take a cup of tea, my dear.'

'I'd best get on. I've to visit my mam and I promised to go into the shop this afternoon.' Lessie squatted to unfasten Ian. The pram's leather straps had long since broken and he was tied in with the woollen scarf she used for him at home. She lifted him out and set him down on his feet, then began to unfasten his knitted coat.

'I'll do that, since you're in a hurry. Off you go and the

tea will be waiting for you when you've finished.'

Lessie stripped off her outer clothes and dug into her worn shopping bag for the sacking apron she wore for heavy work. 'Be a good boy, Ian.'

'He's always a good boy,' Miss Peden told her briskly. 'Go on now, girl. Sooner gone, sooner back!'

The note of crisp command in her voice made Lessie smile as she hurried up to the top floor of the building. Once a teacher, always a teacher. Miss Peden had taught all the Kirkwood family and Lessie had been a special favourite of hers. The two of them had built up a friendship as Lessie grew into maturity, for the retired schoolteacher had no family of her own. It was Miss Peden who had helped to get Davie into night school, giving him extra tutoring when he needed it. It was Miss Peden, still well thought of in the town, who recommended Lessie to ladies who could afford someone to do their heavier housework for them when Donald died and his widow and child were left to fend for themselves.

'Ye're late,' a grating voice said as Lessie topped the final flight of stairs.

'I'm sorry, Mrs Kincaid.'

'Aye, so ye should be. The water's near cold.'

Lessie bit back the suggestion that Mrs Kincaid could easily have waited until she arrived before filling the bucket. In the old woman's view, she knew, tepid water was a fitting punishment for tardiness. Instead, she forced a smile to her lips as she took the bucket that had been waiting by Mrs Kincaid's door, together with a scrubbing brush, a cloth, and bar of soap. Mrs Kincaid stood and watched her work for a few minutes before retiring into her own flat and shutting her polished door.

Outside, the day was grey and chill in spite of the fact that it was May; the River Clyde was sullen, the far shore hidden behind a misty screen. Although she had tied a shawl over her thin coat, Lessie had been chilled on her way from the Vennel. She was glad to work hard now, for scrubbing was a fine way to set the blood coursing warmly through her veins.

The building consisted of eleven flats in all; two on the

ground floor, and three on each of the three other floors. There were six flights of stairs, with a half-landing between each floor. This type of tenement was similar to the home in which Lessie's parents lived. She dreamed of having a place of her own in such a building one day, for each flat had its own sink in the kitchen and there was a water closet on each half-landing. In the Vennel, the water closets were out in the back yards, one to each building. If one was out of order, the residents in that building used the nearest. More often than not there were two dozen families using one water closet.

Scrubbing stairs was an occupation Lessie quite enjoyed, physically exhausting though it was. It freed her mind to wander over the precious months she and Donald had known together, to daydream a little, and to fret over Davie's future and the mysterious estrangement between her parents. No matter how hard she tried not to concern herself, the worrying thoughts kept coming back to nag at her. Lessie cared about her family, she wanted them all to be happy, and she suffered more grief over their hardships than over her own.

When she reached the ground floor she worked her way out to the closemouth, knelt on the pavement to scrub the final step, then tipped her pail into the gutter, her back creaking when she finally stood upright. She swilled some of the dark grey water round vigorously in the bucket to catch up the sediment at the bottom then poured it all out with one final triumphant flourish before making her way back to the top floor, walking carefully to avoid leaving marks on the newly scrubbed surfaces.

Mrs Kincaid studied the soap closely to establish how much of it had been used, then dipped into her apron pocket and counted ten pennies into Lessie's palm. 'That auld miser McAllister didnae answer his door when I went chappin' on it for the money. Ye'll hae tae see him yersel',' she said, and withdrew, shutting her door in Lessie's face.

Nobody answered the middle door on the landing below when Lessie knocked, though it seemed to her that there was a waiting silence on the other side of the wooden panels. She sighed, and trudged down to Miss Peden's flat.

'I'll see to McAllister,' the retired schoolteacher said briskly when Lessie told her.

'I feel bad about it. Mr McAllister's a poor old soul.'

Miss Peden snorted. 'He has to pay his way the same as the rest of us, lassie, and you need the money you earn. You don't scrub stairs for the pleasure of it. Now take that apron off and sit down by the fire. You'll have a fresh-baked scone with your tea,' she added. With Miss Peden it was sometimes hard to tell the difference between a question and a command. The old lady busied herself at the gleaming range, blackleaded every morning except Sundays, and Lessie sat down on one of the two comfortable fireside chairs. She looked with pleasure at the crisp white netting across the window, the heavy red chenille curtains, looped back by day, the matching chenille table cover weighted down by a blue and white bowl of wax fruit. By her feet the companion-set holding poker, brush and shovel glittered brassily in the firelight, and above her head two 'wally dugs' – matching golden-brown, long-eared china dogs – looked down with blank brown eyes. Miss Peden's house was large by Lessie's standards, with two bedrooms and a shared wash-house and little patch of garden at the back. Miss Peden grew vegetables and a few flowers in her section of the garden.

As she handed her guest a cup of tea, the old woman asked, 'How's David's studying coming along?' She always gave Davie his proper name.

'He's doing fine.' Lessie sipped at the hot, well-sugared tea and felt herself relaxing into the soft cushions that Miss Peden had made herself. Ian, already filled to the brim with scones, sat on the floor, playing with a wooden horse kept specially for him.

'Tell him if he's got any problems to mind and come to me. I might not be an engineer but books are books and between us we'll puzzle it out.'

'I wish,' said Lessie, 'that he could be put onto working one of the cranes at the docks instead of loading and unloading the ships. He'd be a lot happier, and that would be more in the engineering line. My da could arrange it for him, but he won't, for all that he knows how much Davie hates the work he's doing.'

'Archie Kirkwood's a stubborn man, one of those folk who believe that it only softens people to give them what they want. But mind you, David's fortunate that his father's an overseer. At least it means that the laddie gets work every day.'

'That bothers him too, being picked out before other men who wait alongside him morning after morning.'

The dock system was a harsh one. Early every morning men hoping for a day or half-day's work gathered at the gate and the overseers of each gang picked out those they wanted. The others usually waited on, enviously watching fortunate workers who had been chosen, hoping against hope that extra hands might be needed. Lessie knew that being picked out every day by his father over men who were desperate for work and might be more skilful dockers than he was, was a humiliating experience for Davie. He had come home with a bloodied nose more than once from a street fight over it.

'Tuts, girl, your heart's far too soft. Someone has to be taken on and it makes sense for your father to favour his own. Besides, if David didn't bring in money, you'd be in an even sorrier state than you are.'

'Ian and me manage fine!' Lessie was stung into answering sharply, and the older woman gave a bark of laughter.

'No need to fly at me. I know you manage very well, but you have to work far too hard for what you get. You look tired – even when you first came in you looked tired. Is it the bairn? Is his whooping cough troubling him at nights again?'

'It's a lot better. I think it's almost gone.' Lessie leaned forward to put a hand lightly, thankfully, on Ian's red-gold head. 'Mebbe I'm just getting old.'

'Away with you! You're not much more than a bairn yourself.'

'I'm twenty now.'

'Imagine!' said Miss Peden dryly, then, 'No, no, lassie,

30

you've not lost that bright glow that always set you apart from the rest of them in the classroom. It's just dimmed, that's all, with the worry you've had. It'll come back.'

'You think so?'

'I know so. There are some who never lose it and you're one of them. Mebbe,' said the old woman thoughtfully, 'this new century'll be your turning point.'

'It's strange to think that we're living in nineteen hundred now.' Lessie touched Ian's head again. 'A new century. I wonder what it'll bring to him – to all of us.'

'A better way of life, surely, for you and your bairn. Mebbe it's time for all of Britain to have some sort of a change. As for me – well, I belong to the last century. Me and the old Queen, God bless her. I wonder if the two of us'll see many more years out.'

The maudlin turn the conversation had taken upset Lessie and robbed her of her brief contentment. She cared little for Queen Victoria, but the thought of being without Miss Peden worried her more than the old lady knew. She glanced at the pretty little enamelled clock on the mantelshelf, finished her tea, and began to bundle Ian into his coat and hat. He gave up the wooden horse placidly, having learned by now that it would be waiting for his next visit. 'If I don't go now I'll not have time to visit my mother and get back to the shop.'

'Here, take a few scones to your mother.' Miss Peden wrapped the scones up in a spotlessly clean dish towel and handed them over. 'You can return the cloth next time. Look after yourself, lassie.'

Edith Fisher, Lessie's older sister, was already in her mother's house with her son Peter when Lessie and Ian arrived. Thomasina greeted the newcomers with her usual cries of joy and Lessie hugged her close. She loved this little sister, the prettiest of the three Kirkwood girls with her soft, dark, curly hair. Thomasina returned the hug affectionately then set about clumsily helping to get Ian out of his outdoor clothes. Barbara watched with a slight softening of her expressionless face, and said when

Lessie handed her gifts over, 'You shouldnae go spendin' your money on us.'

'It's only a few wee biscuits for Thomasina, and the scones are from Miss Peden. Fresh-baked this morning.' Lessie sat down and watched her mother put the biscuits carefully in a cupboard then give her hair a nervous, automatic pat and head for the bedroom, murmuring, 'I'll just give my hair a tidy up.'

'That's the third time since I arrived that she's gone to tidy her hair,' Edith hissed as soon as their mother had left the room. 'I don't know why I come here to be disgraced like this! It was bad enough Da being a drunkard without Ma turning to it as well!'

'She only takes a mouthful each time.'

'Mebbe so, but she can't even let an hour pass without at least one of her mouthfuls.' Edith's voice was accusing. 'You should do something about it.'

'Why me? You and Joseph are older than I am.'

'Joseph!' Edith almost spat the name out. 'In the Bridewell more often than out of it. And it's probably him she's hiding her drink from – he'd have the lot if he could find it. Anyway, you see more of her than I do.'

'What can I do? I can scarcely ask Da to try to stop her, can I? I'd get my ear slapped and you know it.'

'It's not good for Thomasina.' Edith mouthed the final word so that the girl, now on the floor with Peter and Ian, didn't hear her. Her thin colourless lips, so like Barbara's, writhed over the name. Edith, with her pale blue eyes and straight fair hair, was going to look just like her mother in twenty years' time.

Lessie looked round the room. It was spotless, but unlike Miss Peden's little flat it was cheerless, unwelcoming, lacking soul.

'Thomasina and the house are as clean as they can be,' she said.

'Now, mebbe. But what if she gets worse? What if—'

'What if she doesnae get worse?' Lessie interrupted, unwilling to take on any more worry. Edith glared, and would have argued on, but Barbara came back in, bringing with her the unmistakable smell of whisky. She

32

smiled at her daughters with an air of relief.

'I'll make some tea an' we'll toast some bread wi' a wee bit o' cheese, eh? Lessie, you take the toasting fork. I've cut the bread ready.'

'I can't stay long,' Edith told her grimly and Barbara's face fell.

'Och, Edith, I scarce see you these days. You can stay long enough for a cup of tea and some toast, surely?'

'Please, Mama.' Peter's voice was eager. Lessie smiled at him and he flushed and ducked his head shyly.

'Peter, when your grandma's talking to you I'll let you know,' Edith snapped. Deserted by her husband four years earlier when her son was a toddler, she had gone into domestic service at the Warren family's mansion in Gourock, the neighbouring town. She and Peter stayed with Barbara's sister Marion, a childless widow who had had little to do with Barbara since her marriage to Archie Kirkwood, looked on by Marion from the first as unworthy of Barbara. Edith, who had seen how the 'posh' folk raise their children, was determined that her son would grow up to be a little gentleman. Her aunt fully agreed, and between them, in Lessie's opinion, they had turned poor little Peter into a well-dressed miniature adult.

'Besides,' Barbara coaxed, putting the kettle on the range, 'I doubt if Lessie's heard about the new Mr and Mrs Warren arriving from Jamaica.'

Lessie looked up sharply. The name immediately conjured up a picture of a dead face on a dirty pillow, Anna McCauley's hands clutching at her, the money that she had accepted, knowing full well that it was tainted.

The Warrens' Gourock mansion where Edith worked had smooth lawns and huge windows overlooking the broad rivermouth and the lush, wooded shore opposite. For several years now there had been only two elderly brothers living in the house. Now that Frank Warren had succumbed in Anna McCauley's bed, Lessie had assumed that his brother would live on in the family house on his own.

'One day,' Donald had been in the habit of saying when they walked past the Warren gates, Donald carrying Ian, Lessie with her hand tucked proudly into the curve of her man's elbow, 'One day, lass, I'll buy you a house like that. Mebbe this time next year, eh?'

But when this time next year had arrived, Donald was dead, his sparkling blue eyes that could set her heart thumping with just one look closed for ever. Lessie thrust the memories away and asked, 'What new Mr and Mrs Warren?'

Edith smirked, pleased to be the centre of attention. 'The nephew. You'll have heard that Mr Frank died several weeks back—' She broke off, then said, 'It was down your way it happened. Did you not hear about it?'

'I heard something.' Lessie reached down to tug Ian's jersey down at the back, hiding the sudden colour that rose in her cheeks.

'Did you not go to see the funeral procession? A lovely funeral we had. The procession was so long, and we'd to bring in extra staff to see to the meal afterwards. The house was full to the brim.' Edith was smug, as though she had organised it all herself. 'We all thought that that only left Mr James, but not a bit of it. Two weeks after the funeral, who should arrive but Mr Andrew, son of Mr George that died years ago. Brown as a berry he is, for he's been out in Jamaica for years seeing to the family business out there.'

Her voice rattled on about Mr Andrew and the wife he had married out in Jamaica and their twin son and daughter and the house being filled and Mrs Andrew being cold in the Scottish climate. Barbara slipped in murmurs of admiring surprise at the right moments, but Lessie let the long recitation flow by her. She wished that her mother wouldn't feed Edith's vanity by fawning so openly on her elder daughter. Barbara was well aware that it was poor Thomasina and her own supposedly secret tippling that kept Edith from spending much time in her old family home. And Barbara was never invited to call at the Gourock house that Edith and Peter shared with her sister. But instead of being insulted, as Lessie was on her behalf, Barbara worked hard to flatter Edith whenever she did condescend to visit her old home.

Thomasina gave one of her excited shrieks, holding her hands out greedily for a piece of the cheese her mother was cutting, and Lessie was startled out of her private thoughts.

'Sit up at the table, there's a good girl,' Barbara said. 'See, Peter's going to sit nice at the table.'

'Beautiful, she is,' Edith burbled on, raising her voice slightly so that she could be heard above her mother and Thomasina as they all took their places round the kitchen table. 'Every inch a lady. So now we've had to take on more staff – a nurse and nurserymaid for the children, of course, and a lady's maid for Mrs Andrew. The housekeeper says it's like the old days, when Mr James's parents were still alive. She was the housemaid then, in the post I hold now. Peter, smaller bites if you please. Only starving paupers stuff their mouths like that.' She nibbled a few crumbs from her own toast.

Lessie broke off a piece of cheese, popped it into Ian's mouth, open and ready like a fledgling's beak in spite of the scones he had had at Miss Peden's, and wondered how soon she could get away. Draughty though the shop was, it was full of life and interest, free of Edith's sickening snobbishness and her mother's fawning.

Three days later Lessie was washing clothes in the stone sink on the landing, elbow-deep in water patiently heated in a tin bucket on the range. The weather had relented and a glimmer of sunlight had managed to find its way in through the landing window above the sink. She cleaned the window frequently, but as some of the panes were missing and the gaps had been covered with bits of board, not much daylight filtered through.

Ian sat on the floor just inside the open door of her flat, chewing at the last piece of orange. The cough syrup and tonic she had bought with Anna McCauley's money had made a difference to him and the whooping, strangling coughs had almost disappeared. Anna herself had become a nuisance, though. She insisted on assuming that they were now friends, and it seemed to Lessie that almost every time she set foot out of her own door Anna appeared, arms tucked beneath her rounded bosom, ready for a gossip. Today, Anna was out and Lessie was making the most of her absence.

She scrubbed hard at Davie's shirt with a scrap of rough grainy soap, then fisted her hands and used her knuckles to rub one piece of material hard against another. Her washing board, left out in the back yard for a thoughtless moment several weeks earlier, had promptly disappeared and she couldn't afford another. As she plunged the shirt under the surface of the cooling, scumming water, someone came up the stairs at her back and a well-educated male voice asked, 'Are you Anna McCauley?'

Lessie whipped round, wiping her hands on her sacking apron.

'Indeed I am not!' she said indignantly, scandalised to think that one of Anna's clients should mistake her for a prostitute. The shirt slid into the sink. 'She's my neighbour,' Lessie went on, nodding at Anna's door, then she added, as he rapped on it with the handle of his cane, 'She's not in.'

'When will she be back?'

Lessie rubbed a damp forearm over her hot face, tucked a loose strand of hair behind her ear, and saw, in the dim light, that Anna's visitor was far superior to the men who usually came calling on her. This one was immaculately dressed in a suit of dark material, so well fitted to his tall body that it must have been made for him. His bow tie had been tied with casual, careless elegance and atop his high snowy collar, piercing grey eyes surveyed her from a dark square face. A curly-brimmed bowler hat and a silver-handled cane grasped in a gloved hand completed an outfit that must have cost several times as much as all the clothes she and Davie and Ian possessed between them.

'When,' he repeated with a hint of impatience, 'do you expect her back?'

'I've no idea,' Lessie told him, determined not to be

drawn into conversation with one of Anna's clients. 'I'm her neighbour, not her mother.'

He blinked, and she had a feeling that his mouth trembled slightly beneath his dark, well-kept moustache. But instead of leaving, he stood for a moment, tapping the head of his cane against the palm of his other hand, then said, 'Who owns this building?'

'The factor's Lindsay and Ross.'

'How much rent do they charge you?'

He was obviously used to having his questions answered without delay, and she found herself beginning, 'Three shilling a w—' before she stopped herself and said instead, haughtily, 'If you're looking for a place to rent I'd advise you to go to the factor's office. They'll give you the details.'

This time he did smile; she caught it in a sidelong glance. Then the smile was gone as he said, 'It's a slum. How can you live in such a place – and bring up a child?' he added as Ian, covered with sticky orange juice, toddled out to grasp Lessie's skirt and stare, finger in mouth.

The man's impudence infuriated Lessie. 'I don't choose tae live here – nobody would choose tae live here. But some folk have no other place tae—'

Footsteps, light and swift, came up from the close below and Anna McCauley, face rosy from being out of doors, skirt swinging round trim ankles, feathered bonnet set at a jaunty angle on her auburn head, arrived on the landing, her eyes bright as they took in the man standing by her door.

'Are you Miss Anna McCauley?'

She beamed at him. 'I am.'

'My name's Warren. Andrew Warren. I'd like to speak to you.'

The colour drained from Anna's face and Lessie swallowed hard. She might have known the incident of the dead man in Anna's bed wasn't over.

'I came to thank you on the family's behalf for taking my uncle in when he fell ill,' Andrew Warren was saying, and Anna bloomed again, taking her key from her bag, opening her door, ushering him in. She winked at Lessie behind his back, then swept after him and shut the door.

Lessie, left alone, bent and picked Ian up, hugging him tight in her relief. Retribution wasn't about to sweep down on them after all. As she put the little boy down and urged him back inside the flat so that she could get on with her washing, she recalled the sudden widening of Andrew Warren's eyes when he looked down and saw Anna, pretty as a picture, emerging from the dark well of the stairs.

'I just did what anyone would have done,' Anna was saying expansively in her flat, sweeping her hat off, motioning Andrew Warren to the only chair. As she slipped off her shawl and hung it on the nail hammered into the door she glanced at him out of the corner of her eye. He was good-looking, this young member of the Warren family. She wondered what it would be like to lie in bed with him.

He was glancing round the room, taking in every stick of furniture, the black damp patches on the walls, the portrait of Queen Victoria. 'D'you live here on your own?'

She sat down on a stool opposite him, moving gracefully for his benefit, arranging her skirt carefully so that her slender ankles peeped from beneath the hem. 'I've no man living here with me, if that's your meaning.'

'It's an ugly building.'

Unlike Lessie, Anna didn't take offence. 'The factor's a bastard – quick to collect the rent but slow to do anything to help us. If you complain you're put out.' Her voice was cheerful, matter-of-fact. 'But at least I've a roof over my head and that's more than some poor souls in this town can say.'

He glanced up at the ceiling, cracked and dirty and sagging, then reached into his pocket. 'I'm sorry we've taken so long to express our gratitude, but my uncle's an old man and his brother's death has been hard on him. I myself only arrived in Greenock a week or two ago. My uncle and I would like to express our gratitude with this.'

Anna's heart leapt as she saw the notes in his hand. It

was all she could do to stop herself from snatching them. With an effort she managed to take them as casually as they were offered, thank him in her softest, most feminine voice and hold his gaze with her own for a few seconds before he got to his feet abruptly, picked up his hat and said that he must go.

At the door he shook her hand, thanked her again, then went, with a nod to Lessie, still working at the sink. Anna watched him descend the stairs, thinking of the crisp notes lying on the dresser behind her, but thinking even more of the man who had given them to her.

4

The big house overlooking the Firth of Clyde was far too hot. Andrew Warren, returning home for his midday meal, felt as though he was smothering as soon as he stepped inside the front door.

His wife and his uncle were already at the table and as Andrew entered, Madeleine's dark eyes swept up towards him reproachfully. He bent to kiss the cheek that she offered to him. 'Sorry, my dear, I had to attend to something at the refinery. How are you today, Uncle James?'

'Still out of sorts, my boy,' said the elder Mr Warren feebly, although he was making good work of putting his food away, Andrew noticed. James and Frank had been twins; they had never married and had lived all their lives in quiet harmony in the house their father had built when his sugar refinery began to make his fortune. James had been badly shaken by Frank's death and hadn't set foot in the refinery since, leaving all the business to his nephew.

'You should come to the refinery with me this afternoon,' Andrew suggested, taking his place opposite Madeleine. 'We could do with your advice on a few matters.'

'Perhaps next week.'

'At least go out and walk about, or send for a cab and take a ride along the coastline. You could take Madeleine with you.'

Madeleine's elegant shoulders rippled in a shiver. 'It's far too cold to go out, Andrew.' Her voice was petulant and even her attractive French accent sounded sullen. 'This country of yours is the coldest place I have ever known. We will all die of it, my babies and I.'

'If you insist on staying inside all the time and molly-coddling yourself, you're quite likely to die of boredom if nothing else,' Andrew told her, an edge creeping into his voice. 'You can't expect Scotland to be as warm as Jamaica, my dear. You'll become acclimatised.'

'Never!' Her shoulders rippled again, this time in one of the feminine little shrugs that had so captivated him a few short years ago when they first met and he knew at once that he wanted her to be his wife. Today she wore a soft woollen lilac gown decorated from neck to hem with violet bows. The colours suited her rich dark beauty, but the shade of the bows reminded Andrew of the girl in the slum down in the Vennel, the girl with tumbled red hair and wide, long-lashed violet eyes.

He had been thinking of her a great deal in the six days since he had visited her. Aware that it was unseemly to be thinking of another woman in his wife's presence, he put the girl from his mind and said, 'Have the children been out this morning?'

'I said no. The air is too chilled.'

'My dear, we're into June now, this is our summer. You must tell their nursemaid to take them for a walk this after-noon.' Then, seeing the mutinous set of her mouth – a small neat mouth, quite unlike the generous full curve of Anna McCauley's lips – he added, 'I shall tell her myself when I visit the nursery.'

Madeleine glared, but said nothing. When the meal was finished, she rose and left the dining room, followed by James, who muttered something about forty winks in his room. Left alone, Andrew folded his napkin and replaced it carefully in its heavy silver ring, head bent over the task.

It had been a mistake to bring Madeleine to Scotland. He himself would far rather have stayed in Jamaica's sunshine, but someone had to run the refinery and with Frank dead and James apparently sliding comfortably into self-imposed retirement, Andrew had no choice but to stay in Greenock. He got to his feet, telling himself grimly that Madeleine would get used to it. She would have to get used to it.

He yearned for the early months of their marriage, days filled with pleasurable companionship, warm, flower-scented nights of passion. It had all begun to fade with Madeleine's pregnancy, and the shock of producing not one baby but two had put an end to the carefree joy of their marriage. To Madeleine, motherhood was allied with ageing, a fear that dragged her down, and she made no secret of her determination not to have any more children. At first Andrew had been patient with her, finding outlets for his own needs with other women, but six months after the birth of the twins he had requested, then demanded, his marital rights. Although Madeleine remained indifferent to his argument that she was his wife, the woman he loved and wanted, he nonetheless finally availed himself of her body, and had continued to do so, once a week.

It was a cold, unhappy coupling. Madeleine's indifference, her sullen passive acceptance of him, made him feel like an assailant instead of a lover. But having claimed her he could not retreat, although their unloving physical union had become as distasteful to him as it was to her.

The three-year-old twins, supervised by their nurse-maid, were messily spooning lunch into themselves. They greeted him with screams of pleasure, for Andrew liked children and he made a point of seeing his son and daughter several times each day.

They were beautiful children, dark-haired and dark-eyed like their mother. Andrew's hair was also dark, but Martin and Helene both had Madeleine's blue-black tresses. Martin was the heavier, Helene small and dainty.

'Take them out this afternoon,' he told the nurse.

'Mrs Warren—'

'Never mind that, I want them to get some fresh air,' Andrew interrupted, the edge creeping back into his voice.

The woman flushed and said flatly, 'Very good, sir.' He knew very well that she disapproved of fathers visiting the nursery, and preferred to take her orders from Madeleine. Who paid her wages? he asked himself angrily as he left the room and went downstairs again. It was time the nurse – and Madeleine – learned that his orders were to be obeyed.

His wife was lying on the chaise longue in the drawing room, her eyes closed. They opened as he bent to kiss her and a brief frown drifted across her lovely face. 'You'll be back in good time for dinner, Andrew?'

'Of course. I've told nurse to take the children out, and please do as I suggest, Madeleine, and drive out yourself.'

'I have a headache.' The diamond ring he had put on her finger when she agreed to marry him flashed at him as she drew white fingers across her forehead.

'It's little wonder. This house is like a furnace.'

'Your children and I must surely be warm!'

'For God's sake, Madeleine, there are some folk not far from here who have to do without a fraction of the heat you need, even in the winter.' He was on the verge of telling her about the cold clammy tenement slum he had visited in his search for the woman who had taken his uncle into her house, the high cheekbones and fragile, hollowed pale face of the girl washing clothes in a big chipped stone sink on the landing, but her sullenness stopped him.

'This is such an ugly country,' she said. 'Cold and ugly.'

He walked to the window and looked out over the river to the hills beyond. The sky above them was eggshell blue, the sun blessing the water and turning it into diamonds. 'On the contrary, my dear, this part of the Clyde must be one of the most beautiful spots in the world. It is man who makes the ugliness with his factories and mills and slums.' Then he added with a smile, crossing to kiss her, 'Though I must admit that in my eyes the Warren refinery has its own beauty.'

She twitched herself round, away from him, and the rug that lay over her slid to the floor. Andrew picked it up and put it back. His hand brushed against the softness of a breast beneath the wool dress as he did so and she twitched again, almost burrowing into the chaise longue. Madeleine had a beautiful body, satin-smooth hills and softly shaded hollows; at one time he had known it as well as his own. Now it was a strange and alien land that he visited regularly, briefly, with no pleasure other than physical satisfaction.

As he left the house, breathing in the cool air with relief, and climbed into the waiting carriage, he thought of another body, one that he didn't know but could guess at, a promising ripeness beneath a shabby blouse and a skirt with an uneven hem. Every movement Anna McCauley had made had spoken to the sensual side of his nature. He wondered, as he had wondered from the moment he first set eyes on her, if Uncle Frank had really collapsed in the street or if he had collapsed in her sordid, cheerless room. He couldn't blame the old man for seeking a bit of pleasure out of life, and there was something about the confident way the girl had taken the proffered money that made Andrew feel that she was used to being given money by men. All the same, the thought of her sent a pleasurable frisson through his muscles and sinews.

The hooter marking the end of the midday break sounded just as he dismounted from the carriage at the Warren sugar refinery in Bank Street. The row of carthorses outside the loading bay jingled their harnesses and tossed their heads, turning to watch the carters straggling out of the warehouse. The horses knew the routine well and could be trusted to pull their carts down to the docks by themselves then back up to the refinery once they were loaded with great sacks of raw sugar from the ships. The carters could afford to walk in a chattering group behind them.

Andrew crossed the cobbled yard and went into the warm, sweet-smelling world of sugar refining. There was plenty of work for him to see to, for his uncles had not kept up with modern trends and he had a great many plans for the refinery. It was one of several in Greenock; many more had gone to the wall in the past decade or so, and Andrew had no intention of letting the same thing happen to the Bank Street refinery.

But halfway through the afternoon the work palled. His mind wasn't on it today. He put down his pen, stared at

45

it for a long moment, then got briskly to his feet and with a curt word to his clerk left the refinery.

Scorning his carriage, he walked down towards the river, turning left along Dalrymple Street then left again into the Vennel. The landing was vacant this time, the sink empty, its greened brass tap dripping steadily. Anna McCauley opened the door to his knock. Her violet eyes, as lovely as he had remembered them, widened at sight of him, then a small knowing smile curved her full mouth and she tilted her head to one side. 'Mr Warren.'

The wanting that had been flickering through Andrew since he first set eyes on her strengthened as he stood looking at her. There was no need to think of an excuse, he realised that now. So he simply said, 'I had to come back.'

'Yes.' She moved aside, opening the door wide, and he stepped past her into the tiny cold room.

Edith waited impatiently until the corner shop emptied of customers and her sister was free.

'I called in at the house but you weren't there,' she said. Lessie controlled an impulse to inform her solemnly that she'd been here, in the shop. Sometimes Edith's humourlessness and bizarre logic could be amusing, at other times it could be infuriating. Lessie often wondered what it would be like to hear a conversation between two Ediths. They would never get to the point.

'I should be finished in a moment, then we can go and have a cup of tea,' she promised.

'I've not got all day,' Edith protested, then tutted with vexation as a ragged barefoot lad pushed past her to claim Lessie's attention. The boy had the face of an angel that had fallen from Heaven straight into a mud puddle.

'Ha'p'nny o' broken biscuits,' he said gruffly, dumping his coin onto the counter, having to reach up to do so.

'A ha'penny of broken biscuits. You're in luck – we just happen to have some,' Lessie told him pleasantly, picking up a scoop and walking round the end of the counter to the shop door. The place was so small that its goods spilled out onto the footpath and a box of broken biscuits sat outside, perched on a sack of barley and covered with a piece of board to protect its contents from dirt and flies. The child watched greedily as she weighed the biscuit fragments then poured them from the scales into a bag. He took it and did a thoughtful circuit of the small shop before leaving, his blue eyes flickering between the goods and Mrs McKay, who was serving another customer.

'Lessie, I said I've not got all—'

Lessie fluttered the fingers of one hand at her sister, her eyes on the child. 'Just a minute, Edith.'

Near a jar of sweets he stopped, shifted the bag of biscuits from one grimy fist to the other, and looked at the shopkeeper, then at Lessie, who gazed back calmly until his eyes dropped before hers. The corners of his mouth turning down, he humped his shoulders and stamped out, clutching his purchase.

Edith had watched the scene with growing confusion. 'What was all that about?'

'He had it in mind to steal some sweeties. You've to keep your eyes on some of them.'

'The wee rascal!'

'Och, it's probably the only way he has of getting them, poor mite. Even so, he'll have to learn that being poor doesnae mean he has the right to be a thief as well. Anyway,' Lessie finished briskly, knowing full well that if she started fretting over every child that longed for the money to buy a sweet her heart would soon be broken, 'he'd already used up his criminal tendencies for one day.'

'Eh?'

'The biscuits he bought were broken half an hour ago when his elder brother and some friends of his just happened to knock the box over as they were running by,' Lessie explained. 'Broken biscuits cost less and they know it. They break them, then they get one of the wee ones to come in and buy them cheap.'

'I've never heard the like!' Edith's mouth hardened into a thin line.

'No? You'd have heard it long before now if you lived in this part of the town.'

'You should send for the police!'

'Their lives are hard enough without that,' Lessie began to say as Mrs McKay finished with her customer and turned to her.

'Thanks for helpin' me out, hen. Off you go now, you look tired out,' said the old woman, her own face paper-white with exhaustion. Lessie felt bad at leaving her on her own, but Ian would soon be clamouring for food and Edith was impatiently tapping her foot at the shop door.

Mr McKay, a woollen scarf wound round his neck over a shabby jacket, was in bed in the inner room, sound asleep and snoring. Beside him Ian, who had been tucked between the old man and the wall for safety, also snored slightly, lying on his back with his mouth drooping open. His eyelids lifted as soon as Lessie touched him and he beamed a welcome and held his arms out to her. His small body, warm from the bed, nestled against hers and she lowered him into his pram reluctantly.

'I'm worried about the McKays,' she said to Edith as they walked the short distance to Lessie's house. 'His heart's getting worse and she's half killing herself trying to run that shop on her own and look after him. I'm helping out more and more.'

'I hope they pay you for it.'

'Of course they do. But what'll happen if they decide to give it up? I need the money. Besides, it's handy for me and the work's not as hard as scrubbing stairs. And they let me take Ian with me too.'

'Somebody else'll take it over and they'll still need help.'

'It might be a couple with a family. They might have their own help.' But a sidelong glance at her sister's tense face told Lessie that at the moment Edith was uninterested in her problems. 'What was it you came about?'

'I'll tell you when we're behind closed doors,' Edith said primly as she followed Lessie into the narrow close. She seldom ventured into the Vennel, terrified of meeting the thieves and vagabonds she was certain inhabited the place. She preferred to meet Lessie in their mother's house.

'It sounds important.'

'It is.'

Lessie sighed inwardly as she lifted Ian from the pram, hoping that she wasn't in for another burst of complaints about their parents. Edith would not accept the fact that whatever had happened to estrange Archie and Barbara was none of her business, or Lessie's.

'You carry Ian and I'll take the pram,' she said, adding dryly when Edith shied back from the baby, 'He's over the whooping cough now. You'll not catch anything from the wee soul.'

'It's not that.' Edith glanced down at her smart brown jacket and skirt, vulnerable to sticky little fingers and teething dribbles, and said reluctantly, 'I'll see to the perambulator. He'll mebbe cry if I take him.'

Lessie began to mount the stairs, keeping her tongue between her teeth. Edith didn't care for children and lived in constant fear of having her clothing dirtied or crumpled by small clutching hands. Poor little Peter was quite unused to being cuddled and whenever Lessie put her arms about him, even when he had been Ian's age, he stiffened and flinched away just as his mother had done at the thought of carrying Ian. Lessie held her small son closer and decided that Edith wasn't worth fretting over.

They had almost reached the landing, Lessie several steps ahead, Edith struggling with the pram, when a door opened and shut above their heads and light steps began to descend swiftly, almost skimming down.

'It's yourself, Lessie.' Anna McCauley came to a stop and reached out to tickle Ian under the chin. 'Hello, wee man!' She beamed down at Edith, who was getting red in the face because the pram had jammed itself across the stairway and refused to move. 'Here, I'll see to it.'

'I'm quite able to—' Edith began coldly, but the pram was whisked from her hands, deftly disentangled, and handed back. Anna, pretty as a picture in a leaf-green coat with a bunch of darker green satin ribbons at the neck, beamed into Edith's set face.

'There you are. Just hold it straight and you'll be fine,' she said, and was gone.

'I see that . . . woman is still living here.' Edith grimly heaved the pram onto the landing and waited for her sister to open the flat door. 'Does she still have all sorts of men up and down the stairs, visiting her at all hours?'

'I've not seen all sorts of men on the stairs for the past month or more,' Lessie was able to answer truthfully. Andrew Warren could scarcely be described as 'all sorts of men'. Since she had met him, Anna had stopped entertaining anyone else.

'Hmm.' Edith followed her into the small lobby and put the pram into its corner by the wooden coal bunker with a final admonishing shake as though ordering it to stay there and behave itself. 'Don't tell me she's gone and got herself a decent job at last?'

'I've no idea. I've enough to do attending to my own business to worry about hers,' Lessie retorted, putting Ian down and straightening her back with a sigh of relief. He toddled ahead of her into the kitchen, where the kettle simmered on the range. She took her coat off and measured tea from the caddy into the pot, relishing her good fortune in having enough coal to keep the range going. If it hadn't been for Davie's wages she would have had to save what fuel she could afford for the evenings and do without hot food or drink during the day. She was fortunate in so many ways, compared to some of the poor souls who lived in the Vennel.

Edith had settled herself in a fireside chair. 'If she's not entertaining men for money she must have found some sort of work, for that coat cost a pretty penny, even though it's not new.' Edith liked nice clothes, and did her best to ape the gentry when it came to dressing herself and Peter. She and Lessie had been taught by their mother to be good with their needles and they knew all about skilful darning and turning worn garments to make use of the fresh material on the inside.

Lessie said nothing, and her sister waited until the tea was made and poured out before delving into her shopping bag and producing a copy of the *Greenock Telegraph*. 'Have you seen the paper?'

'I can't afford to buy newspapers, Edith. Davie brings one in sometimes.'

'Read that!' Edith thrust the newspaper into her hands, a bony finger tapping a short item near the bottom of one page. Lessie put down her cup, making sure it was well away from Ian's inquisitive fingers, and went to the window to catch what light she could.

Edith waited with pursed lips, and looked scandalised when her sister began to laugh. 'It's not funny.'

'It is! Who else but our Joseph would get into that sort of trouble? Who else would meet a soldier, a complete stranger, in a public house then get so drunk that he agreed when the soldier suggested changing clothes for a lark?'

'You'd think even Joseph would have realised that the soldier was a deserter.' Edith's voice was sour.

'I wish I'd seen him and his cronies waiting in that back room in the pub for the man to come back from his walk, then realising he wasn't going to.' Lessie giggled again, and this time Edith's mouth twitched, then broadened into a smile.

'Then going into the street to look for the man and meeting a policeman instead. I can't imagine our Joseph in uniform – except a prison uniform,' Edith finished, grim again, the amusement stifled almost at birth. 'Seven shillings and sixpence he was fined for receiving the uniform. Seven shillings and sixpence – a good week's wages to most. And him never in work! Where's he going to find that sort of money?'

'He'll get it from somewhere. He's been fined before.' Lessie sobered up and went back to the newspaper. 'I see that the deserter was caught, so at least Joseph'll have got his own clothes back. That poor soul, waiting in prison for men from the War Office to take him back to his regiment in disgrace. I wonder what they'll do to him, and what made his life so bad that he had to run away. P'raps his regiment was going to be sent to South Africa to fight the Boers.'

'You're too soft, Lessie. We all have to face up to the life we choose, even when we didnae choose it o' our own free will. And a soldier has to go where he's sent. Mrs Warren attended a ladies' tea party last week for the soldiers.'

'Oh? Were there many soldiers there?'

'Sometimes, Lessie Hamilton, I don't know whether you're making fun of me or just plain daft! It wasnae for the soldiers themselves and well you know it. The ladies were all stitching clothes to send to South Africa for the men. Mrs Warren came home exhausted.' Edith's mouth suddenly tightened again. 'I saw Mother staggering in the street yesterday.'

'You did not!' Lessie was scandalised on her mother's behalf. Barbara was and always had been a proud woman who had dinned her belief in self-respect into her children – not that Joseph had paid any notice. 'She'd never go out while she was . . . like that!'

'She did so stagger – a wee bit, anyway. I was appalled.'

'What was her speech like when you spoke to her?'

'Spoke to her?' Edith was outraged. 'I crossed the street and managed to get into a shop before she saw me. D'ye think I'd stand talking in the street to her after everyone had seen her near falling against a lamppost?'

'Och, the pavements in this town are a disgrace. She'll have tripped over a paving stone. I've done it often enough myself – and so have you, no doubt.'

Edith took evasive action. 'Why does she have to drink like that?'

'I don't know any more than you do.'

'It started about the time Thomasina was born. It's something to do with her, I'll be bound.'

'Mebbe so, but that's her business, not ours.'

'I don't think she tripped over a paving stone.'

'P'raps she's not well. Did you not think of that instead of running away from your own mother in the street, and her mebbe ill and in need of help and a bit of kindness?'

Edith flushed, and smoothed her skirt. 'She wasn't unwell, I know what I saw. D'you like my new coat?'

Lessie gave in and let the subject be changed. 'It's bonny.'

'Mrs Warren gave it to me. Her maid had the colic so I was sent for to help her to dress. She's got a lovely way of talking, Lessie. It comes from being French. Parisienne,' said Edith reverently. 'And you should see the furnishing in her bedchamber!' She cast a glance round the shabby room. 'The bed alone's near enough as large as this room.'

'It sounds large enough to hold the whole household, servants and all, instead of just two folk.' Lessie was getting tired of hearing about Mrs Andrew Warren.

'It's only for her. Mr Andrew has his own room.'

'They don't sleep in the same bed?'

'The gentry don't need to sleep in the same bed. They've got big houses.'

'Even so . . .' Lessie began, then let her voice die away. She reached for the teapot and refilled Edith's cup, thinking of Andrew Warren, now a regular visitor to the shabby building. The other men who had visited Anna McCauley had arrived and left furtively, heads down, caps or bowlers pulled down over their eyes. They would press themselves against the walls if they happened to encounter Lessie or any other resident, and meeting them always made her feel dirty and ashamed, almost as though it were she, not Anna, who plied a trade in flesh. But Andrew Warren walked into the close and up the stairs with his head high and his shoulders back. If he happened to meet Lessie, he greeted her calmly and civilly, and once he had helped her with Ian's pram. There was an air of strength and confidence about him, a masculinity that spoke of a virile man, surely not the sort to sleep apart from his wife. Did she know about his visits to the Vennel, or did his very openness save him from gossiping tongues?

'Does Mrs Warren keep well?'

'She has a lot of headaches,' said Edith. 'And she feels the cold a great deal after living in Jamaica. She told me herself that she wants to go back there.'

'Mebbe they will.'

'With Mr James turning himself into an invalid and refusing to go to the refinery? Mr Andrew's got to stay here, unless he sells the refinery or gets a manager. Oh, Lessie, you should have seen the gown she wore the other night when they had guests! A crimson bodice and a rose-coloured skirt with a great long train. And golden-coloured lace round the shoulders and the skirt. Silk, the material was. I helped to dress her, and touching it was like dipping your hand into a burn in the summer, all cool and soft . . .'

Lessie let her sister's voice fade into the background. Once Edith started talking about her work and the Warrens, she could babble on happily without need of comment or interruption. Lessie wasn't interested in listening to a long description of fine gowns that she herself could never hope to own. She was far more intrigued by the puzzle of why a good-looking man like Andrew Warren didn't share his wife's bed. True, her own parents hadn't slept together for many years, not since Thomasina's birth, but Edith and Lessie, when they discussed the matter, thought that that might be because they had as many children as they could look after and wanted no more. Though it didn't explain their mother's coldness towards her husband.

But surely the fear of having more bairns than they could feed and clothe wasn't the reason why the Warrens chose to sleep apart? If her Donald had lived, she thought with sudden longing, lifting the teacup to her lips, she would never, ever, have slept alone again, no matter how many rooms they might have had.

5

The pounding on the door made Lessie jump and catch the tip of a finger in the bedspring she was carefully cleaning with paraffin and hot water. Irritated, she put down the cloth she had been using and went into the little hall, sucking at the stinging finger as she went and grimacing at the taste of paraffin from it. Anna McCauley leaned against the door frame, a coat clutched about her body, her hair bundled on top of her head, her face, on this pleasant late summer day, almost beet-red.

A hot, damp hand clutched at Lessie's arm and Anna said, her voice slurring, 'Lessie, ye'll have tae help me!'

It was so reminiscent of the scene several months earlier on the day when Frank Warren died in Anna's bed that Lessie's heart sank.

'Dear God, what have you done now?'

'Are ye alone?' Anna leaned forward to hiss the words and Lessie was surrounded by gin fumes. They clashed with the smell of paraffin and she felt her stomach churn.

'Ian's at my mother's. I'm cleaning the bedsprings to keep the bugs away and I couldna let him near the par—' The words were cut short as Anna pulled her out of her own doorway and started across the landing, her hand still clamped over Lessie's arm.

'What d'you think you're doing?'

'I need yer help.'

Lessie jerked herself free. 'Anna McCauley, if you've got yourself into more trouble, you can find someone else tae get you out of it this time. Away tae your bed and sleep the drink off!'

She turned towards her own open door but Anna,

55

despite her drunkenness, managed to eel round her and get between her and the door. 'Lessie!' Two large tears rose in her lovely eyes and spilled over, followed by two more. 'Lessie, please! I have tae dae it, an' I cannae manage on my own.'

Lessie hesitated, biting her lip. Then she nodded, cursing herself for a fool as she did so. 'Let me shut my own door first, then I'll come across.'

Anna waited instead of going ahead and together they went into her flat. It was the first time Lessie had been in it since Frank Warren's death, and she saw at a glance that it was cleaner than before and more comfortably furnished. Thanks to Andrew Warren, no doubt. But the room was stiflingly hot and stank of gin. A half-empty bottle and a glass stood on the table, and the centre of the room was dominated by a battered tin bath half filled with water. Steam rose lazily from a large kettle on the hob, and two buckets of water stood against one wall.

Anna slipped her coat off. As before, on the day of Frank Warren's death, she was naked beneath it, but this time her soft, slender body was pink and damp. 'Lessie, I'm carryin' a bairn.'

'Andrew Warren's bairn?'

'There's been nobody else these past three months.'

'You've not just found out, surely?' Lessie noticed now that the girl's breasts were full and heavy, her belly beginning to take on a soft curve.

Anna hiccuped and poured a generous measure of gin into the glass. She swallowed, almost gagged, and made a face. 'God, it's terrible stuff! D'ye want some?'

'I do not.' Lessie waved away the proffered bottle and asked, 'How far on are you?'

'Three months. It must've been the first time we were together, or near enough then.' The tears came anew and dripped into the gin. 'If he finds out he'll leave me and I c-couldnae bear it!' Anna hiccuped again, then said, her drunken voice earnest, 'I love him, Lessie. I've tried everything but nothin'll shift it.'

Clumsily, so clumsily that Lessie feared for a minute that the tub would tip over and flood the place, Anna clambered into the water, balancing the glass in one hand. She eased herself down, drawing her breath in sharply as the hot water touched her tender skin, forced to sit in the small space with her knees pressed tightly against her breasts.

'I cannae keep climbin' out tae get more hot water,' she said tearfully, her voice slurring over the words. 'An' if I try tae lean ower tae get the kettle, the damned tub threatens tae tilt an' coup me out. I need ye tae pour more water in for me.'

'I'll not help anyone to get rid of a bairn,' Lessie said firmly.

'It's this or goin' tae the old wifie round the corner,' Anna told her grimly, and took another gulp of gin.

Lessie felt sick. She had heard terrible tales of the old wifie and her methods. Many a desperate young girl or a woman with more than enough children already had lost their lives after visiting the abortionist. 'You'd not do that. You'd not let her—'

'I would.' Anna's voice was suddenly clear and fierce, her gaze level. 'I'd do anythin' tae get rid o' it an' keep Andrew.'

'You'll be found out and sent tae the jail – if you're not already dead by that time.'

Anna splashed a petulant fist into the water, sending a small fountain over the edge onto the linoleum. 'I've got tae get rid of it!'

'Surely you of all folk knew how to prevent this?' Lessie snapped as she wrapped her apron round her hand, seized the kettle, and advanced on the tub. Anna's mind was clearly made up, and anything was better than letting her submit to an abortionist.

'I've always managed before. But that man's no' like other men. No won'er his wife had two instead o' just the one—' Anna broke off with another sharp intake of breath as boiling water trickled into the tub. Steam rose into the air and perspiration ran freely down her face to drip into the water.

'I'll add some cold.'

'You'll not! It's to be as hot as I can bear it.'

'You can't bear it,' Lessie protested.

'I must.' The words were forced out through gritted teeth. 'It's the only way. Here.' She emptied the glass and held it out. 'Fill that up again.'

Lessie took it, filled it, handed it back, and at Anna's insistence trickled more boiling water into the tub. After a few more applications her own skin burned and stung in sympathy, and still Anna stayed where she was, refusing to give up. The level in the bottle dropped steadily and Lessie filled it willingly now, realising that the more Anna drank, the closer she came to lapsing into a stupor. The room was stiflingly hot and they were both perspiring freely. Filling the glass yet again, pouring more water into the tub and watching Anna's face contort as she forced herself to stay where she was, Lessie wondered if this was what Hell was like. If not, the Devil was missing out on a good form of eternal torture.

The ordeal finally ended in a flurry of water when Anna suddenly announced thickly, 'Gaun be—' and erupted from the tub, drenching Lessie with hot water. Anna reached the basin by the window just in time, and as she vomited into it, Lessie hurried to hold her head. The girl's body was lobster-red and almost too hot to touch. As the draught from the ill-fitting window got to her, she began to shiver. Weak as a kitten, she made no more than a token protest as Lessie dried her with a rough cloth and eased her towards the bed.

'Enough,' she said, collapsing onto the mattress. 'We mus've got rid o' the wee bugger by this time.'

Lessie covered her with the blanket and smoothed sweat-soaked hair back from her own forehead. 'Enough,' she agreed thankfully.

Anna mumbled something and was instantly asleep. Lessie went through the laborious process of emptying the tub with a bucket, carrying the water out to the sink on the landing. Then she emptied and cleaned the bowl and after a final glance at Anna hurried back to her own flat.

It was time to fetch Ian home and prepare the evening meal. She lugged Davie's bed, only half disinfected, back into place and dragged the thin mattress onto it. Then she tidied herself and hurried out of the building, wishing as she went that she had never set eyes on Anna McCauley. The woman was nothing but trouble. But Lessie still owed her money, and although Anna herself cared not a jot, to Lessie it was an obligation that bonded the two of them together in uneasy companionship.

As soon as Davie had clattered off to work on the following morning, Lessie fed Ian then settled him down on the rag rug while she filled a bucket with warm water and washed herself from head to toe. She didn't have the luxury of an old tin tub like Anna McCauley's; she and Davie had to make do with the bucket, Davie washing himself thoroughly in the evenings when Lessie was out scrubbing stairs or helping in the corner shop.

When she had dressed herself again she pulled a basin out from under the bed and plunged the contents, strips of cloth that had been left to soak in cold water, into the bucket, rubbing and scrubbing hard in an effort to remove every trace of blood.

What, she wondered as she worked on her knees by the bucket, did rich folk like Mrs Andrew Warren do when they had their monthly bleeding? She couldn't see wealthy women washing their own soiled cloths. Surely they didn't expect their servants to see to the business for them? Squeezing the cloths out, draping them over the range to dry quickly so that they would be out of sight before Davie got back, she decided that they probably just burned them and tore up fresh cloths when they were needed. Wealthy folk were fortunate.

Quiet though she was when she went onto the landing to empty the bucket, she wasn't quiet enough. Anna's door opened so suddenly that Lessie gave a guilty start and water splashed from the bucket onto her foot.

Anna looked ill. Her pretty face was small and waxy, her eyes heavily shadowed. Her hair was still tied up as it had been the day before, long matted red tendrils hanging to her shoulders.

'It's not come,' she said, and the tears welled up again. 'Oh Lessie, what am I to do?'

'Tell the man. It's his responsibility as well as yours.'

Anna blinked, sniffed, scrubbed the back of one hand across her face, and said without emotion, 'God, Lessie Hamilton, you're either daft or you're simple. Men don't have to take responsibilities, they only take their pleasure.'

Lessie tipped the bucket over the sink and saw Anna's envious gaze fixed on the telltale pink tinge of the water sluicing away down the drain.

'Surely he'd not want you to risk your life going to the old wifie.' At the thought, Lessie felt fear grip at the pit of her stomach, right where Ian had nestled trustingly for the nine months before his birth. 'You'll not do anything as daft as that?'

There was a flash of desperation in Anna's eyes, a tremor of sheer terror in her voice. 'What else can I do?'

'Give it a wee while longer. Mebbe the gin and the hot water'll work yet. Give it until tomorrow.' Put off your bairn's death, and as like as not your own death, a little longer, Lessie beseeched silently.

Perhaps it was that unspoken plea that made Anna say as she stepped back and began to close her door, 'Aye, mebbe you're right. Mebbe it'll work yet. But I'll only wait until tomorrow,' she added through the final crack in the door. Then it closed and Lessie was left standing on the landing, the empty bucket in her hand, the last trickle of bloodied water circling noisily into the drain.

She fretted about Anna McCauley all day as she scrubbed stairs then took tea with Miss Peden. She would have liked to ask the old woman's advice, but Miss Peden had never been married and it wouldn't be seemly to talk to her of childbirth, let alone abortion and prostitution. So Lessie carried her burden about with her, finding it much heavier than Ian, recalling over and over again the fear in Anna's eyes when she spoke of the old wifie with her filthy hands and her unspeakable practices.

In the Warren garden the roses were a riot of colour, the grass green and lush, the air rich with the smell of summer and the sound of bees humming round the flower beds. And yet a few miles away in the Vennel it was hard to know what season it was, Andrew Warren thought as he picked his way between the grimy house walls and the gutter with its rich harvest of rotting matter.

The sun had very little chance of finding its way between the buildings and into the dank, narrow street. The people were as pale and undernourished as always, though at this time of year they shivered less. And yet – his thoughts became uncharacteristically lyrical as he neared his goal – this rancid garden had its own blossom, a girl with red hair and violet eyes who, for the moment at least, held him captive. They hadn't arranged a meeting for that day but Andrew had suddenly felt the need to touch Anna, hold her, hear her voice. He hoped that she would be at home.

His step quickened as he turned in at the mouth of the close, almost colliding with Anna's pale, fair-haired little neighbour on her way out, her baby fastened against her body by means of a shawl knotted about them both. His hands went out to steady her and felt her thinness and fragility.

'Forgive me.' He set her safely on her feet, smiled, and went past her into the close, his mind filled with Anna. He was almost at the foot of the stairs when he heard the girl calling after him.

'Mr Warren?'

He swung round, impatient at the delay. 'Yes, what is it?'

She had stepped back into the close, her thin face ghostly in the dim light. 'Mr Warren, I must tell you something.'

He could tell by the quiver in her voice, the way her arms tightened about the child sleeping against her shoulder, that she was nervous. He pushed his impatience aside and said mildly, 'By all means. If there's anything I can do for you—'

'No' for me, for Anna. I'm feared for her.'

'Is she ill?'

'Not ill, but I'm feared that—' She stopped, took in a deep breath, then said swiftly, 'Mr Warren, I'd not talk of other folk's private business tae anyone, so you've no need tae fret about that. But Anna's goin' tae be hurt if she . . . She's carryin' your bairn, Mr Warren.'

For a moment Andrew could only gape at the girl. She moved a step back, as though unsure of his reaction, ready to run if he lifted a hand to her.

'What?' It was a stupid thing to say but it was all he could think of.

'She's carryin' your bairn,' she repeated patiently. 'She says it's yours and I believe her. And she's done everything she can think of tae put an end tae it. But nothing's worked and now she's talking about visiting an old woman who sees tae things like that, only most women who visit her die as well as their bairns an' I'm feared for—'

'Why didn't she tell me?' His voice was loud in the enclosed space and she took a second step back.

'She was frightened.'

'Of me?'

'You've already got bairns of your own. You'll not want this one, Anna says.' Then, her task completed, she fell silent, staring up at him.

'Thank you, Mrs – er—'

'Mrs Lessie Hamilton,' the girl said clearly, taking time over each word, proud of the title. Andrew was suddenly touched by her pride, her dignity.

'Thank you, Mrs Hamilton, for confiding in me. You've no need to worry about Anna. She's my responsibility.'

Lessie Hamilton smiled and her thin, solemn little face was suddenly transformed. 'I thought you'd say that,' she said with satisfaction, then dipped her head in brief acknowledgement and hurried on her way, the child's head bobbing on her shoulder, his body relaxed and boneless in sleep.

Andrew took the stairs three at a time, his feet sure now on the hollowed stone treads. He knocked on the door, waited for a while, then knocked again, insistently, certain that someone was inside. When the door finally opened Anna stared up at him, her hands going at once to her hair, which was loose about her shoulders like a fiery veil.

'Andrew. I didnae think tae see ye today.' She stepped back in confusion as he moved forward into the flat.

'I had a sudden notion to call on you.'

They were in the kitchen now. The place was untidy, clothes strewn about and some dirty crockery lying on the table. Anna turned to face him, her hands still fidgeting with her hair until he took them and imprisoned them in his. She wore a plain blouse and skirt and now that he could see her more clearly he noted the shadowed eyes, the trembling mouth with a bruised, hurt look to it that wrenched at his heart.

'Why didn't you tell me about the child, Anna?' he asked gently.

Her eyes widened, then fell before his gaze, but not before he had seen the apprehension in them. 'How do you know about that?'

'You should have told me.'

'I was feared,' Anna whispered. He had never seen her like this before, stripped of the bravado and the confidence that normally radiated from her. She seemed much younger now, helpless, vulnerable. Madeleine had never moved him as much as Anna did at that moment.

He drew her into his arms, held her close, and said into her hair, 'There's no need to be frightened ever again. And there'll be no more talk of killing my child, d'you hear me? I'll take you out of this place, Anna. I'll find you a decent house where our baby can be born and raised. I'll look after you both. I promise you that.'

6

Beyond the tumble of decks and masts and funnels the river was a broad grey sullen ribbon beneath a grey sky. The bitterly cold January wind ruffled the water surface into flecks of white spume and reddened Davie Kirkwood's nose as he waited at the dock gates with a crowd of other men.

He was cold despite his warm jacket; others in the group, less warmly dressed, were blue and shivering, trying to find shelter in the press of bodies while at the same time remain near the front so that the foremen would see them when they came to pick out the gangs to unload that morning's ships.

'Here, Johnny, take my scarf.' Davie's hands went to his throat and started unknotting the scarf that Lessie had knitted as a Christmas gift but the man beside him shook his head.

'You keep it. I'll get warm enough when I'm working – God willing,' he added, and stamped his feet on the ground. Davie studied him with growing concern. Johnny Lachlan and he had been playmates in the same street for the first ten years of their lives, but Johnny's parents had long since died and his two sisters married and moved far from Greenock. Johnny now lived in a lodging house for men and until recently he had been employed in a small engineering factory as an unskilled worker, sweeping floors and running errands.

He and Davie hadn't seen each other for two years, and as a fresh blast of wind scoured the group by the dock gates, Davie, doing his best to edge between Johnny and the cutting edge of the wind, saw only too clearly how puny and undernourished the man was. He was unfit for the work he so desperately sought.

'Johnny, is there nothing else for you to do?'

His old friend's mouth twisted into a wry smile. 'D'ye think I've no' tried tae find somethin' else? Man, I've begged at every shop an' factory in the toon wi'oot ony luck. Naeb'dy wants an unskilled man. I wish I'd had the brains you have, then mebbe I'd've been able tae go in for the engineerin' tae.' The smile widened; it was genuine, though his eyes were watering with cold. 'Ye'll dae well as an engineer yince ye've got yer papers, Davie. Though mind ye, they've got their troubles tae. Old Mr Beattie that I worked for's findin' it hard tae make ends meet these days. That's why he had tae let me go. An' he cannae afford tae pay skilled men for the factory. I doot he'll hae tae close down soon.'

He stopped and clutched at Davie's arm. 'Here's yin o' them comin'. Wish me luck, man. I need this work awful bad. It's no' the right time o' year tae be stuck for the money tae buy a bed in the lodgin' hoose.'

The muttered conversations around them died away as the men pressed against the gates, each jostling to be in the forefront. With a sinking heart Davie saw that the man striding along the dock in their direction was his father. He knew well enough that Archie, who didn't have an ounce of compassion in his entire body, only wanted able-bodied men. Johnny didn't stand a chance.

Even so, Davie pushed the other man firmly forward until he was against the gates, then tried to ease back himself. It angered and humiliated him to be picked out of the crowd each day by the man everyone knew to be his father. But Archie ignored him when he tried to insist that he be left to take his chances with one of the other foremen. 'Ye're a good worker an' I'll pick out who I please,' he growled each time. Now he walked up and down the cobbles before the gate, taking his time, eyeing the hopeful men who waited for his verdict. In his youth Archie had gone through this humiliation himself day after day and now it was his turn to be top dog. He saw nothing wrong with his attitude – some of the men eyeing him hopefully at that moment would, one day, be in his place and good luck to them.

'I'll hae you, an' you, an' you.' His thick forefinger stabbed at one man after another, moving relentlessly along until, inevitably, it pointed at Davie. 'An' you,' he said without a flicker of recognition, then moved on. 'An' you.'

When he had finished he nodded to the gateman to open the small side gate for the chosen gang. Johnny had not been one of them and Davie, shouldering his way through the crush, trying not to listen to the muttered comments from men who had, once again, watched the foreman's son being singled out while they themselves had been passed over, saw his former friend's head droop, his hands clutch at the bars of the gate before him in despair.

'Come on, man, don't stand there dreamin' when there's work tae be done.' On an impulse Davie caught at Johnny's arm and tugged him through the small gate by his side.

'But I wasnae picked!'

'You were so, I saw him lookin' at ye. Come on,' said Davie relentlessly, and then the two of them were standing on the dock and Archie, suddenly realising that he had one man too many, was swinging round on them, his mouth opening and his hand lifting to indicate Johnny's way back through the gate.

'Ye'll take him as well or ye'll do without me.' The other men picked for the gang were already hurrying towards the sugar ship where they were to work.

'I'll take the men I picked!'

'Ye picked him. I'm no' so sure about me. Mebbe I should go back outside an' wait for the next foreman,' Davie insisted, keeping Johnny by him with a grip on the sleeve of his thin jacket.

Archie's hand fell back to his side. His mouth closed, then tightened. Davie stared back at him, and saw his father waver. He knew that the older man was thinking of Lessie and Ian and their need for Davie's wages. Davie was thinking of them too, hoping that if his bluff was called and he had to go home empty-handed, Lessie would understand. Surely she would understand.

'Come on then, we've not got all day,' Archie said gruffly, swinging away from them, and Davie was free to breathe again. For once he had bested his father.

'Thanks, Davie,' Johnny muttered as they hurried to join the rest of the gang. On the dock by the sugar ship, a row of carts waited. They would take the first batch of unloaded bags to the Warren refinery and the rest of the load would go into the dock warehouses.

'Thanks for what? It was him that picked you, no' me. Stay close tae me, Johnny, I've worked the sugar ships many a time and I know what's tae be done.'

An hour later Johnny had tossed his jacket into a corner and sweat was streaming down his face. To Davie's dismay he was still clumsy in his handling of the large hooks every docker used, one in each hand. He stumbled and slipped over the jute bags that filled the hold, finding it hard to keep a footing on their uneven surface. He had gashed one of them with a hook as he helped to lift it and it had swung up out of the hold leaking brown Demerara sugar as it went. Archie's watchful eyes and his barked reprimands every time one of the men did something wrong were making Johnny nervous; he worked with one eye on the foreman instead of concentrating on what he was doing.

Skilfully, Davie seized another bag and lifted it about a foot off the ground, tensing his back, managing to balance its three hundredweight. 'The rope!' He grated the words at Johnny, who hurried to flip the rope sling under the bag. He fumbled the first time and Davie's back muscles gave a protesting twinge. Then the sling was in place and the dragging weight on Davie was eased. Between them, with Davie doing the lion's share of the work, they packed a dozen bags onto the sling.

The ship's derrick lowered a massive hook down and Davie stepped lightly onto the packed bags, balancing while he guided the hook into the sling. Then he sprang clear and signalled to the hatchman to start swinging the load up.

'You two – outside,' Archie ordered as the bags cleared

the hold. 'Start loadin' the warehouse.'

Davie swore under his breath. The bags were taken to the warehouse manually and he doubted whether Johnny could manage. But there was nothing else for it. They handed their hooks over to another gang and clambered up the ladders, first to the deck, then to the quay, for the tide was low and the ship was now several feet beneath the quayside where a few horses and carts still waited. Davie reached down when he was on the harbour to give Johnny a hand; he scarcely had the energy left to haul himself up the final rungs. Archie watched with sour disapproval, but said nothing.

The cold wind chilled the sweat on their faces at once. Johnny huddled his jacket on and eyed the pile of heavy sacks doubtfully. Then he gritted his teeth and said, 'Gie us a haun', will ye?'

'Take your time now, laddie. I'll balance the bag till you've got the feel of it.' Davie eased a heavy sack onto Johnny's back, steadied him, and watched the smaller, slighter man make his way slowly towards the warehouse, almost doubled under the weight of the bag, his knees buckling. Davie walked over to his father. 'He was doin' fine in the hold. You should've left him there.'

The dockside was noisy with voices and horses' hooves and the clatter of iron-bound cart wheels on cobbles, but a lifetime of experience made Davie shape his words well so that Archie could read his lips.

'It's you that should've left him at the gates. The man's nae use.'

'He's half starved! How can he build up any strength the way he's had tae live?'

'If he's workin' on my gang he'll dae his fair share,' Archie said implacably. 'An' so will you. Get on wi' your work or ye'll be turned away – an' I mean it!'

Seething with anger, Davie strode to the bags and swung one onto his back without waiting for help. He caught the twisted corners, steadied the load, and straightened to stare into his father's cold eyes. Then he turned and went towards the warehouse, passing Johnny on his way back for another bag. Johnny was moving slowly, working his shoulders to ease the pain in them. Catching Davie's anxious glance, he twisted his face into a grin, winked, and swung into an attempt at a jaunty walk.

Men waited inside the huge dim warehouse to take the sugar bag and heave it into its place. Davie hurried out with the intention of working twice as fast as usual so that he could ease Johnny's toil, and saw that the man helping Johnny to hoist a second bag onto his back had done it too quickly so that he was staggering. One or two of the dockers watched, grinning, as the little man reeled this way and that, trying desperately to master the crushing weight that threatened to topple from his back. It was a favourite prank on the docks, where men had to work hard and were only too aware of the dangers they faced every day, the ruptures and damaged joints, the burns from cargoes of salts and lime. But this time the joke was clearly going awry, for in his attempts to stay upright and hold onto the bag, Johnny was staggering back towards the edge of the harbour, his heel catching against a rusted iron ring protruding from the cobblestones.

As Davie sped towards him, his studded boots striking blue light from the cobblestones, he could see the momentum of the heavy sack Johnny carried pulling him back, back, and over the edge of the dock just as Davie's hand reached for him.

There was a double thud from below and a yell of alarm from the open hold.

'Johnny!' Davie threw himself down the ladder onto the deck, then past the burst sugar bag, its contents crunching beneath his feet, and down the second ladder into the hold where a group of men crouched over his friend.

'He caught his head on the edge of the hold as he came down, poor bugger,' someone said, turning a white face up towards the hatch above, ringed with staring men.

Davie took one look and knew the worst. Nobody could sprawl like a discarded cloth doll, head lolling at such a sickening, impossible angle over one shoulder, and still be alive. Davie didn't need to feel for a pulse or a heartbeat. Turning his back on the scene, he scrambled up the ladder again to where Archie had just arrived on the deck.

'He's dead. His neck's broken.'

A muscle jumped in Archie's cheek then he said over his shoulder to the staring men grouped round the open hold, some of them with hats hurriedly snatched off and clutched in their hands, 'Have him taken tae the warehouse an' fetch a doctor.'

'Is that all you've got to say?'

'Accidents happen all the time on the docks, you know that yourself. An' we've still got a ship tae unload.'

His jaw clenched, Davie took a step forward. His father shifted slightly so that his weight was poised properly and waited, his big hands by his sides, ready to curl into fists if need be. Someone touched Davie's arm; someone else said, 'For God's sake, man, he's yer faither!'

Davie hesitated, then hawked deep in his throat and spat, sending a great glob of phlegm onto the deck an inch from the toe of one of his father's boots. As he pulled away from the restraining hand on his sleeve and began to climb the ladder to the quay, he heard Archie's harsh voice. 'Where the hell d'ye think ye're going?'

'Out of here!'

'Ye've no' done yer job yet! Ye'll no' get a penny if ye walk out.'

Davie ignored the voice, almost running from the dock in his need to get as far away as he could from Archie and from poor broken Johnny, shouldering his way through the group of men still waiting for work by the gates, paying no heed to their questions and the voices that called from behind him. All that Johnny's death meant to them was the chance for one of them to take his place.

Davie went to the tenement in the Vennel, needing to talk to Lessie, to be soothed by her calm presence. But Lessie wasn't there; the flat, as clean as she could make it, was empty. So he went back out into the streets and walked, hands fisted in his pockets, eyes on the road, stalking through Greenock and along the coast road and into the neighbouring town of Port Glasgow without noticing where he was. All he could think of was Johnny

– Johnny with his pinched blue face, yearning for enough work to pay for a bed for that night. Johnny alive, determined to cope with a task that was beyond his undernourished strength. Then Johnny crumpled in the hold of a ship, being winched up on a plank of wood, removed hurriedly so that the unloading could continue.

Tears suddenly filled his eyes and he blinked them away, scrubbing his hand over his face and swinging round the nearest corner in case anyone had noticed. Someone who had just stepped from a shop a few feet before him said, 'And what brings you to Port Glasgow, Davie Kirkwood?' and he looked up, dazed and confused, at the lovely woman confronting him, stylish and snug in a dark green jacket and skirt edged with pale brown fur. Red curls could just be glimpsed beneath the brim of a veiled hat decorated with a large bow striped in two shades of green.

'Anna? Is it you?'

She laughed, the clear happy laugh he remembered so well. 'Of course it's me. Oh Davie, it's good to see you!' Then she looked at him more closely. 'What's amiss?'

'Nothin'.'

She had the sense not to ask any more questions. Instead she removed one hand from the huge fur muff she carried and laid it on his arm. 'Davie, come and have tea and see my new wee house. Please,' she insisted as he began to shake his head. 'I'm pining away from boredom and loneliness today, and it's too cold tae stay out of doors. Please, Davie?'

Her violet-blue eyes beseeched him through the veiling that misted her features and made them even more beguiling. Davie hesitated, realised that there was nowhere else for him to go, and nodded. Anna beamed at him and slipped her hand into the crook of his elbow. 'It's not far, we can walk there.'

One or two passersby gave them an inquisitive stare as they went along the street, the tall young man shabby in docker's garb, the woman dressed in fine clothes. But Davie was too sunk in his own misery to wonder what they looked like together, and Anna chattered on about this and that without seeming to expect or need any response from him.

They left the busy street and came to a row of small, neat houses, each with its own little front garden, over-looking the river. Anna opened a gate and said, 'Here we are. I told you that it wasn't far.'

Davie followed her up the flagged path and waited while she rapped on the door knocker. The door opened and she drew him with her into a small square hall where wood and brass shone and the air was fragrant with beeswax. Carpeted stairs led up to the floor above.

'Molly, this is my friend Mr Kirkwood, Mrs Hamilton's brother. We'll have some tea, if you please.' Anna's voice was friendly but firm. She sounded as though she had been used to having a servant all her life.

The elderly woman who had opened the door nodded, looked at Davie without curiosity, and disappeared through a door at the back of the hall. Anna opened another door. 'This is my parlour. Sit down, Davie, while I go and take my hat off.'

The room was comfortable, warmed by a good fire in the hearth. Paintings hung on the blue and white striped walls and ornaments and plants were scattered lavishly throughout the room. The table was covered with a blue chenille cloth and blue velvet curtains at the windows framed the view of the Clyde. At either side of the fire-place stood a solid comfortable chair, and a sofa heaped with cushions was against one wall. A clock ticked softly above it. It was a welcoming room.

Davie hesitated, eyeing the sofa, then opted for one of the chairs, only realising when he sank into its comfort-able depths how tired he was. He leaned his head back, closed his eyes, and was almost asleep when Anna came in, followed by the maidservant with a large tray.

'I should have asked, Davie, if you were hungry. We've toast and muffins and cake, but there's beef and bread in the kitchen if you want it.'

He had instinctively jumped to his feet when the women entered. 'No, this'll be fine.'

'Sit down,' Anna commanded as the door closed

behind the servant. He did as he was told, watching her as she busied herself with the tray. She had taken her jacket off to reveal a full-sleeved blouse of some warm fawn material with a pleated bodice and green velvet ribbon about the throat and wrists. The skilfully cut blouse and skirt and a shawl casually draped about her shoulders all but hid her pregnancy. Apart from some curls round her forehead, her hair had been drawn back loosely into a chignon at the back of her head, exposing her ears and the pearl drops that swung from the lobes.

'Here you are.' She brought him a cup, and as he took it he became aware of her perfume – roses, as always, but a more subtle fragrance than before. Andrew Warren could afford to buy expensive scent for his woman, Davie thought.

'What are you staring at me like that for?' Anna wanted to know as she offered toast.

'You look – different.'

She laughed, lowering herself carefully into the chair opposite his. 'I'm fatter and heavier. Not as able tae skip up and down stairs as I used tae.' She paused, then said carefully, 'Used to.'

'I didnae mean that. I mean . . .' he floundered, then said, 'You look just right in this place.'

Her smile lit up her face. 'What a lovely thing to say, Davie. So you think I make a fine lady, do you?'

'I always did. Are ye happy?'

'I'm very happy,' said Anna at once, and he knew a twinge of jealousy for the man who had the power and the money to give her such pleasure. He wondered how often they sat like this together, Anna and Andrew Warren, facing each other in comfortable intimacy across the fireplace. 'Lessie's been here more than once. Did she not tell you about my wee house?'

'Oh yes.' He knew that Lessie saw Anna only when summoned. Davie wasn't sure whether his sister's continued reluctance to acknowledge Anna McCauley as a friend stemmed from her disapproval of Anna's circumstances, or from envy. Who wouldn't envy Anna this house? Davie imagined Lessie and Ian living here and wished that he could do as much for them as Andrew Warren had done for Anna.

'I hear that there's a man living in my old flat now.'

'That's right. Old Bob Naismith. He's a quiet soul, and civil enough when he's sober.' Davie hesitated then smiled faintly. 'If ye should meet him on his way tae the public house every Saturday afternoon, he passes the time o' day an' his old mongrel dog gives a wee wag o' the tail. Then after a few hours the two o' them come back along the road, old Naismith staggerin' an' cursin' an' shoutin' at everyone he meets an' the dog snarlin' an' makin' runs at folks' ankles on the end of its string. An' it's no' even had a drop tae drink. The next day,' he went on, warmed by Anna's peals of laughter, 'there they are, civil as ye please, tail waggin' an' a'. Wee Ian cries him Mr Nicesmith on his way tae the pub an' Mr Nastysmith on his way back.'

Anna mopped her eyes with a lacy handkerchief. 'Lessie didnae tell me about that.'

'Lessie wouldnae.' Then all at once, unexpectedly, the memory of Johnny lying crumpled in the hold came into Davie's head and he got to his feet and walked clumsily to the window, unseeing, bumping against a corner of the table and setting the china on the tray jangling softly.

'Davie, what is it?'

'Nothin'.' Then, because he didn't want to let what had happened to Johnny taint this safe, pretty, feminine room and he had to say something he said bleakly, 'I don't want tae go back tae the docks again. I don't want tae work wi' my father. I'll no' dae it!'

Anna let the silence stretch between them for a few moments before she said, 'Davie, if you could do anything in the world, what would you choose?'

'Tae be an engineer,' said Davie, his heart in his voice.

She levered herself to her feet and came to stand by his side. Together they looked out at the cold winter's day. 'How long d'you have to go before you've finished your studying?'

'Six months.'

'Could you not find work in a factory now?'

'Who'd take me on?'

'You'll not know until you try,' said Anna. 'Go out and find the sort of work you want, Davie. It's the only way to get out of the docks.'

'An' what if I fail? I'll have tae go back tae the docks wi' my tail between my legs.'

'At least you'll have tried. And you can keep on trying until you succeed. Do it now, this minute. And mind and come back to let me know how you get on. I'd like to see you again.'

He stared down at her, suddenly realising that she was right. There was no rule that said he couldn't aim for what he wanted.

'Aye,' he said slowly. 'Aye. I will. You're right, Anna. There's nothin' wrong wi' failin'. The fault's in no' tryin'. An' by God, I'm goin' tae have a damned good run at it.'

She smiled at him, a smile that warmed him all through, and said softly, 'That's my Davie.'

And all at once he felt that he could move mountains, if Anna asked him.

7

The man who came into the shop to buy matches was vaguely familiar, though Lessie didn't remember seeing him on the other side of the counter before. He had friendly hazel eyes, a square face and fair tumbled hair that teased at the edges of memory until, as she was handing him his change, it came to her.

'Are you not Murdo Carswell that used to go to school with my brother Joseph?'

For a moment he stared and she thought that she had made a mistake. Then his face split into a wide grin. 'By God, it's wee Lessie Kirkwood! What're you doin' in this part o' the town?'

'I live here. And my name's Hamilton now.'

'The pretty ones aye get snapped up before I find them,' said Murdo Carswell in mock sorrow. 'That's why I'm still unwed myself. Dae I know yer man?'

'No, he came to Greenock not long before we were wed. He . . . died a while back.'

'I'm sorry tae hear that, lass.' There was an awkward silence, then he said, 'An' how's Joseph? I've been in Glasgow these past two years so I've lost touch wi' him.'

'Och, he's well enough.'

'Still the same rascal he was at school?'

'Still the same,' she agreed. 'D'ye mind the time a crowd of us went up the braes and Joseph dared you tae have a ride on a big horse in one of the fields?'

His grin widened into a laugh. 'I'm no' likely tae forget that. I thought my arse was broken when the bugger took to its heels and I went flying off.'

'You'd no sense in you at all in those days. You'd take

on any daft dare, and our Joseph knew it. Are you back in Greenock now, or just visiting?'

'I'm back, like the bad penny. I'm workin' as a joiner at Scott's shipyard.' Murdo seemed to be prepared to stay and talk, but the shop was busy and there were customers waiting patiently for attention. He glanced round at them, shrugged, and picked up his matches. 'I'll be sure to look in again, now that I know you're workin' here.'

The memory of his final sunny grin stayed with her for the rest of the afternoon while she served in the shop. Murdo Carswell had been a solemn boy, much quieter than Joseph and the other lads in the 'gang'. He was the only son of a widow who considered herself to be a cut above everyone else and frowned on street games and packs of lads roaming around together. Murdo, though, had defied her, slipping out after school to be with his friends. In order to be more like the other boys, he had, as Lessie had reminded him, been willing and eager to try anything, no matter how dangerous.

She collected Ian from the back room and made her way home to prepare Davie's evening meal.

Murdo's smile seemed a lot readier now, she thought as she peeled potatoes, her hands red with cold. Going to work in Glasgow, away from his mother, had done him good.

'Davie!' yelled Ian with open delight as heavy boots tramped up the stairs. He toddled to the door and Lessie dropped the potato knife and went after him, scooping him onto her hip and opening the door. When she saw Archie standing there her heart somersaulted crazily and she felt the blood drain from her face.

'Davie?'

To her relief her father said, 'Is he no' here?'

'No. I was just expecting him home.' She backed into the kitchen ahead of him and set Ian down. 'I thought when I saw you that he'd met with an accident. Did he not finish along with you?'

'He did no'. The damned fool walked out and left a ship half unloaded.'

'Why? What happened?'

'Ach, some clumsy creature who wasnae fit for the work managed tae get himself killed. But that was no excuse for Davie tae dae whit he did,' Archie said fiercely. 'I came tae gie him the sharp edge o' my tongue, but since he's no' here I might as well be on my way home. Here.' He dug into his pocket and tossed some coins on the table. 'This is what's owin' tae him. See that he gets it an' tell him tae be at the dock gates good an' early tomorrow. There's anither ship due in.'

'You'll stay an' have something to eat?'

'Better no'. Yer mother'll be expectin' me home.' He had stayed on his feet throughout his short visit. Now he ruffled Ian's hair and turned towards the door. 'I'll see mysel' out. Ye could mebbe visit yer mother some time, lassie. She's no' well.'

'What's wrong with her?'

'How should I ken?' Archie demanded grumpily as he left. 'I'm no' a bloody doctor. Just visit her.'

Davie arrived home an hour later, coming into the house quietly, without his usual cheerfulness. He sat down at the table and stared at the money that still lay there. 'What's this?'

'It's your wages. Da brought it.'

He pushed the money away violently. 'I don't want it!'

'Well I do!' Lessie dumped a pot of steaming potatoes down on the wooden table and scooped the money up. 'We need money to pay the rent and buy the food. You worked for it and you earned it.' Then, catching a glimpse of his face, she said more gently, 'Da told me a man was killed today. Is that what sent you away?'

'He—' Davie started explosively, then stopped, clenching his fists on the table. 'He was someone I used to know. I couldnae stay after – after it happened.'

Lessie put a hand on his shoulder, then withdrew it when he flinched away. 'Da says he'll expect you at the gates tomorrow morning.'

'He'll have a long wait. I'm done wi' the docks.'

'Davie, for God's sake! You've got to go back. You cannae give up your work because of an accident. How're ye supposed to live with no wage comin' in?'

'I've found another place.'

'What? Where is it?'

He lifted his head, grim triumph in his face. 'A wee engineering shop in Port Glasgow owned by an old man called Beattie. Jo—' He stopped suddenly then said, 'I heard he needed someone so I went along tae see him. He's no' got much money an' I've no' got my papers yet, an' the way things are just now the place could close down, but I'll dae my damnedest tae see that that doesnae happen – an' I told him that.'

Lessie sank in a chair opposite him. 'You're on the right road now. Oh, Davie, I'm proud of you – and pleased for you!'

He shot a look at her from beneath lowered lashes, then said swiftly, apologetically, 'It's no' as much as I can get at the docks.'

'But it'll be regular, and that's more than you can say for being a docker.' She leaned forward and put her hand on his. 'We'll manage, the three of us. We'll manage fine.'

'Aye,' he said, then with a glance at the clock he jumped to his feet. 'I'll be late for my evening class.'

'You've not eaten yet.'

'I'll have something when I get back,' he said, snatching up his books and departing without changing out of his working clothes. Alone, Lessie got Ian ready for bed, wondering why, when he should be overjoyed at finding the sort of work he wanted, Davie should be so dour and unsmiling about it.

'It's only a cough,' Barbara Kirkwood said impatiently when her daughter called on her. 'Everyone gets colds at this time of year.'

Lessie, helping Thomasina to dress her doll, and almost crushed against the wooden arm of her chair by the weight of her sister's body leaning cosily against hers, asked mildly, 'D'you have any soothing syrup for it?'

'I'll get some if it doesnae stop soon.' Barbara coughed again and wiped her mouth with a handkerchief. Thomasina imitated the dry pecking sound and giggled behind her outspread fingers. Then she snatched the doll from Lessie and plumped herself down on the floor beside Ian.

'It's the poor Queen you want to be worryin' yersel' about. They say she's very poorly.'

'She doesnae need me tae worry about her. She's got enough doctors an' soothing syrup tae cure the ills o' half the folk in the country.'

'Lessie! That's no way tae talk o' your Queen!'

'She didnae hear me, Mam. An' she's had a good long life – everyone has tae die some time. Some earlier than others,' Lessie added sombrely, thinking of Donald.

'You're too young tae ken what it'll mean tae the likes o' me if the old Queen dies. It's the end o' more than just one life. The world'll never be the same again without her.' Barbara coughed again and looked longingly towards the bedroom door. Lessie knew that behind it, in some hidden place, was a whisky bottle.

'Mebbe that won't be a bad thing either, in some ways,' she said, and got another scolding that ended in a further outbreak of coughing.

Within the next week, Greenock, like every other community in the country, was in mourning for Queen Victoria. And yet Lessie, who had had her own private mourning to do some eighteen months earlier, felt the world was beginning to brighten. Although he'd had to work hard in his first week and brought home less than he had from the docks, Davie was happier. He and Mr Beattie, his new employer, got on well together. From the beginning, Mr Beattie encouraged Davie to volunteer ideas and opinions and he was already learning fast now that he was among the machinery he loved. Ian continued to thrive, the whooping cough a dimly remembered nightmare now as he seemed to grow overnight from babyhood to boyhood.

Murdo Carswell soon took to dropping in at the shop and even at the house, his cheerful grin lighting up many a long day. Once or twice, if the weather permitted and Lessie had time, the two of them went walking with Ian trotting ahead or between them, clutching their hands, demanding to be swung off his feet and into the air.

'He fancies you,' Davie said one day when Lessie and Ian returned from a long walk with Murdo.

'Away ye go! He's just looking for a bit of company,' she said swiftly, busying herself with the task of taking off Ian's coat, turning away from Davie, ignoring his dry, 'Oh, aye?'

She enjoyed Murdo's company, but she had put all thoughts of love behind her when she buried her Donald and she wasn't ready yet to think of Murdo as anything but a good friend. Once or twice, when their eyes met over Ian's red head or their hands happened to touch fleetingly, she felt a slight tremor of pleasurable excitement, but each time it was sternly suppressed.

Anyway, it took two to make a romance, and she was quite sure that if a lad like Murdo was looking for more than mere friendship he could easily find it with a pretty unmarried girl unencumbered by a child.

The only cloud on Lessie's horizon as the winter began to drop behind and spring made itself felt, even in the Vennel where there was not a tree to burst into leaf or a patch of soil where a grass blade could flourish, was the money she still owed to Anna McCauley. The rent had to be paid and food had to be bought and now that Davie was earning less, money was even tighter than before. Ian seemed to be continually growing out of his clothes and Lessie scoured the secondhand shops for jerseys and trousers and shoes for him, often buying larger garments that still had some good wear in them, unpicking them, and making them over to fit the little boy.

Edith was good at handing down clothes that Peter had outgrown, but all too often they were impossible. Lessie couldn't bring herself to turn her Ian into a laughing stock by dressing him in the velvet suits that poor Peter had to wear. Guiltily, hoping that Edith would never find out, she took most of the little suits along to the pawnbroker to raise a shilling or two. But even so, she never had enough left over to pay off the debt that continually nagged at her conscience.

In her fine little house with her fine clothes and her

maidservant and Andrew Warren visiting her whenever he could, Anna was becoming bored, missing the bustle and variety of life in the Vennel. As she grew fatter and heavier she took to summoning Lessie for afternoon tea once a week and Lessie, ever aware of the twenty shillings she owed, felt that she had no option but to go to Port Glasgow, busy though she was. Once the debt was paid, she told herself each time she caught the horse tram that ran between the two towns, she need never see Anna again. They were people with entirely different outlooks on life, and now that her former neighbour was living in the house Andrew Warren rented for her, their lives had grown even further apart. At the same time she was uncomfortably aware that as far as Anna was concerned they were friends and would always remain so. Lessie felt she was caught in a difficult situation.

In the early spring Murdo brought an invitation to visit his mother's home for Sunday tea. Lessie stared at him, astonished and flustered. 'I couldn't!'

'Why not?'

'I, well, why does she want to see me?'

He laughed. 'Why shouldnae she want to see you? She's heard me talking about you, that's all. You'll come, won't you? Please, Lessie,' he begged, and she nodded, not wanting to disappoint him yet feeling that she had been caught in a trap.

Mrs Carswell lived with her two unmarried children, Murdo and his younger sister, in the top flat of a well-kept tenement in Roxburgh Street. Her late husband had been a bookkeeper in one of the big sugar houses, a thrifty man who had left his widow well provided for. Mrs Carswell considered herself to be superior to most of the Greenock folk, but she greeted Lessie kindly enough, her eyes travelling approvingly over her guest's best clothes, a blue woollen skirt and jacket over a blue and white striped blouse, with a straw hat decorated with a blue ribbon.

The clothes had originally belonged to Edith and Lessie had ironed them carefully for the occasion, using a damp cloth to protect the material from the hot iron. The blouse was fastened at the neck by a garnet and filigree brooch that had belonged to Donald's mother. He had given it to Lessie on their wedding day and she treasured it. 'One day,' he had said as he handed it over, 'I'll be able to buy you a ring and a necklace to match.' Then he had added, grinning down at her, 'Mebbe this time next year.'

The Carswells and their guest had tea at a table by the window – boiled potatoes and thick glistening slices of cold potted meat with a spoonful of peas carefully measured onto each plate. When Lessie praised the spicy meat, Murdo's mother informed her that she had made it herself, and rattled off the exact price of the shinbone and the beef she had used without a pause for thought.

'Murdo tells me you're a widow like myself, Mistress Hamilton,' she went on as she dispensed tea. 'With a wee boy to raise.'

'Ian's almost two years old now.'

'Murdo was five when I lost his father.' Mrs Carswell made it sound as though she had mislaid the man somewhere. 'I'd four wee ones to bring up on my own, but I pride myself on having done well. Two of them are well married, and Katherine here's walking out with a very nice young man who works in the shipyard offices. It was him who got Murdo into the shipyard. I hope your son grows up to be as successful as my four.'

'I'm sure he will,' Lessie said, adding hastily as her hostess's eyebrows rose, 'This meat's lovely, Mrs Carswell.'

Katherine caught her eye and gave her the shadow of a wink.

They finished off with a syrup tart and as they ate it Mrs Carswell reeled off the cost of the syrup as well as the brand of tea she bought specially for visitors. It was a relief when, the meal over and the table cleared, Murdo suggested an outing. 'Can you ride a bicycle?'

'A bicycle? I've not been on one for more years than I care to remember.'

'You can borrow Katherine's.' Murdo glanced at her clothes. 'You'll manage fine in that skirt. Come on.'

The bicycles, old but lovingly maintained, were kept in a shed in the back yard. Wheeling her machine, Lessie followed Murdo nervously through the close and into the street, quite certain that she would have forgotten everything she had ever learned about bicycling. At first, to the open amusement of the women leaning from their windows and the children playing on the pavements, her machine wobbled precariously and once or twice she had to slap a foot hastily onto the ground to prevent herself from toppling over altogether. But by the time they had negotiated the stretch to the corner of the street her sense of balance was returning and she was able to follow Murdo in a fairly straight line.

Mercifully, he didn't expect her to go far. The Carswells lived further inland than she did, and they only had to turn out of Roxburgh Street and follow the rising sweep of Captain Street to reach the water-filtering system on the higher limits of the town, almost in the countryside. Here, at a stretch of rough winter grass, Murdo dismounted and waited until Lessie, breathless, reached him. He laid both bicycles on the grass and he and Lessie leaned against a drystone wall and looked down towards the river.

It was an exceptionally beautiful February day with more than a promise of the spring to come. The air was as clear and fresh as mountain water, the sky blue, with only a few fluffy clouds on the horizon and the snow-streaked hills on the other side of the river to remind them that it was still winter. The sun had warmed the stones at their backs and woven a broad rope of shimmering gold across the river to link Greenock with Helensburgh. A steam tug and its tow, a sailing ship on the way upriver to its final destination, vanished from sight when they entered that dazzling golden band, then reappeared, the tug as a black beetle, the lofty sailing ship with its masts and spars turned to black lace against the bright background. Then they broke free of it and became themselves again. Here and there brightly coloured paddle-steamers beat the glassy river into sparkling white foam as they fussed from one quay to another.

For some strange reason Andrew Warren came into Lessie's mind. To her left lay Gourock, where he and his family lived in their big house; before her was Greenock, where the Warren sugar refinery was situated, and to the right lay Port Glasgow, where Anna McCauley now lived in a house rented by Warren. Three neighbouring towns, Lessie thought, spanned by the power and wealth of one man.

'What are you thinking about?' Murdo asked at that moment.

'Nothing at all.' She closed her eyes, feeling the sun's warmth on her lids, and promised herself that one day in the summer she would bring Ian to this place, where he could run about and play in the sunshine. Then she jumped as a shadow fell over her lids, Murdo's hands cupped her elbows, and his mouth brushed hers gently.

'Murdo Carswell!' She straightened up, pulling away from the wall, staring in shocked outrage at the face only inches from hers. 'What d'you think you're doing?'

'Kissing you. What's amiss with that?' His breath was soft on her cheek.

'You can't do that – you went to school with our Joseph!'

'School,' said Murdo, his mouth twitching in a suppressed smile, 'was a good long while ago.' Then he kissed her again, this time drawing her into his arms, holding her close, his mouth lingering on hers.

It was the first time a man had kissed her since Donald's death, the first time since then that anyone had held her, apart from the tight clutch of Ian's little arms and an occasional affectionate swipe from his sticky little mouth. It was good to be held by a man again, and Lessie's arms slid round Murdo's back as the kiss deepened. She could feel his heart and hers pounding, and parted her lips as the tip of his tongue slid gently along them. He broke the kiss just long enough to let his mouth taste the angle of her jaw, one ear, the silkiness of her neck, then returned to find her mouth soft and open and eager for his again.

When they finally drew back from each other Lessie said shakily, 'I must get back. My mother's got Ian an' she's enough to do without him under her feet all afternoon.'

One of Murdo's hands brushed back a lock of her hair and tucked it behind her ear. His touch sent a pleasant shiver down her spine. 'We'll do this again, Lessie,' he said, and released her, turning and stooping to lift his sister's bicycle while Lessie, dazed, wondered whether he meant the outing or the kiss.

She was still shaky and somewhat weak about the knees when she knocked at her mother's door a short while later. It opened on a waft of whisky breath and peals of amusement from the kitchen, Thomasina's high-pitched laugh threading its way through Ian's deeper bubbling mirth.

'Ye're earlier than I thought ye'd be,' said Barbara. 'Did your visit go all right?'

'It was fine, but I didnae want to leave Ian for too long.'

In the kitchen Thomasina was dancing round Ian, who stood in the middle of the floor dressed in one of her summer frocks, the waistline almost at his knees, the neck slipping over one of his shoulders. Thomasina's best straw hat was tipped at a drunken angle over one ear and his face was split by a huge delighted grin. When he saw his mother he advanced towards her, skiffing his feet to keep Thomasina's shoes on, and almost tripping over the hem of the frock.

'Bonny wee lassie!' Thomasina screeched, and Ian echoed, 'Bonny!'

'So you are, but a bonnier lad than a lass as far as I'm concerned, ye wee imp.' Lessie swept him up into her arms, lifting him right out of the shoes, and hugged him, then glanced sharply at her mother as she started to cough. 'Have you not got rid of that cough yet?'

'It's goin', it's goin'. It's no' near as bad as it was. My new syrup's helpin' it.' Barbara lifted a dark medicine bottle from a shelf by the sink, found a spoon, and swallowed down several doses of a clear amber liquid. By the time Ian had been restored to his normal self and they were about to go home to the Vennel, Barbara had had another coughing attack and had needed several doses of her syrup. Each time the bottle was uncorked the pungent smell of whisky was noticeable. As she made for the door, Lessie said gently, 'Best not to let Edith see you taking so much of that cough syrup, Mam. She might no' understand.'

Barbara blinked, then gave her daughter a tired smile. 'Ye're a good girl, Lessie,' she said. 'A good girl.'

8

'I'm going to call her Dorothea,' Anna said proudly. 'I found it in a book.'

'It's a lovely name.' Lessie settled the baby more comfortably into the crook of her arm and eased Ian's inquisitive fingers away from the tiny face nestling in the midst of the froth of silk and lace and delicate wool on her lap. 'Just look at her, pet, don't touch. She's too wee to be touched.'

'I sent word for you to come two days ago, Lessie. Did you not get it?'

'Mr McKay's been ill again. I couldnae get away from the shop.'

'I don't suppose Mr McKay was as ill as me.' Anna, rested and beautiful, lying back against a mound of pillows with a shawl about her shoulders, a silken quilt over her legs and her red hair freshly brushed, looked the picture of health and happiness. 'I never knew child-birth could hurt so much, Lessie. I swear I'll never go through that again!'

'It's not as bad as that, and it's easy forgotten. Besides, it's worth it, isn't it, my bonny wee love?' Lessie crooned to the baby, who had opened clear blue eyes. Dorothea yawned and Ian laughed at her then wandered off to explore the room. Lessie watched him carefully. There were so many ornaments in this beautiful bedroom, so many fragile things to tempt inquisitive little fingers.

'Oh, it's worth it now, but never again.' Then Anna's head lifted from the pillow as the door knocker rattled. 'Who's that come to call?'

They heard the servant opening the door then the

murmur of a deep voice. Her face lit up.

'It's Andrew! Here, give her to me.' She held out her arms and Lessie went to the bed and carefully handed the little bundle over. With swift hands Anna arranged the baby's shawl, then she lay back against her pillows again. When Andrew Warren tapped on the door and entered, she smiled at him and reached out her free hand. 'Andrew, I didnae think to see you today.'

'I'd business in Port Glasgow.' He took the proffered hand. 'How are you, my dear?'

'Oh, a little stronger than yesterday.'

'I'm glad to hear it. Good day to you, Mrs Hamilton.'

'Mr Warren.' Lessie had returned to her chair, but she couldn't sit down. If she had known that Andrew Warren was going to visit the house that day she would never have come.

'Here's a fine wee Scotsman, with his red hair. What's his name?' Warren, quite at his ease, smiled down at Ian, who had moved close to his mother's skirt and was staring at the newcomer, one thumb in his mouth.

'Ian.'

'A good Scots name too. And how's our little Dorothea?' To Lessie's astonishment he lifted the baby from Anna's arms and walked over to the window with her, holding her as easily as any woman would.

'She's a wee angel. Scarce a sound out of her.' Anna's voice was smug.

'What d'you think of her, Mrs Hamilton?'

'She's a beautiful baby.'

Andrew's eyes met Anna's over their daughter's head. 'I agree,' he said. 'And she's going to be a beautiful lady one day, like her mother. She's going to have everything her heart desires.'

Lessie, used to men showing no interest in their offspring until the children were old enough to earn money, was dumbfounded by Warren's frank adoration of a child that had not even been born in wedlock. True, Donald had openly delighted in Ian when he was born, but Donald had been special, above other men. She found it hard to believe that a man with Andrew Warren's power and money could care so much for children. But there was no doubt that he did. In fact, he and Anna and the baby were such a complete family, such a happy family, that envy twinged suddenly and unexpectedly, like an aching tooth, in Lessie's heart. As soon as she could she made her excuses, gathered Ian up, and left.

'You'll come back soon to see me?' Anna asked as she was going out of the door. 'I'll be needing your advice now that I've got a bairn of my own to see to.'

'I'll be back when I can.'

Her hand was on the latch of the outer door when Andrew Warren came swiftly down the stairs from the bedroom. 'Mrs Hamilton, I hope that you will continue to visit Anna.' As he stood over her, the little hall seemed even smaller. 'She needs a good friend and it comforts me to know that she has one in you.'

Lessie's heart sank. She had hoped that once the child was born Anna would be too busy, too content, to look for her company any longer. But she couldn't say so, not to this solemn man who adored babies.

'I'll certainly continue to call if Anna wishes it,' she heard herself saying pompously. Miss Peden would have been proud of her.

'Thank you.' He stooped and took Ian's small hand in his. 'Good day, Master Ian. We'll meet again, I'm sure.'

Then he opened the door and ushered them through it with as much courtesy as though they were gentry like himself. She was so bemused that she paid no attention at all to Ian's excited babbling and they were halfway to the tram stop before Lessie discovered the coin clutched tightly in the little boy's fist, where Warren had placed it.

Although he had accepted his new role as the manager of the family refinery because there was no other way, Andrew resented it bitterly. He had always assumed that by the time he was required to return to Greenock from Jamaica to take over the family business he would be the sole owner, with a free hand in the management of the place. But with only one uncle dead and the other determined to become an invalid and at the same time retain his shares and therefore his hold on the refinery, Andrew was in a difficult position. The place needed to be revitalised; the machinery should be modernised or at least improved, but James Warren's attitude to everything that Andrew suggested was one of caution bordering on fear.

'We'll lose every penny we have if you get your way,' the old man grumbled each time his nephew tried to reason with him. 'D'you take me for a fool? I've no intention of losing all my money.'

'But the Continental refiners are seeking to take the sugar monopoly away from the British Isles. You mark my words, Uncle James, if our refinery isn't improved soon, we'll be in danger of falling behind. There are already too many good sugar houses in Greenock being forced to close their doors and dismiss their workers. I don't want it to happen to Warren's as well.'

'This is no time to pour more money into the business. Parliament's just pushed our taxes up to a shilling in the pound, damn their thieving hearts. A fifty per cent increase! At this rate I'll be fortunate if I don't die in the workhouse.'

'We could borrow from the bank. God knows our name's good. We'd have no trouble in raising the capital we need.'

'I'll not go begging to any bank, nor will I be plunged into debt. You hear me, Andrew?' The old man sucked in his lips and scowled. He looked like a large sulky baby and for a moment Warren was tempted to treat him like one, sending him to his bed and making him stay there until he saw sense. But he knew that he had no option but to continue to do the best he could without the free hand that he badly needed.

The workers, too, were unsure of him and slow to give him their trust. He was in the throes of trying to persuade them to set up a scheme whereby they would each pay in a halfpenny a week from their wages so that any man forced to take time off work through illness would be entitled to payment for at least part of his time at home, but the whole process was proving to be as sticky and sluggish as the sugar and syrup mixture they fed into the centrifugal machines to be separated. Although workers in some other firms had started their own 'sick clubs', the majority of the Warren employees were too cautious to part with their hard-earned money. Andrew was working patiently on the younger men, explaining the benefits of such a scheme, in the hope that they would see the light and convince the others. He had even offered to contribute management money amounting to half the sum collected from the workers each week, but he didn't dare tell his uncle that.

But now there was something for Andrew to rejoice over, and rejoice he did, in secret, as he walked from his office to the yard where his small carriage was kept. He had a third child now, a beautiful daughter. He relished the prospect of watching Dorothea thrive and grow, untrammelled by nursery staff who thought that fathers were merely there to provide money and should be neither seen nor heard.

The yard was awash with sunlight that softened and warmed the harsh greys and browns and blacks of the cobbles and the stone walls. Two women came from the warehouse, rolling a huge barrel of kieselguhr between them, struggling to keep it moving over the cobblestones. The melted sugar was poured over troughs of kiesel-guhr, a fine earth almost entirely composed of minute animal skeletons, to cleanse it of impurities before it was crystallised. Although their task was hard, the women were laughing over something, lifting their faces to the sun.

A cart piled high with empty sugar sacks was rattling out of the gate on its way to Boag's factory, which had been set up to wash sugar bags from all the refineries and prepare them for re-use. The old buildings fronting the yard hummed and clanked with the steam-driven machinery that filled them. Studying the buildings while he waited for a stableman to harness his horse to the carriage, Andrew frowned. The plan of the place was wrong; it had been built about a hundred years earlier and a lot of time was wasted in transporting sacks and barrels from one section to another and back again, instead of starting the refining process at one end of the building and completing it at the other.

But the plans he had in mind would take money, a great deal of money. A surge of frustration swept over him as he climbed into the carriage and picked up the reins. He knew the refinery well, knew every stone, every beam, every piece of machinery. Like his father and his uncles, Andrew had begun by working his way through each department. He had toiled in the warehouse, weighing, grading, marking and lifting the great bags of refined sugar; he had served his apprenticeship as a pan floor boy, where the heat generated by the huge vacuum pans was almost intolerable and nobody could bear to wear anything on their feet. He had worked in the char house and as a liquor boy, washing out the big tanks, learning to overcome the queasiness caused by the heavy, sweet, pervasive smell of the sugar. He had spent time in the laboratory, where they tested sugar samples and worked continuously at perfecting the process.

He wondered, as he drove out to Gourock, if Martin would serve such a gruelling apprenticeship before taking over command, then decided with a wry smile that Madeleine would probably fight such an idea tooth and nail.

At nine o'clock that evening James finished reading his newspaper, folded it into a neat rectangle, and announced that he was going to bed. Madeleine had been playing the piano, but when the door closed she rose and came across the room to where her husband sat working at his desk.

'Andrew, I know about your woman.'

The sentence was so blunt, so unexpected, that for a moment he gaped at her. Her lovely face was expressionless, her hands folded demurely before her.

'I won't demean us both by pretending innocence, Madeleine,' he said at last, pushing away the ledger he had been working on and standing up. He felt strangely weak and shaky, as though he had just suffered a mortal blow.

She turned away from him and walked to a sofa, seating herself with that delicate grace that always enchanted him. 'I attend afternoon soirees, I help to raise funds for our soldiers in South Africa. I cannot help hearing gossip. And I have heard that there is a woman, and a house, and a child.'

'Who told you?'

Her shoulders lifted in one of her lovely shrugs. 'That is of no matter. Malicious people sometimes like to carry bad news.'

'It happened—' he started to say, but she held up a hand to stop him.

'I have no desire to know any of the details, Andrew. I only wish you to know that I am aware of the situation.'

'Are you asking me to give her up?'

'Why should I, when I am quite sure that you would only replace her with someone else?'

'You have a cynical idea of men, my dear.'

'I learned from my father. And now I am learning from my husband, am I not?'

Beneath her faint, almost pitying, smile Andrew felt the colour rise to his face.

'I am not a child,' she went on. 'I know that it is apparently not easy for men to be faithful. A man is almost expected to have his paramours.'

'Madeleine—'

'And a woman learns to accept these things. I was taught that by my mama. I do accept, but there are conditions.'

'Conditions?' He could scarcely believe that they were discussing his infidelity in such a matter-of-fact way. He would have expected tears, anger, accusations. He would have welcomed them, welcomed the opportunity to beg her forgiveness, to comfort her and so comfort himself. But that was not what Madeleine sought.

'I am your wife, and I intend to remain so.'

'That's my intention too.'

'My children and I will always come first,' the light voice with its charming accent went on implacably. 'This woman and her child will never come to this house to

95

shame me before my children. My son will inherit his birthright. Any other sons you may have will have no claim to your money or your position.'

Helpless anger had begun to fill Andrew. He was being treated like a badly behaved servant, and he had no way of defending himself, for Madeleine was in the right. 'I would never consider denying your rights as my wife or denying our children their birthright,' he said stiffly.

Madeleine's head bobbed in the slightest nod and the sapphire earrings Andrew had given her only a few months before glittered in the lamplight. 'Then we understand each other. One more thing, Andrew. You will no longer come to my bedchamber. Never again.'

'Madeleine, if I was to give the woman up—'

'Never,' she repeated, and walked away from him, out of the room, her back straight and her small head, piled with the glossy black hair that had never been cut, held high.

The sight of that hair, carefully coiffed and pinned, reminded Andrew of the feel of the soft silky locks in his hands, against his face, his naked body. As the door closed, he strode over to a small table in the corner of the room and fumbled at the whisky decanter, dropping the stopper in his clumsiness. The sound of it bouncing off the inlaid table jangled through him and his hands shook as he measured a generous amount of the liquid into a glass. The stopper had landed intact on the deep carpet and, dazed, he took time to search for it and return it to the decanter before moving to one of the big windows that overlooked the river.

The sun had gone down but a pale pink memory of it remained just above the water. Above that the sky was delicate grey shading into charcoal and the first stars were beginning to glimmer palely. Lights from the boats moved across the water. As Andrew watched, everything blurred and misted and he was horrified to realise that there were tears in his eyes.

Hurriedly, ashamed of them, he scrubbed them away and took a deep swallow from his glass. The whisky burned into his mouth, his throat, his gullet, but brought no comfort. It tasted of his own self-disgust.

He had suggested giving up Anna. Now he turned the thought round, studying it, and realised that he would have done it if that had been what Madeleine wanted. Anna was a joy and a comfort, but she was also an indulgence whereas Madeleine was his wife, now and for as long as they both lived, and he loved her as much as he ever had. He realised this with astonishment, for since the birth of the twins he had come to accept that love was no longer a part of his marriage. He had been wrong; now that he had lost her respect he knew that his feelings for Madeleine had never changed.

He drained the last of the whisky and refilled the glass. If he had only examined his feelings closely a year ago he might have been able, somehow, to win Madeleine back again. Now it was too late; he had lost her through his own foolishness.

The second drink, more comforting than the first, began to wash away the humiliation. He poured a third and returned to the window to watch the last remnants of the sunset fade. He still had Anna. She loved him, depended on him, trusted him. And he had Dorothea. Although he would have relinquished the woman for the promise of his wife's forgiveness, he could never relinquish the child they had made together, his daughter.

He filled his glass for the fourth time.

Lessie's secret fears came true that summer. Mr McKay's health had become so bad that he and his wife decided to give up the corner shop and move to Rothesay on the Clyde island of Bute, where the old man could rest and enjoy what remained of his life.

'I'm sorry, my dear, for you've been such a help to us over the past year.' Mrs McKay's thin fingers kneaded each other nervously as she broke the news. 'But there's nothing else for it. I'll put in a good word with the new owners for you.'

'Is there someone interested?'

'Not yet.'

'It'll likely be someone with a family to help in the

shop,' Lessie said desolately, and went home to fret over this latest blow. There was nowhere near for her to work, and most of the shopkeepers in the town would frown on the thought of Ian tagging with her. The only answer was to find more house-cleaning to do, but there again Ian was the problem. Now that Davie was earning a smaller wage, what little the McKays had paid her, sometimes in goods instead of money, had gained in importance. It meant the difference between managing and going hungry most weeks.

And there was Anna's twenty shillings, briskly receding so far into the distance that Lessie could see no way at all of repaying it. She went about her work that day in a haze of misery, saying nothing about her problems to Miss Peden as she took a cup of tea after scrubbing the stairs. The old lady might offer to lend her money and Lessie felt that she was already burdened with debt. She hoped that she would never again have to owe money to anyone.

She held her tongue when Davie came in at night, full of excitement because Mr Beattie had agreed to an amendment Davie had suggested in one of the machines they were turning out. He had just passed his final night-school examination and was entitled to an increase in wages, but Mr Beattie couldn't afford to pay him more. Rather than try elsewhere, where he might not have the freedom to put forward his own ideas, Davie had decided to stay on for the same money.

'But only if you agree,' he had said to Lessie just two weeks before, when the matter arose. 'It'll be worth it eventually because I'm learning a lot. And if I leave I'll mebbe be out of work for a wee while with no money coming in at all.'

He had looked so hopeful that Lessie had agreed, unaware at that time of the McKays' plans to give up the shop.

That night before going to sleep she ran through her usual prayers in her mind, then added, 'Donald, help me to find a way to look after Ian the way you'd have wanted.' Since her widowhood her prayers had been a mixture of appeals to God and to Donald who, she was certain, would do all he could to put in a good word for her. She sometimes wondered if this was insulting to God, but if so it couldn't be helped. Better to insult God than to ignore her Donald.

She fell asleep at last with the memory of her husband's face, his voice, his touch close in her mind and her heart like a talisman, and wakened in the morning with an idea so startling, so ridiculous, that it could only have been put there by someone else. By Donald, she thought, dazed, scrambling out of bed and knocking on Davie's door to rouse him before getting dressed.

And if it was indeed Donald's answer to her dilemma, she must do all she could to make it work.

9

'Lassie, ye could never dae it!' Mr McKay protested. 'Ye've got enough tae worry aboot wi'oot takin' ower the shop as well.'

'I could, if I gave up the cleaning work. And I'd make enough money to pay you and leave somethin' over tae keep me and Ian, once I got started.' Lessie heard her voice crack and knew that she was almost begging. But she didn't care.

'Even so,' Mrs McKay said gently, her eyes sad, 'there's no sense in us leaving you to look after the shop for us. We need the money we'd get from selling it. My sister in Rothesay's willing tae have us, but we'd have tae pay our way. An' there's the cost o' gettin' over there, an' takin' the bits o' furniture we want tae keep by us.'

Lessie swallowed her disappointment. 'How much are you looking for?'

'Seventy pound, my dear.' Then, at Lessie's gasp of horror, the old man explained in his hoarse, breathless voice, 'The shop an' the wee house are nae' – he paused for breath – 'ours, o' course. They're rented at twelve pound a year. But there's a' the . . . the stock in the shop, an' the goodwill. We bring in seven . . . pound in a good week an' it's . . . customary tae ask ten . . . pound for every pound taken . . . in a week. It's a fair . . . askin' price.'

'D'you need it all at once?'

Mrs McKay glanced at her husband. Years of close companionship made spoken consultation unnecessary for these two; Lessie had often marvelled at the way each knew what the other was thinking, and envied them. It

101

was a gift she and Donald might have shared one day if only he had been spared.

'Fifty pound in oor hands wid jist aboot dae it,' Mr McKay was saying, while his wife nodded agreement. 'An' the rest peyed ower . . . the next year. But there'd be the rent ower an' . . . above that, an' new stock tae . . . tae buy for the shop as ye run . . . oot.'

'It'd be too much for you, Lessie. Best to forget about it,' Mrs McKay urged.

Lessie didn't want to forget about it. The idea fired her with enthusiasm. She took Ian home and gave him a crust dipped in sugar to chew so that she could work out sums on the back of one of Davie's many exercise books. She and Ian and Davie could live in the two rooms behind the shop. As well as being in better condition than her own flat, it would make a small saving in rent. And give her an annual rent of twelve pounds to meet, an inner voice added, and was smartly dismissed. With her own shop she could support Ian and look after him by herself. When he grew older he could be her errand boy and eventually, when she was too old to run the shop by herself, it would be his inheritance. The McKays claimed that the shop could take in six or seven pounds in a good week. To Lessie, that was wealth worth having.

After his first appalled reaction to her scheme, Davie began to catch some of her enthusiasm. They sat together that night after Ian was asleep, adding and subtracting and planning but not getting very far.

'Nae use in askin' Da for the money. Even if he had it he'd no' part wi' it. An' Edith an' Joseph are of no help at all.' Davie dismissed their family in a few words, then went on slowly, 'I could dae more for you if I left Beattie's an' went tae a larger firm that could afford tae pay better wages.'

'You're happy where you are. I'd not hear of you moving.' Lessie tried to tuck up a strand of fair hair that had fallen over her face. 'Besides, I want to do this myself. It was my idea and it should be my worry.'

'There's Miss Peden—'

'I'll not ask her for help.'

Davie sighed. 'You'll have tae, Lessie. She's the only person we know wi' a bit o' money.'

'I'll not be in debt to her!'

'See sense, Lessie.' Davie's voice was suddenly exasperated. 'Ye cannae hope tae take on a shop without borrowing money – everyone in business borrows. Most from the banks, but they'd no' be of any use tae ye. Ye've got tae decide how important this shop is tae ye. If ye want it badly enough, I think Miss Peden'd be the person tae go tae. She'd help ye willingly, an' she'd know ye could be trusted tae pay back the money.'

Lessie started to chew on the end of the lock of hair. 'Mebbe you're right. But I'll only ask her when I can say I've got as much money as I can raise myself.'

'I'll sell my engineering books.'

'You need them.' Davie had slowly managed to put together a library of textbooks. She knew how hard he had worked for each one.

'Not all of them. Not the earlier ones. I'll sell them. Lessie . . .' He hesitated, then said awkwardly, not meeting her eyes, 'There's Donald's good suit still hanging up in the cupboard.'

Two pairs of eyes went to the cupboard door. Behind it was the suit Donald had been married in, and a good winter coat of his that Davie sometimes wore when the weather was bitter. Lessie kept them both well brushed and free of damp. It had always irked her that Donald had been buried in his working suit, but poor people couldn't afford to consign good clothes to the grave and she knew that his spirit would never have forgiven her if she had done so.

'I'll take it tae the pawn tomorrow. And the coat. I'll get them back out before the year's up, for I'll be able tae afford it by then,' she said round a lump in her throat.

'And I'll give you my good suit as well. I can manage without it for a month or two. Until the winter, anyway. Don't take them tae that old twister McConnachie,' Davie warned. 'He always cheats. Go somewhere else.'

'Oh, Davie, ye're a good brother tae me!'

'I should be better. I should be earning what I'm worth

now that I've got my papers,' Davie said gruffly. Lessie leaned forward to put her hand on his and the lock of hair, slightly damp at the end now, fell forward again. She began to lift it back, hesitated, studied it, squinting a little, frowning, thinking, planning.

'What in the world have you done to yourself?' Anna McCauley stared, shocked, as her friend took off her hat.

Lessie ran a hand through her short fair hair and shrugged. 'It was nothing but a nuisance. I decided to have it cut off.'

'I don't believe you.' Anna's voice was blunt. 'Did you have nits?'

Lessie felt her face grow scarlet. 'I did not!'

'Tell me, then, if you don't want me to go on thinking it was head lice.'

Lessie began to refuse, then stopped and bit her lip. Anna would pester her until she got the truth.

'Ian, away out and play in the back garden. It's all right,' Anna added over her shoulder as she opened the door for the little boy. 'Dorothea's out there with Molly watching over her. She can see to two as easy as one. I'm fortunate to have Molly,' she went on, closing the door and returning to her chair. 'She thinks the world of Dorothea.'

Today she was wearing a fawn blouse richly embroidered with violet and green threads on the bodice and sleeves. Her pleated skirt was also fawn, and her red hair was caught up at the back with a jet comb. Lessie, watching her seat herself with easy grace, marvelled at how swiftly Anna had settled into the role of a wealthy young woman. It was very difficult, now, to remember that she had once lived in the Vennel.

'Now,' Anna leaned forward, her lovely eyes wide with curiosity, 'tell me what you're up to.'

Once the story had spilled out, she looked disappointed. 'Is that all? I thought you'd had your hair cut off to please a man.'

'As if I'd do that! Donald didn't ever want me to cut my hair, and I wouldn't have if I hadnae needed the money so badly.' Lessie heard her own voice quiver slightly on the last few words. The business had been far harder than she had imagined. Clean though her hair was, the hairdresser had washed it again, then cut it off carefully, exclaiming in pleasure over the long strands, drying to a soft silkiness, assuring her that he would put it to good use. She had taken the proffered money and left the shop feeling as though she had just sold Ian. Every time she looked into the mirror she felt like a murderer.

'You suit it short,' Anna said thoughtfully. 'Stand up and turn round and let me see it. What does Murdo say to it?'

'It's of no concern to me what Murdo Carswell thinks. I keep telling you, Anna, we're just friends.'

'So you say.' Anna eyed her slyly from beneath long lashes. 'How much more d'you need for the shop?'

Lessie bit her lip again. Donald's good suit and coat had been pawned, together with Davie's suit. Davie had sold some of his engineering books to a secondhand dealer and her beloved garnet brooch had also found its way into the pawnbroker's safe. Davie had gone behind her back and told Miss Peden the whole story, and the former schoolteacher had swept down to the Vennel, marched into Lessie's house, and handed her a twenty-pound note.

'It's all I can raise at the moment, my dear, but it's yours,' she had announced.

'I cannae take your money!'

'I know you'll pay me back when you can. Davie's told me how you feel about loans, but I'm not in a hurry, and surely we know each other well enough by now for you to accept my help graciously. You've done a lot for me, my dear,' Miss Peden had said, her voice suddenly losing its usual steel. 'You've given me friendship and company, and I'm only pleased that at last I can give you something in return.'

'How much more?' Anna asked again.

'I still need twenty pounds.'

'Is that all? I can ask Andrew to give it to you.'

'You'll do nothing of the sort!'

'My dear Lessie, he'd never miss it.'

Lessie got to her feet. 'Anna McCauley, if you dare to ask him for money for me, I'll – I'll never come back tae this house. D'you hear me?'

'For goodness sake, money's money. What does it matter who you get it from?'

'It matters tae me.' It was difficult enough to accept help from Davie and Miss Peden, but Lessie was damned if she would take charity from a man who knew her so vaguely that he would probably walk past her in the street without recognising her. 'I mean it, Anna. I'll not come back, not ever.'

'You couldnae turn your back on wee Dorothea, and her just getting to the interesting stage.'

'Yes I could.'

There was a short silence during which their eyes locked, Lessie's hard and determined; then Anna shrugged and pouted. 'Very well. But you're being very foolish. I don't think you want this shop as much as you say you do.'

Oh, I want it, Lessie wanted to say. I want it so badly that the fear of losing it haunts me every minute of my life. But she kept quiet, for Anna would never understand. As she sat down again and accepted a chocolate from the box by Anna's elbow she wondered yet again how she could ever have allowed herself to be drawn into Anna's web. The two of them were as alike as chalk and cheese, though Anna didn't seem to notice.

'It suits your face like that. I never thought a woman would look so beautiful with short hair.' Murdo reached out to touch it and the back of his hand brushed against Lessie's face. They had cycled up to the water filters again; this time the grass beneath their feet was rich and green and scattered liberally with white and purple clover. Lessie, embarrassed by his suddenly intent look, the way his hand lingered on her cheek, stooped to pick some clover, twisting it round in her fingers, staring down at it because otherwise she would have had to look at Murdo.

'I've been thinkin' about the shop an' you wantin' it so much,' his voice said from above her downbent head, 'an' I was wonderin' . . .' He paused, cleared his throat, then said stiffly, 'I could help ye tae take it over.'

'You've got enough with your mother and sister to look after. You can't go lending money to me. Besides, I'd not—'

'I wasnae thinkin' o' lendin' it. I've got a bit saved up, an' we could live in the rooms at the back. An' wi' me workin' in the shipyard an' you managin' the shop we could dae well for ourselves.'

'We? Living in the back shop? Together?' Lessie stared up at him, the clover falling forgotten from her fingers. 'Murdo Carswell, what d'you think—'

'I'm talkin' o' marriage, Lessie. You an' me. I'd be a good husband tae Ian an' a good father tae you if – I mean, a good father tae him an' a good husband tae—' He stopped, utterly confused, then said, 'Dammit, Lessie, no need tae laugh at a man jist because he gets tongue-tied. I've never proposed marriage tae a woman afore. Oh dammit!' he said fiercely, his face crimson with embarrassment, and turned away to stare hard at the distant river and the familiar shipyard skeleton of cranes etched against the water.

'I'm not laughing at you, Murdo,' Lessie said, small-voiced, angry with herself for having belittled him. 'I just – you took me by surprise.'

'Ye must've known how I felt. Why else would I hae wanted tae keep seein' ye?'

'I knew you liked me, and I like you. But as for marriage – who wants to take on a widow with a child?'

'I do!' Murdo spun round, caught her in his arms before she could move back. 'I love you, Lessie Hamilton. I've watched ye struggle tae make ends meet an' I've wanted badly tae take the worry of it all away from ye, tae look after ye, an' the bairn as well. But it was too early tae tell ye. I was afraid o' frightin' ye, and losin' ye. Now's the right time – now, when we could take over the shop between us an' my wage could support us while ye find yer feet.'

'What would your mother say?'

'My mother?' he asked in bewilderment.

'We have to think of her.'

'No we don't. My father left her well provided for. She'll manage fine. An' she thinks a good deal o' ye. Lessie, don't turn me down. Ye care for me, don't ye?'

She looked up into his hazel eyes, usually carefree and brimming with amusement, but now pleading, afraid of rejection.

'You know I care for you,' she said, and his mouth took hers, preventing her from saying any more. She clung to him, closing her eyes, thinking of Donald. But Donald was dead and she was alive, still young and in need of love and loving and a future. Donald was in the cemetery but Murdo was here, holding her, offering her not only a way to obtain the shop but to know again a way of life that she had thought she had buried in the grave for all time when she buried her husband.

It all fell into place with an ease that told Lessie that it had surely been meant to happen. Mrs Carswell accepted the news that her son and Lessie Hamilton were to marry without making the fuss that Lessie had expected, and within a week or two of hearing about his sister's plans Davie found a room for himself in Port Glasgow, near to the engineering works.

'But there's no need for you to do that,' Lessie protested when he came home and told her. 'You can stay on with us. Murdo, tell him!'

'Of course ye're welcome, Davie,' Murdo said, but to Lessie's mind his voice lacked conviction.

Davie shook his head. 'There's not enough room for us all behind the shop. Anyway, married folk need to be on their own.'

'But Davie—'

He patted her arm reassuringly. 'It's best this way. Besides, I've got plans of my own. I've suggested tae Mr Beattie that he should only pay me enough tae meet my rent and my food. The rest o' my wages are goin' back intae the business. One day there'll be enough o' it tae

108

pay for a junior partnership. Mr Beattie's agreed tae it.'

'God, man, o' course he's agreed!' Murdo said in horror. 'Ye're a fool, takin' less than the money ye're entitled tae! Ye're no' bein' paid what ye're worth as it is.'

'It's settled between him an' me.'

'But the man could cheat ye oot o' your wages an' no' gie ye anythin' in return.'

'Davie,' Lessie said nervously, suddenly aware that Murdo's words made sense, 'wouldn't it be better if—'

'It's all right, Lessie, I trust Mr Beattie an' he trusts me.'

'Ach, gang yer ain way,' Murdo said, 'but ye're a stubborn fool, Davie. Ye'd no' find me workin' for less than I was worth.'

'It'll work out well for me in the end, you'll see,' Davie insisted.

'At least stay with us so that I can make certain that you're eating enough.'

'I told you, I've already taken the room. An' I'll no' have you spendin' a penny o' your money – or your man's – on me.'

His voice was calm, and looking into his clear eyes Lessie knew that there was no turning him. For the first time she realised that her marriage and her venture into shopkeeping closed another door in her life. Never again would she and Davie be as close as they had been. They were moving apart, emotionally as well as physically, and there was nothing she could do about it.

The McKays handed over the shop and went off to Rothesay. The wedding date was set and Anna, after she had met and approved of Murdo, insisted on contributing the wedding gown. Lessie was rushed off her feet reorganising the shop and cleaning out the rooms behind it in readiness for the move. To her surprise Edith offered to help with the cleaning.

'Men are no good at it and there's no sense in asking Mam. She'd only have to bring Thomasina and her fingers would be into everything,' she said, brushing down the walls of the kitchen as though attacking a hated enemy. Peter and Ian were playing in a corner with some toy soldiers Peter had brought with him. 'And I don't see that long-nosed mother of Murdo's going down on her knees to scrub floors.'

'His sister Katherine's offered to help at nights, though. I'd not ask Mam anyway. She's still got that cough, for all that it's summer,' Lessie said from the depths of a cupboard, plunging her scrubbing brush into the pail and thinking with pleasure of the stone sink in the tiny back porch. It would be luxury to have her very own sink.

As she emerged from the cupboard, Edith swiped at another spider's web. 'They didn't keep this place very clean, did they?'

'They did their best. Mr McKay was an invalid, and his wife had more than enough to do looking after him and seeing to the shop as well.' Lessie emptied her pailful of dirty water into the sink and wiped her hands on her sacking apron as the street bell clanged. She had refused to close the shop, and spent each day dashing between it and the back rooms.

'I just hope that wee rascals like the one I saw in the shop thon day don't manage to rob you of every penny of profit while you're trying to do two jobs at once,' Edith said dourly when she reappeared.

'Och, don't worry about them. I've shifted the good biscuits to behind the counter and put the broken ones in a box at the street door. They can knock that one down to their hearts' content and buy the contents cheap, but the best biscuits are safe.'

'You've made a wise decision, Lessie,' Edith said unexpectedly. 'He seems like a good man, Murdo Carswell. You've been fortunate, finding two decent men. God knows there are few of them about and most of us,' she gave a loud disparaging sniff, 'fall foul of the wrong kind.'

Lessie pleated her apron between her fingers, idle for once, then said, 'I know Murdo's a good man, but it's not like the first time.'

'I doubt if it ever could be.'

'When I met Donald,' she said, remembering, smiling at the memory, 'when he first smiled at me, it was as though I'd been completely emptied inside then filled to the brim with warm golden sunshine. When I lost him most of the gold poured away but there was enough left to keep me warm, whatever happened. It's still with me. It'll always be with me. With Murdo there's a good feeling, but it's not like sunshine. I suppose that'll never happen to me again. I suppose—'

'You're altogether too fluttery at times, Lessie. Don't let Murdo hear you talking like that or he'll mebbe have second thoughts about—'

'Look, Mama,' said Peter loudly, pointing. 'There's a baby spider playing in your hair.'

Edith screamed and began to scuttle round in circles, flapping her hands frantically in the air. Lessie stifled a giggle and ran to the rescue, all thoughts of Donald and the past swept aside.

Murdo's mother had graciously invited the Kirkwoods to high tea in her house following the marriage ceremony in the Carswells' minister's house. Only Edith, as best maid, and a shipyard friend of Murdo's as best man attended the ceremony. When the bridal party arrived at the house, the wave of relief from her relatives was so strong that Lessie could almost have touched it.

Her mother, with the faintly desperate look in her eyes that indicated that she hadn't had any of her 'medicine' for several hours, perched uncomfortably on the edge of the sofa, one hand gripping Thomasina, who shifted and squirmed restlessly by her side. Joseph and Archie had refused to attend, for they both hated family get-togethers, but Davie was there, handsome in his best suit, which had been brought out of the pawn for the occasion, and so was Aunt Marion, Barbara's sister. The table in the bay window was laden with salad and cold meats, cakes and biscuits, all presided over by a large silver teapot polished until it blazed in the sunlight.

'So there you are,' Mrs Carswell said as though she had been wondering where on earth they had got to. She came over to kiss her son and then her new daughter-in-law with cool lips that fluttered a fraction of an inch from their faces then withdrew. 'You look bonny, Lessie. D'you not think so, Mistress Kirkwood?'

Barbara's tired face lit up with a genuine smile as she looked at her daughter in the rose-coloured gown that was Anna's gift. 'Very bonny.'

'Thanks, Mam.' As her mother made no move towards her, Lessie went to the sofa, bent, and kissed Barbara's cheek. She felt awkward, because the Kirkwoods were not a demonstrative family, but Mrs Carswell had kissed the bride – or made a pretence of it – and Lessie was determined that her own mother should not be left out.

'Me too, me too,' shrilled Thomasina. Barbara flinched and shushed her, but Lessie laughed and gave her little sister a hug and a smacking kiss. Ian, who had been hanging back, peering round his Uncle Davie's knees at this unexpectedly different mother in her pretty pink dress, lost his shyness and came scuttling to claim his own hug. Lessie picked him up and held him close. Today, at Edith's insistence, he and Peter were both in velvet suits. Beneath the soft material, Ian's wiry little body wriggled and moulded itself against Lessie's as it always did. Still holding him she turned, laughing, and saw Murdo watching them both. She held out a hand and he came to her. My husband, thought Lessie with contentment as their fingers entwined. My man.

He was summoned from her side almost at once to pour out the sherry wine that Mrs Carswell had bought so that the happy couple's health could be drunk. As her son poured, she told the company where she had bought the wine and how much it had cost her. Aunt Marion fluttered and cooed and admired and Mrs Carswell visibly warmed to her, while Barbara's eyes fastened greedily on the pale liquid splashing into elegant glasses, the price of which, Mrs Carswell informed them, she could only estimate since they'd been one of her own wedding gifts. When Barbara received her glass she clutched it, holding herself back with difficulty until the toast was made and she was free to drink. She meant to sip it, but before she could stop herself the glass, which held a pitifully small amount, was empty. Guiltily she glanced at her hostess but Mrs Carswell was too busy talking to Edith to notice and Davie had casually moved so that his body shielded his mother from Mrs Carswell's view.

Lessie watched the little scene, her heart going out to her mother. She wondered again what terrible thing could have happened to make Barbara, the most upright of women, turn to drink as she had. Deep inside her mother there must be a reservoir of unhappiness, hidden away and never shared with anyone, least of all her daughters.

'Thank you, Davie,' she murmured to her brother when he drifted her way, collecting empty glasses. 'Mam needs folk like you to care for her.'

'She cared for us when we were wee and helpless,' he said quietly, then, 'I hope you'll be happy, Lessie. You deserve it.'

'I will be.' The crease between her brows, the crease that had come to stay, deepened. 'You're looking thinner. Are you not eating properly?'

'I'm fine. Don't you start worrying about me.'

'Well, we'd best sit in and eat.' Mrs Carswell shooed them all towards the food, told them where to sit, and urged them to help themselves. Thomasina looked at the food, her eyes like saucers, and reached out greedily. Her mother, ever watchful, caught her hand in mid-stretch.

'Sit by me and be a good lassie, now,' she whispered, tormented with worry in case her beloved youngest child humiliated them all in front of Mrs Carswell and spoiled Lessie's wedding day.

'That's the prettiest dress I've ever seen, Lessie.' Katherine Carswell's eyes rested enviously on the pale pink satin gown, high-necked and trimmed with rose-pink silk net. The skirt, falling at the back in a slight train from a rose-pink bow, rustled slightly as Lessie took her seat. Smiling at her new sister-in-law, Lessie suddenly wished that Anna and Miss Peden, who had given them a handsome china figurine of Rabbie Burns, her favourite poet, could have been there. But as Mrs Carswell had arranged what she called the wedding breakfast, Mrs Carswell was the one who had the right to decide who should attend.

Mrs Carswell senior, Lessie corrected herself, looking down at the new ring on her finger. There were two Mrs Carswells now. It would take time to get used to not being Lessie Hamilton. Her mother-in-law was indulging in her favourite topic, telling everyone what the cold tongue and the cold ham cost, and Lessie wondered if Murdo and Katherine had had to go through this recital every time they sat down at their mother's table. She looked at Murdo, by her side, and he grinned and whispered, 'I'll be glad when this is all over an' we can be alone.'

Barbara took very little food onto her plate, picking at it, her eyes wandering now and again to the sideboard where the half-empty bottle of sherry wine stood. Most of her energy, though, was taken up with making sure that Thomasina behaved herself. Mrs Carswell, Lessie realised with a stab of anger, had ignored the little girl, though she had fussed over Peter and Ian. When they all left the table she drew Thomasina into the circle of her arm and talked to her, letting her sister finger the pretty wedding gown and the tiny pearl earrings that Murdo had given her as a wedding gift.

The party broke up not long after the meal was over, on the pretext that the children were in danger of becoming over-excited and needed to get to their beds. Barbara and Edith and Aunt Marion left together, taking Ian with them. He was going to spend the night with his grandmother. Davie ambled off in the direction of his tiny rented room, and after Mrs Carswell had firmly rejected Lessie's offer of help with the dishes, the bride and groom were free to go to their new home behind the shop in the Vennel.

The shop, which had been closed for the day, was waiting quietly for them in the midsummer evening dusk. Lessie sniffed with pleasure at the mixed smell of meal and tobacco as she went in. She loved the knowledge, each time she stepped into the shop, that it was hers. Hers and Murdo's, but hers to run, because he already had his job at the shipyard.

He locked the door carefully behind them as Lessie moved, sure-footed in the gloom, between sacks and boxes and behind the counter to the door that led to their home. In there, the smell was of paint and carbolic and cleanliness. The best of her furniture and some pieces Murdo had bought shone a friendly welcome at her as her husband struck a match and the gas mantles on the wall came to life with a soft plop.

'Would you like a cup of tea?'

Murdo came to her and took her into his arms. 'You know better than that, Lessie Carswell! I want something a lot better than tea.'

'You mean more of your mother's sherry wine?' she teased him, then squealed as his teeth nipped at her earlobe.

'I mean,' he said, then whispered into her ear, his lips tickling.

'Murdo Carswell!' She pushed him away, fisted her hands on her hips, did her best to look severe, though her whole body was tingling. 'I'll have you know that I'm a respectable married woman!'

'Ach, I'll no' tell anyone if you don't,' said Murdo and swooped, scooping her off her feet and whirling to deposit her on the box bed set into the kitchen alcove. The springs creaked, then creaked again as he joined her.

'Confound it, I'll have tae find a way o' stoppin' that noise afore young Ian moves into the next room,' he said, his fingers busy with the buttons down the front of her gown. The bodice was half opened and the soft warm curves of her breasts exposed when she pushed him away and sat up.

'Murdo, let me take my nice gown off properly.'

'Ye're a terrible tease!' He rested back on his elbows, watching as she scrambled from the bed.

'I made my nightgown specially for tonight.'

'It'll not stay on for long.'

She paused on her way into the inner room and threw a smile over her shoulder at him. 'I'd be disappointed in you if it did – a young lad like you.'

His laughter followed her into the smaller room and made her fingers shake with impatience as she took off her gown and her underclothes, poured water from a jug into a basin and washed herself, then slipped into the nightgown that had been left out in readiness that morning. It was made of muslin, and in the spare moments she had managed to squeeze from preparing the living quarters and running the shop, she had embroidered and tucked it and edged the sleeves and neck with a few scraps of lace Edith had given her.

She picked up the long drawers that lay beside it, pursed her mouth, then tossed the drawers down again, thinking wantonly of Murdo's surprise and pleasure when he discovered that she had come to him with only the nightgown on. She brushed her short hair until it crackled then opened the door.

The kitchen was empty, and from the little scullery that housed the sink came the sound of spluttering and splashing. Swiftly Lessie climbed into bed and drew the blankets round her shoulders. Murdo came through a moment later, in a nightshirt and with his fair hair damp at the front. He stooped and kissed her gently and she said, 'I wish I could have had my hair long over the pillow.'

'You're beautiful just the way you are.' He bent her, carefully unfastening the buttons she had just fastened down the front of her gown. His hand slipped inside and held one breast for a moment, squeezing it gently and rousing her with startling suddenness. Then he turned away swiftly, put out the lights, and came to her.

Lessie had forgotten what it was like to feel a man's solid body dipping the mattress as he got into bed. She had forgotten how wonderful masculine arms felt, reaching through the darkness for her and claiming her. She had forgotten the pleasure of mingled breath on a pillow, the murmuring of private loving words in the darkness. Now, in Murdo's arms, she wondered how she could have borne to be without the intimacies of marriage for so long.

She moved willingly into his embrace, touching him, feeling the deep trembling that shook his body, the blessing of his hands on her skin, drawing the nightdress hem up from knees to thigh, from thigh to hip. She smiled in the darkness when his hand stopped suddenly and he caught his breath then gave a murmur of delight at her unexpected nudity beneath the gown.

Then she raised her hips from the mattress to allow the gown to be drawn up further, gasping at the touch of his fingers and then his lips on her breasts.

The whispering stopped, then the silence of the room was broken by scrambling and creaking as Lessie sat up and drew the nightgown over her head, tossing it carelessly away to land on the floor. It had served its purpose. Murdo writhed and twisted in the bed, too impatient to sit up and take off his own nightshirt properly. She helped him, and at last the cumbersome garment was in her hands and sailing off into the dark.

Then their bodies were touching, lithe and young and impatient. Murdo raised himself above her, his broad muscular body lowering itself on to hers. And at last he was inside her and she was clutching at his hair, clawing his back, crying out in her ecstasy.

At last she was a woman again.

10

Jess Carswell, born on the day the Boer War ended, was as pretty as a blue-eyed rosy-cheeked flower. Her head was covered by a thick mass of dark hair and her soft full mouth and heart-shaped little face captivated everyone except her half-brother Ian who, four months past his third birthday, had little time for babies.

Murdo, who had made his preference for a son clear during Lessie's pregnancy, was spellbound by his daughter from the moment he first saw her. 'We'll have a laddie the next time,' he said, stroking the tiny soft face with his finger. 'In the meantime, this one'll suit me fine.'

Lessie, pale and weak from a long birthing, winced at the thought of having another child and wondered if she and Murdo were going to find themselves at odds over their views on the size of their family. She had always loved Ian, and she already loved this new baby, but she loved her shop as well and she had no intention of giving it up in order to raise a large brood. They had just finished paying off their debt to Miss Peden, and she was impatient already to be up and about again and in the shop. She knew, from the gossip she had heard in the shop, what women could do to prevent unwanted pregnancies. She had heard about vinegar soaked sponges and pessaries made from flour and margarine, and was determined to make certain that there were no more children until she had made a success of the shop. As for Murdo, 'What a man doesnae ken doesnae hurt him,' one of the women advocating home remedies to prevent children had once said in the shop. 'It's us that has tae carry an' bear an'

119

tend tae the bairns, an' the decisions should be oors an'
a'.' And Lessie agreed with her.

Anna came to inspect the new baby within a few days
of the birth. She swept into the room behind the shop,
resplendent in a blue corded silk gown with broad bands
of cream lace let into the bodice, a pert little hat trimmed
with a large blue bow and a curling feather perched on
her red hair, and cast a brief glance into the cradle where
Jess slept.

'She's beautiful, but then who would expect otherwise
with such parents? You and me,' she said, seating herself
in a comfortable chair and drawing off her gloves, 'are
fortunate in having handsome men.'

'You think Murdo's handsome?'

'Oh yes, even though I don't think he approves of me.'
Then she held up a slender hand as Lessie, blushing,
started to speak. 'Don't trouble to deny it, I can see the
truth in your eyes. You never were able to hide your
thoughts, Lessie. Not that your husband's approval
matters. I get on very well without it.'

'Would you like some tea, Anna? If Elma isn't too
busy in the shop she'll make it for us.'

'Don't trouble yourself, I can't stay long.' Anna cast a
look round the room. 'Is there nobody to see to you?'

'Edith comes in when she can, and my mother too,
though I don't like to ask either of them. They've got
enough to do. There's Elma, but the shop keeps her
busy. I don't know what we'd have done without her. I'll
be up and about in a few days anyway.'

'I envy you sometimes, Lessie. You've always got
things to see to, things to do. Times I find it hard to fill
the hours.'

'You've got Dorothea.'

'The maidservant sees to her. I'd not know how to
manage her if Molly wasn't there.' Anna rose and moved
restlessly about the room, picking items up, studying
them without seeing them, putting them down again. 'I've
no friends except you, and I've scarcely seen you since
you took over this shop. And now that his uncle's died
and he's in sole charge of the refinery, Andrew spends far

too much time away from Greenock. Sometimes I think that he only visits to see Dorothea.' Her mouth hardened slightly. 'He worships that child – and spoils her, to my mind. Even when I do see him he can talk of nothing but sugar and the changes he hopes to make in his dull refinery.'

'Davie tells me that Mr Warren has asked him to suggest ways of improving some of the machinery. Was that your idea?'

Anna was by the window now. She peered out into the small back yard where Murdo had planted some vegetables and Lessie had installed a small flower border. 'Your garden looks pretty,' she said vaguely. 'I believe I did mention that your brother was an engineer and might be of help to him.'

'It was kind of you.' Then, as Anna turned back into the room and Lessie saw the shadow in her eyes, the new droop to her mouth, she added, 'Surely you could find some friends to visit and to entertain?'

The lovely mouth lifted to shape itself into a faint ironic smile. 'The sort of people I'd want to know have no intention of mixing socially with a kept woman. As for the rest,' she shrugged dismissively. 'No, I must just look forward to the day when Andrew ends his wandering and settles back in Greenock. If that day ever comes.'

After she left, the room was fragrant with the scent of roses, but Lessie's spirits were low. She lay back against the pillow, wondering why she always felt somehow responsible for Anna's happiness. The woman had everything, and yet in many ways she seemed to have nothing, whereas Lessie's life was full to overflowing. She had two children and a home and a husband to care for now, not to mention worrying over her mother's deteriorating health. If anyone had a claim on what little time Lessie had to spare, it was Barbara, thinner by the week, coughing all the time now, almost dragging herself around the house and out to the shops. Or Miss Peden, still sturdily independent, but looking older and more frail than she had last year.

Then there was the shop. By good fortune a woman

who lived nearby had offered her services during Lessie's pregnancy, and proved to be a reliable and hard-working assistant. Without Elma Buchanan the shop would have had to be closed during Lessie's enforced absence. She had worked behind the counter until the first pains gripped her and sent her, gasping and clutching at furniture for support, to her bed. Elma, tall and angular, grim-faced but scrupulously fair and polite enough to those customers who in her opinion deserved it, had sent for the midwife, seen to Ian, and kept the shop going while Lessie was in bed. Murdo attended to the business of buying in stock from the retailers, dealt with the account books, and spent as much time as he could in the shop when he wasn't in the shipyard. The small wages Elma received were a drain on their resources, but it was better to have the shop bringing in a little money than none at all.

'Thinks she's a fine lady these days, that Anna McCauley,' Elma announced now, tramping into the room and rousing Lessie from the light doze she had drifted into. 'But at the end o' the road we a' find that we've no' travelled far from where we started. Will ye tak' a cup o' tea?'

'If you've got time tae make one.'

'Aye, it's quiet enough oot there for the moment.' Elma measured tea into the pot, added water from the kettle simmering on the range, and went into the scullery to refill the kettle. On her way back she peered into the crib.

'Sound asleep, bless her bonny wee face.' The words were gentle, and so were her eyes, but her voice was as usual – flat and matter-of-fact. Watching her setting out cups, Lessie wondered if Elma would have been different if she had known love and a home and children of her own. It was hard to imagine her in a man's arms. Plain and dour, she lived with her sister, her unemployed brother-in-law, and their five children in two tiny rooms. Elma enjoyed working in the shop and never minded how late she worked. 'It's no pleasure tae go back tae that hoose,' she told Lessie once. 'Fightin' frae mornin' tae night ower money an' the bairns – an' ower me, I ken that fine. If I'd somewhere else tae go I'd be oot o' there today. It's no pleasure tae be bidin' whaur ye'r no' wanted.' She drank her tea standing by the door, ready to dart through it if a customer appeared. 'I like the way ye've got the shop arranged. It's better than the way the McKays had it.'

'It's just a question of finding out how things should be done as I go along.' Lessie sipped at the tea, strong, hot, with plenty of milk and sugar in it. 'I'm missing it.'

'It'll be good tae see ye back behind the counter. Everyone says that,' Elma informed her, then the bell above the street door gave a brisk ting, and she set down her cup and stamped out to atter-d to the customer.

Despite her pretty little face, Jess turned out to be a baby with a will of her own. Unlike Ian she demanded attention, doubling tiny fists and roaring out her anger if she felt that she was being neglected. She liked to linger over feeds and Lessie found herself giving more time to her little daughter than she had planned.

'It's just her way.' Murdo poked a fond finger into the baby's fist, delighting over the way her own tiny fingers curled possessively round it. 'The shop can wait for you. Elma does well enough, though a smile for the customers now and again wouldnae go amiss. An' I can manage.'

'You've enough to do with your own work without having to stand in the shop in the evenings and on Saturday afternoons.'

Murdo shrugged. 'The football season's over so I don't mind givin' up my Saturdays. I'm quite enjoying being a shopkeeper.'

It couldn't be said that Ian was enjoying the changes in their lives, Lessie thought guiltily, remembering the days when it had been just the two of them and she had always had time, between helping in the shop and scrubbing stairs, to spend with her son. He had taken to Murdo from the start and throughout the winter the two of them had gone off to the Saturday football match, Ian riding high on Murdo's shoulder, coming back with his small face glowing from fresh air and excitement. Now, unless Davie dropped in to take him for an outing, he was confined to the pavement outside the shop and the yard at the back. But he was an easygoing little boy and he bore the new limitations stoically, apart from an occasional disgusted glance at the lacy crib when his half-sister started squalling again.

The crib had arrived from Anna's house, together with a bundle of clothes and shawls. 'Now that Dorothea's grown out of them you might as well have the use of them,' she'd said carelessly when she brought them. Lessie had fretted in case Murdo objected, but to her surprise he had been quite pleased.

'It'll save us a deal o' money,' he pointed out. 'An' God knows we need tae save all we can if you intend tae pay the McKays off within the year as you promised.'

Murdo, Lessie had discovered soon after their marriage, had inherited his mother's irritating habit of pricing everything – the food they ate, the clothes they wore, even toys that he himself bought for Ian. But otherwise he was a good man, an attentive, loving husband and a fine father to Ian as well as Jess. And she could never have saved enough to pay off her debt to Miss Peden and to give the McKays the rest of their money without his wages coming in. She could surely put up with one little flaw, she told herself as she laid Jess down in her crib and prodded the potatoes with a fork to see if they were ready.

At the table Murdo was calculating the overall cost of the homemade soup he was eating, smugly taking into consideration the saving made by using ingredients from their own shop. Ian, his audience, had long since lost interest and was busily breaking off lumps of bread and dropping them into his bowl, turning the soup into a satisfying mushy mess.

Jess was a full seven weeks old before Lessie finally got back behind the shop counter one Saturday afternoon. At first Murdo protested, but she waved his arguments aside.

124

'Ian's fair dying to get out with you again. Take him from under my feet and Elma and me'll manage fine.'

Elma had agreed to stay on full-time until a routine had been established. Then she would go back to helping out only when she was needed. The welcome Lessie received from her regular customers touched and warmed her.

'My, Mistress Carswell, but it's guid tae see ye back where ye belong,' the first woman through the door said, adding hastily, with a look at Elma, 'Though we've been very well seen tae, o' course.'

Elma sniffed, but said nothing.

'Ye're lookin' that well, tae. Hoo's the wee yin?'

'She's fine, Mrs Douglas.' Lessie poured sugar crystals from the gleaming scoop into a sheet of paper that she had deftly twisted into a cone, then tucked in the top and handed it over.

'An' I'll hae twa pound o' lentils.'

Ian, waiting for Murdo, was at his favourite game, pushing his small fist hard into the side of the lentil sack then withdrawing it quickly and watching the dent he had made disappear just as fast. Gently Lessie set him aside, taking time to smooth his tousled red hair, and began to scoop out the lentils. Murdo came from the back room and Ian claimed him at once and led him out onto the street, chattering excitedly. Mrs Douglas watched them go, then asked, 'Will yer man be workin' on in the shop noo that ye're back?'

'Mebbe. Now and again when I'm busy with the wee one.'

'Oh aye?' The woman's voice was suddenly flat. 'I'm a wee bittie short the day. Will ye pit it in the book for me, dearie?'

'I'll do that.'

Lessie laughed as she and Elma watched the woman waddle from the shop a few minutes later. 'Some women hate to be served by a man. I mind myself when I first came to live in the Vennel, always hoping it would be Mrs McKay at the counter when I came in here. As if it makes any difference!'

'It does tae some folk.' Elma's voice sounded just as flat as Mrs Douglas's had been.

Lessie fetched out the big black-covered tick book from its usual place beneath the counter and opened it to record Mrs Douglas's purchases. Before putting it away she ran her eyes down the row of shillings and pence, a few written in the assistant's awkward hand, most entered in Murdo's firm black script. 'Folk round here must've been celebrating the end of the South African war. They've been buying more than usual, surely.'

'No' that I've noticed.' Elma turned aside to dust the tops of some jars of preserves. The tick book, a fixture in every small shop, was used to record sums due by the many customers who, through unemployment or illness or grindingly low wages, were unable to pay for goods as they got them. Lessie, well taught by the McKays, dealt with it carefully, forcing herself to turn away those least deserving, least likely to honour their debts when a little money came in. Even so, Murdo had objected to the use of the book at first, seeing it as the road to ruin.

'Look at this,' his finger had stabbed down one page, 'the same folk comin' in again an' again an' no' payin' a penny. Most of them never will, an' then where'll we be?'

'They have to live, and they have to feed their bairns.'

'Exactly. They have tae feed their bairns and we've tae feed ours. It's no' our responsibility tae put food in their children's bellies. I pay my way, why shouldn't they?'

'Och, they'll pay, you don't have to worry about that. The folk round here might be poor but they're not dishonest. They don't like being in debt. They'll pay!'

And pay they did; sixpence here, a shilling there, striving all the time to clear themselves of debt, but never quite succeeding. Only a few of them had ever let Lessie down and when she forced her natural sympathy down and refused, hating herself, to give these few any more tick, they usually cursed her with automatic fluency then took themselves off to find another shopkeeper who would, for a short while, allow them to buy on credit.

People came and went over the next hour, then a little girl, prim and sedate in her dark smock, her hair scraped back until her eyes were almost pulled up at the corners, arrived to buy a pound of best tea.

'How's your mother, Mary?' Lessie smiled down at the serious little face barely visible above the counter, inwardly promising herself that never would her Jess be robbed of her childhood the way this child had been. Like Thomasina, Mary was a late baby born to a middle-aged mother who was now busily raising her to be a middle-aged child.

'She's fine, Mistress Carswell. An' she says,' said Mary severely, 'that she'd be obliged if ye'd weigh oot the tea afore ye pit it intae the paper poke, no' efter.'

Lessie blinked down at her and was stung into retorting sharply, 'I always do.'

'Aye, but yer man doesnae,' Mary snapped back. 'My mither says she's no' gaun tae pay for the paper too. I've tae be sure tae look.'

Lessie swallowed hard, torn between anger and amusement at the thought of this child, scarcely thirty-six inches high, lecturing her. She poured fine dark tea leaves onto the scale, aware of the little girl's pale eyes watching intently until the pound weight on the other side had swung level.

'Does that suit you?'

'Aye,' said Mary, and when the tea had been packed neatly and the paper 'poke' stowed safely in her pocket, she handed over the money and departed, straightbacked.

'Did you ever hear the like?' Lessie asked Elma and the woman she was serving. Elma said nothing; the customer's eyes slid away from Lessie's and she said evasively, 'Some shopkeepers weigh the paper in with the tea or the sugar an' folk don't feel they're gettin' what they paid for.'

'Mebbe so, but it never happened here while the McKays had the place, and it won't while I'm running it.'

'If ye say so, Mistress Carswell,' said the woman, and scuttled from the shop just as Jess's voice was raised in hunger in the back room.

Lessie's tiredness was offset by her pleasure over the

customers' delight at seeing her back in the shop. Perhaps it was because she had been away for too long or perhaps it was the fatigue that blinded her to the true meaning behind the effusive welcome she received from one woman after another. But not until late afternoon when old Cathy Petrie came in did Lessie find out why they were so pleased to welcome her back, and what had been going on in her absence.

'It's this week's saxpence for the tick book,' the old woman said humbly, handing over a coin that was hot from the clutch of her hand.

'Thanks, Cathy.' Lessie opened the book, found the entry, and was about to note down the payment in the 'paid' column when she stopped and looked again at the full entry. The smile faded from her lips.

'Cathy, all that's down in the book for you is a packet of tea and a bag of oatmeal and you've paid two shillings off on them already.'

'Aye, I managed to get some cleanin' work at yin o' the shops, but I couldnae mak' enough tae pay it all off, so Mister Carswell said he'd take saxpence a week till I wis clear. Is there somethin' wrang?' The watery old eyes filled with apprehension.

A cold hand seemed to grip at Lessie's stomach as she looked at the words and figures written in her husband's hand then ran her eyes swiftly over the other entries, her mind adding and subtracting. 'No, there's nothing wrong,' she managed to say calmly despite her growing consternation.

'Here then.' Cathy pushed the sixpence at her. Lessie, aware of Elma's close scrutiny, took the coin and put it into the drawer behind the counter then drew a deep hard line across the entry.

'That's you paid it all off.'

'B-but Mister Carswell said last week that there wis—'

'Mr Carswell made a mistake, Cathy. It's all paid off. Here.' Lessie came round the corner swiftly, snatching items from the shelves and pushing them into the old woman's hands. 'Here's some tobacco for your man's pipe

– and a packet of biscuits and a jar of preserves. Elma, hand me that loaf.'

Cathy looked in horror at her burden. 'But Mistress Carswell, I cannae afford—'

'They're gifts. Off you go, Cathy, and God give you both health to enjoy them. Good day to you.' Lessie almost pushed her out and whirled to see Elma disappearing through the house door. 'Elma Buchanan, you get back here this minute!'

'I think I heard the wean,' Elma said, and kept going. Lessie pushed down the snib on the door; before going into the back shop a sudden suspicion caused her to run her fingers beneath the pan suspended on the weighing scales. A greasy lump of bacon fat dropped from the underside of the pan into her palm. She stared down at it, chewing her lip. It was the custom of unscrupulous shopkeepers to stick a lump of fat beneath their scale pans so that customers received short weight. It was a nasty, deceitful trick that Lessie had sworn never to play on the people who frequented her shop.

'What if a customer comes in?' Elma quavered as her employer closed the kitchen door firmly behind them.

'I've locked the street door. Now, what's been going on?' She folded her arms and waited; although she was a good six inches smaller and about two stones lighter than Elma, the other woman retreated across the room as though afraid that she might be attacked. 'Just what have you and my husband been up to while I've been in here?'

'Mistress Carswell! If you're saying that—'

'Don't pretend you don't know what I mean, Elma Buchanan! Every one of these entries in the tick book are for more money than the goods cost.'

'It wis Mister Carswell that wis in charge, no' me. It's him ye should be speirin'.'

'Mr Carswell's not here, but you are, and you're not getting out of this room until you tell me the truth!'

'All I know is that he telt me tae add a penny on here an' a penny on there when I wrote in the book. When folks argued aboot it he said it wis tae make up for the inconvenience o' havin' tae wait for the payment. He said that a' the shopkeepers dae it.'

'Did he tell you to weigh the tea and sugar in the wrappings as well?' Lessie tossed the lump of bacon fat on the table. 'And did you know the scales had been weighted?'

Elma's face went dusky red. 'Mistress Carswell, it's no' my place tae argue wi' whit yer man decides,' she said, her voice pleading. 'I need the money I earn here. I have tae dae whit I'm telt, whether it's you or him that does the tellin'.'

Jess stirred and whimpered. All at once Lessie felt very tired. 'All right, Elma, nobody's blaming you. But from now on we go back to the way things were before, d'ye hear me? Go on home now, I'll not be opening the shop again today.'

She had to wait until both children were settled for the night before she spoke to Murdo. He and Ian had come back from an afternoon spent down at the river's edge, watching the boats passing, throwing stones into the water, fishing with string and twigs. They arrived home hungry and happy. Their happiness made things all the worse for Lessie; she was on edge all evening. As soon as she was sure that Ian was asleep in the inner room, she faced her husband, the open tick book in her hands. 'What's been going on?'

He glanced at the figures, all scored out now and with the correct amounts written in beside them, and shrugged. 'Everyone charges a wee bit for givin' credit.'

'The McKays didn't. I don't.'

'An' look what happened to the McKays – livin' out the rest o' their lives on the charity o' relatives. Lessie, we're no' runnin' a shop for the benefit of those who havenae the money tae buy what they need.'

'I told you, they pay when they can. There's very few that don't.'

'An' each time someone doesnae pay, each time someone steals from us – for that's what they're doin' – we're expected tae take the loss an' say nothin'? We're surely entitled tae take a penny or two from the others tae cover the losses.'

'It's not their fault that some folk are dishonest.'

'It's no' mine either. But the money has tae come from somewhere. We've all got tae earn as much as we can, as best we can.'

Lessie stared at her husband, shocked by his refusal to see that he had wronged her customers. 'And what about this business of weighing wrapped goods so that you provide a wee bit less for the same money? And the weight on the bottom of the scale pan?'

'For God's sake, woman, a few grains o' sugar, a few leafs o' tea! Who's tae miss that?'

'We agreed before we got married that the shop was tae be my concern. It was tae be run my way. An' I'm not goin' tae make myself rich by clawin' my way ontae the backs o' poor souls like Cathy Petrie that have less than we have ourselves.'

'But that's how the rich become rich! D'you no' understand that I want tae make enough money tae get us out o' this place. I want tae give you an' the weans a nice house, everythin' that you could wish for.'

A sudden memory of Donald saying laughingly, 'This time next year' swept over her. But Donald wouldn't have cheated folk to make the money he needed.

'I'll not condone dishonesty, Murdo, not for any reason.'

His face suddenly dark with anger, Murdo snatched up his jacket and strode to the door.

'Where are you going at this time of night?'

'Out, before I forget mysel' an' take my hand across yer face for what ye just said tae me,' said Murdo thickly, and disappeared into the dimness of the shop. She heard the bell jangle then jangle again as he slammed the street door shut, rousing both children from their sleep.

He didn't come home until late. Lessie had wept, dried her eyes and gone to bed to lie sleepless, wondering if he was going to come back at all. It was a relief to hear the bell, then Murdo cursing softly as he bumped into something. She lay listening to the sounds of him undressing in the dark, then a waft of cold air brushed her back as he lifted the blankets and the mattress dipped beneath his big body.

He whispered her name and she turned to him at once, eager to make up the worst quarrel they had had. His breath was soured with the taint of whisky, but his mouth was warm and eager on hers, his hands demanding, his body taut and hungry. They made love fiercely, silently, smothering their cries against each other for fear of disturbing the children. Then naked, entwined, they slept.

The next morning Murdo was his usual cheerful self. They dressed the children in their best clothes and visited his mother, then walked to the water filters above the town, Jess gurgling in her pram, Ian galloping ahead on an imaginary horse. They were a happy family once more.

Lessie took over the running of the shop again after that and there was no more bacon fat, no more extra pennies added to the tick book, and no more sullen stares from aggrieved customers. Murdo's misdeeds were never again mentioned, and it wasn't until a long time later that Lessie realised that he had never actually admitted that he had done anything wrong.

11

'I drove past your house yesterday,' Anna said casually, her eyes and hands intent on the task in hand. She was carefully wrapping a large multi-coloured velvet ball, a gift to mark little Jess Carswell's first birthday.

'You did what?' Andrew Warren, sprawled in an easy chair by the fireplace, sat upright, almost dislodging Dorothea, who perched on his knee. She gasped then giggled as he caught and held her, believing that he was playing a game with her.

'Anna, you promised me—'

'I promised you that I'd never try to speak to your lady wife or your children. I promised that I'd never go to your door or to your refinery. But surely even the Warrens don't own the road outside their house?'

'Why choose to drive along that particular road?'

'Dorothea and I wanted some fresh air. We went along the waterfront as far as McInroy's Point, then we turned and drove back. Dorothea enjoyed herself. Didn't you, my pet?'

'Yeth, Mama.' Dorothea, busily trying to undress the doll that Andrew had brought back from his recent trip to Liverpool, answered automatically and without interest. Andrew lifted her to the floor and put the doll into her arms.

'Run out into the garden and show dolly the pretty flowers,' he suggested, and the little girl hurried off obediently.

'I saw your son and daughter – your elder daughter,' Anna corrected herself. 'They had been out for a ride too, in their little dog-cart. Such pretty children. The boy will

133

set hearts fluttering one day, just like his father.'

Then, as he said nothing but just sat there, watching her through narrowed eyes, she suddenly pushed the wrapped gift aside and said in a burst of angry words, 'It's us – it's me and Dorothea – that should be with you in your grand house instead of hiding away here!'

'You know that's not possible. We agreed at the beginning—'

'Oh, the beginning!' Anna said stormily. 'I was grateful to you then. I'd have agreed to anything to get out of that rat's nest I lived in. But now I want more, Andrew. I need more!'

'Anna – my dear . . .' He rose and went across to her, but when he tried to draw her into his arms she pulled back.

'I'm not your dear. She is – that woman who lives in your house and bears your name. I've been patient for long enough.' The thoughts that had been building up in her mind since Dorothea's birth over two years earlier broke free. 'I've been patient, Andrew. I've waited, and still she lives in your house.'

'Madeleine is my wife. Martin is my heir.'

'And Dorothea? Is she nothing to you?'

'You know that I adore her.'

'Yes, you do, don't you? Sometimes I think you only come here to see Dorothea.'

'That's untrue. I come to see you both as often as I can.'

'Not often enough!'

'For God's sake, Anna, I'm away from Greenock a lot. I've got a refinery to run, customers to seek. Madeleine and the twins see as little of me as you do.'

'Not quite, surely.' She broke away from beneath his hands, paced the floor, the skirt of her stylish dress making a swishing sound as she made the sharp turn again and again. 'You spend your nights with her – most of them. And she's the one with the right to go about the town with her head held high and folk bowing and scraping to her because she's Mistress Andrew Warren. But not me! I must hide away here, pretend that you mean nothing to me. And what about my child?'

'Dorothea will never want for anything. I told you that the day I found out that you were carrying her.'

She turned, and he thought that she had never been more beautiful than she was now, with her violet eyes burning, her red hair glowing about her perfect face. Motherhood and maturity had improved Anna's looks instead of diminishing them. 'Divorce her, Andrew. Marry me.'

He stared at her in dismay. 'I can't do that.'

'You can. You can do whatever you want. She's got money of her own – a wealthy father, I've heard. And she hates Scotland. Let her go back to her own people, Andrew.' She came to him, put her hands on his arm. The scent of her perfume surrounded him as though the two of them were in a rose garden. 'Then we can be together, you and me and Dorothea.'

He stood motionless, unable to say what she wanted to hear. The light died from her face and she stepped back. 'You care more for her than you do for me.'

'She's my wife, can you not understand that?' Andrew tried again to take her into his arms and was shrugged away. 'Anna, you must see that things have to be left as they are.'

'If she died,' Anna said in a hard, cold voice, her back towards him, 'would you wed me?'

'What's the sense in talking like—'

'Or would I not be good enough for you? Am I just your whore, Andrew?'

'Mind your tongue, woman!'

'You've not answered my question,' she said relentlessly, then as he did not reply, 'Go away. Go home to your lady wife and your son and heir.'

'Anna—'

The door slammed behind her and he heard the patter of her feet on the stairs. For a moment he stood undecided, then shrugged. He well knew Anna's tempers, though there never had been a scene such as this one before. She was best left to her own devices. He let himself out of the house and went round to the back garden where Dorothea was sitting on the grass picking golden-hearted daisies and tucking them into the wide blue sash round the new doll's waist.

Andrew watched her for a moment and wished that he could commission a portrait of her just as she was then, in her pretty frilled white dress, her mouth pursed, long lashes brushing pink cheeks, his dark hair, but with Anna's auburn showing in deep red glints, framing her perfect little face. She looked up, suddenly aware that she wasn't alone, and the daisies were forgotten as she scrambled to her feet, beaming, and ran to him. Heedless of what the grass might do to his dove-grey trousers, Andrew dropped to his knees and caught her in his arms.

'Papa's going away now. Be a good girl and look after your mama while I'm gone. Promise?'

Dorothea nodded and he buried his face for a moment in her soft curly hair, kissed her smooth round cheek. This love-child had given him more pleasure in her two years of life than either of the children he had fathered on Madeleine.

Dorothea, tired of being hugged, squirmed free and went back to pick up her doll. 'Pretty dolly.'

'Not as pretty as you. You're the prettiest little girl in the whole world,' said Andrew, and wondered wryly what his employees and his business colleagues would think if they saw how he, a grown man, doted on this little scrap of a thing.

Anna watched from the open window above, half-hidden behind the curtain in case Andrew looked up. Not that he would, she thought bitterly. He was too engrossed in his precious daughter to care about her. She saw him hold the little girl close and was engulfed by a wave of jealousy so strong that it made her gasp.

She turned away from the window, her arms wrapped tightly about her body, suddenly feeling lonelier than she had felt in many years.

'You've done a good job, Kirkwood,' Andrew said with satisfaction. 'It's running as smoothly as it did before.'

Davie acknowledged the praise with a brief nod as he watched the centrifugal machine, one of three on that particular floor of the refinery. Near the ceiling a large hopper received the massecuite – the sugar and syrup mixture – from the vacuum pans on the floor above. The mixture ran into the centrifugal pans that separated the syrup from the crystals. The great machines set up a throbbing in the floor and the walls, and the heavy sweet smell turned Davie's stomach, more used to the smell of machine oil. He wondered how the refinery workers could bear to be in such an atmosphere all day and every day.

'Aye, she seems to be fine now.' A carefully casual tone hid his pride in his work. Centrifugal machines were notorious for causing trouble; if they weren't charged at the correct speed the baskets started swinging and toppling from their flexible mountings. If the fault wasn't discovered in time and the machine shut down, the basket could slam into the outer monitor case and wreck the entire machine.

The two men, Andrew the taller by a few inches, walked towards the wooden staircase, Davie studying the other machines intently as he passed them, his eyes and ears attuned to the slightest deviation in their rhythm. When they had gained the stairs and started down to the ground floor he said bluntly, 'These machines are old. They'll soon need replacing.'

'I know that.'

'Have you thought of using electric motors?'

'I'd not trust them. My uncles lost money by experimenting with direct-coupled steam when it first came in and they were glad enough to go back to a belt drive. I'm content to stay with it.'

'Electric drive's safer, and more controllable than direct-coupled steam. I've been learning a bit about it, for it's going to be what all modern refineries use from now on.' Davie's voice was crisp and authoritative, as it always was when he spoke of anything connected with his chosen career. Warren eyed him with interest.

'You think so?'

'I know it.'

'They'd cost a deal of money.'

'Aye, but they'd be a saving once they were installed. Belt-driven centrifugals'll always be a problem. You must know as well as I do that you'll never be free of the worry that one or more of them'll come off the mountings and slow the production down.'

'Could you cost the electric motors for me?'

'I could.' They stepped out into the yard and Davie drew in a deep thankful breath. The smell of the sugar was strong out here, too, but diluted by fresh air.

'I'd be interested in seeing what you come up with.'

'It'll take a while, for I've got more work than I can handle, and with Mr Beattie more or less retired I've to see to the paperwork as well as everything else.'

Andrew nodded. 'Would you be willing to look after my present machinery in the meantime, if you're needed?'

Davie's face was still expressionless. 'Aye, I'll do that.'

'I appreciate it.' Andrew held out his hand and for a moment Davie hesitated. Not many men of Warren's wealth and power were quick to shake the hand of ordinary tradesmen and he was taken aback. Then he reached out his own hand, calloused with hard work.

The physical contact between the two men was as brief as Davie could make it. On his first visit to the refinery he had been prepared, almost eager, to hate Andrew Warren. This was the man who possessed Anna McCauley. This was her lover, her protector, the father of her child. The hand Davie had just shaken had caressed Anna's face, her hair, her body as Davie himself longed to do. But he had developed a reluctant respect for Warren, recognising the other's love for his refinery, his determination to keep it going and improve it just as Davie cared for the small engineering shop under his own supervision.

There was guilt in Davie's mind as well, because at least once a month he entered this man's house in Port Glasgow without his knowledge to spend a precious hour in Anna's company. True, they only took tea together and there could never be anything but friendship between them because now Anna was faithful to one man, but to Davie it was enough to be with her. These visits kept him going day after day in the factory; the memory of her smiling at him across the tea table brightened and warmed the dingy room he lodged in. He had many reasons for preferring to dislike her lover. Now he nodded, then swung round and made for the yard gate, stepping out in his need to get away from Warren.

Andrew, watching him go, was impressed by Davie's quick mind and ability. He had made it his business to find out something about the lad before allowing him to deal with the Warren machinery, and had received nothing but good reports. Davie Kirkwood was a fine engineer who had learned his trade through sheer hard work, relying on night school for his paper qualifications. There were some who said that old Beattie's engineering works would have been closed down by now if Davie Kirkwood hadn't happened along. At twenty years of age he was more or less in full charge, working all the hours he could cram into each day and taking little financial reward, choosing instead to plough the profits back into the business to develop it.

There was a lot about the lad to remind Andrew of his sister Lessie, Anna's closest friend and confidante. They shared the same steady gaze, the same way of straight talking. Andrew grinned as he recalled the way the lassie had almost snapped his nose off that first day when he had found her working over the stone sink on the landing of the old hovel in the Vennel, and had asked how much rent she was expected to pay for the privilege of existing there. Anna had told him of Lessie's marriage and the move to rooms behind the little shop. He was glad to hear that her life had improved and glad that Anna had thought to recommend her brother when the refinery was in need of the services of a good engineer.

He wondered, as he walked to the office door, if one day it might be worth his while taking Davie Kirkwood on as an employee. Each time machinery broke down, valuable hours or days were lost, and to Andrew's mind a thriving refinery would be the better for having its own engineer on the premises.

★ ★ ★

Molly put the tray on a small carved table by Anna's elbow and turned to leave the room.

'Take Dorothea with you.'

The little girl shook her head, tucking her fists behind her back as the woman held out a hand to her. 'Doffy stay here.'

'Go with Molly,' Anna ordered sharply, the beginnings of a headache stirring behind her eyes. It was cold outside, too cold for Dorothea to play in the garden. She had been indoors in her mother's company all day, and her prattle was beginning to wear Anna's patience thin.

'Come and help me to make some biscuits,' the maidservant coaxed, but Dorothea's head swung to the left and right so violently that her black curls bounced across her eyes.

'Doffy stay with Mama!'

Anna, recognising the beginnings of a tantrum, gave in. 'Leave her here, Molly. But you're a naughty girl!' she added as the door shut. 'You'd better behave yourself or you'll be put in your bedroom.'

Dorothea thrust out her bottom lip and scowled, looking so like her father that it was all Anna could do to keep herself from slapping the round baby face. Then she plumped down onto the carpet, almost on Anna's feet, and shook the doll she held. 'Bad girl,' she told it in a fierce whisper. 'Bad bad girl!'

Anna leaned forward and poured tea from the delicate little china teapot. Molly had made it just as she liked it – very weak, so that it could be taken without milk. She added sugar, lifted the cup to her lips, and hurriedly returned it to the saucer. It was freshly made and far too hot to drink. She eased herself back against the cushions and closed her eyes, wondering if the spring weather was ever going to arrive. During the past weeks, all but a prisoner in the little house because of rain and cold winds, her growing frustration with the limitations of her life and her resentment against Andrew for his refusal to divorce his wife had almost driven her mad. Dorothea's continual presence, her resemblance to Andrew, had set up a dislike of the child that had grown until she could scarcely bear her daughter's presence. Although she was not yet three years of age, the little girl already, as Andrew never tired of telling Anna, showed promise of the beautiful woman she would become. And as she grew into that beauty, so Anna would age and lose her own looks. Measured as it was now in the growth of her child, time was passing faster than ever before.

'Biscuit?' Dorothea's voice broke in and the pain behind Anna's eyes seemed to leap.

'No!'

Dorothea chewed at her lip, thought for a moment, her plump little fingers combing through the doll's woollen hair, then looked up again, wreathed in smiles as she remembered the magic word. 'P'ease?'

'Naughty girls don't get biscuits.'

The little upturned face went blank with astonishment. Anna closed her eyes again. It was a petty triumph, but it would suffice. Already Andrew was more captivated by the daughter than by the mother. Each time she looked at the child Anna saw her own decay, her descent into lonely old age. The prospect had started to haunt her.

Almost as though she sensed her mother's fears, Dorothea had become more possessive, more determined to be with Anna. In her more despairing moments, Anna even wondered if the woman lying dormant in the little girl and waiting to blossom forth was already aware, already taking delight in Anna's growing uncertainty and fear. She had never wanted Dorothea, she reminded herself, thinking of her desperate attempts to induce an abortion. It was Andrew who had wanted her, Andrew who loved her more than he loved Anna herself. Her thoughts squirrelled round and round and the headache increased.

She was aware that Dorothea had scrambled to her feet, breathing heavily. Anna let her lids flutter open a fraction and saw her daughter gazing up at the table top. One hand released the doll and small fingers began to stalk slowly up the white linen cloth, ready to be snatched back if Anna's eyes opened.

Up, up, the fingers crept, up towards the spot where the saucer stood a little too close to the edge. Steam feathered into the air from the pretty china cup with its border of pink roses and blue forget-me-nots. Anna knew that she should move quickly, pull Dorothea back from danger, but at the same time another Anna, a cold stranger, kept her motionless, watching as the chubby fingers finally reached the top of the table and fumbled around for the plate of biscuits.

'P'ease?' Dorothea said on a breath, anxious not to wake her mother but justifying her actions by using the special word. Anna stayed where she was, watching as her daughter caught the curved edge of the saucer and tipped it over. Watching as the teacup slowly, slowly heeled and the amber tea, still too hot to drink, flowed in a graceful fountain over the edge of the table, missing the spotless white cloth, to spill itself over Dorothea's upturned face.

Lessie, summoned from the shop, arrived to find Anna huddled in a chair in the parlour, her face white, the cheekbones standing out as though she had lost weight overnight.

'She's taken it that bad,' the serving woman murmured when she let Lessie in. 'I had to send for you, Mrs Carswell – she insisted on it. She even made me send a laddie tae the refinery with a note for Mr Warren, though goodness knows what he'll say tae that.'

'I think he'd want to know. How's the baby?'

'Sleeping, poor wee mite. The doctor says her sight's all right, but her bonny wee face'll be scarred.' There were tears in the woman's eyes. 'Such a lovely wee thing, too.'

When the parlour door opened beneath Lessie's touch, Anna's head jerked up; for a moment she pressed back against the cushions, then she left her chair and came to throw her arms about Lessie. 'Oh, Lessie, my poor wee bairn!'

'It's all right. She's going to be fine.' She held Anna, feeling the other woman's body shaking as though in the grip of a violent chill. 'What happened?'

142

'I'd . . . I'd just poured myself some tea—' Anna broke free, turned away, her hands at her face. 'I'd a bad head so I closed my eyes for a minute. I th-think I fell asleep. Then I heard her screaming—' Her voice broke. She recovered herself and said desperately, 'It wasnae my fault, Lessie. It wasnae!'

'Why should anyone think it was?'

'Andrew loved Dorothea. He'll no' love her if her face is spoiled. He'll think I did it on purpose!'

'Don't be daft, Anna!' Lessie took her by the shoulders, deliberately putting a cold edge into her voice. 'You love Dorothea too, don't you?'

The reprimand brought Anna's head up. She drew in a deep breath and clasped her hands tightly together. 'Of course I do!'

'Then why should Mr Warren think ill of you?' Then Lessie said more gently, releasing Anna, 'Take me up to see her.'

'I cannae go.' Anna drew away, shaking her head. 'I cannae!'

'I'll go myself, then. I want to have a wee look at her. I'll not be long.'

The curtains were drawn and the toy-filled bedroom dim. Dorothea, her favourite doll beside her, lay on her back, one fist thrown above her head. All of the right side of her face, including her right eye, was swathed in white bandaging. Beneath it her black hair escaped to pour over the pillow. Her breathing was slow and even, but now and again it caught in a hiccup and a soft whimper.

As Lessie moved to the bed someone knocked impatiently on the front door and almost at once there were steps on the stairs. The bedroom door opened and Andrew Warren came in, sparing her only one swift glance, stepping at once to the other side of the bed to bend over his daughter.

'Dear God,' he said softly, and put a gentle finger into the cupped hand on the pillow above Dorothea's head.

'Let her sleep. She needs to sleep.'

He nodded, removing the finger and brushing it across the exposed cheek so lightly that it was like a breath.

It was a gesture of pure love and tenderness.

'Will she be all right?'

'Of course she will.'

'Thank you,' he said humbly, though whether he was thanking her for her reassurance or accepting it as a solemn pledge she didn't know. Then he looked fully at her for the first time, seemingly surprised to see her there.

'Where's Anna?'

'In the parlour.'

His brows knotted. 'She should be here, with—'

'Mr Warren,' Lessie said firmly, 'Anna's in a terrible state about what's happened. She blames herself, though there's no reason why she should. She needs comforting. You've seen for yourself that the wee one's all right. I think you should go to Anna now.'

For a moment anger flared in his grey eyes, then he turned to the door without a word. Lessie, unsure of what to do, followed him downstairs. In the parlour Anna stood with her back to the window, watching Andrew warily, making no move to go to him as she had run to Lessie. When he reached her, he took her into his arms and at last she let the tension flow from her slender body and sagged against him.

'It wasnae my fault,' she said, as she had said to Lessie.

'I know that, my love.'

From where she stood Lessie could see Anna's face, her eyes wide but seeing nothing. 'Andrew, she'll be scarred,' she said into his shoulder. 'Her wee face – you'll not love her any more.'

'Of course I'll love her,' he said fiercely, his voice muffled. 'D'you think I could ever stop caring for her?'

Anna's eyes closed and two large tears came sparkling from beneath the soft fan of her lashes.

Lessie shifted uncomfortably from one foot to the other. 'I'd best go.'

Anna said nothing but Andrew released her and turned. 'I'd appreciate it if you could stay for a little longer, Mrs Carswell. I must get back to the refinery. I'm sorry, my dear,' he added as Anna gave a whimper of protest and tried to cling to him, 'but I must. I shall come later tonight to see how Dorothea is. Thank you,' he added under his breath to Lessie as he slipped past her.

As soon as the front door had closed behind him, Anna flared into anger. 'How could he? How could he leave me at a time like this?' She raged on, pacing the floor, while Lessie, unsure of what to do for the best, sat waiting for her to work her own way out of her temper. 'It's always the way of it, always! If it's not the refinery he must get back to, it's his children or his precious wife. Why should he always go running back to be with her when it's me he should be married to now?'

'You?' Lessie asked incredulously, 'You think that Mr Warren should marry you?'

'Why not? I'm the mother of his daughter.'

'He already has a wife.'

'Och, she hates Greenock, everyone knows that. She'd be happy to go back to her own people if Andrew would just forget his stupid pride and send her away.'

'For any favour, Anna McCauley, are you never satisfied with what you've got? Money and a fine home and a man who's looked after you just as he said he would, for all that he's got a wife and family of his own. Must you be always girning and wishing for more than you have?'

Anna blinked, her mouth falling open in astonishment. For a moment tears threatened to spill into her eyes, then she blinked them back. 'You've got a caustic tongue, Lessie Carswell!'

'I thank the good Lord for it, then. I'd not manage to keep my customers under control otherwise.' Then Lessie added more gently, regretting her outburst of anger at such a time, 'Don't fret, Anna, just learn to be grateful for what you have.'

'And what do I have? Sometimes I feel that if it wasnae for Dorothea I'd never see Andrew at all.'

'You're being unfair. He cares for you.'

'You think so?' Anna gave a curt little bark of laughter then said with another sudden change of mood, 'Dorothea's fortunate, and so's your Jess. My father never cared about me, from what I remember of him. Did yours?'

Lessie recalled the sound of her father's feet stumbling up the stairs, his flushed face, the smell of drink, the slurred voice and the fear she had known each time he came into the house. He hadn't set foot in her new home; his visits had stopped with her marriage to Murdo, and he was a stranger to her again.

'I must go, Anna. Elma's got the shop and the bairns to see to and I said I'd not be long.'

'Everyone leaves me.' Anna's voice was bleak and her eyes expressionless. 'Nobody stays. You've all got your own lives to live.'

'And you've got yours. Dorothea'll be all right, Anna, and the servant's here. You're not on your own. I'll look in tomorrow.' She hesitated at the door, anxious to get outside but reluctant to leave Anna in that strange mood. 'Will you be all right?'

'I'll have to be, won't I?' Anna retorted in a brittle voice, her head turned away.

As Lessie walked downhill to the tram stop she fretted over what was happening to Anna and what was going to become of her. How long would Andrew Warren tolerate her demands that he put aside his legal wife in Anna's favour? What would happen to her – and to Dorothea – when his patience ran out, as it surely would?

12

To the uninitiated, Port Glasgow, Greenock and Gourock appeared to be one long town, so closely were they linked along the shoreline; but to those who knew better, each community had its own individual stamp. Andrew often walked home from the refinery, as he did one pleasant May evening, his path taking him past the shipyards where some men still worked although the bulk of the workforce had finished for the day. Laughter and the clatter of voices came to his ears from the public houses placed conveniently near to the yards. Leaving the cranes and masts and funnels behind, he detoured to take in the Esplanade, a broad and elegant road where tall houses gazed across their front gardens to where the river widened at the Tail o' the Bank, the edge of a huge stretch of shallows over a sandbank. A cluster of cargo vessels was moored out in the deep water awaiting their turn to unload at one of Greenock's busy harbours.

Once beyond the Esplanade, he entered Gourock, more of a residential area than either Port Glasgow or Greenock. After turning in at the gates of his own house and walking up the drive between great banks of rhododendron bushes, Warren hesitated, hearing the sound of children's voices, then followed the driveway round to the rear of the house where the coachhouse and stables and kitchen-garden lay. Beyond them was a small paddock where a pony had been installed for his children.

Helene was sitting in a canopied swing that had been set up on a patch of grass, singing a nursery song at the top of her voice to a large and beautiful French doll, a recent gift from her mother's parents, which nestled in the crook of her arm. The nursemaid, seated on a wooden kitchen chair nearby, was busy with some mending while Martin, astride the pony, rode up and down the gravel paths brandishing a wooden sword, enacting a cavalry charge. The gardener's lad ambled along behind him, ready to take the animal when its rider grew bored.

Andrew halted at the corner of the house and watched his children. In another month they would reach their seventh birthdays; the babyness had already faded from their faces. They were their mother's children, with Madeleine's rich dark beauty. All too soon Helene would be breaking hearts and Martin being sought after by every society lady with a marriageable daughter in the area. Andrew himself had passed his thirtieth birthday and although he felt no different he realised as he looked at the twins that time was ebbing away and little could be done to halt it.

The nursemaid caught sight of him and jumped to her feet, dropping her mending in her haste to curtsey. The children, alerted by the sudden movement, immediately fell silent and became little adults, Helene slipping from the swing to dip her own curtsey, Martin struggling down from the pony to stand by its head, sword resting on his shoulder as his father advanced.

'Good evening, Papa,' they chorused, eyeing him warily. The days when they ran willingly into his arms were gone. Madeleine had seen to that.

'Good evening Helene, Martin. Are you enjoying yourselves?'

'Yes, thank you, Papa,' they said, still in perfect unison.

Andrew, at a loss for something to say, cleared his throat and glanced up at the sky, where the sun was setting. Unfortunately the nursemaid mistook the movement as a reminder that time was passing. She announced breathlessly, nervously, that it was time to prepare for bed. The children, their faces carefully blank to hide any disappointment they might have felt at having to go indoors, immediately obeyed, Helene hurrying to fetch her doll first. He saw the soft unblemished curve of her cheek as she turned to run back to the maid and his heart twisted within him as he recalled the angry red puckered scar that ran down Dorothea's face from ear to mouth. She had made a good recovery in the three months since her accident and was as much of a delight to him as ever, but each time he saw her scar he was reminded anew of how vulnerable children were. He wanted to call Helene to him, to pick her up and hold her close and safe before it was too late, but the twins had disappeared through the kitchen door, and he was alone.

He couldn't follow them, for it was quite wrong for the master of the house to enter his own kitchen. Instead he walked round to the front door, where Edith, no doubt alerted by the nurserymaid, was waiting, tall and angular and prim-faced.

'Mrs Warren is in the drawing room, sir. Dinner will be served in twenty minutes.'

Madeleine, as slim and as beautiful as the day he had first set eyes on her, was turning the pages of a magazine. She lifted her face for his kiss, presenting him with a smooth cool cheek, then returned to her reading. Andrew half filled a glass from the whisky decanter and sat down opposite her, sipping the drink, watching the way the last shafts of sunlight haloed his wife's hair, the soft regular rise and fall of the lace frills on her bodice as she breathed, the shadow of her lashes on her cheek. Watched, and wanted her with the hopeless yearning that maddened him yet refused to leave him alone.

There were always women willing to lie in his arms – Anna, when he was at home, others when he was away on business. Sometimes he paid for the favours he received, but not often. It was surprising how many well-bred ladies had a streak of the wanton in them, mingled with boredom and a liking for mild sinning. Madeleine had been the first to teach him how passionate some women could be. His blood raced and his body tingled and began to come alive at the memory of that teaching, and he took another mouthful of whisky and forced the memory back. It fought him all the way. Nobody, not even Anna, could slake his thirst for his own wife, the one woman he could not have.

'Dinner will be served soon and I do not like to keep the servants waiting. Should you not prepare?'

He grunted a reply and heaved himself from the chair to make his way up to his own room. As he went, concern over Anna began to niggle at him like a bad tooth. She was unhappy. He was making her unhappy and he didn't know what to do about it. She knew, she had always known, that although he would never desert her or Dorothea, there could be no question of marriage between them.

Washing his hands in the basin of hot water that had been poured out in readiness for him, Andrew sighed and hoped that Anna would have the good sense to see that things must be left as they were. Why did women have to be so complicated?

But he wished, as he made his way downstairs again, that there could have been some way to recognise Dorothea openly as his daughter.

The wind rattled a handful of rain against the windows and in the garden the trees writhed in the grip of a summer storm. It had been a gloomy day and Anna had been glad to draw the curtains early. The gaslight highlighted the gleam of brass and china and glistened on raindrops still caught in Davie's thick hair as he lay back in his chair, eyes closed. She watched him, the restlessness that had gripped her for the past few weeks draining away, leaving her at rest. His presence, the youthful adoration that was still there although he hid it well, always soothed her.

A coal burning in the grate gave a sudden crack and he stirred then opened his eyes and smiled sleepily at her.

'It's a poor visitor that falls asleep.'

'You're tired.'

'Aye, I'm tired. But it's good to feel tired after putting in a hard day at work you enjoy. It's not like the tiredness I felt day after day when I was working on the docks with my father.'

'D'you ever see your family now you're in Port Glasgow?'

'Not Joseph or the old man – I'd not weep if I never saw either of them again. I visit my mother and Thomasina now and then.' His grey eyes darkened. 'My mother's thinner each time I see her, and more tired. Sometimes I see my sister Edith there. And I look in at the shop for a word with Lessie most weeks.'

Lessie. Anna smiled inwardly, for not even clever Lessie, who had tried so hard when they all lived in the Vennel to keep her young brother and Anna apart lest he be corrupted, knew about their friendship. Anna's maid-servant was discreet and it amused her to have a secret. Davie's gratitude when she had recommended him to Andrew Warren had warmed her. It pleased her to know that she had had the power to help him.

He yawned and stretched his arms far above his head, fists clenched. She saw his teeth white against the red of his tongue, watched the muscles cording in his sturdy neck. Something that had been lying dormant for a long time stirred deep within her, a subtle primitive thrill that caught and held her as though her body was controlled by a silken thread.

As Davie completed the stretch and sat up, the little mantel clock chimed and he squinted at it in disbelief. 'Is that the time? I must go.'

'Not yet.' Anna leaned over impulsively and laid a hand on his. For a moment the contact, skin upon skin, made the silken cord tighten and tug again, then he snatched his fingers away, reddening.

'I must. It's not seemly for me to be visiting you so late. Your serving woman'll be waiting to get to her bed.'

'Molly's not here. Her brother's sick and she's gone off to take her turn at sitting up with him tonight.'

Davie's flush deepened as he swiftly got to his feet. 'Then I should never have come into the house. You should've told me!'

'I wanted you to come in. I wanted your company. What's amiss, Davie? Don't tell me you're worried about my good name? There's folk in the Vennel that would tell you I lost that many years ago.'

'Don't talk like that! Don't demean yourself!'

She was going to give him a laughing answer, but the look in his eyes as he stared down at her killed the words before they were uttered. For a long moment they gazed at each other and in that moment the silken thread within Anna became a living thing, tightening and coiling and seeming to draw her, step by step, towards him, although her body stayed where it was, in the chair, hands demurely clasped. She knew by the tightening of his jaw muscles that Davie, too, sensed the insistent tugging. Something that had lain unnoticed for too long had flared up between them, and Davie Kirkwood was afraid.

'I must go.'

'Davie—'

'I must!' He plunged into the hall, wrenching his coat from its peg, pushing his arms into it swiftly.

'Don't go,' Anna said from the parlour door. 'Stay. Stay with me.' The words jerked themselves from her throat and he shook his head, pulling away from her when she reached for his arm. The brief contact, the feel of him, even through the layers of cloth between them, sent sudden heat through her body. 'You know you want to stay with me.'

'For Christ's sake, Anna!' He ground the words out as he tore the door open. The storm, glad of entry, surged in, whipping her skirt against her legs, loosening tendrils of her hair, making the gas flames gasp and dance within the fragile protection of their mantles.

'Davie!'

The door closed and he was gone. The coats that had been set swinging where they hung slowly swayed to a standstill, the gaslight recovered itself, a few wet leaves that had been gusted into the hall flapped limply on the floor like fish torn from their watery home. The invisible thread jerked and tightened and hurt. Anna, alone again, held her aching body in crossed arms, turning to press her face against the flock wallpaper, aware of a low keening deep in her throat that she couldn't stop.

The door rattled and the latch, which had only half caught, slipped open. Hands came from the night and caught her and turned her so that her face was now against a wet coat with buttons that mashed into her soft skin.

'I cannae just leave you like this. Oh God, Anna!' said Davie thickly, and kicked the door shut properly at his back, forcing the wind and the rest of the world out. He tried to tighten his grip on her but she resisted, leaning back to fumble at his coat, his jacket, his waistcoat, wanting him now, with no more waiting. There had been more than enough waiting for the two of them.

The fire ran through her, through her insistent fingers, and caught at him. They staggered, locked together, into the parlour, bumping off the door frame, then the corner of a fireside chair. Their fingers tore and groped, forcing buttons through buttonholes, catching the ends of ribbons and pulling bows apart, dragging studs and hooks and eyes open. His coat, her blouse, his waistcoat, her skirt, his shirt, her chemise flew about the room like large snowflakes, landing where they may.

The fireside rug was rough beneath Anna's back, the flames daubed their two naked bodies with red and gold as they rolled together, now away from the firelight into cool shadow, now back to the heat that was nothing compared to the heat within. As their sweat mingled, his skin slid easily over hers; her thighs were damp with her wanting and his salty body taste was on her tongue. His hands and mouth travelled over her, making her arch her back and writhe with pleasure.

When he finally lifted himself above her Anna opened her body to him willingly, drawing him deep into her, wrapping her arms and legs about him to hold him fiercely captive. Instinctive to each other's desires although it was their first coupling, they moved, paused, moved again, finally reaching their climax in perfect unison. Even after that he stayed with her, edging her round gently so that they lay side by side, their faces touching. He kissed her throat, her ears, her eyes and nose and forehead and mouth with kisses that were butterfly-gentle, then drew his head back and smiled at her.

'I love you.'

'I love you, Davie,' Anna said, and knew that although

she had said it often in her life, and had thought that she meant it when she first said it to Andrew Warren, she had lied. Only when she said it to this man, who had amused her with his clumsy awkward adoration when he was a mere lad, who had until that night been no more than a friend, did she speak the truth.

'We'll sell it, of course.'

'Sell it? We will not! We'll live in it.'

Murdo looked at his wife with exasperation. 'And what about the shop?'

'It's not that far away. I can walk to it and back here each day. The dear Lord knows I've walked the distance many a time, carrying Ian or pushing him in that broken-down old baby carriage. And if we move here, to Cathcart Street,' said Lessie with growing enthusiasm, her quick mind planning ahead as usual, 'Elma could live in the rooms behind the shop and pay us a wee bit of rent out of her wages. She's desperate to get out of her sister's house, for it's far too small for the family as it is without Elma there as well.'

'But think of the money we could make by selling this place. Not to mention the furniture.'

Lessie moved to the empty range and gathered one of the china 'wally dugs' into her arms, hugging it to her protectively, glaring at her husband across its rounded glossy head. 'I'd not consider selling one stick or one thread of Miss Peden's things. She left all that she had to me, God rest her, and she meant us to live here. I know she did, Murdo.'

Then the room, strange and cold without Miss Peden's vital, dominant presence, suddenly wavered and broke up. A tear fell onto the china dog. 'I just wish I'd known, Murdo. I wish I could've been there at the end to keep her company.'

He crossed the kitchen in two long steps and gathered her, wally dug and all, into his arms. 'She didnae know anythin' about it, hen. Ye know what the doctor said, she just went tae sleep an' didnae waken up.'

'I could have vi-visited her that week. I m-meant to,

but what with the shop and M-mam no' being well—'

'Hush now.' He rocked her in his arms, then kissed her forehead. 'You did a lot for her, else why would she leave you her house? Though I still think you should consider sellin',' he added carefully as she sniffed and broke away to scrub at her face with one sleeve.

'D'you not want to move out of the Vennel?'

'Of course I do. An' we will in time. Wi' the money from this place in our pockets—'

Lessie shook her head. 'Miss Peden knew how much I wanted to take Ian out of the Vennel when it was just the two of us. It's why she left me the flat. I'll not go against her wishes, Murdo.' Then she tutted and hurriedly put the china dog down to swoop along the passageway to the door as small boots thudded along the close outside.

'Will you two be quiet? D'you want the folk to think we're a tribe of heathens?'

'There's doos in the yard, Mam!' Ian's nose was red from the cold of a frosty November day, but his eyes shone. 'And the lavvy's just at the back door, not at the other side of puddles the way it is at home!'

'It's a garden, not a yard, and they're pigeons, not doos. They belong to someone who lives up the stairs. You can look at them, but keep out of the way. I don't want anyone complaining about you, d'you hear me? And it's a lavatory, not a lavvy.'

'Piggins,' Jess verified cheerfully, flapping her arms as best she could within the limitations of a long adult scarf covering her fair head then crossing her chest and fastened at the back. 'Lavvy.' She was getting over a cold and Lessie, worried about her persistent cough, insisted on wrapping her up warmly when she took the child out. That was another reason why she was determined to move into Miss Peden's flat; even though the rooms behind the shop were more weathertight than the flat she and Ian had lived in before her marriage, Lessie wanted to get her children out of the Vennel, where an unacceptable proportion of the children died before reaching school age. She didn't want to see that happen to her two.

'Lavvy!' Jess, liking the feel of the word on her tongue, danced around the close repeating it on a higher note each time. It floated on giggles, and Ian joined in the laughter, encouraging her. It was at that moment, to Lessie's horror, that Mrs Kincaid, the old woman who lived on the top floor, the woman who had always made her life a misery when she scrubbed the stairs, rounded the landing above and started down the final flight, pulling on her second glove as she came, her shopping bag over her arm. At the sight of her all Lessie's nervousness flooded back and she snapped, 'Hold your tongues!' so sharply that both children stopped at once and stared up at her, round-eyed. Then, as Mrs Kincaid reached the bottom step, they swivelled to gape at her.

'Good afternoon to you, Mistress Kincaid.'

The old woman said nothing for a moment, looking down her nose at the group by the open door of the flat. Jess, suddenly subdued, moved closer to her mother for protection as the cold eyes ran over her, and Lessie was glad that beneath the protective scarf her daughter was wearing a neat little velvet coat and good boots that had been passed down from Dorothea.

'It's you,' the woman said at last, her voice as forbidding as her look. 'I heard Miss Peden had left you her flat.'

'That's right.'

'I don't know what she was thinking about. I hope your bairns are well behaved. We don't have bairns in this close. We've never wanted bairns in this close.'

Ian, too, had moved to stand against Lessie's legs. She put a protective hand on each child. 'You will have, Mrs Kincaid, and soon. And my bairns are very well behaved.'

'Hmph. Well, there's one blessing, I suppose. The body that's doing the stairs now isnae up to much. At least you'll be handy for that, living here. You can start back at it next week. I'll tell her when she comes tomorrow.'

Lessie gaped at her, feeling the colour flooding into her face. Then Murdo's hand landed on her shoulder, as protective as her own hold on the children.

'My wife'll no' be scrubbin' any stairs for you or anyone else, missus,' he said, his voice courteous but hard. 'She's no need tae skivvy for the likes o' you any more tae earn her food. She's got me now.'

Mrs Kincaid's breath hissed in through her open mouth. She went crimson and seemed to shrivel in on herself. She pushed past them without another word.

'Nasty ol' woman,' said Jess, and Ian nodded in agreement.

'If she doesnae watch out I'll – I'll kick her legs,' he said gruffly, then grinned when his stepfather gave a howl of laughter.

'Ian! Murdo, will you stop encouraging the laddie? Come inside, the lot of you.' Lessie scooped them in and shut the door. Ian scurried ahead into the kitchen; when the others arrived he had drawn the net curtain aside and was peering out of the window.

'Ian! Leave that curtain alone!'

'Och, don't keep on at the laddie,' Murdo told her, his voice roughening. She knew that he was disappointed by her refusal to sell the house. Murdo liked to have money. He had opened a bank account and each week he carefully stowed away as much as could be saved from the shop. They lived on the money he earned at the shipyard.

'He'll have to learn how to behave if we're to live here.'

The curtain fell back into place as Ian spun round, wide-eyed. 'Here? Are we goin' tae live here?'

'Wi' neighbours like the evil-eyed old biddy we've just met?' Murdo added quickly.

Lessie, seeing her daughter's eyes on the china dog, picked it up and put it back on the mantelshelf out of harm's way. 'Aye,' she said. 'Aye, we're goin' tae live here.'

13

Most of Miss Peden's ornaments were carefully packed away, out of reach of the children. Murdo's suggestion that they should be sold met with a firm refusal from Lessie.

'D'you think of nothing but money?' she wanted to know, wounded by the very idea of betraying the old woman.

'I've a family to support. I've no time for sentiment. Better the money than all that stuff takin' up room that we need. My mother says—'

'I might have known that she'd come into it. Well, you can tell your mother that I'll decide what happens in my own house.'

'So that's it, is it? Your house, an' me an' my daughter supposed tae thank you for lettin' us live here, I suppose?'

'Och Murdo, you know I didnae mean it like that! I meant that it's ours, not your mother's.'

As the door slammed behind him, she could have bitten her tongue out. Why, she wondered wearily as she scrubbed Ian's neck and got Jess ready to go out, did Murdo have to set such store by money? But she knew why. Anyone brought up by his mother, with her fascination for pricing everything, would be the same. And it was his only fault. Day in and day out Lessie had seen women with bruised faces and split eyes and even broken arms come into the shop, usually on a Monday after their husbands had been drinking at the weekend. She had seen cowed children who flinched at a sudden movement from an adult. She often felt angry with the battered women, convinced that she herself would never allow a

159

man to treat her in such a way. But no doubt some of the victims had thought the same, once. She was fortunate to be married to a good man like Murdo.

She tugged at the woollen tie of Jess's glove as she remembered how he had said, 'Me and my daughter.' It wasn't like Murdo to make a difference between the children. She had hurt him badly this time.

'Ow!' said Jess plaintively, and Lessie suddenly realised that in her preoccupation she was tying the poor child's wrist up like a parcel.

'Sorry, pet.' She loosened the tie and Jess, her eyes reproachful, mutely held up her wrist so that the red line biting into her white skin could be kissed better.

'You've got a bad mammy, so you have. Come on, Ian, we'll never get to Granny's at this rate. I promised Elma I'd be at the shop by eleven, and it's near enough that now.'

They had only been in the flat for two months and Lessie knew a thrill of pleasure as she locked the door when they left. The knocker and bell pull and wooden panels shone from the polishing she had given them that morning. Out at the back the small patch of ground that belonged to them had been dug over by Murdo in readiness for planting potatoes and leeks and onions and kale – all except a little border that was already bright with the daffodils and crocuses that Miss Peden grew every year. Lessie had wondered whether she would feel at home in the house she had only visited before, but there was a good atmosphere about the little flat, a warmth and serenity that welcomed them all.

Now that Elma was contentedly settled into the rooms behind the shop, she was very willing to take over more running of the place. She was a reliable assistant, and Lessie was glad of that, for as her mother's health flagged, she and Edith had taken over a lot of the household duties in their parents' home. And there was Anna, too, often sending for Lessie on some pretext or another. Dorothea had made a good recovery from her accident, though her little face now carried a red puckered scar running diagonally across her right cheek almost to the mouth. In time, the doctor said, it would fade, but it would never disappear. Dorothea was marked for life.

Since the accident Anna had started fretting over her own health, something that had never bothered her before. She had sent for Lessie several times, and each time, mindful of the assurance she had given Andrew Warren, Lessie had gone hurrying off to Port Glasgow to find Anna seeking her opinion on a new dress, or bored and in need of company. Murdo thought that she was a fool to bother with Anna McCauley, but since that day in the Vennel when the two of them had hurriedly dragged Frank Warren from Anna's bed and dressed him and propped him on a chair, their lives had become entangled. It seemed to Lessie, sometimes despairingly as the increasing demands of her own life made visits to Anna's fine house more and more difficult, that they were bound to each other for life.

Now that her financial situation had eased and the shop was paid for, she had tried on more than one occasion to give the twenty shillings back to Anna and each time it had been refused, or returned slyly as gifts for the children. In Lessie's eyes it was a debt still outstanding, a debt that seemed to have no end to it.

Jess trotted along by her side, chattering happily. Ian scuffed behind them, red head down, continually having to be told to hurry up. He was due to start school at the end of the summer, and he was ready for it, bored at having to be with his mother and sister. There were other children in the street and he had got to know them quickly enough, but in Lessie's opinion he was too young to be left on his own while she visited her mother. Once he was at school, she thought with relief, turning to hurry him yet again, she would get so much more done with only Jess to see to.

Thomasina opened the door and was so pleased to see them that she forgot to step back to allow them in to the narrow hall. It took a few minutes for Lessie to get the three of them in and the door shut. Thomasina was fifteen years old now; if she had been born with a whole mind she would have been starting work now, going out with her friends, giggling about the laddies they knew at work or saw in the street. But instead she was an overgrown child, at home with her mother and scarcely ever out now that Barbara wasn't fit to manage the stairs.

Lessie gave her young sister an extra hug in an attempt to make up for all that she had lost, then went on into the kitchen, where Barbara, her face drawn, was washing clothes, supporting herself with one hand clenched over the rim of the sink while the other kneaded and rubbed as best it could.

'Mam, what d'you think you're doing?'

Barbara lifted a tired face, flushed with effort. 'They'll not wash themselves.'

'You know fine that Edith and me see to the washing for you now.'

'It's things that have to be done right away.'

Lessie hung her coat up on the peg behind the door. 'Thomasina, help Jess off with her coat, hen. Then you can all go and play in the bedroom for a wee while.' She went to the sink and looked down at the old torn strips of sheeting, the pink-tinged water. 'Oh Mam, is it Thomasina?'

'It's no' Joseph,' her mother said with grim irony, staring down at the evidence of her youngest daughter's maturity.

'I thought it might not happen to her.'

'Don't be daft, our Lessie, it's her mind that's no' grown. She's got a woman's body, poor lass, though she's been awful late startin',' Barbara acknowledged.

'Does she know what to do?'

'I gave her a bundle o' cloths an' she seems tae be managin'. Poor wee lamb, she thought she'd sat down on a knife an' cut herself. She was that upset. Then I had an awful bother gettin' her tae hold her tongue. She was all for tellin' her father about it.' Barbara leaned against the sink and sighed. 'It's just another burden sent tae try us.'

'Sit down over here.' Lessie gently urged her mother to a chair and delved into her bag. 'I've brought you some calves' foot jelly. And an orange.'

162

'The orange'll do for Thomasina.'

'I brought one for her too.' Lessie fetched a sharp knife and carefully sliced the orange into small pieces which she arranged on a plate. 'There you are – eat it all before the bairns come through and want it.'

'You shouldnae be spendin' your money on such luxuries. Anyway, I'm not hungry,' Barbara protested, but under her daughter's eagle eye she obediently picked up a piece of glistening orange flesh and put it into her mouth. 'It's – it's pleasant,' she conceded.

'It's good for you, too. You can have the jelly tonight, when Thomasina's in her bed. It's all for you, mind.' Lessie turned her attention to the cloths in the sink, rolling up her sleeves, kneading and scrubbing the material between her knuckles to get rid of the stain. They all knew now that Barbara's 'wee cold' was consumption although nobody used the word, as though feeling in some superstitious way that it couldn't hurt if it wasn't named. Phthisis, the doctor called it. It could be cured but rarely was in streets and tenements where folk used to working hard all the days of their lives just to keep body and soul together couldn't afford to avail themselves of good food and fresh air and rest. It was Lessie's hope that if they could just keep Barbara going until the summer they could take her up to the braes behind the town where good clean air and sunshine might just work its magic. She would have to be carried down to the closemouth, then lifted into a hired cab. Murdo and Davie, maybe her father and Joseph if they were there, could carry her in a kitchen chair. Lessie scrubbed and rinsed and tried not to think of the rage her mother would fly into at the thought of being carried downstairs on a wooden chair instead of going down on her own two feet. That was something that would have to be dealt with when the time came. Nevertheless, she was determined to get Barbara onto the braes with fresh healthy air in her lungs one way or another.

She wrung out the cloths with decisive twists of her wrists and hung them over the fireguard so that they would be dry and folded away before her father got back from the docks. 'Is there anything else to wash while I'm at it?'

'It's all done. Edith was in yesterday morning.'

Lessie reached up to the laden wooden pulley suspended by ropes from the ceiling and touched the clothes that hung there. They had been washed more recently than twenty-four hours ago, but she said nothing as she emptied the sink and dried her hands. She knew that her mother hadn't scrubbed the clothes. She wasn't strong enough.

'Imagine,' Edith had said to her a week earlier, scandalised. 'It's not a man's place to wash and iron. And he doesnae know how to do it properly anyway. There was a food stain on Thomasina's skirt and Mam's blouse was all creased. Why can't he mind his own business and leave you and me to see to things the way Mam wants?'

Lessie had said nothing for there was no point in trying to defend her father against Edith, who had no time for him. But it made her want to cry when she pictured him, slowing now with the passing years, standing in the kitchen after his wife and daughter were asleep, washing clothes in the sink, ironing them with irons heated on the range, doing his best to keep things going. She wondered if her mother was grateful, but even her fairly active imagination couldn't picture that.

'It tastes of sunlight,' Barbara said, showing a rare flash of fancy.

'Murdo says oranges grow in a sunny country. The folk who live there can just reach up and pick them off the trees. Imagine being able to do that!'

'I mind once when I was a lassie, walkin' out in the country. There was a stone wall, an' apple trees on the other side. The branches were hangin' over, all heavy wi' the fruit on them. It was bonny.' Barbara stirred restlessly, pushed the half-empty plate from her, and reached into a small drawer in the cupboard by her chair. She brought out the familiar dark medicine bottle and a glass. There were only a few drops left in the bottle when she tipped it up.

'I'll fetch your medicine. I know where it is,' Lessie said, and went into the bedroom. The children were playing with Thomasina on the floor like puppies, in a giggling, squirming heap. Lessie picked her way round the tangle of moving limbs and bodies and fetched the whisky bottle from the depths of the big dark wardrobe where her mother's and sister's clothes hung.

That was another little mystery that Edith hadn't as yet noticed; although Barbara could no longer go to the wine shop to buy her secret bottles of whisky, there was always drink hidden away in the wardrobe. It could only be put there by her father, Lessie was convinced of that.

She carried the whisky back into the kitchen, filled the medicine bottle to the top and corked it, then filled the glass almost to the brim. Barbara, her face shamed, her eyes lowered, took it and drank greedily. Then she said, 'Lessie, you'll see that Thomasina's all right, won't you – when I'm dead and gone?'

The whisky bottle was cold and hard against Lessie's palm. 'For goodness' sake, Mam, you're not going to die!'

'Och, don't be daft, girl,' said Barbara with tired contempt. 'I'm no' a bairn tae be telt fairy stories, an' neither are you.'

On the way home Lessie decided to give Murdo some boiled ham for his tea as a peace offering. Normally almost everything they ate came from her own shop but she was too tired to walk down to the Vennel, so for the first time she went into the shop at the corner of Cathcart Street. The bell tinged as she and the children went in, and Lessie stared round, her eyes wide with admiration. This shop was far superior to her own. Every inch of space had been carefully utilised, the shelves banked from floor to ceiling and filled with tins and jars and biscuits, sweets, pulses, tea, sugar, jams and sauces and pickles. Behind the counter were tiers of small drawers, each labelled with the name of the spice it held. The floor was covered with thick fresh sawdust that added its own aroma to the tang of coffee beans, which were ranked in marked tins, and a wide variety of cheeses and cold meats was ranged along cool marble shelves.

Great hams, ready for slicing when needed, hung by hooks from the ceiling, and on the long wood-panelled marble counter there were two sets of scales, one of them with a slab for butters and cheeses, a handsome bacon-slicing machine, and – the wonder of all wonders – a large imposing cash register of gleaming brass, with levers to pull down, a cash drawer underneath, and a little glass enclosure on top where tickets jumped up when the levers were manipulated to display the amount of each purchase recorded.

Lessie took her place in the queue, Jess's gloved hand held tightly in hers, and gaped around at the treasure cave she found herself in. Behind the counter Mr Mann, the shop's proprietor, his wife, and their male assistant were each swathed in long snowy aprons. Lessie looked, and marvelled, and thought wistfully of the faded wrap-round flowered pinnies she and Elma had to make do with.

'You, woman – out off my shop!'

It took her a moment to realise that Mr Mann had stopped slicing rich pink bacon and was pointing an index finger straight at her. Everyone in the shop turned to stare.

'Wh-what did you say?'

'Out off my shop,' he repeated, the English words heavy and guttural on his foreign tongue. 'I do not haff to serve you!'

'Willi!' His wife, plump and embarrassed, tugged at his arm, but he shook her off.

'I only came in to buy—'

'I know you!' His voice was booming now and Lessie, her face hot, was sure that half Cathcart Street must hear him. She was aware of Ian gaping up at her, of Jess shrinking back against her skirt, as the man's voice roared on at her, 'I know off your shop. You do not come as honest customer, you come as spy! And I tell you, it is not allowed. Out!'

She went, fumbling for the door, dimly hearing the smug ring of the bell as she herded the children outside, away from the stares and the humiliation, almost running along the road to her own close. By the time they got inside their own front door Jess was crying and Lessie herself was close to tears of anger and embarrassment.

'Nasty man!' Jess wept, then stuck out a small foot, showing a dirty sock wrinkled round her instep. 'My shoe,' she wailed, fresh tears coursing down her little face.

'Oh dear God. Ian, go back and look for your sister's shoe. I'm sorry, lambie!' She gathered Jess up, hiding her own hot face in the child's neck. 'Mammy didnae know your shoe came off. Here, I'll take the sock off and wash your wee foot.'

By the time Ian came panting back, the missing shoe in his hand, Jess's tears had been dried, her foot washed and kissed and exclaimed over, and she was sitting by the fire sucking at a sweet. Lessie wished that she herself could have been as easily soothed and pacified. Her heart was still racing. Frantically, she tried to remember who was in the shop, who had heard her being shouted at. She couldn't remember, for it all had the texture of a bad dream now, a nightmare of pale smudges turned towards her, with only Mr Mann's red face and bristling grey moustache vivid in her mind. She hoped Mrs Kincaid hadn't been there to hear him.

'Mam, why did he shout at us?' Ian wanted to know.

'He wasn't shouting at us.'

'Yes he was, he was pointing at you and—'

'Just forget about it, Ian. Not another word to anyone, and not a word to your daddy, d'you hear me?' The last thing she wanted was Murdo storming along to the corner shop and having a row with the grocer.

She seized the teapot and ladled a generous spoonful of tea into it before filling it from the kettle simmering on the range. As the shock eased, she herself was beginning to simmer with delayed anger. What man in his right mind would think that she was spying? Their two shops were quite unlike each other. Lessie knew what her customers wanted and could afford and it would be madness to try to copy the Manns, even if she had the money, which she hadn't. She had gone into the place as a genuine customer, waiting to make her purchase and hand over her money, admiring the way it was all laid out.

It was nonsense to say that she had been seeking to steal his ideas.

'Mammy, why is Mr Mann called Mr Mann and Mrs Mann called Mrs Mann instead of Mrs Woman?' Ian wanted to know. Lessie gave the contents of the teapot a quick stir and filled a cup, in too much of a hurry to wait for the leaves to steep properly.

'I don't know.'

'Dad says it's because they're forn. What's forn?'

'Foreign. It means they come from another country.'

'What country?'

'Germany, I think.'

'Why did they come here then?'

'I don't know,' said Lessie, and wished, fervently, that they never had.

'Don't go to Jamaica, Andrew. Stay with me,' Anna said frantically into his jacket. He held her close, touched by her feelings for him.

'I have to go, my dear. If I'm to raise the money I need to modernise the refinery I must sell the sugar plantation. And I want to make sure I get a good price for it.'

'But a whole year!' Her arms tightened about him.

'It might not take the full year. I might be back before then.' He knew, though, that that was unlikely. Madeleine and the children were travelling with him, and Madeleine would certainly insist on staying in Jamaica for as long as possible. 'They're waiting for me at the refinery,' he said, suddenly eager to get the farewells over and done with. He hated farewells.

Anna raised a flushed face, her eyes drowned violets. 'Make love to me, Andrew, one more time before you go.'

'With Molly and Dorothea in the house?'

'We can send them out for a walk. Please, Andrew.'

For a moment he hesitated. He was tired, beset by problems at the refinery and by Madeleine's preparations for the journey, which had turned the house into chaos. It would be pleasant to lie with Anna in the soft bed upstairs, a breeze wafting the scent of flowers through the open window. But time was against him. He lifted her hands to his lips and kissed them. 'My dearest, I've neglected both you and our daughter, but it seems now that the days don't hold enough hours for me. I have to go.' Then, as the tears began to spill onto her cheeks he added, 'I'll try to come back tonight, when Dorothea's asleep.'

Hope flashed into her eyes. 'You promise?'

'I'll – I promise,' said Andrew, and she finally let him go.

Alone again, she paced the floor, chewing at her lower lip. It had been a long time, too long, since Andrew had last taken her to bed. Too long ago for him to be the reason why she felt lethargic and irritable and too ill in the mornings to take even a cup of tea. She had taken all her usual precautions, but it was becoming all too clear to her that the sweet secret times spent with Davie, mainly in her room during the maid's time off, sometimes in his lodgings, once on soft fragrant grass on the braes above the town, had rendered their account, and it must be paid.

At first she had thought it would be simple enough to pass the child off as Andrew's. Davie himself mustn't know, for much as she loved him and hoped to belong only to him one day, Anna had been too badly scarred by poverty to turn her back on the comfort she now knew and return to narrow little streets and old damp rooms. And Davie must be free to carry on with his dream of building up the engineering business. Old Mr Beattie had recently died and, true to his word, had left the engineering shop to the hard-working young partner who had saved it from earlier extinction. But there was a lot to be done if it was to prosper, and Davie could never do that if he was burdened with a family to support. For now, until she could go freely to her love, Andrew must be the father of both her children.

When Dorothea was in bed and asleep and Molly sent out for the evening, Anna waited impatiently in the parlour. She had put on Andrew's favourite of all her dresses and the scent of roses stirred the air every time she moved. Upstairs a lamp burned in the bedroom and the covers of the big bed were turned back invitingly.

The mantel clock ticked away the minutes, then an hour, before the door knocker rattled. She ran to open it, fumbling with the latch in her impatience. The lad outside handed her a letter and loped off without a word.

Slowly, the certain knowledge that Andrew was not coming to her forming ice crystals in her belly, Anna closed the door and returned to the parlour, the letter that spelled the end of her safe, comfortable life clutched in her hand.

'My dear,' Andrew had written, his strong handwriting sprawling over the paper in his haste, 'my wife has made arrangements for this, our last evening in Gourock, without my knowledge. I have no choice but to stay with our guests. I have made certain that you will have no financial problems while I am in Jamaica. Kiss Dorothea for me. I look forward to the day when I can be with you both.'

The paper fluttered to the floor. Anna bit hard on the knuckles of one hand to hold back the screams of rage and fear that suddenly filled her throat. Andrew had failed her; by the time he returned, there would be another child, a child that could not possibly be his. Her mind feverishly ran over dates, adding and subtracting, coming up again and again with the same answer. He was no fool; she had no hope, now, of convincing him that he had made her pregnant before leaving Scotland. She recalled the ease of Dorothea's birth, the midwife's admiring comment, 'Ye can birth bairns as easy as shellin' peas.' She remembered how hard she had tried to abort the little girl, and how her body, strong even in those days of deprivation, had defied every effort and finally delivered a healthy child, unaffected by all Anna had tried to do.

Now she must try again, and this time nobody would save her as Andrew had. She would not involve Davie, whatever happened. She would not destroy his hopes and his future; she loved him too deeply to do that. Nor would she go back to the life she had known before. This time, if nothing else worked, she would have to visit the old woman in the Vennel – or someone very like her.

* * *

Lessie was coping with a shop full of customers when the little boy, barefoot and ragged, thrust his way through the crush, leaving a clucking, ruffled trail of women in his wake, and rapped his knuckles on the counter.

'Missus!'

'Wait yer turn,' Elma said sharply, and he turned his hard gaze, old and knowing before his time, on her.

'It's the ither wumman I want tae see.'

'Cheeky wee de'il,' Elma's customer said.

'Needs his backside dichted, so he does,' said someone else.

Ignoring them, the boy ran a flapping-sleeved arm across his damp nose and said to Lessie. 'Ye're wanted in Port Glasgow.'

'Who says so?'

'A lady-wumman. Tell Mistress Carswell she's wanted in Port Glasgow, she says. An' she says ye'd gie me a sixpence for my trouble.'

Lessie went on weighing onions calmly though anger had begun to simmer deep down. This was yet another of Anna's imperious summonses. 'She gave you the sixpence herself.'

He didn't bother to deny it. 'I ran awfu' fast, but. She said I had tae. She said it wis important.'

'Here.' Lessie deserted the onions for a moment, lifted a jar down from a shelf behind the counter, and took out a peppermint ball. It was in the boy's mouth before she realised that it had gone from her outstretched fingers. He turned and eeled his way back out into the street, creating a second avenue of clucks and complaints.

'You shouldnae encourage wee tinks like him,' her customer told her disapprovingly.

Lessie had returned to her work. 'Och, the poor wee soul won't often get a sweetie. And what's one wee sweetie anyway?'

'That's no' whit yer man'd say,' someone grunted. Lessie pretended not to hear the words, or the ripple of agreement that ran through the crowded shop. She knew well enough that her customers didn't like it when Murdo happened to be behind the counter. Since their quarrel shortly after Jess's birth he hadn't tried to impose interest on credit or give short weight, but these women had thin purses and long memories and they didn't trust him any more. More than once Lessie had spotted someone turning away from the door and walking on because Murdo was serving. She handed over the onions, received money, gave change, and turned to the next customer, pushing Anna and her continual demands for attention out of her mind. In the month or so since Andrew Warren had been in Jamaica Anna had got worse.

'Are you not going to Port Glasgow, then?' Elma wanted to know during a lull.

'I am not. It's time Anna McCauley learned that I cannae go running off whenever she sends for me. She's getting to be as bad as a bairn. The times I've gone trailing out there these past few weeks, thinking to find her ill in her bed, mebbe at death's door, and there she was, with some imaginary ailment, just wanting someone to sympathise with her.' Lessie shook her head and felt around the shelf below the counter for a duster. 'She's not got enough to do, that's her trouble. I'll go to Port Glasgow later, when the bairns are in their beds and the shop's shut. For now, I've got work to do.'

By the time she was ready to visit Anna, it was getting dark and Murdo complained about her going out instead of staying in the house to keep him company.

'I'd best go and see what's ailing her this time. If I don't, she'll be in the shop in the morning, getting under my feet. I'll not be long,' she promised, glad enough to get out for a breath of fresh air after spending all her time in the flat and the shop.

At least there was no need to visit Barbara that evening, for Edith was there, Lessie knew. With the entire Warren family away from home Edith had more spare time on her hands than usual and she spent a fair amount of it seeing to their mother, who was more often than not confined to her bed now. Lessie fretted over Barbara's failing strength as she made the short journey by tram to Port Glasgow then started the walk to Anna's house. The planned summer trip to the braes for fresh air hadn't materialised; by then Barbara was noticeably weaker and the very thought of being carried downstairs 'in front of all the neighbours', as she said, as though they would all be standing at their doors watching her go by like a public procession, had agitated her so much that she had coughed up blood. Lessie wished, as she reached the road where Anna lived, that she could have parcelled up some country air the way she parcelled lentils and leeks, and delivered it to her mother.

The house was in darkness. Lessie hesitated at the gate and almost turned away again, then decided that she might as well try the door. There was no reaction to her knock, but when she tried again she caught a thin thread of sound from deep within, like a cat mewling or a child crying. Lessie pressed her ear tightly against the wooden panels and anger flared in her as she heard it again. Surely Anna and the servant hadn't gone out and left the child alone in the dark?

She hurried round to the back of the house, but the kitchen door was firmly locked and there was no light in the window.

Alarmed now, Lessie retraced her steps and was about to go and get help when the gate swung open and Molly came up the path, peering through the darkness at the figure by the door.

'It's yoursel', Mistress Carswell.'

'Where's Anna? Did you go off and leave Dorothea alone in the house?'

'Indeed I did not!' The woman set down the bag she was carrying and fished about in her coat pocket. 'It was my afternoon off. The mistress wasnae plannin' tae go oot, I ken that, for she didnae look too grand when she came home frae the toon this mornin'. I thought she wis comin' down wi' somethin', but she insisted on me takin' my afternoon. She said she'd go to her bed when the bairn was pit doon for the night.'

She finally located the key and unlocked the door. Lessie pushed past her into the house, shouting for Anna, wishing, now, that she had gone to the house earlier. A whimper came from the darkness at the top of the stairs as a match flared and Molly lit the gas mantle in the hall. 'I'll fetch a lamp frae the kitchen.'

Lessie didn't wait for her to come back. She groped her way upstairs, ascending into darkness, following the sound of Dorothea's little voice repeating over and over again, hopelessly, 'Mama, Mama.'

The child was huddled against the closed door of Anna's bedroom, curled into a tight ball. Lessie's hand touched soft cheeks wet with tears, then Dorothea was in her arms, the small body shaking with fear and exhaustion.

Molly, moving swiftly in spite of her bulk, came panting upstairs clutching a lamp in either hand. Their light showed that Dorothea's face was swollen, her eyes puffed with crying. 'Mama,' she wailed, reaching towards the door.

'Take her down to the kitchen, Molly. I'll see what's amiss here.' Lessie managed to take one of the lamps and hand the little girl over without mishap. She waited until she was alone, then opened the door. The room was in darkness.

'Anna?' There was no reply. The air was heavy with a brassy, unpleasant smell, a smell that made Lessie want to back out again, to close the door and let someone else see to things. Instead she advanced until the pool of light she carried illuminated the large bed Andrew Warren had bought for his mistress. At first it looked as though Anna was wearing a dark skirt and resting on top of a dark coverlet, her face half-buried in the pillow, her hands above her head, fingers curled about the brass rails of the bedhead. Then the golden light picked out the dull sheen from the one eye that Lessie could see.

'Anna?' There was no reply, but by that time she hadn't expected one. She reached out and discovered that the skirt and coverlet were not soft, but hardened and stiffened by a great deal of dried blood.

14

'You? Take on Anna McCauley's bairn as well as your own and the shop?' Edith gave a loud sniff. 'You're letting your heart rule your head, Lessie.'

'What else can I do? She's got no one else, poor wee soul. There was a solicitor at the funeral; he'll pay towards her keep, he says, until it's decided what should be done.'

'A solicitor?' Edith's eyes narrowed. 'Is he the bairn's father, d'you think?'

'Of course not! I mean,' said Lessie, suddenly recalling that Edith, who worked for the Warrens, knew nothing of Anna's story, 'I expect he'll be acting for someone else.'

'So the bairn's father must be someone wi' money, then? It's a strange business. Have you no idea who the man might be?'

'Why should I? It's none of my concern.'

'It should be, if you're goin' to take the bairn on.'

Lessie, still in the black clothes she had worn for the funeral, sipped at her tea and tried to change the subject. 'I'm grateful to you for looking after the bairns, Edith. I wish there could have been more to say goodbye to her.'

'Hmmm! She's fortunate tae be buried in a Christian graveyard, let alone having a big send-off.'

'I can't understand it. How could she go to one of those women? It's not as if the bairn wouldnae have had a good home.'

'Mebbe the man wouldnae have wanted this one.'

Lessie, who knew that her sister was quite wrong, held her tongue as Edith helped herself to more sugar and stirred her tea thoughtfully.

'Some folks are strange, and Anna McCauley was aye

more strange than most, in my opinion,' Edith pronounced. 'I can still see her the way she was in the Vennel, painted an' dressed up an' never turning a hair at what folk thought of her with all those men coming and going. At least she died respectable, if you can call being a kept woman respectable. I'd have thought Davie would've come back with you for a cup of tea.'

'He had to get back to Port Glasgow.'

'The Lord knows why he bothered to take time off for the funeral.'

'Davie always liked Anna when he lived with me in the Vennel. It was kind of him to accompany me to her funeral.' She didn't know how she would have sustained the long walk to the cemetery and back or the ordeal of the burial itself without Davie's presence. He had said scarcely a word, but he had been there.

'How could anyone as sensible and hard-workin' as our Davie have liked a woman like that?' Edith said sourly.

'It was the liveliness of her that fascinated him. There were few folk like her in the Vennel.' The memory of Anna, vivacious and laughing, a butterfly amid the grey life they had shared, came to Lessie so strongly that she felt the tears brimming into her eyes. 'Oh Edith, I wish I'd gone to her when she sent that message. She must've visited the – whoever it was – by that time. She waited till Molly's afternoon off and she trusted me to go and look after her. And instead I stayed on in the shop while she—'

'You werenae to know. You said yourself she was aye sendin' for you an' there was never anythin' wrong when you got there.'

'But to turn my back on her the one time she really needed someone – and I never got to pay her the twenty shillings I owed her!'

'For goodness' sake, what would she care about twenty shillings with the money she had? An' I'd be grateful if you'd not cry over my good silk jacket. I loaned it to you on the understandin' that you'd look after it.'

'That wasn't what I meant.' Lessie mopped at her eyes fiercely, fingered the bodice of the jacket and was relieved to find it free of moisture, then took a mouthful of tea. 'I was in her debt. That's another reason why I must see to Dorothea.'

'Sometimes, our Lessie, I wonder about you, I really do!'

Lessie managed a shaky laugh. Edith's complete lack of understanding was better for her at that moment than all the sympathy in the world.

'And what had Murdo to say about another wean to feed and clothe and look after?'

'He'll not have to find the money. I told you, the solicitor's going to pay for her keep until – until something else can be decided.'

'And when'll that be?'

'We'll have to wait and see,' Lessie said, then held up a finger in warning as the door opened and the children came tumbling into the room. Ian was in front as usual, his red hair leading the rest like a pennant, with Jess and Dorothea hand in hand behind him, Jess towing the older girl along possessively. Peter, nine years of age and thin and gangly, came last, standing by the door, cap in hand, until his mother motioned him to a chair by the window. He was at the best school Edith could afford and she was continually boasting about his cleverness. Lessie still felt sorry for him. But at least he had graduated from velvet suits and sailor suits; today he wore a Norfolk jacket and knickerbockers with long black stockings.

She dispensed biscuits, noting how Peter, after a sidelong glance at his mother, passed by the sugary biscuits and chose a plain one, then returned to his chair and perched on the edge, carefully catching crumbs in the palm of his free hand. Ian, on the hearthrug, crunched his way through his biscuit, then wet a finger and used it to snare the fallen crumbs which he then transferred to his mouth. Edith watched, scandalised, almost chewing her lips into mince in her efforts to keep quiet, and Lessie was glad that her sister had come to Cathcart Street to look after the children instead of seeing to them in the spotless, crumb-free house she and Peter shared with Aunt Marion.

Jess, who had taken charge of Dorothea since her arrival, selected a biscuit for her and sat her down in a chair before attending to herself.

'Isn't that a good wee lassie,' Edith said with a side-long glance at Ian, and Jess smirked. Already, halfway into her third year, she knew how to impress grown-ups.

Ten minutes later Edith put her cup down and announced that she and Peter would have to go. Her son immediately rose and thanked Lessie for the biscuit, then pulled on his cap and opened the kitchen door for his mother.

When she had seen the two of them out, Lessie went back into the kitchen and began to gather up the cups. Out of the corner of her eye she saw Jess slip from her chair and go over to Dorothea, who was clutching the beautiful doll she had brought with her on the night of Anna's death, when Lessie had carried her home. The doll went everywhere with her. Jess laid possessive hands on it, and after only a token resistance Dorothea let it go without protest, the corners of her mouth turning down. Lessie almost told her daughter give it back, then decided to hold her tongue. Dorothea must now learn to live with other children and fend for herself.

Jess was on her way back to her chair when five-year-old Ian quietly intercepted her and relieved her of the doll. He returned it to Dorothea, who took it, beaming grate-fully. Then he went back to the hearthrug, impervious to his young sister's murderous glare. It was all Lessie could do to keep herself from giving her son a hug.

In the evening, Davie Kirkwood, still in his working clothes, walked from Port Glasgow back to the Greenock graveyard to stand alone and unseen before the newly filled-in grave. A spray of late-blooming rambler roses, picked by Lessie from the back garden of Anna's little house, lay on the fresh mound, the small, tight many-petalled crimson blossoms and green leaves brilliant against the black earth that hid Anna from his sight. For a long time he stood motionless, listening to the sound of the birds in the trees, the catch of air in his lungs. He well knew the mother plant those roses had come from, remembered Anna only weeks before, in white blouse and green skirt, standing on the lawn, framed by the roses, smiling at him.

Davie stooped and snapped off one of the flowers, heedless of the thorns that plunged into his fingers and drew drops of crimson blood that drained at once into the earth. Carefully he stowed it into his pocket then turned away and walked back to Port Glasgow, to his lodgings. There, he put the flower into a large book to preserve it. Then at last he wept, lying on his bed with the sheet crammed into his mouth so that nobody else in the rooming house could hear him. It was the first time he had cried in his adult life, and it would be the last, for nothing as terrible as the loss of Anna could happen to him again.

He wept until he was drained and empty, then lay motionless, staring unseeingly at the mould-spotted wall inches from his face. The only woman he had ever loved, could ever love, was gone for ever. He couldn't believe that Anna could have died without him knowing it, sensing it. He had seen her just a week before, made love to her, held her and kissed her and laughed with her. They had arranged, when he left, that he would visit her in another ten days' time. Davie would have made it sooner, but Anna had insisted.

'I'll not stand in the way of your work,' she had said, her soft hand cupping his face. He could feel the touch of her fingers now as clearly as he had then; rolling over, he bit fiercely into the grimy sheet to hold back the animal screams of loss and rage that wanted to wrench themselves out of his aching throat.

After a long time he got off the bed and ferreted in the depths of a small cupboard until he found a box. Inside, nestling against a bed of white silk, lay two gold and ruby cuff links. Davie tipped them out into his hand, remembering the day Anna had given them to him, ignoring his protests.

'But when could I ever wear these?'

'When you've made your fortune and we're together

you'll wear them.' She had kissed him fiercely. 'And you'll give me a necklace to match them. We'll make a pretty pair, you and me. Keep them, Davie, they're a pledge between us. If I ever break my word to you, you can sell them and use the money. But I never will.'

Davie's head thumped as he stared down at the expensive baubles. She had broken her pledge. She had gone away from him, so far away that he would never, even if he travelled to the other end of the earth, set eyes on her again. He didn't need anything, other than the rose he had taken from her funeral spray, to remind him of what he had lost. Slowly he turned the cuff links over and over, a sense of purpose beginning to seep into the great hollow space the tears had left behind. All that he had left in the world now was his work and his ambitions – and deep resentment against the man who had possessed Anna more completely than he, Davie, had ever possessed her. Andrew Warren had been her protector until the end. He owned her even in death; Lessie had told him that Anna's death was brought about by a miscarriage, and the child that had killed her had been Warren's child, he knew that. She would have told him if it had been his. He wished to God that it had been his. Somehow, he would have managed to look after her, look after them both. She would have been alive today if the child had only been his.

He clenched his fist, heedless of the pain of the cuff links biting into his palm and fingers. The links, bought with Warren's money, would be sold; the money raised would be used to build a few more steps on the ladder. If it took the rest of his life, Davie Kirkwood was going to become as powerful and as wealthy as Andrew Warren. And then they would see which of them was the better man!

By the beginning of 1905 it was clear to the whole family that Barbara Kirkwood was dying. A ghost of her former energetic self, she was now bed-bound, racked by an increasingly troublesome cough that more often than not stained her handkerchiefs with red spots and splashes, or tossing in the grip of fever. There was nothing they could do but keep her as comfortable as possible.

Her husband insisted on taking over in the evenings when he was at home, growling that he didn't want the house to be cluttered up with folk when he was in it. He had aged a great deal in the past few months, Lessie thought. The belligerence had gone and his shoulders sagged, weighted down by worry. Barbara answered when he spoke to her, submitted to his ministrations when there was nobody else to tend to her, and steadfastly maintained the barrier that had long since been built up between them.

Thomasina cried when they tried to keep her from her mother, and Barbara seemed to be more at peace if her youngest child was in the room with her. Davie visited frequently, but always when his father was out of the house. He too had aged over the past winter, aged and hardened. The swift, youthful smile had gone and his mouth was stern. Somehow he had found the money to invest in better and more modern machinery; the engineering workshop was prospering and gaining a good name among local businessmen.

Joseph, who disliked sickness, had taken himself off to live with some woman down by the docks. 'And good riddance,' Edith said with feeling when she told Lessie the news.

The sisters sat in the kitchen one cold February day, Lessie with a shopping bag full of mending by her side. The children were growing fast and she was hard put to it to keep them in clothes; now that Ian was at school he came home day after day with torn trousers, scuffed boots, elbows poking through holes in his jerseys, and she seemed to be for ever darning for him. Now she knew the true meaning of the caustic Scottish term referring to someone who had prospered and tried to deny his roots: 'I kenned him when his arse wis hingin' oot his troosers.' Ian hadn't quite reached that stage yet, but only because so far Lessie's needle had managed to keep him respectable.

She smiled at the thought, and was about to explain the smile to Edith when a sudden frightened cry of

'Mam!' from the bedroom sent the work in her hands flying to the floor as she jumped up.

'Dear God,' said Edith as Lessie, her heart in her mouth, ran ahead of her sister to the bedroom.

'Mam!' Thomasina, almost hysterical, was trying to pull away from Barbara's grip on her arm. The sick woman was sitting bolt upright in bed, and as her older daughters appeared together in the doorway, her sunken eyes fixed on them and she said in a strong accusing voice, 'Look at her! D'ye see whit ye've done, Archie? Look at yer new bairn – she's no' right in the head!' Weak as she was, she shook poor Thomasina until the girl's head bobbled on her neck. 'Aye, I can tell even now that she's no' right. An' whose fault is it? Yours, Archie Kirkwood!' The words came out in a spray of saliva, the gaze fixed on Lessie full of such hatred that she felt iced water dripping down the length of her spine. Edith, crammed into the narrow doorway with her, shivered and said placatingly, 'Mam, it's all right now. You're safe—'

'Don't you stand there an' deny it, man. You mind thon night ye beat me so bad I couldnae even drag myself tae the bed. I know ye mind it well enough. Ye let me lie there till the mornin', ye drunken bastard!' The cawing voice had dropped to a hiss that was even more frightening than the shouting. Thomasina, still held prisoner, sagged at the knees and fell half on and half off the bed, whimpering. 'Ye kenned I wis carryin' this bairn but ye beat me a' the same. An' now look at yer daughter. Look at her! God damn ye for all eternity, Archie Kirkwood, an' God forgive ye for what ye've done, for I never will. Never!' said Barbara, then the cough came tearing up from her diseased chest, into her throat and her mouth, choking her, silencing her with strings of red-slashed mucus.

As she released Thomasina and sank back onto the pillow, choking and gasping, the paralysis that had held Lessie drained away. She ran to her mother, lifting her up, supporting her, reaching for the pile of clean rags that was kept by the side of the bed. As she soothed and rocked and mopped at Barbara, she was aware that Edith had lifted Thomasina, who sagged against her, sobbing,

'I've been a bad girl, Edie. I've wet in my drawers but I couldnae help it.'

'I know ye couldnae, hen. Come on, now, let's you and me go through tae the kitchen an' get you nice an' dry an' comfy.' Lessie had never known Edith be so gentle and comforting.

When the paroxysm was over, her mother looked up at her with frightened eyes. 'I was havin' a bad dream, Lessie. I woke mysel' up with my shoutin'. What did I say?'

Lessie tossed the stained rag into the bucket kept by the bed for soiled cloths, dipped a fresh clean cloth in a bowl of cool water, and wiped her mother's face gently. 'You were just dreaming.'

'What did I say?' Then, as Lessie hesitated, Barbara said more insistently, 'D'ye hear me? I'm askin' ye what I said?'

There was no sense in lying. 'It was about Da beating you when you were carrying Thomasina, and how she came tae be the way she is.'

Barbara's gaze was vexed. 'So you know now? You and Edith both?'

'Mam, why did you never tell us the truth of it?'

Her mother's lips firmed into a thin line as she held her face up to be dried. 'A good wife doesnae talk tae folk about her man,' she said when the towel had been lifted away.

Edith, who came in at that moment with a mop to clean the puddle from the floor, asked in disbelief, 'Not even tae her own daughters?'

'No' tae anyone. What goes on between man and wife isnae for anyone else's ears. An' I'd be obliged,' said Barbara with weak dignity, 'if the two o' ye would forget what ye heard an' speak about it tae nob'dy. It's no' your concern.'

'No' our concern? And us havin' tae grow up in this house, wonderin' why ye never looked the road Da was on? If we'd known,' Edith pressed on, swishing the mop across the floor with brisk, self-righteous strokes, 'we'd at least've understood what was wrong between the two o' ye. Nae wonder ye turned from him. Poor wee

Thomasina – that was a terrible, wicked thing he did tae her.'

A weak swipe of Barbara's arm caught her elder daughter across the rump. Edith yelped, more with surprise than pain.

'Haud yer tongue!' Barbara hissed through white lips. 'I'll hae no daughter o' mine miscallin' her ain father in my hearin'!'

A final terrifying haemorrhage ended Barbara's life less than a week later. Watching her father standing by the graveside, his big fists clenched on the brim of his black bowler hat, his body wearing his best suit as clumsily as a snail in a crab's shell, Lessie pitied the man. If, as her mother had believed, it was his drunken cruelty that had robbed Thomasina of her right to a normal existence, he had done a terrible thing. But he had surely suffered from it ever since, not only by watching his youngest daughter grow up to become half-woman half-child, but also through his wife's rejection and her drinking. Thinking back to her childhood, to the days when her father had been the drinker and her mother strictly teetotal, she realised that it was Thomasina's birth, and the discovery that she was retarded, that had put a stop to Archie Kirkwood's drinking and at the same time started his wife on the same downward path.

Back at the house, Archie sat uncomfortably on the edge of the chair he had used all his married life and stared into the fire as his two eldest daughters bustled about dispensing tea and sandwiches, cakes and biscuits they had prepared the day before. Thomasina, bewildered and silent, dragged a low stool over to his side and sat down, clutching her rag doll in her arms. Joseph had attended at the graveside but refused to go back to the house. Barbara's sister Marion, crow-like in black, took the other chair where she could coldly eye the brother-in-law she had never approved of. Davie, silent and uncomfortable, stood by the window, drinking tea and refusing food with curt shakes of the head. Murdo sat bolt upright on a hard chair at the table, running a finger now and again round his tight high collar, trying to make conversation and being ignored by everyone but Lessie, who smiled at him gratefully.

As soon as possible she persuaded Peter and Ian to take Dorothea and Jess down to the back yard to play. They went, Peter obediently and Ian unwillingly, his eyes lingering on a plate that still held some cakes. Thomasina shook her head when Lessie suggested that she should go with them, and slipped a hand into the empty calloused palm that lay on Archie's thigh. His fingers jumped slightly at her touch, and for a moment Lessie thought that he was going to reject the girl's hand, but he didn't, though he didn't clasp it either. Shortly afterwards, Aunt Marion announced that it was time for her to go, and both Murdo and Davie immediately declared their intention of accompanying her to the bus stop.

When Archie and his daughters were alone, Edith said briskly, 'Well now, Da, we'll have to decide what's to be done with—'

She stopped short and nodded significantly at Thomasina, who had rested her head against her father's chair and was half asleep. Her free hand was at her mouth, the thumb jammed between her teeth for comfort. The doll had slipped to her lap and Lessie saw, as she took the chair Aunt Marion had vacated, that the bodice of Thomasina's best dress was tight across her young breasts. As her mother had said several months earlier, the girl's mind might be that of a young child, but her body was sixteen years old, and ripening.

'Aunt Marion's too old for the responsibility, and I'm not in the house much, so we can't take her. Anyway, it wouldnae do for Peter to have her living with us. He's growing up.'

'I could take her, Da,' said Lessie, then thinking of Murdo's reaction she added doubtfully, 'though with Dorry living with us just now, and the shop to see to—'

'There's no need for either o' ye to fuss,' Archie said. He had scarcely spoken since Barbara's death and his voice was gravelly, as though it had atrophied at the back of his throat. 'Thomasina'll bide here, where she belongs.'

'That would be the best idea,' Edith agreed, openly relieved. 'I'll ask around, there's sure to be a decent woman willing to take on the job. A widow, mebbe.'

'What're ye haverin' on aboot?' her father asked rudely, and she flushed.

'I'm talking about someone to see to the house and to Thomasina when you're not here.'

'There'll be no decent widow comin' intae my hoose,' Archie growled. 'I'll see tae things mysel'.'

The sisters gaped at each other, then at their father. 'What?' said Edith at last, faintly.

'I said I'll see tae the lassie, an' tae mysel' and the hoose an' a'.'

'But how can a man see to a lassie like our Thomasina? She's a – she's not a child. There are things that—' Edith floundered, then said, 'Have you gone clean daft?'

'Don't you speak tae me like that!' Although the words were spoken quietly they contained all Archie Kirkwood's old fire and fury. Lessie flinched and dull red rose swiftly to Edith's cheeks. Thomasina slumbered on, her dark head brushing her father's arm, for all the world, Lessie thought, like a child trustfully squatting between the paws of a lion.

'Da, Edith's right. You can't see to everything here and work at the docks as well. Nobody expects you to,' she protested more diplomatically than Edith had.

'I'm leavin' the docks. I've got enough put by, an' I'll manage. I've thought it a' oot, so the two o' ye can mind yer ain business. It's my responsibility,' said Archie Kirkwood, his hand lying idle and open in his youngest daughter's tight grasp, 'an' I'll see tae it!'

15

'Eeny meeny miny MO,
'Sit the bairnie on the PO,
'When he's DONE, wipe his BUM,
'Eeny meeny miny—
'You're it!' The rhyme, yelled out by half a dozen shrill voices, broke up in a shower of giggles and the tight-huddled group of little girls scattered in all directions up and down the street, some dodging round Andrew Warren's knees like foam round a rock.

One of them, arms pumping furiously, heels kicking up behind her, almost bumped into him. A laughing little face was lifted for a moment as she veered to avoid him. She was dressed like the others in a plain smock and long stockings but his heart gave a sudden double thump as he caught a glimpse of wide violet eyes and a grooved scar marring her plump right cheek. He swung round, about to call her name, but she was gone, scurrying into a close like a fieldmouse into its hole among the grasses. All the little girls were gone, except for one wee creature who toiled past Andrew screaming, 'It's no' fair, so it's no'! I'm aye the one that's het. It shouldnae be my turn!'

Then she too disappeared and Cathcart Street was empty apart from a knot of smaller children hunkered down on the pavement, intent on some game of their own. They stared up at the tall well-dressed man as he passed, gaped at his brown face, tanned by a sun much stronger than the sun they were used to in Greenock, then went back to their own business as he, in his turn, entered a close.

Anna's friend Lessie was only a name in his memory;

187

he thought that he had forgotten her face, but remembered it as soon as she opened the door. She had put on some weight but she was still slight, and the little worry line between her well-marked brows was familiar.

Her face flushed at the sight of him. 'Mr Warren. I heard you were back. Will you come in?' She opened the door and Andrew walked past her into the house.

'The door at the end there,' she said, then followed him into a kitchen that smelled pleasantly of baking and soup and the scent from a bowl of fragrant pinks standing on a small table by the net-covered window.

'I hope I've not come at a bad time. I went to the shop and the woman there told me where I could find you.'

'Sit down, Mr Warren.' She smoothed her already tidy fair hair with the automatic gesture all women used when they were embarrassed or confused and began to fuss round the large table in the middle of the room, gathering up lists and papers, closing a large ledger, tucking the chair she had been using back under the table. Her hands moved competently, restoring order with every gesture. 'I'm sorry about the mess. I've got the other small shopkeepers to agree to buy in bulk from the wholesalers and this is the day I make up the lists.'

'A sensible idea. Was it your own?'

She ducked her head in a nod. 'It saves us all money, and it works out well, though some of them weren't sure at first, with me being a woman.' A smile crinkled her eyes and banished the worry lines. 'Most of them have changed their minds now, though.' Then, obviously deciding to take the bull by the horns, she perched herself on the chair opposite his, on the other side of the gleaming range, and clasped her hands in her lap. 'You've come about Dorry. Dorothea.'

'I think I saw her out there. She looked happy.'

'She's settled down well. Poor wee lass, it was hard on her, losing her mother like that. There was nobody else to take her in, so I thought—'

'I'm very grateful to you. My solicitor's been looking after things, I believe.'

'Oh yes, he's been generous, but we'd have taken her anyway,' she added hurriedly. 'We didnae do it for the money.'

'Mrs . . .' he hesitated for a moment before recalling the name the solicitor had given him, 'Mrs Carswell, can you tell me what happened to Anna?'

Lessie bit her lip, then said evenly, 'She'd a miscarriage, Mr Warren. That's what everyone was told.' She glanced down at her knotted hands then said in a rush of words, as though wanting to get rid of them quickly, 'But to my mind you deserve to know the truth of it. She must have gone to one of those women that can stop bairns from being born. If I'd known what was in her mind I'd not have let her do it. But—'

'She was carrying a child?' Andrew interrupted, his voice harsh enough to jerk her bowed head up. 'How far on was she?'

'About three months.'

'She must have been more than that!'

When Lessie shook her head he got to his feet, bewildered, his mind reaching back to the previous summer when he had been too busy to visit Anna other than brief calls to see his daughter. He lifted a fold of the curtain, his hand mahogany brown against the snowy net, and stared out at the houses opposite without seeing them or hearing the children's voices; seeing instead the plea in Anna's eyes on that last day, hearing her voice as she begged him to make love to her. Because she was with child to some other man? He knew a sudden surge of anger, then remembered that whatever the truth of the matter, Anna was dead and gone and his main concern now was their child.

'Mr Warren?' Lessie said behind him, her voice uncertain. He turned to her, glad for the moment that with his back to the window his face was in shadow. 'About Dorothea, how old is she now?'

'Four past. She'll be five next March.' Andrew remembered how much he had wanted to acknowledge Dorothea as his own child. The wanting was still there, but for the sake of his wife and all three of his children it was impossible. 'Would you be willing to keep her here, raise her with your own children?'

'Of course. We feel as if she's one of our own as it is.'

'I think it's the best way, at least for the time being. I'll tell my solicitor to increase the payments he makes.'

Colour rose in her cheeks and her chin tilted sharply. 'There's no need. The shop's doing well enough and my husband has a good job at the shipyard.'

'I'd not expect him or you to find the money for an extra child. It's all I can do for her just now.'

The door from the close opened and two voices shaky with laughter squeaked their way along the passage. 'Eeny meeny miny MO, sit the bairnie on the PO—' Then the kitchen door burst open and they surged in, a smaller fair-haired girl followed by Dorothea, pushing and jostling at each other.

'Mammy,' said the little one as they came in, and Dorothea too chimed in, 'Mammy, can we—'

'For any favour,' Lessie shot an embarrassed glance at her visitor, 'will you stop saying that silly rhyme!'

The little girls had already fallen into an abashed silence at the sight of Andrew, staring at him round-eyed, moving automatically to the shelter of Lessie's skirts. She took a small arm in each hand and urged them forward. 'This is Mr Warren. Say good afternoon to him and let him see that you're not the pair of tinks he thinks you are.' Then she said levelly to Andrew, 'This is Dorry – Dorothea – and this is Jess.'

The younger girl rammed a thumb in her mouth and battled her way back into her mother's skirt, but Dorothea came forward, her vivid eyes fixed on Andrew's face, a little puzzled frown tucking her dark brows together. His heart turned over. She was Anna in miniature; although her hair was dark like his, it still held a chestnut sheen, a memory of her mother's glowing russet hair. Andrew achingly wanted her to remember him, but at her age memory was short and he knew that it was best for her to know him only as a visitor. Her life was here now, in this house with the Carswell family. He held out his hand. 'Good afternoon, Dorothea.'

She put her petal-soft fingers in his for a moment, then withdrew them all too soon. 'Good afternoon, Mister Warren,' she said, and the formal title, spoken by the child who had once run to him and hugged him and called him Papa, hurt almost unbearably.

'I must go,' he said abruptly, picking up his hat and stick. 'I've business with your brother, Mrs Carswell. I'm hoping that he'll be willing to help me to modernise the machinery in the refinery.' At the door he paused and asked, 'May I visit from time to time, to see the child?'

'Of course, and don't fret about Dorry. She's well and happy.'

'And in the best hands,' said Andrew, and strode out into the August sunshine before she could see the tears that were threatening.

Murdo grumbled at first over his wife's promise to keep Dorothea indefinitely, but a generous increase in the payments that were delivered regularly silenced him. A few weeks later, returning home from the shipyard to find Andrew Warren in the house, he flushed with embarrassment, keenly aware of the working clothes he wore. Awkward, ill at ease, he sat on an upright chair by the table, since Andrew was comfortably settled in the chair by the fire that was Murdo's by rights, staring at his hands and answering briefly when Warren spoke to him. To his relief their visitor left soon after.

When Lessie came back from seeing him out, Murdo had reclaimed his chair and had the newspaper open.

'I see those suffrage women've been makin' themselves noticed in Parliament again. By God, Lessie, I'm glad ye've got more sense than tae think like them.'

'I do think like them,' she snapped, 'but I've got too much to do to go shouting out at meetings.'

'That's just as well. If I ever hear o' ye makin' a fool o' yersel' like that—'

'It's not only women who can make fools of themselves. You might have been more civil to that man, Murdo.'

'I'll decide who I'll be civil tae in my own house,' he said without looking up, his voice muffled.

She bit back the retort that it wasn't his own house. Murdo hated to be reminded that he lacked complete financial control over his own wife. He had his good points, but all the same, Lessie thought, it was men like him who were making it impossible for women to gain the vote. 'I told you he asked to visit regularly to see Dorothea and I said yes. He's surely got the right to see his own child.'

'I don't see why. She doesnae know who he is. She thinks I'm her father now.'

'Och, Murdo, she's still his daughter. Would you not want to see Jess if you were in his position?'

'I'd no' farm Jess out tae strangers,' Murdo said. 'Anyway, he'll only take the lassie away when he's good an' ready, an' then ye'll break yer heart over it. Ye're storing up trouble for yerself, my girl.'

'He'll not take her. How can he, with a wife an' two children at home?'

'You wait an' see,' Murdo said darkly, and buried himself in his newspaper with a great rustling of pages.

Lessie fetched a knife, ran water into a basin, and began to peel the potatoes. Ever since she had heard from Edith that the Warrens were home – Mrs Warren as beautiful as ever and the twins grown out of all recognition and quite the little lady and gentleman, Edith had gushed – she had been worried in case Dorothea, who had settled into the Carswell household with very little difficulty, was going to be uprooted and sent off to live somewhere else among strangers. She was a happy little girl, undemanding – unlike Jess, who was spoiled by her father – and easy to look after. Lessie had grown to love her and to dread the thought of losing her. It had been a great relief to her when Andrew Warren decided to leave the little girl where she was. Although Murdo complained now and again about being expected to look after other people's brats he had accepted Dorothea and to Lessie's relief he treated her as one of his own.

The thought made her feel guilty about her nagging over his attitude towards Andrew Warren's presence in the flat. Of the three children in Murdo's household, only one was his. It took a special man to care for other men's children. She put the knife aside, dried her hands on her apron, and went over to kiss him.

'For God's sake, woman, what's that for?'

'You're a good man, Murdo Carswell.'

'An' you're gettin' dafter than ever,' he grunted, putting the paper down and brushing her aside so that he could get to the sink. Watching him rolling up his sleeves and grasping the bar of soap, Lessie recalled that a few years earlier he would have seized the excuse to hold her and kiss her and even suggest that they retire to the box bed in the alcove for a wee while before the children came in from their street games. But somewhere along the way, busy with the shop and the shipyard and the house and the children, the magic that had been between them in the early days of their marriage had ebbed away. She supposed that it was only to be expected. It might well have come about between herself and Donald, had he lived longer.

That, she thought as she retrieved the knife from the brown water in the bowl and got on with her work, was what growing older was all about.

Since his wife's death, Archie Kirkwood had taken to visiting his daughter's shop in the Vennel twice a week to buy food. For one thing, it provided a walk for him and Thomasina, and for another he reckoned that he might as well benefit his own flesh and blood with his money than a stranger. But the main reason, the need to see Lessie frequently, was one of the many secrets Archie kept to himself. Edith was uncomfortably like her mother as she had been in the days since Thomasina's birth, grim-mouthed and unforgiving. Lessie, on the other hand, was a reminder of Barbara in the early days when Archie had met and courted her. She too had been slim and fair, kindly, gentle, quick to smile. That was why Archie had started to call on her after Donald Hamilton's death; she would never know, for wild horses wouldn't have dragged the admission from him, how much he had treasured those peaceful hours in the damp room in the Vennel, away from Barbara's continual silent condemnation. He had missed them after her marriage; he had no reason to believe that Murdo Carswell was a bad husband to Lessie, but from the first there had been something about the man that Archie mistrusted and disliked. He didn't feel comfortable with his new son-in-law.

But now that he and Thomasina were on their own, Archie hankered for brief contact with Lessie again, and his visits to the shop provided them. He took comfort in her cheerfulness, her gentleness, the smile that lit up her thin face.

'You know that Ian would be glad to bring the food to you, don't you, Da?' she asked, all unknowing, as she packed the basket neatly in that deft, economical way she had. 'You don't have to come all the way down here every time.'

'Don't want me an' the lass in yer shop, is that it?' Archie barked at her.

Her eyes were hurt when she looked up from her work. 'You know fine that that's not what I mean! You look tired and I just thought it would be easier on you if Ian carried the shopping. He's used to it now that he works for me on Saturdays.'

'I can manage fine.' He fumbled in his pocket and produced some coins. 'An' ye can gie me the right change – I'll no' take charity just because I'm no' at the docks any more. I can afford tae pay my way. An' add on the price o' her sweeties.' He nodded at Thomasina, who had hurried round to the back of the counter as soon as she preceded him into the shop and was carefully measuring some sweets out of a large glass jar into the scales, her tongue poking out between her teeth as she struggled to measure the right amount. She loved to use the scales.

'I can surely give my wee sister a poke of sweeties now an' then,' Lessie protested.

'No' when your man's out o' work an' no' bringing' a pay intae the hoose. Is there no word o' a job for him yet?'

Lessie bit her lip. 'He's sure to get something soon.'

'He should be helpin' you in here while he's idle.'

194

'He was here earlier. He went after a place he heard about in the Lithgow yard.'

'Oh aye?' said Archie, who had seen his son-in-law idling at a street corner with a group of men not ten minutes earlier. 'I doubt if he'll get it, for the gaffers in Scott's and Lithgow's joiner shops drink together. Any man that falls foul o' one o' them'll no' be taken on by the other.'

'Mebbe Murdo'll be lucky,' Lessie said without much hope.

'He should've kept his tongue atween his teeth an' no' answered the gaffer back. When I was workin' on the docks I'd have nothin' tae dae wi' a man known tae have a temper. They're nothin' but trouble,' Archie said sharply, then turned to Thomasina. 'Come on, you, time we were home.'

'Careful, pet, you're going to have the scales overflowing.' Lessie gently eased the jar from her sister's hands. 'That's right. Now pick up the paper and twist it into a poke the way I showed you.'

Flora, the young girl Lessie had taken on to work in the shop part-time with herself and Elma, sniggered at the sight of a grown woman behaving like a child and was silenced by one look from beneath Archie's lowered brows. Patiently, Lessie helped Thomasina to wrap up the sweets and put them into the shopping bag she carried.

'Will you not come through the back for a cup of tea, Da? You look as though you could do with a bit of a rest before you've to walk back home.'

Archie would dearly have liked to accept, but he had had a bad night and he wasn't feeling well. He was anxious to get home again before the pain that had become a part of his life in the past six months or so came back, so he shook his head and made for the door. Thomasina immediately scurried after him, pushing her hand into his, turning to wave to her sister with the shopping bag, which almost hit another customer in the face.

'Come on!' Archie said, then added placatingly as his youngest daughter's lower lip trembled, 'It's time for Bonny's tea.'

At mention of the budgerigar he had bought for her a year earlier, Thomasina brightened and trotted happily by his side, stopping now and then to fish a sweet out of her bag and pop it into her mouth. She had chosen raspberry balls and frequently, as she sucked and chattered, a ribbon of pink saliva drooled down her chin. Each time, Archie put down his heavy bag and wiped her mouth with a handkerchief kept specially for the purpose. Thomasina's mother had always kept the girl immaculate and since she had gone, it had become Archie's self-imposed task in life to make sure that though her poor head might be in disarray, Thomasina's outer shell was always beyond reproach.

It was a task that had become increasingly harder in the four years and two months since Barbara's death. He knew that Lessie would help if asked, and so would Edith, though in her case he would have to suffer comments about her knowing fine and well that he could never manage and it only being a matter of time before he discovered the obvious for himself. But he had taken the task on for life when Barbara was forced to lay it down, and he would die before he would seek help from anyone. Aye, he thought grimly, he'd die first.

As they drew nearer home, Thomasina skipped ahead. Some people turned to stare at her while others, those who knew the Kirkwoods, either smiled kindly or turned their heads away, pretending that they hadn't seen the 'daftie'. Archie opened his mouth to call her back, but just then the pain he had hoped to beat home swooped down on him, hammering at his chest, and he gasped and put down the bag. He leaned against a wall, perspiration breaking out on his forehead. If he waited for a minute, if he rode the pain, it would go. It always did, though it shamed him to ride it when his instincts told him to fight it, to force it out of his body, out of his life. It had no right to be there, no right at all.

'Da!' Thomasina was back, tugging at his hand, her breath on his face sweet with raspberry. 'Come on, Da, Bonny's hungry!'

'Wait a . . . a minute,' Archie said through stiff lips. She was fretting him, making it difficult for the pain to go. But at last it began to ease as he knew it would, and he was able to pull himself away from the wall and pick up the bag. Not far to go now, he told himself, gearing up weakened muscles for the task of getting home.

He took the stairs to the house carefully while Thomasina, who had raced ahead, hung over the stair rail watching him, impatient to get indoors to feed her pet. Toiling up one step at a time, one hand gripping at the banister, Archie remembered the far-away days when he had scaled these stairs without even noticing them. Old age was a right bugger, he thought as he reached the landing and felt in his jacket pocket for the key.

By the time he got into the kitchen, Thomasina was at the cage, spilling birdseed everywhere in her haste to fill Bonny's dish. The bird chirruped a greeting then watched her, his head cocked. Archie sank into his chair and rested for a while before getting up again to clean up the spilled grain, unpack the bag and put the groceries away, and make a meal for them both. Afterwards Thomasina helped him to wash the dishes and played with her doll while Archie read the paper he had bought.

'That Lloyd George's set the cat among the dogs wi' his new taxes,' he said with dour amusement. 'The rich dinnae mind payin' for new weapons, but the bit aboot payin' for a pension for the old folk sticks in their fat craws. Hell mend them, for I'll never see their precious pensions.'

Thomasina, buttoning her doll's coat the wrong way, paid no heed. Watching her downbent head, Archie was shocked by a wave of love for her, almost as intense as the earlier pain that had gripped at his heart. In the past four years he had come to know Thomasina well, well enough to realise that he could never leave her to fend for herself. He couldn't bear to think of her in the workhouse, or even dependent on her sisters for charity. Edith had pointed out that the girl could perhaps manage to hold down a post as a kitchen maid but Archie would have none of it. His wee lassie would never have to slave morning to night for rich folk that cared nothing for her. Besides, who would protect her? Her mind might be weak but her body was mature and she was prettier than either of her sisters. The thought of a man taking advantage of Thomasina's trusting nature made him want to spew.

He knew that he wouldn't be able to hide the chest pains from his other daughters for much longer. He hadn't bothered going to see a doctor – he hadn't the money to spare, for one thing, and for another he knew well enough what he would be told. He knew, too, that he wouldn't be able to look after Thomasina for much longer.

It was time, Archie decided as he sat there listening to the child-woman crooning to her doll, to do something about it. Time to put his plan into operation. It had been forming in his head for a long time now, since he had first noticed the growing intensity and frequency of the crippling attacks. His heart, damn it to everlasting hell for its weakness, was going to give up on him, but nothing and nobody decided things for Archie Kirkwood. He, and not his heart, would make the final decision.

He had pondered over the rights and wrongs of what he planned to do, thought long and hard about the alternatives, and had made up his mind. And that was all there was to it. He cleared his throat, rustled the newspaper, and turned to another page, strongly aware of the warmth of Thomasina's body against his leg as she sprawled on the floor with her doll.

'Time for bed,' he said gruffly when he had read every single word, even the advertisements. Thomasina got up obediently and went into the bedroom, reappearing half an hour later with her nightgown on and a hairbrush in her hand. She gave it to him then whisked round and sat on the floor again, her back to him. His hard-skinned hands loosened her dark brown hair and he brushed it until it crackled and shone. After that he wet a flannel and washed and dried her face.

'I want juice,' she said, as she did every night.

'Aye, ye'll get yer juice. Dae I ever send ye tae yer bed wi'oot it?' He fetched the bottle of lemonade, half filled a mug, then after only a moment's hesitation he reached into the back of the cupboard, up on the top shelf, and brought out a small brown bottle. Uncorking it, he shook several drops into the drink, then a few more. When he turned round Thomasina took the mug from him and drank its contents down, trusting as always, apparently unaware of any change in the taste. Archie sat and watched, hands fisted tightly on his knees.

'Night night, Da.' She put the glass down, wiped her mouth on her sleeve before he could stop her, and came to kiss him, her lips cold on his stubbled cheek from the drink. He held her for a moment then let her go. When she had padded off to bed he washed her glass and lit his pipe.

An hour passed, then another, before he tapped the pipe out on the range, collecting the dottle from the bowl in one calloused hand and brushing it into the glowing coals that had become the only source of light in the room now that it was almost dark outside. He lit a candle and went into the bedroom; Thomasina lay on her side, the bedclothes up to her waist, her hands clasped about her doll. He bent over her and saw that her eyes weren't quite closed; the whites gleamed through a slight opening. He put a hand on her cheek. It was still warm, but soon it would cool and harden.

Carefully, Archie Kirkwood arranged his daughter's silky hair over the pillow, remembering how he had delighted in doing the same thing with Barbara's long hair when they first married. He went back into the kitchen, tiptoeing, although no amount of noise would rouse Thomasina again. The bird cheeped at him, rustling along its perch. He checked the cage to make sure that there was ample seed and water.

'Mrs Connelly'll be along in time tae see tae ye, never fear, Bonny,' he told the bird. The motherly woman who lived across the landing had fallen into the habit of taking Thomasina into her house once a week to teach her to bake. Archie knew fine that it was just the woman's kindly way of giving him a wee while on his own, but much as he hated charity he had given in. It was good for the lassie to have a woman's company now and then, and

Thomasina loved her baking lessons. Wrapped in a big pinny Mrs Connelly kept specially for her, she sprinkled flour and mixed in water and currants, returning home each time bearing an apple pie or a plate of fluffy spicy scones. Archie always pretended to believe that she had made them all by herself.

The front door wasn't locked; Mrs Connelly would be able to get in when there was no answer to her knock in the morning. Archie was sorry to give the woman so much trouble, but he knew that she had a good, sensible head on her shoulders. She wouldn't run off in a squawking panic as some folk might.

He took out the small bottle of whisky he had been saving and uncorked it, then stopped, the bottle tilted over the glass Thomasina had used. He put it down, picked up the lemonade bottle instead, tilted it in its turn, hesitated once more then, suddenly angry with this indecision at a time when he had made the greatest decision of his life, he put the lemonade bottle away, poured out a generous amount of whisky, added a further generous amount of laudanum from the brown bottle, and drank deep. The spirit burned its way down his gullet and into his stomach, leaving in its trail a satisfying glow that he had long denied himself, but never forgotten. He drank again, emptied the glass, put it down by the laudanum bottle, then blew out the candle and settled back in his fireside chair, his eyes on the pale square of the window, and waited for the silence and the peace to claim him.

'The selfish old bastard that he was!' Edith said fiercely on the following afternoon. Her eyes were dry, and blazing with vindictive anger. 'Imagine what poor Mam would have said if she'd known about the polis coming round and all the neighbours gossiping. He might have thought about what this would all do to the rest of us. I don't care one whit about him, but to kill poor wee defenceless Thomasina the way he did—'

'That's enough, Edith!' Lessie's voice was too loud, she knew that. It clanged through her father's kitchen like a cracked, ugly bell. Murdo put a restraining hand on her arm as her sister's head whipped round, her face blotchy with rage.

'You're surely not going to condone what he did? It was murder!'

'He didnae want tae leave Thomasina alone. She'd already lost Mam; he did what he thought had to be done.' Lessie's fingers dug into the high back of the chair – her father's chair. He and Thomasina were gone from the flat, carried downstairs in wooden boxes, past staring, whispering neighbours. Davie, ashen-faced, had gone with them to make arrangements with the undertaker.

'The man was wrong in the head! We should never have let him keep Thomasina. We should have taken her from him. If I'd only known—'

Lessie turned so sharply that she banged against the birdcage. It rocked violently and Bonny clung to his perch as Murdo moved swiftly to steady the stand. She kept going and didn't stop until she was in the bedroom, the door closed behind her.

The window pane was cool and hard against her palms. It was a sunny day and the sky was blue. A knot of women stood below her at a closemouth in the opposite building, arms folded, mouths busy. Every now and again one of them turned to stare up at the house where Archie Kirkwood had killed himself and his daft daughter. Lessie stared back without seeing their inquisitive eyes, their clacking mouths.

When someone tapped softly on the door she ignored it. It opened, and she turned, steeling herself to face her sister.

'She's gone, stormed out in a temper,' Murdo said, closing the door behind him. 'We should go too. The bairns'll be home from the school soon.'

'You go and see to them,' Lessie told him, walking to the bed, sitting on it, stroking the pillow that still held the dent made by Thomasina's head.

'Lessie, come on. There's no sense in stayin' here.'

'I'll be home in a wee while.'

'D'you want me to stay with you?'

Yes, she wanted him to stay with her. She wanted, in

this house of death, to be held and comforted and told that somehow everything was going to be all right. But more than anything, she wanted that comfort to be given freely, without her having to beg for it. So she said, carefully, 'Suit yourself.'

'Aye, well, the bairns'll need to find somebody at home. I'd best go. You'll not be long?'

Lessie shook her head without looking up at him. The door opened and closed and she heard his feet carrying him away from her along the oilcloth in the hall, then the outer door opened and closed and he was gone.

She picked up Thomasina's pillow and folded her arms tightly round it. 'Oh, my poor wee innocent lassie,' she whispered into the cold material that still smelled of Thomasina's hair. 'Oh, Da!'

Then the tears came, and she cried and cried for her sister, who had never been allowed to know what life was about, and for her father and the terrible anguish he had had to suffer alone. And for herself, because Murdo had gone home to see to the children and she had only a pillow for comfort.

16

'He can't have gone! He can't!' Jess's voice was tremulous, her blue eyes glittering with unshed tears. 'My daddy wouldn't go away and leave me!'

'He's left all of us.' Lessie fought to keep her own voice flat and emotionless. Inside she was quivering with shock and outrage and a terrible sense of shame, but she would have died rather than let the three children know that. Waiting for them to come home from school, she had been working hard at forcing her own emotions away so that she could confront her children when the time came, and tell them calmly that Murdo had walked out of their lives.

Jess started to sob. It was Dorothea, the puckered scar standing out against her sudden pallor, who put an arm round her. Ian, silent and ashen-faced until then, stepped forward to face his mother, his voice belligerent. 'It's your fault!'

'Ian!'

'It is. It's your fault. You were too busy with the shop to think about how he felt after he lost his job.' His thirteen-year-old voice was breaking; it see-sawed up and down comically but Lessie didn't feel like laughing. His eyes, Donald's eyes, were hard as they held hers.

'Hold your tongue!'

'You didn't care about how he felt. I know you didn't. He told me. Now he's gone away and it's all your—'

For the first time in his life, Lessie hit her son. She hit him hard, all her anger and grief behind the blow, swinging stiff-armed from the shoulder. He was the same height as she was now and her open palm caught him

203

squarely across the face, rocking him back, jerking his face away from her, turning off the flow of words. He stumbled and fell against the corner of the table, then steadied himself. Sheer shock had stopped Jess's crying; she and Dorothea stared, wide-eyed and appalled, at the red mark burning across Ian's face.

There was a moment's silence in the room before Ian turned and blundered towards the door, tore it open, and went into the hall.

'Ian, come back here!'

The outer door banged and she ran to open it again. 'Ian!'

'He's off down the street as though a band of thieves were after him,' said Andrew Warren mildly from the close. 'If I hadn't given him right of way on the steps I think he'd have carried me along with him.' Then his voice sharpened. 'Is there something amiss? D'you want me to chase after him?'

'No. Best leave him.'

She sagged for a moment against the doorframe and Warren put a hand on her shoulder. 'What is it?'

'You'd best come in before the neighbours hear me, though they'll know soon enough.' She led him into the kitchen where the two girls still stood, clinging to each other, Jess's face streaked with tears.

'Go into your bedroom for a wee while,' Lessie told them, and as they went, Andrew's eyes followed Dorothea with the hunger that Lessie had come to know well. Then as the door closed and they were alone, she said flatly, 'Murdo – my husband – he's left us.'

His face went blank with shock, then he asked, 'D'you have any whisky in the house?'

She nodded towards a cupboard. 'I'd as soon have tea, myself.'

'You can have both.' Andrew waited until she had made tea and poured two cups, then he added a generous dose of whisky to her cup. She sipped, and grimaced.

'It'll do you good. D'you want me to fetch someone – a neighbour, or your sister?'

'My sister?' Lessie gave a short yelp of laughter. 'Oh,

Edith's going to gloat over this!' She took another sip and this time the hot strong mixture was comforting. The steam warmed her face and obscured her vision. Then she realised that her eyes were misty with tears. 'I hit Ian,' she said, her voice shaking. 'I've never hit him before.'

'He must have deserved it, then.' Andrew was in the chair opposite, his own teacup in his hand, leaning towards her, elbows on knees. It wasn't until later that she realised that he hadn't helped himself to whisky. 'D'you want to tell me what happened?'

It was a relief to talk about it, and there was no point now in keeping anything secret, so she told him how moody Murdo had become in the long months of unemployment, how he had grown to resent the family's dependence on the money she earned.

'But I offered to find work for him in the refinery and he turned it down.'

'He wanted to stay in the shipyards,' Lessie lied. When she had mentioned Andrew's offer, Murdo had rounded on her.

'It's bad enough living in my wife's house without having her begging for work for me as well,' he had told her savagely, snatching at his jacket and slamming out of the house, as he always did when they had words.

'Mebbe I did give the shop more attention than I gave Murdo,' she said shakily, her fingers turning her teacup round and round and round. 'Mebbe Ian's right—'

'Never mind about Ian, he'll come back in his own good time. Tell me about your husband,' Andrew's calm voice broke in, and she stared down into her cup, half empty now.

'Nothing seemed to be amiss, no more than usual. I'd to go to the warehouse this morning to order this month's provisions for me and the other shopkeepers, and Elma that works in the shop had the toothache so she was at the dentist. Murdo was to keep the shop going till I got back from the warehouse but when I got there it was closed, the door locked.' She bit her lip, remembering. 'There was a letter on the counter. He's gone off to England to get work in the shipyards there. And—' this was the hardest part to tell, 'Flora – the lassie that used to work in the shop, only I had to turn her off after Murdo lost his job because we couldnae afford to pay her – she's gone with him. And the drawer was empty. The takings were gone. He said in the letter that he'd taken the shop money and half the money in the bank because it was his . . . his due.'

She finished the tea and put the cup aside. 'Elma arrived and opened up the shop and I came back here. His clothes were gone. He must've known for a while what he was going to do and waited till the right moment.'

'D'you want to go after him? Try to get him back?'

Her head came up proudly. 'Indeed I do not! But it's hard on the bairns. He aye thought the world of Jess and he's the only father that Ian and Dorry—' She stopped abruptly, and Andrew finished the sentence for her.

'That Ian and Dorothea knew. He's been good to Dorothea, I'll give him that.'

'He's been good to them all. They're going to take it hard, mebbe harder than me, poor wee souls.'

'Well now,' Andrew said crisply, setting down his untasted cup. 'My sympathy won't fill bellies and stock shelves. How d'you stand financially? Is there enough to keep you going?' He got to his feet and stood looking down on her.

'Aye, for the moment. But the shop'll need restocking next month and I doubt if I'll have the money I need for that. We've depended too much on Murdo's wages coming in and it's been hard since he lost his job. There's only enough to pay the shop rent and keep us going in food for a few weeks.'

'You could get credit at the warehouse.'

She shook her head. 'I'll not start that. For one thing I'll lose my discount, and for another it means I'd be in debt to the wholesalers and that's something I've avoided from the first.'

'Would you let me help?'

'No!'

'But after all you've done for Dorothea—'

'You've paid for her keep.'

'I can increase that, at least.'

'I'll not take more. It's not necessary.'

'So you'd as soon starve, and let your children starve along with you, than accept help?'

'It'll not come to that. It's kind of you,' she said gently, determined to retain her hard-won independence but at the same time unwilling to throw his generosity back in his face, 'but I'll not be beholden to anyone. This is my problem, and I'll work it out myself.'

'That leaves a bank loan as your only option.'

She nodded. 'I'll speak to the bank manager tomorrow.'

'At least let me go with you and stand as guarantor for you.' Then as she opened her mouth to protest he added swiftly, 'I'll lose nothing, for I know that you'll pay the loan back yourself. My dear woman, you can't expect to go through life without letting friends help you at all.'

She rested her head on the back of her chair, suddenly aware that she was feeling very weary. 'Thank you, Mr Warren, it's generous of you.'

'Not generous enough. I wish you'd let me do more for you,' he said, and left. Walking back to the office he decided that Lessie Carswell was one of the most remarkable women he had ever met. He had watched her cope cheerfully with her family and the shop and the added burden of his illegitimate, motherless daughter, and minutes ago he had watched all the contentment and serenity leach out of her, leaving her wan and tired. Yet always there was that inner core of steel that had sustained her through desperate poverty and the loss of her first husband. It would undoubtedly continue to sustain her through the loss of a second husband and the struggle ahead.

Murdo Carswell, he thought as he turned in at the gates of the refinery, was a fool to walk away from such a woman.

When he returned home that night Ian refused to talk about Murdo. He spent as little time as possible in the house, and when he spoke to Lessie he avoided her eyes. Tall and rangy, his red hair curly and reluctant to submit to a brush, he looked so like Donald – and yet to all intents and purposes he was Murdo's son, she realised with pain. It was as though they had both betrayed Donald, she by marrying Murdo, Ian by accepting him so whole-heartedly as his father.

As she had expected, Edith almost gloated over Murdo's departure and went on at such lengths about men not being trustworthy that it was all Lessie could do not to scream at her to hold her tongue. Peter, as quiet as ever, was working in the counting house at the Warren sugar refinery now and his mother pointed to his success as an example of how well children did without the disrupting influence of a father.

Lessie had to force herself to go to the shop the day after Murdo left. It was hard to face her customers' inquisitive eyes, hard to fend off nosy questions and to pretend she didn't hear the whispers, but it had to be done, and the sooner the better. Flora had lived only a few closes away from the shop and by the time the shop opened the next day everyone in the area knew the girl had run off with Lessie Carswell's man. Few of the folk in the Vennel could afford to buy the local newspaper, but their grapevine was much more efficient than any paper.

Standing behind the counter, Lessie kept her head high, looked her customers straight in the eye, and dared any of them to say a word. Most had the sense to keep quiet, though the whispering from those waiting in the queue and the inquisitive glances through the open door from passersby were hard to bear. Lessie coped with it all until the early afternoon when a woman known throughout the Vennel for her malicious tongue said to other waiting customers in a voice that rose above a discreet whisper, 'I aye kenned he wis a scoundrel ever since he cheated us a' that time she wis birthin' the wean.'

Lessie laid down the ladle she had been using to measure porridge oats into the scale. 'Did you have something to say, Mrs McQueen?'

Everyone turned and gazed at the culprit, who went scarlet and said, 'I was havin' a private conversation.'

'About my man?' Lessie challenged.

'From whit we hear, he's no' yours ony mair.'

'For once, you heard right, Mrs McQueen. He's run off and left me, and taken Flora Paterson with him.' Lessie put her hands flat on the counter to stop their trembling. She knew that her face was red but mercifully her voice was steady. 'And as far as I'm concerned, bad riddance to him. Well, you all know about it now and I'd be grateful if you'd have the decency to do your whispering and sniggering outside my shop and not in front of my face.'

There was a murmur of approval and almost everyone turned to glare at Mrs McQueen.

'You're quite right, hen,' old Cathy Petrie spoke up. 'Men's no' worth the bother, that's whit I say.'

'It's a' right saying that at your age, Cathy,' a plump young woman, recently married, called from near the doorway. 'Ye had yer fill o' them afore ye started runnin' them doon.'

'By God an' I wis filled mair often nor I wanted tae be, I'll tell ye that,' Cathy shot back, and in the great roar of bawdy laughter that shook the shop Mrs McQueen slipped out and took her custom elsewhere. Lessie laughed as loudly as anyone else in a bid to keep back the tears, and from then on she had no more trouble with gossiping tongues.

In spite of her brave words and the calm way she dealt with the situation in front of the children, she missed Murdo desperately. Lying alone in the bed she had shared with him she tossed and turned and longed for him, only now realising how seldom they had made love in the past year or more. Preoccupied with the shop and the children and the house, too tired when she finally climbed into bed to think of anything but sleep, she hadn't noticed that he scarcely ever reached out for her in the dark any more.

Now that he had gone and she was alone, her body ached for him and she was tormented by thoughts of him and Flora together, in each other's arms. She meant what she had said to Andrew Warren: she wouldn't seek

Murdo out, or beg him to come back. If he wanted to be free of her, there was no point in trying to get him to change his mind. But she kept hoping that he would find out for himself that he had made a mistake. If he came back to her she would welcome him in with open arms. But he never did.

Davie had gone to Glasgow on business and knew nothing of Murdo's disappearance until he got back a week later. He went to the flat at once, and finding it empty, strode down to the shop. It was a quiet time of day and Lessie was free to take him into Elma's kitchen at the back, leaving the other woman to deal with the customers.

'Where is he? I'll go after him. He cannae be allowed to walk out on his responsibilities!'

'He's in England, where he can earn good wages in the shipyards doing the same work he was doing here. Ian got a letter from him the other day.' Lessie sighed. 'I had to go to see his poor mother. At least he's written to her as well. She's humiliated beyond bearing.' No point in telling Davie how the older Mrs Carswell had tried to free herself of her hurt and shame by blaming her daughter-in-law. When a man ran off, it always seemed to be his wife's fault. It was the unfair way of the world.

'And what about you? What about him humiliating you by going off with a lassie that worked in your own shop?'

'Davie, there's no sense in going on about it. Give folk's tongues a week or two and they'll find something else to wag about.' Outside, it was a glorious August day, but inside the room, inside herself, everything was cold. 'Oh Davie, sometimes it's hard being grown-up, isn't it? There's Mam gone, then Da and poor wee Thomasina. And now Murdo, for all that I'll—' To her horror her voice broke. At once Davie was by her side, his arm about her.

'Don't fret, Lessie,' he said gently. 'I'll look after you, all of you.'

She gave a sniff and straightened up, moving away from him. She had cried silently each night when the children were in bed, but had promised herself that there would be no tears in front of anyone. 'Indeed you will not, Davie Kirkwood. You've got your own life to lead.'

'Now that I've got a wee place of my own, you an' the bairns could move in with me. I'm doin' well now. I could support you.'

'I've no doubt that you could, and I'm proud of the way you've turned out, Davie, but I can manage fine. You did your share of supporting me before I got the shop. Anyway, is it no' time you were thinking of getting yourself a wife?'

Davie's jaw twitched. 'I've no intention of gettin' wed.'

'Why not? You're doing well for yourself, you should marry and have a family of your own.'

'Och, don't nag at me, Lessie. I get enough of that from Edith. Anyway, it's you we're talkin' about, no' me. How are you goin' tae manage for money?'

'The bank's giving me a loan.'

'I'll stand guarantee for you,' he said at once.

'There's no need. Mr Warren's already seen to that.'

He stared at her. 'You let Andrew Warren speak for you?'

'He made the offer and I accepted. Why not? I thought you got on well with the man.'

'I've done some work for him,' Davie's words were as hard as pebbles, 'but I don't like my sister bein' beholden tae him.'

'I'm not beholden. I'll pay off the loan and that'll be an end to it.'

'And if you can't pay it off?'

'I'll pay it off!'

They scowled at each other for a moment, then the anger left Lessie. 'Davie, don't let's fall out about this. Don't spoil things between us just because of Andrew Warren.'

For a moment she thought that he was going to disregard her, then he nodded stiffly, making an effort to smile. 'Aye, you're right. But if I'd Murdo Carswell between my two hands right now I'd squeeze the life out o' him for what he's done tae you!'

'That wouldnae be any sort of answer and you know

it.' She put her hand on his arm, smiled up at him, 'We'll manage, the bairns and me. We'll manage fine.'

On his next visit Andrew Warren went over the shop books with her, giving advice and helping her to plan ways of saving money.

'You've got a good business head on your shoulders,' he commented. 'You could do well, given time. You could build up your shop, buy another, then another.'

Lessie shook her head, closing the ledger. 'I only started as a shopkeeper because I'd to support myself and Ian. I'll leave the ambitions to you and to my brother Davie.'

'But money's there to be made. Why shouldn't you make it?'

'Some folk have a burning drive in them to make money, Mr Warren. Davie, for one. But most of us just live our own lives and feel quite content to get by on just filling our needs. It would never do for us all to be one thing or another, but I know which crowd I belong to,' Lessie said firmly. 'I'd not want the stramash of chasing after riches.'

Andrew blinked at her in some surprise, but said no more.

It was hard work, caring for the shop and her family on her own; at times Lessie lay awake at night worrying about whether or not she was going to manage to pay the next instalment of the bank loan and stock the shop and pay the rent and keep the children in clothes and food, but each month she found herself getting by, though it meant that Miss Peden's ornaments and the handsome 'wally dugs' and her own precious garnet brooch went back into the pawnshop for long periods. It embarrassed her acutely to have to pawn her benefactor's possessions, but Lessie was fighting for survival and she couldn't afford to be fussy about such matters.

Around her as she worked and worried, the world moved on through 1913 and into 1914. There were stormy scenes over the proposal to grant Home Rule to Ulster. The decision by Asquith's government to scrap the Franchise Bill caused the suffragettes to step up their militant fight for the vote, including hunger strikes by women thrown into prison for their beliefs. The Government retaliated by bringing in the Cat and Mouse Act, giving authorities the power to release hunger strikers then re-arrest them once they had recovered their strength.

To Lessie, serving women who as often as not bore blackened eyes and bruised faces and split lips, dealing with wan children bandy-legged from rickets, these concerns were like vague messages from a far and unknown country compared to the business of stocking and renting her shop.

Captain Robert Scott and his team died in the frozen wastes of Antarctica without reaching the South Pole and Lessie managed to persuade Ian, the clever member of the family, to stay on at school instead of leaving as soon as he reached his fourteenth birthday, offering to pay him five shillings a week to deliver goods for her in the early mornings and evenings and at weekends as an incentive. How she was to scrape up the money she didn't know, but she was determined to manage it. To her great relief the boy agreed. Ever since Murdo's going, there had been tension between them. Murdo wrote to Ian, who jealously guarded the letters and said nothing about them to Lessie. Jess, too, received an occasional letter; each time her pretty little face flushed with pleasure and she almost drove Lessie out of her mind chattering on about her father's new job, the room he and Flora had rented, their plans and ambitions. But Jess was an indifferent letter writer and rarely got around to answering, and gradually Murdo's letters to her dwindled and stopped. Caught up in the exciting business of growing older, she didn't seem to notice.

Germany's peacetime army grew. The Panama Canal was officially opened, then one day a foreign archduke and his wife were shot dead during a visit to a small distant country and Lessie looked up from weighing out lentils and giving change and balancing her ledgers to discover that everyone had begun to talk about a war.

'It wouldnae come to that, surely?' she asked Andrew Warren on his next visit. He helped her with her books as a matter of course now, and to her great relief he approved of her way of cutting prices on some goods to attract more affluent customers who might otherwise have got their groceries from further afield. It was a scheme that Murdo had strongly opposed.

Andrew looked tired and worried. 'It may well come to it from what I hear. My daughter's school in France has closed down. I would have sent for her in any case, she's safer at home at such a time of unrest.'

'But they're cousins, our King and the German Kaiser. Surely they'd not go to war with each other?'

The corners of Andrew's mouth quirked up in a brief smile. 'They'd not be the first family to fall out.'

'Thank goodness Ian's too young to fight if it comes to it,' said Lessie, and could have bitten her tongue out when she remembered that Martin Warren, now at a good school in Glasgow, was old enough to go into the army. 'Not that there's any chance of it happening,' she added briskly.

'My son's hoping that it will. He's been a member of his school's Officer Training Corps for some time now and he likes the idea of being a warrior. But let's pray that you're right. What's Ian going to do with his life now that you've got him to stay on at the school?'

'He wants to be a chemist, if you please.'

'A chemist?' Warren was taken aback.

'It's something he decided on a few years back. Murdo and his mother encouraged him. They liked the idea of having a professional man in the family.' The ghost of a smile brushed her mouth.

'And what do you think of it?'

Lessie folded her hands in her lap and eased her shoulders against the back of her chair. 'I want him to be happy. And if that's what makes him happy then so be it. That's why I talked him into staying on at school. I'm trying to save towards the day when I might have to find the money to pay college fees.' She laughed, and released one hand from the other to push back a stray wisp of fair hair that had drifted across her face. 'I never in my life thought I'd hear myself saying that!'

'I could help.'

'Indeed you could not. It's not your worry.'

'For God's sake, Lessie, will you never let anyone offer assistance?' She didn't know when he had started using her first name, it had just happened, not long after Murdo's desertion. 'If the lad wants to go to university it'll take money. I've got enough of that to see to my own family and help yours as well. D'you not think you've earned it, the way you've looked after Dorothea?'

She felt her face stiffen. 'You pay for Dorry's keep as it is. And I'll not take charity.'

'You're the most infuriating, stubborn woman I've ever met!'

'It's the only way to be, for the likes of me,' said Lessie, and refused to discuss the matter any further.

To his mother's fury Martin Warren left school and joined the army as soon as Britain declared war against Germany. 'It won't last,' he pointed out to Madeleine when he came home to break the news and announce that he was about to leave for England to train as an officer. 'I want to do something interesting before I go to university then settle down in the refinery. If I don't go now it'll be over and I'll have missed it.'

Men who had been in the Reservists disappeared from Greenock's streets; not only men – delivery vans and horses were commandeered and fuming merchants who had led the way into the twentieth century with smart new motorised vans had to resort to delivering their goods by bicycle and cart once again. The carts themselves, and those trams still pulled by horses, moved at a sedate pace, drawn as they were by old animals too near the end of their useful working lives to interest the War Department.

Only a matter of weeks after war fever had swept the country came the reality. Scores were killed and hundreds wounded when the British Expeditionary Forces were defeated at Mons; then the cream of the Russian army was defeated on the East Prussian border. An appeal was launched for another half million volunteers and all at once it began to look as though the war against Germany might not be over by the end of the year after all.

17

Lessie wearily turned the corner into Cathcart Street after a busy day in the shop, the basket of provisions dragging at her arm, then lifted her head at the sound of tinkling glass. Across the road from where she stood the Manns' handsome corner shop was a mess, with every window out, glass all over the pavement, the display shelves just inside the windows empty and hanging drunkenly from broken supports. A few men were loitering about, watching Mr and Mrs Mann sweeping broken glass from the pavement. Children stood staring and groups of women hovered at each closemouth, arms folded and heads together in eager talk. Nobody was helping the grocer and his wife.

'What happened?'

The woman Lessie asked, a neighbour from the next close, shrugged her shoulders. 'A crowd came doon frae the town an' went for their shop.'

'Why?'

''Cause they're Germans, that's why,' the woman said in surprise. 'We're at war wi' their sort.'

'Not with the Manns!'

'He's got the same name as the Kaiser. They're a' foreigners. Ye cannae trust foreigners these days,' was the uncompromising answer. Disgusted with the woman's attitude, Lessie marched home, deposited her heavy basket on the kitchen table, and tied an apron round her waist. Then she seized a broom and a shovel and went out again, exhaustion forgotten as she made for the corner.

Mr Mann eyed her warily as she approached, scattering

217

children before her. He had a bruise on his forehead and blood was drying and crusting at the corner of his mouth. 'Vat do you vant?'

'I've come to help.'

He drew himself up proudly. 'Ve do not need help from you.'

'Vilhelm!' His wife, her eyes puffed with crying, tugged at his sleeve.

'You do so need help,' Lessie told him roundly, and started to wield her brush. For a terrible moment she thought that the grocer was going to grab her by the collar and send her packing in front of everyone, just as he had done when she first moved into the street, but after a moment's indecision he turned away and got on with his own work.

Ian and Dorothea arrived and were set to work when they came to see what their mother was up to. An hour later the pavement was clear, the glass safely stowed away in boxes in the small back yard, the windows boarded up.

'Did they spoil much of your stock?' Lessie asked, and the grocer's swollen mouth grimaced.

'Zey took everything. Vy do zey do zat to us? Ve haff been here for many years. Ve do not'ing to harm zem.'

'I can send stuff up tomorrow morning from my own wee shop, and I'll get in touch with the other shopkeepers and ask them to spare what they can. It'll not be much, but it'll help you to stay in business until you can get more supplies in from the warehouses.' The Manns had refused to become part of the group that Lessie bought stock for.

'I vill not take charity.'

'For any favour!' she said, disgusted. 'It's not charity, it's help. We're not all mindless fools, some of us want to help.'

'Vy do zey do zis to us?' he asked again. 'Ve are not German, ve are Sviss.'

'I'm sorry,' Lessie said, and knew that the words were empty, useless, in the face of the hatred and cruelty that had suddenly been unleashed on this middle-aged couple who only sought to earn a living far from their own home.

With borrowed provisions from her shop and from others, the corner grocery opened its doors on the following day. The windows were replaced but a week later they were smashed and the shop vandalised again. This time the Manns had had enough. They left the shop boarded up and vanished from Cathcart Street. Some said that they had been taken away by the military to be put into a camp for aliens. Some said that they had stolen out of Greenock in the dead of night and gone off to Germany, taking with them military secrets.

'How could a grocer and his wife find out military secrets, let alone go off to Germany whenever the notion took them?' Lessie asked, exasperated. 'Anyway, they come from Switzerland, not Germany. He told me that himself.'

The man she was talking to looked at her as though she were simple in the head. 'They're a' foreigners,' he said.

'He's shamed me, Lessie. Shamed me in front of the whole town! What have I ever done to deserve this?'

Edith gulped her tea, set the cup back in its saucer with almost enough force to smash it, and groped in her bag for a handkerchief to press to the end of her reddened nose. 'Why?' she asked piteously, her voice muffled by the handkerchief. 'What's got into the laddie?'

'There's nothing wrong with not wanting to kill folk, Edith.'

'That's what Peter says. But he's not even religious!' Edith's voice broke. 'He says he doesnae even believe in God so he's not got that excuse to fall back on. And there's me workin' for the Warrens an' Master Martin off to France soon to fight the Germans while my son stays safe at home. D'you think he's soft in the head and I've never noticed before?'

'Edith Fisher, he's a decent, honest young man who's decided to stand by his own principles and chosen a hard road to walk. You should be thinking about him, not yourself!'

Edith shot to her feet, tears forgotten, glaring at her

sister. 'If he is wrong in the head it's you he gets it from,' she snapped. 'You were aye strange, you and Davie both. I've no doubt he'll not be going off to France either. I'm mortified, so I am!' And she flounced out, tussling in the doorway with Jess, who was just coming in.

'What's up with her?'

'Don't call your Aunt Edith "her". She's upset because Peter won't volunteer to fight in France.'

Jess helped herself to a biscuit. At twelve years of age she was already ripening into maturity and beauty. 'He's in for a rough time, then, and it'll serve him right.'

'Jess!'

The girl shrugged and took a second biscuit. 'I'm only telling the truth. Folk don't like young men who shirk their duty to their country. If everyone was like Peter, the Germans'd get everything their own way.' Her blue eyes brightened and she changed the subject. 'Can I go to the La Scala tonight, Mam? There's a really good film on.'

'I'll see. Leave those biscuits alone, will you! And go and see if the washing's dry. If it is, bring it in from the line,' Lessie ordered, and frowned as her daughter sauntered from the room, her heart-shaped little face bulging with the biscuit she had just crammed into her mouth. Jess was shallow and self-centred, altogether too interested in posing before a mirror and reading women's magazines and sitting in picture houses. Lessie worried more about her than about Ian and Dorry. Ian was practical and sensible, although the old warmth between them had never quite recovered from the boy's accusations after Murdo's desertion. As for Dorothea, she was quiet and biddable, and Andrew had already decided that she should become a schoolteacher.

But Jess – Lessie sighed as she gathered up the teacups and put the biscuits back into their tin. Jess was no scholar. She loved spending money, but as yet there was no indication as to how she was going to earn it when the time came.

A training camp was set up in Wood Street and the Greenock folk became used to the sight of the soldiers swaggering about the streets in their clumsy and often ill-fitting khaki uniforms. Men in ordinary civilian clothes without the armband that showed that they had volunteered and were waiting their turn to go became objects of suspicion, sneered at and on occasion treated roughly.

When he came home on leave before going off to France, Lieutenant Martin Warren was welcomed like a hero. His mother held parties so that she could show him off, and when he toured the refinery to make his farewells, darkly handsome in his uniform, the women employees, regardless of age, gaped in unashamed admiration.

'Not away yet?' Martin asked, pausing by Peter Fisher's desk in the counting house.

'No, Mr Martin.' Peter got to his feet and resisted the temptation to say 'sir'. He had to work hard all the time to overcome the upbringing his mother had given him.

The deep brown eyes beneath the peaked hat were sympathetic. 'Not fit enough?'

Peter swallowed. 'I don't believe in killing.'

Martin Warren blinked, long dark lashes briefly sweeping cheeks that still bore the bloom of naive youth. His eyes hardened, but his voice remained level when he said, 'Sometimes it has to be done, old chap. And someone has to do it.' Then he turned on his heel and left, presenting a broad, upright, khaki-covered back.

Peter was used by now to seeing people's backs. He was used to being ignored in shops while men in uniform or bearing armbands were attended to before him. He was used to sudden silences when he entered public houses or departments in the refinery or even the house he had grown up in. Aunt Marion was as upset as his mother at his decision, and the two of them only spoke to him when they had to. Even the food they dumped down before him tasted different, as though it had been prepared by someone who didn't care. He had always been a loner but he had never known until now what it was like to be an outcast.

Despite the fact that his own son had gone to fight the enemy, Andrew Warren was kind enough to Peter. He

continued to employ him and to talk to him when the
occasion arose as though everything was as it had been
before and there was no war. And there was one other
ally, an ally Peter had been unaware of until he happened
to meet her in the street one evening.

His first impulse on coming across his mother's sister
was to mutter a greeting and hurry by, but Lessie caught
hold of his sleeve and he had to stop.

'Peter, I've not seen you for many a long month.' Her
hazel eyes crinkled into a smile and he twisted his stiff
mouth up at the corners in polite response. Peter was
unused to smiling and a complete stranger to laughter.

'Hello, Aunt Lessie. How are you?'

'Och, I'm fine. Getting older, like all the rest of us. Are
you off to night school?'

'No, just out for a bit of a walk.'

'I'm on my way home from the shop. Come with me,
Peter. It's a long time since we had a visit from you.'

He stared down at her, astonished, then began to shake
his head. 'I'd best—'

'Come on.' She took a firm grip of his arm and began
to walk. Short of struggling free he had no option but to
accompany her. 'I'm getting a crick in my neck looking
up at you, and it'd be more comfortable if we were both
in chairs. Here, you can carry my shopping bag for me.'

She chattered all the way back to Cathcart Street,
apparently oblivious of the pointed stares passersby
directed at Peter, the audible remarks from a group of
women who were standing outside their closes, arms
folded, enjoying the last warmth of the October evening.
From the river a boat's siren sounded and a sharp-eyed
seagull on a chimney stack high above the road answered
it with a harsh scream.

Ian was out delivering goods to shop customers and Jess
had gone to the cinema with her best friend, but Dorothea
was at home, curled up in an armchair in the kitchen. She
got up when Lessie ushered Peter in and put down her
book, smiling at him.

'Make a cup of tea, pet,' Lessie told her, taking her coat
off. 'And we'll have toast. You'd like some toast, wouldn't

you, Peter? You'll find a pot of strawberry jam in that bag you've got. Take your coat off, man, and sit down in that chair, it's the most comfortable. Give him the toasting fork, Dorry, he can see to the bread for us.'

There was a warmth and cheerfulness about the little kitchen that Peter had never found in the house he had been raised in. It began to seep into his bones as he watched Dorothea and Lessie bustle about. He caught the girl's eye, and she smiled shyly at him. She had none of Jess's vitality, but her violet eyes and the auburn sheen in her dark curly hair gave her a quiet beauty. As she stooped to put a plate of bread slices near to his hand he caught sight of the puckered scar that bisected her right cheek. He vaguely recalled his mother saying something to her aunt about that scar and the pity of it, spoiling the girl's chances of marriage. Peter disagreed; Dorothea was too pretty to be marred by a mere scar.

They drank strong scalding tea and ate hot toast and strawberry jam and Peter felt the wound inside, continually aggravated by the results of his decision not to be part of the war, heal a little. He told them something of his job at the refinery and listened to Dorothea talking about school and Lessie's description of the day she had just spent at the shop, and was glad that he had met his aunt. Now and then, as she talked or listened, one hand went up to push back the strands of soft fair hair that kept falling across her face. The sparkle in her hazel eyes and the smile that came readily to her lips made him suspect that his Aunt Lessie would never really look old. Not like his mother, with her mouth narrowing by the year and her dark hair liberally streaked with grey.

When she had finished her tea, Dorothea went off to do homework in the room she shared with Jess. Stacking dishes in the sink, Lessie said quietly to her nephew, 'Are they hard on you, son?'

He didn't have to ask what she meant. 'Mr Warren's very understanding, but the rest of them – and my mother and Great-Aunt Marion – don't even try to grasp what I'm saying. Is it so hard, Aunt Lessie? Is it difficult to believe that some folk just cannae bring themselves to kill other folk?' His hands tightened round the cup he was holding. 'They think I'm scared. They think I'm a coward.' His voice broke on the last word and he swallowed hard. 'I'm not scared about what might happen to me. We all have to die sometime.'

'I know you're not frightened for yourself. You never were, not even as a wee laddie. You aye faced the world and I admired you for it.'

He gaped at her in amazement. 'I wish I'd known that.'

'That's why I'm telling you now. Your mother was too hard on you, Peter. She never meant to be, it was her way of bringing you up properly.'

'She's ashamed of me. And so's Great-Aunt Marion. I'm going to move out, Aunt Lessie. I'll find myself a room to rent somewhere.'

'I wish we'd space for you here, son, but with the girls growing up . . .'

He shook his head. 'It's kind of you but I'd not come here even if you had the room. I'd not want to bring shame on you or get you into trouble with your neighbours.'

'Don't you worry your head about that, I can handle the neighbours!'

He laughed. 'I think you can. But I need to be on my own.'

'You'll come here when you're in need of company?'

He nodded, looking down at the hands clasped between his knees. Then he said suddenly, 'I'll tell you what scares me. I get nightmares about it sometimes. It's not so much killing lads like myself, though that's bad enough. It's what would happen if I didn't manage to do it properly. What if I hurt someone sore and he was left to die slowly, in agony? I cannae get the picture of it out of my mind, and I – I c-couldnae—'

To his horror he felt the tears spill down his cheeks, dripping onto his hands. He tucked his head low so that she couldn't see his face and felt her hands on his shoulders. Then she was on the arm of the chair, turning his face into her body, holding him. She smelled of scented soap and her breast was soft. Peter Fisher pressed his cheek into it and sobbed, deep wrenching sobs that had been waiting for too long for release.

'I'm s-sorry—'

'Sshh,' said Lessie, holding him tightly, rocking him. 'No need to be sorry, laddie. You have a good cry. God knows you've earned it.'

Dorothea had never heard a man crying before. In the small bedroom through the wall she listened, the exercise book she had been writing in forgotten; listened, and felt her heart break with pity for the man who wept so despairingly in the next room.

As time passed, the ordinary people of Britain became familiar with foreign names that had been unknown to them before. The Dardanelles. Gallipolli. Ypres. The liner *Lusitania* was sunk by German torpedoes and the appeals for fresh volunteers continued. In the first two months of the war the required minimum height for a man applying to become a soldier had dropped from five feet eight inches to five feet five inches. A month later it dropped by another two inches, resulting in a great surge in recruitment among men from the poorer areas of Greenock, men who were wiry enough but hadn't grown tall because of poor nutrition in their youth. Some of them volunteered in Greenock's own battalion, the 3rd (Highland) Howitzer Brigade of the Royal Field Artillery, and in the Greenock Naval Company.

The townsfolk grew used to the skirl of the pipes as lines of men marched from the training camp to Fort Matilda Station where they entrained on the first leg of their journey to the trenches in France. Peter, who had found himself a room in the Vennel, grew more and more morose, seeing nothing of his mother and sometimes staying away from Lessie's house for months at a time.

As the men left, the women moved in to keep offices and factories and transport going. There were fewer bruised faces among Lessie's customers and a new air of confidence straightened many a woman's shoulders once she became her family's breadwinner. Those with small children found child-minders among elderly relatives and neighbours and went into munitions or offices or manned the tramcars and buses. They earned good money, though the price of tea and some other goods began to rise, taking with them the cost of living. A lot of domestic servants, too, went into factories for better money, but Edith Fisher stayed loyal to the Warrens.

'It's not seemly for women to do men's work,' she said sternly, and when Jess asked with studied, wide-eyed innocence how the country was to be run in wartime without the help of its women, she snapped back, 'That's for the Government to decide, miss. That's what they're there for.'

'But the Government's decided that w—' Jess began before a warning glare from her mother made her subside.

Andrew Warren, who had lost a fair number of his male workforce, offered Ian a job in the sugar refinery laboratories with the refinery paying for evening chemistry classes at the Technical School. Ian, who had become restless at school, accepted at once and settled in happily.

In August 1915 Dorothea came home just before the new school term started and announced, pink-cheeked and defiant, that she had found herself a job in a small cotton mill in Port Glasgow. Lessie stared at her, dismayed. This was not what Andrew had planned for his daughter.

'But Dorry, we – I wanted you to stay on and become a teacher. You know that!'

'Ian's the brainy one of the family. I'm not nearly clever enough to teach. And since you won't let me work in the shop with you I decided that I'd find something for myself.'

Lessie thought of what Andrew's reaction would be and said in a voice that was not to be defied, 'You can go right back to Rattray's, young lady, and tell them you've changed your mind and you're staying on at the school!'

Dorothea, normally a biddable girl, glared back at her foster mother, her mouth mutinous. 'I'll not do it, Mam. I'm too old for school. I want to earn my own money instead of costing you.'

When Lessie broke the news to Andrew on his next visit he reacted just as she had thought he would. 'You shouldn't have allowed it. You should have ordered her to give up the job and stay on at school!'

'I tried, but she'd have none of it. In any case, I'm not so sure that we've got the right to dictate to young people when it comes to their own lives. We don't own them, we can't force them to do as we want. If you're so set on your daughter being a schoolteacher, you try to tell her what to do!'

'I should have taken her to live with me in Gourock and be damned to what Madeleine thought. I've a good mind to do it now.'

'You'll not get my consent to it, and surely I've got a right to have my say. Dorry's just at the age where she needs to know where she belongs. When the time comes for her to know the truth she'll need to be told properly and given time to come round to the idea, not just snatched out of my life and into yours because you disapprove of what she's doing with herself.'

They glared at each other for a moment, then his face relaxed into a reluctant grin that was startlingly youthful in spite of the touch of silver over each temple. 'I might have known she'd have plans of her own. For a moment there I forgot that she's Anna's daughter too. Very well, let her be – for the moment.'

'There's one good thing; now that she's earning there'll be no need for you to go on paying her keep.'

The smile disappeared. 'Don't talk nonsense, Lessie Carswell,' he said stiffly. 'As long as she's under your roof I'll support her. I've no intention of stopping.'

A flutter went through the young ladies of the town when Captain Martin Warren came home on leave early in 1916. In the past year he had matured into a handsome, confident man who wore his uniform with accomplished ease. Both his parents were taken aback when he announced that he was thinking of making the army his career.

'I know that you were counting on me joining you in

the refinery, Father,' he said as he and his parents waited for their guests to arrive for an evening soiree Madeleine had arranged solely to show off her soldier son, 'but the life I've led since this war began has broadened my horizons. I enjoy being in the army. When this lot's over and done with I could apply for a posting anywhere in the world.'

Madeleine, as lovely as ever despite the silver streaks scattered through her thick hair, put a hand on his arm. 'But my darling, Helene and I have worked our poor fingers to the bone knitting and sewing and holding bazaars, your father has lost half his workforce and now that the Government's controlling the buying of sugar he has to work hard to make sure that the refinery gets all it needs. We've scarcely enough servants left to keep the house going. Surely we've all done enough for this war without losing you altogether to a military life!'

'D'you know what I saw this morning in the town?' Martin asked, straight-faced, 'A woman, delivering coal. Carrying a bag of coal into a close on her back.'

Madeleine went white to the lips and drew herself to her full height. 'No doubt she was too ignorant to know how to knit or sew or run bazaars. Or are you making mock of us, implying that your sister and your mother should be doing more, descending to working-class level?'

'Of course not. I'm quite certain that you do more than your fair share as it is. And you know I'd never mock my little maman.' Martin reverted to the old French name that he and Helene had dropped as they grew into adulthood. Madeleine's eyes softened and she reached both hands out to him.

'Change your mind, my darling. Come back to us when this terrible business is over.'

Martin threw an imploring look at his father. Andrew, standing by the drawing-room window watching the sun go down over the river, put his own disappointment aside and said gently, recalling Lessie Carswell's comments about Dorothea's decision to work in the mills, 'My dear, Martin's a man now. He must make his own decisions.'

Madeleine pouted, an expression that had delighted Andrew in their youth, but one that looked decidedly out of place now that she was into middle age. 'I might have known better than to ask you to intervene. You never have cared overmuch about what happens to your children,' she said icily, and swept from the room with a rustle of skirts.

Left alone, father and son looked at each other wryly. 'Sorry, Father.' Martin gave a Gallic shrug of the shoulders. 'I made a mess of that. I should have told you both separately. I might have known she'd be upset.'

Andrew looked at his son and felt a sudden surge of love for him. He bitterly regretted the way he had allowed Madeleine to put a wedge between himself and his children as they grew into adolescence and adulthood. If he hadn't been so immersed in developing the refinery he might have recognised the danger in time and moved to avert it. But now it was too late, and all he could do for his son was to support him – and pray to God that Martin lived through the war and had a future, no matter what he might choose to do with it.

'Is it very bad?' he asked, and the young man shrugged again.

'Oh, you know – like the curate's egg, I suppose. Good in parts.' He grinned, then sobered for a moment. 'The bad parts can be hellish, though. The noise, and losing people one's grown to know and care about. But it's got to be done. We've been lucky with the gas in my area, no problems from it so far. And I like the comradeship, the sense of belonging. I'm sorry about walking away from the refinery, though, I know it'll make things difficult for you.'

'Don't worry about that. You can never be happy if you're not doing what you want. In any case,' Andrew added wryly, 'I still consider myself to be a young man and I intend to live for a good many years yet. You may well have finished with the army by the time your turn comes to inherit the refinery.'

A motor car came chugging up the driveway and came to a halt at the door. The horn tootled unmusically and

Helene, slim and elegant and beautiful, burst from the front door and threw herself into the arms of the young man who climbed down from the driving seat. By happy chance her current boyfriend, a naval officer, was on leave at the same time as Martin.

'They look pleased with each other,' her twin said as the couple, arms entwined, moved out of sight towards the front porch.

'They are. I think that this might be the right man for your sister. Bob would make a good husband.'

'He will as far as Mother's concerned. His family's got plenty of money. Which reminds me – I suppose she's got someone lined up for me this evening? Pretty, I hope?'

'Pretty face, elegant background, beautiful bankbook,' Andrew said, and as they laughed together he wished without much hope that Madeleine might spare him some time with Martin this leave.

In June 1916 the Military Service Act came into force and Peter Fisher was summoned to face a service tribunal to explain why he wasn't yet serving in the army. He stood before Andrew Warren's desk, pale-faced but determined, and asked for time off to attend the tribunal. 'If I don't attend they'll come for me, and that'd upset the running of the refinery, sir.'

Andrew sat back in his chair, studying the young man thoughtfully. He had learned from Lessie that his counting house clerk was his parlourmaid's son, though nobody, including Edith, Madeleine and Peter, was aware of his knowledge. 'Do you intend to go into the army?'

'No, sir.'

'They can offer you a non-combatant role as a clerk or a stretcher bearer.'

'I don't believe in the whole business, Mr Warren.'

'Do you belong to the No-Conscriptions Fellowship or some such organisation that might give you backing?'

'I've got my own beliefs. I don't need to join any organisation.'

'I see.' Andrew paused, then asked quietly, 'You know what'll probably happen to you, Fisher?'

'Yes, I know. If you wish,' said Peter levelly, 'I'll hand in my notice now and get out of your way.'

'I've no intention of accepting it.' Andrew rocked his chair back on its hind legs, chewing at his lower lip. 'I could transfer you to another department and claim that you're necessary to the refinery.'

A flush rose to the pale face on the other side of the desk, almost obscuring a large yellowing bruise on one side of the tense jaw. 'It's kind of you, Mr Warren, but I've no intention of hiding. I'd prefer to stand by my beliefs.'

'I see. What happened to your face?'

'I walked into a lamppost.'

'It's easily done.' Andrew's voice was dry. 'Tell me, did you turn the other cheek?'

Peter's eyes widened with surprise as he looked down at his employer, then a faint smile twitched at his mouth. 'I don't believe in that, sir. I gave the lamppost as good as I got.'

'I'm glad to hear it. Tell the chief clerk that you've got my permission to take the day off. On second thoughts,' Andrew said as Peter turned towards the door, 'leave it to me. I'll tell him myself.' He wasn't a fool, he knew well enough that the only time the other men in the refinery spoke to Peter Fisher was to ridicule and revile him. He knew, from Lessie, how the young man had been turned out from one squalid lodging house after another. No doubt he had run into quite a few 'lampposts' as well. Better that the day off came as an order from the refinery owner himself.

Davie Kirkwood, now thirty-three years of age, was also called before a tribunal, but since the Government had taken control of engineering in the interests of the war effort, and Davie had seen the way the wind was blowing in good time and had turned his interests to serving the shipyards, he proved easily that his continued presence in Port Glasgow was far more important than his presence in the French trenches.

For Davie, the war had come just at the right time.

When rumours of war were flying around the country and being discounted by most people, he had carefully started to build up his small company with money borrowed from the banks. Now, with Government backing, he had managed to buy another small engineering shop and had combined it with his own. He had also contracted enough business to keep both his shops going for three years and the loans were being paid back.

To his sister Lessie's annoyance he had not yet married, though with a third of the men of marriageable age away from home there were plenty of bonny women to choose from. For Davie there had only been one woman, and now that she lay in the cemetery, out of his reach but never out of his heart and his thoughts, all his ambition was concentrated on becoming as wealthy and as powerful as the man who had, to Davie's mind, owned her.

It was for Anna that Davie schemed and worked and saved, only for Anna. Jeers and threats and the white feathers the older women handed out to healthy young men not yet in uniform were of no importance to Davie Kirkwood; he accepted the feathers with a bow then let them fall from his fingers and walked on, leaving the donor feeling that she, and not he, had been mocked.

In the first months of the war, as soon as the drive for recruits began to take hold, Joseph Kirkwood had vanished from the town. His sisters and brother had no knowledge of where he was, and whether or not he had been called up or managed to escape being put into uniform.

'But you can be certain,' Edith said darkly when his name was mentioned, 'that our Joseph wouldnae risk his precious skin for anyone. If you ask me, we've all seen the last of him – and good riddance to bad rubbish!'

As he expected, Peter wasn't as fortunate as his Uncle Davie when it was his turn to go before the tribunal. They contemptuously dismissed as unfounded and unpatriotic his refusal to fight and in due course the letter ordering him to report to barracks in Glasgow arrived. When he ignored it, two grim-faced police officers arrived at his lodgings early one morning and bundled him off to the police station. There, he was handed over the military police, taken to Glasgow, and locked in a tiny empty guard room when he refused to put on the uniform that was handed to him.

He lay in the night-dark on the cement floor, tightly curled up to keep out the worst of the cold, his body aching from the rough handling he had received, and tried to sleep. There was worse to come, he knew that well enough even without the graphic warnings the guards had given him.

He hadn't had time to say goodbye to his mother, or to Lessie. Not that his mother would have wanted to see him, for they had become estranged months earlier when he steadfastly refused to change his mind.

But he regretted not being given time to see his Aunt Lessie once more.

18

It began to seem, as 1916 gave way to 1917, as though the war had always been there and always would be there. In France thousands were dying. Death was indifferent to age and nationality, and it seemed to Lessie as she worked on in the shop and looked after her house and her family that the old men who planned and manipulated the war and stayed at home while the younger generation marched out to do their bidding were just as indifferent.

'Mebbe they should give women more than the vote,' she said once to Jess as the two of them dragged a sack of grain across the shop floor to rest against the counter. 'Mebbe they should let them have a turn at running a few countries. Women know more than men about the value of one single life. They'd no' stand by and see thousands cut down in their prime. They'd find some way to stop it.'

The bag was where they wanted it. Jess, panting with effort, straightened up and stared at her mother. 'You've changed your tune. You werenae even interested in the suffragettes, and now listen to you!'

'I was never unsympathetic to them, just busy with my own problems. But a terrible war like this one makes everyone think harder about what's important.'

'Hmmph,' Jess said, and went to put the kettle on for a cup of tea. She had been at odds with her mother ever since leaving school three months earlier, when Lessie had decreed that she should come and work in the shop.

'Elma's rheumatism's got a lot worse and now that Ian's at the refinery I need someone fit and strong to help me.'

'Why me? You wouldn't let Dorry work in the shop, and now she's enjoying herself in Rattray's Mill and I'm miserable here. It's not fair!' Jess had whined, but Lessie had been adamant. Jess, spoiled from the beginning by a father who had then gone waltzing off and left her, never thought of anyone but herself. She immersed herself in women's magazines, lingering over the photographs of models. She turned her aptitude for sewing to making her clothes as fashionable as possible, brushed her long fair hair one hundred times every night, went to bed with her pretty face layered with cream that left grease stains on the pillows, and walked about the house with books balanced on her head in an effort to acquire a stately grace. Lessie had finally decided that it was time her daughter learned that growing up carried responsibilities with it.

Jess had had no option but to do as she was told, but she let her annoyance show in no uncertain way. It sometimes seemed to Lessie that Dorry, Anna's daughter, was a more loving child to her than either of her own. She blamed herself, when her spirits were low, for marrying Murdo and giving Ian a father to replace the one he had never known. Without Murdo around she could have kept Donald alive for Ian. They might have retained the closeness that had been so precious to her during his first few years and had never returned after Murdo left.

But if she hadn't married Murdo, beautiful, enchanting, maddening, selfish Jess wouldn't have been born. Sometimes Lessie thought that that might not have been a bad thing. Her daughter came through from the back shop to hand her a cup of steaming hot tea. 'I gave Elma's face a wipe with the flannel and sorted her pillows and gave her her tea,' she said and Lessie felt guilty at wishing Murdo, and therefore Jess, out of her past.

Some of the men who had set off from the Vennel with hearts high at the beginning of the war were back home again, manoeuvring themselves on crutches because one leg was missing or maimed beyond repair, or with an empty sleeve pinned across their chests. Some were blinded or deafened, some so badly scarred that they were almost unrecognisable, some had their lungs permanently damaged by mustard gas. Their womenfolk – wives, mothers, sisters – took on the task of caring for them as well as earning and seeing to the house and the children.

Some men would never come back; day after day the telegrams arrived: Missing in Action, Killed in Action, Died of Wounds.

One customer came wandering, dazed, into the shop, telegram in hand, disbelieving, needing to share her disbelief with other women rather than with her wide-eyed, wondering children. 'It's like the pawn,' she said bitterly after displaying the briefly worded form. 'They take your man and they give you a ticket for him.' Her face, often marked by a heavy fist in the past, was ashen and desolate as she stared down at the telegram. 'But ye cannae redeem him, no matter what ye're willin' tae pay. Ye can never redeem him.'

Tears began to slide slowly down her face and the other women stood gawping at her, huddled in their shawls. One reached out a hand then drew it back, as though touching the widow might infect her and put her own husband, still alive as far as she knew, into danger. Lessie went round the counter and put an arm about the weeping woman, drawing her to a chair, her own eyes moist.

Peter occupied Lessie's thoughts a lot and she worried about him as though he were one of her own. Once the army discovered that it could do nothing to change his mind, he had been handed back to the civilian authorities, taken to court in Glasgow, and was serving a prison sentence. She received the occasional scrawled note from him, written on prison paper and containing the minimum amount of news. She only knew where he was, not how he felt, what it was like, how he was being treated. She could only guess the answer to these questions, and her guesses frightened and chilled her. She wrote every week, filling her letters with love and caring and support, and sent parcels of food and warm clothing from time to time, but they were never mentioned in his notes and she had a suspicion that they were never given to him. All the same, she kept sending them, just in case.

She said nothing to Edith, who never let Peter's name pass her lips. It was as though Edith had never had a son. Andrew Warren had tried to find out more, but conscientious objectors had no friends, and the authorities remained tight-lipped and unwilling to help in any way.

'It'll probably be worse for him than it would be in France,' Lessie said wretchedly when Andrew reported his failure.

'That's the idea. They want to make life so hard that the men'll decide to opt for army life instead.'

'It's not fair.' Without realising it Lessie resorted to Jess's habitual complaint. 'He's such a gentle laddie. All he's doing is protesting against having to hurt other boys like himself.'

A tear rolled down one cheek and Andrew Warren took an involuntary step towards her, his arms reaching out. Then they dropped to his sides as Lessie scrubbed at her face and stiffened her back and said, 'Well now, this isn't going to balance the books, is it? Andrew,' she had started calling him by his Christian name in private, after a great deal of coaxing on his part, 'I was looking at this ledger last night, and there seems to be more money free this month than usual.'

'That's because you're doing more business. Even with prices going up, the women who use your shop are earning more money now that they're doing men's work and getting decent wages for it. Then there's Ian and Dorothea bringing something in, and you've been shrewd in the way you've handled the shop.'

'That's thanks to you and your advice.'

'Nonsense, I just listened to your ideas and gave you the bit of encouragement you needed to put them into practice. Now it's all starting to show results.'

The cleft between her brows deepened in a way that he had long since begun to find endearing. 'It seems wrong to be making more money than I need at a time like this.'

'Your brother wouldn't agree with you from what I've heard,' he said without thinking, and was rewarded with a cool glare.

'My brother works very hard. Besides, he's dealing with companies. I'm dealing with folk.'

'Lessie, when this war's over – and one day it will be – the men'll come back to claim the jobs the women are keeping open for them. The women'll go back to being dependent on their husbands again and there might not be so much money then for shopkeepers such as you. Make the most of it while you can, my dear. Invest it, make it work for you.'

'How can money work?'

'You lend it to various companies for their own use, and in return they undertake to pay you interest, an annual percentage of the sum you've invested. The capital – the amount you first loaned to them – is still yours, and the money's earning more money for you instead of lying in a bank.'

Her mouth had dropped open. 'I've never heard the like!'

Andrew hid a smile and said solemnly, 'Most wealthy people live by investing their money and collecting the interest.'

'You think I should do that?'

'If I were you I'd invest a small sum, see how things go.'

'Could I invest it in your refinery?'

He was taken aback. 'You could, but I'd not advise it.'

'Why? Is it not doing well?'

This time he allowed the smile to spread across his face. This was indeed the most interesting woman he had ever come across. 'It's doing fine, but it would be a worry to me if your hard-earned money was in my charge. I'd as soon you talked to your bank manager. He could advise you.'

'If I do, can I ask your opinion on whatever he says?'

'Indeed you can,' Andrew assured her, and she nodded, satisfied, and turned her attention back to the ledger.

In January 1917 Ian celebrated his eighteenth birthday and within two weeks he was on his way to France as a member of the Medical Corps. For the past two years he had taken night classes in First Aid as well as his chemistry classes in preparation for the day when he would join the army.

Tall and broad in his khaki uniform, his red hair glowing like a beacon in the cold February morning, he hugged Lessie on the station platform and said, 'Don't worry, Mother, I'll soon be back. This time next year it'll all be over.'

The old familiar phrase brought the tears she had been fighting back into her eyes. 'Oh, Ian!'

'I'll be fine. I'm only going to be an orderly, they won't be pushing me into the trenches with a gun. They've got more sense than to do that, I'd probably shoot my own mates by accident.' He turned to his sister. 'If you get to America before I come home, Jess, give my love to Mary Pickford.'

Jess had never forgiven him for catching her in front of the mirror one day, acting out one of the famous film star's more dramatic scenes in a film that had recently been shown in Greenock. She sniffed disdainfully and eyed a young couple who were locked in each other's arms a few yards away. Scenes like that were being enacted all over the station platform – men in uniform, tearful women. It was romantic, Jess thought, and wished that she had a soldier in uniform to bid farewell to. Not Ian – someone who looked more like Douglas Fairbanks.

'Ian!' There was a flurry further down the platform and a hand clutching a hat waved high in the air. People stepped hurriedly out of the way and some were nudged aside as Dorothea came flying along, her coat flapping open, her dark hair escaping from the bun at the back of her head. She reached them and stopped, fanning herself with her hat. Her eyes were bright and her face rosy with her run through the cold air. At first glance the scar down her cheek looked like a thin ruffled strip of pink ribbon that had come loose from her hair and drifted across her pretty face as she ran. 'I thought I was going to be too late!'

'Dorry, just look at you!' Scandalised, Lessie began to tidy the girl up. 'You didn't run through the town like that, did you? What would people think? And why aren't you at work?'

Dorothea pushed the busy hands away, her violet eyes fixed on Ian. 'I asked for time off. I couldn't let you go without saying goodbye.'

'You said goodbye to him this morning,' Jess pointed out. She was beginning to shift from one foot to the other and eye the clock. She had seen an advertisement in the *Telegraph* the night before; a smart assistant was wanted in a well-known dress shop in Gourock, the ability to sew an advantage, must be willing to learn. She was impatient to get her mother on her own, to convince her that she, Jess, would be much better employed in a dress shop than working in the little corner shop in the Vennel.

'It's not the same as saying goodbye properly at the station.'

'You're covered in cotton fluff,' Ian pointed out with amusement. Dorothea looked down at herself and laughed.

'I didn't stop to brush it off. I'll be much tidier when you come home, I promise.' Then, as the order came to board the train, she threw her arms about the young soldier and kissed him on the cheek. 'I'll write to you. Take care, come home to us.'

He held her briefly, then turned to his young sister and, finally, to his mother. 'Don't worry, I'll be fine,' he whispered, and for a moment he was the old Ian, Donald's son, Lessie's precious firstborn. Then the warmth of him left her embrace and he was gone, just another arm in the forest of khaki-covered arms reaching out to wave as the train slowly moved off.

Rattray's cotton mill was small and stuffy. It smelled of oil and it was so noisy that the workers could only communicate with the people who sat back to back to them by leaning backwards so that their shoulder-blades touched and bellowing. Wisps of cotton continually eddied in the air like tiny flower petals, landing wherever they pleased – on hair, eyelashes, and clothes. When

Dorothea changed out of her working clothes in the evenings she had to carry them out to the back yard and shake them vigorously; when she brushed her long dark hair in the bedroom they shared, Jess complained about the fluff that was teased from its strands.

She worked in the winding shop, winding spun cotton onto bobbins which then went off to loom shops all over the country to be woven into cloth. It was monotonous work requiring continual attention: all too often one of the three threads being combined on the one spindle broke and the ends had to be cut with the knife each winder carried, then blended back onto the spindle. But Dorothea liked the mill. She liked the independence it gave her, the knowledge that she was earning her own keep. Although she was as much a part of the Carswell family as Ian or Jess, there had always been a part of her that knew that she stood alone, without her own parents to care for her. Her father, Lessie had told her, was unknown, her mother a friend and former neighbour of Lessie's. Sometimes, on the rare occasions when Dorothea caught the scent of roses, she fleetingly recalled pictures of another life, a small garden, a beautiful red-haired woman in pretty clothes that rustled. But she wasn't a romantic like Jess and she didn't speculate on her real parents very often, preferring to live in the present.

The mill was mainly staffed by women on war work, together with some men too old or frail for war service and a few lads who were too young to go into uniform. Many of the women were already known to her as customers in Lessie's shop. Two of the men who worked in the place had been invalided out of France: Johnny Morning, who supervised the winding shop, had only one foot now, and stumped about the place on crutches, and Robbie McKinlay, who tended to the machinery, looked ten years older than his thirty years because he had been one of the first of the British Tommies to be gassed in the trenches. His sentences were jerky and breathless and he was often off sick, but he had been a good worker before the war and Mr Rattray had, as promised, made sure that he would have a job to come back to.

Seeing the two men every day made Dorothea fear for Ian, but she kept her thoughts from Lessie, who had enough to worry her, and from Ian himself, writing him long amusing letters about her work in the mill, any gossip she happened to hear around the town, the film she and her friend Aileen had gone to the previous night, and Aileen herself, with her frizzy brown hair and bold brown eyes, her sturdy body and quick mind.

When Johnny Morning decreed that the women in the winding shop could only have three minutes away from their looms to answer the call of nature, it was Aileen who brought angry colour to his face by suggesting with a sweet smile that he could cut the time limit to two minutes by providing buckets, to be hung on the ends of the machines.

'Then we'd no' have tae move far from our seats at all,' she said, and Johnny stumped out, followed by gales of female mirth.

On the following day, his three-minute rule, written out and signed by his own fist, was firmly pinned to the privy door. Aileen coaxed a pencil stub from someone and wrote beneath his signature, 'A man's ambition's very poor, to put his name on the shithouse door.' The notice disappeared within the hour, and after that a lad was stationed halfway up the stairs with Johnny's pocket watch in his hand, to time the women as they climbed past him to the privy, each with her own comment to make into his ear so that his face was permanently crimson.

'Och, that Johnny Morning wis a sour-faced bugger afore ever he lost his foot,' Aileen said blithely when Dorothea voiced sympathy for the overseer. 'My ma used tae work here an' she could tell ye a tale or two aboot him. I see nae sense in feelin' sorry for him now. When's he ever sorry for us?' Then she added with a toss of her head, sending a cloud of cotton into the air, 'You're too nice, Dorry. Ye'll never make yer way in this world bein' sorry for every bugger you meet.'

'I've got used to the sound of the machinery all the time.

At the beginning it was so deafening that I never thought I would.' Lying on his bunk, Orderly Ian Carswell of the Medical Corps stopped reading his foster sister's letter and wondered if he himself would ever get used to the noise he lived with now, the muffled but continual pounding of the guns, the crack and boom of explosions, the bark of orders, and, worst of all, the continual sound of suffering. He was at one of the advance dressing stations where the men were brought in for emergency treatment before being sent up the line to the casualty clearing stations and base hospitals – or to their graves. By this time he should have grown accustomed to the moaning and the cursing and the screaming, but he hadn't. Every time he went on duty he had to pause for a second outside the tent flaps and brace himself to enter.

Today the noise of the guns and the bombs was louder, without as much as a few minutes' blessed silence. For the third time the Allies were doggedly fighting for control of Ypres and the ambulances were almost nose to tail on the tracks between trenches and hospital tents, lining up to disgorge their quota of stretchers then turning at once, wheels slipping and splashing in the khaki-coloured watery mire, to head back towards the trenches for another load of wounded, dead and dying.

Someone shook his shoulder roughly and yelled in his ear that he was wanted back in the wards because there was another surge of incoming wounded. Ian came to himself with a jerk of fright and realised that he had fallen asleep reading Dorothea's letter. Running outside, slipping and slithering through the mud, he stuffed the letter into his breast pocket. At least the rain had stopped, though the sky overhead was grey and menacing. But the mud was still there. It was always there, Ian thought irritably, splashing through it. On more than one occasion, men left outside the overcrowded wards, their stretchers placed on the duckboards that were supposed to provide a firm path over the mud but rarely did, had sunk into it and drowned, too weak to save themselves.

'Orderly!' someone called as soon as Ian appeared in the big marquee tent that did little to prevent the rain, when it came, from dripping through the canvas onto the wounded. He made his way between beds, past stretchers laid on the ground because there was nowhere else to put the wounded, to the doctor who had beckoned him with a hand that looked as though it had gone rusty with other men's blood.

The canvas walls vibrated to the sound of explosions. The ward was crammed with surgeons, nurses, orderlies like himself, walking wounded stoically waiting their turn. Others writhed and cried out on stretchers and beds, or lay, already treated and drugged against pain, white-bandaged and silent, eyes closed in merciful oblivion or open and staring in confusion and bewilderment at the bedlam that surrounded them. The strong disinfectant the nurses doused the wards with was mingled now with the stench of blood and putrefaction and vomit.

'Hold him,' the doctor said tersely, his own face drawn and ashen with exhaustion. Ian obediently put his weight on the shoulders of a fair-haired lad who was struggling against the hands that tried to help him, hoarsely shouting. He looked too young to be out of school, let alone fighting for his country. His uniform tunic was a ragged mess, some of it ground into the large bloody hole in his chest.

'It's all right, you'll be all right,' Ian told him, lying through his teeth, and the boy glared up at him and struggled harder to get away from the restraining hands and the pain and the sudden mess that had been made of his body and his world. A nurse appeared, hypodermic in hand, and in a moment or two the boy relaxed, his blue eyes closing, and Ian was free to answer another call for help.

Hurrying from one bed to another, his fingers brushed against his tunic pocket and felt the outline of the letter, folded again and again into a small square so that there was no danger of it falling out and being lost. Dorry's letters always bore a faint floral scent. He appreciated the letters he received from Lessie and Jess, but he had begun to look forward especially to hearing from Dorry, who never missed a week and who always seemed to manage to enclose a slice of Greenock, a breath of real life and sanity, between the pages. Sometimes he thought that without her letters he wouldn't be able to cope with the life he led now. 'Tell me about everything,' she wrote each time, but he never could. Instead, he wrote about the better moments, the friendships, the learning, the satis-faction of seeing critically wounded men bandaged up after emergency treatment or surgery, well enough to go on down the line and, hopefully, survive. It would be wrong to let any of his womenfolk know what the war was really like. It would be wrong to expose Dorry, with her shy smile and her gentleness, to the appalling cruelties of life, the terrible things that men filled with hate or fear or a determination to survive no matter what happened to others could do to fellow human beings.

'Orderly!'

With difficulty Ian made his way to the door, to where a doctor and nurse were kneeling beside a stretcher that had just been brought in. The nurse, scissors in hand, was trying to cut the sleeve of the patient's jacket.

'Nearly stood on the poor bloke's face,' the stretcher bearer was saying, looming over the trio. 'If he hadn't let out a groan I'd have missed seeing him. God knows how long he'd been lying in that shell hole. It's a wonder he didn't drown. I don't know how he managed to keep his head out of the water.'

'Let me.' Ian dropped to his knees beside the nurse and took the scissors. The man was an officer; his uniform jacket, sopping wet and thick with clay, was of good cloth and difficult to cut. Specially made for him, Ian thought as he worked, carefully sawing at the material without cutting into the skin beneath. Not like those poor Tommies who had to take whatever uniform they got, whether it was too tight or too loose, too long or too short. He had got into the habit of avoiding looking into faces; it helped to think of the dead and dying men as units rather than people who had been snatched by war from the business of living. But this time his eyes rested briefly on the face above the jacket he was mutilating. The officer's skin was grey with shock and loss of blood and it was easy to understand how the stretcher bearers had almost missed him in the mud. Black hair still dripping dirty water had been pushed back by someone from a face that looked very old, the skin tight against sharp protruding bones, the mouth a thin line, holding back its pain and its secrets.

The doctor's hand was on his patient's wrist, feeling for a pulse. 'He's still with us.'

Ian eased open the sleeve and the shirt beneath it. The wounded officer's arm was icy cold to the touch and slashed with a deep long cut from elbow to wrist. It had stopped bleeding and the lips of the wound were purple and puffy, the bone glinting dully from deep within. Ian moved aside and watched as the doctor's hand deftly travelled over the horrific wound.

'Sword slash. We might manage to save him. Find a bed for him, will you?'

'Over there,' Ian said tersely, and the wounded man moaned as the stretcher was lifted. As they eased him onto the narrow cot, the label pinned to the man's shoulder flipped over and Ian stared at the hastily scribbled words, then at the face.

The last time he had seen this man had been in Greenock, when Martin Warren, now quite unrecognisable as the handsome, confident young man he had been that day, had toured his father's sugar refinery to say goodbye to the workers.

19

Lessie's heart sank as she came in from the pleasant August evening and found Edith in the kitchen with Dorothea, her long, normally solemn face a mixture of expressions. Clearly she had important news; Lessie already knew what it was, and was grateful when Dorothea cut in ahead of her aunt, insisting that Lessie sit down and have something to eat.

'I'll have something later, pet. For now I'd love a good hot cup of tea.' Lessie kicked off her shoes and sank into her usual fireside chair with a sigh of relief.

'Why d'you have to stay open so late these nights?' her sister wanted to know.

'Because most of the women have work to go to during the day. The evening's the only time they've got free to do their shopping.'

'It's too much for you. You're not getting any younger.'

'It's kind of you to remind me,' Lessie said caustically. Not that she needed reminding on that particular evening. Her feet and legs ached, her head ached, and she felt as old as Methuselah.

'And you should have more help in the shop anyway. You've never replaced Jess yet. If she were my daughter,' Edith nagged on, 'I'd not have agreed to her going to work in that fancy dress shop. Not when your need's greater.'

'It's easier to do without her than to put up with her sulks when she's crossed. And with Ian away in France, I'm as well working than sitting at home worrying about him.' Lessie sipped at the hot tea and felt stronger, able to face her sister and ask, 'What brings you to Greenock, Edith?'

'You'll not have heard that Mr Martin—'

'We know about it,' said Dorothea, then flushed, catching Lessie's warning look just too late. The anticipation drained from Edith's face.

'Who told you?'

'Someone in the mill,' Dorothea said swiftly. 'And I ran to the shop in my dinner hour to tell Mam.' In actual fact Andrew Warren himself had told them, arriving at the flat early that morning, hollow-eyed with lack of sleep but restless with the need to talk to someone – to Lessie, Dorothea realised, and had quickly removed herself and Jess out of the house, off to work, leaving the two older people alone.

'I might've known word would travel fast. I came here as soon as I could.'

'That poor laddie – and his poor family,' Lessie said. 'How are they?'

'Mrs Warren's taken it very badly, and so's Miss Helene. We had to fetch the doctor for the mistress and she's in her bed, with nobody allowed to visit her. Mr Warren – well, nobody ever knows what's going on in his head. He keeps things to himself. Mind you, it must have been hard on him, trying to comfort the mistress and her screaming at him that he didn't care about what had happened to poor Mr Martin. She'd have nothing to do with him, so he just turned about first thing this morning and took himself out of the house and off to the refinery as if it was an ordinary day. Out of her mind, she was. We're wondering in the kitchen if she'll ever be right again.'

Dorothea had taken Lessie's cup and refilled it. Lessie bent her head over it, the steam warm on her cheeks. Andrew hadn't said a word to her about his wife that morning. He had just told her, calmly and without emotion, about his only son's death, and then the minute the door had closed behind the two girls, he had given a great shudder and been unable to stop shaking. She had taken him into her arms the way she had held the customer who had brought in the telegram announcing her husband's death in the trenches, and had held him until the trembling eased. Then she had made some tea, with whisky in it for Andrew, and sat on in her kitchen, long past the time she should have been in the shop, letting him talk about Martin as a baby, a toddler, a schoolboy.

'I'll have to go or I'll no' get the last tram back to Gourock,' Edith was saying. 'That's with waiting for you for so long, Lessie. Oh, before I go, our Peter's signed on in the army at last.'

'What?'

'I thought that'd surprise you.' Her sister's voice was smug. 'I got a letter from him this morning. He's finally seen the error of his ways. I knew he would.'

'Is that what he said?'

Edith gave a small shrug of the shoulders, rising to her feet and looking about for her bag. 'He says he couldnae stand up against them any more, whatever that means. The main thing is that he's done it. I don't know how I could have faced the Warrens today if I hadnae had that letter. I'd have been too ashamed. Which reminds me.' She paused at the door. 'D'you ever see our Davie?'

'Now and again. Not often.'

'There's another one that's got out of going to fight.'

'He's doing important work for the shipyards, Edith.'

'Aye, and making a fortune at the same time, from what I hear.' Edith sniffed, then said, 'While young lads like poor Mr Martin and your Ian – and my Peter too,' she added smugly, 'are fighting and dying for their country.'

'Don't talk about dying, Aunt Edith,' Dorothea said sharply, and Edith's eyebrows rose.

'You mind your manners, miss. Working in that mill's not good for her, Lessie. She's become impertinent since she went there. Anyway, I'm right in what I'm saying. Davie should think black burning shame of himself, but I don't suppose he will. Nor Joseph – I'm sure he's managed to keep out of the fighting too, wherever he is.'

'She's got a wicked tongue at times,' Dorothea said when Edith had gone.

'Dorry! That's no way to speak of your elders.'

'Being elder doesn't mean she's better. Why do Mr

Warren's visits have to be such a secret?' Dorothea wanted to know.

'They're not a secret. It's just that it's his business who he calls on, not anyone else's. If he wants to tell Edith, it's up to him, not us. I think I'll away to my bed, Dorry.'

'Not until you've had something to eat,' the girl said firmly, starting to set the table.

'I'm not hungry.'

'That's because you're past hunger. It's not much, some potted meat and cold boiled potatoes. It'll not take a minute to fry them up for you. And I'll make fresh tea.' Dorothea touched a spill to the fire and used the flame to light the gas mantles. Part of Greenock was lit by electricity now, but not Cathcart Street. 'What d'you think Peter's up to, joining the army after all he said about it?'

Lessie remembered the few scribbled notes she had received from her nephew. 'I think it's as he said to his mother. He just hadn't the strength to stand up to them any longer, poor laddie.' She sighed, then got up and looked into the mirror hanging on the wall between the two china wally dugs she still thought of as Miss Peden's. The little frown between her hazel eyes had deepened and other lines had begun to spread out from the corners of her eyes and her mouth. She put a hand up to her hair, which was still fair, then noticed that the skin on the back of the hand was beginning to lose its elasticity. It took a moment's mental arithmetic to recall that she was thirty-seven years old now. Time wouldn't stay still for anyone, and in Lessie's case it had flown by unnoticed while she struggled for survival.

'D'you think I'm beginning to look old, Dorry?'

The girl left the frying pan and came to stand beside her, their heads almost touching. Lessie felt herself age as she compared her own face with Dorothea's fresh bloom. The younger woman had some of her mother's beauty; tonight the soft gas light teased auburn glints from her rich dark hair and when she smiled, the sparkle in her large violet eyes brought Anna to life again.

'Never! Mind you, you could do with a bit of colour

in your face, and mebbe a nice modern hairdo.'

'Away you go, I've not got the time for that sort of nonsense!'

They were laughing as the door opened and Jess came in from a late evening at the shop where she had been taking part in a special fashion display to raise funds for the war effort. Smartly dressed, her pretty nose wrinkling appreciatively at the aroma of fried potatoes sizzling in the pan, she demanded some as well.

While Dorothea sliced another potato for her, Jess sat at the table chattering about the compliments she had received while modelling the gowns. To Jess the war, like anything else outside her own life, was a minor matter.

Ian and Dorothea climbed on, leaving the town behind, stopping once they had gained the hill fields to rest for a moment. Below them the River Clyde, dotted with vessels of all sizes, was folded and tucked between hills and fingers of land that thrust inquisitively into its waters. Gourock's grey stone skirts spilled down the hill and spread comfortably along the shoreline, with shipyard cranes outlined against the water here and there. They could hear the sound of the town's church bells calling through the clear autumn air, summoning worshippers to morning service.

They sat for a companionably silent five minutes before Ian stood and held out his hand. Dorothea sighed, but took it and let him hoist her to her feet. She turned her back on the river and followed him on up the hill. In another half-hour they were over its crest and on the downward walk to Loch Thom, the nineteenth-century reservoir that provided all the water needed by Greenock's residents and had, in the previous century, supplied power for its many mills and factories before electricity took over the running of the machinery. The loch, a flooded valley, lay in a great stretch of moorland cupped by the hills that fed it with burn water and rainwater. On its banks they found themselves a sheltered cranny surrounded by broom bushes that had now shed their golden blossoms. Dorothea spread out her jacket to sit on and Ian dropped onto the grass and opened the bag he had carried, dispensing sandwiches and lemonade.

'It's good to see so much green,' he said appreciatively, looking around at the springy grass, the trees and bushes, the clumps of reeds that fringed the loch like long eyelashes. 'It's like another world. You don't know how much you have until you leave it behind.'

He had said very little about France since coming home, and Lessie and Dorothea, aware that his leave was all too short, hadn't asked questions. Jess hadn't been interested enough to ask.

He slept when they'd finished eating, and Dorothea sat by him, her long legs tucked comfortably beneath her, watching the movement of the water and enjoying the peace of the place, so different from the noise and rattle of the mill. The loch, ruffled with tiny wavelets whipped up by the wind, looked like a stretch of dove-grey silk that some giant hand had carelessly tossed down among the hills. A bird called and was answered by another. The breeze rustled through the nearby bushes.

Ian woke suddenly, startled from sleep by the muffled thump of the guns, the noise of the wounded and dying. He stared around, bewildered at finding himself on the grassy lochside in the sunshine, with no noise but the birds and the soft lapping of small waves among the reeds. With a sigh of relief he unlocked tense muscles and lay back, waiting for his racing heart to slow down, watching Dorothea as she worked on a daisy chain, her head bent over the small white and gold flowers. She turned to smile down at him, then went back to her work. She had loosened her hair and the sunlight had become entangled in it, outlining her head in a halo of glittering bronze.

Ian put his arms behind his head and watched her, drinking in her graceful serenity. In three days' time he would be on his way back; every moment of this leave was precious, something to be stowed carefully away in his head and used as a charm, later, against the horrors he would once again have to face.

He had gone to the refinery on his second day in Greenock to see his former workmates and to tell Andrew

Warren about his son's final moments. The man had listened impassively, his eyes hooded, then said, 'Thank you, Ian. I'm pleased to know that at the end he was with someone who knew him.'

'There was no pain, sir. No suffering.'

Andrew firmed his lips and nodded, clearly unable to trust his voice for a moment. Ian was sorry for him. From what he had heard, Mrs Warren had voluntarily become an invalid since her son's death. He wondered if his own mother would go the same way if anything happened to him, then decided that she would be more likely to bury herself in even more work. He hoped to God that she would never be put in that position. He admitted freely to himself, if to nobody else, that he was afraid of dying. He had seen enough to know how hard dying could be for young men wrenched from life before their proper time. He wanted to live, to savour the days and the years, to grow old and acquire wisdom and knowledge, to have something to look back on. He wanted this moment, with just himself and Dorry and the blue sky and the water, to go on for ever. He wanted . . . With a shock that almost took his breath away, he realised that he wanted Dorry with a wanting that had crept up on him, letter by letter, during his time away from her.

'We should be thinking of getting back,' she said at that moment, regret in her voice. She put the daisy chain she had made about her wrist; it was too long and it swung gently as she began to repack the bag. Ian, dazed with his discovery, sat up and stopped her with a hand on her arm. 'Dorry.'

'What?' She glanced at him and her eyes widened in startled confusion as they met the look in his. Soft rose stained her cheeks and she knelt up, pulling away from beneath his hand. 'I told Mam that we'd be back by—'

'Dorry.' He too got to his knees, both hands on her shoulders now, his voice insistent. 'Look at me.'

She started to say something, then fell silent. Her eyes lifted to his and his heart began to speed up again. A man could drown sweetly in that deep pool of violet light,

Ian thought, stunned by poetic notions he had never entertained before.

He reached out, cupped the soft hair at the back of her neck, and kissed her. He only had time to register that her mouth was soft and warm and sweet before she pulled back so sharply that she almost overbalanced and he had to tighten his grip to steady her.

'Ian!' She tried to twist away from him, but he held her firmly. 'You can't!'

'I can – we can. Listen to me, Dorry,' he said hurriedly as she shook her head in denial, lashing his cheek with her soft flying hair. 'You're not my sister. We were raised together, but we're not brother and sister!' Words that had been forming themselves in the back of his mind during the past terrifying, threatening months, longings that had somehow been woven into him, tumbled out half-formed, unplanned. 'D'you understand me? I never thought of it until I was away, till I was in France and your letters began to mean so much to me. I didn't think of you not being my sister until then. But you're not, Dorry, you're no relation to me. We're free, both of us, to choose. And I choose you.'

She stopped struggling, looked at him, her eyes moving over his face as though she were seeing him for the first time. His hands dropped from her shoulders to her fingers. He lifted them to his lips then slipped the daisy chain from her wrist and gently arranged it on her dark sun-kissed head. 'I choose you,' he said again and stooped towards her. This time she responded, and her hands and her face and her sweet soft mouth, opening beneath his, tasted of the same floral scent that had wafted from her letters.

'Pneumonia. That's what it says on the death certificate, but the truth of the matter is that she died of a broken heart.' Flakes of January snow still clung to Andrew Warren's coat as he stood in the middle of Lessie's kitchen. A week earlier he had buried his wife; in the past six months, Lessie thought, he had aged a great deal, though his shoulders were still broad, his back still straight. The striking tan he had brought back to Greenock all those years ago had long gone, but even so there was still a hint of more exotic places about the planes of his face and the clarity of his eyes, as though the hot sun and lush foliage of Jamaica were still in his blood.

His hands fumbled with the brim of the hat he had just taken off. 'She was never truly happy after I brought her here, Lessie. She never settled. Perhaps I should have stayed out there, found other work and let the refinery be sold. Or put it into a manager's hands as she wanted, and gone back. But I felt that it was my duty to stay here. I put my family and its traditions first. I let her down.'

'You did what you had to.'

'It's hard to lose a child,' he said without seeming to hear her. 'It doesn't seem right to go on living when your own flesh and blood – your own creation – has gone before you. I knew how Madeleine felt after we lost Martin, though she'd not believe me when I tried to tell her that.' His grey eyes travelled the room without seeing anything. 'God, Lessie, they're all vanishing. Only yesterday I was a young man with my life in front of me, and now they're gone – my uncles, Madeleine, Anna, Martin. All I've got is Helene. And Dorothea, but I lost her too, when her mother died. I wish now that I'd had the courage to take Dorothea into my own house when she was younger.'

Lessie knew a moment's unease. Dorry was a human being, not a figurine to be pushed into the space left by Martin Warren's death. 'You'd only have made your wife more unhappy if you'd done that. Best leave things as they are, Andrew.'

'I suppose so. But there are times when I . . .' He sighed, then said, 'But it's wrong of me to speak to you like that. You've lost folk too, and here I am expecting you to listen to me and put up with my girning.'

'You're not girning. Men are too harsh on themselves. Everyone needs to speak their hearts instead of their minds now and again.'

'You never do.'

She thought of Donald and her parents and laughing, trusting Thomasina – and of Murdo, not dead but lost to her. 'Not to you, mebbe, but others have to put up with my complaints.'

'And you've heard enough of mine,' Andrew said, suddenly brisk, making an effort to push his troubles aside. 'Have you heard from young Ian lately?'

'He was fine last week when he wrote to me. He's hoping that mebbe this year'll be the one that sees the end of the war.'

'Who would have believed at the beginning that it would last so long or take such a toll? We were so conceited, weren't we? So – British. So sure that no foreigner could vanquish us. Well, we've got more than we'd bargained for.'

When he had gone, Lessie walked down to the shop, her mind on Ian – and on Dorothea, who had a new bounce in her step and a new sparkle in her eye these days. Nothing had been said, but Lessie had a shrewd idea that her son and Anna's daughter had come to an understanding during Ian's last leave. She wondered, uneasily, how Andrew would react if his daughter fell in love with one of his employees, then decided to leave the worry of it aside until it happened. If it did, she had a feeling that both Ian and Dorothea would be capable of facing the consequences of their actions.

Six months after his wife's death Andrew Warren took Lessie's breath away by inviting her to be his partner at a business dinner to be held in the Town Hall.

'What? You're havering,' she told him bluntly, and he roared with laughter.

'You don't believe in mincing your words, do you, Lessie Carswell? I mean it. Will you accompany me to the dinner?'

'Certainly not! The very idea of it! You the owner of one of the town's largest refineries and me with my wee shop in the Vennel. We'd be the laughing stock of the place.'

'I'd like to see the man or woman that would dare to

laugh at either of us. Lessie, I'm serious. It's in aid of war savings and I'll be expected to attend. I'd like you to be with me.'

'It's only been half a year since your wife died.'

'Even so, I'll be looked for. The world's changed, my dear, there are no such luxuries as an official year of mourning now. God only knows the world would be in mourning for evermore if there were, these days.'

'Why don't you take your daughter?'

'Helene would be bored, and she'd show it and embarrass me. Besides, if I must go I'd as soon enjoy myself by going with someone of my own choosing. Lessie,' he said in exasperation, 'have you not done much more for me than I could ever do for you? Let me pay off some of my debt by taking you to the dinner.'

When they heard about it, Jess and Dorothea, far from agreeing with Lessie that the whole thing was preposterous, astonished her by taking Andrew Warren's side.

'The ladies have started coming into the shop for their gowns already. Mam, just think of it,' Jess said, her lovely little face flushed with excitement, 'the richest folk in the area – all the businessmen and their wives. And you in the middle of it all! You can tell us about it afterwards – wait till I tell them at the shop that my mother's going to be there.'

'That's just it, all those rich folk and me. I'd stick out like a sore thumb!'

'Not if we helped you with your hair, and your clothes,' Dorothea said, and Jess chimed in with, 'Go on, Mam, you can't say no. When will you ever get a chance to go to something like this again?'

'Never, I hope,' Lessie told her daughter, but she could hear the surrender in her own voice, and judging from the gleeful looks they exchanged, so could the girls.

The interior of the shop Jess worked in was like a luxurious house and Lessie was hard put to it not to feel awed as she stepped through the glass doors and onto the thick carpet. There were comfortable chairs and sofas, mirrors, soft lights, and racks to the left and right of her held beautiful gowns in all colours and materials. It was like walking into a rainbow, she thought bemused, as Jess swept towards her, pink-cheeked with excitement, slender and elegant and older than her fifteen years in a black dress with snowy white lace at the neck and wrists, her fair hair pinned stylishly on top of her small head. Seeing her daughter in a different setting for the first time, Lessie felt her breath catch. It was no wonder that Jess's employers used her to model their gowns.

'Ma – Mother,' Jessie corrected herself smoothly, 'this is Miss Forsyth. She's going to help you to choose a gown for the dinner.'

The tall, grey-haired woman who came to Jess's side was so imposingly regal that it was difficult not to hold out a hand to her. 'Whatever you do, Mam,' Jess had said that morning before hurrying off to work, 'don't say how d'ye do and shake hands with anyone. You're a client, and clients don't do that.'

Miss Forsyth was already casting a practised eye over her. 'You're right, Miss Carswell, I think the deep blue would be just the thing for your mother. This way, madam.'

Lessie was ushered into a cubicle, stripped to her best underclothes, and dressed in the deep blue gown. Then Miss Forsyth turned her towards a mirror and stepped back. 'What do you think, madam?'

Lessie looked, and looked again. The face was familiar, so was the fair hair drawn back in a bun, but the dress was so breathtaking that for a moment she couldn't speak. It was made of deep blue silk embroidered with tiny silver flowers. The bodice ran from shoulder to waist in a V shape with an inset of pale blue chiffon studded with tiny pearls. The skirt was slightly hobbled, falling from the high waist to the knees in two tiers then gathered at the centre to fall to a slight split at ankle length.

'The skirt needs taking up just a little,' said Miss Forsyth, dropping to her knees with the ease of an ardent churchgoer, as though worshipping the hem of the dress with pins, each one darting into the right place with skilled speed. 'But otherwise it seems to be a perfect fit.'

She put in the final pin and rose to her feet, a faint smile brushing her pale mouth. 'You wear clothes very well, madam. There are gloves to go with the gown and we can provide a chiffon boa and silver shoes to match the embroidery.'

'It's – it's beautiful!'

Miss Forsyth swept the curtain back and Jess, who had been hovering outside impatiently, stood stock still, her mouth falling open. 'Oh, Mam,' she whispered after a moment, completely forgetting her role as a cool assistant, 'you look lovely!'

The smile touched Miss Forsyth's mouth again for just a second before she said briskly, 'The shoes, Miss Carswell, and the gloves and boa, if you please.'

When Lessie was dressed to their satisfaction, both women walked round her as though she was a statue, murmuring their approval, Jess in control of herself once more.

'The hair,' Miss Forsyth said, 'and the face . . .'

'My sister and I will see to that,' Jess assured her as Lessie twisted round to see the back view in the mirror. The back of the bodice was like the front, though it was highlighted at the waist by a rosette in pale blue chiffon and the skirt tiers were shaped in two points which complemented the line of the gown. When the inspection was finally over, she took the dress off carefully, reverently, and got into her own clothes while Jess bore the blue gown off to the back regions where someone waited to take up the hem and make it perfect.

'As to the cost,' Miss Forsyth said in a discreet murmur.

'How much?' Lessie asked bluntly, on more familiar ground now.

The woman named a sum that almost rocked her back on her heels, then said, 'As you are related to a member of our staff and this is a special occasion, we can deduct a small percentage. And it could be paid in weekly instalments of, shall we say—'

'I'll pay the full amount, thank you, and I'll pay it all when the gown's ready for me,' Lessie said firmly, and was gratified to see surprise and chagrin in the woman's eyes.

'Nobody's going to patronise me,' she told herself grimly as she went back into the street and headed for the nearest tram stop. 'If I must do this, I'll do it the right way.'

Thanks to Andrew Warren and his sound financial advice over the years, she was in a position to buy her own gown and pay the same price as the richest lady in the finest house in Gourock. Donald, she thought as she boarded the tram, would have been pleased.

20

When Andrew came to collect Lessie on the night of the town hall dinner, he stood motionless in the middle of the kitchen, elegant in his formal evening suit, his eyes travelling slowly over the woman who waited for him. Lessie felt colour rise to her face as she saw the admiration in his gaze. Jess and Dorothea exchanged a look and smiled.

'You look like royalty,' he said at last.

'I feel like Cinderella with two fairy godmothers,' Lessie told him with a shaky attempt at sarcasm. She was quite shocked herself by her new appearance. Her hair, normally drawn back into a loose bun at the nape of her neck, had been softly curled round her face at the front and piled high in a chignon on the crown. Her lips had been reddened, her cheeks softly dusted with rouge, and a single-strand pearl necklace, unexpectedly loaned by the formidable Miss Forsyth, clasped her long slim neck. The girls had even shaped and buffed her nails and made her cream her hands every night and sleep with them in gloves for a week.

'You look very beautiful,' Andrew told her after he had helped her into the back of his chauffeur-driven car.

'I feel very nervous.'

'No need to be. I'll look after you.' He covered her gloved hands with one of his. At that moment the car stopped, and Lessie said with a giggle, 'We're here. I told you I could have walked – we're only a matter of yards away from the house!'

'Tonight,' Andrew promised her, 'you're doing everything in style.'

The town hall was already thronged with people. They had to wait in line until their names were called and they were welcomed by the Provost and his wife. Long lines of tables awaited them in the main hall, the linen covers crisply white, splashed with colour from the vases of flowers placed at regular intervals down their length. Silver gleamed, glassware sparkled and threw back colour at the chandeliers overhead.

As they were shown to their table, Lessie was uncomfortably aware that heads were turning, people murmuring to each other. She knew that they were wondering who Andrew Warren was escorting.

As though he was reading her mind, the elbow she was holding squeezed her hand against his side briefly, reassuringly. 'Remember that they all wondered about Cinderella too,' he murmured. 'And she turned out to be a princess.'

She laughed, then lifted her head high and looked back at the starers, feeling secure in Andrew's company.

The food was delicious, but afterwards she scarcely remembered any details, much to Jess's and Dorothea's annoyance. Wine helped to ease her nervousness, though when the waiter came round again with the bottle she put her hand over her glass as she had seen someone else do. One glassful was quite enough for a woman who was unused to drink.

After the meal, there were speeches and announcements of donations to the appeal for money for the war effort. Andrew's name was read out, followed by an impressive amount. People in the vicinity smiled their approval at him, and at Lessie. Then another name and amount caught her attention.

'That's our Davie the man's talking about!' she hissed to Andrew.

'It is indeed. He's probably here tonight.'

'Davie? Here?'

'He's become quite a well-known businessman in the town. Didn't you know?'

As they rose later to move into another large room where musicians waited she caught sight of her brother at the other side of the hall. He saw them and nodded to them.

'I'd no idea he had become well known,' Lessie marvelled. 'He never says much about himself when he visits me.'

'Oh, he's done well. He's got a good head on his shoulders. He was the man who first suggested new centrifugal machinery for the refinery, and eventually installed it. I've got cause to be grateful.'

Davie came to talk to Lessie when she was sitting on her own later in the evening. Watching him crossing the floor towards her, as smart as Andrew in his evening garb, but having to work hard at looking as elegant, she felt the old affection sweep over her. She hadn't seen Joseph for years, and might indeed have passed him in the street these days without recognition if he returned to the town, but Davie still had a special place in her heart.

'You're mixing with the posh folk tonight, my lad,' she said as he reached her.

He shrugged. 'It's one of the things I must do now that I've got my own business. It means nothing.'

'And what about the lady you're with? Don't tell me she means nothing.'

Davie glanced over his shoulder to where his dark-haired partner was dancing with an older man. 'I've told you before, our Lessie, none of your match-making.' The old grin broke up the normally solemn lines of his broad face for a moment. 'She's the daughter of one of my best customers – that's him dancing with her now. A man needs a partner when he goes to these soirees, that's all.' Then he said with an undertone of steel in his voice, 'You're a fine one to talk. I was surprised to see who you were partnering. I didnae realise you were so friendly, the two of you.'

'Mr Warren keeps in touch for Dorry's sake. He asked me to partner him since it's only six months since he lost his wife.'

'Is that all there is to it?'

'It is. But that,' said Lessie with spirit, 'is my own business.'

He grinned again. 'Still the same sharp-tongued Lessie, underneath. But on the surface you're beautiful enough to be more than a match for any of the fine ladies here. I wish I'd thought to ask you to be my partner.'

'Kirkwood,' Andrew loomed over them, holding out his hand to Davie, 'good to see you again.'

The smile vanished from Davie's face as he got to his feet, putting his hand forward. 'Warren.'

'Will you and your partner not join us?'

'Thank you, but we're with a party of folk. I'd best be getting back to them. Lessie,' said Davie with a curt nod, and left them, weaving his way in and out of the dancers with ease.

If Andrew noticed Davie's sudden coolness he didn't remark on it. But Lessie puzzled over it for the rest of the evening.

'I'm so close to home that I might as well get into this car and out again through the other door,' she protested later as the diners spilled out through the town hall doors into the summer night.

'We'll do the thing properly,' Andrew said firmly, handing her into the back of the car. 'And thank you,' he added as they moved off. 'You turned a duty into a pleasure.'

'I enjoyed it, once I got over the nervousness. When I think back to the days when I cleaned stairs for a living, who'd ever have thought then that I could go to a dinner like that?'

'You worked for your money, like all the other people there. You deserve tonight as much as they do – more than most. Look at me, for instance. I was born into my livelihood. You had to find yours wherever you could.'

The car stopped and he detained her with a hand on her arm until the chauffeur got out and opened the door for her. In the dark close, Lessie fumbled for her key in the tiny bag she carried, then Andrew's hand came down and claimed it.

'I've enjoyed this evening, Lessie. You should come to Gourock to see the house some time, perhaps meet Helene.'

'No, Andrew.'

'Why not?'

'You know why not.' She had often been alone with him in her kitchen, but never before had she been as aware of him as she was in this dark corridor with nobody there to see the two of them. 'We're from different lives, you and me. And you'd best be going back to your car. The driver'll be wondering what you're up to.'

He laughed, then leaned towards her, the faint smell of hair cream and good tobacco wafting round her. For a moment she tensed, certain that he was going to kiss her, then she heard her key in the lock and the faint creak of the door being edged open. 'Good night, my dear,' said Andrew. 'Thank you for a very pleasant evening.'

In the kitchen, where a light had been left burning for her, Lessie realised with embarrassment and annoyance that she was trembling. She was far too old for such silliness, she told herself briskly, taking off the chiffon boa and putting it over the back of a chair. And yet the faint dizziness she was experiencing woke happy recollections of past loving and courtship. She caught sight of herself in the mirror over the mantel and saw that she was smiling, flushed, almost pretty with her hair curled softly about her rosy face. Then the smile faded as she saw an army-issue envelope propped against the mirror, unopened, her name scrawled on the front.

For a moment she thought that it was from Ian, then she saw Peter's name and an unfamiliar unit scribbled on the back. She ripped it open hurriedly and saw that it held only a few lines, written as though in haste, or when the writer was under strain.

'Dear Aunt Lessie, I'm sorry not to have written to you earlier. I was too shamed. They won, Aunt Lessie. I couldn't let them do to me what they had done to others I saw. So I'm in France and I have a gun and I'm no better than they are after all. My mother is pleased. I'm sorry. Peter.'

All the young man's agony and shame reached out to Lessie from the few words. The dance forgotten, she dug in a drawer for the notepad and pen she used to write Ian's letters and sat down at the table, ignoring the clock that ticked the night hours away. Her letter was brief, for there was no point in overwhelming the lad with the love she badly wanted to give him. And she had the sense to realise that too affectionate a letter might well break down the wall he must have been forced to build round himself, brick by painful brick, in order to cope with the sheer burden of living. She tried to convey as much love and sympathy in her words as she could while at the same time keeping the letter cheerful and matter-of-fact; more than an hour later, with several sheets of paper discarded and burned in the last ashes of the dying fire, she completed her difficult task and rose stiffly to wash her face vigorously with soap and water, cleaning away every vestige of the make-up the girls had put on hours before. Then she went into Ian's room, which she was using in his absence, took off the fine gown and stowed it away carefully in the wardrobe. After that she took the hidden pins from her hair and brushed it hard until it fell down her back, then braided it. She was ashamed of the way she had dressed like a lady and gone out and eaten good food and enjoyed herself while young men like Peter – and Ian – were risking their lives so far from home and from those who loved them.

Jess and Dorothea were disappointed when they came into the kitchen the following morning and found the usual Lessie, her hair swept back into a bun, making the porridge.

'You could have kept the curls for several days,' Jess pouted, 'then I could have done your hair for you again. You looked lovely.'

'Did you not see the way Mr Warren looked at you when he came into the room?' Dorothea chimed in.

'Like Douglas Fairbanks in a film I saw last week,' Jess said dreamily, and was quelled by a look from her mother.

'He thought you were lovely too, I know he did. Did you have a good time?'

'I had a grand time, thank you, Dorry.' Lessie ladled

porridge into their plates and fetched the milk jug from its place on the shelf, removing the beaded muslin cover that protected its contents. 'But this is a new day and the dance is over.'

'Mam, why don't you let me do your hair again?' Jess coaxed, stirring milk into her porridge. 'You've got nice hair – you should look after it.'

'I do look after it. It's washed regularly, and brushed every day. As to the rest,' said Lessie evenly, pouring boiling water into the teapot, talking to Andrew Warren and the small rebellious spark deep within herself as much as to the two young girls who sat at the table, 'we're all as God meant us to be, and He meant me to be a shopkeeper. I'm an ordinary woman and I see no sense in trying to change.'

In October Dorothea and her friend Aileen were moved to the mill's weighing room. It was quieter there, with no need to shout or lip-read. The loading bay was situated directly beneath them and a large square hole in the middle of the floor gave access to the hoist which brought the bales of cotton up to be weighed. Each bale was numbered and its weight recorded in a large ledger, and once its contents had been spun into yarn, they, and the waste from the bale, came back to be weighed again and checked against the original weight.

The repartee of the young lads who handled the bales and rode up and down on the hoist with them kept Aileen entertained all day. Dorothea's thoughts were with Ian for most of the time. He was still alive, still unhurt, and from all that was being said, the war was as good as over. She slept with his letters under her pillow now and re-read them whenever she got the opportunity. It was a wonder that Jess hadn't noticed her dreaming over them, but Jess was doing more and more modelling and trying to persuade her mother to allow her to take a job in one of the big Glasgow shops; she was too preoccupied with her own dreams to notice what was going on under her pretty little nose.

Soon, Dorothea thought as she entered figures in the

book, for she was the neater writer of the two and the task fell to her, soon Ian would be home. Perhaps he would propose to her properly and they would get married and—

'Cheeky bugger you are, Aileen Lennox,' one of the lads shouted as his laughing face disappeared below floor level on his way down in the hoist.

'My mam doesnae breed buggers!' Aileen retorted swiftly, getting the last word in as usual. The door banged open and the winding shop overseer put his head in and glared at her, catching the final sentence.

'Dorry Carswell, Mr Spiers wants to see you in his office. Now!'

The two girls stared at each other. 'Ooh, Dorry, what've you done?'

'I don't know. D'you think I've been entering the figures wrong?' Dorothea felt as though a cold hand was clutching at her stomach. She wasn't like Aileen, care-free and able to cock a snook at authority.

'It's almost clocking-off time. Want me to wait for you?'

'No, it's all right.' If she was in for a scolding or, even worse, dismissal, the last thing Dorothea wanted was sympathy.

She tapped on the door of the manager's office on the ground floor and Mr Spiers himself opened it, stepping aside to let her in.

'Miss – er – Carswell, Mr Warren would like a word with you. I'll – er – ' He scurried out, closing the door carefully behind him. Dorothea stared at the tall figure by the window. He could only be the bearer of bad news.

'Mam,' she said, her mouth suddenly dry. Then, even more fearfully, 'Ian?'

'There's nothing wrong,' Andrew said quickly, coming forward, his hands outstretched. 'Nothing at all, my dear. In fact, I hope that it's the opposite. Sit down, Dorothea.'

He guided her into a chair then leaned back against Mr Spiers' desk, clearing his throat before he said, 'Dorothea, there's something I must tell you. I've been giving it a lot of thought lately and it's my belief, now, that you should have known it a while ago . . .'

It wasn't like Dorry to be late. Normally she was home by this time, setting the table, peeling potatoes, chattering on about her day at the mill, willing to listen to anything Lessie had to say about the shop. Jess, complaining at having to do the potatoes, fretting about ruining her hands, was a poor substitute.

Just as Lessie was about to go out to the closemouth to see if Dorry was in sight, a car door closed in the street outside and Jess, dripping dirty water, abandoned the basin of potatoes and flew to the window.

'It's Mr Warren come to call – and he's brought our Dorry home in his car!' Her voice sharpened with envy. 'Trust her to get all the luck!'

'Mr Warren? At this hour? Jess, put the basin out of sight, dry your hands.' Lessie ran to the mirror to tidy her hair. The close door opened and suddenly Dorothea was in the kitchen, her eyes hard, the old scar standing out against the pallor of her face.

'Dorry, pet, what's happened? Has there been an accident?'

Dorothea stepped back, away from Lessie's reaching arms. 'Is it true?' she said in a hard voice Lessie had never heard from her before. It shook with shock and anger. 'Why didn't you tell me about – about who my real father was?'

Andrew came into the kitchen behind her, his eyes wary but defiant. 'I thought it was time she knew, Lessie. I want everyone to know the truth.'

Lessie, the blood draining from her heart, took a step or two towards Dorothea, her arms outstretched, but the girl moved back again, shaking her dark head vehemently, dislodging drifts of cotton that had been caught in the curls.

'You should have told me!'

'Dorry, I – we decided that it was for the best that we wait until you were older. Didn't we?' Lessie angrily challenged Andrew, who had the grace to colour and glance away for a second. In the background Jess, forgotten, gaped in astonishment at the drama being played out in front of her disbelieving eyes.

'I thought it was time Dorothea knew everything. She's not a child any more and I want her to come and live with me, to be openly recognised as my daughter. I've waited for too long,' Andrew said, his voice slightly unsteady.

'And you think I haven't waited for a long time to know the truth?' Dorothea suddenly blazed at him. 'All those years you visited, and I never knew that I was your daughter! All those years, wondering. And neither of the two of you bothered to tell me!'

Andrews eyes were anguished. 'I wanted to, but I couldn't, not while my wife was alive. I know I've left it late, but I've never stopped wanting to acknowledge you. Let me make it up to you now, Dorothea!'

'Dorry, you must do as you think best. You'll always have a home here, if that's what you want.'

The hurt and bewilderment in the girl's eyes made Lessie feel as though a knife had been plunged into her own heart. 'Oh, I'll go with him, since he's my own flesh and blood. Whatever you say, I've no rights to this house any more, have I?'

'Dorry!'

'I'll just collect some of my things,' Dorothea said, and turned on her heel.

'Jess, go and help your – go and help her.'

Still gaping, Jess did as she was told and Lessie, heedless now of the mess the kitchen was in and the fact that she hadn't washed her face or brushed her hair since coming home from the shop, rounded on Andrew Warren, so angry that she could have lifted her fist and struck him. 'How could you? How could you do such a thing to the lassie? We discussed this, did we not? We agreed that—'

He flinched, but stood firm. 'I'm lonely, Lessie.'

'To hell with your loneliness! We agreed that when she was told it would be done gently. Surely I've earned the right to be considered as well!'

'Would you have given your consent to her being told

now? I doubt it. I've lost Martin, I've as good as lost Helene now that she's engaged to be married – not that I ever had her as a daughter,' said Andrew bitterly. 'I need to have someone of my own to care for.'

'So that's it, is it? You're claiming Dorry, turning her life upside down, just to satisfy your own need? You could have bought yourself a dog!'

His face went scarlet, and suddenly he was as angry as she was. 'For God's sake, she's my daughter!'

'And mine too, as good as!' They were quarrelling in fierce whispers so as not to be overheard by the girls. 'I've raised her from babyhood. How d'you think I feel, losing her like this?'

'You're not losing her. She'll visit you, and so will I, just as I always have. Lessie, try to see things my way.'

'How can I?' she began hotly, then stopped as the bedroom door opened. When Dorothea, carrying a small bag, came into the room, Lessie was stirring fiercely at a pot of broth on the stove and Andrew stood gazing out of the window. He turned and smiled at the girl, his mouth stiff, his eyes bright. 'All ready? Come along, my dear.'

At the door Lessie put her arms round Dorothea and kissed her on the cheek. 'This is still your home, love. Come here whenever you want to,' she whispered, but the girl stood stiff and unresponsive in her embrace then turned without a word and followed her father.

Lessie and Jess stood at the closemouth watching as the chauffeur opened the car door and Warren stowed his newly claimed daughter into the back seat as though she were made of delicate porcelain. Children playing on the pavement and women leaning out of their windows and gossiping at the closemouths stared as the door closed on the two of them and the gleaming car moved smoothly away from the pavement.

Dorothea glanced back once, her white expressionless face blurred behind the glass. Then the car turned a corner and was gone, taking a piece of Lessie's heart with it.

'Why her?' Jess wanted to know as they went back

into the house. 'It was just like a film, but why should it be her and not me? Dorry always has all the luck. No wonder she was your favourite. I might have known she'd be the rich one and not me, oh no, I'm just—'

'Hold your tongue if you don't want a good skelp across the ear,' said Lessie, and her daughter subsided with a gasp of astonishment and outrage.

'And get on with the potatoes,' Lessie went on as they went into the kitchen. 'We still have to eat.' She lifted the lid of a pot, stirred its contents without knowing what she was doing.

'I suppose there's one thing,' Jess said after a moment, chopping vicious lumps off the potatoes, reducing them to half their original size. 'I'll get the bedroom to myself.'

21

As though to warn people not to be too optimistic about the future now that the tide of war seemed to be turning, one of the most virulent forms of influenza ever known swept the country like a scythe through grass. It took the oldest and the youngest and the weakest. It took Elma, who had worked valiantly for Lessie for so many years.

Lessie wept for her friend as she followed the coffin to the cemetery, then returned home and dried her tears and got on with the business of running the shop and fumigating the two rooms beyond to clear them of the influenza virus. She turned them into storerooms and took on a woman widowed in the war, one of her staunchest customers.

In November the town, like every other town and village in Britain, erupted into colour and noise, its streets thronged with people who, forsaking their Scottish reticence for once, hugged and kissed complete strangers in celebration of the end of the Great War.

Ian was safe, Peter was safe, and for Lessie and Edith, at any rate, there would be young men to welcome home, eventually. But Lessie's joy was dulled by the other loss she had just suffered, for to her Dorothea was as much her child as Ian and Jess. The girl had come back twice to the house in Cathcart Street since her move to the Warren house, elegant in her new clothes, her hair fashionably coiffed by Helene Warren's hairdresser. She had changed inside as well as outside; in a few weeks she had built up a wall between herself and Lessie and remained firmly behind it, no matter how hard Lessie tried to regain their former affection. She had collected the rest of her belongings and tucked the two letters waiting for her from Ian carefully into her pocket.

'Have you any word of when Ian's coming home?'

'Not yet. It'll be a while before they're all back where they belong. Will I tell him, when I next write?'

Dorothea shook her head and the feather on her wide-brimmed hat moved languidly. 'I'll tell him,' she said, and went back to the big house in Gourock, leaving behind only a trace of expensive scent.

Jess fumed with helpless envy over her former sister's new clothes. She wasted no time in removing every trace of Dorothea from the small bedroom they had shared for so long and renewed her demands to be allowed to move to Glasgow where she could get a better job with more chance of modelling.

'Miss Forsyth's willing to give me a good reference and a letter to a friend who's supervisor of one of the largest dress stores,' she nagged. 'I'm sixteen and a half, it's time I started to travel. Anyway, it's terrible here with folk knowing about Dorry. They come into the shop and stare at me and whisper to each other. And they snigger!'

The news of Dorothea's parentage and her entry into the Warren household had indeed been a talking point in the town, but only for a short while, as Lessie crisply pointed out to her daughter. It had quickly been superseded by the armistice, which was of far greater importance. She knew well enough that she would soon lose Jess too, for there was little she could do to keep the girl at home now that she was old enough to make her own decisions. But she managed to persuade her to stay until Ian came back. She couldn't bear the thought of being alone in the house. All at once it seemed as though her life had gone out of control and taken a turn onto a road that she followed against her will.

Andrew still called every week, ostensibly to report on Dorothea's progress. He brought small gifts with him – a box of sweets, hothouse grapes from a business colleague's glasshouse, a tiny bunch of delicate snowdrops early in January, the first that had appeared in his garden. Every time he came, Lessie was aware of his eyes on her, guilty, hopeful of forgiveness. She soon realised that there was no point in letting her anger over his thoughtlessness cause a permanent rift between them. They had been friends for too long, they owed each other debts of gratitude. They were linked, too, by Dorothea, just as they had been linked by Anna. The gifts of fruit reminded her poignantly of the days when her father and Davie brought stolen oranges from the docks for wee Ian; they also reminded her that folk needed folk, and there was no sense in turning her back on a friendship that had in many ways come to mean a great deal to her.

'Dorothea's fine,' he assured her over and over again. 'Naturally it'll take a while to get used to a different way of life, but she's fine. And I can offer her so much – more than I was ever able to offer Anna.' His eyes softened, looking beyond her to the window, and she knew that he, too, was recalling days long past. 'She's like her mother in so many ways, Lessie. I'm reminded of Anna every time she looks at me.'

Lessie said nothing, but wondered if he realised that nobody could fully take the place of someone else. Nobody, particularly Anna's daughter, could be expected to follow the path planned, step by step, for her.

'I know you miss her, but surely it's my turn now,' he said just then, confirming her thoughts.

'It's nobody's turn, Andrew, can you not understand that? The lassie's a living, breathing human being, not a doll!' Then the snowdrops, fragile and beautiful in the little vase she had found for them, caught her eye and she softened her voice. 'I know how you feel, you've stood back from her for a long time and denied yourself. I don't blame you for wanting her. But she must be free to live her own life.'

'She will be. I know that you miss her, but you'll soon have your son home.' There was faint bitterness in his voice and she knew he was thinking of his own boy.

'I'm not sure whether Ian'll settle back to his old life, and at his age I'd not expect to have him with me for much longer. Mebbe I need a new interest in life. The woman I took on in poor Elma's place is worth her weight in gold. I'm scarcely needed in the shop now.'

'It's time you had a rest and a chance to think of yourself for once. We're none of us getting any younger, Lessie, and you don't need to work as hard as you used to, surely?'

'I'm not a horse ready to be put out to graze!' she protested hotly, and he laughed. But his words rankled, and when he had gone she turned them over in her mind, finding them condescending and typically masculine. It was true that the need to work wasn't as sharp as it had been. Jess was earning, Ian would find his old job in the refinery waiting for him when he came home, Dorry had gone. Thanks largely to Andrew's advice over the years, Lessie had managed to put by some money.

She went back to the ledgers laid out on the kitchen table, running her finger down columns of figures, turning pages, checking figures. Since Dorry had left, since the end of the war that had kept them all living on a knife-edge for four long years, she was restless and there was a need to take her life in hand. The shop in the Vennel was ticking along very nicely, thanks to Doreen's efficiency and to the assistance of a girl who had been taken on two months earlier and had proved to be well worth her wages. Since the end of the war, there had been a new affluence among her customers. They bought luxury foods now, items like tinned salmon and cream biscuits, and the takings had risen impressively.

The germ of an idea began to tickle at the back of Lessie's mind. She put the ledgers away, brought them out, glanced over them again, then with a sudden surge of purpose she put on her hat and coat and left the house. There were folk to see, plans to pursue. There was a new idea to be followed up.

Two days later, the groundwork laid, she took a five-minute walk from the shop in the Vennel to a single-end apartment buried in a warren of narrow streets. Here, she had been told, the Manns, who had once run the gleaming, successful corner shop in Cathcart Street, lived, still in Greenock although their shop had remained boarded up and padlocked during the war years.

The stairs were dingy, the building smelled of boiled cabbage, and the door Lessie knocked on was badly in need of a coat of paint. After a long pause, steps came dragging and shuffling to the door and it opened a crack.

'Vat you vant?'

'Mrs Mann? It's Lessie Carswell, from Cathcart Street. Can I come in and talk to you and your husband?'

There was a long pause. The woman, breathing heavily, seemed to be unsure of what to do, then a mumble was faintly heard and slowly, reluctantly, the door opened just wide enough for Lessie to slip in through the gap.

The single room smelled as though it were the source of the building's entire cabbage stench. It was cold and dank and dim, most of the dull January afternoon light kept out. At first Lessie thought that the one narrow window was curtained. After a great deal of panting and shuffling a match was lit and shakily applied to a stub of candle and she saw that the window was covered with pieces torn from cardboard boxes, nailed haphazardly over the gap where the glass had been. Rags were stuffed between the pieces of board in a vain attempt to keep the wind out.

She looked round in dawning horror at the black, mouldy patches on the walls, the empty grate, the bottle and the lumps of bread and cheese on the rickety table, the single shabby blanket on the alcove bed.

'Vat do you vant with us?' A hoarse voice, thick with phlegm, brought her attention to Mr Mann, huddled in a chair by the fireplace. At first she didn't recognise him, for he had shrunk to about half his original size and was almost hidden from view deep within the shabby coat that he wore. He was no longer the big handsome man in the snowy apron who had shouted at her in front of her neighbours and ordered her from his shop. But his eyes were the same, dark orbs glittering defiance at her from under an incongruous red woollen hat that had been dragged over his head and right down to his thick grey eyebrows. His wife, small and stooped, was also huddled into a coat, and on her head she wore an old felt hat, stripped of its former flowers or feathers, over greasy grey hair that escaped in wisps here and there. She had moved to behind Mr Mann's chair, her hands tightly gripping its back. Lessie didn't know whether the woman was sheltering behind her husband or poised to defend him.

'Mr Mann, d'you remember me?'

'The voman vith the shop. The voman,' he said reluctantly, as though the words were being dragged from him, 'who offered help ven the mob took our living from us.'

'Yes.' There was one other chair, an ordinary kitchen chair, in the room. Lessie moved to it and sat down, so that she and Mr Mann were on the same eye level. The chair shook and rocked under her weight, and she dug her feet into the sticky floor to balance herself. 'I believe you still own the shop. Are you not thinking of opening it again now that – now that it's all over?'

'Vat vith, lady?' There was no mistaking the sarcasm in his voice. 'Ze money ve no longer earn? Ze rent ve had to go on paying? Ze health your damned town took from us?'

'I'm surprised you stayed on in Greenock after what was done to you.'

'Ve had nowhere else to go. Our children,' a knotted hand in an old fingerless woollen glove emerged from the folds of the coat and gestured clumsily, 'zey also had persecution because zeir blood is not British. How could ve go to zem?'

'Are they still in Britain?'

He nodded, a tired dipping of the head. 'Still here. Vere else vould zey be? Zey sink of zis country as zeir home.'

Lessie felt the chill of the place seeping into her bones. The smell of age and illness and stale cooking and despair was beginning to grip at her throat. 'Mr Mann, I've been to the factor who owns the building where your shop is. He's willing to transfer the rent to me. I want to open it up again. Would you sell me whatever's still in the shop, and the goodwill?'

Mrs Mann jerked suddenly, and was still again as a rusty mirthless laugh rumbled in her husband's chest. 'Goodvill? You zink zere is any goodvill left, voman?'

'You'll get it for next to nothing,' the bank manager had said in his brisk unemotional way earlier that day, folding his hands on the desk before him. 'What's left inside will be in a terrible condition. You'll have to put a deal of money into it. Offer them the lowest amount possible, Mrs Carswell. It's my belief they'll snatch at it. They're not in any position to bargain.'

Lessie's mind raced, adding and subtracting, considering the amount the bank was prepared to lend, the weekly income from the shop she already had, the amount she would doubtless have to spend on the new shop. When she finally spoke she named a sum which would probably give the bank manager apoplexy and would cut her own financial margin uncomfortably close. But it was a sum that would allow the Manns, once a respectable and respected couple in Greenock, the chance to travel to wherever their family were picking themselves up, repairing the damage done by the war. A chance for them to pay their own way, to hold their heads high again, if they were willing to make the effort.

Mrs Mann's outline jerked again and she put a hand on her husband's shoulder. The old man ignored her. 'Vat? Vat you say? You're mad, you know zat, voman?' he said at last. 'You sink ze ruins of our shop could be worth so much?'

'It's what I'm willing to pay.' Lessie got to her feet. 'I can come back tomorrow for your answer if you want to think it over.'

'No.' His voice stopped her as she reached for the door handle. 'Ve take it.'

'Good.' She went back to him, held out her hand. At first she thought that he was going to ignore it, then it was taken in a chilly clasp that was all skin and bone. Even the wool of the glove he wore was dank against her skin and it was all she could do not to wipe her fingers against her skirt when he released them.

'I'm sorry,' she said at the open door. Sorry that two people who had worked so hard had come to this, sorry that a decent couple who had only wanted to make Scotland their home had been humiliated and defeated in a way far more cruel than the day Mr Mann had ordered her out of his shop.

'Ve are not Germans,' his voice said bleakly out of the gloom. 'Ve are Sviss. Not bad people. Never bad people.'

The following day Lessie turned the key in the padlock and walked into the remains of the Manns' shop, followed by a local joiner who had been invited to name a price for the work that needed doing.

'God, woman, ye've a big heart takin' this on,' the man said, pressing in behind her, looking at the desolation that had once been a smart little shop. He crunched through the debris on the floor towards the windows, taking a claw-headed hammer from his belt as he went, and began to wrench at the planks of wood that had been nailed over the broken windows. They gave easily and daylight flooded the interior, showing the full extent of the chaos wrought by the mob, and by the years that had elapsed since. Something scuttered into a corner and Lessie gave a yelp of fright, then stamped hard on an empty patch of floor to discourage any other little creatures that might have taken up residence.

The marble counter was still there, the wooden panels on the sides dull but intact. So were the spice drawers she remembered, and the two lots of scales, one with a porcelain platform for weighing cheese and butter. And behind the counter, to her great delight, she found the handsome cash register, lying on its side, the empty drawer open, but as far as she could see undamaged. A good cleaning should see it as right as rain. As more of the planks came off the windows and more of the shop was revealed, she stood in the middle of the devastation, looking round at the empty shelves, the hooks waiting for pink and white hams to hang from them, seeing the shop once more as it had been and could be again.

I'll buy a white apron, she thought. I'll hire a young man home from the war and in need of a job. I'll buy two white aprons—

'Ye've a big heart,' the joiner said again.

'Can the place be put right?'

He ran a hand over the marble counter then down a

panel like a groom examining a horse. 'Aye, but it'll take a wee while, and it'll cost you.'

'Could you do it? I'll pay you as you go along.'

He shrugged then nodded. Lessie beamed at him through the dust motes that had been stirred up by their presence. The restlessness had gone and in its place was determination.

'Can you start tomorrow?' she said.

Only her pride kept Dorothea from admitting that she was wretchedly unhappy in the handsome Warren house in Gourock. Everything that had given her life shape had gone – her work at the mill, the security of being one of the Carswell family, her sense of belonging. In their place were only loneliness and bewilderment. She felt like a kitten that had been taken from its mother, put into a pet shop, then bought and taken to its new owner's home. There wasn't even the comfort of having butter spread on her paws to be licked off, she thought drearily in those first terrible early days.

Andrew Warren, the man who had suddenly turned out to be her father, had been kindness itself, and she was aware of his eagerness to make her happy, make her feel at home in this large, beautiful house he and his daughter Helene inhabited. But he was away all day and every day in the refinery and beautiful dark-eyed Helene, as shocked and confused as Dorothea herself at the sudden change in circumstances, made no secret of her resentment and rage.

'You're not my sister,' she told Dorothea coldly on the first day they found themselves alone together. 'I have never had a sister and I have no wish to have one forced on me now.'

Dorothea had glared back, refusing to let the other girl see how intimidated she felt. 'I already have a sister. Her name's Jess and I don't need you any more than you need me. If it was left to me I'd not have set foot in this house!'

But it had not been left to her or to Helene, and Andrew, when he realised that there was a coolness between his two daughters, had ordered Helene to make the newcomer welcome. The command, given in front of Dorothea, had only made matters worse. Helene did as she was bid, taking Dorothea to her hairdresser and to the dress shops she herself frequented, telling the people who worked there to see to it that her half-sister – said in a cool, contemptuous little voice – was suitably attended to and provided with the correct clothes. And she took Dorothea to afternoon tea parties, introducing her in the same glacial tones.

Dorothea, unable to refuse to go out because it would have gone against her father's wishes, trailed along miserably, keenly aware of the inquisitive looks cast on her everywhere she went, the whispers and the stifled amusement. Andrew Warren was too important to be denied, and so his new daughter was included in every invitation extended to Helene.

Aileen, with her quick wit and warmth, had vanished from Dorothea's life; a few days after moving to the Warren house she had gone along to the mill at clocking-off time to see her friend, who had come out of the gate arm in arm with two of the other women, talking and laughing. The trio had stopped short at sight of Dorothea in a stylish new jacket and hat that had been bought that very day. After a pause, Aileen had detached herself from the others and sent them on their way while she herself stood waiting for Dorothea, running her eyes up and down the new jacket and skirt.

'What're you doin' here?'

'I thought I'd walk along with you.'

Aileen snorted, dislodging some flecks of cotton from her shabby coat. 'Walk wi' me? Ye're surely too high and mighty for that now!'

'I didn't want it to happen,' Dorothea burst out in an agony of helpless fury. 'I didn't want to stop working in the mill!'

'More fool you, then. If it was me, ye'd no' find me within a mile o' this bugger o' a place. Don't embarrass me – go an' spend yer money,' said Aileen, shrugging off the hand Dorothea put on her arm and moving off. 'Ye don't belong here any more, Dorry, an' there's nothin' more tae be said.'

She had gone back to Cathcart Street a few times, but the people who lived there looked at her the way Aileen had, as though she were a posh lady going slumming. Jess, for all Dorothea's brave words to Helene, had been no comfort at all. Her lovely heart-shaped little face hard with jealousy, she had passed barbed remarks that had finally driven Dorothea out. Mam – Aunt Lessie – Mrs Carswell – poor Dorothea had no idea now of how to address the woman who had raised her since babyhood – had checked Jess sharply, with little success, and had looked as wretched as Dorothea felt. Even so, they had no way of comforting each other. Dorothea had been betrayed and they both knew it.

On the first day in the Warren household she had been pathetically grateful to see a familiar, though unloved and unloveable, face when she wandered into the drawing room. Edith Fisher, in cap and apron, was dusting the room, so intent on her work that she jumped when Dorothea, in a rush of pleasure, said, 'Oh, Aunt Edith, I'm so pleased to see you!'

The plain face beneath the unbecoming cap was suddenly suffused with blood. 'Dor— Miss Dorothea. Can I help you, miss?'

'Aunt Edith—'

'My name is Edith, miss.'

'But—'

'Aunt Edith?' a light amused voice asked from the door and the two women whirled to see Helene Warren standing there, elegant in a walking dress, drawing gloves over her slender hands. 'You may go, Edith. You can continue your work in here later, when the room is free.'

'Yes, Miss Helene,' Edith said with all the dignity she could muster, and fled, the duster clenched in her hand.

'Aunt Edith?' Helene said again, putting emphasis on the first word.

'She's my – my foster mother's sister.'

'Dear me, what a confusion the house is in. What other little revelations do you have for us, Dorothea? Is the cook perhaps the sister you boasted about? And the chauffeur your cousin?'

Dorothea, her face flaming, pushed past her tormentor and fled to her room, followed up the stairs by silvery laughter. From then on she and Edith avoided each other, Edith because her pride had been wounded, Dorothea because she loathed having to treat the woman she had known as an aunt for so many years like a menial.

At night she cried herself to sleep in the lovely bedroom she now had all to herself, lonely in the soft bed, used to Jess fighting to take the lion's share of mattress and blankets.

The only thing that kept her going was the thought of Ian's return to Greenock. She wrote to him every week as before, longing to pour out her unhappiness but drawing back from it because she had no way of knowing what sort of miserable life he himself might be leading and she didn't want to burden him with her own unhappiness. Instead she wrote cheerful letters, telling him only the facts – that Andrew Warren, her real father, had taken her to live in his house. She didn't refer to her own feelings in the matter. When they were together again, when she was safe in his arms, she would pour out the truth, tell him how unhappy she had been. And he would, she hoped, tell her that there was nothing to worry about any more, that he was going to look after her and make her happy and provide a proper home for them both to share.

He, too, made little reference to the new situation. His letters became few and far between, and not as long as they had been, but she put that down to the ending of the war and the preparations his unit were making to return home with the last of the wounded.

It was February 1919 before he got back, and Dorothea, reluctant to go to Cathcart Street where she no longer belonged, waited impatiently for him to come to her. But day followed day and lengthened into one week, then two, and there was no sign of him, no word.

22

At last, in an agony of worry and need, Dorothea was forced to go to Cathcart Street in search of Ian. The house was empty but she found Lessie in the corner shop supervising the replacing of shelves that had been torn from the walls. The place had been swept clean and the rubbish removed; new glass windows were in place, the smell of fresh paint hung in the air and Lessie looked happy, her hands full of lists and plans.

Everyone was happy, Dorothea thought, hesitating in the open doorway, happy because the war was over. Helene was expecting her new fiancé home soon and even Andrew's pain at losing Martin had been eased by Dorothea herself. Perhaps now that Ian was home it was her turn to be happy.

'Dorry.' Lessie had turned and noticed her. The old warmth showed in her face and her voice and Dorothea smiled nervously in answer.

'It's looking grand.'

'I'm hoping to open it for business in two weeks' time.'

'How's Ian?'

Lessie's smile faltered. 'Oh, he's fine. Back at his old job in the refinery.'

Dorothea nodded casually, as though she already knew that. As soon as she could, she left the shop and walked back along Cathcart Street, towards the refinery. She reached it a few minutes before the noon whistle was due to blow, releasing the workers for an hour. An icy wind was gusting along the street, tossing old pieces of newspaper against her smart new shoes and slender ankles. She stepped into a shop doorway, glad of the fur-trimmed coat she wore.

The whistle shrilled and almost at once men and women began to emerge from the refinery gates, some alone, others in twos and threes, some silent, others laughing and talking. It reminded Dorothea of the mill and reinforced her sense of loneliness.

Her eyes took in each figure emerging from the gates, and brightened when, at last, Ian appeared, alone and striding out, his collar turned up against the wind. He was hatless and his red hair glowed against the grey refinery wall. She stepped out onto the pavement and waited for him, her heart beginning to beat faster. He walked with his head down and didn't notice her until she said his name, then his head jerked up and he stopped in his tracks.

For a brief moment he was the Ian she had always known, the Ian she had fallen in love with that sunny afternoon on the banks of Loch Thom. Then his blue eyes cooled and his face was wiped of expression.

'Miss Warren,' he said politely, as though greeting an acquaintance.

'What d'you mean, "Miss Warren"? It's Dorry you're talking to, you daft lummock!' She laughed and tried to tuck her hand into the crook of his elbow, but he stepped back, his face wary.

'It's my employer's daughter I'm talking to. You shouldnae be here,' he said, and tried to walk past her. She barred his way, blood stinging her cheeks.

'Ian, you surely don't think that me living in Gourock's going to make any difference to us?'

'It makes all the difference! D'you not see that?'

'But you said – you said, that day at Loch Thom—' Dorothea felt as though the only solid piece of ground left beneath her feet had started crumbling away.

'We have to forget about Loch Thom. Sometimes,' Ian told her, his voice hard, 'the past should be left where it is. Goodbye, Dorry.' And with that last bitter use of her old name he walked away and left her alone on the footpath, weeping, not caring who saw the tears staining her cheeks. He didn't turn his head, but walked faster, swinging round the corner and out of sight.

As the last sight of him disappeared, she swung round and began to walk just as fast in the opposite direction, grief taking refuge in an anger that soon stopped the tears. Never ever again would she let anyone humiliate her as he had just done. Never again would she let anyone get close enough to touch her heart then break it. How dare he, she raged, how dare he talk to her like that?

A car passed then drew up. As she came level with it, the uniformed driver jumped out and opened the rear door and her father called to her from the warm interior. She sniffed, hoping that her tears had left no marks, and got in beside him. The door clicked shut and the car slid off again.

'What were you doing here?'

'Just walking.'

'My dear child, it's a cold day for that. You look as though you're frozen through.' He gave her a sidelong glance then said, 'I hope you remember that we're going out to a social evening at the Latimers' tonight?'

'No, I hadn't forgotten,' Dorothea said indifferently. The Latimers were old friends of Andrew's, with three sons in their early twenties. One of them was still in the army, but the other two were back home.

'You'll enjoy it. Time you got to know some young people,' Andrew said, patting her hand. Dorothea gave him a wan smile then stared out of the window. The car was gliding through Gourock now; it passed a shop window where two mannequins posed stiffly, one dressed in black, the other in deep red. They flashed across Dorothea's vision then were gone, leaving behind the memory of sleek, smart clothes, a memory that lingered through luncheon and gradually solidified in her mind into a decision. Since she was no longer Dorry from Cathcart Street, and since she could never, she felt, become the Dorothea that Andrew Warren wanted her to be, why should she not take on a new personality, one that couldn't be hurt by others, one that belonged to her alone? The more she thought of it, the more she realised that taking her future into her own hands was her only chance of survival.

That afternoon Dorothea went into the town and had most of her long hair cut off and the rest shaped so that it cupped her neatly shaped head in a cluster of dark bronzed curls. Then she crossed the road to the dress shop she had noticed earlier from the car. For a moment, as the doors closed behind her, shutting her into a warm, perfumed world, she faltered as her eyes fell on Jess, almost unrecognisably chic in black. She had forgotten that her foster sister worked here. She pulled herself together and started across the carpeted floor, a smile pinned defiantly to her mouth, but Jess, after one appalled glance, had disappeared from view into a back room, leaving the other assistant to deal with Dorothea.

'Can I help you, madam?'

Dorothea reminded herself of the new personality, lifted her chin and said coolly, pitching her voice loud enough to be heard in the back shop, 'I'm looking for a dress to wear tonight at a dinner party. You can send the account to Mr Andrew Warren.'

Two women looking through a rack of clothes turned and stared at her, then at each other, moving with one accord to the other side of the rack so that they could peer and whisper unnoticed. The sales assistant flushed, cast a quick glance at the doorway Jess had melted into, then recovered her professional smile and led the way to a rack in one corner. Dorothea flicked through them and thought of how much she would have revelled in owning any one of them a few short months earlier, when she had been plain Dorry Carswell. She rejected them and turned, her eye caught by a flash of colour. 'Let me see that one.'

It was brought to her and spread out over a chair for her inspection, a lace and chiffon gown in violet, low-waisted and sleeveless, with silver embroidery across the straight neckline and tiny silver balls edging the ankle-length hem.

For a moment Dorothea, remembering Jess's tales of modelling clothes for some of her customers, was tempted to ask that the gown be modelled for her. But even the new Dorothea couldn't be so cruel. Instead she tried it on herself and found that her first impression had been right – the violet of the gown matched her eyes exactly. Ian would have loved her in that dress. But Ian wasn't going to get the chance to love her, not any more. There were other men in the world, Dorothea thought desolately, then defiantly. Her father was wealthy; she could have her pick of men, men who could offer her far more than Ian Hamilton.

'It's beautiful, madam. It could have been made for your colouring.'

'I'll take it. Have it delivered to the house at once,' Dorothea said carelessly and went on to pick out silk stockings and underwear to go with it. Then she dashed her signature across the order form the girl proffered. There was no need to give an address, everyone knew where Mr Andrew Warren lived.

She returned home an hour later to find the dress waiting in her room. She stripped off her afternoon clothes, ran a deep bath, scented it with a handful of salts, then lay in the comfortingly hot water, eyes closed, making plans until the water began to cool and she had to climb out and wrap herself in a huge soft towel that waited close at hand.

She had a pleasing body, she decided later as she posed before her full-length mirror. Slim without being bony, her pink-nippled breasts and her hips rounded and firm, her legs long. Freed of its usual burden of curly hair, her neck was a slender column with her neat-featured face and newly sculpted head poised proudly above it.

She slipped into the satin underwear she had just bought, cream with violet ribbons and lace at breast and knee, then put her dressing-gown on and sat down before the dressing-table mirror, opening the parcels she had brought back with her.

She had never tried using eyebrow liner and rouge and powder and lip paint before, but she had watched Jess experiment with it many times. Now she tried to remember what the girl had done, leaning forward to stare into the mirror, raising her eyebrows, opening her eyes wide, frowning and pouting and smiling as Jess did, trying to find out which feature was her best and which needed artificial aids to beauty.

It was as well that she had decided to give the rest of the afternoon over to the business of making up her face, she thought an hour and a half later, surrounded by the items she had bought, a pot of cream half gouged out, the towel she had used to wipe off the first disastrous attempts lying like a discarded rainbow on the carpet. But at least she had learned by her mistakes. Jess wasn't there to help her and Helene certainly would never have done so. Helene, under duress, had politely told her to make use of her own ladies' maid, inherited from her mother, whenever she wished, but that was out of the question. And she wouldn't dream of summoning her aunt, although it was part of a parlourmaid's duties to assist any ladies of the house who might have need of her. Apart from a natural reluctance to ask for Edith's help, Dorothea couldn't picture her being able to do any better than she herself had. She studied her face, noting the faults that still had to be rectified, applied more cream, wiped her face with a corner of the towel, then started again.

As she worked she heard the front door open and Andrew Warren's deep voice rumble faintly in the hall below. Some time later the door to his room opened and shut, then Helene's arrogant voice called out to her maid and the pipes gurgled discreetly as her bath was run. Helene wouldn't dream of seeing to her own bathwater.

As the hands of the delicate little clock on her bedside table indicated that it was almost time for the Warrens to leave the house, Dorothea stood again in front of her full-length mirror, well pleased with what she saw there. The dress was simple enough to show her figure to advantage, her breasts just lifting the material demurely and the bobbles at the hem flattering her slim ankles. Her shoulders were smooth and creamy, almost matching the pearls about her neck and those swinging from her earlobes. Like the dress, the soft pink lip paint on her mouth and the rouge she had dusted on her cheekbones only emphasised the brilliance of her eyes beneath brows that had been brushed into shape with oil.

Dorothea gave herself a mirthless smile and watched the painted lips in the mirror curve up. The new Dorothea, she thought, then frowned. Dorothea was the name her parents had given to her, Dorry was the name Lessie had bestowed on her. Neither name fitted this new personality.

'Thea,' she said softly, and smiled again, with faint pleasure. Thea was just right for the elegant beauty before her.

There was a tap at the door and Edith came into the room. 'Mr Warren and Miss Helene are—' she began, then stopped, her mouth hanging open.

Thea Warren swung away from the mirror and picked up her evening bag and wrap from the bed, aware as she did so of the scent of violets, the new eau de cologne she had bought, wafting around her. 'I'm ready. See to that, will you?' she instructed coolly, indicating the mess on the dressing-table, the towel on the floor. Dorry would never have had the nerve, but Thea had. Thea could do anything.

Edith, still gaping, stepped aside to let her pass and she went to the stairs, her nerve almost failing her at the last moment as she saw her father and half-sister waiting down in the hall, Helene pacing with impatient little jerky steps. For a moment Dorry surfaced, gripping the banister tightly, yearning to run down the stairs and out of the house and all the way to Greenock to the safety of Lessie's love and Ian's arms. But she had no claim on Lessie now, and Ian had rejected her, she reminded herself, forcing Dorry away, bringing Thea again to the fore, loosening her grip on the polished wooden rail finger by finger.

She took a deep breath and began to descend slowly, one step at a time, concentrating on keeping her back straight and her head high, a faint smile on her lips. The Warrens, disbelieving, watched her come down the last few steps, Helene's dark eyes wide with astonishment, Andrew stiffening as though his first reaction was anger, then forcing himself to relax as his younger daughter came towards him across the hall, her eyes defiant.

'You look – very striking, my dear,' he said, then moved to open the door. 'Shall we go?'

Lessie's new shop opened in March 1919 and thrived from the first day. She spent a great deal of time in it herself, and took on two assistants, a young man newly returned from the war, a former shop assistant with some experience of the grocery trade, and a girl fresh from school. With pride, Lessie dressed the two of them, and herself, in long white aprons that were changed and washed every second day. A lad who lived in the next close took on the job of messenger boy.

'You'll not listen to reason, will you, woman?' Andrew asked with wry amusement when he visited the shop after it had opened. 'I said you should take more time to yourself, not take on extra work.'

She stroked her hands over the cool marble counter. 'Don't fret, I'm not setting out to challenge Thomas Lipton. This'll do me. But who wants to sit back just when the war's finally over and folk are picking up their lives again? It occurred to me when I cast my vote for the very first time a few months back that this is a time for moving forward, not sitting back.'

He nodded and turned towards the door, opening it then pausing so that a woman burdened with a large basket and two small children could enter. Lessie walked round the counter and followed him, nodding a welcome to the harassed customer. On the pavement Andrew stood back and looked up at the wooden panel above the door which bore her name in bold white letters.

'You should have the shop's likeness taken, with you and your employees posing outside.'

'I'll think about it.'

'Lessie, are you certain you can manage? If you ever find yourself in need of a loan—'

'I'll go to my bank, not to my friends,' she finished the sentence sharply, then relented. 'If there's one belief me and my brother Davie share, it's that we shouldnae walk

294

before we can crawl. Don't fret, Andrew, I'm fine. And I'm grateful to you for giving Ian time off to go to England.'

He brushed her thanks off with a quick movement of the hand. 'The boy's fond of his father, it's natural that he'd want to see him.'

'His stepfather,' Lessie corrected him swiftly, adding, 'though the only father the lad knew, I suppose.'

'From what Ian said, Carswell hasn't got long. D'you still miss him, Lessie?'

She considered for a moment. 'To tell the truth, I feel now as if Murdo died when he left us. It was hard at first, but now I've no feeling left for him, apart from the natural pity I'd have for anyone in his place. And life moves on, never backwards.'

'Lessie, does Dorothea ever visit you?'

She thought of the last time she had seen Dorothea, the day when Ian had returned for his midday meal with a face dark as thunder and remained in a foul mood for the best part of a week. She had a fair idea that the two young people had met each other and that the result had been heartbreak for them both.

'Not for a while.'

'She's never at home, never still for a moment. It's as though she's decided to pack an entire lifetime into every moment. She's – she's changed, Lessie.'

'What can you expect? You whisk her away from the house she was raised in without giving her time to get used to the idea of being your daughter, then you expect her to stay just as she was. She'll be fine once she's worked things out in her own mind.'

But she wished she had more faith in her own words as she watched him walk off in the direction of the refinery.

She had a second visitor that day, but she was so busy that at first she didn't notice him waiting in the background. Rob, her senior assistant, went over to deal with him and came back to murmur, 'There's someone wants a word with you.'

She looked up and saw the man for the first time, thin,

wearing a suit that looked as though it had been made for someone else, light brown hair just a little longer than the fashion of the day dictated showing beneath a cap. At first she wasn't sure of his identity, then as he turned and his grey eyes met hers, she knew that it was Peter, home at last.

'See to my customer for me, Rob. I'm just going along to the house,' she said, her hands flying to the strings of her apron. 'I'll not be long.'

She went round the counter and put a hand on Peter's sleeve, noticing how he flinched slightly beneath her touch, just as he had done as a child. 'It's good to see you! Come along to the house and have a cup of tea.'

In the kitchen he sat in the fireside chair she indicated and looked around as she busied herself with kettle and teapot.

'This place is much the same.' It was the first time he had spoken; his voice sounded rusty, as though it wasn't used very often.

'It's much the way it was when Miss Peden used to own it. I loved it then and I didn't see the sense of changing it when it became mine.' She turned to face him, her hands clasped before her. 'How are you, Peter?'

'I'm . . .' he gave the appearance of seeking for words, 'I'm still in one piece and that's more than can be said for most.'

'I know. You'll have heard about young Martin Warren?'

'He's just one of thousands – millions. Dead, maimed – it makes a man shamed tae still be alive. My mother seems tae think I'm a hero, just because I'm still alive.'

She made the tea and put a cup into his hands. He stared down at it.

'Are you going back to the refinery?'

His head, shaggy now that the cap was off, swung slowly from side to side.

'So you're looking for work?'

'My mother's looking for work for me. I don't see the sense of it.'

'We've all got to support ourselves,' Lessie said, letting a sharp note enter her voice.

It worked. He lifted his gaze from the cup and asked simply, 'Why?'

'In order to live.'

'Aunt Lessie, they gave me a gun. I kept it by me all the time. I carried it, I slept with it, I damned near stirred my tea with it. They taught me how tae love it more than I've loved a human being in my whole life.' Tears glistened in the depths of his eyes. 'I didnae just carry it and love it, though, I used it. I pulled the trigger and I don't know if I killed or maimed, but I'm sure I must have. I did my bit. And now you all think I should just go on as if everything in the world's back together again.'

'Peter—'

'My mother wanted me tae go back tae the refinery, tae take orders, do as I was told.' He jerked suddenly in his chair and hot tea spilled over his hand. He didn't seem to notice it. 'I've done what I was told. I've taken orders. I let them put the gun intae my hand because I hadnae the courage tae fight them. It was easier tae fight Germans, lads I didnae know and couldnae see most of the time. That's why war's so easy, did ye know that? Because the further away ye are from the enemy, the more stripes ye've got, the easier it is tae kill. Or better still, tae get other folk tae dae yer killin' for ye. It gets tae be like a game.' Again the jerk; this time the cup tilted and fell to its side in the saucer, emptying itself over his hand and his clothes. Lessie started to move towards him then stopped, riveted by the agony in the grey eyes lifted to hers.

'D'ye see what I mean, Aunt Lessie?' Peter demanded. 'D'ye see why I cannae take any more orders? The folk that give them are the folk that end up givin' out guns an' turnin' ordinary nobodies like me intae machines that pull the triggers an' think nothin' of it. I cannae let them dae it tae me any more!'

'I see, Peter. I see.'

'Then I wish tae Christ ye'd explain it tae my mother an' make her understand!' For the first time he noticed the spilled tea, righting the cup and putting it on the table, brushing spots of liquid from his clothes, apparently impervious to the scalding he must have got from the hot tea. 'I'm sorry.'

'Don't worry about it.' Lessie picked up a towel and moved to rub off some of the worst stains, but he got up and backed away, towards the door.

'I'd best go. She'll be wondering. She always wonders if she gets home an' I'm no' there. Deserted. Absent without leave. They shot the deserters, did ye know that? Oh, more than a few of the poor souls that died in the war had their own side's bullets in them.' He blundered out and Lessie was alone, left with the eerie feeling that Peter had been killed on the battlefield, and the man who had just left was only a caricature, an empty husk of the lad who had, so long ago, sworn that he would never hurt a fellow human being at the behest of his country's leaders.

23

Ian stayed away for a week and came home grim-faced with the news that Murdo Carswell was dead. He said no more and Lessie asked him nothing, but she heard from Jess that Murdo had been living alone; Flora, the young woman for whom he had deserted his family, had long vanished. Jess's former affection for Murdo had also vanished, and she scarcely reacted to the news of his death.

'He didn't care enough about me to stay, so why should I care about him?' she said with chilling logic.

A month after he got back, Ian came to Lessie and told her that he wanted to leave Greenock.

'I want to study medicine, Mam.'

'Go for doctoring?'

'It's something I've been thinking about ever since I was in Europe. My chemistry studies and my war experience'll help. I talked it over with Father during his last days and he thought I should go ahead.'

'But how will we manage it? It'll cost a deal of money.'

'I'll go to Glasgow, try to enrol in the university. I've got my school certificates and my chemistry certificate from the night school; they'll count for something, and so will my time in the army, no doubt. I'll find somewhere cheap to stay and get work that'll fit in with my studies. There'll probably be a job of some sort in one of the hospitals, and there are some scholarships for students in need of them. Father left me some money – not much, but it'll help, and there's the money paid to me while I was in the army. I put most of it by and kept it safe.'

'What about Dorry?'

Ian's fair skin flushed scarlet. 'What's she got to do with it?'

'I thought that the two of you – when you came home on leave that last time—'

'You thought wrong.' He got to his feet. 'She's a rich man's daughter now, he'll be looking for her to marry money.'

'Dorry's got a mind of her own.'

'And so have I.' Ian tossed the words over his shoulder as he left the room. 'I'm not a social climber. I'll not court any woman who's considered to be above me!'

His bedroom door slammed and Lessie wisely gave him some time to get over his anger before she took a small notebook from the drawer where she kept her account books and tapped on the bedroom door, opening it only when she heard his muffled permission.

He was sitting on the bed, a chemistry textbook in his hand, an exercise book covered with strange symbols and squiggles on his knee.

'Here.' She handed him the little book and he leafed through it then looked up at her incomprehendingly.

'What is it?'

'The money I got from the War Office while you were away.'

Ian pushed the book back at her. 'That was for you, to make up for missing my wages.'

She kept her hands by her side, refusing to take the book back. 'I didnae need it. I managed fine, as you can see for yourself. I thought at the time that it would mebbe do for you and – and your lassie when you decided to settle down. Now it seems it's to be put to a different use.'

'I could manage without it.'

'I've no doubt you could, being my son. But it's yours, and if doctoring's what you want to do, you'll need all the money you can get.'

'Mam,' he said as she reached the door. The little notebook thumped to the floor and the exercise book pages flapped as he got up and came to give her a clumsy, embarrassed hug.

'Thanks, Mam, I'll not forget this.'

For a moment she held him; for a moment he was her laddie again. Then his embarrassment reached and infected her and she pushed him away. 'Och, for any favour just take it and stop your havering,' she said gruffly, and left him.

When Ian left Greenock in August, Jess, who had achieved her ambition and found a job modelling and selling clothes in a large Glasgow dress shop, went with him. All at once Lessie was alone and grateful for the new shop, which filled her days and her evenings as well, since she was still working between the other shopkeepers and the wholesalers, and a great deal of paperwork and mental arithmetic was required to keep everything going.

In September Davie Kirkwood set Greenock on its heels by announcing his engagement to the daughter of one of the town's shipyard owners, the young woman Lessie had seen him with at the dinner in the town hall.

'I knew it,' she crowed when he came to the house to tell her. 'I knew she was the right one for you!'

'Ach, women always say that. Although the gentry cannae say the same thing – it's set the cat among the pigeons, a man like me marryin' intae their ranks,' Davie said with a certain grim satisfaction.

'She's a fortunate lassie, getting a hard-working man like you. And I'm glad you're going to have someone to care for.'

'God, woman, don't go getting sentimental about it!'

'Are you happy?'

'Happy? I'm pleased about it, if that's what you mean,' said Davie evasively. 'Come April I'm going to walk down the aisle of St George's North Church with the daughter of one of the town's most successful men on my arm.'

'I wish Mam had been alive to see it!'

'And I wish,' his voice was grim, 'that the old man was alive to see it. After all he thought of me, this would surely stick in his gullet!'

Ishbel Wilson, twenty years old and sixteen years younger than Davie, was a pretty young woman with glossy black hair and large, deep blue, expressive eyes. When Davie brought her to the house in Cathcart Street to meet his sisters, she looked round Lessie's kitchen with fascinated interest. It was clear that she had never been in such a small house before. Edith, who had been invited along to meet her future sister-in-law, simpered and twitched and all but curtseyed when the girl complimented Lessie on her 'quaint' home.

'You should see the place where Lessie and me used to live,' Davie told her, but Edith added hurriedly, as Ishbel opened her mouth to ask questions, 'Don't bring up the past, Davie, the future's what we should be talking about. Where are you planning to live when you're wed?'

'David's bought a house in Newton Street,' said Ishbel lightly.

'Newton Street?' Edith squawked, and Lessie felt her mouth dropping open. Newton Street was on the hill behind the town, a spacious tree-lined avenue with large houses set in their own gardens to either side. Newton Street was for affluent folk. She caught Davie's eyes and saw the glint of humour in them. He was enjoying his sisters' reaction, Lessie realised, and pulled herself together.

'It'll be big, then,' she said calmly. 'It'll take a deal of looking after.'

'My mother's training some servants for me. And we'll need gardeners, of course. But we'll manage.'

'Oh aye,' said Davie. 'We'll manage.'

Lessie was relieved when the visit ended; Ishbel seemed to enjoy herself, but Davie was strangely remote, and Edith's almost servile attitude turned Lessie's stomach. When Ishbel left, she turned at the door to flash a smile of farewell, and just for a moment Lessie was reminded of Anna McCauley. Ishbel's long-lashed eyes were deep blue rather than violet blue, but there was something about them, something about the quick way she turned her head over her shoulder, that had belonged to Anna as well.

'Well, who'd have ever thought of it? Our Davie marrying intae the gentry an' living in Newton Street!'

Edith exclaimed as soon as Lessie went back into the kitchen. 'He must be doing well for himself. Mind you, she's the only child in the family, so the man that marries her'll stand tae inherit a deal of money one of those days. Imagine it being our Davie!'

Lessie let her prattle on. It seemed clear to her that the girl doted on Davie, but there was still that air of reserve about him, a certain distant courtesy in the way he talked to his fiancée that made Lessie wonder if Ishbel had indeed managed to break through to his heart, or if the engagement had come about simply because Davie felt that it was time he had a wife, someone to give him entry into local society.

'It'll be a big society wedding,' Edith was saying at that moment, unwittingly fanning Lessie's uneasiness. 'We'll need tae get ourselves dressed up, you and me.' Then she added, casting a disparaging glance round the kitchen, 'I told you we should all have met in Aunt Marion's house in Gourock, did I not?'

'It was Davie's idea to bring her here. Anyway, what's wrong with this place?'

'The likes of Ishbel Wilson's not used tae sitting in the kitchen with the range and the sink right in front of her eyes. At least they're out of sight in the scullery in Aunt Marion's house. And she's got a gas stove and not an old range like you.'

'There's nothing wrong with this flat. If she's marrying our Davie she'll have to get to know us as we are.'

'She said this place was quaint. That means—'

'I'm not bothered about what it means,' Lessie cut in, suddenly exasperated with her sister. It did not matter to Edith whether or not Davie was marrying for love. All she cared about was the look of a thing, not the meaning behind it. Whereas to Lessie, he was still the warm-hearted youth who had handed her his wages from the docks and taken very little back for himself, the youth who had come home exhausted and yet forced himself out to night school to slake his burning thirst for knowledge and betterment.

She wanted him to be happy, but for some reason she

couldn't understand, he had built such a barricade about himself in those early years of struggle that she had no way of knowing if he was truly content. Even though he could now afford to buy a house in Newton Street and marry into the gentry, she worried about him.

Ian and Jess came to Greenock for their uncle's wedding, Jess so elegant in a fur-edged velvet coat and flower-pot style hat trimmed with satin ribbon that Lessie scarcely recognised her when she walked into the shop. Staff and customers alike gaped as Jess elegantly moved round the counter to give her mother a kiss on the cheek, clearly enjoying the stir she was creating. Even her speech had changed; now she shaped her words with great care, cultivating a deeper tone than usual.

'I can only stay until the morning after the wedding,' she told Lessie when they were in the house. 'There's a dress showing that afternoon and I promised to be back for it.' Then the reserve broke. 'Look, Mam.' She delved into her bag and produced a handful of glossy photographs which she scattered across the table. A dozen or more Jesses stared up at Lessie, some pouting under the broad brims of elegant hats, some smiling above soft fur, some wide-eyed, one with a flower nestling against her cheek.

'Are they all you?'

'Of course they are.' Jess giggled, just as she used to do. 'I'm photogenic. I'm hoping to get my picture into a fashion magazine soon. Oh, Mam, I'm having a lovely time, it's all just what I wanted!'

'I hope you're not posing for the wrong sort of photographs, my lady.'

'What d'you mean?' Jess asked demurely.

'You know very well what I mean. Some of these models in pictures I've seen need to have their bottoms smacked.'

'Oh, Mam, whatever sort of pictures do you look at then?' Jess giggled again. 'I'm a fashion model, I pose to show off clothes and nothing else. Not that I've not been asked,' she added pertly, scooping up the pictures.

Murdo, Lessie thought with an unexpected moment's sadness for his death, would have been delighted with his beautiful, successful daughter. Especially with the money she seemed to be earning.

Ian, who arrived later that day, was altogether too thin for Lessie's liking. When she said so, he brushed her off with an impatient, 'Don't fuss, Mam, I'm fine!'

He had managed to get a small scholarship and a job as a night porter at Glasgow Royal Infirmary, and with the additional help of the money he and Lessie had saved during his war service he was just managing to make ends meet. He had a room in a tenement building not far from the infirmary, and had found his first year as a medical student hard but exhilarating. His blue eyes glowed when he talked about his studies and his work in the infirmary. Jess wrinkled up her pretty nose and opened one of the fashion magazines she had brought with her, but Lessie sat late into the night listening for as long as he was willing to talk. For a few hours, at least, she felt that she had been allowed to peep into the strange new world her son had chosen to live in, and his enthusiasm made her certain that he had made the right choice after all.

In spite of his assurance that he got enough to eat, she noticed that he wolfed down everything she put before him, and she was glad that she had thought to lay in plenty of food. He would have a good breakfast the next morning, she decided – porridge, sausage and fried potatoes and two eggs.

He ate it all, while Jess nibbled at some toast and sipped a cup of weak tea. Then to Lessie's relief he announced that he was off to get his hair cut before the wedding. She hadn't wanted to antagonise him by pointing out, when he arrived home, that it was too long.

He returned, red hair smartly styled, in good time to get into his best suit. It was looser on him that it had been before he went to Glasgow, Lessie thought, but again managed to hold her tongue. It was difficult, but she was learning.

She had bought a slim green dress for the wedding, with

a satin-trimmed overtunic. Her brimmed hat, made to sit at a jaunty angle on her head, was a paler green with a dark green feather. Jess nodded approval when she saw it. 'A good choice, Mam. You've got the proper slender figure to show it off.'

Jess wore a cinnamon velvet cape edged with dark silky fur over a brown silky dress patterned with cinnamon rosettes. The skirt was draped and a snug-fitting cap in cinnamon with a tiny brown brim made the most of her fair hair and blue eyes. The colours would have looked dowdy on most women, but on Jess they were just right, enhancing her beauty as green leaves enhanced a perfect rose.

Davie had insisted on sending a chauffeur-driven car for them, and for Edith, who arrived as they reached the church door.

'Oh no, would you look at her?' Jess murmured as her aunt approached on Peter's arm. 'Can she never forget that she's a parlourmaid?' Edith had on a new outfit, a coat and skirt in her usual black, with a white blouse. Her son towered over her, and Lessie realised for the first time that Edith seemed to have shrunk into herself. She was getting older – they all were, Lessie thought with a pang as she smiled at the newcomers. A powerful smell of mothballs surrounded Peter, who was wearing a black suit that was too small for him. Lessie was quite sure that it had been borrowed from some neighbour; clothes and household items travelled continually between folk with little money to spare, and as often as not a single decent hat served for all the women in one street, decorating this head or that at funerals, weddings, christenings and any other special occasion that might arise.

They were ushered to a pew near the front of the crowded church, which was filled with flowers. On the way down the aisle, Lessie noticed Andrew sitting with his two daughters. Her heart sank. She hadn't realised that the Warrens would be there. Ian didn't seem to notice them. When Davie appeared with his best man, his eyes sought out his relatives and he gave them a stiff nod before taking up his place before the altar. He looked sternly handsome in his morning suit.

The minister arrived, the organ started playing, and everyone rose as the bride floated down the aisle on her father's arm in a cloud of white silk and lace and orange blossom, attended by two flower girls before her, two pages to hold the long, heavily embroidered train falling from her shoulders, and six bridesmaids.

To Lessie the service seemed to go on for ever, but at last Ishbel and Davie, man and wife, moved to the vestry to sign the register. They emerged arm in arm, Ishbel glowing and Davie handsomely solemn, to lead their guests from the church.

As they filed out into the April sunshine Lessie, holding Ian's arm, felt him stiffen suddenly as a slender figure with a halo of dark red hair beneath the wide brim of her hat moved out of a pew and up the aisle in front of them. Looking up at her son she saw that his face was expressionless, his eyes hooded.

The reception was held in the bride's family home, where a huge marquee had been set up in the garden for the guests. It was a lovely day, and Edith's eyes bulged with disapproval when Jess carelessly tossed aside her cape to reveal the draped top of her dress with its short sleeves and low back. Three strings of pearls clasped her throat and more pearls dangled from her small ears on silver chains.

Jess was just as disapproving of her aunt. 'You'd think she was here to serve the folk, not as a guest,' she murmured to her mother as Edith moved, crow-like, through the crowd. 'Could you not have taken her in hand, Mam, and made her buy something decent to wear?'

'Your aunt's a grown woman, she can wear what she wants.'

'And as for Peter, did you ever see anything that looked as helpless and hopeless as he does? Someone ought to—'

'That's enough, Jess.' Lessie's voice was suddenly chilly. 'Peter's a fine lad who never seems to get a decent word from anyone.'

Her daughter pouted, shrugged, and said no more.

There were so many people present that it was easy enough for Ian and Dorothea to avoid each other. Watching, wondering, loving them both and worrying about them, Lessie saw how time and again their paths seemed to be converging, and how time and again they both managed to veer away without apparently noticing the other. Dorothea came to talk to her when Ian was well out of the way. The girl's face was subtly made up to disguise the faint scar on her cheek, expensive scent wafted round her, but it seemed to Lessie that her expressive violet-blue eyes, so like her mother's, were shadowed and carried hurt in their depths. Her mouth, however, was fixed in a bright permanent smile.

'Are you enjoying yourself?'

'It's all very nice. How are you, Dorry?'

One shoulder was elegantly lifted. 'I'm very well. I call myself Thea now, didn't you know that?'

'I heard. But to me you'll always be Dorry.'

For a moment she thought that she had broken through the carefully built up defences; then Dorothea blinked hard and the smile painted itself back into place. 'Excuse me,' she said, 'I've just seen someone I want to talk to,' and she eeled gracefully through the crowd, presenting a slender, beautifully clad back to Lessie, who wanted, all at once, to run after her foster daughter and catch her by the hand and take her home to Cathcart Street.

'Dorry's looking well,' she said brightly to Andrew when they met.

'She prefers to be called—'

'I know about that. And I said, Dorry's looking well.'

A broad grin lit up his face. 'You never change, Lessie. She's fine, but trying to get to know her's like trying to guddle trout. Did you ever do that?'

'I was always too clumsy. But Davie was good at it.' She remembered kneeling on a grassy bank with Donald in their courting days, watching Davie stretched full-length a little further down, his shirt off, one arm in a running burn almost up to the shoulder, a rapt inward-looking expression on his face as his hand, out of sight below the surface, gently tickled at the belly of a plump trout drowsing in the shadow of the bank. She remembered the way he suddenly tightened his grasp and rolled over on the grass, whisking his arm high above his head so that the trout flashed in his fingers like a rainbow in captivity. She remembered squealing as she and Donald were showered with water, the quick way Davie dispatched the fish by banging its head against a stone. She even, for a brief moment, remembered the taste of it when Donald and Davie had cooked it over a fire made of twigs. Then she came back to the present, the crowded garden, and Andrew Warren.

'And it seems he's still got the knack,' she finished briskly. 'He's guddled himself a bonny fish today.'

This time Andrew laughed so hard that several people turned and stared. One of them, Lessie noticed, was his daughter Helene, her lovely face disturbed by a frown as she saw her father with someone of no account.

Lessie bit her lip, and would have turned away if Andrew hadn't taken her arm. 'Come and look at the garden,' he said. 'I'm tired of all these folk. You'll have heard that I'm making a lot of changes at the refinery?' he went on as they walked. 'I've always wanted to modernise it, bring in new machinery and change some of the departments round so that the refining process moves sensibly from one area to another without the sugar having to be carted back and forth. It's a big job and it's taking all the money I've got. I'm going to have to sell some shares, but it's still going to be worth it.'

'You're looking tired. You surely don't have to be there all the time?'

'No sense in leaving things to other folk who might make the wrong decisions.' He steered her down a gravel path to where a small bench had been placed in a wind-free corner. They sat down and stayed there in a companionable silence for some time while behind them, nearer the house, the people who had been summoned to celebrate Davie Kirkwood's marriage and his entry into local society sipped champagne and chattered. The sun was warm; Andrew leaned back and closed his eyes, while Lessie watched some early butterflies flit through the banks of daffodils and hyacinths that still bloomed in brilliant splendour.

After a while she turned and looked at her companion. His dark hair was well streaked with silver and there were new lines between his eyes and at the corners of his mouth, but he was still a handsome man; if anything, maturity had enhanced his looks. But now that his face was at rest, his tiredness was more obvious, she thought compassionately, suddenly realising that he had become as much a part of her life as her own children. He was dear to her, this man who had fathered her foster daughter.

At that moment Andrew's hand moved, searching for hers, finding it, covering it. 'You're so filled with energy, Lessie,' he murmured without opening his eyes. 'And yet you're such a peaceful woman to be with at times.'

She said nothing, and they sat on for a while, her hand in his, under the April sky.

24

Shortly after Davie and his bride left for Italy on their honeymoon the influenza which was still haunting the country claimed Aunt Marion, Barbara Kirkwood's sister. Edith, who took over her tenement flat, was quick to suggest that she and Lessie should consider setting up house together.

'It would save money for us both and it would mean company for you,' she said as they washed dishes together in the tidy little Gourock flat after the funeral. The boiled ham meal that was obligatory at Scottish funerals was over, the few mourners had departed, and only the clearing up was left to do.

'I'd not get much company with you at the Warren house most of the time and me at one shop or the other,' Lessie pointed out, drying a gilt-edged cup rich with blue flowers and green leaves.

'It's still better to be in a house where there's more than just yourself,' Edith argued. 'A lived-in house.'

Lessie said nothing, carefully setting the cup down on the wooden coal bunker that, topped with oilcloth, acted as an extra work surface. In Cathcart Street her coal bunker was outside the back door, but Aunt Marion's flat – Edith's flat, now – boasted a tiny separate kitchen known as a scullery which housed the gas cooker, sink and bunker. It meant that when the coalman called, sheets of newspaper had to be laid down all the way from the door of the flat so that he wouldn't leave black marks on the linoleum, and every surface and item in the scullery had to be wiped free of coal dust after his visits. But even so a scullery was considered by the tenement dwellers who made up most of Scotland's population to be a step up the social scale.

This house had never been what Lessie would call lived-in. It had a chilly, forbidding air about it. She pitied Peter, who had had to do his growing up in such sterile surroundings.

'It suits me to be in Cathcart Street. I'd be too far away from both the shops here.'

'I was thinking about that. If you gave them up you'd have enough money to live on, would you not? We could mebbe do up the living room here, get rid of some of Auntie's old furniture so that you could bring some of yours.'

Lessie gave her sister a sidelong glance. Edith never gave without receiving more back, and it had suddenly become plain that she was more interested in renovating the house than in offering Lessie a new home.

'I've no intention of giving up the shops. They're both doing well and I mean to see that they do better.'

'All you're interested in these days is making money.'

'All I'm interested in,' Lessie countered sharply, placing the last blue-flowered saucer atop the pile of clean saucers, 'is keeping a home for my children to come back to whenever they want, and paying my way. I know there's a pension for old folk now and no doubt I'll be very grateful for it one day, but I've got a good few years to go yet and I still have to earn my living.'

No point in telling Edith her guilty secret, the first exciting dabbles into the stock market that Andrew had told her about so many years ago. Lessie had discovered that her love of figures and order was to her advantage, and she had started investing a percentage of the little money she saved each year instead of putting it all into the bank as before.

Edith dried her hands and started to put the china away, her fingers gentle as she came to the blue-flowered set. 'Aunt Marion always kept her things nice. I'll make another cup of tea.' As she filled the kettle she said over her shoulder, 'I'd not depend on your two to come back if I was you. Children today are ungrateful, with no thought to what their parents have suffered for them.'

'I don't see why you should be so harsh on Ian and Jess.'

Edith sniffed and put two cups and saucers – not the pretty ones, Lessie noticed – onto a tray. 'You'll find some milk in a jug in the larder. Let me tell you, Lessie, none of today's young folk can be trusted. Look at that Dorry of yours – Miss Thea, she calls herself now, if you please. Gone completely wild, that one. She should think black burning shame of herself, so she should, after the way you brought her up. Out till all hours, painting her face, showing her legs, and making eyes at every young man that comes into the house.'

Lessie fought to keep sudden anger under control. 'From what I hear, that's the way all the rich young folk behave nowadays. Is she that much different from Mr Warren's other daughter?'

Edith sniffed again and tucked a crocheted cosy over the teapot. 'We'll have our tea in comfort through in the room. I'll grant you that Miss Helene does some of those things,' she went on once they were settled on either side of the fire and she was pouring the tea. 'But she's gentry. Dorry's not.'

'She is now. The poor lassie probably thinks that if she doesnae behave like the rest of them she'll be laughed at for being different.'

Edith put the teapot down then folded back her skirt to let the fire's heat get as close as possible to her wool-covered knobbly knees. 'There's a difference between behaving like the rest of them and going a lot further than the rest of them.'

'Och, Edith! Dorry's a good girl, she'll settle down in her own time.'

'You're forgetting whose daughter she is.'

'Mr Warren's. We all know that now.'

'She's that Anna McCauley's daughter too, that's what I'm getting at. And if you ask me she's taken after her mother. I mind well enough the way that one used tae carry on with all sorts of men. Blood will out, and bad blood won't be denied.'

'That's enough, Edith. Dorry's a good girl and I'll not hear her miscalled!'

Edith shot her sister a glance from beneath lowered lashes then said sulkily, 'No need tae fly into a temper. You'll find out soon enough how it is with young folk. You're too trusting, Lessie, you always were. Too quick tae see the best in folk.' Then, after a long silence broken only by the ticking of the clock, she burst out, 'Lessie, I'm that worried about Peter!'

'What's amiss with him?' Peter had attended his great-aunt's funeral but had left with the other mourners, sliding out of the door before Lessie had a chance to talk to him.

'What's amiss?' she repeated as Edith said nothing but stared down into her tea. When her sister finally looked up, Lessie was shocked to see tears in her eyes.

'The polis were at the door last night asking about him.'

'What?'

'A big constable with a moustache.' Edith's cup rattled faintly in its saucer as she put it down. 'Wanted tae know where Peter was the night before. He went away when I said the laddie had been here, at home.'

'And was he?'

'Of course he was! I'd no' tell lies tae the polis, not for Peter or anyone else!'

'So he hadnae done anything wrong.'

'Not that time, but they know him, Lessie,' Edith wailed, a tear escaping to trickle down her cheek. 'The constable said tae tell him they were keeping an eye on him. Thank God Aunt Marion was safe in her coffin in her room and not sitting here tae see the shame he was bringing down on us!'

Lessie leaned over and touched her sister's hand. It was dry and rough.

'It's just like the old days when the polis came looking for Da – and Joseph too. He'll go just the same way as our Joseph,' Edith wailed. 'Named in the police court reports in the *Telegraph* for all tae see, having tae pay fines and go tae the jail. I'll not be able tae show my face in the street! And what'll the Warrens say?' She withdrew her hand from beneath Lessie's and fished in her pocket for a handkerchief. After scrubbing at her eyes and blowing her nose she went on more calmly, 'After all I've done for him! He could have gone back intae the office at the refinery when he came home, but would he? Oh no, not Master Peter! He's been in one job after another and he's lost them all. He'll not keep his mouth shut or his hands tae himself. My Peter that looked so nice in his wee velvet suits and was clever at the school and never said a bad word tae anyone. He's working on the docks now, did you know that? A common labourer just like Da was.'

'Edith, he'd a hard time during the war.'

'So did other folk and they've not disgraced their mothers.'

'Peter had it harder than most. He's unsettled, that's all. Give the laddie time.'

'Give him enough rope and he'll hang himself, more like,' retorted Edith, stuffing the handkerchief back into her pocket, snatching up the teapot and dashing more tea into her cup. She hurled a spoonful of sugar in after it and stirred the brew so viciously that it was as well she hadn't used the delicate china. 'It's what I was telling you before – he's just ungrateful. They're all ungrateful! Nothing'll ever be the same again. They're going tae ruin this country, the young ones!'

To mark their first wedding anniversary, Davie and Ishbel Kirkwood held a dance at their grand house. Davie himself came to the shop to hand Lessie two white envelopes.

'Mebbe you'd see that Ian and Jess get these. I'd just as soon not have bothered, but Ishbel wants to have some folk of her own age about. She's even booked one of those terrible American-style jazz bands.'

'You can't blame her for wanting that sort of party, she's young yet.'

'I suppose so. I'd have been just as happy having you up for the evening. I feel comfortable with you.'

'I was there just the other week. You must let your wife have her own way sometimes.'

'It seems to me,' said Davie dourly, 'that she gets her own way most of the time. Her father spoiled her and she expects me to do the same.'

Lessie eyed him thoughtfully, then changed the subject. 'Jess is in London just now, she's working for a big modelling agency there. But I'll try to get Ian to come down for your party. It's time he had a bit of pleasure. He works far too hard in my opinion.'

'A man cannae work too hard. It's what we were born for.'

'You sounded just like Da then,' Lessie said without thinking.

Davie scowled and said sharply, 'I'm nothing like him!' then turned on his heel and left without another word. She watched him go, the usual little frown tucking itself between her fair brows.

Ian, looking tired and strained but refusing to be fussed over, came to Greenock to attend the party, and with him came Jess, in a coat of corded blue velvet with a huge fur collar and a tiny hat perched on top of her fair head. She brought more photographs, taken this time during modelling sessions in London, and chattered on incessantly about the wonderful time she had had in the city and how she just couldn't wait to go back there. Her lovely long hair had been shingled – 'Everyone's doing it, Mother' – and Ian was amused to hear that Douglas Fairbanks had been supplanted in her affections by a young actor named Rudolf Valentino.

'I've heard about him. A gigolo, a smarmy ladies' man.'

'He is not!' Jess flashed. 'I went to see him in *The Four Horsemen of the Apocalypse*, and he's the most handsome man in the world, and the best actor. You're just jealous!'

'I would be if he could remove an appendix without having to open the patient up first,' retorted Ian, and ducked as his sister threw a cushion at him.

'For goodness' sake, you two, when are you going to grow up?' scolded Lessie, secretly revelling in the all-too-brief pleasure of having them both under her roof again.

Her eyes popped when her daughter came into the

kitchen on the night of the dance. 'Jess Carswell, you're surely not going into company looking like that!'

Jess glided over to the mirror and peered into it, running the tip of one finger round the outline of her glossy red lips. 'Why not?'

'You're scarcely decent!'

'Oh, Mother! Ian, what do you think?' Jess appealed to her brother as he came in tying his tie. He watched as she revolved slowly in front of him, a bird of paradise in a crimson silk short-sleeved dress that hugged her slender figure and fell in skilful folds from hips to mid-calf. Jess's shoes were crimson and black and a crimson band about her head sported a curling black feather.

'You look all right to me,' he said at last, without much interest, and Lessie knew that she had lost the battle.

The lights were blazing in the Kirkwood house, the open windows letting out strains of jazz music when Ian and Jess stepped from their hired car. Jess's feet began to tap on the gravel at once and she hurried up the stairs ahead of her brother, eager to join the party. He handed over their invitations and his coat and followed her more slowly across the foyer and into the large drawing room at the front of the house.

The sliding doors between drawing and dining rooms had been folded back; a wooden dais had been set up against one wall to hold the band, who were playing enthusiastically. The carpets had been rolled back and the furniture pushed against the walls, and the middle of the floor was already filled with dancers.

Ishbel and Davie were standing by the door to greet their guests; Ian had a brief word with his uncle and the pretty girl who was now his aunt although only a few months older than he was, then he joined his sister.

'Looks like a good evening,' Jess said, then with a change of tone, 'Isn't that Dorry?'

Ian spun round and for a moment the blood stopped in his veins. Dorothea was at the other side of the room, dancing with a tall fair-haired man, laughing up into his face, one slim hand on his shoulder. She was dressed in violet, a lacy dress that seemed to drift about her body. Like Jess's, it was short-sleeved and short-skirted. As her partner swung her round, Ian saw that the bodice was cut low in the back to show her smooth white skin. Below a broad cream satin sash that hugged her hips, the dress fell in floating panels of various shades of lilac, violet and purple to a jagged hem. On her short bronze hair, feathers in the same shades as the skirt nodded in a cream band.

'What a wonderful dress,' Jess said enviously. 'It must have been made specially for her. I never would have thought that Dorry could be so stylish. Come on, let's talk to her.'

'You can if you want to.'

'You're not still sulking about her going to live with the Warrens, are you?'

'It makes no difference to me.'

'Then why are you behaving like a spoiled kid?' Jess wanted to know. 'If I'd had the chance I'd have gone like a shot. And I doubt if you'd have missed me the way you seem to miss her.' Then she shrugged. 'Please yourself, I'm going to talk to her.'

Left on his own, Ian made his way to the bar that ran down one corner of the room and helped himself to a glass of punch. He drank it slowly, his eyes roaming round the room, returning again and again to Dorothea, who was talking animatedly to Jess now that the dance was over. Jess indicated him; Dorothea glanced across and waved, a casual, disinterested wave. Then she turned back to Jess, her face vivid and happy. Ian drained his glass, and went to find a partner for the next dance.

The evening drifted along on a cloud of laughter and music. Balloons were released from the ceiling and greeted with cries of delight that turned to shrill squeals when some of the men started popping them with lighted cigarettes. The sky outside darkened and the first stars appeared. Ian danced with one girl after another, took someone in to supper, danced again. Occasionally he and his partner of the moment danced past Dorothea, who never seemed to notice him, but was always clasping her partner about the neck, laughing and chattering and enjoying herself. She had no shortage of escorts, Ian noticed. All at once he wanted to get out of the house, away from the revellers, the music, the sight of Dorothea being happy with other men.

Jess and he had scarcely exchanged two words all evening. She, too, had had no problem finding partners. When Dorothea disappeared into the hallway hand in hand with the fair-haired man Ian had seen her with earlier, he decided that he had had enough. He sought out his sister and drew her away from the group she was with. 'Let's go home.'

'Why? I'm having a wonderful time and it's still early.'

'I'm fed up with the whole business.'

'Off you go, then. I'm staying here,' she said, and swung back to her friends.

He shrugged. Jess was old enough to look after herself. In the foyer it was cooler, and a little quieter. Several couples could be glimpsed in shadowy corners, in each other's arms, and there were bursts of stifled laughter now and then from the stairs where several groups perched. Ian was looking about for a servant who could find his coat for him when he noticed Dorothea's escort striding alone from the door leading to the conservatory, his handsome face flushed and scowling. He brushed past Ian and disappeared back into the drawing room.

Ian hesitated, glanced at the front door, then at the conservatory. She was probably fine, he told himself. If he went to make sure of that she would only laugh at him. He would just be giving her the chance to hurt him as he had, of necessity, hurt her when she accosted him outside the refinery gates over a year ago. But he knew that she had had several drinks, and obviously her partner had tried to take advantage of that. Perhaps he should make sure that she was safe before going home.

He bit his lip, then walked across the hall and reached out towards the door handle.

The conservatory was large and humid. Water dripped softly somewhere, but apart from that the place was pleasantly quiet and Dorothea inhaled the lush spicy smell of green growth, her arms wrapped about her body, trying to still the trembling deep within. She shouldn't have hit Jack so hard. He had been an amusing escort for some time now, but no doubt he would never speak to her again. On the other hand, she told herself, close to tears, he had had no right, no right at all to assume that—

She swallowed hard but the lump in her throat wouldn't go away. She felt dizzy and wished that she hadn't had so much to drink. Drinking was a smart thing to do, but she had never really cared for it. She took a good long look at herself and wondered if, after all, Jack had been so wrong in assuming that she would do whatever he wanted. She had led him on just as she had led other young men on. Usually she was able to back away before she got herself into danger, and usually the men were gentlemanly enough to leave it at that. But Jack, too, had had a lot to drink tonight, and he was quite a bit older than she was. No doubt he knew more about women than most of the immature youths she went out with. No doubt he was unused to a woman saying no.

She felt sick. She wanted to go home. She turned round, staring through the dim light at the green jungle about her, unsure, for the moment, where the door was. She located it and had taken a step towards it when the greenery at her back rustled and she spun round, eyes wide, suddenly aware that she wasn't alone.

25

Davie Kirkwood hated jazz. He hated having his house invaded by crowds of shrill-voiced, empty-headed strangers. He would have been happy to stay away, to spend the evening in the factory office going over the books, but Ishbel had insisted on his being there, playing the host. It was all right for Ishbel, she enjoyed this sort of nonsense; as soon as he could manage it, Davie had retreated to the peace of the conservatory with a glass and a bottle of good brandy, which was now almost empty. He was aware that he drank quite a lot these days, but he could hold his liquor and he needed something to make life bearable.

By the time he had returned home from his honeymoon, Davie had become bored with his young wife. He had courted her because he felt that it was time for him to marry, to have a wife by his side as he advanced into society. Ishbel herself had been the key to that society, to respectability. People who wouldn't have looked at Davie before had to accept him now because of his wife. And his father-in-law's wealth had been another reason for marriage to Ishbel. The success of his business, largely thanks to the war, wasn't enough for Davie Kirkwood. He still had a lot of ambition and he still had a score to settle. Ishbel and her family's money would help him in that direction too. He might be invited nowadays to the same events as Andrew Warren, he might be Warren's equal in business, but even so resentment still smouldered deep within and he wasn't done with the man yet.

Thinking of Warren made him think of Anna. Not that there was a day that passed without thoughts and memories of her. Marriage hadn't eased the pain of her loss;

at first there had been something about Ishbel – her liveliness, perhaps – that had seemed to Davie to have faint
echoes of Anna McCauley, but no more. His wife had
none of Anna's vitality or her courage, and certainly
none of her passion. Davie had found that out within
hours of their society wedding. He poured more brandy
into his glass and drank it down.

Dimly, he heard the sound of the door leading to the
house opening and closing, then there were whispers
and a distant giggle, followed by a scuffling sound and
the sharp echo of someone clapping their hands together
– or a slap. He neither knew nor cared which, he only
realised that some of his wife's confounded guests had
found his hiding place, and he stayed still, hoping that
he wouldn't be discovered and required to make genteel
conversation. When the door opened and closed again
and the place fell silent, he assumed he was alone again.
With relief he settled back in his wicker chair, shook the
bottle to find out how much remained, and was about to
pour more brandy into the glass when he heard a light
step and his nose caught the sudden scent of roses, the
perfume Anna had always worn.

Quietly, not daring to hope, he put the bottle down and
got to his feet, parting the branches before his face. In the
shaft of moonlight that lit up the path before him he saw
a young woman, her back to him. Alerted by the sound
he made, she turned; the movement, the bronze gleam
from her hair, and the glimpse he had of wide eyes set in
a face shaped just like Anna's set Davie's heart racing. Part
of his mind told him that what he saw was a drink-
induced mirage, but all the same he reached out and
found his fingers touching warm flesh, catching an arm,
pulling the girl closer. It was Anna – her height, her
build, her face looking up at him, lips parted and eyes
huge and dark in the moonlight. But he knew the true
colour of those eyes. They were violet-blue.

'Oh God,' said Davie hoarsely, dragging her into his
arms, rejoicing at the feel of her, the warmth of her, the
sweetness of her held close to his heart after all the empty
years. 'Oh, Anna!'

* * *

Ian didn't stop to find out the identity of the man struggling with Dorothea. All he knew was that someone was holding her, kissing her, and that far from kissing him back she was fighting to free herself, whimpering like a child in the grip of a fearsome nightmare. He charged towards them, snatched at the man, tore him away from Dorothea, spun him round and hit him with all his might without giving him time to defend himself. In the instant before his fist connected and the other man crashed back into the greenery to the accompaniment of rending branches and agitatedly whipping leaves, he saw that it was his Uncle Davie. But it was too late to stop the blow and he didn't want to stop it anyway. At that moment he would have struck down the Archangel Gabriel if he had found him in the same situation.

Without giving the older man a second look he whirled, stooped, and plucked Dorothea from the ground where she had fallen when Davie had been wrenched away from her. 'Are you all right?'

She clung to him, sobbing his name over and over again. Her feathered band had disappeared and her short, soft hair lay against his cheek. Ian half carried her to a bench and, detaching her grasping fingers, sat her down. He plunged into the shrubbery and located his uncle, lying on his back, with the strong smell of brandy about him. Running skilled fingers over Davie's head and face, Ian satisfied himself that though unconscious and with a growing knot on his jaw, Davie was in no danger and owed his slumber more to drink than to the blow. Then he gathered Dorothea up from the bench and hustled her out of the conservatory and across the large foyer. A serving-man materialised in front of them, his face carefully expressionless as he took in the dishevelled young couple, the girl in tears, the man tousled and angry. 'Can I be of assistance, sir?'

'Just get out of my way,' Ian told him, and managed to open the front door. With one arm about her waist he got Dorothea down the steps and halfway down the drive before she wrenched herself free and staggered to the

bushes, where she sank to her knees and vomited. He
followed her and held her head, then helped her to her
feet and wiped her mouth with his handkerchief.

'You'll feel better now. Come on.'

'Where – where are we going?'

'I'm taking you home.'

The night chill had gone some way to sobering her. She
pulled away from him. 'I want to go back to the party!'

'Why? Because you were having a good time?'

The sarcasm in his voice did more than anything else
to clear the last of the drink-induced confusion from her
head. 'You've got no right to—'

'Someone has to. You're not fit to look after yourself.'

'How dare you!'

'Don't be a fool, Dorry,' Ian said wearily, and started
on down the drive.

She hesitated, then ran after him. 'Go back to the
house and ask them to telephone for a car.'

'I've just knocked out my uncle. I'll have to go back
there tomorrow and have it out with him once he's
sobered up, but not before. We can walk.'

'All the way to Gourock?'

'It'll do you good, Dorry.'

They had gained the gate now. Ian started out along
the road, walking fast. She had to run to catch up with
him. 'My name is Thea!'

'Your name is Dorry.'

'That was before.'

'Before what?' Ian wanted to know, stepping out, not
looking at Dorry struggling to keep up with him.

'Before I knew about – before you turned your back on
me.'

'I'd no choice.'

'You had a choice! You didn't have to turn away from
me, leave me alone the way you did!' Then she said, her
voice shaky, 'I'm cold.'

He stopped so suddenly that she almost bumped into
him, and pulled his jacket off. He put it round her and
fastened the buttons, his face remote, his brows drawn
together, before moving on.

324

'You've been behaving like a fool, Dorry. D'you know that?'

'What does that matter to you?'

'It matters!'

'Why didn't you tell me that it mattered when I needed to know?'

'Because – for God's sake, Dorry,' said Ian in anguish, 'can't you understand anything? Can't you see that it could never have worked out once you became a rich man's daughter?'

'I can't understand how anyone can just walk away from the person he's supposed to love. Perhaps I have been behaving like a f-fool, but what else was there for me to do? I'd n-nobody after you left me, Ian. Mam wasn't my mam any more, Jess and Helene both loathed me, even Aunt Edith w-wouldn't have anything to do with me.' The tears had begun to flow again; her body shook with them and she stumbled on the pavement, unable to see where she was going. 'It's all been terrible. I've n-never been so alone in my whole l-life!'

He stopped, and again she walked into him. Ian looked down at her, at the downbent head, the slim shoulders shaking beneath his jacket. 'Oh, Dorry,' he said helplessly, shaken by such a wave of love and longing that it could no longer be denied. She lifted her face to his and he saw that it was wet with tears and almost misshapen, in the moon's light, with the grotesque effect of smeared make-up.

She gave an almighty sniff, then said with as much dignity as she could muster, 'My name's n-not Dorry. Not any m-more. It's Th-ea.'

'Not to me, Dorry.'

'Th-thea!'

'Dorothea,' he said, taking out his handkerchief again and carefully, tenderly, wiping her face. 'Dorothea. My darling Dorothea.'

He ran a finger gently down the line of her scar, then drew her into the shadow of a gatepost and into the shelter of his arms, and kissed her wet eyelashes, her nose, her lips, again and again and again.

★ ★ ★

Dorothea refused pointblank to stay in Greenock when Ian went back to Glasgow, even though her father had given his consent to their engagement.

'I'm not going to be separated from him again,' she told Andrew mulishly, and he finally had to give in. She also refused to accept more than a token amount in financial support.

'I have to get used to earning my own living again, Father,' she insisted, and finally Andrew obtained a post for her in the offices of a Glasgow sugar refiner he knew.

'She's obstinate,' he complained to Lessie.

'So was her mother.'

'Not like that. If you ask me, Lessie Carswell, she's learned it from you. I don't see why she had to go to lodgings in Glasgow when she could have been living in comfort here. We're not that far from the city, she could have seen as much of Ian as she wanted to without having to move away from Gourock.'

'They're young and they're in love. Let them enjoy their lives for as long as they can.'

'You talk,' said Andrew, 'as though being in love is a privilege that only belongs to young folk.'

'Mebbe it is. When we get older we're too busy just trying to survive to think of such things.'

'Oh Lessie, Lessie,' said Andrew, studying her with a disquieting light in his eyes. 'What am I going to do with you? There are times when I know that you've still got a lot to learn yourself.'

It seemed to the Greenock folk that Davie Kirkwood had a midas touch. Aided by financial support from his wife's family, he began to expand even further after his marriage, buying up small engineering shops and extending his business interests to take in other small companies such as Rattray's spinning mill, where Dorothea had once worked. A year after the party which had ended with Davie being found unconscious in his own conservatory, an empty bottle by his side and a tender blue lump on his jaw, he prepared to make the largest killing of his career.

326

Lessie first heard of it when Andrew came charging into the shop in the Vennel, his face dark with anger.

Her mouth went dry at the sight of him and she abandoned her customer without so much as an apology. 'Ian? Dorry?'

'They're fine.' His voice was clipped, cold. 'I must talk to you.'

All the women waiting to be served, and the assistant behind the counter, were gawping at him now. Lessie pulled her pinny off, asked Doreen if she could manage on her own for a while, then snatched her coat from its peg behind the inner door and hurried from the shop, hearing the buzz of inquisitive talk break out at her back as she went. Andrew was pacing the narrow footpath outside. As soon as she emerged, he took hold of her arm and started to walk, not up into the town as she had expected, but down towards the river, splashing through the puddles that were always to be found in the Vennel no matter how warm and sunny the day might be.

'I've got a shop full of customers back there – not that you noticed,' Lessie said breathlessly as they barrelled along.

'Did you know what that damned brother of yours was up to?'

'Davie?' He could scarcely mean Joseph, who had never returned to Greenock after disappearing at the beginning of the war, nor contacted his brother or his sisters. 'What's Davie done?'

'I've just had a visit from my lawyer,' Andrew said grimly. 'It seems that your brother's out to take the refinery away from me.'

She stopped short, staring up at him. 'You're not serious!'

'Do I look as though I'm joking? For God's sake, Lessie, what's the man playing at? Are you certain he said nothing to you?'

They were down at the docks now. Across from where they stood a ship was being unloaded, only its upper decks and grimy funnels visible above dock level. A line of lorries waited where once there had been horses and carts.

'Nothing. But how—'

'At your brother's wedding I told you that I'd had to sell shares to raise the capital needed to modernise the refinery. I retained forty-eight per cent and the other shares were parcelled out to ensure that no one person could buy more than a safe amount. It seems that Davie bought some under various names and since then he's been calling on shareholders, buying up their shares. Now he holds thirty-seven per cent.'

'Not as many as you hold.'

'Not yet. But fifteen per cent of the shares are un-accounted for. If he gets his hands on them, he has the controlling interest. He can take over and force me out, if he's a mind to.'

'And if you get your hands on them you're safe?'

'Assuming I can find the holder or holders before he does. Assuming that I can top his offer.' He hesitated, gnawing at his lower lip, staring at the far shore of the river without seeing it, then said, 'Almost all my money's tied up in the refinery, Lessie. Helene's wedding cost a great deal and I've no doubt that with his father-in-law's wealth behind him your brother will be in a position to offer more than I can at the moment. I'm done for, Lessie.'

'Mr Wilson might not agree to giving Davie the money to buy you out.'

Andrew gave a short grim laugh. 'Old Wilson won't hesitate to back him, for all that he's known my family all his life. To him, business is business and the Warren refinery's worth having, especially after all the work I've put into modernising it over the past few years. But why my refinery? Why should he be so hellbent on putting me out of business and doing it in such an underhand way?'

'Because I'm a businessman and the Warren refinery's worth the having,' Davie said coolly when Lessie asked him the same question. 'I've put in a fair amount of work on the place over the years and I know its value.'

The two of them were in the study of his house, Davie behind a massive desk, Lessie opposite. The air was rich with the scent of his cigar.

'Davie, the Warrens began that refinery well over a hundred years ago. It means more to Andrew than a collection of buildings and machinery. More to him than it could ever mean to you.' She knew that she was begging, and hated herself for it. But she desperately wanted to prove to herself that the old Davie was still there, still reachable behind all the trappings of wealth and power. 'It's his whole life.'

'And making money's my life.'

'Och, you don't need to make any more. You've got as much as any one person could ever want.'

Good living had begun to make its mark on Davie. He was putting on weight, there was a florid tinge to his face now, and his mouth had hardened. 'You might have forgotten what it was like to be poor, Lessie, but I haven't. I'll never have enough money.'

'I've forgotten nothing, including how good you were to me and Ian after Donald died and how hard you worked for us. But you don't need the refinery.'

He eyed her coldly across his desk. 'If you've come to ask me to give up my plans, you've had a wasted journey. Why should you worry about Andrew Warren anyway? Save your pity for folks that need it.'

'Folks like you? Why d'you dislike the man so much, Davie? What has he ever done to you? He gave you work when you needed it badly, he's always been fair to you.'

Davie's colour deepened and he ground out his cigar in an ashtray. 'You'd not understand.'

The question was out before she even knew that it was in her mind. 'Has it got anything to do with Anna McCauley?'

Taken off guard, he gaped at her for a brief moment before recovering himself. 'Why should it?'

'You'd a soft spot for Anna all those years ago when she lived on the same landing as us in the Vennel. But it was Andrew Warren who won her.'

'Aye, because he had money.' Her brother's voice was suddenly grating and bitter. 'And you wonder why I'll never have enough? If I'd had it then—'

'What difference would it have made? You were

just a laddie. Anna never took you seriously.'

'You think not?' said Davie, and all at once the missing piece fell into place in the puzzle that had been Anna McCauley.

'Davie, were you the man she was seeing before she died?'

'Who told you there was another man?'

'Nobody. Nobody needed to.' Then she said quietly, 'Anna bled to death after aborting the child she was carrying.'

'You mean that she'd tried to get rid of it?' When she nodded, he said explosively, 'You see? Warren's child, and she didnae want it because it was his. He killed her as surely as if he had put his hands round her throat!'

'Not Andrew's child, Davie. It couldnae have been his. He was certain of that when he came home from Jamaica and heard about it. I believed him then, and I still do. That's how I knew there had been someone else.'

He lunged forward as though he was going to throw himself across the desk at her, his face draining of colour then as swiftly flushing again until it was brick-red. 'Mine? But she didnae . . . I knew nothing—'

'You were struggling to keep the engineering works going, Davie.' It was all clear in Lessie's head now. All she had needed to know was the identity of the child's father. Once she had that, she knew why Anna had had to have an abortion. 'You'd nothing to offer her at that time except the sort of life Andrew Warren had rescued her from. She couldnae face that again, and she couldnae face him with someone else's bairn in her arms when he came home from Jamaica.'

Davie's mouth twisted as if he had just bitten into something unbearably sour. 'When I'd enough money I was going to take her away from him. And his bairn, too; I'd have taken the bairn willingly, for her sake.' Now that his secret was a secret no longer, the words spilled out. His hands, linked on the blotter, were shaking. He looked at them, then up at Lessie. 'It was his bairn she was carryin', no' mine! His, an' it killed her!'

'You're wrong, Davie. You've nursed your hatred all

these years and you were wrong. You cannae blame him.'

'Anna!' The word was torn from Davie's throat and his eyes flooded with sudden tears; he got up so violently that his chair fell over, and lurched to the window. Lessie rose and went to put her hand on his arm.

'Davie, it all happened a long time ago. No sense in raking up the past. No sense in hating Andrew now for something that wasnae his fault.'

His arm jerked back from beneath her hand as he swung round on her, his wet eyes blazing. 'You think anything's changed? She was mine, and he held her because he had money and I hadnae!'

'The only thing that held Anna was her own fear of going back to the sort of poverty she'd known in the Vennel. You'll drive yourself insane if you go on letting bitterness fester in your head, Davie.'

'Mind your own business!' He had his emotions under control again. 'You can beg all you like, beg on your knees if you want to, but I'll not change my mind. I'm going to have that refinery. I'm going to let Andrew Warren know what it feels like to lose the most important thing in his life!'

'You still need the other fifteen per cent.'

He walked past her and picked up the fallen chair, his movements sharp and vicious. 'I'll get it. I can offer more than he can, once I find the holder.'

'Davie, let the matter end here and now. For my sake if not for Anna's.'

'What's Warren to you?'

'A good friend. Dorry's father.'

His lower lip stuck out, reminding her strongly of their own father in one of his tempers. 'You'll be able to tell him you've done your best for him. I hope he's grateful. But it's not enough.'

'It will be.' Then she took a deep breath and said, 'That fifteen per cent you're looking for – I hold it.'

For a moment he gaped at her foolishly, then found his voice. 'You?'

'I bought the shares in my broker's name when Andrew was modernising the refinery.'

'Does he know?'

'Not yet.'

Davie's hands were white-knuckled on the back of the chair, the light of the hunter in his narrowed eyes. 'I'll give you double what they're worth on the market just now. I'll give you whatever you want for them.'

'They're not for sale.'

He released the chair and caught at her arms, his fingers digging in. 'Damn it, Lessie, you're my sister! You said yourself that I'd done a lot for you and Ian when you'd nothing, and nobody to lean on. It's your duty to sell to me!'

It was her turn to pull free. 'I'll not help you to seek revenge on a man who's done you no wrong.'

'You'd turn from your own flesh and blood for the sake of someone who probably thought you werenae even good enough to clean his boots in the old days?'

'The old days are gone,' she flashed at him. 'It's now we're talking about!'

'You can never escape from the past. Lessie, I'll give you whatever you want for those shares.'

'I'm not like you, Davie. I only need enough, not everything in the world.'

'I'm your flesh and blood,' he said again.

'Sometimes,' said Lessie, suddenly bone-weary, turning towards the door, 'flesh and blood doesn't count for much.'

'You and Ian would've starved if it hadnae been for me.'

'I'd rather have starved than seen what you've turned into.'

'Lessie!'

She didn't answer, didn't turn round. There was a sudden clatter as he swept everything off his desk with a violent movement of his arm. 'You bitch!' she heard him say as she opened the door and stepped out into the foyer without looking back.

26

Glasgow was never silent, even on a Sunday afternoon when the shops and markets and factories and offices were shut. The single room Ian Hamilton rented near the Royal Infirmary was right at the top of an old tenement building but even on a Sunday he could still hear cars rumbling down the narrow cobblestoned street below where horses used to pull carts. Trams groaned and rocked their way along the nearby main road, children shrilled at their games, and women leaning comfortably on cushions propped on windowsills or standing at the closemouths called to each other and erupted now and again into peals of laughter.

He stretched, yawned, and said reluctantly against Dorothea's silkily smooth back, 'It's time I was getting up. Time to go to work.'

'If you must.' She turned and smiled at him. Her hair was tousled and she was beautiful.

He bent his head and kissed the soft slope of each breast lingeringly. 'And you'll have to get up too. Time you were back where you belong.'

'This,' said Dorothea, reaching out to stroke her hands seductively down his naked body, 'is where I belong.' Then she squealed as he threw the blankets back and let cold air into the cosy little nest they had made for themselves. 'Ian! It's freezing!'

'Get up, woman.' He crawled over her and stood upright on the faded linoleum, reaching for his clothes, feeling his skin tauten in the chill air. 'You'll have to get back to Mrs Prissy before she starts wondering if you've been kidnapped.'

'It's Mrs Plessey, and I wish I didn't have to go back there.' Dorothea crawled reluctantly from the bed. 'Why can't we get married now and live here together?'

'Because I won't marry until I can support my wife,' he told her for the umpteenth time, forcing himself to avert his eyes from the hills and valleys of her nude body. He didn't have time to take her back to bed, much as he wanted to. 'And I'll not have you living in a hovel like this.'

'You're being daft. With what I earn we could manage. We could find somewhere a wee bit—'

'I want us to do more than manage. I saw what happened to my mother and stepfather because of the need to bring in more money.'

Dorothea, a stocking dangling from one hand, came up behind him and put her free arm about his waist. Her cheek was soft and warm against his back, through the material of his shirt. 'That'll never happen to us.'

'I won't let it happen to us. Not much more than another year and I'll be through. Then we're going to have the best marriage there ever was.'

She sighed, released him, and shook the kettle to make sure there was water in it before putting it onto the tiny gas stove and lighting the ring. 'Why did I have to fall in love with a stubborn man?'

'Because I'm irresistible,' said Ian, shrugging on his jacket and attacking his red hair with a brush. Between them they tidied the bed then gulped down some hot strong tea before leaving the room and clattering hand in hand down flight after flight of the stone stairs, and running along the dark close. The group of women clustered at its mouth split to allow them through then reformed at their back, nodding and whispering to each other.

'They're talking about us.'

Ian put his arm about her. 'That lot talk about everyone.'

'D'you think they know what we've been doing?' Dorothea asked with a giggle.

'Probably. But I hope to God your father doesn't.'

Her heels pattered briskly on the paving stones by his

side. 'I don't care. I know what I want, and I want you.'

They paused at the corner, where their paths separated. 'I do love you, Dorothea,' Ian said through a sudden lump in his throat. 'When I think how close I came to losing you—'

'Hush!' She touched the corner of his mouth with the tip of one finger, a touch as light as a butterfly's wing, yet erotic enough to send a tingle of pleasure and wanting through his body.

'Tomorrow night? I'm off duty.'

She made a face. 'I've got a class.' To fill in her evenings, when Ian was more often than not working or studying, Dorothea was taking classes in shorthand and typewriting and bookkeeping at night school to help her in her job. She enjoyed her work at the sugar refinery; when she visited Greenock she always made a point of going to the family refinery, asking question after question, getting to know the business inside out.

'I'll get some studying in then and meet you outside afterwards. We'll buy a fish supper between us.'

'Good.' They looked at each other one last time, then reluctantly split up, Dorothea heading for the boarding house for young ladies that Andrew Warren had insisted she stayed in, Ian striding off to Glasgow Royal Infirmary where he worked as a night porter.

The rain had stopped and although the sky and water were still dull on that March day, the sky had managed to lighten from slate-grey to dove-grey. A shaft of sunlight pierced the clouds to form a shimmering circle, a large golden sovereign far out in the Clyde. Beyond it the soft blue hills on the other side, folded and tucked neatly, guarded the hidden entrances to Loch Long and the Holy Loch. A filmy scarf of mist tossed carelessly down by some giant hand was caught between two of the hills, giving them a silvery lustre.

Lessie studied it, entranced, and Andrew Warren had to say her name twice before she turned away from the window, smiling at him. 'It's beautiful. You're fortunate to have such a splendid view.'

'I spend many an hour at the windows myself. But for now, come and pour the tea.'

She moved to the low solid table conveniently set beside a comfortable couch and poured milk into delicately fluted china cups. On the opposite side of the fireplace where a cheerful blaze crackled, Warren watched her. 'It's good to see you here at last,' he said.

'It feels strange.' Getting out of the car he had sent for her, standing on the gravel sweep before the front door, she had almost panicked, almost turned and run down the drive and out into the road. It was fortunate that Andrew himself had opened the door at that moment to rescue her from such a ridiculous flight.

'You should have been in this house long ago,' he said firmly, leaning forward to accept his cup from her hand.

'I remember walking past it with Donald and Ian, and Donald saying that this time next year we'd have a place just like it.' She smiled at the memory. 'It was his favourite saying – this time next year. It kept me going many a time after I lost him, thinking that this time next year things might be better, might be worth waiting for. But neither of us ever dreamed that one day I'd actually be inside the house, sitting here and pouring tea like a lady.'

'And looking as though you belong here,' he said quietly. Glancing up, she caught the look in his eyes and felt foolish colour rise to her cheeks.

'I'd certainly not be here if Edith was still working for you.' Lessie thought of the way Edith would have reacted if she had come into this room in her maid's uniform and seen her sister sitting like a lady of leisure, and felt the corners of her mouth turn up in a broad smile.

'It's thanks to her that I've finally got you to cross the threshold, so I should be grateful. Even though it irks me not to be able to call in at Cathcart Street when the mood takes me.'

'I'd no option but to take her in, Andrew. She's my own sister, and I could scarcely leave her on her own after that heart attack. I don't have the time to run back and forth to Gourock to keep an eye on her.'

'It can't be easy for you.'

'She's not a bad patient,' Lessie said swiftly, but Andrew was right; there was little pleasure to be found in her home now that Edith was lying in regal state in the box bed in the kitchen, demanding attention and finding fault.

'You should have let me pay for a nurse companion to see to her in her own home.'

'You've done enough, settling a regular pension on her. Most employers don't bother, no matter how long folk've worked for them.'

'I didn't do it for her as much as for you. And before you fly up like a turkey cock at me, I'll never be able to make it up to you for the way you saved the refinery.'

'Och, that didn't cost me anything.'

'It cost you the good money Kirkwood would have paid you for those shares. Far more than I did. And then there was having to decide between us – between your own brother and me.'

A cloud drifted over Lessie. She had heard nothing from Davie since their quarrel and didn't expect to. She knew that she had lost him for ever now. Somewhere along the hard road he had created for himself, Davie had become an unforgiving man. She sipped at her tea then said, 'I couldn't go along with what he was going to do. It wasn't fair.'

'I just thank God that you went behind my back and bought those shares. Thanks to you I hold over fifty per cent now and I'll keep them. I've learned my lesson.'

Lessie finished her tea and put down the cup. 'I must go.'

'Not yet.'

'Edith'll be wondering where I am. I've got a meal to prepare.'

She got up a little stiffly, thinking wryly that her age was beginning to tell. But when Andrew stood up to take her hands in his, his tall body unfolded itself effortlessly. 'Come and have a look round the house before you leave. I thought women always wanted to see round houses,' he added in surprise when she shook her head.

'It wouldn't be right, me poking about the place.'

'My dear woman, Helene's safely tucked away in her husband's house down in Dumfries, and I can assure you that Madeleine's ghost isn't stalking the place.'

'Even so, it wouldn't be right.'

Warren shrugged and sighed. 'I still haven't got the measure of you,' he said resignedly, then to her surprise he stooped and brushed his lips along the line of her cheekbone. 'But thank you for being you, Lessie.'

In the car on the way home Lessie lifted a gloved hand and pressed her fingertips lightly against the place his lips had touched, half pleased and half afraid. Pleased because over the years, and particularly since they had been alone, their grown children scattered, Andrew had become very dear to her. Afraid because the look she sometimes glimpsed in his eyes made her wonder if he read more into their friendship than there could ever be. Men hated being alone, they took it harder than women, but the common sense that had kept her going throughout the ups and downs of her life told her that there could never be anything more for either of them. The very idea was a nonsense and she put it firmly from her mind as she stepped from the car. She thanked the uniformed chauffeur and rounded the corner to walk down Cathcart Street. She couldn't take the chance of letting the car deliver her right to her own close. Lessie knew her sister well enough to realise that Edith would be shocked and humiliated by a friendship between her sister and her former employer. Edith's snobbishness reached into every aspect of her existence.

'Where have you been?' she wanted to know as soon as Lessie stepped into the kitchen. She lay in the box bed in the alcove as Lessie had left her, with not an added crease in the pillow or the coverlet. She must have lain like that, motionless, all afternoon. 'I've been choked for want of a cup of tea. I thought you'd have been back before this.'

'I was just visiting.' Lessie hurried to where the kettle simmered on the coal range, not stopping to take off her coat. The doctor had said that Edith could get up and do things for herself, providing she rested often, but

Edith, who felt that she had spent more than enough time caring for others, had opted for total invalidism and the luxury of someone tending to her for a change. Peter had left Greenock by the time his mother suffered her heart attack, and so far Lessie had been unable to trace him. Edith seemed indifferent to her son's disappearance. 'He'll turn up again like a bad penny,' she said peevishly when he was mentioned. 'He was never any good. If you ask me he inherited more from Joseph than from me.'

'When are you ever going to get rid of that monster and put in a gas cooker?' she wanted to know now, scowling at the gleaming range.

'I'm quite happy with things as they are.'

'It's old-fashioned, and it takes far too much cleaning. Who were you visiting?'

'Just an old friend,' said Lessie.

Just before Ian began his final year as a medical student, Dorothea got her way, and the two of them came down to Greenock for their wedding. As Andrew escorted his daughter down the aisle, radiant in ivory satin and lace, her face glowing beneath a circlet of orange blossom, Lessie let tears of joy run unashamedly down her face, much to Edith's annoyance. Her sister, who had consented to rise from her sickbed to attend the ceremony and was wearing the same black skirt and coat and white blouse she had bought for Davie's marriage, nudged her painfully in the ribs with a bony elbow. 'Stop shaming me in front of all the folk,' she hissed.

'I'll cry at my son's wedding if I want,' Lessie hissed back, and smiled through her tears at Andrew as he stepped away from the altar, his task done.

'I've got a name of my own at last,' Dorothea confided to her new mother-in-law at the reception in the Warren house. 'First it was McCauley, because that was my mother's name, then Carswell when I lived with you, then Warren, but none of them belonged to me. Now I'm Dorothea Hamilton, and it fits me fine.'

'I hope that being Mrs Hamilton brings as much happiness to you as it did to me, and for a great deal longer,'

Lessie said, and Dorothea suddenly threw her arms about her and hugged her.

'Oh Mam,' she used the old title unselfconsciously, 'I'm so happy!'

Davie and Ishbel attended the wedding, but Ishbel was on her own at the reception. Davie nodded formally to Lessie when the guests left the church, but didn't speak to her. Although she felt that she had done the right thing in helping Andrew to keep the refinery, she missed her younger brother, and mourned him too, for to her he was dead and a stranger inhabited his body and used his name. They had each selected a certain road in life, she thought sadly, and their roads no longer ran side by side.

'Davie's got to get back to the factory,' Ishbel apologised on his behalf at the reception. 'He's so wrapped up in work just now.'

Lessie put a hand on her arm. 'I know he's busy. Don't worry about it.' In the four years of her marriage, Ishbel's eyes had lost their sparkle, her mouth had taken a downward turn at the corners. Lessie felt sorry for her, realising that her life couldn't be easy, and was relieved when Jess, who had come up from London where she now worked, took charge of her young aunt and brought a smile to her face. Jess was beautiful in a low-waisted vivid orange dress with a dramatic orange-embroidered black panel down the front from neck to hem and deep black cuffs to the sleeves. Several long strands of pearls were looped about her slim neck and her narrow shoes were orange with black heels. Heads turned wherever she went; she was featured frequently in fashion magazines now, and in great demand in the fashion world.

It was hard to believe that she had once been an ordinary little girl, playing in the Greenock streets with the other children. Lessie felt, each time Jess visited, as though she were holding an exotic butterfly in her hand – brilliant, fragile, settling for only a moment and impatient to be off again. She was proud of Jess, and she loved her, but she had lost the girl almost as completely as she had lost Davie. Their former closeness had long since faded. She felt that of the two girls, Dorothea was truly her daughter.

For years now, Jess had had no need of a mother.

Ian and Dorothea settled in a neat little house in Glasgow, Andrew's wedding present to them. Although Ian was still a student they managed to scrape by on his scholarship and the money Dorothea had saved from her job. To Dorothea's fury Ian refused point-blank to allow her to go back to work, even for the final year of his studies. 'I'll support my own wife,' he insisted. 'You got your way about marrying before my finals, and I'll have my way about this.'

'I'm used to working,' Dorothea told Lessie mutinously during a trip to Greenock. 'I liked working in the refinery. They'd have kept me on and I'd only just become the manager's secretary. We could fairly do with the money, too, though he's almost proud of being poor and getting by. I don't know why he's so stubborn.'

'Some men hate the thought of their wives having to go out to work. It makes them feel inferior.' Even as she said the words, Lessie wondered if Ian was testing his young wife, making her prove to his satisfaction that she could manage without the Warren money.

'And it makes women feel inferior to be dependent on a man. Mam, I've got the housework done in a morning, and I'm not the sort to spend all my days embroidering or visiting.' Then Dorothea added guiltily, 'You'll not let him know what I've been saying, will you? I don't want to hurt his feelings. I love him and I'm so happy with him. I don't mind doing without things and having to be careful with the housekeeping money, really I don't. I just wish I'd more to do with my time, that's all.'

Two months later she and Ian arrived together in Greenock, eyes shining, to announce that Dorothea was pregnant.

'That'll keep her busy,' Lessie said with relief to her sister when she returned with the news from the Warren house where the young couple were staying for a few days.

'Fetch me that calendar,' Edith ordered, and Lessie obediently brought the calendar from where it hung on a nail.

She watched her sister mumble through it, brows furrowed, and said dryly, 'Nine months, Edith. They were wed in August and the bairn's due early in June, Dorry says. They'll not shame me – or you.'

'Hmmm.' Edith relinquished her grasp on the calendar. 'It's gey quick, all the same. They'd have been better to wait for a wee while. At least until he'd finished his studying.'

'Love and bairns don't go by the calendar,' Lessie told her sister solemnly, and Edith scowled at her. 'They'll manage, and it's good to see them so happy together, making plans. It minds me of when Donald and me were waiting for Ian to be born. They say that the time passes slowly, but I never noticed it myself. With Jess I was busy with the new shop, and with Ian every day of the nine months just seemed to fly past. Happiness'll do that for Dorry and Ian too. D'you not mind it yourself, Edith, when you were carrying Peter?'

'I mind the heartburn and the backache and the discomfort. And I mind being left on my lone wi' a bairn tae raise.'

'Were you ever happy, Edith?'

Her sister's mouth pursed like a prune. 'I did my duty by Peter and by my employers and by Mam. I've nothing to reproach myself with. Life's not for enjoying – not for the likes of us, anyway. It's a hard business an' I'll not be sorry when the time comes tae lay down my burden.'

'Och, Edith, don't be so depressing! You've got years ahead of you yet.'

Edith shook her grey head. 'Life must go before life comes.'

'That's an old wife's tale!'

'There's truth in it, you mark my words, our Lessie. There's a new life to come now and before it does a life has to go. It'll be mine,' said Edith, almost smugly.

'You'll live to hold Ian's bairn in your arms, I'll make sure of that, if only to prove to you what nonsense you're talking,' Lessie said firmly. 'I'll make a nice cup of tea before I go along to see how they're managing in the shop.'

342

* * *

Edith Fisher's iron will held to the end. Despite Lessie's determination to prove that there was no truth in old wives' tales, she came home from the shop in the Vennel four months later to find her sister lying dead in the box bed, her hair in two iron-grey plaits on her shoulders, her hands clasped across her stomach.

For a few minutes she sat by the bed, looking at the sallow face on the pillow, certain that the half-closed lids would suddenly fly open and Edith's complaining voice would ask what had kept her, and if there was such a thing as a cup of tea going. But the silence deepened and she knew that she was alone, and that Edith, like Mam and Da and Thomasina and Donald, had finished with this life. She got to her feet, patted her sister's clasped hands, and went out to seek help.

Edith was laid in the cemetery close to the other family graves. Standing by the grave, Ian and Dorothea on either side of her, Lessie looked up as the minister's voice droned on and saw Andrew, who had taken time from the refinery to attend the funeral. As their eyes met he smiled faintly; she nodded in return then let her gaze travel on, round the small semi-circle of mourners, to where Davie stood alone, hat in hand, staring sombrely down at his sister's coffin. She wondered if he was remembering the old days when they had all been children.

There was movement beside her as Ian stepped forward to take one of the ropes, his young face solemn above his dark clothes, his hair a flaming beacon in the graveyard. Davie came forward too, and the undertaker's men held the other ropes as Edith Fisher was lowered to her final rest. They sang 'The Lord's My Shepherd', and as Ian's strong bass voice and Dorothea's clear alto soared above the others with the words, 'In His house for evermore my dwelling place shall be,' Lessie had a sudden picture of Edith, not resting in that heavenly mansion, but working her way grimly from room to room armed with a tin of polish and a cloth. For a terrifying moment she thought that she was going to giggle, right there at the graveside, and shame Edith for eternity, then scalding tears came instead, and at last she wept for her sister, not only for her death, but for the grey days of her life, and for all the pleasure Edith had somehow missed in raising her son.

Where Peter was on that day when his mother was being buried, Lessie had no idea. Nobody had been able to trace him and Edith had died without a final sight of him. Jess, too, was missing; she had an important modelling assignment in London and was unable to get away in time for the funeral.

The psalm ended and Lessie stooped, lifted a handful of earth from the pile by the grave, and scattered it over the coffin. Then, the tears drying on her cheeks, she turned away.

Davie hurried off without speaking to anyone. He looked straight ahead as he was driven off by his chauffeur.

'I thought Ishbel would have been here too.' Dorothea clutched Ian's arm as she negotiated the pebbly drive; she was in excellent health but the growing baby had made her top-heavy and clumsy on uneven surfaces.

'She's in France on holiday with her mother,' Andrew told her. 'She's more often away from her home than in it.' He shot a sidelong glance at Lessie then said, 'There's talk that the marriage's foundering.'

'I thought you'd more to do than listen to idle gossip,' Lessie said sharply, and stalked ahead of the others towards the entrance. Her Davie might be as dead to her now as Edith but she'd not allow folk to miscall him. She had never told a soul, and never would, about his love for Dorothea's mother, a lost love that had soured and warped his whole life; since discovering the truth of it herself she had come to understand more about her brother and to pity him with all her heart. But her understanding had come too late; Davie had mourned Anna on his own for many years, and didn't need or want anyone to share his secret. The very fact that Lessie knew of it had probably been enough in itself to make him turn away from her.

Just before she reached the drive leading down to the street she glanced to one side and saw the little stone that marked Anna's grassy grave halfway along a row. Every year, on the anniversary of Anna's death, Lessie laid flowers on the grave – twenty shillings' worth of flowers. She always would, for as long as she herself lived.

27

Morag Anna Hamilton was born at the end of May 1924, a few weeks before her father graduated as a doctor. She was a sturdy baby with her father's red hair tempered to a rich auburn by her mother's dark colouring, but with her mother's and grandmother's unmistakable violet-blue eyes. Holding her, looking down into those beautiful large eyes, Lessie felt her heart jolt, as though she had taken a step back in time.

She and Andrew had travelled up to Glasgow together to see the baby; on the train back to Greenock that evening it was Andrew who put their shared thoughts into words.

'She's the image of Anna.'

'What?' Lessie, who had been watching the countryside flash by and remembering with pleasure the utter happiness in the little house she had just left, took a moment to return to the present.

'Wee Morag.' Andrew, opposite her in the swaying compartment, folded his hands over his silver-topped cane and rested his chin on them. 'She's the image of Anna. It's as if she's come back to us.'

'It's strange how the mixture of Ian's red hair and Dorry's dark hair's just caught the colour Anna's was. And she has her eyes, there's no getting away from it.'

He grinned across the compartment at her, a boyish grin with mischief in it. 'D'you realise that Morag links us together for all time? We're grandparents now, with a shared grandchild.'

'I suppose we are,' she agreed with amusement. 'Being a grandmother doesnae make me feel any older.'

'You look younger than ever, to me.'

'It seems just last week that I went to Port Glasgow to see Dorothea for the first time. D'you miss Anna still, Andrew?'

His eyes softened, seeing beyond the carriage walls, looking into the past. 'I wish to God she'd not died so young, or died the way she did. Anna deserved better. But if I was to be honest – and I always have to be honest with you, Lessie – I'd have to say that I don't think that what was between her and me would have lasted.'

For a moment she wondered if he knew something of Davie's involvement with Anna, then he went on, 'It was a physical affair as far as I was concerned, and I think my money was more of an attraction to her than I was. Oh, I liked her dash and daring and her love of life, and I admired her courage. But if it hadn't been for Dorothea, I doubt if I'd ever have set Anna up in her own house. If it hadn't been for Dorothea I might even have stopped seeing Anna by the time she died.' He paused, then gave a rueful laugh and admitted, 'I loved my wife more than I ever loved Anna. But I didn't realise it until it was too late. I'll always regret that. Always.'

'It's good to have loved, though. To have it to look back on, and remember.'

'It's good to be in love at any age. And better to have love now than in the past.'

'You're an old romantic, Andrew Warren!'

He laughed as the train whistled shrilly and rocked round a corner. 'And you, Lessie Carswell, are altogether too practical for your own good – or mine.'

Two weeks later they were back in Glasgow for Ian's graduation. Sitting in the lofty university hall, Andrew unselfconsciously reached out to take Dorothea's hand in his left and Lessie's in his right as Ian, solemn in his robes, stepped forward to accept the scroll that entitled him to call himself Dr Hamilton from that moment on. Just as unselfconsciously, Lessie let the tears run down her cheeks. Edith would have been furious if she had seen them, but Edith wasn't there.

Ian started working as a junior doctor in the infirmary

where he had worked as a porter, able at last to support his wife and his little daughter without recourse to Dorothea's savings or the occasional financial gift from her father.

In May 1926 Britain was hit by a general strike. It was bitter but soon over for most of the strikers, though the miners stayed out and the subsequent drop in coal supplies forced local factory owners to close down and lay men off. To Lessie it was a strong reminder of the hardship she herself had gone through after Donald's death. She opened up a 'tick book' in the Cathcart Street shop and extended the list of debtors in the Vennel shop.

'They'll pay when they can, and if we don't give credit to our customers they'll try elsewhere – and stay elsewhere when things improve,' she told her staff, and taught them to distinguish between fly-by-night customers who would never honour their debts and those who could be trusted to pay off their accounts when they could. Mindful of the way Murdo had once treated customers who owed money, she kept a close watch on the financial dealings of both shops and made sure that nobody was charged interest on their debts.

Poverty held Greenock in its choking grip. Soup kitchens were set up, but despite their own misery the local people were generous to the miners' bands that marched through the town, hungry and suffering men dependent on their own class for aid in a country ruthlessly prepared to starve them and their families into submission. Rallies and meetings were held throughout the country and at one such rally in Well Park there was a riot when the police moved in to arrest two men speaking in the park without official permission. One man was taken but the other fled with the help of sympathisers before he could be arrested.

'The word going round is that the missing man's called Peter Fisher,' Andrew told Lessie, his brow furrowed.

Her heart gave a double thump. 'Edith's lad? Here, in Greenock?'

'So I've heard. I didn't see him myself but I'm told that he gave a fine stirring speech before the constables got there. You've had no word from him?'

She shook her head. 'I hope I will, though. Surely he'll come to me.'

'He's a wanted man, Lessie.'

'D'you think I'd give my own nephew away? Anyway, I've no doubt that he was speaking in support of the poor miners and their families, and I've no quarrel with that. I hope he comes to me,' she said again.

'Probably not. He'll not want to get you into trouble.'

Andrew was right. Although she waited anxiously for several days and woke in the night at the slightest noise, always hoping for a gentle tap on the door, the sound of fugitive footsteps in the close, Peter didn't turn up.

Towards the end of the year, relief to able-bodied unemployed men was scaled down and Lessie's tick books began to fill up rapidly.

'How would the Members of Parliament like it if they were expected to feed and clothe and house their families on one pound and fifteen shillings a week?' she raged helplessly. 'It must cost them more than that to keep their wives in hats!'

'You're beginning to sound like one of those communists,' a customer told her, grinning.

Lessie shot back, 'If the communists believe in keeping folks' bellies full and giving them the right to work, then good luck to them!'

The coal strike finally came to an end in November 1926, and only then because the miners were so weakened by the hardships of their long and arduous strike that they had no option but to accept reduced wages and longer hours. The mills and factories went back into production and Greenock began to try to get back to normal.

Shortly after Morag's third birthday Dorothea suffered a miscarriage and was ill for several weeks. Lessie hurried up to Glasgow and looked after the family until Dorothea was on her feet again. Then, at her suggestion, Dorothea and Morag travelled back to Greenock with her for a holiday. Ian was left behind in Glasgow.

'I can't just take time off whenever it suits me,' he said.

'You look tired,' Lessie argued. 'You could do with some sea air yourself.'

'I'm fine, but I'd like Dorothea to have a good rest. She needs it. She took the baby's loss badly, poor lass. Look after her for me, Mam, I can look after myself,' he insisted.

It had been agreed that Dorothea and Morag, now an energetic red-headed bundle, should stay in the Warren house. Lessie took time off from the shops and as Dorothea's strength returned, the two women went for long walks along the river road, Morag trotting ahead of them. They sat talking for hours in the Warren house or in Cathcart Street and Andrew took them on a day-long river trip on the Clyde paddle steamer *Juno*, to the beautiful Kyles of Bute.

Although Lessie had lived all her life within sight and smell of the Clyde, this was her first trip on the river, and she was as excited as Morag, clambering down the companionways to see the great engines pounding as they forced the paddles through the water, hurrying up and up to the top deck where she stood by the rail, one hand holding her hat on her head, the other clutching Morag's small fist, watching as the steamer was manoeuvred skilfully alongside a pier, or gazing back at the foaming white wake unravelling itself behind them like the long lacy train on a magnificent gown.

Andrew watched her with amusement. 'You're like a child yourself, Lessie. You never lose your sense of wonder at new things.'

'Life's too short as it is,' she retorted. 'I'd lose a lot of pleasure if I started taking things for granted.'

Jess arrived on an unexpected visit, smoking cigarettes that she fitted into long elaborate holders and talking enthusiastically in a voice that had taken on a slight English drawl about Greta Garbo and Mae West and P.G. Wodehouse, who had apparently written funny books that were 'all the rage, darling', about a butler named Jeeves. It was hard for Lessie to believe that she had given birth to this elegant, worldly woman and raised her in the rooms behind the shop in the Vennel. Jess had recently flown to Paris on a modelling assignment and hoped to return soon. Paris, she said, was invigorating and absolutely the only place to be.

'I can't understand why you're not married by now,' Lessie said one evening, marvelling over the way her vividly beautiful daughter seemed to light up the kitchen simply by being in it. Jess shrugged elegantly.

'I've no intention of marrying. I'm an independent woman. I'm enjoying life far too much to devote it to one man.'

'You'll change your tune when the right man comes along.'

Jess fitted another cigarette into her holder. 'That's a sweet thought, Mother, but it's for the likes of Dorry, not for me. One day when I'm too old to model any more perhaps I will marry – but he'll have to be rich and able to support me in luxury in my old age.'

She brought with her a portable phonograph and a box of records, and the small flat was filled every day with seductive male voices singing, 'Ain't She Sweet', 'Ol' Man River', and 'I Can't Give You Anything But Love, Baby'.

Lessie tolerated the records, and secretly grew to like 'Ol' Man River', but she refused point-blank to allow Jess to buy her a wireless.

'Why not, Mother? It'd be company for you now that you're living on your own.'

'I'm not in the house all that much, and when I am I appreciate the peace and quiet,' Lessie said firmly. 'I couldnae be bothered with all the fuss of a box talking and singing at me.'

'You don't have to switch it on if you don't want to.'

'Then what's the sense in having it at all?' Lessie asked triumphantly, and Jess glared and blew smoke from both nostrils, for all the world like a small angry bull.

When Jess hired a small Austin open tourer and insisted on taking her mother, sister-in-law and niece for a 'spin', Dorothea and Morag accepted eagerly, clambering into the little car without hesitation, but Lessie hung back.

'You mean you can drive this thing by yourself?'

'Of course, Mother,' Jess told her impatiently. 'I drive all over London. There's nothing to it. Climb in and let's go.'

Cautiously Lessie got into the small high seat at the back with Morag clutched tightly to her side. Jess, in a bronze silk jersey suit with a tight-fitting cap of the same material and colour pulled over her shingled head, released the brake and moved off with a triumphant throaty bray from the horn that brought all the Cathcart Street residents to their windows and Lessie's staff and customers to the door of the corner shop. As they proceeded along the street Lessie, holding tightly to Morag's skirt with one hand and the side of the car with the other, thanked the Lord that old Mrs Kincaid who had lived on the top floor had long since died. She could just imagine the woman's harsh disapproving stare and her comments that she had always known that the Carswells were the wrong sort of residents for the street. To her surprise Jess turned out to be a confident and accomplished driver, and before the drive along the coast to Largs and back was over, Lessie had relaxed and was enjoying herself.

Two days later she arrived back from the corner shop to find the short hallway filled with rounded energetically waggling bottoms and slender backward-kicking legs. Jess and Dorothea had their hands flat against the wall at shoulder level, elbows bent, and their feet in the middle of the passageway. Jess was singing breathlessly and the two of them were twisting their feet and kicking their legs back from the knees. Morag, jiggling about between them with a doll dangling from one hand, was screaming with excitement.

'Da – da-da – kick – da-da – da-da,' Jess panted as Lessie walked in.

'What on earth?'

The gymnasts peered at her over their shoulders, then slumped against the wall, giggling. 'It's the Charleston,' Dorothea managed at last. 'It's a dance.'

'Lord's sake!'

'It's all the rage, Mother,' Jess chimed in. 'I'll show you. Out of the way, Morag.' She held her hands in the air and launched into an intricate sequence of kicks, wiggles, and foot twisting, her red-tipped fingers fluttering as though playing an invisible piano that was suspended from the ceiling.

'It's great,' Dorothea enthused.

'It's daft!'

'Not with the proper music. Come on, Mother, try it.'

'I will not!'

'Yes you will. Come on.' Dorothea seized her hands and planted them on the wall. 'Now put your feet back here so that you're bending forward. Now twist your left foot as if you're – er – squashing a cockroach.'

'And while you're doing that, kick to the side with your other foot,' Jess instructed. They took up their positions on either side of her. 'Ready? Da – da-da – and twist-kick, twist-kick, that's it, Mother, you've got the rhythm – da – da-da.'

Twisting, kicking, waggling her bottom, Lessie wondered again what Mrs Kincaid would have made of it all. Then she decided that she didn't really care. She was having a good time, Dorothea was getting better, and that was all that mattered.

Jess went back to London but Dorothea stayed on. Ian came down whenever he could, which wasn't as often as Lessie would have liked. As her health improved, Dorothea began to spend time with her father at the refinery, leaving Morag in Lessie's care. The little girl adored her gran's shops and was content to sit for hours, if Lessie was busy, with a bowl of barley and some twists of paper and a tiny ladle and scales that Andrew had bought for her, playing at shops in the corner while the customers came and went.

'There always seems to be more to do in Greenock,' Dorothea said one night when she had gone to Cathcart Street on her own to visit Lessie. She sat on the rug before the range, looking fit and relaxed.

'I thought it would be the other way round.'

'In Glasgow there's the house, and Morag, and going to the shops, and seeing a few friends. Here there's the river and the boats – and the refinery. I've enjoyed helping Father in the office.' Dorothea hesitated and looked down at her hands, twisting her wedding ring on her finger. 'I enjoyed working before we got married. I was good at it. Sugar refining's interesting.'

'You must have inherited the Warren mind.'

Dorothea smiled fleetingly then looked back at her hands. 'I've been on at Ian to let me go back to work but he'll not hear of it.'

'He probably thinks you've got enough to do.'

'He's wrong, then. There's not going to be any more children, Mam; they told us that when I lost my baby. And with Morag starting school fairly soon I'm going to find time heavy on my hands. I'm not like Helene, I can't fill my time with charity work and afternoon teas and sewing parties. I want to do something, to have a life of my own. I wish Ian could understand. But he thinks—' She stopped abruptly, then said, 'He thinks that's what destroyed your marriage – you working all the time, especially once his stepfather was out of work. Some men just don't take kindly to being supported by their wives.'

Lessie remembered Ian's accusations when Murdo left them and felt a return of the pain she'd known then. 'But lassie, I had to work. There was no sense in letting you all starve in order to save Murdo's pride.'

'I know,' Dorothea said, staring down at the rug so that Lessie could only see the top of her dark bronze head. 'I know.'

'I'm going to miss her,' Andrew said as they stood on the platform watching the train carry Dorothea, Ian and Morag back to Glasgow.

'We both will.'

'She's got a damned good head on her shoulders, has Dorothea. I'm proud of her, and glad I didn't lose touch with her when she was growing up.'

Together they turned and walked from the station, back to their everyday lives.

28

In a faraway American thoroughfare called Wall Street,
ruined businessmen, if stories were to be believed, were
raining down the sheer slopes of high buildings like the
tears down the faces of the thousands who had lost all their
savings in the financial slump. The crash was so tremen-
dous that it echoed across Britain and unemployment
soared, but thanks to Andrew's advice and her own
shrewd instincts, Lessie managed to salvage most of the
money she had had invested. But things were nonetheless changing in Lessie's world.

The Vennel had existed in Greenock for over two
hundred years, and was part of the original town. By 1931,
tenements that had been built to hold a fraction of the
numbers who now burrowed into them like mice were
rightly and finally deemed to be grossly overcrowded
and in a poor state, with inadequate facilities for the
men, women and children who lived there. A Housing
Enquiry was held and Greenock Corporation was granted
a Compulsory Purchase Order that spelled the end for
the Vennel.

The building that housed Lessie's shop was bought out
and the shop forced to close. As it happened, one of the
girls who worked in the Cathcart Street shop had just left,
so Lessie found room there for the two women who had
worked in the Vennel.

'It's not a problem for me, not now,' she told Andrew
as they sat in her kitchen one evening. 'It's sad, losing the
wee shop and the rooms behind it. They were the saving
of me years ago. But the folk that live in the buildings'll
be found better accommodation now, and the job of

bringing the place to the ground and building new'll give work to a good number of poor souls who've been idle for too long.'

'Will you look out for another shop?'

Lessie considered, then shook her head. 'No. Mebbe it's time to take your advice and have more time to myself.'

He stared at her and his brows knotted together over grey eyes that were as clear and direct as they had been when she first met him. 'Woman, you've never taken sensible advice in your entire life. Why should you start now?' Then he said gruffly, taking his pipe from his mouth and contemplating the glowing bowl, 'I think you need another interest.'

'Jess has taught me to dance the Charleston and Amelia Earheart's already flown the Atlantic. What's left for me to do?'

Andrew didn't laugh. Instead he laid his pipe down carefully, got up, took a turn about the room, then said, 'You could marry me.'

'What?'

'You could take me in hand. And don't tell me I'm daft,' he added swiftly as she opened her mouth to speak. 'If I am it's only because I've waited all this while to ask you.'

'Andrew, it could never work!'

'Why not?'

Lessie floundered, and realised that her heart was skipping along at a ridiculous pace and her face was probably the colour of a tomato. She groped for words. 'You're one of the Warrens, and I'm—'

'You're a local businesswoman, a woman who's looked up to far more in this town than you realise. You're self-made, Lessie; you started with nothing but determination and you've worked damned hard for what you've got. You raised three children – one of them mine – and did it on your own for most of the time,' said Andrew almost angrily. 'The Greenock folk have got more sense, most of them, than to judge people by what they were born into. They appreciate good hard work. I doubt if I could have done half what you have, given your beginnings. So that takes care of whether or not you're good enough. Anyway, to hell with what they might think. It's me that should be worrying about my own worth—'

'You've got nothing to worry about!' she said hotly.

'—but I'm not even going to think of that, because I know what I want – and you're what I want, Lessie,' he finished, running out of steam at last.

'But I'm fifty-two years old!'

'And I'm sixty-two years old. You don't believe all that nonsense about love only belonging to the young folk, do you? Let them think that if they want, but they don't have the experience or the wit to know what love really is.' His voice softened. 'It's being old enough to know your own mind. It's watching someone mature and grow into her own special beauty in spite of what life throws at her. It's wanting to warm my hands at the glow she gives off and be with her and take care of her for all the days left to me.'

Tears came suddenly to Lessie's eyes and Andrew misted, wavered, and broke up. 'You should have been a poet,' she began to say mockingly, but her voice, too, wavered and disintegrated. She felt his touch on her, felt him drawing her to her feet, moving his hands to cup her face.

'My dearest, dearest Lessie, don't cry,' he whispered, and kissed her. His mouth was soft and warm at first, his grey moustache harsh on her face. Then his lips firmed, parted, and her own mouth opened beneath his in response as his arms moved to hold her.

She had thought that passion was long gone from her life, even before Murdo left her. It was an emotion that surely belonged to the heady days of courtship and early marriage, something that couldn't last. But now she discovered that it had only been lying dormant, and despite the half-century she had already spent in the world it was as clear and strong and wonderful as it had ever been. Nobody could have found it except Andrew Warren, she thought as she clung to him in the clock-ticking peace of her little kitchen, returning kiss for kiss, tasting his skin on her tongue, letting her fingers know the texture of his thick hair and the strong solid breadth of his back beneath the tweed jacket he wore.

When they finally drew apart they were both breathless. Lessie reached up and touched his cheek, smoothing away the dampness left by her own tears. His eyes were blazing with triumph as he smiled down at her.

'Now try to tell me you don't love me, Lessie Carswell.'

'I hate a man who always thinks he's right,' she said, her voice still shaky, and he laughed.

'I promise you, my love, that from now on we'll take turns in being right.'

'What's Helene going to say?' Lessie asked later, when they were seated on opposite sides of the range again. She had made fresh tea and the hot strong brew brought the taste of normality back to a life that had suddenly taken on the feeling of a fairytale.

'I'm not bothered about what Helene says. She's comfortably settled in her own home in Dumfries and I'm old enough to do as I please. I think Ian and Dorothea will approve. And Morag. Especially Morag. Now she'll have her gran and her grandpa together under the one roof. If you've got any more reservations, my love,' he added, eyes creasing with laughter, 'just tell yourself that we're doing the right thing by Morag.' Then he leaned forward and caught her hand in his. 'Let's go to Glasgow tomorrow and tell them – they should be the first to know.'

'Not yet, Andrew. Give me time to – to get used to the idea.' What she really wanted was time to relish her new happiness, to hold it close and marvel over it in secret before it became the property of other people.

'I'm off to London on Saturday. It's supposed to be a week-long business but I could get it over in five days, I'm sure. We could go to Glasgow together on the following Saturday to tell them.' Then his hand tightened on hers. 'Come to London with me, Lessie.'

'I couldn't just up and leave the shop.'

'Yes you could. When did you last have a holiday? When did you ever have a holiday?'

Lessie, taken aback, had to admit that she had never in her life taken time away from her duties and from Greenock.

'Then come to London. We'll see the sights together and when I'm at meetings you can go shopping for your trousseau. We'll choose a ring, too.'

'Andrew, don't rush me along at such a rate! Anyway, your trip's all been planned. I might not get a room in your hotel and I'd be frighted to stay in a big city like that on my own.'

'I always book a double room,' Andrew said diffidently, not meeting her eyes. 'I find single rooms claustrophobic.'

'You mean we'd share a – a—'

'A bed, Lessie. That's what you're trying to get your tongue round. Why shouldn't we book in as husband and wife? Nobody in the hotel would know the difference.'

'I'd know the difference!'

He came to kneel by her chair, taking the cup from her hands and putting it gently to one side. 'I love you, Lessie. I've loved you for years. I don't want to be apart from you any more.' Then he added with mock seriousness, 'If you're scared that I'll change my mind about marrying you after I've had my way with you—'

'Don't be d—' She bit down on the word, then said, 'It wouldn't seem right. Not in a hotel, with the folk there thinking we were wed and our own kin knowing nothing about it.'

He sighed and got to his feet with a slight cracking of joints. 'Very well, but as soon as I get back we're going to Glasgow to tell Ian and Dorothea, even if I have to drag you away from your bacon-slicer in front of all your customers and cause a scandal in the town. Then we'll buy a ring and we'll have a party in my house, and tha 's when we'll tell the rest of the world.'

She nodded, almost in tears again, loving him all the more for his understanding. 'I'll buy a fine dress for the party while you're away.'

'And a wedding dress. I want you to buy your wedding

dress soon, Lessie. That way I'll know that you're really going to be mine.'

'I'll go to Glasgow for it.'

'Buy the best and have the bills sent to me.'

'I'll do nothing of the sort,' she said at once. 'I can afford to buy my own clothes.'

He grinned and gave in. 'If you must, but just remember that once my ring's on your finger, it'll be my right – and my pleasure – to pay for them. Don't take money with you, my darling, this damned country's thrown so many honest hard-working men out of employment and into hopelessness that some of them can scarcely be blamed for taking any opportunity they can find to lay their hands on some money.'

'I've got my own chequebook. You can't run two shops and buy in supplies for other grocers without the use of a chequebook these days.'

'Another thing, you can be thinking of our honeymoon while I'm away. Anywhere you want, Lessie. What about a cruise?' he said enthusiastically. 'France and Spain, the African coast, Jamaica. Oh, Lessie, I'd love to see Jamaica again, with you by my side!'

When he had gone, with one last reluctant kiss, Lessie felt as though she had been caught up in a whirlwind, tumbled about for hours, then dropped back into her kitchen. Dazed, she peered into the mirror and saw the same well-remembered face peering back at her. Her fair hair glittered silver here and there, but it was still soft and in good condition. Her face had rounded out a little and the worry lines that had reigned between her eyes for as long as she could remember had been joined by fine lines stretching along her forehead and radiating from the corners of her eyes and mouth. She had never been one to try to fight against the passing years, using paint and powder as allies. But her skin was still quite good, and her eyes, tonight, were wide and luminous, her mouth softened by Andrew's kisses.

The thought of these kisses, of his arms about her, the look in his eyes as he said goodnight to her, made her feel as though she had shed thirty years. She remembered talking to Edith while they were getting the rooms behind the shop in the Vennel ready for habitation, describing her love for Donald as something that had filled her up with warm liquid gold. Tonight the gold was back, glowing through every fibre of her.

She was so fortunate, Lessie thought as she began to wash the teacups they had used, to have found such love twice in one lifetime.

The next day she was certain that the customers in the shop and the staff working with her behind the counter must be able to tell at a glance what had happened. Dorothea and Jess would certainly have known, so it was a good thing that neither of them were in Greenock. But apart from being told once or twice how well she looked, nothing else was said and she was able to nurse her secret in peace.

Andrew called in briefly on the evening before his London trip. He came in the door shaking his head, a vexed frown between his brows.

'All the years I've walked along this street and into this close and knocked at this door and never given a thought to who might see me and what they might think. But tonight I found myself skulking along and nearly looking over my shoulder because of what's happened between us.'

'I know.' Lessie giggled. 'We're a pair of silly old fools.'

'It's a great feeling, isn't it?' He took a small box from his pocket. 'This is for you – until we get a ring.'

Inside the box a delicate little brooch in the shape of a gold leaf with tiny diamonds along the stem lay on white velvet.

'Oh Andrew, it's beautiful!' Then she said nervously as she lifted it from its box, 'They're not real diamonds, are they?'

'Only very small ones.'

'It must have cost a fortune! I can't wear it!'

'Of course you can. You must. I told you, it's a stand-in engagement ring.' Strong though his fingers were, they were also deft and gentle enough to pin the brooch onto the jumper she was wearing. As his hand brushed against the curve of her breast it hesitated briefly, and Lessie felt weak with longing for him. She wished, then, that she had agreed to go to London with him. But it was best to leave things as they were.

Andrew secured the brooch and stood back. 'There. I chose an autumn leaf because we've found each other in September, and I suppose some folk might say this is the autumn of our lives. Although I fully intend us to celebrate our golden wedding together when the time comes.' His lips were hard and warm on hers, his arms strong about her. 'Look after yourself for me, Lessie,' he whispered before releasing her. 'The next five days are going to be the longest of my life.'

Lessie had only been to Glasgow a few times in her life, once with Donald, once or twice with Edith or Jess or Dorothea. She had never visited the city on her own and it took three days for her to muster up enough courage. With Andrew's brooch pinned on the lapel of her coat to give her added confidence, she left Greenock early one morning by train and emerged into Glasgow's busy streets just as the shops began to open, clutching her handbag firmly, her mind buzzing with all that she had to do before returning home.

First, she went to the nearest hairdresser's, where she firmly resisted the suggestion that she should have her hair shingled. Instead, it was washed and trimmed then softly drawn back into a chignon at the nape of her neck, with a fringe over her forehead. The style, softer than her usual bun at the back of the head, flattered the shape of her face.

'You have lovely hair, madam,' the hairdresser said, and Lessie, suddenly reminded of the day she had sold her hair to raise money for her first shop, was glad that she had insisted on retaining its length.

Feeling a little bolder now that the first step had been accomplished, she walked back onto the street, fingering Andrew's autumn-leaf brooch, then plunged into the first large store she came to.

It took her three hours to complete her task. She

bought a green crepe georgette dress gently draped about the hips and falling in a flared skirt to mid-calf length, with a plain neck and bodice and short sleeves. That, she thought, eyeing it in the full-length mirror, would do for the party that was to be held in Andrew's house. The colour suited her hazel eyes and she allowed herself a smug moment to note that the elegant lines of the gown emphasised a figure that was still slim despite her advancing years. With the dress came a long coat in the same colour, snug-fitting in the bodice and waist and flaring slightly at the hem. It was fastened with a large ornate button at the side.

For her marriage she selected a cream wool crepe suit with a fashionably short low-necked jacket embroidered on the pockets and cuffs with bronze stitching. A plain bronze-coloured silk blouse completed the outfit.

By the time she had selected shoes and handbags to match both outfits, as well as cream gloves and a brown cloche hat with a scalloped brim and a side knot of bronze flowers for the wedding suit, she had run up a bill that would have kept the entire family well fed for a month in the days when she was struggling to raise three children. She brushed her fingertips against the leaf brooch then took out her chequebook and filled a cheque in with hands that, for a wonder, didn't tremble and betray her uncertainty as she had expected.

Back on the street again, leaving her purchases behind to be delivered, she drew in a long breath and felt some of the day's tensions draining away. She had managed everything, and now she was free to go home. But first, she thought, she would celebrate her success with a cup of tea.

The tearoom was quite busy when she entered, but she found a table for two in a corner and sank gratefully onto a chair.

'A lunch menu, madam? We're still serving lunch.'

Lessie hadn't realised that it was early afternoon. Several of the people at nearby tables were enjoying a full meal, but although she hadn't had any food since leaving Greenock she was too excited to feel hungry. She ordered a pot of tea and a scone, then sat back and looked round the room, thinking idly of her purchases, hoping that Andrew would approve, eager to see his reaction to the wedding outfit.

Then all thoughts of clothes were swept from her mind as a family party in the middle of the room rose from their table and she had a clear view to the far corner where a man sat hunched over a cup of tea, his head almost sunk onto his chest. He was turned away from her, but even so there was something familiar about the thin body in the long shabby coat, the light brown hair, in need of cutting, the almost gaunt line of the jaw. Lessie got up and forged her way across the room, bumping into an empty chair in her haste to get to him.

'Peter?'

Peter Fisher's head jerked up. For a moment his grey-blue eyes stared blankly, then slow recognition dawned.

'Aunt Lessie?' he said disbelievingly.

'Oh, Peter, it's so good to see you!' She pulled out the other chair and sat down; her knees had suddenly become so weak that she didn't think they were going to support her much longer. She reached across the table, past the half-empty cup, and put a hand on his. His skin was calloused and his nails were bitten down to the quick.

'What are you doing in Glasgow?'

'Just – doing some shopping. Where have you been? I heard you'd been speaking in Greenock. Why didn't you come to see me?' She blinked hard to keep back tears, knowing that that was the last thing he would want to see.

He bit his lip and stared down at the table. 'If you know I was there you'll know that the polis were after me. I could scarcely lead them to your door.'

'I'd not have minded. I'd—'

'Your tea, madam.' The harassed waitress loomed over them, her reproachful eyes telling Lessie that her feet hurt and she had more to do than chase around the tearoom looking for folk who should have the sense to stay put and not move to other tables.

'I'll have it here. And bring another cup – no, wait,' Lessie said swiftly, 'I think I will have lunch after all. I'm starving all at once. You'll join me, Peter? Two plates of bacon and egg and sausages and tomatoes,' she rattled on, not giving him the chance to refuse. 'And we'll have some chips with it, and a plate of hot toast and a plate of scones as well.' Then when the girl had moved away, she said gently, 'Peter, son, did you know that your mother had died?'

'I heard,' he said gruffly. 'When I was in Greenock.'

'It was her heart. She stayed with me for the last months. It was a peaceful ending when it came. I tried to find you, but nobody knew where you were.'

'I was in Newcastle – or Manchester. I cannae mind now.'

'So you've been travelling around a lot?'

He nodded and told her something of the life he had been living, finding work where he could, living rough when there was no money.

'There are plenty of us doing that these days,' he said bitterly. 'Men that fought all through the war for their country, praised for their valour then thrown on the scrapheap when they werenae needed any longer.'

Their meal came and while he ate hungrily Lessie, who had no appetite at all, cut her food up neatly and made a pretence of enjoying it. When Peter's plate had been emptied and wiped clean with a piece of toast, she pushed her own plate over to him, saying briskly when he hesitated, 'Eat it up when your auntie tells you to. You're still a growing laddie.'

He grinned, showing teeth that had gone bad with neglect, and started to eat. Lessie ordered another pot of tea and a plate of cakes and went on listening. Peter had become involved in politics and had, she gathered from a few disjointed words, spent time in prison for his beliefs.

'Oh, Peter! And to think that all this time there's been money waiting in the bank for you.'

He blinked at her in disbelief. 'For me?'

'Your mother was thrifty; she had a bit put by. And Aunt Marion's house was bought, not rented. I sold it and the money's been lying in the bank, waiting for you.'

'I don't want it.'

'Don't be silly, man!'

Peter chewed on his lower lip then said, 'I don't feel that I've a right to her money. I let her down.'

Rage flooded through Lessie. 'For God's sake,' she said, loud enough to turn a few heads at the nearby tables. She lowered her voice, leaning across the table towards him. 'If anyone let anyone down it was Edith, not you. I know she was my own sister and we shouldnae speak ill of the dead, but what chance did you ever get? Having to go to school in velvet suits, never getting a proper childhood, not being understood when the war started and you had the courage to stand up for what you believed in.'

'I lost that courage, though.'

'And no wonder, with what you must have had to suffer. You didn't shirk doing what you had to do once you went into uniform. If our Edith had had any sense she'd have thanked God every day for blessing her with a son like you. And you think you're not entitled to her money? If you ask me, it's little enough compensation for what you've been through.'

During her tirade he had at last lifted his head and looked straight at her. His eyes had started to glisten and he blinked hard to clear them. When Lessie stopped, there was a silence, then he said gruffly, 'I wish I'd been your son.'

'So do I, Peter. I always wished it and I always will.'

'Even so, I don't want the money.'

'And I don't want the responsibility of it. You can give it away or make a fire with it or spend it on sweeties for all I care,' she said, getting a faint smile from him. 'It'll be yours to do with as you want. D'you know where the nearest Bank of Scotland is?'

'Aye, but I'm no' a customer of theirs,' he said wryly.

'That doesnae matter.' She got to her feet, nodding to the waitress to bring the bill. 'Take me there. I'll sort it all out.'

Within an hour she had seen the manager, made him telephone to her bank in Greenock to confirm that she was a respectable customer and not a madwoman, written the largest cheque she had ever signed, and opened an account for Peter, who stood silently by her side throughout.

'I don't think I'll be staying in Glasgow,' he said when they emerged into the street again. 'And it's not a good idea for me to have a bank account. Folk can be traced through bank accounts.'

'You'll have to give it three days, then you can take the lot out in cash and close the account,' Lessie told him briskly. 'I've hinted to the manager that that's what you'll be doing. After that, what you do with the money's your own business, and now my conscience is clear.' She held out her hand. 'I hope I'll see you again, Peter. You know you'll always find a welcome in my house.'

To her surprise he ignored her hand and bent to kiss her cheek. For a brief moment his fingers were painfully tight on her shoulders. 'Goodbye, Auntie Lessie,' he said, his voice hoarse. 'God bless you.' Then he turned and was gone, slipping into the passing crowd as though he had trained himself to vanish from sight swiftly.

On the train home she sat in a corner seat, staring out of the window, seeing nothing but Peter's thin face, the way he had attacked the food she had bought for him. He hadn't once asked about his cousins or anyone else from Greenock. She had said nothing to him about the family, guessing that part of his defence against a world that had treated him too harshly was the rejection of people who had once mattered to him. She knew that she would never see him again, probably never find out what happened to him, unless he did something that got his name into the papers. She hoped, for his sake, that that wouldn't happen. She hoped, too, that he would never find out that Aunt Marion's house had been rented, not bought as she had told him.

As the train rocked along on its way home she wondered what would have become of Peter if the war had never happened. He would still be working in the refinery, maybe married by now, with a nice wee home of his own and some children. He would have made a good father, would Peter. The war, she thought, had a lot to answer for. There were more casualties of battle than those who carried the physical scars for all to see.

'A terrible shock to his family,' the man beside her said, raising his voice slightly as the train rattled over some points. He and his companion, who sat opposite, were dressed in sober office clothes; they had entered the carriage together and opened their respective newspapers at once, conveying pieces of news back and forth to each other.

'You never know when your time's coming,' the other man agreed. 'Is there a family?'

'A daughter – two daughters, I believe. His only boy died in the war.'

'I wonder what'll become of the refinery?'

'He's done a great deal for it, I've heard. A good healthy business in spite of the current—'

The word 'refinery' had stabbed into Lessie's brain like an icicle, scattering all thoughts of Peter. 'Excuse me,' she interrupted, and almost snatched at the newspaper only a few inches away. She saw the headline almost at once. 'Greenock Refiner Dies'. And underneath it in stark black letters was the report of how Greenock businessman Andrew Warren had become ill at a meeting and been taken to St Thomas's Hospital. He was dead on arrival. It was believed, the newspaper informed Lessie imper-sonally, that Mr Warren had suffered a severe stroke. His family had lived in Greenock for . . .

The words started to slide together then dance around the page. There was a buzzing in her ears as though her head was filled with bees. She looked up and saw that the two men and the elderly couple who had been dozing in the far corner were all staring at her with varying expres-sions of astonishment and disapproval.

'I'm sorry.' She returned the paper, crumpled from her tight grasp, to its rightful owner and said lamely to the staring eyes, 'I'm – I was acquainted with the Warrens.' Then she turned away from their murmured sympathies and stared out of the window again, this time listing all that she saw carefully in her mind in an attempt not to break down in front of her travelling companions. A group of houses, cows in a field, a horse pulling a cart along a lane, a farmhouse, a river.

When she left the station, the *Greenock Telegraph* news boards by the entrance had 'Death of Local Refiner' scrawled over them. Lessie turned away and walked aimlessly, travelling up one street and down another until after a long time she found herself on one of the quays by the river's edge. Men were unloading a ship further along, but where she stood it was quiet, with only gulls for company. Grey water, echoing the gathering clouds in the sky, lapped against stone steps several feet below her.

Andrew had promised her a golden wedding anniversary and then he had gone away, and now she was so frighteningly alone that her whole body shook with the terror of it. He had gone, leaving her with only a small autumn-gold leaf to mark their September promises to each other, only the memory of a few – too few – kisses and caresses and some wonderful, half-formed plans that had died with him.

No, she corrected herself sharply. He had left her with far more than that. She had the memories of over half a lifetime of friendship and comfort and support. He had given her more than any other human being, even Donald, had ever given her. If it was true that people lived on as long as others remembered them, then Andrew would continue to exist for many years, and many more years after that, for as long as anybody remembered Lessie herself. He was a part of her, a part that death could never touch.

The thought comforted her briefly. She tried to hold tightly to it but it was whipped away in a sudden storm of remembering the way he had kissed her and held her. He had asked her to go to London with him to share his bed there, and she, like a fool, had declined. Now she would never know what it was like to lie in his arms, to belong to him. Stupidly, blindly, she had denied that special loving to them both. Because of her stupidity Andrew had died alone and now she must live alone, without him.

She stood on the quay for a long time, until early night came, bringing the rain with it, until the wavelets below were freckled with rain and the ground round her feet was dark with it and her face was wet with it. Or tears. Or both.

29

A pile of boxes was delivered on the following morning, boxes bright with the Glasgow store's emblem. Lessie, her hair brushed out and restored to its usual bun at the back of her head, pushed them deep into the recesses of the huge walnut wardrobe that had belonged to Miss Peden. She would never wear the clothes and the hat and the shoes now, never look at them again.

Dorothea and Ian arrived, bringing Morag with them, less than an hour after the delivery man had gone whistling out of the close. Ian's face was sombre, Dorothea's ashen. She started to cry as soon as she saw her mother-in-law, and Ian deftly scooped Morag up and carried her out. 'Come on and look at the pigeons,' Lessie heard him saying as the door closed on Morag's wondering little face, looking back at her mother over Ian's shoulder. 'When I was a wee boy I liked looking at the pigeons. We called them doos . . .'

'It must be just as hard for you, Mam,' Dorothea sniffed when her tears began to subside. 'I only knew him as my father for a few years. You knew him for such a long time.'

'Aye. I'll miss him,' Lessie said quietly. In the long wakeful hours of the night she had decided that there was no point in telling anyone about the plans she and Andrew had made together. What was over was over.

In the church, which was filled to overflowing for the funeral service, she watched dry-eyed as Andrew was carried past her in his coffin. She had done her weeping on the day she heard the news and in the terrible never-ending night that had followed. In the cemetery she looked among the crowd of mourners for Davie but didn't see him. Ishbel had left him two years earlier but he still lived in the big house in Newton Street, alone except for the servants. Ishbel had left the district; Lessie had heard that she had gone off with another man, a man less buried in his work and more able to give her the loving she needed, and that her father had signed a considerable slice of his wealth over to Davie as the purchase price of a discreet divorce, to prevent him from causing a scandal and dragging Ishbel's name through the local mud. Lessie wasn't entirely surprised by her brother's absence, for she was quite sure that he had never been able to bring himself to stop hating Andrew for having been Anna's lover.

The greatest test of her strength came when she had to go into the Warren house and sit in the drawing room that reminded her so strongly of Andrew's warm, vital presence. The drawing room, she thought, looking around, that she might have entered as mistress, if the fates had been kinder. She shook her head when a black-gowned housemaid offered tiny delicate sandwiches, but although she disliked drink, she took a glass of sherry wine from a proffered tray. Holding it gave her something to do with her hands, and she felt that she needed the comfort of alcohol on that day of all days.

Helene, elegantly stylish in black, acted hostess, ordering the servants around with the impersonal confidence of one who has been conscious of her own superiority all her life. Apart from a cool little nod of recognition she ignored Lessie, who wished, for one impish moment, that Helene had known how close they had come to being stepmother and stepdaughter. The young woman would have hated that.

Lessie lifted her glass, studied its pale golden contents, said in her mind, 'To you, my dearest,' and drank the wine down.

Dorothea and Ian had to stay on to hear the reading of the will, but Lessie left as soon as she possibly could, using Morag as her excuse for hurrying back to Cathcart Street. As she stepped onto the gravel drive outside, she let her breath out in a long shaky sigh of relief. The ordeal was over and now she would be free to mourn in peace and privacy.

She fetched Morag from a neighbour's house and spent the rest of the afternoon playing with her. The little girl's cheerful grin and incessant chatter was an antidote to the strains and tensions of the past week, and for the first time since Andrew's death Lessie found herself laughing again. She gave Morag her tea, bathed her and dressed her in her little nightgown, then tucked her into the box bed. Morag loved it, and always insisted on sleeping there when she was in Cathcart Street. Lessie always shared it with her, for it was high and there was a danger of the little girl rolling out of it in the middle of the night. She read her way through half a storybook before Morag's eyelids finally lost the fight and closed. She drew the curtains across the alcove to shade the child from the light and started tidying up the kitchen.

She knew as soon as Ian and Dorothea came in that something had happened. Ian's mouth was grim, while his wife, looking pale and distressed, fidgeted with her bag, her gloves, the cup of tea that Lessie put into her hands.

Andrew, it seemed, had left a few bequests to members of his household staff; and everything else – the house, the money, the refinery – he left to his daughters.

Lessie felt dismay run her through like a sword. How would Ian react to his wife being wealthy in her own right? It made sense for Andrew to leave everything to his own flesh and blood but when the will was written and signed he had had every intention of living for a very long time. Had he died an old man, Ian and Dorothea, mellowed by middle-age and many years together, would have been more able to cope with her inheritance. But it had all happened too soon – too soon for her son and daughter-in-law as well as for herself and Andrew. Looking at Dorothea's strained face, Lessie saw that her thoughts ran along the same lines as her own.

'So now Dorothea and Helene have to decide whether to sell the refinery as well as the house, or whether to try to find a trustworthy manager to run it for them,' Ian was saying, his voice taut with reaction. 'It's going to take months to sort out. A sale would make sense, but this might not be a good time to sell a business, with the country in a depression. Dorothea, if you ask me—'

'Not now, Ian.' Her voice, too, was tense. 'I need time to think about what's best.'

His brows tucked together. 'Helene didn't have any trouble in making up her mind. She wants to sell, lock, stock and barrel. You're surely not thinking of keeping the house on, are you? Apart from the fact that my work's in Glasgow and I don't want to move from the Royal, I couldn't afford the upkeep of a house that size. And I'm certainly not going to live on my wife's charity.'

Dorothea, who hadn't touched her tea, put the cup aside and got to her feet. 'It's been a long day. I think I'll go to bed. Was Morag all right?'

'She's been as good as gold.'

Dorothea peered between the curtains drawn round the box bed then went out of the room without another word. Scowling, Ian followed her. In bed later, with the heat from Morag's curled-up body reaching across the mattress towards her, Lessie could hear her son's voice murmuring through the wall, with an occasional brief word from Dorothea. She wished that Ian would leave the girl alone to think things through instead of trying to force her into a swift plan of action.

They left for Glasgow in the morning, Dorothea still quiet, Ian still moody, and Morag as bright as a button. Lessie stripped the beds and put the sheets in to soak, then went along to the shop, stepping into its aroma of sawdust and coffee and cheeses with relief. Being back in her usual routine was like putting soothing salve on a burn.

Dorothea and Ian were rarely far from her mind for the next few weeks. She felt a niggling anxiety about them, and kept telling herself that it was none of her business and they were sensible enough and loving enough to come to some agreement over her daughter-in-law's newfound wealth.

But when Dorothea arrived unexpectedly at the house

one evening, alone and with an air of nervous defiance about her, Lessie's heart sank.

'Where's Ian – and the bairn?' She tried to keep her voice light as she led her daughter-in-law into the kitchen. 'Did you come down on your own?'

'Morag's in Gourock and Ian's in Glasgow.' Dorothea sat down on the edge of a chair and said in a rush of words, 'Mam, leave the kettle. I don't want tea. I – I've decided to take over the refinery and run it myself.'

'What?' It was Lessie's turn to sit down, abruptly. 'But how can you?'

'I've thought hard about it and I believe I can do it. I learned a lot about sugar refining when I worked in Glasgow, and when I was staying here after the – after I lost the baby.' Dorothea's hands twisted and turned in her lap, her gold wedding ring catching the light. 'I've read books about it too. My father reorganised the refinery so well that it can be run more easily now. I'll do things the way he did them, and that'll keep me on the right lines.'

'And what about Ian?'

Dorothea's hands were like trapped butterflies now. Lessie longed to reach out and still them, cover them with her own and calm them. 'He's staying in Glasgow. That's where his work is.'

'Oh, Dorry!'

'I know it's not the best way to run a marriage, but I can't go on sitting in the house day after day, watching my life go by and never doing anything with it. It's got worse since Morag started school. And Ian refuses to let me go back to work. I have to find out if I'm any good at making sense of the refinery and my own life, Mam. Helene's agreed to rent me her half of the house for the moment – the money my father left me will cover that. And she's agreed to give me six months with the refinery. A meeting of the other shareholders has been called, but I think I can persuade them to let me go ahead. If I can make a success of it in the next six months I'll buy Helene out and buy her share of the house. I've put Morag into a school down here for the time being.'

'You've done that already?'

Dorothea coloured and the scar on her cheek showed as a faint white line. 'I've been down here for over a week. I wanted to find out if things would work before I told you, and I wanted to find out if I could be apart from Ian.'

'And you've discovered that you can.'

Dorothea's flush deepened. 'He's not tried to persuade me to go back to Glasgow. He'll come down to see us when he can and I'll take Morag to Glasgow often to visit him.'

'Is there not some other way the two of you can work this out together?'

'If there is, we can't think of it. It would be just as bad if I went along with Helene and sold the refinery. You know that, don't you? I'd be rich and that would make Ian unhappy anyway. This way when he sees me working to keep it going, and managing to care for Morag as well, he'll mebbe accept things and come down to work in one of the hospitals here so that we can be together again.' Then she said in a rush of words, 'Mam, I know it's difficult for you, being Ian's mother and my foster mother. But I need you to help me. It's all very well having a housekeeper but I can't concentrate on the refinery without knowing that Morag's all right. I need to know that she's got you as well as me.'

It was on the tip of Lessie's tongue to say, 'She'd be better with her two parents, be it in Glasgow or Greenock,' but she held the words back. This crisis was between Ian and Dorothea, and only they could work it out.

'Aye, I'll help you,' she said instead, and Dorothea's lovely blue eyes suddenly sparkled with tears.

'Thank you, Mam,' she said, and hugged Lessie fiercely.

When she was alone again, Lessie fingered the gold leaf brooch, which she wore all the time, and whispered to the empty room, 'Oh, Andrew, my darling, what have you done to our children?'

One thing Lessie refused to do, and that was to move into

the Warren house. The thought of being in Andrew's home now that he himself was gone was quite unbearable. Dorothea's argument that it would make things easier as far as Morag was concerned and that it was time Lessie enjoyed a little comfort did nothing to sway her.

'I need to be near the shop, and I'm quite happy in my own wee house. Morag can come here whenever she likes, and there's nothing to stop her staying here now and again.'

Morag was delighted with the new arrangement. To her, being in Gourock was the same as being on holiday. Even attending a new school had a temporary air to it, and she was able to see her beloved gran every day. On most afternoons the housekeeper met her out of school and brought her on the tram to Cathcart Street, where she 'helped' in the shop, then went back to Lessie's house and had her tea. Then either Lessie took her home or she was collected by the housekeeper. Occasionally Dorothea herself came from the refinery in Bank Street to claim her daughter, but more often than not she was too busy.

It was hard work, taking over the reins from Andrew Warren, but as far as Dorothea was concerned this was her chance to prove herself and she was determined not to fail. Through the business contacts she had slowly built up over the years Lessie learned, by dint of a question here, a listening ear there, that her daughter-in-law was giving a good account of herself and winning the grudging admiration of men who had been quite convinced, at the beginning, that sugar-refining was not for a woman.

'I can't see why they should be surprised,' Dorothea said with a grim smile when she heard what they were saying about her. 'After all, it's women who buy sugar and use it, not men. Why shouldn't women deal with the business of refining it too?'

At first she looked so tired and drawn all the time that Lessie fretted about her. But once she settled in at the refinery Dorothea began to bloom. There was no denying that being busy suited her. Her eyes sparkled, her skin glowed, and even her hair seemed to take on more of a red lustre. She moved and spoke with renewed purpose, and Lessie began to see more of Andrew in her than ever before. He would have been proud of his illegitimate daughter, she thought, then wondered what he would have said about what was happening to Dorothea's marriage. She doubted if he would have been happy to know that he had been the unwitting cause of the enforced separation.

Ian came down often to visit his wife and daughter, staying in the Gourock house at first; then after a few months he began to stay with Lessie instead.

'I don't feel comfortable in that house,' he told her. 'It's too big for me, too fancy. I'd just as soon be in Cathcart Street. After all, it's where Morag spends a fair amount of her time.'

Dorothea may have blossomed during their time apart, but Ian had not. He looked older, more withdrawn, and a tiny frown, not unlike the frown-lines Lessie had carried since Donald's death, had etched itself between his brows. When they were all together Lessie saw how Dorothea watched him, saw the shadow on the younger woman's face, and wondered each time, with renewed hope, if Dorothea had realised that her marriage meant more to her than her business. After all, she had proved herself. Perhaps it was time for her to install a good manager and go back to being a wife and mother.

Ian, she gradually noticed, tended to avoid meeting his wife's eyes – and his mother's too. He kept his own counsel well, only unbending with his daughter.

'Would you not think of coming back to stay in Greenock?' Lessie asked him on one visit. 'We need doctors just as much here as they do in Glasgow, and you'd be near Dor— near Morag.'

'I like working in the Royal,' he told her at once, snapping the words out. 'There's no reason for me to move. And Morag seems happy enough with the way things are.' There was no more to be said on the subject.

During the winter, bad weather and an increased work-load at the hospital meant that his visits became few and far between. When the spring came, the visits stayed at their winter level.

In the summer of 1932 Dorothea went off to Glasgow, asking Lessie to look after Morag in her absence.

'Are you not taking her with you?'

'We've things to talk about, Ian and me,' Dorothea said awkwardly. 'We need to be on our own.'

For three days Lessie waited impatiently, praying that Ian and Dorothea were working out some form of compromise. She loved them equally and she wanted nothing more than to see them both happy. It vexed her that Ian had been so indoctrinated by Murdo, the only father he had known, as far as working wives were concerned. Murdo had been happy enough for her to keep the shop on; indeed, he had loved money too much to think otherwise. It was only when their marriage had soured for him, when he was embittered by his own unemployment and needed to justify his infidelity and eventual desertion, that he had cited the shop as a rival instead of a means of financial support. She wondered what he had said to Ian in the letters he had continued to send, and during his last days, when Ian was with him. Her son had never given her any information and she would have bitten her tongue out rather than ask. Whatever it was, it had been one-sided and unfair, and although she rarely admitted it to herself, she was hurt at Ian's acceptance of it, especially once he matured and became more aware of the complexities of human nature.

Dorothea returned one evening to a rapturous welcome from Morag, who was ready for bed.

'Let me stay one last night,' she clamoured, and her mother laughed and nodded.

'One last night, then. But I want you to come home tomorrow. Daddy's sent you a present. I'll give it to you tomorrow.'

She hugged her daughter, tucked her into the box bed, and read her a story with such an air of serenity that Lessie dared to hope. When Morag had fallen asleep and they were sitting together by the range, the bed curtains drawn, Dorothea said quietly, 'Helene and I are selling the house, Mam.'

'You're going back to Glasgow?'

'No, I'm buying something smaller, more suited to Morag and me. There's a house for sale in Brougham Street, here in Greenock. It has a back garden and it's small enough for the housekeeper to run it on her own.' Keeping her gaze fixed on Lessie's face she went on levelly, 'I'm buying Helene's refinery shares too.'

A chill ran through Lessie. 'And what about Ian?'

'He insists on staying on in Glasgow. He'll not consider moving down here, or living with a businesswoman.' A faint smile touched Dorothea's mouth but not her eyes. 'He doesn't see how a woman can have two loves, her husband and her career, though men do it all the time.'

'Oh, Dorry.'

'Don't ask me to give it all up and go back to him on his own terms, Mam, please.' Dorothea's voice shook and she put a slim hand to her mouth for a moment. The tiny sapphire on the engagement ring Ian had given her glittered in the gaslight. 'I couldn't go back to being a housewife, any more than he could bear to live on my money. Mebbe we're both too proud for our own good. I just know that these past seven months or so I've come alive. I can't give it all up now, not even for—'

In a graceful, fluid movement, she slipped from her chair to her knees on the rug and put her arms about Lessie, her dark bronze head in Lessie's lap.

'I wish women didn't have to make decisions like this,' she said, then her voice broke and Lessie held her as she cried her heart out.

Without saying a word to anyone, Lessie went up to Glasgow on the following Saturday, trying not to remember, as she walked out of Central Station into Hope Street, the last time she had been in the city and the happiness she had carried with her then.

She caught a bus to the end of the road where Andrew had bought a house for his daughter and son-in-law, and was fortunate enough to find Ian in. She had been prepared to camp on the doorstep until his return if the house had been empty.

He came to the door in waistcoat and shirt sleeves, his

eyes flaring in astonishment as he saw his mother standing on the step. 'What are you doing here?'

'I've come to talk to you.'

'You're lucky to find me at home. You should have telephoned first.'

'You know fine that I hate telephones. And if I had made myself use one you'd have found some excuse to prevent me coming here,' she told him dryly, going before him into the little living room. Some neatly taped boxes were lined up under the windows and another box, open and half filled with books, stood before a chair. More books were piled close by.

'What's all this?'

'I'm sorry about the mess.' Ian ran a hand through his red hair. 'I'm moving out. The house belongs to Dorothea – she can do as she wants with it.' Then, to forestall the words that were trembling on her lips, he asked, 'Can I get you some tea?'

She nodded, and looked around as he went to the kitchen. The bookshelves were half-empty; some pictures were missing from the walls.

'Ian.' She went through to the kitchen, which bore the unmistakable signs of a house with no mistress.

'I'll be through in a minute, Mam,' he said impatiently, but she was already at the sink, turning on the taps, stacking dirty dishes.

'I'll just do these things first.' She seized the kettle, which had just boiled, and emptied it into the sink then refilled it and handed it back to him. 'Put that on for the tea.'

Twenty minutes later the kitchen was neater than it had been and they were back in the living room, facing each other across a low table as Lessie poured tea.

'Did Dorothea send you?' he wanted to know as she handed him a cup.

'She knows nothing about this. She'd not have let me come if she'd known. Dorry has her pride.'

He nodded, his eyes fixed on the spoon that was circling round and round in his cup.

'It was pride that almost ruined your lives before, Ian;

I don't want to see it happen again. Can the two of you not come to some sort of agreement?'

'We've talked and talked about it, and there's no agreement to be reached. I'll not live off my wife.'

'You can earn a good salary in the Greenock Infirmary, and you'd surely not find it hard to get a post there.'

'I like the Royal, I like living in Glasgow. It's a woman's place,' said Ian doggedly, 'to be where her husband's living is.'

'That's nonsense, and it's old-fashioned too. Surely you can see that? And what about wee Morag? Does she not matter at all?'

Colour rose to his face. 'Of course she matters. D'you think I'm happy about being away from her for most of the time? I'll go on seeing her whenever I can. But a child of that age needs its mother more than its father, especially a girl.'

Lessie could see her hopes drifting away. 'So you're just going to let your marriage break up, after all the misery you both went through before you found each other again?'

'We've both changed since then, Mam. I need a wife who believes in me and wants to be with me more than anything else. Dorothea needs—' there was a sudden harsh twist to his mouth, ' – she needs to be free to follow her own dream. I certainly don't think she needs marriage as much as she once thought she did. We married in good faith, Mam; we meant to keep the vows we made. But we've both changed and there's little you or I or Dorothea can do about that. It's all decided – it's over.'

'Not,' said Lessie clearly, vigorously, 'as far as I'm concerned. I don't know what nonsense Murdo put into your head about working wives, but he was wrong.' Ignoring the way her son's mouth suddenly tightened, she surged on. 'Murdo liked money and he'd no objection to getting it from the shop. If I hadnae worked we'd all have starved when he lost his job at the shipyard. There's nothing wrong with Dorry running the refinery if she wants to. Would you rather have her sitting at home

384

growing more and more unhappy? Is that what you want for her? And what would Andrew think of this sorry business? The last thing he had in mind was breaking up your marriage.'

For a moment the cold, implacable expression on Ian's face reminded her disquietingly of the way Davie had looked when she refused to sell him her refinery shares. 'You've had your say, Mam, but it doesn't make any difference to what's happened,' he said, and went over to the bookshelves. 'I've got a lot to do,' he said over his shoulder, lifting a bundle of books down.

'Ian, come back to Greenock with me. Talk to Dorothea again, let me help in any way I can. It's not too late.'

On his knees before the box, he looked up at her. 'You mean she's not told you?'

'She's told me nothing, except that she's staying on in Greenock.'

Ian smiled wryly. 'It was loyal of her to keep quiet, though it means I'm the one who'll have to tell you. I thought you were here because of . . .'

For two pins she would have boxed his ears. 'What are you havering about?'

He got up, sticking his hands into his trouser pockets and fixing his eyes on the floor. 'I'm moving in with someone, Mam,' he told the carpet. 'We were friendly with her and her husband when we came here first. Robert died almost two years ago, and since Dorothea went back to Greenock, Ruth's been a good friend to me. She's got her own house, and she has no interest in a career. She's – I'm in love with her, Mam. So there's no sense in trying to get me and Dorothea back together again. I told you, it's all over.'

30

While her schoolfriends went through all the miseries of growing into womanhood – greasy hair, spots, agonising over a figure that was too plump or too scrawny – Morag Hamilton blossomed like a rose. By the time she reached her fourteenth birthday she was of medium height, slender without being thin, and blessed with a clear creamy skin, glowing red hair cut in a neat, casual bob, and the beautiful violet-blue eyes she had inherited from her maternal grandmother and mother. Even in an unflattering school blazer and knee-length gymslip, with a round-brimmed velour hat held in place by an elastic strap under her chin, Morag was striking.

Throughout the thirties Lessie had watched the girl grow with a mixture of pride and concern; although Morag looked older than her years, there was an emotional vulnerability about her. And despite her happy nature there was a rebellious streak apparent in the girl as she grew older, a reminder of Anna McCauley's disregard for what others might think. If there was any escapade at school, any breach of discipline, Morag was involved, and Lessie lay awake at nights sometimes, worrying in case the girl should one day take a wrong turning and live to regret it.

She had had a great deal to do with her granddaughter over the years, for since her divorce, Dorothea had become more and more involved in the refinery and it had been left to a series of housekeepers and to Lessie herself to see to Morag's upbringing. The girl lacked for nothing as far as material comforts were concerned; she went to the best local school, she had a generous allowance, and she lived in a comfortable home, but she and her mother weren't close.

Dorothea, who had lost weight and taken on a severe, classical beauty as she matured, loved her daughter in her own way but simply didn't have much time to spare her. She had made a good job of running the refinery, proving to herself and to everyone else that a woman could be just as sharp at business as any man. She tended to treat Morag as she treated her employees – with kind, efficient firmness.

With her mother more often than not at the refinery, Morag spent most of her free time in Cathcart Street, either assisting her grandmother in the shop or in the house. It was Lessie who heard all about Morag's hopes and dreams, her worries and her triumphs, the confessions of wrong-doing, the crush Morag developed at thirteen years of age on the new young art teacher. It was Lessie who comforted her when things went wrong and celebrated with her when they went well.

Ian had married Ruth, the widow he had turned to for consolation when Dorothea chose commerce instead of domesticity, and now he lived in contented harmony with her and their three children in Glasgow. Morag was always welcome at his house but as she grew older she chose to see less of her father and stepmother.

'They're so – so cosy,' she told Lessie, her nose wrinkling as they worked together to make the Christmas pudding. She was fourteen and a half years old, and the Christmas pudding ritual, started the first Christmas Dorothea and Ian had spent apart, had become a precious event for both Lessie and Morag. 'Ruth's very kind, but nothing exciting happens in their house. I get bored.'

'What about your brothers and your sister? You enjoy being with them, don't you?'

Morag stirred mixed fruit in with flour. 'They're childish,' she said with lofty disdain. 'The boys are football mad, and the last time I was there Catherine was too busy with her pony to be any fun. It seems to suit Daddy but it's not for me. No wonder Mummy didn't stay with him. I know she's wrapped up in her work, but at least she's enthusiastic about it. And she's much more beautiful than Ruth. Ruth's running to fat.'

'So will you be if you don't stop picking at those sultanas, my girl.'

Morag grinned, took one last handful of fruit, then attacked the stirring of the pudding with relish, scowling down into the mixture, her face closed and her brows knotted as she made a wish. Lessie dusted flour from her hands and washed them, glad that the girl was there to deal with the stiff mixture. Her own hands had lost some of their strength now, and sometimes during the night they ached with rheumatism. It seemed no time at all since she had been wringing out wet clothes over the stone sink in the Vennel, and now and then she railed at the way time had crept up on her and aged her when she was too busy to notice what was going on.

As usual, she spent Christmas with Dorothea and Morag in their comfortable house in Brougham Street. Over the years Dorothea had made several attempts to get Lessie to give up the Cathcart Street house and move in with her, even offering to buy something larger so that Lessie could have a suite of rooms to herself. But Lessie had consistently refused; she loved the little flat that Miss Peden had left her, and it was convenient for the shop where she still spent the greater part of each day.

'Besides,' she told her daughter-in-law, 'I like to be independent. I don't want to be beholden to anyone.'

'You'd still be independent, with your own bedroom and sittingroom – and a proper indoor bathroom, not to mention your own kitchen and outside door if you want them. As for being beholden,' Dorothea went on, unconsciously echoing her father's words of so long ago, 'I owe you much more than a home for the rest of your life. I could never have made a success of running the refinery if you hadn't been so understanding and looked after Morag so well for me.'

The housekeeper, a local woman, was spending Christmas with her own family; Dorothea, who hadn't lost her domestic skills, had made the soup and dealt with the turkey and trimmings. Lessie contributed the pudding and

Christmas cake, as usual, and Morag's undoubted artistic talent had gone into decorating the house, which was bright with paper chains and bells and a magnificent Nativity centre piece that she had made herself.

Her gifts to her mother and grandmother were framed portraits of themselves, painted in secret from memory. She beamed as she saw the astonishment in their faces.

'Darling, it's wonderful!' Dorothea, elegant in dark green satin trousers with a high-necked cream lace blouse under a small jacket the same colour and material as the trousers, kissed her daughter then went to prop the painting on the mantelshelf, standing back to admire it. Her own fine-boned face looked serenely back at her from a cloudy pearl-grey background; the bronze high-lights in her rich dark hair, which was dressed in her usual soft chignon, were just the right shade, as were the long-lashed violet eyes coolly staring out of the canvas.

'I'd no idea that you were so talented,' Dorothea marvelled.

Morag flushed with pleasure. 'Open yours, Gran,' she urged.

The last piece of wrapping paper fell away and Lessie gazed down at a neat rounded face set in a halo of white hair, drawn back and fastened at the back of the head. The mouth was slightly curved in a smile, the face touched liberally with laugh-lines – and two deeply grooved worry-lines between the tidy eyebrows. The hazel eyes that looked out of the portrait were amused, kindly, and yet there was a trace of habitual worry about them that toned with the lines above. In the portrait she wore a dark blue blouse, her favourite, and pinned to the collar, gleaming against the material, was the little autumn leaf brooch.

'What d'you think, Gran?' Morag's voice prompted, then Dorothea's hand, slim and well cared for, the nails tipped with bright red, reached over Lessie's shoulder and lifted the painting.

'This is good too.' She propped it up beside her own. 'In fact, it's excellent. It's so like you, Mam.'

'Is it?'

'Oh yes, Gran. It was easier than Mummy's – I had to

have several tries at hers, but I could draw you in the dark with my eyes closed, I know you so well.'

'And you don't know me?' Dorothea's voice was slightly edgy, but Morag seemed quite unaware of the tension.

'You change so much, Mummy, but Gran – well, she's always Gran, isn't she? What d'you think?' she repeated, slightly anxious now, and Lessie fumbled for the right words.

'It's – it's lovely, dear. I just – it's strange, seeing yourself.'

'It's the image of you,' Dorothea assured her, adding, 'Now then, who wants a drink? A small sherry, Mam?'

'Since it's Christmas,' Morag began.

'And since you're fourteen, you'll have ginger wine,' her mother told her.

'But I'm in my fifteenth year, and I look older than I really am. Just a little sherry, Mum.' Their voices rattled on around Lessie, and her portrait gazed down on her from the mantelpiece.

It wasn't until she was back home and had had another look at it that she realised why it had disturbed her so much. It was good, as Dorothea had said. It was like her – a quick glance in the mirror proved that. But it was the portrait of an old woman. A woman with fifty-nine years of hard living behind her – more than half a century. It wasn't, she realised with sharp dismay, the woman Andrew Warren had known and loved. Soon she would be older than he had been the last time they were together.

Lessie sank down onto a chair and her fingers unconsciously groped for the leaf brooch, as they always did in a moment of crisis. Where, she wondered in panic, had the years gone? What had she done with them? It was as though they had been stolen away from her while she was too busy to keep an eye on them. As far as she was concerned she was still the same Lessie who had scrubbed floors to keep herself and Ian in the Vennel. Apart from a touch of rheumatism she was the same Lessie who had left her parents' house eagerly, radiantly, to become Donald Hamilton's wife. Panic stirred in her again as she realised that there was nobody left who remembered that

Lessie, with the fair hair and the young face. Nobody except Davie, and she never saw him now, even though he still lived in Newton Street.

Then, mercifully, the panic began to subside as her usual common sense fought its way to the surface to remind her that time affected everyone, not just her, and that there was still plenty of it left. Stiffly, she got up and made a cup of tea, and by the time she climbed into bed, Morag's gift, painted with love, had been hung on a nail hammered into the kitchen wall.

Jess came home for a few days on the following Easter, as beautiful and vivid as ever. Although she was well into her thirties Jess, Lessie thought as she watched her daughter, would never change. She would always be beautiful, confident, crackling with energy. She had been in America on a modelling assignment, travelling on the *Queen Mary*, and arrived laden down with gifts and full of wonderful stories. Morag hung on her every word and after Jess had gone, the girl was in a restless mood and talking of leaving school at the end of the summer term.

'I thought you were staying on and going to art school?' Lessie protested, and Morag shrugged.

'That'll take too long. Aunt Jess started her career by working in a dress shop. I could do the same.'

'Your Aunt Jess had little choice. I couldn't afford to pay for school fees, but your mother can. Why a dress shop, anyway? You don't want to be a model like Jess.'

'No, but I could learn about design, work my way up the way she did. I need to get some experience of life if I'm to be an artist. And Aunt Jess has certainly experienced life.'

'She'll change her mind once she starts work,' Dorothea said when Lessie appealed to her. 'She'll be glad enough to go back to school by the end of the year. Let her try her wings.'

In June Lessie opened her door to find a young man standing in the close. 'Mrs Carswell? My name's Elder, Colin Elder.'

The name was faintly familiar, but it wasn't until he

went on, 'I teach art at your granddaughter's school,' that she could place him as the teacher Morag had had such a crush on over the past year.

He came into the kitchen, hat in hand, and beamed round the small neat room. 'This takes me back – we've a kitchen like this at home.'

'You're not from Greenock, Mr Elder?'

'No, I was brought up in Perth. I live in a boarding house here.' He went over to her portrait. 'This is Morag's work.'

'It was her Christmas gift to me.'

He studied the portrait closely for several moments in silence. Lessie left him to it and poured water from the steaming kettle into the teapot, then took the caddy down from the high mantelshelf and opened it.

'It's good,' Colin Elder said at last, standing back from the picture. 'It's been painted with love, I can see it in every brush stroke.'

'Sit down, Mr Elder. You'll have some tea?'

'Thank you.' He put his hat on the table and watched as she bustled about the kitchen, making tea. 'I hope you don't mind me calling, Mrs Carswell, but I know that Morag's fond of you. She often comes up with some remark of yours in class.' His open young face broadened into a grin. 'In fact, your sensible sayings have often been the saving of me when I was trying to explain things to my class and not making a very good job of it.'

By the time the tea was made and Lessie was seated across the table from him she had decided that she liked Morag's Mr Elder. He was younger than she had expected, with smiling brown eyes and curly brown hair that looked as though it defied any attempt to flatten it. He was dressed casually in a pale blue shirt and a fawn tweed jacket over brown trousers.

When Lessie remarked, as much to herself as to him, 'I always thought that folk judged advancing years by noticing how young the policemen were getting, but it seems to me it's the teachers we should be looking at,' he threw his head back and laughed.

'My mother told me this would happen. She's always

fretting about me looking too young for my profession. I'm twenty-four, Mrs Carswell, and this is my first job. But I've not had much trouble in getting my classes to behave themselves and listen to me.'

'From what I hear from Morag you seem to be able to hold their attention without having to shout or threaten. The teachers at the school I attended all seemed to be as old as Methuselah and as crusty as homemade bread,' Lessie started to say, then stopped herself. 'But it's my granddaughter you've come to talk about, not my past.'

His face was suddenly solemn as he leaned across the table, his big square hands clasping his cup. 'She says that she intends to leave school at the end of term.'

'Aye. She wants to work in a dress shop and learn something about design from the beginning.'

'She's making a mistake. She's not a designer, you can tell that from the portrait there. I'm told that a teacher – especially an art teacher – is lucky if he gets three or four talented pupils in a lifetime's teaching. I consider myself to be very fortunate to have Morag in my class during my very first year. She's got talent, Mrs Carswell, but she has a lot to learn, too. I've been looking forward to at least another year of working with her, steering her towards art school. I'm not long out of the place myself and I know what they're looking for and how to release it in your granddaughter. Believe me, dress designing's not for her.'

'Her mother thinks she should be left to find that out for herself.'

A frown tucked itself between his brows. 'I know, I went to her before I came to you. Her argument is that Morag can still go to art school once she's got this restlessness out of her soul. But what I'm afraid of is that by that time she'll have taken the wrong road. I want to use that restlessness, Mrs Carswell, to harness it and make it work for Morag. She'd be making a mistake if she left school now. From what I can gather, you might be the one who could influence her.'

'I doubt if I could influence her as much as all that.

Morag's got a mind of her own, Mr Elder. You'd have a better chance than me.'

'People of her age tend to do the opposite from what their teachers advise. I'd not want to damage her future by charging in where I'm not welcome.'

'From the way she's been speaking of you these past nine months or more I doubt if you'd be charging in.' Then, as his brown eyes asked a puzzled question, she said with amusement, 'Did you not know she had you on a pedestal, Mr Elder?'

'I did not. Oh, there are some girls who make it obvious – we're warned to expect that and told how to deal with it. But Morag – she's always been too sensible for that. She's mature for her age, downright aloof at times.'

Lessie smiled wryly. 'Not when she's talking about you in this house, I can assure you. Morag's a right mixture at the moment; everyone who knows her sees a different side to her. If I were you, Mr Elder, I'd find the chance to have a wee word with her. Tell her what you've told me, that you'd like to have another year of teaching her and getting her ready for college. I think she'd listen to you.'

When he was leaving, she asked, 'What sort of pictures do you paint, Mr Elder?'

He grinned down at her ruefully. 'I only dabble, Mrs Carswell. I've enough sense to know that my talent's for teaching, not for becoming a famous artist. My pleasure's going to be to see others do what I'd have loved to do myself.'

'Tell Morag that,' said Lessie, and thought to herself when he had gone that her granddaughter was very fortunate to have met up with such a dedicated teacher. She was glad that she had met him, for she'd been slightly worried about the adoration in the girl's eyes whenever she mentioned Mr Elder. Morag was suffering from the lack of a father in her life. Although she still saw Ian, he belonged to his new family now. It was inevitable that the girl should latch on to a male teacher at an age where girls were just as likely to have crushes on the female teachers. Lessie was glad to know that Colin Elder was a sensible, modest young man.

She never found out what the teacher said to Morag;
her granddaughter said nothing about any conversation
between them. She merely announced, as the summer
term drew to a close, that she had decided to stay on at
school after all and begin to prepare a portfolio for
submission to Glasgow School of Art when the time
came.

Morag had grown up against a seething, shifting tapestry;
during the thirties so much happened in the world that
sometimes it seemed to Lessie as though the globe they
lived on had begun to spin faster through the heavens,
scattering the wits of its inhabitants as it revolved.

With the death of George V, the decision by the new
King Edward VIII to relinquish the throne for the love
of an American divorcee, and the subsequent appointment of his quiet young brother as King George VI,
Britain found itself with three kings in quick succession
during 1936. The country was in a deep industrial depression and that same year, unemployed, hungry and frantic
men marched from Jarrow to London to ask for the right
to work to support their families. The tick book had
come into its own once again in the shop at the corner
of Cathcart Street and unemployed men hung around the
Greenock streets, their faces grey with worry and
becoming more gaunt every week. There had been trouble
in Russia and Abyssinia and a war between Japan and
China as well as a bloody civil war in Spain, but the
most worrying news of all was the rise of a young man
named Adolf Hitler in Germany and the subsequent
terrorising and imprisonment of Jews in that country.

Reading about shops being looted and helpless, innocent men, women and children attacked in the streets of
Germany, Lessie was sharply reminded of Mr Mann and
his wife: their frightened faces on the morning she helped
them to clean up the mess hooligans had made of their
shop in the early days of the war; their poverty when she
had sought them out to offer to buy the business; Mr
Mann's insistent, bewildered, 'Ve are Sviss!'

Why, she wondered as the stories of atrocities continued

to appear in the newspapers, did folk have to treat other folk like that? Was evil a disease that could strike wherever it wanted and never be denied? Why did other nations allow these things to happen and say nothing?

Throughout the thirties, too, the British Government continued to build up the country's defences. Even when Prime Minister Neville Chamberlain waved a scrap of paper and said that Britain and Germany had come to an understanding and there would be 'peace in our time', Lessie found herself doubting the man, much as she wanted to believe him.

'Sometimes,' she told Morag, 'politicians are awful daft. They seem to be playing some sort of game where they have to go by the rules instead of thinking things out for themselves. If they'd only use the brains God gave them they might see what's coming in time enough to do something about it.'

'Don't fret yourself, Gran,' the girl advised her serenely. 'There's nothing folk like us can do about it.'

'Mebbe not, but we're the ones that have to pay for their silly games, every time,' Lessie said with rare gloominess.

31

In September 1939 the German army marched into
Poland, and Britain declared war on Germany. Lessie
watched, her heart sinking, as the Territorials, their
young faces shining with patriotism and determination,
marched off to war led by the skirl of the pipes. She had
seen it all before, at the beginning of the 1914 war that
was supposed to end all wars.

Her younger male assistant, who had started straight
from school in the shop as a messenger boy, went off
almost at once with the Territorials; the older man had
been gassed in the 1914–18 war and was unfit to serve
this time. Children scampered off to school with square
boxes containing their gas masks looped on string over
one shoulder and thumping on the opposite hip. They
proudly dragged their new identity discs from beneath
their shirt and blouse collars and displayed them in the
shop, little realising that the small metal label was
intended for identification purposes should they have to
be dragged from beneath rubble after an air raid. This war
was going to be fought in the air as well as on the ground
and at sea, and air raid shelters were being scooped out
of back yards, blackout curtains installed, brown paper
or tough netting being stuck on windows to prevent glass
being blown in when the bombs fell, as fall they must.
Greenock was a shipbuilding town and would surely be
a target. Some children were bundled off to live in the
country, where they were considered to be safer. Brick
baffle walls were hurriedly erected at the pavement's
edge in front of each tenement close in an attempt to limit
damage from bomb blast, causing all sorts of scrapes

and bruises at first when children heedlessly scampered out of the closes and rebounded off the walls, or adults bumped into them in the enforced blackout at night now that street lights were forbidden.

'Thank goodness your building's got electric light now,' Dorothea told Lessie. 'At least if it's blitzed you'll not have the danger of escaping gas.'

'You're right,' Lessie said, grateful that her daughter-in-law, normally so sharp, had completely overlooked the fact that some of the other residents in the building had gas cookers. She herself still used the neat, gleaming little range that had been there since Miss Peden's days, and worked as well as when it was new.

Ration books were introduced to quell the rush of panic buying and offset the difficulty of shipping in food-stuffs from abroad, and Lessie spent a great deal of her working day clipping coupons and doling out ridiculously small amounts of butter and margarine to her listed customers. The River Clyde filled with ships, crowding the popular anchorage at the Tail o' the Bank, the deep water area skirting a great sandbank.

Nineteen forty arrived and all at once the town was filled with foreign sailors, predominantly French, young lads brightening the grey streets with the bright red 'toories' on the top of their white caps. The locals and the foreigners eyed each other warily at first across the barricade of two different languages. The local stationers' sold out of French/English phrase books within days, and funny stories of confusions between the incomers and the townspeople swept from one end of Greenock to the other.

After those first apprehensive days the invasion turned out to be friendly, and Scottish hospitality was offered generously to the young men. Dances were held for them and canteens opened for their use when on shore leave. Much against her mother's wishes Morag volunteered to work in one of the canteens after school and at weekends.

'They need people who can speak French, and I can.'

'School French,' Dorothea pointed out disparagingly.

'I can get by, and that's more than most folk can say.

Anyway, I want to do something to help,' Morag argued, and her mother eventually shrugged her shoulders and gave way.

As soon as Morag began working at the canteen, her restlessness eased. She might still be a schoolgirl, but now she had something else to do, something that made her feel useful. She was proud of her ability to speak to the sailors in their own language, and Dorothea told Lessie with relief that her school reports were improving and she was doing particularly well in the French class.

At the beginning of April Morag came to Cathcart Street and asked her grandmother diffidently if she could bring a friend to visit.

'A school friend?'

Morag coloured and stared past Lessie's shoulder at one of the wally dugs on the mantelshelf. 'No, it's – he's a French sailor.'

'Oh.'

'He's awful nice, Gran, and he's far away from home and everyone else is asking them home, only my mother wouldn't approve, I know she wouldn't.'

'That's only because you're still so young, lassie.'

Morag's eyes blazed violet fire. 'I'm not saying I want to marry him! He's a friend, that's all, but Mummy wouldn't see it that way. She'd fret about it and think it was wrong and probably make me stop working at—'

'Tuts, girl, I didnae say you couldnae bring him here,' Lessie interrupted. 'Of course you can. Goodness only knows these poor lads need some friends, with their families across the water being threatened by the Germans.'

Morag launched herself across the kitchen and hugged Lessie so hard that she almost took the breath from her. 'Oh, thank you, Gran! I'll invite him to tea next week, will I?'

Georges reminded Lessie strongly of Peter when he shyly followed Morag into the kitchen the following week, his cap clutched in both hands, his eyes flickering nervously around the room. Although Peter's hair was brown and Georges' was fair, although Peter's eyes were grey and Georges' brown, there was the same air of uncertainty, of not belonging, that immediately tugged at her heart.

'Come in, laddie, come in and sit yourself down,' she said briskly, waving one hand at the chairs waiting round the table and making for the simmering kettle. Food and drink made up a universal language.

As the meal progressed the boy slowly lost some of his initial shyness. In the short time he had been in Greenock, anxious to fit in, he had picked up a few English words. He and Morag laughed comfortably together when he said something wrong, or when she made a mistake in her French. He carefully and gently put her right each time and she repeated the correct word or phrase several times, until he nodded smiling approval. They made a good pair, Lessie decided when the meal was over and she sat with her knitting by the range, watching the fair head and the bronze head close together as they studied her one and only photograph album. There was affection between them but it was youthful and natural and she didn't see it as a threat, only something that could be good for the two of them at this time of uncertainty and stress.

'Of course,' she said at once when Morag asked if she could bring Georges again. 'Whenever you like. He'll not be here for long anyway, I expect his ship'll be refitting at the moment.' Then she added cautiously, 'But should you not take him to meet your mother?'

Morag's face set in mutinous lines. 'She'd only insist on inspecting him and questioning him and he'd feel uncomfortable. He likes it here, with you. He says it reminds him of his own home in Tours. I'd as soon leave things as they are. You'll not tell her about him, will you?'

'It's not my business to tell her.'

'Anyway,' said Morag, 'she's so busy these days, it's best to leave her alone.'

Georges came often to Cathcart Street over the next few weeks. He and Lessie found ways of communicating despite the language barrier, and to Morag's amusement Lessie even began to pick up some French words. The three of them spent happy hours working on a large and intricate jigsaw puzzle that Morag brought from her own home, or sat companionably listening to the wireless that Jess had insisted on buying for Lessie the Christmas before war was declared. Sometimes, when music was being played, the young couple pushed back the big table and danced. Watching her granddaughter, seeing her happiness and contentment, Lessie grew to dread the day when Georges had to leave Greenock. He and Morag had already promised to write to each other but even so, life was cruel these days for young folk, and nobody could tell what the future held.

It made her uncomfortable to be aiding Morag behind Dorothea's back, but at the same time it was good to see the girl so contented for once. Although she knew well enough that her daughter-in-law would disapprove of the friendship if she knew of it, Lessie gave permission when Morag asked if she could go with Georges to a Saturday night dance being held in one of the church halls. Dorothea was in Glasgow on business and it had already been agreed that Morag should stay overnight with Lessie.

'But you're to be back here by ten thirty, mind. I cannae have you staying out too late. The Lord knows I'm deceiving your mother enough as it is.'

Morag's cheek was soft against Lessie's. 'I promise, Gran, and thank you!'

On the night of the dance Georges came to collect Morag, his young face solemn with the importance of the occasion. As he and Lessie waited in the kitchen for her, he said awkwardly but earnestly, 'I promise you, madam, zat I come from a good family. My maman teach me to respect young ladies. I respect Morag very much.'

It was clear that he had carefully learned the little speech beforehand, probably from a comrade with a better command of English than Georges himself. Touched, Lessie smiled at him.

'I'm sure you will, laddie. I trust you.'

Then Morag burst into the kitchen, her eyes sparkling, her hair brushed into a gleaming auburn cap about her neat little face, wearing a pretty white crepe blouse and a swinging silky skirt that Lessie knew she had altered herself from some pre-war clothes of her mother's. Looking at the awe and pride on the French boy's face, the way his eyes lit up as he scrambled to his feet, Lessie knew that she could indeed trust him to look after her precious granddaughter.

Morag arrived home at twenty-eight minutes past ten, bringing a waft of cool night air in with her, launching at once into a description of the dances, the music, the people who had been there.

'Where's Georges?' Lessie had two mugs waiting, each with a spoonful of cocoa and a spoonful of her precious sugar in it. She moved the pan of milk, which had been heating slowly at the side of the range, onto the metal plate that covered the fire.

'He had to get back on board. But he walked me right to the door first.' Morag brushed her fingertips across her lips without realising that she was betraying the memory of goodnight kisses.

'In that case I'll have his cocoa. Morag, pet,' Lessie said carefully when their drinks were in front of them and Morag's excited chatter finally began to slow down, 'Georges'll be sailing away soon.'

'I know that.' The happiness was wiped from the girl's face as she slowly stirred her cocoa.

'And you're not sixteen yet.'

'Almost sixteen.'

'Too young to know your own mind.'

Morag took a sip from the mug then put it down. 'Gran, I'm not rushing about like a chicken with its head cut off, falling in love and thinking about the rest of my life. I'm just being happy for now, d'you not see that? Now's all we've got, me and Georges.'

'Aye, lassie.' Lessie reached out and put a hand over her granddaughter's. 'I know that. I just wondered if you did.'

On the last day of April a dull boom shook the town. Windows rattled in their frames, dogs started barking hysterically, folk rushed to their doors in panic.

It was a half day, so the shop was shut and Lessie was doing some ironing in her kitchen. She set the iron on its heel and ran to the closemouth to see women and children gathering all up and down the street, and passersby stopped in their tracks, everyone staring anxiously up into the cloudy sky.

Feet pounded on the stairs behind her and two of her neighbours, one clutching a baby in her arms, joined her. 'God help us, it's an air raid!' the girl whimpered, but an older woman out on the pavement said briskly, 'There's no' been ony sirens. Anyway, they'd no' come ower in daylight.'

'Look!' Someone pointed, and they all craned their necks and saw a mushroom-shaped cloud rise slowly above the rooftops.

'It's somethin' doon by the river,' someone said, and another voice chimed in, 'Yin o' the ships – a mine, mebbe?'

'How could the Nazis get a mine intae the Clyde?' someone scoffed. They could hear a clamour from the river now, the frantic blaring of sirens and klaxons, the jangle of a bell as a fire engine or an ambulance raced along a street somewhere. The smoke continued to rise ominously into the sky, the fringes beginning to fuzz as they met the wind, though the body of it remained solid.

'Whatever it was, some poor souls must've copped it,' someone said and Mrs Delaney, who lived above Lessie, crossed herself and whispered, 'God have mercy on them.'

Lessie, watching the smoke towering over the rooftops, felt a shiver run through her, as though someone had walked over her grave.

The clamour of ships' sirens died away, but a few hours later there was another explosion, and again the floor shook beneath Lessie's feet.

All afternoon rumours flew about the town, but by early evening they solidified into something more positive, despite the fact that the stretch of river by the docks had been closed to the public ever since the first explosion. One of the ships anchored at the Tail o' the Bank had

blown up. It was understood that a torpedo had slipped
from its housing during maintenance work and exploded
on contact with the deck. While nearby battleships and
oil tankers up-anchored and moved as quickly as possible
away from the fiercely burning ship, other boats had
gone scuttling out from Albert Harbour to give what
aid they could. But there was little anyone could do.
Shells stored on the ship had exploded with the heat, and
in a few hours she had gone down with heavy loss of
life.

Something within Lessie knew without being told that
the stricken ship was the *Maille Breze*, the Free French
destroyer Georges served on. She waited, expecting
Morag to come to her after school, but there was no sign
of the girl, and shortly after the second explosion Lessie
put on her hat and coat and set off for Dorothea's house.
She had just reached the corner of Cathcart Street when
Dorothea's car swept in to the kerb beside her and the
driver, an elderly man called out of retirement, got out
and handed Lessie a letter. Petrol was rationed and most
car owners had resigned themselves to keeping their cars
off the road until the war was over, but because of the
refinery Dorothea was allowed enough fuel to keep her
car on the road. Lessie ripped open the envelope, read
the few words on the sheet of paper inside, and got into
the car.

In the small but elegant house in Brougham Street
Dorothea, ashen with worry, came to the door as soon
as she heard the car, almost dragging Lessie in. There was
a half-empty glass, a packet of cigarettes, a lighter and an
ashtray piled with cigarette butts on the little table by
Dorothea's favourite chair. As soon as Lessie walked
into the room Dorothea lit a fresh cigarette.

'It's Morag, Mam. I can't do a thing with her.' She
paced the floor, her slim body taut with worry. 'Her
headmistress phoned the refinery this afternoon to say that
she had run out of school without asking permission. I
worried myself sick for three hours before a policeman
brought her home. Apparently she'd been making a
nuisance of herself at the hospitals, demanding to know

the names of the poor men being brought in from that ship that blew up this afternoon.'

'Where is she?'

'In her room. I wanted to fetch the doctor, but she went hysterical at the very idea. She won't talk to me. Mam, what's going on?'

Lessie took off her coat, noting with vague surprise that she still wore her apron. She sat down and told Dorothea the whole story, making no bones about her own part in it. As Dorothea listened, her face went white with anger, her eyes hardening and the slight scar on her cheek standing out as a streak of rose-pink beneath her carefully applied make-up.

'Morag – and a French sailor? And you allowed this? Condoned it behind my back? Dear God, woman, she's only a child! I credited you with more sense than that!'

'He's – he was a decent lad, Dorothea.' Lessie knew now that Georges must be dead. 'They spent most of their time together in my house.'

'Most of the time? And what about the rest of the time?'

'D'you not trust your own daughter?'

'Not with foreigners! I knew when I let her work at that canteen that there would be trouble, but I'd no idea that her own grandmother would connive at it. She's not sixteen yet!'

'And he was only eighteen. They were both children, both in need of friendship. Can you not see that, Dorothea?'

There was a tense silence. Dorothea stubbed her half-smoked cigarette viciously into the ashtray. 'Oh, what's the use of arguing about it now? What's done's done. I asked you to come here because I can't get any sense out of her. I thought you might, since the two of you have always been close.' She swung towards the window, though with the blackout curtains fastened securely against the night there was nothing to see. 'You'd best go to her,' she said over her shoulder.

Morag's room was bright and pretty and still heart-rendingly childish. Morag herself was sitting on the edge of her bed, hunched over a battered old teddy bear clutched in her arms. She didn't look up, and her body was rigid and remote when Lessie put her arms about her.

'Morag, lass.'

'He's dead.' The girl's voice was dry, harsh, old. 'I went to the hospitals where they took the wounded but he wasn't anywhere. He's dead.'

'In wartime—'

'He didn't die because of the war!' Morag dragged herself from Lessie's embrace, hurtled to the other end of the room. There was no trace of tears, just a face as white as snow and eyes that burned into Lessie's. The teddy bear, tossed away, rolled beneath the pink-frilled dressing table. 'He died because of an accident! We were going to go for a walk tonight and coming to you afterwards. But now he's dead!' She put her hands to her face then said wonderingly, pitifully, through her fingers, 'How can things go on being the same when people you care about aren't in the world any more?'

Lessie remembered thinking the same thing when Donald and her parents and Thomasina and Anna died. So many people, left behind. Thomasina had been much the same age as Georges. It was cruel, at Morag's age, to suddenly come face to face with death and loss.

'I know what you're going through, lovey. You'd feel better if you'd talk to your mother, let her help.'

'And have her going on at me because I went out with a foreigner?'

'She'd not do that.'

'She'd better not,' Morag said fiercely. 'I'm glad I went out with him. I'm glad we knew each other, and she's not going to make me say any different!'

'I'm glad too. You were a good friend to him just when he needed friends. Morag,' Lessie coaxed, but the girl backed into a corner, shaking her head.

'You can't make it better, Gran. Don't try to pretend that it's like the time I fell off my bike, or the time I lost my coral bracelet. Nothing can make it better, only bringing Georges back. You don't understand!' Her voice rose to a wail. 'How could you understand? You're too old to know what it's like to care for someone and lose them.'

'Stop it!' Without realising what she was doing Lessie stormed across the room and shook the girl by the shoulders. 'D'you think I was always like this? D'you think I was only put on this earth tae be your grandmother? I've been young like you and I've had my hard times just as you will. And I've lost folk that meant more tae me than my own life!' She heard herself going on like a harpie, heard the Vennel accent creeping back into her voice, but couldn't stop the words. Morag's anguish had unlocked sorrows that had been thrust deep down, out of sight but never out of mind. 'This is what life's all about, lassie, and age has little tae dae with it. Losin' folk ye love can hurt as much as fifty-five as it does at fifteen!'

'Why did it have to be him?' Morag's swollen face was reddened and ugly with grief, her mouth twisted. She wrenched herself free with such force that Lessie staggered back and almost fell over a chair. The very air in the room seemed to crackle between grandmother and granddaughter. 'He was only eighteen! Why should he be dead and someone as old as you still be alive?'

The words were like a dash of cold water in Lessie's face. She looked into her granddaughter's blazing eyes and knew full well that nothing she said at that moment, either in anger or in love, would reach the girl; knew, too, that the warmth that had been between them for fifteen years was over and things would never be the same again.

She turned away and walked out of the room, back to the lounge where Dorothea still paced, another cigarette burning down between slim red-tipped fingers.

'Well?'

'You'll have to be patient with her, Dorry. Let her come to terms with the laddie's death in her own time.' Lessie reached for her coat, which she had laid neatly over the back of a chair. She felt completely exhausted, hollow inside, and raw, as though she had been scrubbed out with a stiff-bristled brush.

'Sit down, Mam,' Dorry said, her voice gentler. 'I'll make us a cup of tea.'

'I'd just as soon get home. I'll walk,' she added as Dorothea went to the door.

'Don't be silly, of course you'll not walk. I told Hamish to wait for you. I'll not risk you breaking your ankle or falling in those dark streets. I've got enough trouble without that.' Dorothea caught her arm as Lessie stumbled. 'Are you all right?'

'I'm fine. Don't fuss me, Dorry,' Lessie said automatically, wanting only to get back to the safety and comfort of her own home.

By the time she got there she was shivering, as though coming down with the 'flu. When she got inside the door, after fumbling her way through the black close, she took out the little bottle of whisky that she kept in the kitchen cupboard and made herself a hot toddy. The glass rattled against her teeth as she drank; when it was empty she crawled into the box bed fully dressed, unable to face the short journey to her own room.

She fell into sleep without realising it and woke in the early morning to the discomfort of creased clothes and a pillow damp with tears she didn't know she had shed.

She woke to the certain knowledge that she had lost Morag and was alone once more.

As the weeks passed more details about the *Maille Breze* came out, bit by bit. About thirty of the French sailors on board had been trapped in the mess deck by a buckled fo'c'sle hatch and all attempts to free them as the fire crept towards them had been in vain. Finally a doctor had lain on the hot metal plates of the upper deck and reached down to the open portholes below with a syringe, injecting a strong sedative into the arms held out desperately from below, trying to ease the young men's final moments. The cries from below had all ceased before the would-be rescuers scrambled clear to save their own lives.

Soon afterwards the fire had reached the magazine near the mess deck and after a final explosion the destroyer had gone down, coming to rest on a sandbank. Her mast reached out above the water, a mute reminder to the people of Greenock, though no reminder was needed, of the youngsters who had met such a cruel end far from their homes.

Lessie hoped against hope that Georges had been among the half-dozen who had died mercifully quickly on deck in the original explosion. She hoped – again without believing it possible – that Morag wouldn't come to hear of the terrible plight of those trapped on the messdeck. She thought of Georges' family, of the 'maman' who had brought him up to be so respectful to young ladies, and wondered if they had heard of his death. But in June when the remnants of the British army were frantically scooped from the beaches of Dunkirk, from the very jaws of the powerful German army that had poured across France and now became its triumphant masters, she thought to herself that the news of Georges' death had probably not had time to reach his parents, and trusted that living as they were now under the German jackboot they took comfort in believing that he, at least, was free and safe.

Just after France fell, Ian enlisted in the Royal Army Medical Corps. He took Ruth and their children from Glasgow to Inverness, where Ruth's sister lived, then came to Greenock to say goodbye to his mother. He had put on weight since his second marriage and there were streaks of grey over his temples.

'Why, Ian? You've already served in one war and you've surely got important work to do in Glasgow,' Lessie said to him as he sipped the cup of tea she'd insisted he drink before he left.

'I'm needed more by the army than the infirmary just now. They can spare me. When I was an orderly I mind standing by many a time watching some poor laddie dying before the surgeon got to him and not able to do a thing to help him. This time I'll be the surgeon, this time I'll know what to do. With any luck I'll see most of them recovering. Anyway,' he gave a short laugh, 'I'm getting a commission. Captain Ian Hamilton. And I can't let Jess have it all her own way. Imagine our Jess, of all people, driving an ambulance! Have you heard from her?'

'Aye, she's the only person I know who can make the blackout and the air raids sound funny.'

'She'll be good for the morale of the poor blighters in her ambulance – mebbe that'll take their minds off the way she drives it.'

'Have you seen Morag and Dorothea?'

'I saw them before I came here. Morag's grown ten years older in as many weeks. I could scarce get a word out of her.'

'You heard why?'

'Aye. Poor lassie, she's too young for such grief.'

'She's a survivor. She'll work it out in her own way, given time.'

'I hope so. Dorothea's looking wonderful; running her own business suits her. I believe,' said Ian thoughtfully, 'that giving her a divorce was the best thing I could have done for her. Marriage was too limiting for her. She turned out to be her father's daughter after all. Mam, you're looking tired. Why don't you go and spend some time in Inverness? Ruth would be glad to see you.'

'I'm fine. And there's the shop to see to.'

Ian gave an impatient wave of the hand. 'Surely the folk that work in it could see to things for you for a wee while. You need a holiday.'

She shook her head. 'I'm not used to holidays.'

'At least think about it.' Then he looked at his watch and a brisk note came into his voice. 'I must go, Mam. I've to be in Glasgow by three.'

'You'll write?'

'Of course I will. Keep in touch with Ruth while I'm gone.'

'Take care, son.' She wished, not for the first time, that the Scots weren't such a dour race. It wasn't the done thing for a mother to hug and kiss a grown son, even when he was going off to war.

'I will,' said Ian, and left her standing alone in her kitchen.

The shop demanded a lot of time and attention, which was just as well because Dorothea was busier than ever and Morag didn't come to Cathcart Street any more. When grandmother and granddaughter met occasionally over Dorothea's tea table, Morag, who had taken the step between childhood and womanhood on the day the French ship exploded, was pleasant enough but as remote as an acquaintance.

'It's not right,' said Dorothea, who had got over her anger with Lessie. 'You were the one who helped her to see this boy behind my back, and now she's punishing you for it. I'm going to have to talk to her.' The two of them were in Dorothea's lounge; after a silent evening meal Morag had left for the canteen, where she had insisted on continuing after Georges' death.

'Leave her, Dorry. Mebbe it's because I was part of their friendship that she can't feel comfortable with me.

And she's right, it's hard to understand why old folk are left alive when young folk at the beginning of their lives have to die.'

'That was a terrible thing to say to you.'

'She needed to pass some of her hurt on to someone else. It was too much for her to carry on her own. Leave her,' Lessie said again, her hands busy with her knitting, her voice calm. 'She has to take her own time about things.'

It was a relief to Lessie when Jess came from London for a few days, as fresh and pretty as ever in spite of the London bombings, brightening up the house with her very presence. As always, she turned everything that had happened to her, including ambulance driving during air raids, into an amusing story, though her eyes were shadowed and her lovely face pale with weariness.

On the fourth day of her visit Lessie, who had left her daughter sound asleep when she left for the shop in the morning, came back to find her standing over the range, wrapped in one of Lessie's own aprons. The flat was filled with the appetising smell of liver and bacon and onions. A candle, kept on the mantelshelf for emergencies, burned on the kitchen table, which was set with the best china.

'I thought I'd make a meal for you, for once,' Jess said lightly.

'Where did you get the food? I've not collected my meat ration yet.'

'I managed to coax a little more out of the butcher. You'll have to live on potatoes for the rest of the week, but tonight we dine in style. Take off your coat, I'm going to dish up the soup now.'

'I didnae know you could cook,' Lessie marvelled half an hour later as they spooned up the remains of a rhubarb sponge made from eggless sponge and a handful of rhubarb that Jess had sweet-talked from a neighbour.

'Darling, I can do lots of amazing things these days. The restaurants are pretty awful now, so I've had to learn to fend for myself. And last month a friend who was supposed to give a talk on wartime cookery to a group of

414

housewives went down with laryngitis, so I had to do it for her.'

'You?'

'Don't look so surprised,' Jess reprimanded. 'She wrote it all down for me and I was an absolute riot. I even got interested in it and tried out some of the recipes for myself. They worked very well.' There was a pause before, dropping her gaze and toying with the salt cellar, she said abruptly, 'Mam, I've met someone. His name's Philip – Philip Lorrimer.' Then she added self-mockingly, 'Major Philip Lorrimer, of course. I'd not have settled for anything less than a major.'

'Where is he?'

'In London. We met during an air raid, of all things, and when the all-clear went we just kept on seeing each other. He's based in London at the moment, but,' her fingers released the salt cellar and twined with the fingers of her other hand, 'he'll probably be going away soon.'

'How special is he?'

Jess looked up, her eyes bright with memories and secrets. 'More than anyone else has ever been. I just wanted to tell you. Isn't it ridiculous, falling in love at my age? I'm thirty-eight, for God's sake!'

Andrew's face, his voice, the touch of his lips, suddenly came clearly to Lessie and filled her with longing for him. 'It's not just the young who fall in love, Jess.' She heard a tremor in her voice and wondered if her daughter, normally as sharp as a pin, had heard it too. But Jess was too caught up in the wonder of her own happiness to notice anything.

'And there was me, thinking I'd finally reached the age of common sense.' She made a face, laughed a bit shakily, then said, 'It's bad judgement, isn't it, being footloose and fancy free during peacetime, then falling for someone when there's a war on and nobody knows who's going to survive it.'

'I think that's why people do fall in love during a war – they need a commitment.'

'I just wish it hadn't happened to me. What can I do about it, Mam?'

'Go back to London and to your major and enjoy each other while you can.'

Jess laughed again, reaching out to capture one of Lessie's hands in her own. A tear fell onto their linked fingers and she gave a huge unladylike sniff before saying, 'I knew you'd say something sensible. You always do.'

As the year wore on the list of local war casualties in the *Telegraph* continued to grow. Some of the young men who had gone marching off were back home again, some missing limbs, some blinded or deafened or shell-shocked into a stunned bewildered silence. The Royal Air Force launched offensives against Berlin and Hamburg and Hitler retaliated by sending his own bombers to devastate London. Lessie lay awake at nights fretting over Jess, who continued to drive her ambulance and sent reassuring letters regularly. Once or twice Lessie phoned her; she sounded as cheerful as ever, although her major had been sent overseas.

Coventry was severely damaged by bombing, then Birmingham, then Liverpool. 'They're making their way up towards us,' someone said gloomily in the shop. 'You'll see. They'll not forget about us.'

Nineteen forty-one arrived, marking the close of the first full year of war with no sign of the early ending that had been confidently prophesied fifteen months earlier. The sirens still sounded in Greenock, but not often. Twice a stick of bombs, possibly from some plane shedding the last of its load before heading for home, landed in the town, but there was no full-scale attack.

When the sirens wailed their eerie warning to the town one moonlit night in March, Lessie, who had been sitting alone listening to the radio, switched it off and listened anxiously for the sound of aircraft engines. She could hear the occasional dull thud as the anti-aircraft guns on the hills above the town and across the river began to fire, but that was all. She put the lights out, went into the coal-black hall, moving with the ease of someone who has lived in the same place for so long that even a blackout can't do more than blunt the edge of familiarity, and pulled on her coat before slipping out of the door.

'Who's there?' a familiar voice barked from the close-mouth.

'It's me, Mr Delaney, Lessie Carswell.'

The man made room for her and together they stared up at the moon floating serenely in a cloudless sky. Searchlights prodded their long fingers up from the ground, sweeping back and forth, and the guns thudded in the hills. There was the faint drone of massed engines from above, but although Lessie narrowed her eyes she couldn't make out any planes.

'They're high,' her neighbour said. 'Passing by over-head. They're after some other poor bugger tonight, if you'll pardon the language, Mrs Carswell.'

The throb of aircraft engines died away, the guns fell silent, the lights were switched off. They could hear other guns firing, further away.

'The all-clear'll go in a minute,' Mr Delaney said, and nodded his satisfaction as he was proved right within minutes. 'We can get to our beds now. It's not our turn. Not yet.'

The bombers had been making for Clydebank, a ship-building town further up the river, close to Glasgow. They returned to their target on the following night, like a dog returning to a buried bone, and by the time they had finished with it the town had been appallingly and ruthlessly ravaged, with hundreds of 'Bankies' dead or wounded. Only a handful of houses had escaped without any damage.

In May the enemy planes returned, this time unleashing their savagery on Greenock while Lessie crouched in a makeshift cave comprised of two upended armchairs pushed against the big kitchen table. Holding a cushion tightly over each ear to try to keep out the worst of the continuous, terrifying din, she recited the multiplication table at the top of her voice, then went on to the poems she had learned at school, nursery rhymes, street songs, songs she had heard on the radio; anything that came into her head, anything that would take her mind off the whistling noises of the bombs coming down, and the

417

way the floor shook beneath her with each one that fell.

It was a long, clamorous night, filled with the throbbing of heavy German bombers, the dull thud of anti-aircraft guns, the high-pitched whistle of bombs coming down, then the crash of their arrival. The building surely couldn't stand up to such punishment, Lessie thought, and was instantly reminded of the floors above her, poised to give way and crush her.

'Don't be daft!' she ordered herself in a shaky voice, and found some comfort in summoning Andrew's memory to keep her company. The thought of him, and her great need for him at that moment, brought tears, but at least they were tears of grief and not of fear.

Finally, exhausted, she fell into a doze and was jolted awake by a fist thundering on the door. Confused and startled, thinking at first that she was in her bed, she bumped her head on the underside of the table when she tried to get up.

'Mrs Carswell! Are you in there?'

She shook her head hard to clear it and managed to fumble her way out from beneath the table, clutching at the torch when her hand found its familiar shape.

'I'm coming!' she yelled as Mr Delaney's fist started assaulting her door again. Still dazed with sleep she collided with the coatstand which went down with a clatter, and at last reached the door, waiting until he was inside before switching on her torch. 'Has the all-clear gone?'

'Five minutes ago. Did ye no' hear it?'

'I must have fallen asleep.'

'Asleep? You're a cool yin,' he said admiringly, then, 'Are ye all right? Yer voice is awful hoarse.'

'I think I've got a summer cold coming on,' lied Lessie, feeling her cheeks grow hot. It would never do to let him know that she had been sitting all alone under her own table singing to herself. She reached for the light switch, but nothing happened.

'I think they got the power station,' Mr Delaney said. 'God, that wis a bad night! We're lucky tae have survived it. If ye're sure ye're all right, Mrs Carswell, I'll get

418

away tae my bed. It'll be a busy day tomorrow.'

Dorothea, as smart as ever in spite of a night without sleep, arrived in Cathcart Street while Lessie was finishing off her morning cup of tea.

'It's terrible,' she said as soon as she walked in. 'The whole town – they're still putting the fires out and trying to find missing folk. Mam, I was worried sick about you! You'll have to come to us tonight.'

'I'll do nothing of the kind. If I'm going to die I'd as soon die in my own house, among my own possessions.'

'But they might come back. They bombed Clydebank for two nights. Mam, will you listen to sense for once?'

'I'm not in my dotage, Dorry, so don't speak to me like that,' Lessie snapped. She had a headache and there was a tender lump on her skull where she had collided with the table when Mr Delaney had wakened her abruptly after the raid. 'I've got a shop to run, and as long as it's standing I'll be here to see that it opens on time in the mornings. I'm not going to let Adolf Hitler get in the way of my work.'

All morning customers filed into the shop, dazed with shock and lack of sleep, adding their own contribution to an ever-growing list of death and injuries and damage. The shipyards, the prime target, had been badly hit. The Westburn sugar refinery had been damaged and at the height of the blitz melted sugar had been seen running down the gutters. The distillery had received a direct hit early in the raid, and the inferno caused by about three million gallons of whisky catching fire had attracted the bombers back to that area, which was almost flattened. The incendiaries, one woman reported in wonder, had looked like flaming fire falling out of the sky, and people scrambling to the hills behind the town for shelter away from burning buildings had been machine-gunned by low-flying German planes.

In a tenement building in Dunlop Street the blast from an exploding bomb had dragged the feathers from an unfortunate canary sitting in its cage in a close where its owner had trusted in the baffle wall to protect her and her pet from the bombing.

In the afternoon Lessie left the shop to her assistants and went to have a look for herself. Glass crunched under her feet and the air was still heavy with the reek of smoke and charred wood and cloth, mingled with the sweet caramel tang of burned sugar and the reek of whisky. In some places shop windows had been blown out and tins and boxes were still strewn over the pavement. The pavement in front of a painter and decorator's smashed window was a magnificent rainbow of brilliant colours where the tins had burst and their contents run together. Here and there smoke still trickled sullenly from a gaping window or a battered roof; parts of the pavements were roped off because of the danger of falling masonry.

People stood and stared in disbelief, or picked among the ruins of a tenement, searching for any possessions that might be intact and worth salvaging. Water arced from hoses into buildings that still smouldered; men worked in one street she passed to shore up a building that was in danger of sliding into the abyss where its neighbour had stood only the day before. Lessie looked at it all, appalled, wondering what possessed folk to do such terrible things to each other.

Since the beginning of the war an old shopping bag had served as Lessie's emergency holdall. Each night she filled it with a box containing her important papers, a torch, a clean handkerchief, candles, matches, some first aid essentials, a box of biscuits and a flask of hot tea. She was stoppering the flask on the night after the raid when Morag came to the door, slipping into the hall as soon as the door opened wide enough. The power was still off and, in the light of the candle Lessie carried in a saucer of water, Morag's hair gleamed like a polished chestnut beneath her woollen beret.

'Gran, I've come to take you to Brougham Street.'

'I told your mother—'

'I know you did, but you've got to come!' The girl's thin face was determined. 'I'll not have you here all alone.'

'Does Dorothea know where you are?'

'I've been at the canteen. I sent a message to tell her I was coming to fetch you.'

'But Morag—'

'Gran, please!'

Lessie hesitated, but only for a moment. It was the first time in over a year, since the young French sailor's death, that Morag had made a move towards her. The girl's concern brought a lump to her throat.

'All right. I'll just fetch my bag and my—'

The familiar banshee wail of the siren cut across the words, and they stared at each other in horror before Lessie said briskly, 'It looks as though we're both going to have to say here, lassie.'

'But you don't have a shelter.'

Lessie drew her granddaughter into the kitchen. 'We'll manage fine without one. The other folk in the building go to Mrs McBeth's house across the close, but I'm happier here. Give me a hand—'

Together they dragged the two armchairs into position in the centre of the kitchen and upended them so that they formed a solid wall between the table and the window, to give protection from flying glass if the window should be blown in. Lessie scooped back the curtains across the alcove bed, brought out armfuls of pillows and blankets, and tossed them under the table together with her emergency bag, then fetched an extra torch. The siren was still sending out its urgent warning and there were other sounds, too, now – the thump of the guns, the ominous broken drone of hundreds of big heavy planes reaching the end of their long journey.

'Under the table with you, lassie.' Lessie anchored two quilts to the top of the table with the coal scuttle, the pouffe and two stools, so that they hung down like a curtain.

'It's cosy in here,' Morag said from beneath the table. 'Cosier than our garden shelter at home.'

'I spent a lot of time designing it,' Lessie said, and was rewarded with a soft giggle. She blew out the candles and crawled in beside Morag, puffing as she went. 'Dear God, I'm getting too stiff and too old for this sort of nonsense!'

Morag's hands reached out for her, drew her down onto a nest of pillows and blankets. 'You're not too old,' she said fiercely. 'Gran, I'm sorry I said that you were.'

'Wheesht, lassie. Don't fret yourself about that. I am old, there's no getting away from that.'

'But it wasn't fair of me to say it,' Morag said with a gulp. 'It wasn't your fault – what happened to Georges. I should have—'

The floor vibrated and the windows rattled as a bomb exploded somewhere close. Morag screamed and Lessie held her closer, switching on one of the torches with her free hand, illuminating their snug little shelter. 'It's all right, pet, you're all right.'

Morag's eyes were huge and brilliant in the torchlight. 'It s-sounds so loud. You don't hear them so loud in our shelter.'

'Noise cannae hurt you.'

They sat for a while, listening. Tonight was going to be just as bad as last night. The bombs were coming down thick and fast. She thought of Dorothea, who must be worried sick about Morag.

'Gran,' Morag asked at last, tentatively, 'that night that Georges – that the ship blew up – you said that losing someone was as bad at fifty-five as at fifteen. Did you . . .?'

Her voice died away into an inquisitive silence. For a moment the raid was forgotten as Lessie floundered for the right words. For years she had longed to tell someone about Andrew, to be free to talk about him. But once it was shared, a secret was no longer a secret. Even in the telling it could lose some of its magic. And anyway, Morag was too young as yet to hear that particular secret.

'Don't you be so nosy, miss,' she said at last, and Morag giggled again.

'Does that mean you're not telling?'

'One day, mebbe, when we're both older.'

The aircraft continued to drone overhead, wave after wave of them, and there were muffled explosions, mercifully far away. Heavy booted feet thundered by the window, then the floor shook again. That bomb had landed quite near to Cathcart Street, Lessie thought, tightening her arms protectively about her granddaughter.

'Are you scared, Gran?'

'A wee bit. I'll tell you one thing,' Lessie said wryly, 'I'll never tread on a cockroach again, not now I know what it's like to be cowering on the floor, never knowing when a big boot's going to land on you. When I think of the cockroaches I killed in the very first house I lived in after I was married . . .'

The bombs fell and she talked on, about Donald and about Ian's babyhood and about the people who had lived in the street, talking herself hoarse to keep the girl's attention away from the death that was being flung down on them from the night skies.

Then suddenly the world was wrenched apart by a crash that shook Lessie's teeth in her head. She and Morag flew into each other's arms and the girl's screams of terror corkscrewed through her ears. The floor thundered beneath them then calmed as there was a great rending, roaring noise from a short distance away. The noise faded at last, giving way to an agitated tinkling over by the mantelshelf, where the wally dugs and the clock and a little pair of matched vases stood. For a moment there was silence before Morag said shakily, tears and laughter in her voice, 'We're still alive! Gran, we're all right!'

'Of course we're all right. We'll always be all right.' The torch had fallen off its perch on the top of Lessie's emergency bag and was shining its beam uselessly up at the underside of the sturdy table. She rescued it and lifted a corner of the quilt. The room looked its usual self.

'It couldnae have been this building,' she said in relief. Then, sharply, struck by a terrible thought. 'Morag, which direction d'you think the noise came from?'

'That way, I think.'

'The shop. Dear God, what's happened to my shop?'

'Gran!'

Without stopping to think Lessie scrambled out from under the table and got to her feet, fumbling in the darkness for the door. 'Stay there, Morag. I have to go and see if anything's happened to the shop.'

'Gran!'

As she reached the hall there was another explosion, too far away to do more than make the building vibrate. The front door opened and Lessie scrambled out into the close, which was erratically lit by flashes of light and an ominous dull glow reflecting against the inside of the baffle wall.

She reached the closemouth, almost running into the temporary brick baffle wall, bringing herself up in time, using it to steady herself, straining her eyes towards the corner where flames were beginning to lick greedily up from the ground. It must have been the shop that time!

'Gran!' Morag said breathlessly, snatching for her and finding her. From above came a menacing whistling noise. Folk who had been outside during raids spoke of the whistling sound the bombs made as they fell.

'Get back into the house, Morag!'

The whistling cut out; there was a pause, as though the world was holding its breath, then it really did split apart. Somebody or something gave Lessie a hefty shove in the chest and she went staggering back, reaching out in search of something to catch onto, in search of Morag. But there was nothing but a deep black well with no more noise, and no bottom to it.

33

The shop was gone, and so was the tenement she had lived in for most of her life. She was lucky to be alive, they told her in the hospital. Running out just before the bomb fell at the back of the building, she had been caught by the blast and thrown back against the brick baffle wall, sustaining concussion and severe bruising, but no broken bones.

Morag, behind her, had been thrown clear of the wall and had escaped with scratches and bruises. 'Oh, Gran,' she wept when she and Dorothea came into the hospital ward, crammed with blitz victims, 'I thought you were dead! I thought we'd lost you!'

'You'll have to work harder than that to lose me,' Lessie whispered, and summoned up a smile. Talking and smiling were hard work; all she wanted to do was to lie still and not have to think, or even be. Her hand lay in Morag's warm clasp, and she could scarcely find the energy to return the pressure of the girl's fingers.

'They found your bag, still there under the table,' Dorothea told her.

'The shop?'

'It's gone, Mam. Most of Cathcart Street went last night.' So had poor Mrs Delaney, but Dorothea kept that to herself for the time being. 'You'll be out of here in a couple of days, then you'll come to stay with us, Mam. There's plenty of room.'

She was lucky, Lessie thought when they had gone, lucky to have family, to have somewhere to go. She should be grateful, but she only felt tired, and very old. She had never felt old before. It was a frightening sensation.

Mercifully, the enemy planes didn't return and she was able to sleep that night, a confused sleep that had her battling enormous cockroaches in the Vennel one moment, with Ian, tied into a chair with a scarf, contentedly gumming away at a sugared crust, and in the shop the next minute, dealing with a continuous queue of customers. Mam was there, and Da, and Thomasina filling a paper poke from the sweetie jar, and Peter, pale and silent. And Anna, who blurred and changed into Dorothea, who glowered at Lessie with her beautiful violet eyes and said, 'He was only eighteen! Why should he be dead and someone as old as you be alive?'

She woke with a start to find herself in the quiet, dimly lit ward, and tossed and turned until the lights went on and the nurses' heels clicked up the long crowded ward to start preparing their patients for the day.

The cuts and bruises healed but the fire that had blazed at the core of Lessie's being for sixty-two years had been quenched on the second night of the blitz. She sat in the comfortable lounge of Dorothea's house, or in the garden if the weather was good, and couldn't be bothered to think about her future. One day she would have to stir herself, but each time she said so Dorothea replied firmly, 'You've done your bit, Mam. You've raised three of us and worked all your life. You deserve a bit of mollycoddling.' And Lessie was content to accept her decree.

Morag spent a lot of time with her grandmother, pathetically anxious to make up for the rift that had been between them for a year. She and Lessie went out for walks by the Clyde, worked on a jigsaw, played cards together. Morag chattered on about school and her work in the canteen, and she painted Lessie again, a replacement for the picture that had been destroyed in the blitz. For the sittings Lessie wore the little autumn leaf brooch, which had been in the emergency bag rescued from the tenement ruins. Looking at the picture when it was completed, then into the mirror, she saw that although this time she had sat for the painting, Morag had again worked from memory, and turned out an almost perfect replica of the original, depicting her grandmother as she had been before the blitz. The woman in the painting was serene, with the hint of a smile in her eyes and at the corners of her mouth; the woman who looked back at Lessie from the mirror was years older, with the humour and the strength gone from her face.

Occasionally she woke in the night or the early morning, wondering what had happened to her. Never in her life had she been so helpless and hopeless, she told herself, recalling her mother's favourite criticism. A neighbour who didn't work every hour of the day to keep herself and her house and her family clean and decent had always been dismissed by Barbara Kirkwood as 'helpless and hopeless'. Not worth fretting over. What would her mother think of her now, Lessie wondered, and knew that she should start taking control of her life. But not yet; later maybe, when the war was over and they all knew what lay ahead of them. For now, she hadn't the energy. Adolf Hitler, it seemed, had got the better of her after all. Perhaps Dorry was right, perhaps she had reached the age where she should just give in and sit back and enjoy the rest of her life. Not that she was enjoying any of it at the moment. She was just drifting, like one of those big silvery barrage balloons that had been put up to foil enemy aircraft.

Day followed day and summer gave way to early autumn. The invincible German battleship *Bismark* was sunk and the Germans invaded Russia. In October Lessie's sense of duty made her rouse herself and pay her annual visit to Anna's grave. Morag accompanied her, and Dorothea insisted on sending them in the car. Without it, Lessie could never have managed the long driveway from the gate to where the first of the gravestones stood. At the top of the drive they left the car and Morag took her grandmother's arm, accommodating her long strides to suit Lessie's slower, shorter steps. It was a grey day with a chill wind blowing in from the river. In addition to her thick school coat, Morag wore a dark blue woollen beret pulled down over her bright hair and a long matching scarf looped about her neck. Lessie's shopping bag hung over her arm and bumped against her hip with every step; a large bunch of chrysanthemums picked from Dorothea's garden nodded their lush bright heads over the top of the bag.

They took a path to the left and visited Andrew's grave first; he and his wife lay beneath a handsome marble stone, one of several marking the graves of other Warrens, including Frank, who had died so ignominiously in Anna McCauley's bed in the Vennel. There was no grave for Martin, who had been buried in France, but his name and the years of his birth and death were on his parents' stone.

Morag took the jug they had brought to fetch water from the stand-pipe and watched as Lessie arranged flowers in the urn that stood at the foot of the stone.

'I don't remember him, but Mummy says we got on very well together. I wish he'd lived long enough for me to get to know him properly.'

'So do I,' said Lessie, getting to her feet slowly.

Anna's grave was some distance away, near the wall. As they walked towards it Lessie suddenly noticed a sturdily built man standing motionless before it, grey head bowed.

'Morag, take the jug over and fetch some more water, will you?' she asked quickly, shaken out of the lethargy that had become her constant companion since the blitz, and went on alone towards the man, who didn't lift his head as she neared him. It was only when she stopped by his side and said, 'Hello, Davie,' that he looked up.

'Lessie?' He had aged a great deal since she had last seen him, but then so had she. His hair was completely grey now, as grey as his cold and piercing eyes, and all the lines of his square face dragged down. There was nothing left of the good-looking, laughing young man who had shared her home in the Vennel.

'I wondered who left them every year,' Lessie said, nodding at the bunch of crimson roses lying on the grass that covered Anna McCauley.

His jaw twitched but he only said, 'How are you?' His voice was harsh and stiff, as though it wasn't used much for conversation.

'Well enough. And you?'

'I heard you'd lost the house and the shop in the blitz.'

'I'm living with Dorry just now.'

'I heard,' said Davie, then turned his head sharply as Morag, carefully balancing the jug of water, appeared at the end of the path. 'Who's that?'

'My granddaughter.' And Anna's, she was going to add, but something stopped her. Perhaps it wasn't a good idea to interest Davie in Morag – not if he still retained his obsession with Anna. Looking at the roses, Lessie knew that he did.

'I'll say good day then,' he said, and swung round on his heel, walking away from the approaching girl, striding out as though anxious to escape from them both.

'Who was that?' Morag wanted to know in her turn as she knelt by the grave, drawing her gloves off with her teeth so that she could pour the water carefully from the jug into the urn Lessie had put on the grave on the first anniversary of Anna's death.

'Someone your grandmother Anna and I used to know, long ago. Put the flowers into the water for me, will you? And the roses too.' Lessie handed over the chrysanthemums and watched as Morag's slim fingers arranged them, working among the brilliant blooms with a deft, sure touch. All at once she felt very tired, and anxious to get back to the safety and comfort of Dorothea's house.

Lessie could just make out Davie, between the tombstones, leaving the cemetery. 'Next time round I'll make sure things'll be different for him – for us all,' she thought, then remembered with a pang that there would be no next time round; life only happened once, and some mistakes couldn't be undone.

'Imagine roses in October. They must have been growing in a sheltered spot.' Morag's hand reached out for them.

'Be careful,' Lessie said, her eyes on the gate. 'Be careful. Roses have thorns.'

The ringing of the phone in the hall woke Lessie from an afternoon nap in her chair by the sitting-room window.

She hadn't had a phone in her house or even in the shop, and the jangling bell always made her jump. Looking at the clock she was appalled to find that she had slept two hours away since coming back from the cemetery. The sky outside had been grey when she dozed off, but now there was a shaft of sunlight lying across the carpet, stretching almost to her feet, and when she got up stiffly and followed it to the window she saw that the clouds had rolled back and the sky was blue.

The phone had stopped ringing; Dorothea's voice, clear and decisive, floated from the hall. 'She's resting and I don't want to disturb her. Yes, of course she's fine, just worn out with everything that's happened, that's all. She was out this morning and when she came back she was so tired that I didn't even have the heart to waken her for her lunch. Look Jess, you're not supposed to use the phone for long chats just now, or haven't they told you that in London? When she wakens I'll tell—'

'Is that Jess?'

There was a pause, then Dorothea called back, 'Yes, Mam. She's only phoning to ask after you.'

'Tell her I'm coming,' Lessie said, then muttered irritably under her breath as her legs, stiff from inaction, refused to carry her across the room quickly enough. In the hall Dorothea, her immaculately made-up face disapproving, held the receiver out to her.

'Did the phone waken you? I though it would.'

'Jess?' Lessie hated telephones, and was never sure how loudly she should talk into the receiver. Jess's voice, with its usual undercurrent of laughter, travelled blithely across the miles between London and Greenock.

'Mam? How are you?'

'Never mind how I am, how are you?'

'I'm fine. Why shouldn't I—' There was a silence, as though someone had just clapped a hand over Jess's mouth, then a sudden gasp before she said, the laughter gone, 'Oh Mam, Philip's missing. Somewhere in Africa. Mam,' said Jess, her voice broken, 'I can't bear it, not on my own. I want to . . . Can I come home?'

'Of course you can, pet. Right away.'

There was a huge inelegant sniff and a choke from the other end of the line before Jess said, 'I'll not be able to get away for another three weeks, but I just needed to know that it's all right. I know Dorry's house won't be big enough for us all, but if you could find a place for me to stay, somewhere near you . . .'

'I'll find somewhere. Just come as soon as you can.'

'I'll let you know the date. Oh, Mam,' said Jess with a shaky laugh, 'falling in love's hellish, isn't it?'

'Not always,' said Lessie, reaching out to her daughter with her voice instead of her arms. 'Just sometimes.'

'She's coming to Greenock, isn't she?' Dorothea asked when the receiver had been replaced.

'Philip's missing. She needs to be with her own folk.'

Dorothea's brows knotted. 'I'm sorry for Jess, but even so, Mam, you're not strong enough to cope with this sort of thing.'

'Nonsense,' said Lessie firmly. Someone needed her again; for the first time since babyhood Jess needed her. 'Nonsense,' she repeated, and her mind, rusty from disuse over the past six months, began to crank into action.

'I could mebbe borrow a camp bed from someone, if you don't mind sharing with her,' Dorothea offered.

'You've done enough, Dorry. It's time I got myself sorted out.' Lessie looked round the room for her handbag and found it stuffed down the side of the chair she usually sat in. She claimed it then made for the door.

Dorothea followed her out into the hall. 'Mother, where are you going?'

'To the housing people,' said Lessie, one arm in the sleeve of her coat. 'I'm surely entitled to a wee place now that I've been bombed out.'

'But—'

'I need to have somewhere of my own for when Jess comes home. If she's had no good news by then she'll take a lot of looking after.'

'Mam, you're not fit to start house-hunting and worrying about Jess.'

'I'm perfectly fit. You've been good to me, Dorry, but

431

it's time I got on with my own life.' The coat was on now and Lessie was buttoning it, remembering the way small Jess used to stand stoically, her face screwed up with boredom, while her coat was buttoned for her.

'But—'

'Leave her alone, Mother,' Morag said from the kitchen door where she stood, a potato in one hand and a knife in the other. 'Gran knows what she's doing.'

'I'll be back by teatime, Dorry.'

'At least let me send for the car!'

'I've got two good legs. It's time they started doing some work again.'

'Can I come with you, Gran?'

'If you want.'

Morag thrust the potato and the knife at her mother, snatched her jacket from its hook, and hurried after Lessie, who was opening the gate. She offered her arm and Lessie was glad to take it.

'A room and kitchen would do me fine,' she said as the two of them, close-linked, set off. 'Jess won't be able to stay for long. Mebbe I'll look out for another corner shop when she's gone away again – just a wee one would do.'

'There's sure to be something, Gran.' Morag's voice was enthusiastic, happy. The blood began to surge through Lessie and creaking muscles began to stretch. She drew a deep breath, felt the autumn air flood her lungs, and thought with pleasure of the challenge that lay ahead. It would be good to have a place of her own again, and perhaps a business to occupy her energies.

It would all take time but, God willing, she had enough. There was always tomorrow, she told herself as she and Morag, shoulders touching, turned the corner.

There was mebbe even next year.

34

The chill, grey November wind cutting its way in from the river sent crisp packets and bus tickets whisking among the people standing on a stretch of waste ground alongside Lamont's shipyard. It was 1968 and the new Cunard liner the *Queen Elizabeth II*, recently arrived from John Brown's yard in Clydebank to be fitted out in Greenock, was attracting crowds of sightseers.

Morag Elder kicked away a sheet of newspaper, greasy with the memory of fish suppers, that was making amorous advances to her left ankle, buried her hands deep into the pockets of her thick jacket, and looked round anxiously for James and Elizabeth. Spotting them through the crowd, standing together, gaping up at the magnificent bulk of the liner in the dry dock a short distance away, she felt free to do a bit of gawping herself.

Product of the Clyde, where the finest shipbuilders in the world could be found, the ship was a sight worth the seeing. She soared up from the cradle that supported her massive keel, challenging the sky, looming above the streets and houses. From this angle, her bows flaring out overhead, it was impossible to see the magnificent white superstructure and the men working there, poised halfway between heaven and earth.

The Elders – Colin, Morag and their two younger children – had driven over from their home in Glasgow, taking the road over the hills so as to get the best possible first sighting of the new liner. And what a sight it had been. Even James and Elizabeth, wrangling in the back seat, had gasped then fallen silent as the ship came into sight below them, its bulk turning Greenock into a toy town.

'If she fell, Mum, she'd crush the whole town!' James had said at last, in an awed voice.

'She wouldn't fall, would she, Mum?' his thirteen-year-old sister had asked, her voice tense.

'Of course not. They can't afford to let something as beautiful and as costly as that just fall over,' Colin scoffed.

'If she did, she'd not land on Gran's house, would she? Not on Gran and Malcolm?' Elizabeth had had little time for her elder brother when he was at home, but now he was out of the house and living in Greenock with their grandmother her fondness for him had grown by leaps and bounds.

'We-ell . . .' James, who was about to put his name down for a mathematics course at Glasgow University, started measuring distances with his hands, then had the sense to fall silent when Morag screwed herself about in the driving seat and glared at him. But the damage had been done and it had taken a full five minutes after they finally found somewhere to park the car to convince timorous Elizabeth that it was safe to venture near the enormous ship.

'She is a queen, isn't she?' Morag marvelled. 'She knows fine and well that we've all come to pay homage. She looks as though she's graciously holding court.'

'She's fantastic.' There was awe in her husband's voice, then sudden bitterness. 'I just wish they'd had more tact than to name her Elizabeth the Second.'

It was a sore point with many Scots. Only their famous Clydeside yards had been good enough to entrust with this new ship and her older sisters, the *Queen Elizabeth* and the *Queen Mary*. But their pride had been soured by the naming of the liner. The first Elizabeth had been ruler of England alone; the current monarch was in actual fact the first Queen Elizabeth of Great Britain, not the second.

'They did say that it meant second to the old liner, not to the Queen.'

'Aye, and you can believe that if you like!' Colin grunted. She moved closer, slipping her hand into the crook of his elbow. After a moment he relaxed and grinned down at her. Although he was in his mid-fifties and there was more grey than brown in his hair, his face was still open and youthful. 'Okay, love, I'm not going to start doing my Scottish Nationalist bit today. It's not the ship's fault that she's been caught up in a row.' He craned his neck. 'Did you ever see such beautiful lines? Think of the craftmanship that went into making that, Morag. They've got a lot to be proud of, these men.'

The wind gusted, bringing with it a fine smirr of rain. Morag, who had considered her soft green sweater and navy trousers and heavy jacket adequate when she left the house, shivered. She dug into her pocket and took out the deep lilac silk scarf Colin had given her for her last birthday, her forty-fourth. He had bought it because, he said, it matched the colour of her eyes. As she tied it about her throat, Elizabeth, finding the mighty liner just too much to take in, sought out her parents and announced that she was hungry.

'We're not due at your mother's for another forty-five minutes, and you know how the matriarch hates folk to land on her before she's ready,' Colin said as the four of them eased their way out of the crowd and back to the car.

'We'll go somewhere else first, then.' Morag unlocked the driver's door, tipped the seat forward to let her son and daughter get into the back, then got in herself and leaned across to open the passenger door. Colin preferred not to drive if he could avoid it; he had been invalided out of the Second World War with a smashed right arm, and although twenty-five years had passed since then and he could use it fairly easily, it tended to ache if he drove for too long. It had put paid once and for all to any hopes he might still have had of progressing as an artist himself, but he was content enough to teach, and immensely proud of his wife, who had, with his support and encouragement, become a successful and well-known artist. He loved to tell people that he had been the first to recognise her potential, in those long-ago innocent days when she had been a pupil in his art class in Greenock.

The rain had only been an empty threat; the windscreen

was clear as Morag drove further into Greenock then turned the car up the hill, into a residential area. 'She loves me,' James's amazingly deep singing voice boomed from the back seat, and Elizabeth at once joined in, harmonising with practised skill, 'Yeah, yeah, yeah!'

The interior of the car was comfortably warm after the chill of the dockside. Morag, who was a Beatles fan herself, hummed along with her children and noticed that there was a streak of blue paint down the side of her right forefinger. It had taken her two hours to spot it; it would take her mother, always elegant despite her sixty-seven years, two seconds.

In the back seat James and Elizabeth had started squabbling again. Morag turned into Newton Street, drew in to the side of the road and switched off the engine. She could have taken the car to the top of Lyle Hill but it would do them good to walk. 'Everybody out.'

'Mum! We've only just got in!' With exaggerated groans the children – she would have to stop thinking of them as children, Morag realised with a pang, they were both teenagers now – struggled out of the back seat, making heavy weather of it. She waited, swinging the car keys from the blue painted finger.

'Straight on up the hill.' She snatched a swift glance at herself in the wing mirror as she bent to lock the car door. She had been too busy finishing a commissioned painting to go to the hairdresser for a few weeks and her coppery red hair, which had grown long enough to swing about her face and annoy her while she was working, was tucked beneath a restraining fabric band. She pulled the band off and let her hair swing free.

Colin had waited for her. He took her hand and pushed their linked fingers deep into the pocket of his duffle coat. 'Think of the money in this street alone,' he said, nodding at the large houses lining both sides, most of them well back from the pavement and hidden from curious eyes by trees or shrubbery.

'They were built by people who made their fortunes in the area – or retired here, where they could look down over the Clyde.'

'Like him, poor soul,' Colin murmured as they halted to let a middle-aged woman in a navy coat and hat emerge from a gate a few feet in front of them, pushing a wheelchair. She gave them a slight nod of thanks and began to wheel her charge, a very old man muffled in rugs and scarves, round them and along the pavement. Smiling down at the man in the chair, Morag met a pair of chilly grey eyes set beneath thick white brows. The eyes suddenly widened, held hers for a few seconds in an intense, almost intimate stare. The yellow-white moustache fluttered but the mouth beneath it was only capable of making inarticulate sounds. A gloved hand fluttered like a wounded bird trying to fly, then subsided helplessly back onto the rug that covered his knees.

'Yes dear, that's right,' the woman said with automatic and impersonal cheerfulness as she pushed the chair past them. Morag was left with the strange feeling that the old man had recognised her – or thought that he had recognised her.

'Newton Street,' she said thoughtfully as she and Colin, still linked, walked on. 'I remember Gran talking about a brother who lived here, but I don't think I met him. He was a recluse and they didn't have any contact with each other. He wasn't at her funeral.'

'A skeleton in the family cupboard?'

'I don't know. He was very rich, I'm sure she said that.' She shivered, then said decisively, 'He must be dead by now. Gran was seventy-one when she died, and that was eighteen years ago.'

'You've got an amazing family,' Colin said, not for the first time. 'You keep telling me that they all sprang from modest beginnings, yet your grandmother amassed a fair amount of money just by running corner shops and your mother's wealthy. Not to mention your Aunt Jess being Lady Lorrimer down in London.'

'That was only because Uncle Philip was knighted for his services as a Member of Parliament.'

'And now you spring another wealthy relative on me. I wonder who he left all his money to?' Colin mused as they toiled up the hill after James and Elizabeth.

'Some fortunate cats' home, no doubt.'

By the time they reached the top of the hill James had left the road and scrambled up to the highest point, calling to his father to come and see the liner far below. While Colin went to join him Elizabeth slipped a hand into her mother's and together they walked along to the huge white stone anchor on its plinth. Elizabeth went through the gate in the low fence and began to translate the French inscription on the plinth, brows knotted the way her father's did when he was trying to work something out. 'To the – memory of—'

'—the sailors of the Free French navy.' Morag's French was still good. 'The French sailors who came here during the war, and died before it was over.'

'Were there a lot of them?'

'A lot. All of them young and far away from home.' Her fingers strayed to the little gold and diamond autumn leaf brooch that had once belonged to her grandmother. The second portrait she had painted of Lessie Carswell wearing it hung on the studio wall of her Glasgow home. She and Colin had moved out of their rented tenement flat and bought their roomy house when Malcolm was three years old, using the money Morag had inherited from Lessie to pay for the house and for the studio Morag had had built in the garden. Nobody, least of all Morag's mother Dorothea, had had any idea until after her death that Lessie Carswell had amassed so much money by a mixture of thrift, good business sense, and an amazingly shrewd knowledge of the intricacies of investment.

Morag's red hair whipped about her face as she walked to the front of the monument, hands thrust deep into her pockets, to look down over Cardwell Bay and the Clyde. Lessie had lived to be a great-grandmother and had been proud of Malcolm, now being groomed by Dorothea to take over the sugar refinery. She had died quietly one day in her armchair in the small flat behind the corner shop she owned a few streets away from Cathcart Street, and had never known James and Elizabeth, or how well Morag herself had done. On the other hand, perhaps she did know. Probably she did, Morag thought, because nothing had ever slipped by her. She wondered for the umpteenth time what her grandmother had meant when she spoke about loving and losing being hard at any age. Morag had never found out after all; that was a secret that Lessie had kept to the end.

Her stomach rumbled, reminding her that time was passing and they were due soon at her mother's house for tea. They would all be together again for a few hours – Dorothea and Colin and Malcolm and James and Elizabeth. Then there would be a lazy weekend and on Monday she would start the task of preparing for her next exhibition.

She turned, her eyes on the memorial. So many years had passed, but Georges was still young, unchanged, though not as clear in her mind as he once had been.

'I'm hungry,' said James, arriving in a whirl of arms and legs. His father was only a few yards behind him.

'We all are.' Morag held out a hand to her daughter. 'Coming, love?'